The Wingless Boy

The Wingless Boy

THE FLEDGING OF AZ GABRIELSON
AND
PIRATES OF THE RELENTLESS DESERT

Jay Amory

The Fledging of Az Gabrielson copyright © Jay Amory 2006
Pirates of the Relentless Desert copyright © Jay Amory 2007

The right of Jay Amory to be identified as the
author of this work has been asserted by him in accordance
with the Copyright, Designs and Patents Act 1988.

This edition first published in Great Britain in 2008 by
Gollancz
An imprint of the Orion Publishing Group
Orion House, 5 Upper St Martin's Lane, London WC2H 9EA
An Hachette Livre UK Company

A CIP catalogue record for this book is available
from the British Library

ISBN 978 0 575 08371 4 (Trade Paperback)

1 3 5 7 9 10 8 6 4 2

Typeset by Input Data Services Ltd,
Bridgwater, Somerset

Printed in Great Britain by Mackays of Chatham plc,
Chatham, Kent

www.orionbooks.co.uk

The Orion Publishing Group's policy is to use papers that
are natural, renewable and recyclable products and made from
wood grown in sustainable forests. The logging and manufacturing
processes are expected to conform to the environmental
regulations of the country of origin.

The Fledging of Az Gabrielson

CHAPTER I

The Groundling Exhibit

The airbus touched down outside the Museum of Arts, Sciences and History and opened its door to let out thirty students from High Haven senior school. Some of them rushed straight for the museum entrance, propelling themselves with quick, eager thrusts of their wings. They couldn't wait to get started. Others were less keen. They couldn't think of anything duller than spending the day looking at stuffy old exhibits and listening to lectures from droney-voiced curators. They drifted across the landing apron using the bare minimum of effort to stay aloft. A few even walked, to show just how unenthralled they were.

Last to step off the airbus was Az. He, too, walked, but not because he was trying to look cool and nonchalant. He would gladly have flown, had the option been open to him. Shoulders slumped, hands in pockets, Az dragged his feet all the way to the building entrance, where Miss Kabnielsdaughter, the form teacher, was marshalling her pupils and counting heads.

'Quizzes!' Miss Kabnielsdaughter announced, and began doling out mimeographed sheets of paper. A groan rippled among the students. 'Well, you didn't think I was just going to let you dawdle around aimlessly, did you? I know you lot. Given half a chance you'd sit in the museum café all day drinking coffee, or else sneak off to hang around in the Seven Dreams Mall. Whereas I expect you to make good use of your time.'

'Hanging around in the mall *is* making good use of our time, miss,' said one joker.

Students laughed but Miss Kabnielsdaughter ignored the wisecrack. 'Now, you'll find fifty questions relating to items in the museum. Simple observation will provide the answers, though be warned – I've thrown in a couple of tricky ones to keep you on your toes. Azrael?'

Miss Kabnielsdaughter handed Az his sheet.

'You do as many as you feel able,' she said in a slightly lowered voice.

Az narrowed his eyes. 'I can manage, miss. I don't need special treatment.'

'Even so. Unlike at school, the museum isn't adapted so that you can get around easily. I'll understand if you can't cover quite as much ground as the others.'

'I can manage,' Az repeated firmly and stuffed the questionnaire in his back pocket. 'I'm not a *completely* hopeless case.'

Miss Kabnielsdaughter debated whether to scold him. She didn't mind wit but normally she would not tolerate backchat from any of her pupils. With Az Gabrielson, however, you had to make allowances. Though she did her best to treat him the same as everyone else, she couldn't help feeling sorry for the poor kid.

'Off you go,' she said to the whole class. 'We rendezvous on the mezzanine at lunchtime. That's one o'clock sharp.'

The students flowed through the arched entrance portal and dispersed in groups of three and four. Brushing past Miss Kabnielsdaughter, Az set off on his own.

Spherical in shape, the Museum of Arts, Sciences and History was divided into ten levels. Each hoop-like floor ran around a cylindrical atrium which was capped at either end by a vast circular window made up of concentric roundels of glass. The museum's upper levels were devoted to technology and culture while the lower levels dealt with famous events and figures from the Airborn race's past. Most of Az's classmates rose through the atrium to view exhibits such as the Casmaronson brothers' prototype biplane and the waxwork effigy of the celebrated concert harpist Talia Israfelsdaughter.

Az, however, gravitated in the opposite direction. There was a narrow, zigzagging staircase at the rim of the atrium for the benefit of the elderly and infirm. Az followed it downward until he could go no further.

Few visitors ever bothered with the bottom floor. Today, in fact, Az was alone there apart from a middle-aged man clad in black, who was wafting around on the far side.

From a previous trip to the museum with his family Az knew that this floor dealt with the earliest days of the Airborn – the period immediately following the Great Cataclysm when the survivors of that worldwide disaster built the sky-cities and moved up into them in order to escape the shadow of the cloud mass which was slowly blanketing the planet's surface. Various models and dioramas showed how the sky-cities were constructed, a feat of engineering as brilliant as it had been rapid. Architects had innovated and labourers had toiled, all of them inspired by the urgency of the crisis to find solutions to monumental problems and work like they had never worked before. Columns had risen from the ground at impossible speed; cities had branched out at the top, each different in design, each unique, some functional, some bizarre, some perched on a single column, some on several.

But there was one particular exhibit that Az remembered from before and was drawn to now. It was a scene depicting how life must have been for those who hadn't migrated into the sky-cities, those who'd remained below. The Groundlings.

It consisted of a replica of the interior of a small wooden shack, home to a family of four. The furniture was crude, little better than nailed-together planks, and the sole source of heat and light was an open hearth that fed up into a brick chimney. Flames made of orange silk fluttered above a heap of fake coal and licked around the base of a copper cauldron suspended from a hook. Through an open doorway a landscape backdrop could be glimpsed, an artist's impression of dense, damp forest beneath a menacing overcast sky.

The family themselves were waxwork representations of a father, a mother, a teenage daughter and a very young son. The father was sharpening the blade of a wood-chopping axe with a whetstone, the mother was cooking, the daughter was teasing wool from yarn on a spinning wheel, and the son was playing with a furry four-legged animal which, according to the information caption in front of the exhibit, was a domestic pet called a 'cat'. All four were dressed in rags and looked weary and malnourished. The parents looked especially haggard. Their troubled expressions seemed to say they knew what the future of their race was going to be, as if they had some inkling that this harsh, gloomy, primitive existence of theirs was going to wear them out and grind them down and that the coming generations would dwindle and decline and soon there would be no more Groundlings left.

Az felt pity for them, but more than that he felt a terrible, aching pang of empathy.

Because the Groundlings were wingless.

That was what fascinated him about the exhibit. That was why he stood now with his thighs touching one of the sections of velvet rope which cordoned off the exhibit; why he stared at the detailed tableau of Groundling domesticity, absorbed, transfixed. The waxwork Groundlings resembled the Airborn in every respect but one. They had arms, legs, heads, torsos – no wings. They looked normal yet incomplete. They looked, in short, like Az.

Lost in contemplation of the exhibit, Az forgot about everything else, including Miss Kabnielsdaughter's quiz. He became so oblivious to his surroundings that he didn't hear the other person on the floor, the black-clad man, float up behind him on slow, stealthy wingbeats. He didn't even realise that the stranger was hovering at his back, close enough to whisper in his ear, until the man did just that.

One word.

Softly spoken.

A single syllable.

'Freak.'

3

CHAPTER 2

The Man With The Crimson Spectacles

Az almost jumped out of his skin. He whirled round to face the stranger.

The man was small and slender but well-proportioned; handsome, if a little hawkish-looking. The dark suit he was wearing appeared tailor-made and expensive. The feathers of his wings were combed into neat, almost obsessively neat rows. The most striking thing about him, however, were the crimson-tinted spectacles which perched on the bridge of his nose. Behind the lenses his eyes shone like a pair of setting suns.

'What did you just say?' Az demanded. His body was tingling all over with shock. And with anger.

'You heard,' the man replied.

'Say it again.'

'Very well. Freak.'

The man smiled as he said this, revealing thin, sharp teeth.

'You've got a nerve,' Az said, jabbing a finger at him. 'What gives you the right to go around calling someone else a freak? What gives you the right to criticise anyone's appearance – *four-eyes?*'

'I'm merely stating something I see through these very useful spectacles of mine, which correct a small defect in my vision,' the man said, unflustered, 'and what I see through them is a young man with a very *large* defect. Namely no wings. I presume you were born this way.'

'So what if I was?'

'You didn't lose them in some dreadful accident?'

'No, I did not,' Az said with an aggressive sigh. 'But its got nothing to do with you anyway, so why don't you just pluck off and leave me alone!'

The man smiled again, briskly and without warmth.

'How interesting, then, that you should be standing here,' he said, 'looking at an exhibit about Groundlings. A boy born without wings looking at a lost race of people also born without wings. Perhaps ... perhaps you're wondering if you might be related to them.'

'We're all related to them. The Airborn were Groundlings once. We evolved to suit our new environment.' Az said this as though he were explaining it to a simpleton.

'Except you didn't. Does that make you a throwback maybe? Is that the

4

word to describe you? No, all said and done, I think I prefer "freak". Much more straightforward and to the point.'

That did it. Az had had as much as he could take. A few jibes and taunts he could handle. He was used to it. Kids his own age could be unthinkingly cruel. So could some adults. But this man was being deliberately malicious, and Az was not going to stand for it.

He did something he knew he would regret but had to do anyway. He balled his hand into a fist and took a swing at the stranger ...

... who avoided the punch as if he had known Az was about to hit him even before Az did. A single forceful pulse of his wings drove him backwards out of Az's reach.

Az blinked, then lunged at the man.

The man darted sideways with effortless ease.

Az stumbled forward and recovered his balance just in time to catch a blow from the man's left wing. It wasn't especially hard – little more than a swat. Still, it had sufficient force to knock him to the floor. Stunned, he staggered to his feet. The side of his head smarted, but he ignored the pain, more determined than ever to inflict some kind of reprisal on the man.

He had been thrown close to the Groundling exhibit. His gaze fell on the axe being sharpened by the waxwork father, but he knew it was just a flimsy confection of wood and paint. However, the short brass poles which held up the lengths of velvet rope in front of the exhibit looked sturdy and useful. Az snatched up the nearest one, twisting it at the same time so that it unhooked itself from the loops at the ends of the ropes it was attached to. Then he turned towards the man, brandishing the pole like a club.

'Oh really!' the man snorted, as if he couldn't believe his opponent would stoop to such a low tactic. 'I thought this was going to be a fair fight.'

'It is now,' Az said. 'I'm the one without wings, remember? This evens things up.'

The man's crimson-shaded gaze flicked from Az's face to the pole and back again. 'You could break a bone with that.'

'You could break one with your wing.'

'I bet you wouldn't dare, though.'

Az gritted his teeth. 'Try me.'

The man barked a laugh. He was hovering half a metre off the floor. He could swoop at any moment. Az tightened his grip on the pole.

'Azrael Gabrielson!' said a loud, shocked voice, echoing across the atrium. 'What in the name of all that's high and bright are you up to!?'

Miss Kabnielsdaughter flew across the open space to land near Az and the man. She had three students in tow, all of them front-of-the-classroom

5

types, teacher's pets. They looked smirkingly amused at Az's plight, whereas Miss Kabnielsdaughter was just plain aghast.

'Defending myself,' Az said. 'This bloke attacked me. I didn't do anything to him. It was entirely unprovoked.'

'Is this so?' Miss Kabnielsdaughter asked the man.

He alighted on the floor and dipped his wings in a gesture of humility. For some reason Az thought the man would admit the truth and back up his version of events. How could he not?

But in the event, perhaps unsurprisingly, he didn't.

'Of course not, madam,' he said. 'What a ridiculous story! There I was, minding my own business, enjoying the many delights of the museum, and all of a sudden I find myself viciously set upon by this . . . this hooligan.'

'You – you plucking liar!' Az burst out. '*You* started it. You know you did.'

'Az!' snapped Miss Kabnielsdaughter. 'Language!'

The man shrugged at her, as if Az's swearing simply proved his point. Az was clearly an out-of-control teen thug with no manners and no respect for his elders.

'But this isn't right,' Az protested hotly. 'What he said didn't happen. He's just trying to shift the blame. He—'

'He, Az,' said Miss Kabnielsdaughter, cutting in, 'isn't the one waving a piece of museum property around in a threatening manner, which inclines me to put more store by his claims than by yours.'

'But – but—'

Put the pole down, Az. Put it down now and apologise to the gentleman.'

'No.'

'Do as I tell you.'

Sullenly Az let the brass pole drop onto the floor. It made a satisfyingly loud, resounding clang. 'I won't apologise, though.'

'Do you want a Censure?'

'Don't care.'

Miss Kabnielsdaughter studied his expression and knew he meant it. The threat of a black mark on his report card, along with a note to his parents, really didn't bother him.

She let out a sigh. 'I am sorry, sir,' she said to the man. 'Azrael can be one of our more difficult pupils. He has his unruly moments. If you wish, you may file a complaint with our principal, but I'm hoping you'll be good enough to overlook the whole episode.'

The man deliberated, then nodded. 'Consider it forgotten, madam. After all, I was a hot-headed, impulsive lad myself once, believe it or not. I understand that some youngsters aren't always in control of their emotions.'

'I'm most grateful to you. And so should you be, Az.'

'Huh,' said Az.

'As a matter of fact,' the man added, 'I'd ask you to be lenient with him. Don't punish him on my account. No harm's been done, after all.'

'If you're certain.'

'I insist on it.'

'Very well,' said Miss Kabnielsdaughter. 'All the same, Az, I feel the only way to ensure you stay out of trouble is if you don't leave my sight for the rest of the day. Have you even started on your quiz? Because it looks to me like that piece of paper hasn't left your back pocket since you put it there.'

Az wanted to protest some more. He didn't want to be cast as the villain here. Fine if he had done something wrong, but he hadn't. Quite the opposite. He was completely innocent. It was all so unfair! And the man's patronising forgiveness only made it worse.

But Miss Kabnielsdaughter's stern expression brooked no further argument. She had made up her mind about the situation and nothing was going to change it.

The teacher's pets tittered as Az tugged out the quiz and sidled over to join them at Miss Kabnielsdaughter's side. With a further, final apology to the man, Miss Kabnielsdaughter led them off in a group, making for the staircase.

At the last moment Az turned and fixed the man with a fierce, glowering glare.

In return the man with the crimson spectacles gave a sly wink.

To Az, still fuming with the injustice of it all, the wink seemed like an insult but also, somehow, a promise.

It seemed to say: *You and I haven't seen the last of each other.*

Az, though, firmly hoped they had.

CHAPTER 3

The Ultimate Pulling Machine

Michael picked Az up after school.

Az's brother was ten years older than him and worked as a test pilot for Aerodyne Aeronauticals over on the west side of town, not far from Valhalla Mansions, where he lived in an all-mod-cons bachelor pad. The job was a prestigious and demanding one, but nevertheless Michael made a point of leaving the research and development hangar mid-afternoon, whenever he could, in order to collect Az from outside the school gates. That way Az was spared from having to use public transport for the journey home. The other children could fly to wherever they needed to go, if they wanted to, but for Az there was always the long wait at the airbus queue and then the embarrassment of having to sit with all the infants and old people on the bus, surrounded by mothers with squalling, barebacked babies and by pensioners with wrinkled faces and grey feathers and weakened wing muscles. And the stares. Inevitably, whenever he was in public, there were stares.

Whereas travelling with Michael was always a hoot, not least because Michael was a helicopter fanatic. He got through them at a rate of knots, one every six months, always purchasing the newest sports model when it came out and selling off his old one second-hand. Helicopters were where most of his spare money went, and he usually bought Aerodyne because of the employee discount, but not always. It depended on the specifications – airspeed, power-to-output ratio, manoeuvrability and, above all, looks.

For Michael, a 'copter had to look good. It had to be sleek, trim, with fins and ailerons in all the right places, with rotors that shimmered as they spun. And it had to turn heads, especially girls' heads. Girls were Michael's second main interest. They were where the rest of his spare money went. In fact, he got through girlfriends at an even greater rate than he got through helicopters. His relationships with two-seater, rotor- powered aircraft invariably outlasted his relationships with members of the opposite sex.

Currently Michael was piloting the latest offering from Aerodyne's main rival marque, the AtmoCorp Dragonfly 750. The open-cabbed Dragonfly afforded near-silent flight thanks to its razor-thin blades and shrouded tail rotor. It was streamlined to within an inch of its life, had an iridescent indigo paintjob, and danced in the air as lightly as a dust mote. It was, as Michael put it, 'the ultimate pulling machine', and this was no idle boast. He had owned the helicopter for less than a month and managed to date three different women during that period, two of them simultaneously.

For a while, as he and Az darted through the ups and downs and sidelongs of the city, they chatted about jetball. Their team, the Stratoville Shrikes, was doing very badly in the league, and both brothers feared relegation at the end of the season. The thought of the Shrikes lapsing from Division One to Division Two was almost too depressing to contemplate, and the brothers agreed that the blame for the team's present losing form could be laid at the feet (and hands, and wingtips) of Iaoth Zeruchson, the Shrikes' upper forward, who was failing to score even when the most glaringly basic opportunities presented themselves.

'That featherbrained moron,' Michael said. 'All those sponsorship deals have gone to his head. Thinks he's too good for the game now, that's his trouble.'

'Yeah,' said Az. 'Last week against the Cumula Collective Harpies he was worse than useless. Neriah Tenth-House had him marked from first whistle to last. She was on him like a tattoo.'

'She *is* pretty lethal. Anyone who says women can't play jetball has obviously never seen Neriah Tenth-House in action.'

'But then what about that vertical toss that Zeruchson missed? Finally he manages to slip past Tenth-House for a moment, there's an open frame, it's a sitter – and he still misses! Even I could do better than that.'

'You know what? I reckon you could and all.' Michael thrust the joystick down, and the Dragonfly fell into Anvilhead Avenue with giddying, stomach-churning speed, missing a gyro-cab by inches. The gyro-cab's pilot flipped Michael the bird, and Az chortled, and so did Michael. In a helicopter Az came as close as he would ever get to true flight, and his brother always did his best to make the experience as exhilarating and breakneck as possible.

'In fact,' Michael continued, as they straightened out along broad, four-lane Sunbeam Boulevard, 'I think we should get a surgeon to transplant Zeruchson's wings onto your back, and you can show him a thing or two about jetball.'

'I wish, Mike,' said Az, with feeling. 'I really do.'

Michael glanced over at his little brother. 'Sorry, that was stupid of me. I was only making a point.'

'No, no, it's not that.' Az knew Michael wouldn't have dreamed of saying anything deliberately to hurt him. 'I'm just a bit sensitive at the moment. Something happened on our trip to the museum today. I was standing at this exhibit and then ...'

'Then what?'

Az realised he didn't want to rake up the whole episode with the man with the crimson spectacles again. He had only just got over his feelings of anger and humiliation and he was enjoying the flight with Michael. Why ruin it?

Instead, he changed the subject slightly.

'Groundlings,' he said. 'That's what's on my mind.'

'Oh ho,' said Michael. 'You were down on the bottom floor of the museum again, weren't you? Looking at those waxworks. I remember this from last time. That exhibit put you in a funny mood all day, and its done it again.'

'Well, maybe. It just got me thinking. I mean, who were they? Groundlings? What were they like? And what happened to them?'

Michael looked askance at Az, then threw the Dragonfly into a tight turn around a corner, pitching the helicopter over almost onto its side. When they righted, he said, 'You know as well as I do. They died out. That's what the historians say. They stayed down below to oversee the machines that gather the essential raw materials and feed them up to the sky-cities, but after a while they realised that the machines run themselves. There was nothing more for them to do. So they just sort of . . . faded away.'

'We know that for certain?'

'Yes. No. Sort of. Put it this way, we don't know any differently, and there's no way of checking since no one can go down below the cloud cover. You'd die if you tried. You can't fly through it. On your own or in an aircraft, you'd get shaken to pieces by the turbulence. But its pretty obvious that nothing can have survived on the ground. It's all lightless and poisoned down there, and . . . oops, hold on.'

Michael decelerated sharply, having just spied a member of the Alar Patrol on traffic duty at a six-way intersection ahead. He gave the Patroller a wry salute as the Dragonfly buzzed past at precisely 1 kph below the speed limit. The Patroller's reaction was unclear, because his face was hidden behind his helmet visor. However, he clenched his lance a little more tightly and shook his wings, making the broad gold hoops that pierced their upper arches flash in the sun. The action implied that he had spotted Michael going too fast but was prepared to let him get away with it this once.

'And you know where you can stick that lance of yours, my friend,' Michael said through a cheesy grin, hardly moving his lips. The moment he was out of the Alar Patroller's sight, he throttled forward again, pushing the Dragonfly back up to its previous velocity.

It was clear that he considered the earlier conversation finished, and Az let it lie. Michael, much though Az loved him, was not a great thinker, not prone to dwelling on the big issues the way Az did. Sometimes Az envied him for that.

For the remainder of the journey Az leaned his head out from the cockpit and peered at the cloud cover below, wondering. It wreathed the planet, this layer of vapour. It hid sky from ground and ground from sky, a permanent white nebulous shroud, the aftermath of the Great Cataclysm, that time of terror when fire fell from the sky and the whole world shuddered.

The cloud cover never broke, never parted. Occasionally it was smooth and flat, more usually it was whipped and tormented. At night you might see dim flashes of light flickering within it – electrostatic discharges – and hear the faint rumbles that accompanied them, like the gurgling of a hungry stomach. The cloud cover was perpetually present, the base of the Airborn realm, and nothing penetrated it except the gigantic stems of the sky-cities, on which the automated supply elevators forever rose and fell.

Generally among the Airborn there was the feeling that they should be grateful for the cloud cover's existence. It meant they never had to view the ground beneath, never had to be exposed to the ugliness that must lie down there. The cloud cover was like a bandage over a wound.

That day, though, Az would have given anything just to be able to peel it back for a moment and take a peek beneath – see what was under it, see who was under it maybe.

Just to know. Just to be sure.

CHAPTER 4

Serena, Lady Aanfielsdaughter

It was widely agreed that the smallest of all the sky-cities was also the most beautiful. More ornate than Pearl Town, more dazzling than Prismburg, the Silver Sanctum was a miracle of structural whimsicality and extravagance. Its every tower was festooned with a dozen lesser towers. Its every stained- glass window was an intricate, brilliant mosaic of colours. Building was linked to building by a network of bridges and walkways, and every building within was a maze of corridors and pillared rooms, each grander and more imposing than the last.

There was no traffic in the Silver Sanctum. You winged your way around, or walked. Nor was any business allowed to be conducted inside its limits. There were no shops, no bars or restaurants, no commercial premises of any kind. The Silver Sanctum was the administrative headquarters for the entire Airborn race, and a place for thought and contemplation and sober decision-making. It was home to people who preferred to live without any distractions and superfluous demands on their time. Only the wisest heads dwelled there, the clearest minds, the sharpest intellects.

Serena, Lady Aanfielsdaughter, certainly fitted that description. Hailing originally from the city of Zenith, born of fowl-farming stock, Lady Aanfielsdaughter had never had any ambition in life but to join the ranks of the great and good who circulated through the Silver Sanctum's halls and debating chambers. From a very early age she had known that she was destined to govern, and at the first available opportunity she had left Zenith and begged a lift to the Silver Sanctum, where she had thrown himself on the mercy of the first resident she met.

This happened to be Asmodel, Lord Urielson, and Lord Urielson happened, by immense good fortune, to be in need of a new permanent secretary, his previous one having recently left in unfortunate circumstances (pilfering from petty cash, a minor crime but even the smallest misdemeanours were frowned upon at the Sanctum). Recognising something in Serena, an alertness, a special quality of keenness, not to mention a bewitching charisma, Lord Urielson offered her the position; and from there, through diligence and obvious talent, the girl had worked her way up through the hierarchy of power until, eventually, indeed inevitably, she reached the top.

Now in her mid-sixties, Lady Aanfieldsdaughter was regarded, by all who knew her personally and by any who knew *of her*, as the cleverest and subtlest-minded of the Silver Sanctum's inhabitants. The Silver Sanctum was run by committee, or rather by numerous committees and subcommittees, so there was no such thing as an absolute ruler, no single person to whom everyone else deferred. But had there been such a role, Lady Aanfieldsdaughter would undoubtedly have filled it. She was the one whose opinion always counted, the one to whom the serious political issues were always brought for consultation. If Lady Aanfieldsdaughter suggested something, even hinted at some idea, it was invariably considered official policy and put into effect. A simple yes or no from Lady Aanfieldsdaughter could affect the lives of nearly three million people.

What this great woman had learned over the years, however, was that with increasing responsibility came increasing uncertainty. For all that she appeared a confident and authoritative leader, Lady Aanfieldsdaughter was actually anything but. Within her roiled a confusion of doubts and fears. The more she had found out about the workings of the world during her rise to prominence, the less contented she had become. There were days, now, when she sat alone in her lavish apartment and looked back on her childhood at the fowl farm and wept. If someone had told her she could return to Zenith tomorrow and pick up exactly where she had left off, she would have jumped at the chance. Mucking out the chicken coops, fending off the geese who always came at you hissing viciously when you entered their pens, putting up with racket of the peacocks wailing in their cages all day and night – she wouldn't have minded one bit. Give up all this luxury and splendour for the stinky, impoverished lot of a fowl farmer? In a flash she would have, if she could.

This morning Lady Aanfieldsdaughter knew she had to keep such remorseful thoughts at bay. There was a crucial decision to be made today and, in order to make it properly, she needed to be as untroubled and unpreoccupied as possible. At first light, she went for a soar around the Silver Sanctum's topmost pinnacles. There were few better methods for de-cluttering one's brain and reinvigorating one's heart than to loop and swoop for half an hour above this most majestic of sky-cities, especially when the rays of the rising sun were striking it from the side and giving its metallic surfaces a burnish of glowing pink. A flock of swifts joined her for a while, swirling around her and chirping. She laughed as they zoomed playfully close then darted away again.

She then spent the breakfast hour engaged in debate with a dozen of her juniors, discussing some fine point of legislation. The purpose of the debate was not to settle anything but simply to hone their thinking skills and keep hers in trim. Cerebral gymnastics.

Next, she went for a wander through the city, meeting groups of colleagues along the way and dipping in and out of their conversations. This was an opportunity for her to gauge the mood among her peers, and the results, she was unsurprised to find, were not encouraging. There was a distinct atmosphere of unease. Everyone in the Silver Sanctum was aware that an awkward situation was developing, a volatile and very possibly dangerous situation. Even when no one was mentioning it directly, it lurked behind what they were saying. Lady Aanfieldsdaughter had taken it upon herself to resolve the crisis if she could. In the eyes of everyone she spoke to she saw a gleam of hopefulness, directed at her. They wanted her to succeed. How they wanted her to! For if she failed . . .

But the consequences of failure were too terrible to imagine.

Finally, around the middle of the morning, Lady Aanfieldsdaughter flew to her office for a scheduled appointment which she was both looking forward to and dreading.

Her personal assistant, Aurora Jukarsdaughter, informed her that her emissary had already arrived and was waiting for her. Aurora held open the door which connected the antechamber to Lady Aanfieldsdaughter's office with the office itself, and Lady Aanfieldsdaughter strode through.

The emissary rose to greet her.

'Milady,' the man said, with a bow and a smile. A brief, sharp-toothed, and not very engaging smile. His eyes flashed like rubies behind his crimson-tinted spectacles.

'Mr Mordadson,' said Lady Aanfieldsdaughter. 'Tell me, what have you discovered?'

CHAPTER 5

The Only Candidate For The Job

'The boy,' said Mr Mordadson, 'is a loner. That much I could gather from the fact that he was on his own when I accosted him at the museum, and background enquiries confirm it. This, of course, is likely to be a consequence of his, for want of a better word, condition. He feels different from his peers and therefore, by choice, sets himself apart from them.'

Lady Aanfieldsdaughter had stationed herself at the office windows, which were tall and opened out onto a broad balcony. Her hands were behind her back, her wings crossed and furled. Her gaze was fixed outward, on the far horizon. From this angle and altitude you could see nothing but a perfect blue firmament, an azure eternity.

'Milady?'

'Go on. I'm listening.'

'Right. Well. I have to admit that, in person, I found him quite hard to "read". So much of our body language is conveyed through our wings, isn't it? All those little physical tics and mannerisms which we give as a matter of course, without even thinking about it, he can't. All the same I received a clear impression of a high degree of intelligence coupled with a strong-mindedness bordering on wilfulness. There appear to be discipline issues.'

'Discipline issues. Is that how the educational establishment refer to bad behaviour these days?'

'Apparently so. Again, this is something I dug up with a little surreptitious snooping around. It seems Az has had more than his fair share of Censures and detentions over the course of his academic career. Nothing too serious, scuffles in the schoolyard now and then, the occasional flunked exam. But again, I'd say his winglessness was probably at the root of it.'

'No run-ins with the Alar Patrol?'

'Oh no, nothing like that. He's not one of those juvenile delinquent types. Just a very troubled teen.'

'And you pushed him, in order to see how he would respond?'

'I did indeed. I provoked him verbally. I was, as a matter of fact, somewhat unkind.'

To judge by the casual smile that accompanied the remark, Mr

Mordadson didn't seem any too troubled by his actions.

'And he stood up to me,' he went on. 'Didn't bat an eyelid, and full credit to him for that. There aren't many his age who would have done the same, shown that kind of backbone, especially to an adult. Eventually I goaded him to the point where he came at me with a right hook. It would have been quite a good punch, too, had it connected. And he'd have done a lot worse, had he had the opportunity. Aggressive tyke, he was.'

'And you believe this to be a good thing?'

'Naturally, milady, yes. He'll need to be tough and assertive. Very much so. It's a valuable trait for him to have if we're going to use him for what we want to use him for. Nevertheless . . .'

Lady Aanfieldsdaughter looked round. 'Nevertheless what?'

'Milady, it isn't my place to query your judgement. Far be it for me to suggest that your plan won't work. However, I do think—'

'You have a better plan?' Lady Aanfieldsdaughter said brusquely.

Mr Mordadson's smile this time was a quick, nervous one. His wings drooped a fraction.

'Not as such,' he replied. 'It's merely – in my view, this is a significant burden to be placing on such a young pair of shoulders. Not to mention the potential physical risk to the boy himself.'

'You yourself just said that he's tough and assertive.' 'Correct. But he's only sixteen. You're asking a great deal of a sixteen-year-old.'

'And he can always refuse to do what we ask of him, or his parents can on his behalf. I don't expect him to take part in the mission unless he volunteers to. I can't force him. I won't.'

Lady Aanfieldsdaughter then turned and made her way to the centre of the room, where an ancient teak desk resided, an object that was huge and dark and heavy and in every way redolent of the ground. Seating herself behind it, she picked up another gift of the ground, a multifaceted chunk of amethyst that served as a desk ornament. She hefted it in her hands, watching mauve and lilac highlights play across its surfaces.

'The thing is, Mr Mordadson, we don't really have a choice here. There's no one else we can ask. The boy isn't simply the most suitable candidate for the job, he's the *only* candidate. I know there's that other person similarly afflicted, wingless, the one who lives over in the Cumula Collective, but she's how old? Eighty?'

'At least. And frail as a twig.'

'Exactly. She wouldn't last a minute, and even if she was in good health, that Cumula lot are so ferociously independent, they probably wouldn't agree to allow her to go.'

'Quite. But still, milady, we could keep searching. We may turn up someone else. Maybe a double wing amputee. You never know.'

'No,' said Lady Aanfielsdaughter with finality. 'We don't have the time. Like it or not, we're going to have to go with this lad. So it's up to you now. I want you to pay a call on him at home and convince him to come and meet me.'

'That may be tricky. I left him with a distinctly negative impression of me. Perhaps if *you* were turn up in person . . .'

'Not an option. We need to keep this operation as low- profile as possible. If I were to appear on his doorstep and someone spotted me and recognised me, there'd be talk. Neighbours would want to know what Lady Aanfielsdaughter was doing in the area. Tongues would wag, rumours would start, and we can do without that. No, I'm afraid it's down to you, Mr Mordadson. I need you to bring him here. However you manage it, get me Azrael Gabrielson.'

CHAPTER 6

A Familiar Visitor

The model of Troop-Carrier *Cerulean* was taking shape. Az and his father, mainly his father, had been busy constructing it over the course of several weeks, off and on. The balsa wood framework was complete, and today they were pasting sections of light blue tissue paper over the largest part of the model, its balloon. The tissue paper emulated the canvas covering of the real *Cerulean*'s balloon. Attaching it was a delicate, painstaking process, like fitting skin to a skeleton.

'Easy with the glue,' Gabriel Enochson warned his son. Too much and that bit of paper will go soggy and rip.'

Az wiped off the excess glue with a cloth, then passed the piece of tissue paper to his father, who laid it over the airship's nosecone and gently tamped it into place.

They paused a moment to admire their handiwork. The balloon was covered on one side. The model was really starting to look like the military vessel it copied, or at any rate it was really starting to look like the picture of Troop-Carrier *Cerulean* which was tacked to the wall next to the workbench.

'We can start painting the control gondola when this is done,' Az's father said. 'Then the next job's putting together the propellers, although those are going to be fiddly, I warn you. So is the Prismburg insignia on the tailfins. That's going to be pretty hard to get right. I'll do a few preliminary sketches first, for practice.'

'Good idea, Dad.'

'You could have a bash at it yourself, you know, Az.'

'I could,' Az agreed without enthusiasm, 'only . . .'

'Only this is very boring for you, isn't it?' said his father. 'Come on, be honest.'

Reluctantly Az nodded. 'I enjoy spending time down here with you and everything. Really. I'm just not . . .'

'Not twelve years old any more,' Gabriel Enochson finished for him. 'I know. And I know you're helping me make this model just to indulge me. I tell myself it's for you but really it's for me.'

'Well, a retired man like you has to have little hobby-type projects to keep you busy.' Az pointed to the tools that could be found in their dozens around the basement workshop, racked on the walls, and the various items of equipment – a lathe, a vice, a band-driven jigsaw – the legacy of his father's long career as a maker and mender of clocks. 'Otherwise all this stuff would go to waste. Like Mum says, "Gabe, you need to be doing something, otherwise you'll be under my feet all day and annoying me."'

Az's mimickry of his mother's fruity tones drew a furtive smirk from his father. Gabriel Enochson glanced upward.

'Let's pray she didn't overhear,' he said. 'You still like *Cerulean*, though, don't you, Az? I'm not wrong about that, am I? That hasn't changed.'

'Oh yeah. *Cerulean's* pretty cool.'

'And here's me under the impression that the young are always into whatever's now and newfangled and "in". Michael and his helicopters, for example. And yet you're fascinated by a big old obsolete airship. Why is that?'

Az peered at the picture of the lighter-than-air military vessel. From the moment he first learned about *Cerulean* he had felt a strange affinity for her. She seemed at once so grace- less and so fragile, with her massive balloon and her helium- filled gas cells and her propellers on their spindly mountings. She had no wings. She looked like something that couldn't – shouldn't – fly. And yet she did. Beautifully.

Also, she was the only one of her kind. Every other military vessel like her had been decommissioned and broken down for parts years ago, after the signing of the Sky-City Pact of Hegemony, part of a worldwide demonstration of abhorrence for war and the vessels of war. *Cerulean* alone had been spared that fate and was now a museum piece, a tangible reminder of an age when the sky-cities used to fight among themselves. She was unique, the last survivor of a time gone by.

A lumbering, ungainly, wingless thing which defied appearances by being able to fly – yes, Az could certainly relate to that. Troop-Carrier *Cerulean* was both something he understood and something he admired.

But he felt a little foolish trying to put this into words, so all he said in answer to his father's query was: 'I just like her, that's all.'

The old man gave a wry, quiet grin, in a way that suggested he knew what Az had really meant to say. 'Maybe one day we should go and take one of those tourist trips in her.'

'Maybe,' Az said.

His father had made the offer many times before, but Az invariably wriggled out of accepting it. He feared they would go to Prismburg and take a short flight on board *Cerulean* and it would be a letdown. It wouldn't measure up to how he imagined. She wouldn't be all he thought she was. Perhaps it was better simply to dream about *Cerulean* and never have that dream dashed.

They had just resumed work on the model when the doorbell rang upstairs. Both of them cocked their heads and listened out. Michael had promised to drop by this evening for supper, but it was still a bit too early for that. Most likely it was one of Az's mother's friends, or else a door-to-door sales rep, of which High Haven seemed to have an endless supply. They hawked everything from floor-mops to life insurance, encyclopaedias to toothpicks, and somehow made a living at it, even though no householder was glad to see them.

Az's mother went to open the front door, her footfalls passing directly overhead on the hallway floor.

The voice that issued down from the front doorway was courteous and soft. It was a man's voice, and Az heard his mother being addressed with full formality – forename (Ramona), maiden name (Orifielsdaughter), then married surname (Enochson). The visitor was evidently keen to make a good first impression.

A sales rep then, as he had suspected. One of those rare ones who did their homework before calling by.

As Az continued to listen, however, it dawned on him that he knew that voice. He couldn't quite place it, but he was sure he had heard it before, and just recently.

The man had a lot to say to Az's mother and was hardly allowing her to get a word in edgeways. He apologised for disturbing the lady of the house and wondered if he might beg a few moments of her and her husband's time.

Az felt the hackles on the back of his neck rise. Who *was* this? Why did the voice make him feel so uneasy?

His mother called out, 'Gabe? Would you come here a second?'

Az's father shrugged. 'Coming, dear!' To Az, he added softly, 'Wonder what this is about.' With a couple of flap-thrusts of his wings, he rose to the trapdoor in the basement ceiling. He hovered there, wings beating, as he undid the latch. Then he hauled himself through and closed the trapdoor behind him.

A low, muffled conversation followed between Az's father and the visitor, and it was while this was going on that something clicked in Az's head. He remembered where and when he had last heard this visitor speaking. It had been just a couple of days ago.

The man at the museum. The man with the crimson spectacles.

Az went to the ladder which was his means of getting out of the basement, and clambered stealthily up and put his ear to the trapdoor so that he could hear more clearly.

'. . . talk with your son on a matter of the utmost importance,' the man was saying. 'I can't put it any plainer than that. Perhaps if you could see your way to inviting me in . . .'

'Gabe?' said Az's mother. 'What do you think?'

Az heard his father ruffling his wings. 'Maybe if the gentleman were to show us credentials of some sort . . .'

'Oh, but of course. Silly me,' said the man. There was the sound of pockets being patted. 'I have something . . . yes . . . here. I assume that will do.'

Az's mother gave a small gasp, then said, 'Come on through to the living room.'

'And the young man himself? I take it he's home,' the visitor said, as the front door was closed behind him.

'He's downstairs,' said Az's mother. 'Let me give him a shout. Az!'

Az waited a moment, so that it wouldn't look as if he had been eaves-dropping, then levered open the trapdoor and climbed the last few rungs of the ladder, emerging into the hallway.

'Az, there's someone here to see you. He's—'

'I know who he is,' Az said, eyeing the man coolly. 'We've met.

'Really?' said his father. He was puzzled by his son's obvious hostility towards their guest. 'Why didn't you tell us about this, that you'd met someone so prestigious?'

Az hadn't mentioned anything at all to his parents about his encounter with the man at the museum. Once he'd calmed down about it, he had decided he just wanted to put the whole matter behind him. He counted himself lucky not to have got a punishment. He was in trouble at school often enough and one less Censure for his parents to fret about was no bad thing.

'He didn't seem very prestigious at the time,' he said. 'And I'm not sure he is.'

Gabriel Enochson's puzzled expression deepened. 'Well, you're wrong. See?'

He held up a small leather wallet to show Az. Within the wallet was set a silver badge, a feather overlaid on a circle. The circle represented the world and had several dozen tiny embossed dots on it, representing sky-cities.

Az recognised the emblem. Who wouldn't?

The seal of the Silver Sanctum.

'My name, Az, is Mr Mordadson,' said the man, 'and I come on urgent business. Azrael Gabrielson, the Airborn race needs your help.'

CHAPTER 7

Face-off In The Living Room

Oh please, Az thought. *This is a joke. This is ludicrous.* How could the man sitting opposite honestly expect him to agree to go to the Silver Sanctum with him? Without explaining exactly *why* he should go with him?

'You'll have to take it on trust,' Mr Mordadson said, looking very comfortable in the family's best armchair. 'In matters of state, one must take great care what one does and doesn't say. In this particular instance, I'm afraid I'm forbidden to reveal anything specific. The whole issue is far too delicate. What I *can* tell you is that our future – all of our futures – may well depend on your agreeing to participate. I'm asking you, Azrael, and you, Mr and Mrs Enochson, to consider what's good for all of us.

'I appreciate,' Mr Mordadson continued, focusing on Az, 'that you and I got off on the wrong foot. I'd be grateful if you could erase that incident from your memory and we could start anew. I am, I hope you'll soon come to see, not a needlessly unpleasant man. I had a job to do then. I have another job to do now.'

The smile he gave desperately wanted to be likeable, but it was all too reminiscent of his other, charmless smiles.

'How *can* I trust you?' Az retorted.

'Now, Az,' said his mother, 'he's carrying the Silver Sanctum seal. I don't know what went on between the two of you before, but the seal gives Mr Mordadson absolute governmental authority.'

'Yeah? For all we know he stole it, or it's a fake.'

'Az!' said his father. 'How can you say such a thing!'

'No, no, its quite all right, Mr Enochson. Perfectly understandable, under the circumstances. I was testing young Azrael the last time we met, to see what stuff he's made of. What I did wouldn't have endeared me to him in the least. On the plus side, it proved to me that he's up to the task we have in mind for him. It proved it to Lady Aanfieldsdaughter as well.'

'Lady Aanfieldsdaughter,' breathed Az's mother. 'You work for *her?*'

'Indeed I do, madam. Directly answerable. I am, you might say, milady's strong right arm.' Mr Mordadson bent forward and took a sip from the cup of fragrant tea which Az's mother had prepared. The gesture implied a casualness about his close professional relationship with that most august and revered personage, Serena, Lady Aanfieldsdaughter.

'But – well – Az, there's no question, then. You must do as Mr Mordadson says. You must go with him.'

'Must I? Why?'

'I'm sorry, Mr Mordadson. This attitude of his . . . he's a stubborn one sometimes.'

'Stubborn is fine, Mrs Enochson. Don't apologise. At the heart of a stubborn person lies a strong spirit.'

'Does this,' said Az's father, 'this "task" you have in mind for Az – does it by any chance have to do with Az being different from other kids the way he is?'

Mr Mordadson nodded gravely. 'Let's just say it requires someone with his special talent.'

'Special talent!' Az snorted. 'Huh! Why not just come right out with it: you want me to do something for you because I'm wingless.'

'It is, yes, because of your unfortunate lack of wings. More than that, though, I'm not at liberty to divulge.'

'It's because I'm a – what's that word again? – freak.'

'As I explained—'

'Darling,' Az's mother cut in, 'put aside your feelings for the moment. Regardless of what happened earlier, Lady Aanfielsdaughter herself has summoned you. You simply cannot refuse.'

'Can't I?' said Az, and stood up. 'I think I can, and I will.'

'I was afraid of this,' said Mr Mordadson, standing up too. 'Azrael, if you won't come with me of your own accord, I regret to say that I'm going to have to make you. I was hoping we could do this without resorting to physicality, but apparently not. Most regrettable.'

So saying, he reached across to grab Az. Az yanked his arm out of Mr Mordadson's grasp. Mr Mordadson made a second lunge, which was thwarted by Az's father placing himself in between them.

'That's enough, Mr Mordadson. You've crossed a line. Seal or no seal, you can't just saunter into my house and abduct my son. I won't have it.'

'Oh yes?' sneered Mr Mordadson. 'And what are you going to do about it? Are you going to stop me, *old man*? I doubt it.'

It was a harsh jibe but true. Az's father was not in the prime of life, and his health was not brilliant. You could tell by the state of his wings – the yellowness of their plumage, the missing feathers (gone like much of the hair from his head). His joints often ached, and he moved slowly and found it an effort to fly any great distance.

He was, in other words, hardly a match for someone like Mr Mordadson. If it came to a tussle between them, there was no question who would win. Both knew it.

Still, Az's father did not budge. He glared defiantly at Mr Mordadson, who peered sneeringly back through his crimson spectacles. Each man waited for the other to make the next move. Tension crackled in the air.

Perhaps they would have stood there for ever, holding each other's gaze. Perhaps the situation in the living room would have remained as perpetually static and unchanging as the tableau of Groundling life at the Museum of Arts, Sciences and History: Az's father and Mr Mordadson facing off against each other, Az hunkered behind his father, Az's mother frozen with anxiety in her chair.

Then someone entered the room and broke the spell. 'Hello, hello,' said Michael, sauntering in. 'What's going on here then?'

CHAPTER 8

Journey To The Silver Sanctum

High Haven fell away behind, diminishing into the distance. Bent round in his seat, Az watched it recede. The roughly dome-shaped agglomeration of buildings, which seemed huge and pulsing with life when you were in it, shrank and shrank until he could block it from view just by raising a hand. From afar the city, balancing on its quartet of supporting columns, looked like a tiny paper sculpture, extraordinarily delicate.

Then it was gone, swallowed in sky haze.

Az turned forward. Ahead, Mr Mordadson's monoplane was making its way sedately along the airlane. It was a Metatronco Wayfarer, a boxy little thing, the kind of vehicle that accountants and office managers flew, a reliable, unexciting ride that got an excellent kilometre-per-litre ratio but was dull in every way, right down to its name. It wasn't a patch on Michael's Dragonfly for speed and elegance, and Michael soon became impatient with having to tootle along in its wake.

'Come on, Az, let's have a little fun,' he said, with a wicked look on his face. 'Let's show our friend Mr Mordadson what a *real* aircraft can do. Buckle up!'

Az was already strapped into his seat but he tightened the belt anyway in eager anticipation.

Michael checked that the airlane ahead was clear, then poured on speed till the helicopter's nose was right up to the Wayfarer's tailfins. He made sure Mr Mordadson had seen them in his rearview mirror. Then he abruptly cut power to the rotors so that the Dragonfly plummeted.

Az's stomach rose into his throat as they free-fell. Fifty metres down Michael re-engaged the rotors and soared up under the Wayfarer. At the same time he stamped on the anti-torque pedals, spinning the Dragonfly on its vertical axis so that it was facing the other way round. He re-entered the airlane in front of the Wayfarer, hurtling along in reverse. They were travelling at the same speed as Mr Mordadson, so for a while the Wayfarer and the Dragonfly were nose to nose. Az could see Mr Mordadson through the plane's windscreen. He was gesticulating wildly, flapping a hand at Michael to get out of the way, and beeping his horn. Michael waved cheerily back, and Az followed suit. Both brothers were laughing hard.

They laughed harder when Mr Mordadson attempted to overtake. He pulled to one side, and Michael steered the same way, blocking his path. He pulled to the other side, and again Michael matched him.

Finally, infuriated, Mr Mordadson hit the flaps and reduced speed almost to a standstill – any slower and he would have been in danger of stalling. Seeing this, Michael decided to perform one final stunt, the kind only a experienced test pilot would dare attempt. He throttled forward, and the Dragonfly dipped its nose and aimed straight for the Wayfarer. At the very last second, when it looked like a midair collision was inevitable, he flipped the helicopter upside down and shot over the plane. The rotor blades were mere centimetres from the Wayfarer's cockpit canopy.

Michael righted the Dragonfly and fell in behind Mr Mordadson again. For a while both aircraft droned slowly along, until finally Mr Mordadson understood that Michael was finished with his fun and games. The Wayfarer accelerated till it was at cruising speed once more, and every so often its driver shot a scowling glance in the rearview, to let Michael know what he thought of *that* kind of behaviour.

'Serves you right,' Michael said, as though Mr Mordadson could hear him. 'Shouldn't fly such an old piece-of-guano junker, should you?'

Apart from this little episode, the five-hour flight to the Silver Sanctum was uneventful, and Az had plenty of time to think about things.

Above all he wondered what would have happened if Michael had not turned up early for dinner. Would Mr Mordadson have got into a fight with Az's father? Would he really have forced Az into his plane and flown him to the Silver Sanctum against his will?

Az feared the answer to both these questions was yes, and this led him to think that whatever situation it was that required his services, it must indeed be a dire one if Mr Mordadson was prepared to use extreme measures like assault and kidnap in order to get hold of him. He could not for the life of him fathom what Lady Aanfielsdaughter wanted him for, and this uncertainty made the prospect of meeting the great woman, which would otherwise have been a thrill and an honour, somewhat daunting.

Michael had truly arrived in the nick of time, and it was lucky he had. Mr Mordadson had backed off the moment Michael came into the room. Clearly it was one thing to threaten an old man, quite another to tackle a young, fit, well-winged fellow like Az's brother. With Michael's arrival the balance of power in the living room had undergone a subtle but significant shift, not in Mr Mordadson's favour.

Az's mother had quickly filled Michael in on what was going on. In response, Michael had said, 'Az isn't going anywhere, not if he doesn't want to. I mean it.'

'Perhaps,' Mr Mordadson had replied, 'we could come to some sort of accommodation ...'

'If it involves you getting straight out of my family's house, then fine, I don't have a problem with that.'

'No, what I meant was, perhaps Azrael might be able to see his way to accompanying me if he were to have a chaperone.' He gestured to Michael. 'Yourself, for instance.'

There had been some discussion amongst the family, and eventually it had been agreed that Az should journey to the Silver Sanctum, but only on condition that Michael went with him every wingbeat of the way, to look after him.

Az himself had been able to overcome his reluctance because, with his big brother beside him, he felt there was very little that could go wrong.

Three hours into the trip they made a scheduled stopover at a way-station, a vast snowflake-shaped structure which was kept aloft on a cushion of air generated by a half-dozen horizontal fans. They docked at one 'arm' of the snowflake and an attendant in overalls came out to refuel both aircraft and polish the windshields. Michael expressed dismay at the price the waystation was charging for aviation fuel, and the attendant shrugged and said there had been problems with deliveries. He hoped it would sort itself out quickly, but in the meantime there was no alternative: prices had to go up.

It became a moot point anyway, thanks to Mr Mordadson's Silver Sanctum seal. He showed it to the attendant, who studied it and then said, with a wince of reluctance, 'Right. The Sanctum. Well then, consider the bill settled.'

'Not bad, this working-for-the-government lark,' Michael commented to Az as they went inside the waystation to buy refreshments and visit the toilets. 'Flash that seal and its freebies all round. Unlimited everything. I could get used to it.'

In front of them, Mr Mordadson overheard. 'Mr Gabrielson, the chance of someone like you ever qualifying to join the Silver Sanctum is, I'd say, somewhere between remote and impossible.'

'Ooh!' Michael said. 'Snarky!'

'Simply being honest. And while I'm about it, no more antics when we get back in the air, please.' It was half request, half warning. 'You have a valuable passenger on board, remember.'

Michael chuckled, unabashed. 'Fair enough, Mordy. On condition that you admit that top-prop beats front-prop any day.'

'But helicopters are so much more costly to run than planes.'

'But so much more agile in the air.'

'But they reek of frivolity and waste, and they— Oh, never mind. Why am I wasting my breath? If it'll satisfy you, I'll say it. Top-prop beats front-prop.'

'Good man,' Michael said, and patted Mr Mordadson's wing in a manner that was calculated to irritate, and did.

Az was elated by the lack of respect Michael was showing Mr Mordadson. It made him feel far less intimidated by the man, almost to the point where he could forgive him. Almost.

A couple of hours after that, the Silver Sanctum hove into sight.

Pictures Az had seen did not prepare him for the breathtaking loveliness of the place. Unlike other sky-cities, which were often sprawling and unruly creations, the Silver Sanctum was small and self-contained. It was virtually a single edifice, a shining vision of metalcraft and spires, a work of art.

The beauty of the Silver Sanctum, however, did not make Az any less nervous about his upcoming meeting with Lady Aanfielsdaughter.

CHAPTER 9

The Belvedere Vineyard

They were met on the Silver Sanctum's perimeter landing apron by Aurora Jukarsdaughter, Lady Aanfielsdaughter's personal assistant. Aurora had long, curling, black hair, and the swan-whiteness of her wings contrasted exquisitely with the darkness of her complexion. She was more than attractive, she was glorious, and Az could tell that Michael was smitten by her. As soon as Mr Mordadson introduced them to each other, Michael dropped his voice and did a certain trick with his eyes, making them go wide and limpid. This, as he had often told Az, never failed with the ladies.

It did with Aurora, though. She seemed more amused than impressed by Michael's attempts to charm her. When he arched his wings slightly, to give himself more height and show off the blue-black magpie feathers that were stitched into his plumage, a laughing look came into Aurora's eyes, suggesting she didn't think much of fashion statements like that. When he oh-so-casually asked her if she had ever flown in a Dragonfly, she looked as if she was trying to stifle a yawn.

Az knew her indifference would only make Michael more determined than ever. Aurora was now a challenge, and he wouldn't stint in his efforts to pursue her.

In the meantime, however, there were more pressing matters to be attended to.

'Lady Aanfielsdaughter is expecting you,' Aurora said. 'She's up in the Belvedere Vineyard. I'll show you the way.'

Michael scooped Az up in his arms. Aurora took flight, and Michael followed. Mr Mordadson fell in behind. In procession they dived through a round gateway and followed a twisting, turning, circuitous route between various buildings. A team of window washers, suspended in midair from helium balloons, waved to them as they went by. They gained height till they were near the summit of the city, passing over tower tops and spires. Michael kept pace with Aurora the whole way. Although he had the extra weight of Az to carry, he was doing his best to make it seem as if this was no effort.

They arrived at a tower which was capped by a hexagonal area of grass crisscrossed with trellises. Leafy vines swathed the trellis wires, and Az saw grapes hanging in thick, ripe clusters.

Someone was standing alone in the midst of this garden. She was a tall, slender, aristocratic woman with a mane of white hair and a long, tapering nose. As Aurora led the three of them – Az, Michael, Mr Mordadson – down to land, the woman did not rise up to meet them. This would have been the polite thing to do, but instead she remained firmly footed on the grass. Az wondered why, then realised that Lady Aanfieldsdaughter (for that was obviously who the woman was) was staying put for his benefit. By making a point of not flying, she meant to set Az at his ease.

Michael lowered Az to the grass. Lady Aanfieldsdaughter strode forward.

'Azrael Gabrielson, it's a pleasure to make your acquaintance.'

They shook hands, and Az noticed that Lady Aanfieldsdaughter had eyes of the purest, most piercing blue. *Stratospheric blue*, as it was known.

Lady Aanfieldsdaughter turned. 'And you are . . .'

'His brother,' said Michael.

'Ah, of course. It's Michael, isn't it? Here to keep an eye on him, I take it. Doing your fraternal duty. Most commendable.'

Michael was thoroughly disarmed. Az had seldom seen his brother stunned or lost for words, but he was now. Lady Aanfieldsdaughter knew his name and had complimented him. Michael's mouth gaped and he looked like he might need to sit down.

'Now then,' Lady Aanfieldsdaughter, turning back at Az, 'may I say how grateful I am that you agreed to come, Azrael. I've heard many good things about you. If it's not impertinent, I'd like to ask a couple of questions.'

'No. I mean, yes. I mean, it wouldn't be impertinent. Fire away.'

The corners of Lady Aanfieldsdaughter's mouth twitched. 'Fire away I shall. Firstly, you've never had wings, correct?'

'Never.'

'Any idea why?'

Az was surprised to find that he wasn't peeved by this line of enquiry, as he might have been. It was the way Lady Aanfieldsdaughter was asking the questions – she wasn't prying, she was curious, genuinely interested to know the answers. Compare and contrast with Mr Mordadson's approach at the museum.

'Our parents are pretty old,' Az said. 'My mum was well into her forties when she had me, my dad just fifty. The doctors think that had something to do with it. Kids of older parents can be born with illnesses, defects, that sort of thing. Quite often they're born dead, so I suppose I should consider myself lucky.'

'You're normal in every other way?'

'Yeah, I think so. I've been to see all sorts of specialists. I have the nubs on my back. Pinfeathers should have sprouted from those when I was a baby. They just ... didn't, and none of the specialists could figure out why.'

'Do you miss not being able to fly?'

'I don't know. I don't think "miss" is the right word, because to miss something you have to have had it and lost it, don't you? I'd love to be able to fly, of course I would. But I can't, so that's that. I did once, actually. Sort of.'

Lady Aanfielsdaughter raised her eyebrows. 'How so?' 'Well, my dad, he used to make and fix clocks for a living. He's very good with his hands. He can build stuff, invent stuff – and one day, for my fourteenth birthday, he made me a pair of wings. He put together this kind of backpack, a harness with these wings attached on armatures. The wings were made out of metal. Copper. Every joint, every feather – copper. So, as you can imagine, the whole contraption weighed a tonne, and he stuck it on my back, strapped it on, and the idea was that I would put my hands through these loops on the underside of the wings and flap them and fly. Only ...'

The wings had been too heavy. Far too heavy. Az recalled very clearly his father and Michael tossing him out into space, and then moments of plummeting, a sickening vertiginous downrush, the terrible sense of being out of control, utterly helpless. The weight of the wings had rolled him over onto his back, and he had plunged face upwards, down past his house, down into the street below, then further down, falling, falling, nothing to be done about it, buildings hurtling up past him, traffic, people, the city letting him slip through its gaps ...

Above him, Michael shouting: *Go limp, Az! I'm coming for you!*

Michael swooping, his arms outstretched, his wings pressed flat against his back.

'... only, it all went a bit wrong,' Az resumed. 'Michael managed to catch me in time. If he hadn't, well, I'd probably have gone through the cloud cover and ended up splatted on the ground.'

'A hair-raising experience,' said Lady Aanfielsdaughter.

'Just a bit.'

'I imagine it might have put you off the whole idea of flying.'

'It put it into perspective. I'd like to be able to fly, just not in that way. I'd like it to be on my own terms. But' – he shrugged – 'it's not going to happen.'

'And you don't resent your father for building you the wings?'

'Oh no. He did it because he loves me and because he wanted to grant me my greatest wish. He did me a favour, in fact, since now that wish isn't nearly so important to me any more.'

'Do you think, Azrael ...'

'Call me Az. Nobody calls me Azrael unless they're cross with me or I don't like them.' He said this while flicking a glance in Mr Mordadson's direction.

'Az it is then,' Lady Aanfielsdaughter said. She had spotted Az's glance and who it was aimed at. 'Do you think, changing the subject a little, that on the whole you're happy with your lot, Az?'

'On the whole, yeah. Sometimes it gets me down but mostly – mustn't grumble.'

'Because, now that I've met you, I'm firmly convinced that there's a reason you were born as you are. I don't mean a medical reason. A higher purpose. Let me explain ...'

CHAPTER 10

Wine And Soil

Lady Aanfielsdaughter laid an arm across Az's shoulders and drew his attention to the vines all around them.

'These are some of the finest grapes around,' she said, 'and they produce a most excellent wine, which we make here in the Silver Sanctum ourselves. It's a hobby of ours, something to while away an idle hour. I myself, when I have the odd spare moment, come up to this garden to do some pruning or picking. Others do the pressing, the distilling and the bottling, and then we all enjoy the fruits of our labours over an evening meal. Delicious, I promise you. I might even go so far as to say ambrosial!

'This is the Silver Sanctum's own small version of the cultivation areas you'll find in every sky-city – the orchards, the nurseries, the greenhouses, the crop plazas. And what are the essential ingredients that keep plants alive? Sunlight, of course, which we have a constant supply of, and water, which our vaporisation vats furnish us with. But also earth. Soil.'

She bent down to the roots of one vine and dug up a handful of earth, then let the brown granules trickle through her fingers.

'Soil, though, doesn't last for ever.' She brushed her hand clean. 'Its nutrients are soon used up, and we can fertilise it with guano to extend its life but that's not enough. So we need to import fresh soil, which of course comes from the ground. All this is somewhat obvious, Az, I know. I can tell by your expression that that's what you're thinking. "What *is* the old bat wittering on about? I learnt all about it in Biology ages ago."'

Az shook his head, but he was blushing. Lady Aanfielsdaughter had read his mind.

'I'm telling you all this, Az, to illustrate the fact that we Airborn rely on what we can get from the ground. Not just soil, but other raw materials. Fossil fuels, ores, you name it. The copper your father made those wings out of. We live up here in these magnificent, lofty sky-cities, three, four kilometres high, but we're far from self-sufficient. The ground supports us in more ways than one. We need its natural resources.

'But this is a fact which we're apt to forget. We're not directly involved in the gathering of the raw materials. We rather take it for granted. Seldom do we think about where the natural resources come from and how they get here, and indeed I'd go so far as to say that most of us never think about it at all, because we never need to.

'Unfortunately, we're going to *have* to think about it, Az. It's a truth we're going to have to confront, all of us, and soon.

'Because, you see, there's a problem.'

Lady Aanfieldsdaughter paused to allow her words to sink in. She was no longer genial. Her face was now utterly serious, her mood deadly earnest.

'A problem?' said Az.

With the system of supply. There have been disruptions. Shortages. Deficits. Nothing to get alarmed about, at least not yet. You yourself may well not have noticed. It's unlikely anyone in the general population has.'

Az thought of the raised price of aviation fuel at the waystation.

'So far the trouble appears to be confined to here in the Central Sector ofthe Western Quadrant,' LadyAanfielsdaughter continued. 'It hasn't spread any further than this region. Still, the data is worrying. We in the Silver Sanctum have collated statistics from the supply-arrival depots at every sky-city in the Sector, and the conclusion is unavoidable. Sporadically, we have not been receiving as much from the ground as we should.'

'What is it, a fault with the machines?'

'It could be, it could be. We've not yet been able to pinpoint the cause. Nor do we know yet whether this is a temporary glitch or something more sinister. We simply don't have enough information to work that out. Only when we do will we be able to formulate a response strategy.'

'And how do you plan to ...'

Az's voice trailed off. All of a sudden everything was beginning to make sense. Mr Mordadson's remarks to him at the museum. His winglessness. Why Lady Aanfieldsdaughter had summoned him.

Lady Aanfieldsdaughter was scrutinising Az's face. She could see Az putting two and two together.

'You want me,' Az said slowly, 'to go down there, don't you? You want me to travel down to the ground and find out what's happening. That's it, isn't it?'

Serena, Lady Aanfieldsdaughter, gave a sombre nod. 'That, Az, is it. We believe that you, out of the entire Airborn race, are the one person who might be able to survive on the ground. Owing to your unique attributes, you are the only one of us who could stand a chance.'

'But I'm Airborn, like anyone. The only difference is I don't have wings.'

'True, true, but you're accustomed to moving without flight and to operating in two dimensions rather than three. Not to put too fine a point on it, you're to all intents and purposes a Groundling. That aspect of our racial heritage has come to the fore in you.

Throwback, Mr Mordadson had said.

'In physiological terms,' Lady Aanfielsdaughter continued, 'it's unlikely there's anybody more suited to surviving conditions on the ground than you.'

'But,' said Az, 'if it's as toxic down there as everybody says it is . . .'

'You wouldn't be expected to stay down there for long. Just long enough to reconnoitre and build up an impression of the situation, then report back.'

'And I'm not a machinery expert . . .' A practical talent with machines was something Az had not inherited from his father. Something *else*, along with wings.

'Az, these are valid objections and you're entitled to raise them. I'm not ordering you to do anything. I'm *asking* you to. I'm asking you at least to consider it. I don't expect you to give me an answer straight away. Go off and mull it over. Discuss it with your brother. You're under no pressure whatever, and nobody will think any the less of you if, after thinking about it, you come back and say no. Please believe me when I say that. What I would like, though, is a reasonably quick decision. By tonight, say?'

Lady Aanfielsdaughter instructed Aurora to escort Az and Michael to the Silver Sanctum's guest quarters. Az's brain was in a whirl as, cradled in Michael's arms, he was borne aloft from the Belvedere Vineyard. So much was happening at once. There was so much to think about.

A decision by tonight?

For all his bewilderment, Az already had an inkling what his choice was going to be.

CHAPTER 11

A Brief Dialogue

Mr Mordadson sidled over to Lady Aanfielsdaughter.

'Forgive me, milady,' he said, 'but I couldn't help noticing that you were somewhat *selectively* honest with the boy.'

Lady Aanfielsdaughter let out a rueful sigh. 'I had to be. I told him as much of the truth as I dared, but I had to withhold a few salient details.'

'Why? I would have thought that, if he's to make an informed decision, he ought to know everything.'

'That would have been fairer on him, yes. But frankly, the less he knows, the better. He needs to go down there with an open mind. It could be what will save him if he gets into difficulties. That and his own resourcefulness. Besides, with his brother standing there I couldn't just blurt out everything. The fewer people who are in on the secret, the more likely it is that the secret *stays* a secret.'

'It's your call, milady.'

'Yes, it *is* my call, Mr Mordadson.' Lady Aanfielsdaughter was irritated. 'And I'd appreciate it if you'd remember that. You may not realise this, but its far harder to give orders than it is to take them.'

'I apologise.' Mr Mordadson flattened his wings.

'No, I'm sorry too. I shouldn't have snapped. It's just – this whole business is so trying.' Lady Aanfielsdaughter rubbed her temples, wincing as though in pain. 'What the old adage? "Uneasy lies the head that wears the crown." That's never felt truer than now. After all, I could well be about to send a teenager to his death.'

'Let's hope not.'

'Let's. But do you want to know a funny thing? I like Az. I like him a lot. He reminds me of myself at that age. Bright and full of fire, and just needing something to channel it into, a focus for all that restless inner energy. Misgivings aside, I don't think we could have asked for a better recruit for the job. I think he'll perform it admirably.'

'Assuming he agrees to do it.'

'If I've read him right,' Lady Aanfielsdaughter said, 'then I don't think we need have any worries on that score.'

CHAPTER 12

Another Brief Dialogue

'She's crazy about me,' Michael said, after Aurora had left the room. 'I can tell. She's giving me all the signals. Crazy.'

Az hadn't noticed any significant change in Aurora's attitude towards Michael while they were on their way over to the guest quarters, but he said nothing. If she *was* crazy about him, she was disguising it well.

'What should I do, Mike?' he said, crossing over to the balcony. From here the view of the Silver Sanctum was spectacular: gleaming canyons of streets, with wrought metalwork everywhere, so intensely detailed that the eye could scarcely take it all in. Two birds of paradise flapped by, looking utterly at home with their extravagant plumage of velvety golden heads and long, swooping pink tails.

'Do?' Michael had decided to try out one of the twin beds in the room. He flumped into it face-down. The mattress nearly swallowed him. Now that's what I call soft,' he said in a muffled voice. He rolled over. 'Well, what do you want to do?'

'Obviously I want not to have to visit the ground.'

'Fine, then you don't. Just like Lady Aanfieldsdaughter said.' Michael paused, shaking his head. 'Lady Aanfieldsdaughter. We were just talking to Lady Aanfieldsdaughter! Can you believe it, Az?'

Az smiled indulgently at his brother. 'No, you're right, I don't have to. Except that I do.'

Michael looked up with a frown. 'Eh? I don't get it.'

'You heard her. She said it was my ... my higher purpose. My destiny, almost. It's why I don't have wings.'

'Uh, well, maybe. I thought that was a bit highfaluting of her, myself. You know politicians. They can get very flowery sometimes, especially when they're trying to convince somebody about something.'

'I know. But look at it this way, Mike. You're not me. With the best will in the world, you have no idea what it's like to be me. If I can do something useful, if I can find some virtue in the fact that I don't have wings, then really I should. I must.'

'But there are risks ...'

'There are risks all the time for me. My whole life is a risk. I could fall

37

off a pavement by mistake, any day of the week, and that would be that. A single misstep, and 'bye-bye.'

Michael hopped up off the bed and came over to Az.

'So you're sure about this, little bro.'

Az forced a smile. 'Not really, no.'

'But . . .'

'But it's got to be done.'

Michael reached out and engulfed him in a huge hug.

'You're a brave little plucker, you know that, don't you?'

'. . . crushing me, Mike . . . can't breathe . . .'

'Oops.' Michael let go. He stepped back, and a musing look came over his face. 'And it's good that you're so brave, because it's going to make me look even better in Aurora Jukarsdaughter's eyes, isn't it? The hero's big brother.'

'Well, as long as *you* get something out of it,' Az said, with a lopsided grin.

Michael cuffed him with a wingtip.

What Az nearly said then, but didn't, was that an idea was forming at the back of his mind. It was, as yet, the merest glimmer of a suspicion, but it seemed valid and plausible. Lady Aanfielsdaughter had kept something from him, some crucial piece of information. And if it was what he thought it was, then a trip down to the ground would make sense of many things and, from his own personal point of view, be more than a little interesting.

Assuming he survived the conditions down there, or even the journey.

CHAPTER 13

The Astral Dome

The refectory was lit by what appeared to be a million candles. Their glow reflected off the mirror-bright metallic panelling on the walls, so that the whole of the chamber was ablaze with illumination, right up to the vault-ribbed ceiling. The dazzle took some getting used to. For the first minutes of the meal Az found himself having to squint, but eventually his vision adjusted.

They ate butter-laced asparagus stalks for starters, followed by pigeon pie and then a second main course of swan steak served on a bed of spicy rice. Az and Michael were in the privileged position of having seats at the top table, where the seniormost residents of the Silver Sanctum sat. Around them were Lord this and Lady that, a plethora of grey-feathered nobles whose names Az had forgotten almost as soon as he had been told them. He managed to hold his own in conversation with them, but sometimes the talk at the table turned to arcane political matters which he couldn't follow, so he kept quiet then and sipped his wine. The wine was, as Lady Aanfieldsdaughter had promised, ambrosial, and after a couple of glasses of it everything took on a warm fuzziness. A trio of harpists were playing in a corner, providing background music, and to Az, as he got tipsy, the rippling ebb and flow of their arpeggio notes became lullingly hypnotic.

Finally dessert came, nectarine soufflé, and after that Lady Aanfieldsdaughter stood up, thanked the assembled worthies for their company at their meal, and invited Az and Michael to accompany her to the Astral Dome. The three of them walked out of the refectory, and as they went Az sensed that every eye in the room was on him. People were watching him go past, some of them trying to disguise it, some not. He felt an incalculable weight of expectation pressing on him. This helped sober him up.

The Astral Dome lay at the top of a tower to the north of the city. Its walls and ceiling were a hemisphere of transparent crystal, and the moment Az stepped into it he felt he was actually part of the heavens. Star clusters glittered brilliantly around him. It seemed that there was nothing to stop him reaching out and running his hand through the universe as though it were an upturned pool of water.

39

Then Lady Aanfieldsdaughter switched on a series of lights recessed in the dome's base. All at once, through a trick of refraction, numerous sets of lines appeared overhead, flaws deliberately introduced into the crystal. They formed an array of irregular geometrical patterns which linked the stars together in their constellation shapes. Powered by an immense, hidden system of clockwork, the dome revolved slowly in time to the turning of the heavens, and its angle could be adjusted by means of gimbals, so that the lines and the stars always corresponded.

Az passed several happy minutes identifying constellations by name. He recognised Agor the Vulture and Tift the Bat, and there was the Huntsman, Jophiel, with his falcon on his wrist, and there was the pilot Metatron. The dim, pale band that traversed the sky was the wake of Metatron's aircraft, a cloudy furrow which this mythical entity renewed every night as he crossed east-west from horizon to horizon. He navigated by the True Star, the bright, sparkling scintilla of light that remained constant at the apex of the firmament, the fixed point around which all the other stars pivoted.

'Now, Az,' said Lady Aanfieldsdaughter, breaking in on his heaven-gazing reverie. She switched the lights off and the stars reverted to their natural randomness. 'I really need to know. I've been patient all evening, but ... an answer. Yes or no?'

Az turned to her and gave an emphatic nod.

'You're aware of the dangers? The possible consequences?'

Another firm nod.

'Very well.' Lady Aanfieldsdaughter looked gratified, although not wholly glad. 'Then tomorrow you'll be travelling to Heliotropia.'

'Why Heliotropia?'

'That's where the supply disruption has been worst. Might as well send you into the heart of things, where the problems will be at their most apparent.'

'And will you be going there with me?'

'Unfortunately not. There's no escape for people like me. Government is a prison sentence!' She laughed. 'But we'll meet again when you return, Az. Have no doubt about that. You'll be brought straight to me to report what you've found out.'

They shared a firm handshake.

'Best of luck.'

'Thank you,' said Az, hoping fervently that he wouldn't need it.

CHAPTER 14

Heliotropia

The holiday resort of Heliotropia was one day's journey away. They travelled there in convoy with Mr Mordadson. Aurora joined them on the trip, which Michael was delighted about, but she flew with Mr Mordadson in his Wayfarer, which he was less delighted about. There was, of course, no room in the Dragonfly for her, unless Az gave up his seat, and Michael wasn't going to ask him to make that sacrifice. Nevertheless, Michael would dearly have loved some time alone in the helicopter with Aurora so that he could continue to, as he put it, 'work his magic' on her.

Heliotropia perched atop a single column and was designed along the lines of a flower, with dozens of flat radial arms arrayed like petals around a disc-shaped hub. Each 'petal' was a strip of hotels, while the hub contained souvenir shops, swimming pools, funfairs, cabaret theatres, and casinos, plus a few nightclubs, many of them with a rather risqué reputation. Heliotropia, being the highest of the sky-cities by a margin of nearly a kilometre, was also the coldest, but what it lacked in ambient temperature it gained in proximity to the sun. For anyone wishing to get a tan and not waste time about it, this was the place to come. After just quarter of an hour shivering semi-naked on a sun lounger, you'd be browner than if you had spent a couple of hours doing the same at a lower, milder clime.

Az and Michael had no opportunity to sample any of the recreational delights on offer in Heliotropia, however. No sooner had they arrived than they were being shown into the city's underbelly.

'Huh, brings back memories,' said Michael as they descended beneath the streets via an access shaft. 'Six months working the supply elevators. I really felt like I'd done my bit for society after *that*. You've got all this to look forward to when you turn twenty-one, Az.'

Az, in Michael's arms, nodded, thinking that his winglessness would probably excuse him from his mandatory stretch of community service – and then thinking that he might not even reach twenty-one, if something went wrong today.

He was starting to get anxious, for the first time since agreeing to Lady Aanfielsdaughter's request. He had been able to put it out of his mind before, but now it was hitting home. The ground. He was about to travel

41

down to the ground. His mouth felt dry and his stomach had tightened into a hard, painful ball.

Michael sensed the tension in his brother's body. 'You can pull out any time, little bro. It's never too late. Just say the word.'

'I'll be fine,' Az replied, although he wasn't sure whether he was trying to convince Michael or himself.

At the base of the shaft, a tunnel led off at right angles. It was dimly lit and not much broader than the average wingspan. From far off came a thrumming sound, vibrating along the tunnel's length.

'Now then, you probably should put these on.'

This was said by the supply-arrival depot supervisor, who had led Az, Michael, Aurora and Mr Mordadson down here. The 'these' he was referring to were sets of zip-up gauze wing covers, which he produced from a wall locker.

'One size fits all,' the supervisor went on. 'They'll keep the dust and grime off your feathers. None necessary for you, of course,' he said to Az.

Az would have come back with some smart-alec retort, but he was too preoccupied to think of one just then.

Everyone who had wings sheathed them in gauze. Then they trooped off along the tunnel on foot, the supervisor leading the way. The further they went, the louder the thrumming sound became, until soon it was like a bass note on a concert organ, deep and resonant.

'Don't remember there being this much noise,' Michael commented to Az.

The supervisor overheard. 'That would be because Heliotropia has all its supply elevators confined to one spot. Since the city has just a single column, all of its elevators – a hundred or so – are grouped around it. The mechanism to run that many of them is, as you can imagine, of a pretty considerable size, hence the noise. You'll see for yourselves in a moment.'

They did. The tunnel terminated, and Az found himself entering the biggest room he had ever been in. It was cylindrical, and he estimated that at least three jetball hoopdromes could have fitted comfortably inside it, one on top of the other. The ceiling was so high up as to be all but invisible. The opposite wall looked impossibly distant.

At the centre of the room – although *room* seemed much too diminutive a word to describe this place – there was a raised area, circular in shape and buttressed with girders. It took Az several moments to work out what he was looking at. This was the summit of Heliotropia's column, the point on which the entire city rested.

Even as he assimilated *that* fact, his eye was drawn to the complex arrangement of pulleys and cables that filled much of the open space above the raised area. Huge wheels revolved, suspended in an intricate steel framework. Counterweights the size of airbuses rose and fell. It was a gigantic spiderweb of mechanical activity, all to facilitate the raising and lowering of the elevators on their tracks spaced around the circumference of the column.

'Remarkable, isn't it?' the supervisor said, with a gloat of professional pride. The sky-cities' designers certainly didn't think small. The elevators work on a gravity-driven system. One descending helps another rise. It's the closest thing you'll ever get to perpetual motion. And you know what? Right up above us, over our heads, tens of thousands of holidaymakers are gadding about, having fun, enjoying themselves, none of them caring a jot about any of this. Nobody gives a hoot what goes on right beneath their feet. Makes you think, eh?'

Mr Mordadson, for one, didn't seem to be in the mood for rumination just then.

'What about all those workers?' he asked, pointing to clusters of men and women dotted around the supply-arrival depot floor, near the elevators. 'It doesn't suit us to have them around. We don't need any witnesses.'

'They'll be going off-shift quite soon.' The supervisor consulted his watch. 'Couple of minutes' time, in fact.'

'Not exactly doing a lot of work, are they?' Michael observed.

The workers were dressed in olive-green overalls and had wing-covers on. The majority of them were just sitting around, apparently waiting for something to do. Each time an elevator arrived, they glanced at it, then resumed their lounging.

Not all of them were idle, however. Az spotted two people in flight, daubing grease on the pulleys. He saw another at the controls of a hover-lifter, practising how to manoeuvre the little vehicle. There was an unladen pallet on the hover-lifter's forks, and the worker was trying, with great care, to lodge it into a distribution bay in the wall, a couple of hundred metres up off the floor. The 'lifter's fans swivelled this way and that as he tried, and kept failing, to insert the pallet correctly.

'Well, that's because nothing's coming up right now, is it?' said the supervisor. 'There's nothing to unload. We have periods like this, when the elevators keep turning up with empty pallets and everybody just has to twiddle their thumbs. Only, I have to say, it's been happening rather a lot lately. Whole shifts will go by, and no coal, no crude oil, no timber, no soil, nothing. Heliotropia has enough to be getting by with for now. Our stockpiles are OK, and there's plenty of money in the city coffers to buy in anything we're running low on. Still, it's a bit worrying. But of course, that's what you've come here to—'

A klaxon sounded, and the workers immediately took to the air and swarmed towards a far-off exit.

Departure

One after another, in sequence, the elevators heaved up through apertures in the floor and rolled their doors open, revealing dark, featureless interiors. Up close, Az noticed that their metal sides were covered in patches of rust, and here and there the corrosion had eaten through, leaving small jagged holes. He noticed, too, that many of the elevators creaked and shuddered as they moved.

None of this made him any more thrilled at the prospect of travelling in one.

'Downward journey time will be best part of an hour, by my estimate,' said the supervisor. He was talking to Mr Mordadson. 'That's only an educated guess, though. Could be a great deal longer. Then you want to allow him how long to look around? Two, three hours?'

'That would seem adequate,' said Mr Mordadson.

'After which he can come right back up. So a six-hour round trip, let's say. Seven, to be on the safe side.'

'And you'll be here all the time? Outside the elevator?'

'All the time,' the supervisor confirmed. 'The moment he resurfaces, I'll whisk him out of sight before anybody spots him. That's as long as he comes up on the exact same one. You think you can do that, boy? Come back on the same elevator?'

'Yeah,' said Az drily, 'I reckon I can manage that.'

'And we,' said Mr Mordadson to the supervisor, 'will wait for you and Azrael up in your administrative offices. I don't need to remind you, do I, that the Silver Sanctum is counting on your discretion in this matter.'

'You don't.'

'Or that a good turn done for the Silver Sanctum is always reciprocated.'

'Just pleased to be of service, that's all,' said the supervisor, although it was obvious he didn't mind the Silver Sanctum being in his debt. It might come in handy someday, to be able to call in that kind of favour.

'Good, good,' said Mr Mordadson.

'The lad ...' The supervisor eyed Az. 'He does understand that the ground isn't a healthy place for a human to be? I mean, he's clear on the fact that *you just don't go down there*, right? Not and live.'

'He is,' Az said, who was fed up with the way the supervisor kept talking about him in the third person, as if he wasn't even there. 'He's also clear on the fact that he's going to chicken out if we don't get on with this right away.'

'Yes. OK. Fair enough.' The supervisor brisked his palms together. 'Here we are then, next elevator in line to arrive, coming up. Doors'll remain open till I release this lever here. The lever re-engages the drive ratchet, and descent commences. If you've goodbyes to say, now's the time to say them.'

Az turned to Michael and was alarmed to see that his brother was struggling to hold back tears.

'You're coming back,' Michael said, with conviction. 'Seven hours' time, we'll be seeing your ugly mug again.'

'Count on it,' said Az.

'Go on then. Stop faffing about. Sooner you leave . . .' sooner I return. Mike, if anything does go wrong, you should tell Mum and Dad—'

Nothing's going to go wrong.'

'Still, you should tell them I love them and they're not to blame. For anything. They carry this guilt around with them, guilt about me. They don't ever say anything about it but I know they do. And they don't need to. There's no reason to.'

'Tell 'em yourself, squirt.'

'All right. I will.'

Aurora Jukarsdaughter leaned close and gaze Az a peck on the cheek. She even smelled beautiful, the scent of her skin like lilacs. 'Good luck, young man.'

Az couldn't resist a chance for mischief. 'You realise my brother fancies the socks off you, don't you?'

'Az!' hissed Michael, exasperated.

Aurora's teeth sparkled as she laughed. 'I had noticed. He's not subtle, is he?'

'Not very.'

Michael buried his face in his hands. 'I've changed my mind, Az. *Don't* come back. Ever.'

'Azrael?'

Now Mr Mordadson stepped forward. He looked oddly hesitant, ill at ease with his emotions.

'Be careful,' he settled for saying. 'And be observant.'

'Will do.'

'You're not alone,' Mr Mordadson added, his eyelids closing behind his spectacles in a slow, meaningful blink.

'Uh, right,' said Az, thinking that the last thing he needed right now was a heartfelt expression of moral support like this from Mr Mordadson.

Or was he trying to imply more than that?

This wasn't the time to dwell on it. Az about-faced. The elevator had risen and halted. An empty pallet had rolled out of it and now the elevator was waiting, doors agape. From within, a dark, burnt odour drifted out, the smell of functionality and necessity.

He stepped forward.

'Ready?' said the supervisor, hand on the lever.

Az swallowed and nodded.

'Then here goes.'

Az entered the elevator.

The lever fell with a clank.

The doors trundled shut with a clunk.

The elevator gave a groan and started to sink.

CHAPTER 16

Down

Through a rust hole in the elevator's roof, Az watched Heliotropia recede above him.

The sky-city's underside was veined with sewage pipes and garbage conduits, like some complex, interlocking tubular puzzle. It was possible to discern a pattern, however, and the pattern became clearer the further Az descended. Everything ultimately led towards the column, fed into it, and continued down inside. The column served as a gigantic waste disposal chute, along with its many other functions.

Gradually Heliotropia darkened, until soon it had become a silhouette against the firmament, a vast black flower, and Az couldn't make out details any more. He found another rust hole, this one at chest height in the right-hand-side wall of the elevator. Through it he could see the cloud cover. The sun was low, and the cloud cover, where it wasn't in Heliotropia's immense lengthening shadow, had started to take on evening hues. Soon the peaks would be pink, the troughs purple. After that its surface would become a uniform dark grey.

The cloud cover was still some way below, but rising fast.

Az was alone.

The feeling swamped him – *engulfed* him. Everything he knew, everyone he loved, was up there. Up in Heliotropia, up in High Haven. Up in the world of the Airborn. He was beneath them, and getting further away with every passing second. He was separated. Isolated.

Then came fear.

There was no way out. He was trapped in the elevator till it reached the ground – and then what? What awaited down there?

He fought the urge to scream and hammer at the doors of the elevator. As if there was someone outside to hear him and let him out!

The elevator gave a sudden, heart-stopping lurch, then continued as before. That put paid to any ideas Az had about pounding on it. He lowered himself into a corner and sat there with his knees to his chin, keeping himself small and still. He didn't want to do the slightest thing to interfere with the elevator's progress. He knew that it must have made the trip up and down the column a million times without a hitch, but what if this was the occasion when it finally malfunctioned? What if, by a stroke of appalling misfortune, it got stuck, or even broke free of its track and fell?

A long time passed before Az's thoughts settled into any semblance of order again. There was no point in panicking. It was far too late for that. He might as well try and enjoy the ride, even if it turned out to be the last ride he ever took. No, *especially* if.

By that point the elevator was drawing level with the cloud cover. Carefully Az got up and pressed his eye to the chest- high rust hole again. This close to, the agitation of the cloud cover was clear to see. Wisps of vapour twisted upward from the surface, forming spirals and cones that dissipated rapidly. Deeper down, the clouds flurried and swirled. Currents were visible, surging powerfully around in immense streams and eddies.

It swallowed him suddenly. One moment, Az was beginning to wonder if the elevator was ever going to reach the cloud cover. Next moment everything outside went hazy, then blank grey.

The air turned clammy, so that Az could see his breath. The interior of the elevator darkened, the air got clammier still, and then the elevator started to shake. Winds had begun to batter it, hurling themselves at it from front and sides. The doors whumped inward every time a particularly powerful gust struck. The floor under Az's feet juddered. It seemed such a frail thing, this metal box he was in. Too frail to withstand the cloud cover's fury. If it wasn't wrenched loose from its tracks, it might just get crushed to pieces.

Fear returned, and Az resorted to prayer. He didn't believe in God. Who did? A few strange folk who gathered in community halls to hold hands and mumble about a Superior Being, that was who. A tiny minority of superstitious weirdos who clung to the notion that Someone watched over the Airborn race from on high and looked after them, whereas anybody with an ounce of sense knew that the Airborn were clever enough and organised enough to look after themselves, thank you very much.

For all that, Az had always been intrigued by the notion of God. He wanted to believe that his being born without wings was part of some divine master plan, that there was a meaning to it, it wasn't just a random genetic accident. Lady Aanfielsdaughter, perhaps knowingly, perhaps not, had touched on this hope of Az's when she had referred to Az having a 'higher purpose'.

Everyone wanted to feel special, didn't they?

So, silently, he prayed. Eyes tight shut, he strung together a few rambling, desperate pleas, as the elevator trembled and rattled in the cloud cover's tempestuous grasp.

Please let me live.

Please, if you're up there, let me live.

CHAPTER 17

Groundfall

A while later, the shaking stopped and calm was restored.

Az opened his eyes and found himself in darkness. He groped his way to the rust hole. Outside, all was murk and gloom. He couldn't tell how high he was. He had no idea how long he had been in the elevator. It would take an hour, the supervisor had said, to get to the ground. But the supervisor had just pulled that figure out of thin air. He didn't actually know.

Az felt as though he had been in the elevator for ever and would always be in it. The journey was an eternity.

He noticed that he was feeling slightly dizzy but he put it down to the trauma of going through the cloud cover. It wasn't a wholly un-pleasant sensation and a couple of deep breaths were enough to clear his head.

Then, below, he spied lights.

There was just a handful of them, a smattering. It was as if he was looking down at a lone constellation, a group of stars on the ground. For a brief, exhilarating moment he thought he might even be going up again and the lights were real stars. Somehow he had managed to avoid visiting the ground. A reprieve!

But of course this wasn't so. He was still travelling downward.

What were they then, those lights?

As he got nearer to them, he perceived that they were scattered across the surface of a dark, looming structure of some kind, and that they shone with an uneven flicker.

Nearer still, he realised that the lights were glows from the mouths of several tall chimneys. There were furnaces burning down there and the lights showed where the furnaces were being vented. Above each glow a thick black plume of smoke arose, churning up into the air.

As for the structure, it was an agglomeration of buildings that spread around the foot of the column and outward, visible to Az as a jumbled mass of roofs, some curved, some jagged, plus those chimneys. It was hard to make out the structure clearly by the uncertain orange light of the furnaces, but even so Az had never seen anything so haphazard before, so apparently thrown together. The whole thing looked as if it had grown rather than been constructed, as if it had sprung up around the column's base like some kind of fungus.

The elevator seemed to be moving faster. Maybe this was just an optical illusion as the ground came closer, or maybe gravity's hold on it was stronger here. Whichever, Az felt it rushing to complete the final section of its journey. The last few minutes of the descent were a swoop, a throat-tightening plunge.

At the back of Az's mind was the thought that he should not inhale, or at least should inhale shallowly. The smoke from those chimneys. Poisoned air. Toxic.

But no. There was nothing he could do about that. He was either going to die now or he wasn't.

The elevator sank into the structure, entering some sort of shaft. The sounds it was making changed, becoming at once confined and echoey.

Then it started to decelerate, easing itself bit by bit to a stop.

When it finally did halt, Az felt distinctly unsteady on his feet. Inside, he was still going down. He had been in the elevator for so long that his body had adjusted and now needed to *re*adjust. It had to get used to the idea of being motionless once more.

The doors divided, rolling open to reveal . . .

. . . an empty pallet, hurtling along rails, straight towards Az's shins.

CHAPTER 18

Going Through The Motions

He leapt aside just in time. The pallet slammed home inside the elevator. Had Az reacted a split-second more slowly, it would have pinned him against the back wall, crushing his legs.

He scrambled out of the elevator and scanned frantically around. Where there had been one hazard, there might be others.

In every direction he saw machinery. He was in a chamber that was not unlike the supply-arrival depot. It wasn't quite as vast, and the level of illumination was dim to the point of being nonexistent, coming as it did from a set of skylights located way up in the ceiling. But there was the same impression of constant mechanical commotion, and here the noise was even louder and more disorientating than above, at Heliotropia. In fact, the racket was such that Az's ears could barely take it. Things were working – ponderously, repetitively working. Pistons thump-whumped. Flywheels whirled. Gear chains as thick as a man's torso went scrolling through systems of cogs. Great pendulum-like weights shot downward and slowly rose. And everywhere, pallets were shuttling around, either rolling along rails or else being plucked from one spot and transported to another in the jaws of cranes, which glided along tracks mounted on the ceiling joists. There were squeaks of metal grinding on metal, sudden eruptions of steam from valves, the occasional shower-burst of sparks – all of which added to the near-deafening din.

Az thought two things. First of all, that his ex-clockmaker father might feel right at home here. It was like being inside an enormous timepiece. And second of all, that he himself wanted to get out. The dizziness from earlier had returned, worse than before, no longer pleasant in any way, and even if the cacophony around him wasn't the cause, it definitely wasn't helping. He needed to find a quieter spot if he could.

He staggered away from the elevator, which had closed its doors and was ascending back towards the ceiling. He made a mental note of its location within the chamber, hoping against hope that when the time came he would be able to find it again. In an odd way he felt an affinity for that particular elevator, over all the others. After all, it had got him here safely, more or less. He owed it a debt of gratitude for that.

Fighting the dizziness, he ventured through the – what would you call this place? Supply-departure depot? Somehow, because it was automated, it didn't seem to merit a name. He threaded a wary path between the various devices. A pallet came swinging towards him, hoisted by a crane. He ducked and it passed over his head. A jet of steam nearly scorched his backside. A piston thrust itself out at him unexpectedly.

If he hadn't known better, he would have thought the machinery had taken a dislike to him and was on the attack.

Eventually he reached the sanctuary of the chamber's outer wall. Three metres up there was a gantry, which could be reached by a metal ladder. Connected to the gantry by a door was a room with a row of viewing windows – some kind of monitoring gallery. Once, long ago, the Groundling equivalent of the supply-arrival depot supervisor might have looked out from that gallery to observe the machinery as it laboured away. Now no one did any more.

Az climbed the ladder and took a breather, leaning on the gantry's safety rail and watching the vista of robotic industry in front of him. From this vantage point he could see more clearly than ever how the machines weren't achieving anything. They were meant to be filling the elevators with essential supplies for Heliotropia but there were no raw materials anywhere to be seen. The pallets were conspicuously bare. Yet still the machines went through the motions, loading the elevators with nothing.

It was a starkly depressing sight, a vision of mindless futility. All that effort and energy, to no end.

The dizzy spell finally passed. The door to the gallery was made of steel and secured by a heavy lever-type handle. It was hard to open, much as you might expect of a door that hadn't been used in centuries. Az grappled with the handle, which was stiff to the point of being almost unmoveable. He pushed down on it with all his might, and in the end, with a sharp, protesting screech, it shifted. He pushed again, grunting with the effort, and all at once the handle gave, the door sprang open and he tumbled through. He closed it behind him, relieved to be able to shut out the deafening 'ruckus in the chamber.

Inside the gallery were banks of consoles with levers, dials, switches and gauges on them, an array of instrumentation glinting faintly in the gloom. Az pictured Groundlings manning the consoles, perhaps touching a knob here, a lever there, with the growing realisation that what they were doing didn't seem to make any difference. The machinery on the other side of the windows went on regardless. The Groundlings must have sensed they were becoming redundant.

Mustn't they?

A race that had collectively lost the will to live. Was it possible?

Az was beginning to wonder.

Another steel door led out from the gallery. Reasoning that the interruption to the flow of supplies must be occurring somewhere further up the production line, Az knew he had to delve further into the building to investigate.

This door opened far more easily than the last, and he found himself in a passageway that was bathed in murky red light. As his eyes accustomed themselves to the crimson glow, it occurred to him that this must be how Mr Mordadson viewed the world through his tinted spectacles: everything blood-coloured.

Not nice.

It also occurred to him that the lighting must be for somebody's benefit. If, as he and all the other Airborn had been led to believe, there were no Groundlings any more, wouldn't the bulbs have burned out long ago and not been replaced? So far Az had seen nothing but abandoned automation. However, his half-formed suspicion – the one he had refrained from voicing to Michael – was still there, and the presence of the working lights helped give it strength. It was gradually coalescing into a conviction, although as yet he lacked absolute, clinching proof.

He headed off along the passageway. The dizziness returned briefly. His brain woozed and the walls of the passageway flexed and pulsed around him. He halted. But as before, the sensations passed and he felt OK again. Perhaps Lady Aanfielsdaughter was right. Physiologically he could cope with the rigours of being on the ground in a way no ordinary Airborn person could.

The passageway turned a corner, and not long afterward Az emerged into a chamber of similar dimensions to the first one but far quieter. Here, there was only a distant rumble to be heard, emanating from the other chamber. In this chamber nothing was moving. What apparatus there was stood inert. Huge pieces of machinery hulked to the rafters but were inactive.

This appeared to be the place where items were deposited onto pallets and transferred by conveyor belt through a connecting conduit to the chamber where the elevators were. And if nothing was operational here, then here, logically, was where the problem lay. Here or in the conduit.

Az strode into the room, flooded with a sense of satisfaction. Mission not quite accomplished but almost. He couldn't believe it had been so easy. (Well, perhaps not easy, but straightforward.) All he had to do was check around, identify where the hold-up was, then head back to the elevator and report to Lady Aanfielsdaughter. After that, it was up to Lady Aanfielsdaughter and everyone else at the Silver Sanctum to sort things out somehow. Az would have done his bit. The problem would be someone else's.

He explored the chamber thoroughly, examined every machine, but was unable to find anything obviously awry. There wasn't a jam anywhere in the system. None of the machines appeared to have broken down. They just weren't *on*.

Maybe the power was out. There was power elsewhere but maybe a fuse or a circuit-breaker for this particular chamber had blown.

Further investigation brought Az to an exit at the far end of the chamber. He took it. He was starting to feel bold. He would have some stories to tell Michael and their parents when he got back!

He was in another red-lit passageway. Right or left? He chose left.

The passageway twisted around several right-angle corners. Az came to a T-junction and went left again. He knew he must be careful not to lose his bearings. He promised himself if he arrived at another junction he would turn back. This place was a maze.

An entrance appeared. It consisted of two doors, each adorned with a set of designs. Etched steel panels depicted arrows pointing upward and an Airborn figure, wings and arms outstretched, gazing serenely down.

What did that signify? Why Airborn?

Intrigued, Az nudged one of the doors open and went in.

There was no light in the room apart from the faint red illumination borrowed from the passageway outside. Az glimpsed vague shapes – something like a bed in the middle of the room and a large square portal with an ornate frame set into the far wall.

On the bed there was a man lying down.

Az froze.

The man didn't stir. Either he was fast asleep and Az's entering had not woken him, or . . .

Gradually Az's eyes adapted to the dim light. He could see the man was on his back and naked except for a white loin-cloth. His hands were folded across his stomach and his wings lay flat, forming the outline of a heart around him. Az looked for the rise and fall of the man's chest. There wasn't any.

The awful truth dawned. He was looking at a dead body.

CHAPTER 19

Anatomy Of A Dead Man

Steeling himself, Az went further into the room. He didn't want to examine the corpse more closely, and yet he knew he had to. His curiosity must be satisfied, even if it meant going to within touching distance of death.

He tiptoed up to the bed, which he could now see was not a bed at all but a kind of gurney, similar to the ones that sick people were moved around on at a hospital. There were castors on the ends of its legs.

The man was very skinny. His face was whiskery, his hair was thin and lank, and the veins were prominent through his pale skin, twisting around his bones like vines around posts. He was old, or rather had been old when he died.

Who was this? Was he perhaps Az's predecessor, someone who had come to the ground before him to investigate and had not returned? Lady Aanfieldsdaughter hadn't mentioned sending anyone else on this mission first, but then why would she? It would hardly have helped her cause if she'd told Az, 'In point of fact, the last chap didn't make it back alive. Still willing to go?'

The explanation didn't quite hold water, though. It failed to account for why the man was lying there on the gurney, quite clearly having been placed in that position. And his wings. His wings were strange. The way they sat so flat on the gurney – it just didn't look right. There was no thickness, no solidity to them.

Squinting, Az studied the wings and realised that they weren't actually wings at all. They were just feathers arranged around the body to resemble wings. An assortment of feathers, too, not uniformly white. There were grey ones, half-white half-brown ones, even a few black ones. They'd been placed on the gurney in such a way to make the man look as if he was Airborn.

And yet he was not.

Groundling.

Had to be.

'Yes,' Az hissed to himself.

So there *were* Groundlings after all. His suspicion had been correct. Contrary to popular Airborn belief, they hadn't died out. This one might be defunct, but someone else had placed those feathers around him, therefore the race as a whole remained alive. And that fact was common knowledge to those in the upper echelons of Airborn life. Lady Aanfielsdaughter knew it and Mr Mordadson had hinted at it with his 'You're not alone' remark, a kind of oblique warning to Az, a way of preparing him for what he might find down here.

While Az was coming to terms with this, the dizziness returned with a vengeance. All at once his head was reeling. His stomach was churning greasily. Nausea rippled through him in waves.

And then from the passageway outside came the sound of voices.

Too dazed and disorientated to know what else to do, Az scanned about for somewhere to hide. He didn't want to be caught with the body. Whoever these people were, if they found him peering at the dead man, what would they think? What would they *do?*

A hasty hunt around the room revealed a closet. There were clothes hanging inside – robes of some sort – and bottles on a shelf containing a clear fluid. Az crawled in and tugged the closet door shut. The catch slipped and the door swung open, though only a little way. He didn't have time to try and shut it properly again. He heard a switch being thrown. Bright light flooded the room. Two men had entered.

CHAPTER 20

Archdeacon Corbelgilt

Az peered through the open crack of the closet door. His head was swimming and he felt on the brink of passing out. Still, he couldn't help but gaze in amazement at the two arrivals. Living Groundlings, in the flesh.

Both of the men were clad in robes, just like the ones hanging above him in the closet. The robes were black with symbols embroidered on them in scarlet and gold. One of the men had more symbols on his robe than the other and, where the other had just a plain skullcap, he wore an ornate item of headgear. It was a tall arch-shaped hat with a golden arrow on the front, pointing upward like the arrows on the door.

This man was clearly the more important of the two. The other man addressed him with deference and, Az thought, with a certain amount of fear. The more important man was also the fatter of the two, by quite some margin. He was, indeed, obese. His body was a massive quivering sphere, his head was as round as a jetball, and he wheezed as he walked, his stubby little arms working hard to keep him balanced. If he had been Airborn and winged, he might well have been too heavy to fly.

'Your grace,' the second, much thinner man was saying, 'everything is prepared. The body is feathered, as you can see, and the mourners will be arriving shortly.'

'Have they paid tribute?' the obese man with the ornate hat enquired. He spoke through his nose, with a haughty air, as though it was beneath his dignity to discuss such mundane, practical matters.

'Naturally, your grace. A tithe of the deceased's estate, such as it was, has been presented to the Chancel actuaries. Unfortunately, of course, the obligatory bodyweight's worth of offerings has *not* been provided. The family were unable to obtain anything suitable. I'm assured they tried, they made every effort, but ...'

'The pickets.'

'Indeed, your grace, they were hindered by the pickets. Nothing is coming out of any of the local commercial premises unless it can be guaranteed that it's going to the people and not to here.'

'This blasted industrial action, Deacon Shatterlonger,' the obese man said with a heartfelt, contemptuous sigh. 'When is it going to end? It cannot be allowed to continue much longer. Do the people not realise the danger to their souls?'

'I wish I could give you an answer, Archdeacon Corbelgilt. All I can say is, the militancy out there is getting worse by the day. Wretched Humanists! Stirring up trouble wherever they raise their heathen heads. One can only hope that common sense will soon prevail.'

'*Faith* and common sense.'

'Yes, your grace, that's what I meant. Faith and common sense will prevail. Otherwise ...'

'Otherwise we're damned, all of us,' said Archdeacon Corbelgilt. 'No salvation, no life after this life. The disfavour of the heavens will be upon us. We shall none of us rise to join the Ascended Ones.'

Deacon Shatterlonger's face was a picture of misery, mirroring the sentiments of his superior. 'Perhaps if your grace were to deliver one of your trademark rousing sermons at the ceremony ...'

'Already composed.' The Archdeacon tapped his temple. 'Memorised and ready. Usually I would be wary of intruding on the grief of mourners, but today I cannot allow myself such niceties of conscience. The situation demands that the Chancel restate its case in the strongest terms possible. The people *must* be told that the Humanist cause is wrong and insupportable, and they must be encouraged to carry that message out into the community.'

Az struggled to make head or tail of what he was listening to. It didn't help that he felt close to fainting and that there was a buzzing in his ears which made the conversation seem as though it was coming from a hundred metres away. Also, the men spoke with a thick accent which stretched some words out and shortened others. For instance, *raring* sounded like it had at least three R's in the middle of it, while *encouraged* came out as *incard*.

Mainly, though, Az didn't get certain references. Humanists? Salvation? Chancel? Ascended Ones? It was like a whole new language.

'Ah, here we are,' said the Deacon. The sound of shuffling footfalls could be heard in the passageway outside.

'Your grace,' he added softly, pointing to Corbelgilt's hat. 'Your mitre. A tad lopsided.'

Archdeacon Corbelgilt hurriedly straightened the hat, then composed himself, putting on a polite, pleasant face.

More Groundlings filed into the room, thirty or so in all, and Corbelgilt greeted each with a handclasp and a condescending tilt of the head. There were men and women of all ages, and a few children, and the majority looked sombre and sad. One elderly woman, whom Az took to be the dead man's widow, was especially distraught. Her eyes were red-rimmed and she was barely looking where she was going – a couple of younger relatives had to guide her by the elbows. When she caught sight of the body on the gurney, she burst into fits of sobbing. The archdeacon moved to comfort her, whispering something reassuring in her ear.

The mourners took their places in the room, lining up facing the body. Deacon Shatterlonger moved to a position close to Az's hiding place. Archdeacon Corbelgilt, meanwhile, stationed himself next to the gurney.

He raised his hands.

'Let us begin.'

CHAPTER 21

The Ceremony Of Ascension

The next few minutes were a blur for Az. He tried to keep up with what was going on but there were shooting stars exploding across his vision and the buzzing in his ears had become a deep drone. It was all he could do simply to stay conscious.

Archdeacon Corbelgilt intoned long sentences, punctuating them with formal hand gestures. He was talking about the dead man, describing his life, saying he had been a good person and a hard worker, and anyone who was good and worked hard would deserve a place in the glorious hereafter of the skies.

Then came something he called the Rite of Unction. The archdeacon signalled to Deacon Shatterlonger, and the latter turned and opened the closet door.

Az looked up blearily, expecting Shatterlonger to catch sight of him and let out a yell of surprise.

In the event, the Deacon didn't spot him on the floor of the closet, half-obscured by the hanging robes. Instead, intent on his task, he removed a bottle from the shelf and shut the door.

As before, the catch didn't hold and the door swung silently ajar.

Archdeacon Corbelgilt took the bottle, which was small and made of frosted glass. He unstoppered it and poured a quantity of oil into his cupped hand. He drizzled this over the dead man's chest in a pattern – an arrow shape, Az thought – at the same time uttering some phrases about 'fragrant smoke' that would 'transport the body to its new and better incarnation' and be 'favourable to the noses of those whose company the deceased is to join'.

In the meantime, Deacon Shatterlonger slid open the portal in the wall, exposing a chute. Distantly Az heard a sound like an immense fire.

Furnace, he thought.

Then there was singing. The archdeacon led the mourners in a cyclical, lugubrious melody, the lyrics of which reiterated much of what he had already said. Each verse ended with the lines:

> This is our one intention —
> To rise in true Ascension

The song concluded, and a solemn Deacon Shatterlonger took hold of the gurney and rolled it over to the chute. He undid a latch and, with the archdeacon's assistance, raised one end of the gurney's top section. It came up on a hinge until it reached a steep enough angle, whereupon the dead man slid off, disappearing down into the chute head first, feathers and all

As the body vanished, the man's widow let out a despairing wail and sagged. If not for the relatives on either side of her, she would have collapsed.

The gurney was restored to its original position. The portal was closed. Archdeacon Corbelgilt then announced that, before he gave everyone his blessing to depart, he had something to say concerning the current 'undesirable industrial situation'.

This would have marked the beginning of his rousing sermon, if Deacon Shatterlonger hadn't at that moment reopened the closet door to return the bottle of oil to the shelf.

Unlike before, this time the Deacon *did* spot Az.

The cry of surprise he let out was girlishly high-pitched, and was accompanied by a crashing and a splattering as the bottle of oil slipped from his fingers and shattered on the floor, releasing a cloyingly pungent reek.

'What is it?' Archdeacon Corbelgilt snapped.

Deacon Shatterlonger didn't have a chance to reply. Az, summoning all the strength and speed he could muster, leapt from his hiding place, darted around the Deacon's legs, and made for the exit. He veered between the startled mourners, while behind him Archdeacon Corbelgilt shouted, 'Who is that boy? What was he doing in there? Stop him! *Stop him!*'

Az hurled himself through the double doors and dashed off along the passageway.

He didn't know which direction to go in. He couldn't think straight. His only thought was: *escape.*

He ran.

Along red-lit passageway after red-lit passageway.

Ran and ran.

Hoping he was headed towards the elevators.

Ran and ran and ran.

CHAPTER 22

In The Shadow Zone

Den Grubdollar's voice crackled through the speaker tube.

'Bless my bum, Cassie! You'm asleep up there, girl?'

Cassie's head twitched and she straightened up in her seat. Not asleep, no, but she had fallen into a daze. It had been a long, hard outing, and she'd spent all of it at the controls of the murk-comber. She was exhausted.

She snatched the speaker tube off its hook to reply: 'Wide awake and grinning, Da.'

'Then hit full floods. It'm nearly duskfall, in case you hadn't noticed.'

'Hitting full floods, straight up.'

Cassie reached above her head and clicked a series of switches. Outside, the Shadow Zone was in gloom – not the usual gloom but the deeper, denser gloom that showed the day was nearly done. With each switch she threw, a floodlight on *Cackling Bertha*'s hull came on, injecting a cone of yellow brilliance into the greyness. Through the windscreen well-defined shapes appeared, their outlines flat like stage scenery. Here, a gnarled, stunted tree. There, an outcrop of rock. Cassie could no longer see as far as she could with her naked eye, but everything in the immediate vicinity of the murk-comber was much more clearly visible.

The floodlights put an extra demand on *Cackling Bertha*'s batteries, and her engine automatically stepped up its output to compensate. The noise she made went from a throaty chugging to a higher pitch, from *hughh-hughh-hughh* to *hehh-hehh-hehh*. This pattern then began to break up, becoming irregular. A faulty drive piston, which no one had never been able to fix properly, threw the engine's timing out whenever there was a strain on the system.

All at once *Bertha* was making her signature sound, that wheezy, broken, choking rhythm that resembled an old woman's laugh.

Cassie sat back in the driving seat, comforted by what she was hearing. She had grown up with *Bertha*'s cackle. It was music to her. She had spent all her life near, on, or in the murk-comber. A foetus in the womb, listening to its mother's heartbeat, could not have been as soothed as Cassie was by the stuttering, on-off exclamation of glee that came from *Bertha*'s engine when under pressure. The massive, caterpillar-tracked vehicle beneath her seemed perpetually eager to work. There was nothing *Bertha* liked more than to have to make an effort.

Cassie grasped the dual control sticks and steered around the rock outcrop. Then she huffed into the speaker tube's mouthpiece and demanded a status update.

From their observation nacelles on each corner Cassie's family responded one after another, in order of seniority – first her father, then her brothers, Martin, Fletcher and Robert. Nothing to report. No bounty visible. It looked like they were going to return home empty-handed.

'Keep she steady, Cass,' Den warned. 'Ground gets soft round here. There'm boggy patches that could swallow we up without so much as a burp.'

'Don't worry, Da. Eyes is peeled like grapes.'

'Mind them is.'

Cassie stifled a huge yawn and blinked several times owlishly. Her stint at the controls had lasted nearly eight hours, the longest uninterrupted period of driving she had ever done. The effort of staying focused and alert for all that time was taking its toll on her, but she refused to give in and ask for a rest. One of her brothers would have gladly taken her place – but she was the best driver in the family. Her father said so. They all knew it. And there was no way she would give any of them an excuse to think otherwise. She had that special touch with *Bertha*. Maybe it was a female thing, all girls together.

The terrain ahead undulated. This was, as her father had just reminded her, one of the Shadow Zone's most treacherous regions. There were swamps that looked like solid ground – lakes of mud with a crusty, dried surface which would crack like an eggshell beneath the fifty-tonne weight of a murk-comber. It was said that the swamps could be up to two kilometres deep, but this was highly unlikely. Fifteen metres was nearer the truth. Even so, *Cackling Bertha* would still disappear without a trace in fifteen metres of mud, and the Grubdollar family with her. Cassie could not afford to lose concentration.

It was a mark of the family's desperation that they were in the area at all. But after several days on the trot without so much as a glimpse of an item of salvage, the Grubdollars had to go where few others of their kind would dare. Murkcombers didn't run on thin air, and neither did the people who owned and operated them. The Grubdollars needed money – for fuel, for food – and when the pickings got as slim as they had recently, that meant taking risks.

In the distance Cassie spied the lights of the Chancel, where all salvage went to, if salvage could be found. The Deacons paid well but only for results. They didn't extend credit. If you failed to come up with the Relics they were after, you didn't receive a penny.

She entertained some very uncharitable thoughts about the Deacons, and about Archdeacon Corbelgilt in particular. Cassie wasn't a Humanist herself, far from it, but she could see that the Humanists had a point. For all these centuries the Deacons had held sway over everyone. Tucked up in their Chancels, they were keepers of the key to the next life. They had used and abused that position. They were rich and powerful, and jealously guarded their wealth and their dominance. You couldn't—

Bertha gave a sudden, sickening lurch to the left. Cassie, with a curse, slid the control sticks into neutral, and the murk-comber halted. What had she been thinking? She had let her attention drift. Idiot!

'What were that?' said her father. 'Cass?'

Not answering, Cassie peered out. She couldn't tell if *Bertha* had run into a soft patch or just a ditch of some sort. The ground look pretty firm. She hoped—

Bertha lurched again, and Cassie knew her hope was in vain. A soft patch! Swamp!

Immediately, she slammed both control sticks into reverse. It was an instinctive reaction but, as it happened, the wrong thing to do. *Bertha* let out a steep roar and Cassie could feel through the left-hand stick that the track on that side was not gripping. A jet of mud squirting forwards into her line of vision confirmed it. *Bertha* slewed round clockwise, her right-hand track propelling by itself, the left one useless.

Cassie thrust both sticks into neutral and *Bertha* stopped turning.

For a moment nothing happened. Then, with an almighty *gloop* from outside, *Bertha* began to list to the left. She was side-on to the swamp, half in it, half out. And she was starting to sink.

Panic seized Cassie. She shot a glance at the roll meter mounted on the dashboard – a ball, marked off in five-degree increments, housed in a water-filled glass globe. It was reading 10° off the lateral plane. 15° now.

Bertha was going down, tipping to the left with steady, ponderous inexorability. It wouldn't be long before she overbalanced and rolled onto her side, or perhaps even further than that, onto her roof. And it was happening too quickly for the family to evacuate. If *Bertha* went under, the Grubdollars would go under with her, and then all that would be left for them to do was wait as the mud oozed in through chinks in her bodywork. Wait to drown, if they didn't suffocate first.

Cassie heard Robert yelling, 'Do something, sis! Get we out of here!'

But Cassie didn't know what to do. She could only stare helplessly at the roll meter, while leaning rightwards in her seat to stay vertical. The roll meter was reading 20°, edging towards 25. All her brothers were shouting into their speaker tubes.

'Shut up, you lot!' their father ordered.

They shut up.

'Cass,' said Den Grubdollar.

'Da.'

'Listen to I. Listen to my voice. Keep cool. Focus. Us doesn't have traction on the left but us still does on the right. Use that.'

'How?'

'Go forwards with the right track, reverse the left.'

'But that'll spin *Bertha* back the way she came and us'll just end up nose-first in the—'

'Not if us is lucky. There might be enough grip on the left to push we halfway clear, and then, at the crucial moment, when I tell you, you hit both sticks full into reverse. Got it?'

'All right, Da. I'll try.'

'Good girl. You can do this.'

Cassie manipulated the sticks as advised. *Bertha* responded with a gutsy rumble and began to pivot round anticlockwise. It was slow, slippery going. *Bertha* slithered constantly, shuddered, threw up a huge splattering plume of mud ... but gradually she was hauling herself out of the swamp, her left track digging into increasingly solid ground.

'Come on, good lady,' Cassie murmured, 'my dear, my lovely, come on, come on, come *on*.'

Then, abruptly, *Bertha* was free of the mud, both tracks in full contact with terra firma – and straight away she began to rotate into the swamp again, this time angling her right flank towards it.

'Now, Cass!' shouted her father.

Cassie thrust both sticks against her knees and *Bertha* skidded backwards, fishtailing like crazy, then gained traction, reversing smoothly. Cassie watched the swamp recede into the distance, its churned-up edge already flattening out, soon to form a fresh dry crust and pose a hazard to the unwary once again. She braked only when she had put several hundred metres between it and *Bertha*. Then she sat and took several big, deep breaths to calm her racing heartbeat.

Her brothers started jabbering, all three of them at once, veering between relief and rage.

Den told them to be quiet, then asked his daughter how she was doing.

'I be fine,' Cassie replied.

'Good. It were a near thing but you came through.' The praise was cautious and reserved. Cassie knew she would be in for a stern talking-to later, but for now her father simply wanted his children to understand that the crisis was past and they were safe and sound. 'Maybe you'm done enough driving for one day, girl. Martin and you swap places.'

With mixed feelings Cassie vacated the driver's pod and elbowed through the murk-comber's crawl-ducts to the rear right observation nacelle. She met Martin coming the other way. All he did was give her a sarcastic wink as he squeezed past.

The wink said that none of her brothers was going to let her forget this. They'd be ragging her about it for some while. She probably wasn't going to be allowed to drive again for some while, either.

She resigned herself to that.

'Head for town, Mart,' said Den, with a sigh. 'Let's call off today as a bad job.'

Martin brought *Bertha* around and started homeward at a stately trundle.

Cassie, glum in her observation nacelle, stared dully at the retreating landscape. Not even *Bertha*'s cackle could console her at this moment.

That was when she saw him.

Flickering into and out of the beam of a floodlight.

A boy.

At first she thought she had imagined him. Must have.

But there he was again, further away now, running in a line perpendicular to *Bertha*'s course. And then Cassie spotted a series of pale, skulking shapes loping along after him, a couple of hundred paces behind.

Verms. Verms on the hunt.

'Da,' Cassie said into the speaker tube, urgently. 'Da, us has to stop. There be someone out there, and him's in trouble.'

CHAPTER 23

Verm Attack

What they actually were, verms, remained open to debate. The creatures they most resembled were rats – large, hairless rats with puckered little slits where there had once been eyes, till nature decided these were surplus to requirements. At the same time, they grunted like pigs and worked in packs like dogs. Their blindness, and the fact that they lived in underground burrows, made everyone think they must somehow be related to moles. Their large, semi-translucent ears suggested there was bat somewhere in their family tree.

It could be that they were some ghastly hybrid of all these species, misbegotten things, grotesque evolutionary fusions.

Whatever their origin and ancestry, though, verms were uniquely suited to life in the Shadow Zones. They didn't require light to see by, they thrived in dirt and sogginess, and they were very unchoosy about what they ate. In fact, when there was no other source of food available, quite often they ate each other.

Of all the many hazards you might encounter in a Shadow Zone, a pack of hungry verms was by far the worst. They mostly stayed clear of the main roads to the Chancels because the noise of traffic hurt their sensitive ears. But step off the road, venture out onto the open plain, travel across a Shadow Zone on foot, alone, without the protection of a murk-comber around you – you were asking to become verm dinner.

As, it seemed, this boy was.

To Cassie, now ensconced in one of the front observation nacelles, the boy didn't even realise he was being stalked. Nor did he understand that *Cackling Bertha* was a potential source of safety. He was blundering and stumbling heedlessly along, while the verms were gaining on him with every second. If he had known they were on his trail, he would surely have been running. Not that anyone could outrun verms once those creatures accelerated to top speed.

Martin had spun *Bertha* around and locked her on a course that would intersect with the boy's, as long as the boy kept going in a straight line. Robert and Fletcher, meanwhile, were down in the loading bay, kitting themselves out in retrieval suits. Cassie wanted to do something more than simply sit there like a useless lump, so she clambered back through

68

the murk-comber and hauled herself up into the roof turret, where she found her father hunched at the controls of the javelin launcher. He had the verms in his sights and was swivelling the barrel of the launcher in order to keep them there. His thumb was over the trigger, but he would take the shot only if he had to. Javelins were expensive and the Grubdollars couldn't afford to deploy one unless it was absolutely necessary.

'What be him up to anyway?' Den said, glancing over his shoulder at Cassie. 'Out taking a nice evening stroll?'

'How should I know, Da?'

They both heard Martin let out a hiss of exasperation. 'Him's only gone and turned the wrong way. Back here, you bugger! *Towards* we, not away!'

The boy had veered off to the side, having suddenly noticed *Bertha*'s approach and taken fright. The verms, sensing his panic, picked up their pace. Ordinarily they would have been scared off by a murk-comber coming so close to them, but bloodlust overrode their natural caution. They were thinking about their prey, nothing else.

Cassie could hear them even above *Bertha*'s engine. The verms were squealing and yipping in their excitement. There were at least two dozen of them and they moved flowingly, the whole pack operating like a single organism, twenty-odd animals thinking as one. Now they were mere metres from the boy, and they broke into a sprint, a last burst of speed before the fatal pounce.

'Da ...'

'I know, Cass.'

Den took careful aim and fired. The javelin sailed straight and true, spearing the verm who was running at the head of the pack. The creature somersaulted forwards and tried to get up, but the javelin had impaled it through the ribcage, the barbed tip poking clean out the other side. The verm was already dead, it just didn't realise yet. It snapped its jaws uselessly at the protruding haft of the javelin, then rolled over and lay still.

The effect on the other verms was instantaneous. They swarmed around the corpse of their fallen packmate and began devouring. The boy was temporarily forgotten. The verms had been distracted by the scent of blood from a fresh kill.

'That should hold they,' said Den, 'for a bit.'

Cassie, without needing to be asked, selected a new javelin from the rack behind her and slotted it into the groove of the launcher, while her father primed the air-pressure pump for the next shot.

With the verms otherwise engaged for now, Martin was able to put *Bertha* between them and the boy, using her bulk to block him from their view. By this time Robert and Fletcher were ready. The loading bay hatch went up with a clang and they emerged from the murk-comber's belly in their padded retrieval suits, with their helmets and their chainmail gloves on. They made for the boy as quickly as the cumbersome suits would allow, wading through the air like it was water. As they caught up with him, he turned and stared, apparently unable to comprehend who or what they were. Then, just like that, he keeled over. Fletcher caught him before he hit the ground, hoisted him over his shoulder, and began lugging him back to *Bertha*.

Cassie checked on the verm situation and was appalled to see that they had finished feasting and were on the prowl again. All that was left of their dead packmate was a few bloodied bones and some twists of intestine. With gore-smeared chops the verms picked their way anxiously towards *Cackling Bertha*. Their snouts were up and sniffing. They were back on the boy's scent.

'Dammit, look at that,' said Cassie's father. 'Them's gone separate ways.'

Some unguessable instinct had prompted the pack to split into two and go around *Bertha*. They were still keeping a wary distance from the murkcomber but they were close enough to make a clean shot difficult. The angle from the roof turret to them was too steep.

'Electrify *Bertha*'s hull?' Cassie suggested.

'Thought of that,' said her father, 'but them'd have to be a whole lot nearer. Touching her, in fact. Nope, there be nothing else for it now. It'm up to those two lads. Them needs to get a wiggle on.'

Robert and Fletcher were certainly heading for the murk- comber as fast as they could. They knew they were in danger, but perhaps not how much danger. They certainly had no idea the verms would be coming at them from two directions at once.

Cassie had an urge to hammer on the glass of the roof turret and yell at her brothers to hurry up. With their helmets on, however, they would never hear her. They probably wouldn't see her either, since the helmet visors gave them such a restricted view.

There must be *something* she could do.

Decisively, she spun round and hurled herself down the ladder that led from the turret to the loading bay. Above, her father shouted, 'Cass, where'm you off to? No!' But it was too late. Sliding down the uprights rather than using the rungs, she reached the foot of the ladder in an instant. Crossing the loading bay, she grabbed the first pair of chainmail gloves she could find and shoved them on. Then she headed for the open hatchway, just as Robert and Fletcher came staggering up to *Bertha*'s side.

The dank, foetid stink of the Shadow Zone filled her nostrils as she leapt to the ground.

'Cass!' Robert cried, voice muffled by the helmet. 'What'm you doing? Get back inside!'

'The verms!' she replied. 'Them's going to—'

All at once, her warning was redundant. The divided verm pack appeared, half of them to the front of *Bertha*, half to the rear. With a rush the two half packs converged on the group of humans at *Bertha*'s flank, yelping with ravenous glee.

Robert lunged for the loading bay, Fletcher following with the boy.

Then Fletcher tripped. His foot struck a rock and he crashed to one knee. The boy tumbled from his arms.

Fletcher was back on both feet almost straight away. The brief hiatus, however, nearly cost him his life. He bent over to scoop up the boy, unaware that there was a verm just a metre or so away from him. The creature's hindquarters were coiled. It was tensed to jump.

And jump it did. It sprang at Fletcher's neck, jaws wide, fangs bared, and would have torn his throat out ...

... had Cassie not thrust a chainmailed fist in the way.

The verm clamped its mouth shut on her hand. The pressure was immense. Her hand was bring crushed. She could feel the small bones in there grinding together. The verm was hanging off her arm by its teeth, gnawing at the chainmail, desperate to bite through. It was grunting with effort and frustration. Grey slobber leaked from its mouth onto the glove. The stench of its breath! Like rotten meat and rancid vegetables and wounds gone gangrenous.

Cassie was repulsed, nauseated. She had to get the verm off her any way she could. She shook her arm violently, but the verm held fast. She punched the side of its skull with her other fist. That nearly did the trick. The verm yowled in protest, but still would not budge.

Nothing else for it.

Cassie jabbed a rigid index finger into its ear.

The verm quivered in agony. Cassie dug her finger further in. The verm shrieked in pain and indignation. Hooking the finger, Cassie wormed it around in the creature's ear canal, using the chainmail to scrape and scour the delicate inner tissues.

At last the verm let go, falling to the ground and writhing there, helpless with agony. Blood was streaming out of its ear. Blood was also dripping from Cassie's finger, along with scraps of flesh. Fighting her disgust, she looked up. Her struggle with the verm had lasted just a handful of seconds, although it had seemed much longer. Robert was leaning out of the loading bay and Fletcher was passing the boy to him. Fletcher then leapt aboard *Bertha* and stretched out a hand to Cassie.

'Come on, Cass. Quick!'

Cassie took a couple of steps towards him. Then her father appeared in the hatchway, brandishing a javelin.

'Duck,' he said, in a tone of voice that didn't expect her to disobey.

She didn't. She ducked.

The javelin shot over her head, and she heard a shrill howl behind her.

She didn't look round. There had been a verm at her back, about to attack. Now it was an ex-verm. Good. She leapt for the hatchway. Robert and Fletcher grabbed her wrists and she went flying into the loading bay, crash-landing on her chest. There was a huge, resounding *clunk* as the hatch came down. This was followed by a series of slobbering, snacking sounds from outside as the verms turned on another dead packmate, as before, and feasted.

'Be you OK, kids?' Den asked.

Robert, Fletcher and Cassie all announced that they were fine.

'Cass,' said Fletcher, 'I owes you one. Thanks, girl. That verm'd've had me, straight up, if not for you.'

Nodding, Cassie removed the gloves and began massaging her mauled hand. It ached and was reddened in that way that promised bruises later. But that didn't matter. What mattered was that she had saved Fletcher's life. By doing so, she also felt she had redeemed herself after nearly killing the whole family earlier. Her father, at any rate, was looking at her forgivingly – as forgivingly as someone with Den's craggy, grizzled features could. He was perhaps even proud of her, although he was never the kind of man to say such a thing.

He grabbed a nearby speaker tube. 'Martin? Us is all aboard, safe and sound. Let's go.'

As *Bertha* started to move, Den turned and peered at the boy. 'So who be this then, what'm caused us so much trouble?' He nudged the sprawled, unconscious body. 'Dead to the world. But breathing still. Wet through, too. Grab a blanket for he, will you, Cass? There'm a girl. Cover he up and keep he warm. Can't have the lad perishing of rattle-lung. And once us is back in Grimvale, us can look for somebody who might know who him be.'

CHAPTER 24

Waiting

In the administrative offices of the supply-arrival depot at Heliotropia, a clock ticked slowly. Distressingly slowly, as though seconds here took ten times as long to pass as they did anywhere else. Michael sat, stood up, paced, sat down again, went outside for a breath of air, came back in, sat, tapped his teeth with his fingernails, tried to amuse himself by reading documents on the supervisor's desk (till Mr Mordadson told him to stop it), spent a few minutes de-fluffing his wings, another few minutes picking at a loose bit of cuticle on his thumb, another few minutes thinking about work and the fuselage stress-fracturing problem that was giving the Aerodyne design team so much grief on the new model ...

None of it made the time go any more quickly. Michael, not a naturally patient person, hated waiting, and this wait was especially difficult. It was nearly eight o'clock. Az was due back around midnight. What if he didn't come back? How was Michael supposed to break the news to their parents? They hadn't a clue what Az was doing, why Lady Aanfieldsdaughter had wanted him. If it all went wrong, if Az failed to make it back, Michael would not only have to cope with that fact, but he would have to return to High Haven and explain everything, and then his mother and father would no doubt want to know how he could have let it happen, how he could let Az, his own brother, their only other son, travel down to the ground. They would be angry. They were likely to blame *him* rather than anyone else.

Aurora Jukarsdaughter intruded delicately on his thoughts. 'Maybe we should go and get something to eat. Michael?'

'Mmm?'

'Something to eat?'

'But—'

'Don't worry,' said Mr Mordadson. 'I'm not hungry. I'll stay here. You two go off.'

In a restaurant somewhere along one of Heliotropia's garish main avenues, beneath the flashing, cascading brilliance of a multiplicity of coloured lights, Michael shared a meal with Aurora. At any other time, under any other circumstances, he would have been overjoyed and would have been chatting her up for all he was worth. Now? He toyed with his food, and his conversation with the beautiful girl across the table was desultory at best.

Still, somehow he managed to glean a little bit about her. She was exceptionally intelligent, having graduated top of her year at Cloud 9 University, with honours. The Silver Sanctum had recruited her straight from there, and she was evidently on the fast track to the highest levels of government. Otherwise, why would she be Lady Aanfielsdaughter's personal assistant?

Next to her, Michael felt like an underachiever and a bit of a dimwit. After all, what as he? A test pilot, yes. And it was a glamorous occupation but it hardly required much use of your brain and it had a limited career span. You couldn't stick at it much past 35, when your reflexes started to slow. And then what? You were too young to retire and too old to start again from scratch. You were washed up. Weren't you?

'I think that's the first glimpse I've had of the real Michael Gabrielson,' Aurora said as he outlined these doubts and insecurities. Her smile was nothing short of dazzling. 'I think I like him. Much more than the Michael Gabrielson you normally present to the world.'

The remark buoyed Michael up considerably. He felt, at that moment, that he could have flown even if, like Az, he'd had no wings.

The recollection of his brother dampened his spirits again. Az, down there on the ground, alone ...

'Cheer up,' said Aurora, gently patting his hand. 'He's going to be fine.'

Some dreadful gut instinct, however, was telling Michael otherwise.

CHAPTER 25

Grimvale

Rain had set in by the time *Cackling Bertha* reached Grimvale – the kind of creeping, insidious rain that was going to last all night and probably well into the next day, rain that fell without hurrying, a humid seep from the sky.

In Grimvale Forest the boughs of the thin, scraggly pine trees sagged and dripped like the limbs of exhausted, sweaty labourers. *Bertha* trundled along an old, paved road, her track links clanking. The route took her past several lumberyards, and outside the entrance to each there was a Humanist picket. The Humanists didn't look very happy to be there in this weather. Gathered round blazing braziers, they stood with hunched backs, warming their hands. Some had waterproofs on, others had draped tarpaulins over their shoulders. By the light of the braziers Cassie saw eyes staring out from beneath hoods, aiming surly looks at the murk-comber. The Grubdollars were not breaking the goods embargo; they weren't transporting materials to the Chancel. They were, however, employed by the Deacons to scavenge in the Shadow Zone, and so in principle they weren't on the picketers' side.

Or so the picketers thought, till Martin hooted *Bertha's* horn in a show of solidarity. Then there were raised hands and clenched-fist salutes around the braziers, as the picketers saw that this wasn't just any old murk-comber but *Cackling Bertha*, and were reminded that at least one person aboard her was sympathetic to their cause.

Each time Martin hit the horn, Den shouted at him to pack it in. But Martin would not be stopped, and Fletcher backed him up, arguing that it was his right to support the picketers if he wished.

'This be a family after all, Da,' Fletcher said, 'not a dictatorship.'

'I'll dictate *you* in a minute,' their father growled. The threat didn't make any sense but it was menacing nonetheless. 'Straight up, if your ma were alive today to see two of her boys showing Humanist tendencies ...'

'Be'n't she alive, Da?' said Fletcher, as sarcastically as he dared. He wouldn't have been so bold if his father had been directly in front of him, rather than at the other end of a speaker tube. 'Be'n't she watching down on us from above the clouds as one of the Ascended Ones, in her new body, with her new wings?'

Whatever Den might have replied to that, was lost beneath another blast on *Bertha*'s horn. Now Martin was sending a friendly message to a picket outside a coalmine which stood on the fringes of Grimvale Township itself. In response he got a low, ragged cheer from the picketers.

A short while after that, the Grubdollars arrived home. The property consisted of a large courtyard where they could park *Bertha*, with just enough space on every side to allow maintenance and repairs to be carried out on her. Her loading bay hatch opened directly onto a raised concrete dock, which extended out from a storage area where tools and spare parts were kept and where, also, salvage was stockpiled before being taken to the Chancel.

While Robert closed the huge portcullis gate that secured the courtyard, Den carried the still unconscious boy across the dock. He took him up via a spiralling iron staircase into the family's living quarters, which surmounted the storage area, and there, in the lounge, stripped off the boy's damp clothes, leaving just his underpants on. He laid the boy's semi-naked form out on the creaky-springed couch and got Cassie to fetch a fresh, dry blanket for him. Then he spent several moments peering down at the youngster with a puzzled frown.

'It'm odd,' he said, scratching his stubble-covered chin. 'Him just doesn't look like him's from around here. Doesn't look rough enough around the edges, if you see what I mean. Delicate, kind of. And those clothes as well. Them's decent clothes, more decent than you usually see. Likely as not him's come from the Chancel or some such. But that still begs the question: what were him doing out in the Zone?'

'What about a doctor?' Cassie asked. 'Shouldn't us get him medical attention?'

'At this time of night? You'd be lucky. Besides, doctors costs money. If the lad takes a turn for the worse, then I'll think about it. But otherwise us can look after he, don't you think?'

Cassie didn't answer that. She had a feeling only one of the family would be doing any looking after, and it would be her.

'Now, how about some supper?' said her father. 'Can't speak for anyone else but I be famished.'

Cassie heated up some Last Chance Stew, which was an accumulation of leftover bits and pieces from previous meals that she couldn't afford to throw away and couldn't think of anything else to do with. Her verm-gnawed hand ached, so she had to do the work single-handed in more ways than one. She set bowls of the stew before her father and brothers at the kitchen table and watched them slurp it down so fast they barely seemed to taste it. They shovelled in mouthfuls of bread and butter at the same time, and glugged down pint-pots of beer. There was no conversation till the meal was finished and bellies were full, and then Martin broke the silence by letting out a long, resonant belch.

'Not bad,' he said, smacking his lips. 'Gets better with every warming, in fact. It'm got kind of a more *lived-in* flavour now.'

Cassie knew this was the nearest thing she would get to a compliment on her cooking. Mostly her family took her culinary efforts for granted. Never a word of thanks escaped their lips for the time she put in at the stove, although she was sure that if she served them up something truly disgusting they wouldn't hesitate to tell her what they thought about *that*.

'Now Fletch,' said her father, as he sat back, loosening his belt a notch, 'you happens to notice something about that lad next door when you was carrying he?'

Fletcher looked puzzled. 'What do you mean, Da?'

'Well, maybe it be as I don't knows my own strength, but it seems him don't weigh nearly almost anything.'

'Can't say as I were in a way to notice such a thing,' Fletcher said, 'on account of there were a pack of verms snapping at the seat of my trousers at the time. But now's you mention it . . . him weren't what you might calls heavy.'

'It be a mystery all right,' Martin said, although his tone of voice suggested it wasn't a mystery that intrigued him much. With a quick glance at Fletcher, he shoved back his chair and stood up. 'Da, OK if me'n Fletch heads off to the pub? I mean, if there'm nothing you needs us for . . .'

Den Grubollar's eyes went hard and narrow. 'The pub, eh?'

'Yeah, Da,' Fletcher said, standing too. 'Just for a pint or so, like.'

'Any particular pub in mind? You wouldn't be heading down to the Logger's Head, say, by any chance?'

Cassie watched her two brothers exchange a furtive look.

'Well, might be the Logger's Head, might not,' said Martin, airily. 'Can't say as us has decided.'

'Sounds to me like you has. And this'm be the Logger's Head where it just so happen them Humanists is holding a rally this evening?'

Again a furtive look, although both brothers were wearing guilty expressions now.

'Go on then,' their father said with an irritated growl. 'You be old enough to know your own minds, even if you be'n't old enough to know better. Them's a dangerous lot, them Humanists, I'll tell you that. Trying to upset the status quo, them are, and it'm be the ruin of us all if them succeeds. There'm a balance in the way things are. Be'n't perfect, but it be a balance nonetheless, and it'm lasted this long because it works. You go about upsetting that at your peril. But why listen to your old da?

What's *him* know about anything? Only raised you all on his tod, him did. Only ...'

Martin and Fletcher, by this point, were long gone. Den's voice trailed off as he acknowledged that he was delivering his lecture to a pair of empty chairs.

Cassie looked over at Robert, who had his head down and was subjecting the surface of the kitchen table to intense scrutiny. Neither of them knew what to say. Their father hated the fact that his two older sons had fallen under the Humanists' sway, and there had recently been some savage rows between him and them on the topic. He understood that the family was going to stay together only if Martin and Fletcher were allowed the freedom to pursue whatever political beliefs they wanted. Equally, those beliefs could end up tearing the Grubdollars apart anyway. Sooner or later Martin and Fletcher might come to the conclusion that murk-combing on the Chancel's behalf was not compatible with Humanism, and would refuse to carry on working in the family business.

So Den was in a no-win position, and that pained him.

'If their ma could see they ...' he said finally, with a sigh. And that was that. Subject closed.

For now.

CHAPTER 26

The Humanist Rally

'Half,' said Alan Steamarm. 'One half. One half of everything we dig out and chop down and drill for and smelt and refine. One half of it goes up in those elevators. One half of our worldly goods disappears into the clouds. And what for? What do we get in return?'

He paused, allowing the questions time to echo around the room. The rally was extremely well attended. The function room upstairs at the Logger's Head was packed, and there were people on the landing outside, craning their necks to get a view through the doorway. Not only that but there were people downstairs in the bar who hadn't been able to get up to the first floor at all. Steamarm planned to chat with them later, informally. He made a mental note: *next time, arrange a bigger venue.*

'I'll tell you what we get in return,' he said. 'Nothing. Absolutely nothing. Nothing but false hopes and empty promises. The Deacons tell us that making these sacrifices is the only way to guarantee our passage to the next life. They insist this is true. They've been insisting it since time immemorial. But then, they would, wouldn't they? They're no fools. Their position, their status, depends entirely on them being intermediaries between us and what's up there.'

He made a gesture that was a parody of a Deacon's blessing – hand held loosely open, a skyward flourish. It got a ripple of laughter, the audience marvelling at his nerve.

'And they make sure they get their cut from us. A tithe from us when we die. And in return for ten per cent of our savings, ten per cent of our worldly goods, plus a bodyweight's worth of supplies – in return for this *taxation*, there's no other word for it, this *taxation* – they carry out their mumbo-jumbo with the oil and the feathers, and up in smoke we go ... and then they go back to sitting snug and smug in their Chancels and laughing at us behind our backs. Mocking our gullibility. They can't believe we keep falling for it, and yet we do. We want to believe in a next life, we want to become Ascended Ones, we want to ensure this for ourselves and our kin, and that's what they take advantage of. That's how they've been exploiting us for centuries. Centuries! And do you know what I say?'

Steamarm raised his voice, and also a fist.

'I say, "No more!" I say, "Enough!" It's time we stopped letting them get away with it. It's time we kept everything that's ours for ourselves and stopped giving half of it away. The ones who are up there above the clouds – let them fend for themselves. Let them go without. I, for one, don't want to join them after I die, assuming that's what actually happens. Not if it means I buy my next life at the expense of people in *this* life. That's not fair. It's never been fair.'

The crowd were grumbling and chattering indignantly now. Steamarm had them in the palm of his hand. He could feel his rhetoric spreading through them, one to another, like a flame, firing up their resentment, igniting dormant grudges. It was a delicious sensation, this ability to motivate audiences, to rouse them to anger. Steamarm was becoming quite addicted to it.

'Brothers, sisters,' he said, bringing his speech to a conclusion, 'the hour is almost upon us. I've been touring the region, and I've been keeping in touch with my fellow Humanist leaders, and let me tell you, there's a groundswell building up. All across the Westward Territories, we're mobilising, and it won't be long before we're taking assertive action. Pickets are just the start. The next step is insurgency. I invite you, I *urge* you, to join me in the struggle. Together, united, we can overthrow the tyranny of the Deacons. We can expose their religious so-called orthodoxies for the lies they are. We can usher in a new age – a fairer, wealthier, more rational age. And we can all be happier and freer as a result. What's ours should be ours. That's the Humanist motto, the movement's call to arms. What's ours should be ours. Let's make that statement come true. Thank you.'

Tremendous applause followed, whistles and foot-stamps adding to the deafening din of handclaps. Steamarm accepted the ovation with a reluctant bow, as if he wasn't – OK, he *was* worthy of it. Before the applause could die down completely he made his exit, passing through the ranks of the audience. By the time he reached the door his back was sore from all the slaps it had received.

Downstairs, Steamarm mingled with the Humanist supporters who hadn't managed to attend the rally. There was no shortage of offers to buy him a drink, but as it happened, his beers were on the house tonight. The pub landlord was doing a roaring trade thanks to all the extra customers whom Steamarm's presence had attracted. The least he could do in exchange was give Steamarm free booze.

Steamarm was accosted by a couple of young men, brothers, who introduced themselves as Martin and Fletcher Grubdollar and said how sorry they were that they hadn't got the chance to hear him speak upstairs. They'd arrived at the pub too late. They wanted him to know, however, that they were ardent Humanists. They said they felt that in this day and age there was no worthier cause a person could follow.

'Us deals with them Deacons on a daily basis pretty much,' said Martin. 'Right bunch of stuck-up ponces them is, too. It'm like, sometimes you gets the feeling them's doing we a favour just speaking to we.'

'Wouldn't mind seeing that lot out of a job,' added Fletcher, 'even if it means us is out of a job too. Us can always find something else to do. It'm the principle of the thing, be'n't it?

'You work in transportation, then? You'm ferrying stuff to the Chancels?' Steamarm wasn't ordinarily the sort to use grammar like *you'm*, but he had learned long ago the value of careful mimickry. In one-to-one conversations people responded well if you met them at their own verbal level.

'Nope, not transportation,' said Martin. 'Murk-combing.'

'Really?' All at once the two Grubdollar brothers had Steamarm's undivided attention. He wasn't just making polite chitchat with them any more. 'That's a tough business to be in, straight up. Those Shadow Zones are pretty perilous places.'

Fletcher gave a manful shrug. 'Hard work but it pay the bills.'

'You must be fascinated by some of the items you retrieve. Pieces of machinery, detritus from above ...'

'Relics, as the Deacons calls it.'

'Indeed.'

'It'm fallen a long, long way. Most of it gets mashed up on impact. But still, us has seen some strange bits and bobs, hasn't us, Fletch? Like, pages from books. Shoes. A saucepan.'

'Pair of lady's undergarments,' said Fletcher. He and Martin sniggered at the recollection.

'And perhaps a body or two?'

'That us has, Alan. By the way, I can call you Alan?'

'Of course you can, Fletcher.'

'Yes, us has retrieved bodies,' Fletcher went on, 'although there never be much left by the time us finds they. Verms has gnashed most of the tasty parts. But the Deacons pays top whack even for a broke-up skeleton. Then there was that time us hauled part of a car, or something like, out of a soft patch.'

'Some kind of flying vehicle, it were,' Martin chipped in. 'Got a tidy little sum for that, us did.'

'So it'm a funny old game, murk-combing, but us likes it enough. Though not so much as us couldn't live without it.'

'It doesn't trouble you, then,' said Steamarm, 'that we live in a world where objects fall out of the sky on us and we're supposed to treat them as holy artefacts?'

'Earns we a wage, them objects,' said Martin. 'But now you mention it, yeah, it do trouble we. Which is why us is all for Humanism. You know, because why should us have to put up with being the underlings? The underclass? Them's what gives so much and gets back the privilege of living in' – he searched for the right word – 'somebody else's trash bin?'

'I couldn't have put it better myself. "The privilege of living in somebody else's trash bin." I shall use that phrase in a future speech, Martin. Thank you.'

Martin preened with pride.

'So you own your own murk-comber, I take it.'

'Yes. Well, sort of. It'm our da's, and it were his da's before him. But us all works with it, the whole family, so I suppose you could say it belongs to all of we.'

'That's good, that's good.' Steamarm was studying both brothers with avid interest now. 'Boys, how are you off for drinks? You seem thirsty. Let me get you something. And then I think us needs to talk, us three. Us needs to sit down in a quiet corner and have a good long chinwag ...'

CHAPTER 27

Housebound

Cassie wasn't sure why she volunteered to watch over the boy. She was bone-weary and her nice, warm bed was calling to her. It seemed like the right thing to do, however. If the boy came round in the middle of the night, in a place that was unfamiliar to him, it would help if there was a friendly face beside him. She realised, too, that if she didn't play nursemaid, nobody else was going to.

She drew up an armchair next to the couch, huddled under a blanket, and promptly fell asleep.

She was roused, briefly, by Martin and Fletcher returning home in the small hours. They were drunk, to judge by the way they yelled at each other while clearly under the impression that they were whispering.

She sank into sleep once more, assuring herself that if the boy woke up, she would sense it and wake up too.

Then: daybreak. Outside the lounge window the sky was brightening to its customary hazy grey pallor. It was still raining. Droplets rattled softly against the panes. Cassie hauled herself from the chair and stretched various kinks and knots out of her body. She flexed her injured hand and found that it was in better shape than she'd expected. Overnight, bruising had formed, U-shaped purple patches on the back and palm denoting the pattern of the verm's teeth, but the hand was functional and didn't ache too badly any more.

The boy remained comatose. Cassie prepared toast and tea for everybody, and there was the usual groggy breakfast around the kitchen table. Martin and Fletcher were obviously hung-over, and their father commented on this, saying he hoped they were feeling rotten because they deserved to. Neither of them could muster a comeback, but Cassie did catch Martin firing a surreptitious grin at Fletcher, which Fletcher returned. She said nothing, but it was clear the two brothers were sharing some kind of secret.

'What be us up to today?' she asked her father. 'Off into the Zone again?'

He nodded yes. 'Got to keep trying. Our luck'll surely turn soon. Except that you, girl, be'n't coming with we. You be staying at home today.'

'What!' Cassie couldn't believe her ears.

Her father jerked his head in the direction of the lounge. 'Someone has to keep an eye on that boy till him recovers. You'm best qualified for the job.'

'But – but—'

'Going to leave he to the tender mercies of one of your brothers, eh? Don't think so. Sorry, lass, no arguments. You be staying and that be final.'

Cassie bristled at the injustice of this. She couldn't help but think she was being punished in some way for the near-disaster yesterday.

Her sense of outrage was not at all lessened by Fletcher saying, with a smirk, 'Better you in charge of he than in charge of *Bertha*.'

'Yeah,' Martin chimed in, 'though likely as not you'll kill he just like you nearly killed *we*.'

'Buggers! Buggers the lot of you!' Cassie yelled, and stormed out of the room.

After *Bertha* left with the four male Grubdollars aboard, Cassie sulked in her bedroom, refusing to pay attention to the boy. Since he was the source of all her woes, she got a petty satisfaction out of ignoring him. But eventually the novelty of sulking wore off, so she went round the house tidying up and putting away. The only rooms she left untouched were her brothers'. Being young men, they appeared to enjoy living in squalor, surrounded by a knee-deep debris of unwashed socks, dirty teacups, and worse. Every so often one of them would complain about his own mess, as though it was someone else's fault. Seldom did the complaint lead to positive action, however.

Her father was a different story. Cassie didn't mind cleaning up after him. Not only did he at least make some effort to keep his room in order, but as a widower there was a helplessness about him when it came to domestic matters. The wife who should have been looking after him was not around to do so any more, and Cassie could tell that he still missed her, even after twelve years. In so many ways he missed her.

While she was straightening the counterpane on her father's bed, Cassie's gaze fell on the framed picture of her mother that sat on the dressing table. It was a mezzotint etching which had been commissioned by her mother's parents, Cassie's grandparents, as a gift to her on her twenty-first birthday.

Orla Grubdollar had been a very pretty woman. Not beautiful, but she had a kindly face and a mischievous twinkle in her eyes, which the artist had skilfully captured. It was often remarked how like her Cassie looked, but Cassie couldn't see the resemblance herself. Mirrors showed her a slightly chunky girl, round-faced, with a tendency to frown and with a crop of wayward hair that didn't fall in an elegant sweep like her mother's in the picture. She would have liked to look like her mother but doubted she did or ever would.

Rattle-lung had taken Cassie's mother when Cassie was just three years old. Within a week of contracting the disease, Orla Grubdollar was dead. Cassie could remember nothing about this, and very little about her mother in general. She had no visual memories of her to fall back on, just a collection of faint, non-visual impressions. A voice, trilling a song. A certain fragrance. The enfolding embrace of two warm arms. And the only reason she even knew that these were impressions of her mother was because whenever she thought about them she felt a deep, sharp pang of yearning. If not for that, she would have assumed they were things her imagination had conjured up to fill the space where her mother should have been.

For better, for worse, Cassie was the mother in this family now ...

A creak of couch springs roused her from her reverie.

The boy was lying in the lounge with his eyes wide open, staring around. How long he had been like this, awake, Cassie had no way of knowing.

She stifled her resentment of him just enough to sound civil. 'Oh, hello there. Hungry?'

The boy frowned, puzzled. He let out a cracked, dry sound from his throat. Some kind of question, but Cassie couldn't make sense of it.

The boy tried to frame the question again, but it was no good. He was too hoarse.

'Thirsty?' Cassie asked.

He managed a nod.

She brought him a glass of water and tipped it up to his lips.

'Just sips,' she said, but the boy seized the glass and gulped the whole lot down.

Next thing Cassie knew, he was puking on the floor.

'I said just sips,' she sighed, and went to fetch a cloth.

By the time she got back, he had lapsed into insensibility again. She mopped up the vomit, glowering at him all the while.

A little later, he came to again, and she tried him with the water again. This time he sipped, as instructed, and was able to hold it down. She reheated what remained of the Last Chance Stew and fed him a few spoonfuls. This, too, he held down. She didn't try to engage him in conversation; it seemed he hadn't the energy for that yet, and she had no great urge to chat with him anyway. She concentrated solely on helping him get his strength back. The sooner he recovered, the sooner he would be out of the house and not her problem any more. Then life could return to normal. The boy was an imposition and she wanted him gone.

He slept once more. It was midday, and by now Cassie was beginning to get a little stir-crazy, so much so that she decided to launder the boy's damp clothing, just for a distraction.

As she rinsed out his shirt in the sink, she remembered her father's remark about the boy's clothes. 'More decent than you usually see,' he had said, and he was right. The stitching on the shirt was finer than any Cassie had ever beheld, and the cloth it was made from was glossily smooth and had a good, tight weave. The clothes which she and her family and everyone she knew wore were much coarser. Only someone with money could afford a shirt like this, which gave credibility to her father's assumption that the boy came from the Chancel. But there weren't children at the Chancel, were there? The youngest age at which a novice could join was twenty-one. The boy was a good half-decade shy of that.

She held the shirt up to the window to get a better look at it, and noticed something odd. In the back of it there were two long slits which had been sewn up, starting from where the shoulderblades sat and going almost the whole way down to the shirttail. The stitching there was not the same as everywhere else: it had been done with a different thread, and by hand rather than by machine.

Why would you alter a shirt this way?

No, that was the wrong question.

'Why would you *make* a shirt with two long slits in the back?'

Cassie asked herself the question aloud without realising it. She also answered it aloud.

And her answer stunned her, and at the same time raised a host of fresh questions.

'For wings,' she said. 'You'd make it like that to fit wings.'

CHAPTER 28

Genesis Of A Revelation

'*Somebody's* responsible for this!' snarled Michael. 'And I know who!'

'Calm yourself, Michael,' said Mr Mordadson. 'Please. There's no need to go flying off the handle.'

'No need? *No need?* Pluck you!'

Red-faced, wild-eyed, Michael lunged for the Silver Sanctum emissary. He couldn't see straight. He was blind with distress and anger.

With a flicker of his wings, Mr Mordadson darted out of Michael's way. As Michael hurtled past, Mr Mordadson grabbed his wrist and his wing root. *Flip, shove, thump* – Michael was on his belly on the floor, with Mr Mordadson on his back, holding him down. Michael squirmed, but the combination of arm-lock and wing-lock was unbeatable. For all that Mr Mordadson was slender and none too tall, he possessed a surprising strength and nimbleness.

'Combat and self-defence training,' he said to Michael. 'I was in the Alar Patrol before I joined the Sanctum. I have the hoop scars in my wings to prove it, in case you doubt me.'

'Let me up, you four-eyed bustard!' Michael snarled.

'I will if you promise to be a good boy and behave yourself. You're upset, and I quite understand why. Believe me, I'm as concerned about Azrael as you are.'

'Az is dead! He should have come back twelve hours ago, and he hasn't, and he's dead!' Tears sprang to Michael's eyes, and all at once he was sobbing helplessly, burying his face in the administrative office's carpet. 'My ... little brother ...'

'Michael,' said Aurora, kneeling beside him, 'no one meant for any of this to happen, but there were risks. Az knew that. We all knew that.'

'Easy for you to say ...'

'No, not easy, Michael. Not in the slightest. But still, it has to be said. And Michael ... there's something else.'

Mr Mordadson levelled his gaze at her. 'No, Aurora. I don't think we should tell him.'

'And I think we should. It's only fair.'

'Tell me what?' said Michael.

Aurora, still holding eye contact with Mr Mordadson, said, 'There's a very good chance Az isn't dead.'

'Huh?'

'It could be that he's been ... detained somehow.'

'Detained? What are you talking about, detained?'

'Mr Mordadson's going to release you, and you're going to sit down quietly, and I'm going to explain something to you. All right? And you're going to listen, that's all you're going to do. No histrionics. No fisticuffs. Do we have a deal, Michael?'

'... Yeah.'

Moments later, Michael was in a chair, rubbing the arm which Mr Mordadson had twisted behind his back, and Aurora was speaking to him, and what she had to say astonished him and dispelled the weariness of a sleepless, fretful night, and cut through his grief, and even gave him grounds to be slightly optimistic.

'There are Groundlings?' he said at the end. 'Still?'

'There are. There always have been. It's just been convenient for us to forget that fact.'

In hindsight, the revelation wasn't as shocking to Michael as it had first seemed. Somewhere deep down, on a subconscious level, he had known it all along. Yes, automation could account for the flow of supplies to the sky-cities. It *could*. It was plausible enough. But it didn't really stand up to scrutiny. Machines, unattended, left to themselves, couldn't do everything. They needed overseeing, maintenance, human involvement. As someone involved in aeronautics Michael understood that as well as anyone, if not better than most.

'So it's all just some lie we've been fed,' he said. 'A Silver Sanctum conspiracy. "The Groundlings died out." So that we don't have to think about them, don't have to remember all the time that there are people down there beneath the cloud cover ...' He shuddered. 'What can it be like down there? I can't imagine.'

'You're looking at it from the wrong perspective,' Aurora said. 'It isn't a conspiracy. It isn't a case of government influencing public feeling. It's a case of public feeling influencing government. What came first was the Airborn race gradually forgetting about the Groundlings. They slipped from our memory. Whether it was deliberate or not, we stopped being mindful of them.'

'Aurora used the word "convenient",' said Mr Mordadson, 'and that's it in a nutshell. It didn't sit well with people, thinking that there were other people slaving away on their behalf, down below in constant twilight, after the Great Cataclysm. So it became easier – preferable – *convenient* – to imagine that they weren't down there, to say it was machines doing the work and the people themselves had died out.'

'Life up here is wonderful,' Aurora said. 'We have everything we could need, and more. We have luxury. Perpetual sunshine. We work and play, sleep and love, blithely, almost without a care in the world.'

'The Airborn are happy,' said Mr Mordadson. 'We don't even wage wars any more. We seem to have progressed past that, finally. The last conflict between sky-cities was nearly half a century ago, wasn't it? And it was over in seven days and all but bloodless.'

'The Week's War.' Aurora and Mr Mordadson had fallen into a pattern of taking it in turns to speak. 'And there's been peace ever since.'

'And the Silver Sanctum's job is to make sure that state of affairs remains. But it's also to make sure that the Airborn continue their lives of, well, of blissful ignorance.'

'So, while the Sanctum doesn't actively promote the story that the Groundlings are extinct, it doesn't actively deny it either. It lets people continue to believe what they wish to believe. It allows the collective amnesia about the Groundlings to persist because there's nothing to be gained by dispelling it, nothing except distress and disharmony.'

'It's official now, of course. Places like the Museum of Arts, Sciences and History state as fact the myth that there are no more Groundlings, and their exhibits foster the impression of a backward race of beings, not quite sophisticated enough to survive. We choose to let this inaccuracy go uncorrected.'

'In fact, outside of the Sanctum itself, the continued existence of Groundlings is a complete secret.'

'But it's not a conspiracy,' said Mr Mordadson, reiterating Aurora's earlier remark. 'The term suggests a policy of actively hiding the truth, whereas its actually a policy of passively allowing the truth to fall into disuse. Not the same thing.'

'You see, Michael?' Aurora said. 'And now you're in on the secret, and now you understand why it's possible that Az is still alive.'

'The Groundlings,' Michael said, tonelessly. 'The Groundlings have him.'

'They may well do.'

'Well, what ... ? I mean, if they do, then ... then what can we do about it? Can we get him back?'

Suddenly he shot to his feet.

'The elevators!' he exclaimed. 'I'll go down and look for him.'

'No, Michael,' said Mr Mordadson.

'Just try and stop me.'

'Oh, I will if I have to.' The smile Mr Mordadson gave then was profoundly unnerving, not unlike the leer of a skull. 'And you know I can. I used minimum force to restrain you last time. You wouldn't want me to resort to maximum force. Trust me on that.'

Michael eyed him, weighing up the options. Male pride growled at him not to back down. Common sense, however, gently suggested that he would be wise to heed Mr Mordadson's warning.

'All right.' He resumed his seat. 'Why not, then? Why can't I go down?'

'Several reasons. First and foremost, you have wings. You'd stand out a mile. You'd perhaps make a target of yourself. Az's lack of wings is a sort of camouflage, enabling him to merge with his surroundings. He could pass for a Groundling, you could not. And we can't allow the Groundlings to know yet that we Airborn are interested in them and what they're up to.

'Because . . .'

'Because, Michael,' said Aurora, 'if you think about it, why are supplies being disrupted? If it isn't a mechanical breakdown . . .'

Michael made the leap of logic. 'It's the Groundlings. Doing it on purpose. They're angry.'

'Angry, and worse. Possibly mutinous. Possibly starting a rebellion.'

'Rebellion,' said Michael tonelessly.

'We spoke of war a short while ago,' Mr Mordadson said, 'and of our half-century of peace. We're very much afraid, at the Silver Sanctum, that that period may be about to come to an end. In the most devastating manner imaginable.'

CHAPTER 29

Flight

It all seemed like a dream, a sequence of events he had no control over and just had to go along with. At times it wasn't even a dream, more like a nightmare, and there was nothing he could do to snap himself out of it. A nightmare that was actually happening.

As he fled from the room where the Ceremony of Ascension was being held, Az's main impulse was to get back to the chamber with the elevators and jump aboard the first one that opened its doors to him.

He was disorientated, however. His brain felt clogged and muddled. He took a wrong turn. Several wrong turns, indeed. Next thing he knew, he was stumbling through a set of rooms that were sumptuously furnished and decorated. There were marble floors, rich red velvet curtains that hung in opulent swags and were trimmed with gold tassels, oil paintings in beautiful frames, gleamingly polished wooden chairs and tables, teak-cased mantel clocks that would have made his father's mouth water, and shelf upon shelf of leather-bound books. One room led to another, and each was grander than the last. Az found it hard to reconcile all this luxury with the functional, machinery-filled areas he had seen elsewhere in the building. It didn't make sense, having industry and elegance in such close proximity . . . did it?

By the time he reached a fourth room, it dawned on him that he wasn't getting any nearer to his destination going this way. He backtracked dazedly. Sometime later he was in a corridor and realised he had no memory of how and when he had got there. He must have faded out for a while and kept going through sheer instinct alone. There was a vibrant hissing sound in his ears. He couldn't tell if it was real or imagined, coming from outside him or within. His vision was filled with blotches of light that swelled and popped like soap bubbles. At the back of his skull a low ache had set in.

'There! There he is!'

The voice that barked these words belonged to one of the two men from the ceremony, the thinner one, Deacon Shatterlonger. Accompanying him were two more Deacons. Shatterlonger was pointing, straight-armed, at Az.

'Stop right there, whoever you are. The Archdeacon would like a word with you. Why were you eavesdropping on us? How did you get in here?'

Az began backing away. He didn't fancy having 'a word' with Archdeacon Corbelgilt. Not in the slightest.

'I told you to stop!' Shatterlonger motioned to the other two Deacons. 'Well, go on. What are you waiting for? Get him.'

The two Deacons moved towards Az. They were neither of them especially big men but their robes lent them a sinister, crow-like look, and they strode with menacing purpose.

Az turned and . . .

Another fadeout. He was on a raised steel catwalk. That hissing sound from earlier was now a surging. On either side of him were arrays of huge sealed metal vats, each with the words SEWAGE TREATMENT painted on the side in bold capitals amid streaks of rust. About three metres below him there was a brick channel, like a large half-drainpipe, through which a torrent of brownish water sluiced. He was aware of a rotten odour in the air, and dimly his brain deduced that this was where the waste-water downflow from Heliotropia ended up.

Then he realised that the three Deacons were closing in on him along the catwalk, Shatterlonger coming from one direction, his two colleagues from the other.

'Chase over,' said Shatterlonger, who was looking flustered. There were spots of bright pink in his sallow cheeks. 'We've got you now. Just come quietly. I swear no one means you any harm, boy.'

Az would have liked to believe this but somehow couldn't.

He was cornered. There was no escape route. Or was there?

He pictured himself clambering up onto the catwalk handrail.

No, that's crazy, don't do it.

He pictured himself swinging over and dangling off the other side, above the brick channel.

You don't know where it goes.

He pictured himself letting go and dropping.

It was only when he hit the water below that he realised he hadn't imagined this feat. He had actually done it.

The torrent snatched him like a fist and whisked him along with it, away from the Deacons. They shouted at him but he could barely hear above the liquid tumult engulfing him. He tumbled, sank, rose again, somersaulted, flailed, fought to keep his head above the surface, choking on the water's brackish stink, gasping as it sluiced sickeningly down his throat . . .

All at once everything went dark. The channel had become a tunnel, a full pipe. In the enclosed space the surging of the water took on a roaring echo. Az truly believed he was going to drown. He could no longer tell which way was up. He sped along helplessly in the torrent's clutches. Each time his arm happened to strike the side of the tunnel he grabbed out in the hope that there might be something to cling on to, but there was just brickwork. It was slippery-slimy and there were no fissures in it nor any projecting bits, nothing that might serve as a handhold.

The tunnel appeared to be angling downward, getting steeper; the torrent was getting faster.

Then Az was falling.

A huge *splash*, and he was underwater, completely immersed and plunging deeper and deeper, still being rolled this way and that by currents which seemed to take a cruel pleasure in toying with him. He kicked with his legs, lashed out with his arms ... and gradually the water relaxed its grip and stopped tossing him about. He rose as fast as he could, but not fast enough, it seemed. Air. He needed air.

He broke surface, and heaved in a lungful of air.

... fadeout ...

He was slogging through muddy shallows, wading up onto dry land. He could barely see a thing. The darkness around him was total. There was perhaps a vague distinction between the ground underfoot and the sky above – the latter marginally less black than the former.

The ground.

He registered that he was outdoors, down on the very ground itself, out in the world beneath the Airborn's world. But it was a fact he would have found difficult to digest even if he had been in good shape, and he was in anything but good shape. He had a pulsing headache, and somehow he couldn't catch his breath. He was soaked to the skin and starting to shiver with cold. All in all, just keeping walking was the most he could manage. He was down to the core of himself, a creature operating almost solely on instinct.

Walk. Move.

The ground had pebbles that rolled treacherously when trodden on. It had unexpected clefts and cracks that tripped you. It had roots that snagged at your ankles.

Where are you going?

No idea.

The ground had noises, too.

Footfalls. Like a crowd of people, running shoeless, softly. People ... or animals?

And a deep, reverberating rumble ... like someone chuckling very hard?

And sudden, sharp, blinding lights.

And creatures that looked like men but with thickset bodies and no faces. A pair of them, coming towards him, haloed by the fiercely bright lights. Creatures with metallic hands that reached out and—

Nothing.

Blankness.
Afloat.
Numb.
Voices.
Mumbling.
Silence.
Calm.
Soft.
Light.
Face.
Girl.
Speech.
Enquiry.
Water.
Sick.
Sleep.
Wake.
Girl.
Food.
Doze.
Awake.
Room.
Girl.
Girl talking.
Talking to him.
Girl in room, talking to him.
'Nice to see you again. Back with we. Who'm you be then?'

CHAPTER 30

Not A Very Good Spy

Az tried to clamber off the couch.

'Have to ... Have to go. Get to ...'

A wave of light-headedness washed over him and he sank back onto the cushions.

'Rest, be what you has to do,' said the girl, drawing the blanket up to his chin. 'Lay still and rest.'

'But—'

'But nothing. You'm in no fit state to go gallivanting about.'

Az acknowledged it with a feeble nod. 'What's wrong with me? I feel terrible. I've felt like this virtually since I ...' He was going to say *since I arrived in the elevator*, but amended it to: 'Since I don't know how long.' Lame, very lame.

'Well now,' said the girl, 'I be'n't no doctor, but it may have to do with you being out in the Shadow Zone, wandering around all soaked through. Recipe for catching rattle-lung, that be.'

Az struggled to make sense of what she was saying. Her dialect and thick accent weren't helping matters. 'Rattle-lung?'

'Everyone knows someone who knows someone who caught rattle-lung and died. You do, on account of you's met I.'

'Oh yeah, rattle-lung,' Az said, pretending he understood now. He added, 'I misheard, that's all. Thought you said something else.'

'Be the dampness, you see. The clammy air.'

'Yes. Obviously. And someone you know died of it?'

'My ma.'

'Oh, I'm sorry.'

'It'm all right. I weren't much more than a nipper. Don't hardly re-member she at all. So, you be having a name?'

'Hmmh?'

Az had been studying the girl. So this was what a proper Groundling looked and sounded like. Not one of those Deacons, who were clearly an elite – privileged members of the species. Here was the authentic version, the real deal.

She was brown-haired and dark-eyed, although her complexion was contrastingly pale, her skin so white that in places the veins showed through. She had a sturdy build, with strong arms and a chunky jawline. In spite of that she wasn't in any way unattractive. In fact she was rather pretty.

Her clothes were plain: a suede jerkin over a shirt made of some rough material, and a pair of leather trousers cross- stitched down the sides. (In that respect, at least, the curators at the Museum of Arts, Sciences and History had got their facts right. Groundlings did favour simple dress.)

Age-wise, Az put her at sixteen, same as him. She seemed far more forthright than the sixteen-year-old girls he was familiar with, however.. *Those* girls were all secrets and giggles, and made out they were more grown-up than they were. *This* girl didn't seem to have time for that sort of behaviour.

'A name. I asked what you'm being called. Come on, it be'n't a difficult question, surely.'

Az debated how much he could reveal without giving away that he was an Airborn spy. Probably it would be OK to tell her his name. There would be nothing suspicious about that. Besides, he was still too foggy and fuddled in the head to come up with a convincing alias.

'Az.'

The Groundling girl's forehead puckered into a frown. '"Ash", did you say?'

'No, Az. Az Gabrielson.'

She laughed. 'Az Gabrielson? What kind of name be that?'

Az offered a noncommittal shrug. 'It's the one I was given. And you're ...'

'Cassie Grubdollar.'

He couldn't keep his eyebrows from rising a centimetre or so. 'Well, you're one to talk. What kind of a name is Cassie Grubdollar?'

'Nothing wrong with it,' Cassie Grubdollar replied with a haughty glare. 'Be a good, traditional Westward Territories name, it be. Straight up.'

Az said, 'Well, anyway, now that we've established that we both have funny names ...'

'No, *you* does.'

'I'm trying to change the subject. You said you found me in ... the Shadow Zone?'

'Yup. Ambling around, you was, like some kind of sightseer or something. Didn't seem to realise you had a pack of verms on your tail.'

'Verms.' Az tried to make it appear as if he recognised the word, hoping Cassie would go on to explain it, unprompted. He didn't think he was making a very good job of this spying business. Then again, nobody had seen fit to inform him that there would be people down here and that he might have to concoct some sort of cover story for himself.

'Yes, verms. Me and my brothers, and our da, we saved you from they. You'd have been verm dinner if not for we.'

'Then I'm very grateful to you. Thanks.'

'And us has been looking after you ever since. Or rather, *I* has.'

'Again, thanks.'

A teasing note entered Cassie Grubdollar's voice. 'I's got to say, Az Gabrielson, you doesn't speak like someone what comes from round hereabouts.'

'Oh?'

'No, more like someone what comes from quite a ways away. And here's I, mentioning rattle-lung and verms and that, and there you be, looking just as like you never heard of such things.'

'I have. Honestly.'

'Don't lie. Want to know what I think? Actually, it be'n't what I *think* so much as what I *know*. *I know* what you be, Az Gabrielson, and where you be from.'

Az felt a peculiar blend of anxiety and relief. 'Really?'

'You be one of they.'

'One of . . .'

Cassie gestured upwards. 'They up there. The Ascended Ones. Although, why you's here and where your wings be – that'm a puzzle. A puzzle which maybe you wants to clear up for I, yes?'

CHAPTER 31

Not Such A Bad Spy After All

Az considered clamming up. It would certainly have been easier to do so, but it would also have been pointless. Saying nothing was tantamount to admitting everything. Cassie Grubdollar had seen through his paltry efforts at bluffing. Admittedly he had underestimated her. He had thought that someone whose grammar was so muddled must be muddled in the head as well, but that was clearly not the case.

In any event, he was left with nothing to fall back on but the truth.

It couldn't be the whole truth, though. He couldn't, for instance, tell her he was a spy. If he did, she would no doubt hand him over to the Groundling authorities. She would feel duty-bound to, because that was what you did with spies, wasn't it? Turned them in, let whoever was in charge deal with them. Weak as he was right now, there was no way he could stop her doing that if she felt like it.

'Can I trust you?' he asked.

Cassie cocked her head to one side. 'No idea. Can you?'

'I don't suppose I have a choice, under the circumstances.'

'No, I don't suppose you has.'

'OK then. I *am* from "up there".'

She nodded with the satisfaction of someone proved correct. 'But you doesn't have wings.'

'No, I doesn't – I *don't*.'

'Why's that? Them fall off or something?'

'No, nothing like that.'

'An accident, then.'

'Accident of birth. I was born this way. I'm not the only person I know of who was, but we're exceptionally rare. Everyone else is winged. I just got unlucky, I guess you could say.'

'You'm got no wings and you live way up high up there. Be'n't that a bit scary?'

'Certainly is. I've got used to it, but sometimes – quite a lot of the time, in fact – I have to be careful what I do. One mistake, and it's a long way down.'

'So what be it like up there? I mean, the Deacons tells we there be these amazing, beautiful cities, and there'm dazzling sunshine all the time, and people is as kind and friendly as can be. Be it like that?'

'More or less, yes. We don't all get along constantly. Wouldn't need prisons and the Alar Patrol if we did. It isn't perfect. What is? But there haven't been any wars, not lately. And the sky-cities – well, they are beautiful, most of them, there's no denying that.'

'Tell me about they.'

He gave a verbal sketch of his hometown High Haven – the bustling central avenues, the quieter outer suburbs, the way the buildings all latticed together, over, under, around.

'A three-dimensional town,' said Cassie. 'Imagine that. And so this all balances on, like, the columns?'

'Cantilevers arch out from the tops of the columns, and they support some buildings, and those buildings support other buildings, and so on. A big framework, branching out. Somewhat like a tree. Although most of the cities have more than one column, so a tree with several trunks.'

'Yeah, that'd be sort of how I pictured they. And open sky above?'

'Blue sky.'

'Blue sky,' she echoed wonderingly. 'And you see the sun? I mean, properly. It'm more than just this pale circle? And the moon too?'

'And stars.'

'Stars.' It was almost a sigh. 'The Deacons, them talks about stars now and then. Bright twinkles of light, like sparks from a furnace. Oh, it'm true. It'm all true. Tell I more.'

He told her more. He described school, jetball, his brother's helicopter – all these everyday things which to Cassie seemed impossibly exotic.

'Now, your turn,' he said. 'What's life like down here?'

'You's seen, hasn't you?'

'Some of it. Not much.'

'It be grey. Always grey. Sometimes lighter grey, sometimes darker. But always grey. The clouds is always there, like a lid over us, and it rains a lot, like it'm raining now.' She shrugged. 'I don't know what else to say. It be'n't great. But this be just the first life. There'm the next life waiting for us up above, and if us is good and us sacrifices materials and keeps the Deacons pleased, us'll get there after we die.'

'You'll' – what was the phrase he had overheard in the Chancel? – 'Ascend?'

'Straight up.'

'How does that work, exactly? Ascension? The Deacons burn your bodies and ...'

'... and the smoke rises and what happens then is Reconstitution, it'm called. The smoke enters the womb of a pregnant lady above, mingles with the foetus what be growing inside her, and that be how you gets born again. With wings. *Not* with, apparently, in your case. But usually with.'

99

Az pondered this. It didn't strike him as very plausible. Perhaps, at a molecular level, it was conceivable that a few atoms of smoke from a cremated Groundling cadaver could form part of an Airborn foetus's makeup, if, say, the expectant mother happened to inhale them. But that was assuming the smoke even got that far and wasn't dissipated in the cloud cover.

No, frankly the whole idea seemed bogus. A con, perpetrated by the Deacons on ordinary people. A way of manipulating the existing situation to their advantage.

'It'm faith, see,' Cassie said, perhaps sensing what was going through Az's mind. 'You has to believe in it. You has to believe you'm going to become Ascended when you die. It'm what makes life, and death, bearable. Otherwise ... Well, there be'n't no "otherwise", really. Although there is according to them Humanists. Them argue that us doesn't Ascend and become Reconstituted, that that be all a load of Chancel baloney, and that you lot up there's just people like we – with wings, but just people – and you doesn't think about us or care about we one little jot. But that be'n't' true, right?'

'No,' said Az, lying (convincingly, he hoped). 'No, we're concerned about you. We think about you a lot.'

'That be why you'm down here then?'

He hadn't anticipated this particular question, although perhaps he should have. So far, he felt he had been doing pretty well. He was actively gathering information. He was learning about Humanists and Deacons and suchlike, and it would all be of immense interest to Lady Aanfields-daughter if – no, when – he managed to get back up above the cloud cover. He was, in short, making a better job of being a spy than he had initially thought.

He stalled for time. 'Me? Erm ... What do you mean?'

'You'm down here 'cause you'm concerned. Be that it?'

'I'm ... down here ... because ...'

Think, Az, think!

'Because I was curious. Look at me. I have no wings. I'm like one of you. So I wanted to see ... to see if I might fit in down here. Fit in better than I do up there.'

His speech gained momentum. Here, at last, was his cover story.

'I sneaked onto an elevator. Strictly forbidden, of course. I could have got into terrible trouble. But I had to take a look. I had to see for myself. Often I've felt that I don't belong in a place where everyone else can fly and I can't. Whereas down here, maybe I could belong.'

Yes, that was it. Good work.

'And?'

'And what?'

'What conclusion has you come to? Does you?'

'Belong? Not sure yet. I've hardly had a chance to look round and see the place. You're the first person I've actually spoken to. But now that I have, and given how you've taken care of me . . .'

She smiled.

He smiled back.

It seemed, in that moment, that they shared something, that something passed between them, although Az could not accurately interpret what it was. An understanding? Or was it something more than that?

It occurred to him that this girl, Cassie, might have taken a shine to him. To her, after all, he was an ordinary boy. Up in the world of the Airborn, girls seldom gave him a second glance, and when they did it wasn't so much second glance as double take. *Oh look, he hasn't got any wings.* And then they would either ignore him or subject him to stares of embarrassed pity.

Whereas down here he was outwardly no different from anybody else. He wasn't abnormal. He was equal.

Therefore, down here, might he not have a similar effect on the opposite sex as Michael did up there? Might he not be as irresistible to Groundling girls as Michael was, usually, to the Airborn variety?

It wasn't beyond the realms of possibility.

CHAPTER 32

A Human Relic

Had Az known what was actually going through Cassie's head, he would have been considerably crestfallen. She wasn't entertaining romantic notions about him at all.

Basically what she was thinking could be boiled down to a single word. *Relic.*

Not to put too fine a point on it, Cassie was thinking money. She was looking at Az, not as a boy, but as a transferable cash asset.

The Grubdollars had found him in the Zone, after all. They had scavenged him fair and square, in accordance with the Code of Murk-Combing.

How much would the Chancel pay for him? Not just any old Relic from above, not some random scrap of debris, but a living, breathing person. A genuine, honest-to-goodness Ascended One, in more or less perfect condition. What kind of sum might *he* fetch?

A small fortune, she thought.

Truly, the family's luck *had* turned.

For the rest of the day she tended to Az solicitously, without a hint of resentment any more. She spoon-fed him more stew. She brought him a basin of warm water and some soap so that he could wash himself. She presented him with his clothes, laundered and pressed, and waited outside the room while he put them on.

She wasn't simply nursing him, of course. She was guarding him as well, like a security man outside a bank vault.

By mid-afternoon Az had regained some of his strength. He no longer complained of dizziness and there was colour back in his cheeks.

'Think I'm safe from rattle-lung?' he asked at one point.

Cassie said she reckoned so. 'Though you was courting it, slopping around in the wet in the Zone like that.'

'The Zone. The Shadow Zone. What *is* it exactly?'

'Well, it be where us works, for one thing.'

'Doing what?'

'Us, me and my family, us is in the murk-combing biz. Us and *Cackling Bertha.*'

'Who's she?'

'Strictly speaking her be an it, but her's a she to we. Our murk-comber. That big damn vehicle us was in when us found you. Us trawls around in the Zone in she, looking for Relics.'

'Relics being ...'

'Stuff that falls from above. Bits and bobs. Anything.'

She could see Az thinking hard about that. 'And what do you do with these ... Relics?'

'Sells they to the Deacons. Us pays for a licence to go in the Zone, and in return gets the privilege of the Deacons buying off we whatever us finds there. It'm not a great living but it'm what us does.'

'And then what happens to the Relics?'

'Deacons stores they away in their Reliquary. All goes in there.'

'And you can only sell it to the Chancel? No one else?'

'Against the law to. And against the Code of Murk-Combing. The Deacons gets it all.'

'Bit of a cartel, isn't it?'

'You mean unfair? That be'n't the half of it. You can only buy one licence, and the Chancels is very strict about their territory. You can't play one Chancel off against another to get a better price. Be all sorts of trouble if you tried. Lose your licence, apart from anything.'

'So I'm sort of ... a human Relic, you might say.'

Cassie was startled. Had he guessed what she was planning for him?

'You might,' she replied, buttressing the words with a light laugh.

'Huh.'

The idea seemed to amuse him, but nothing more. Cassie was relieved. But there was also a first small stirring of guilt inside her.

Around teatime Az said he felt well enough to brave a few tentative steps. Although the effort left him weak and breathless, he was delighted, and Cassie echoed his delight.

A tour of the Grubdollar abode followed, and was necessarily brief, because it wasn't a very big house. In essence, it was a first-floor flat, its rooms hunkering under the roof.

Az summed up the place – decor and layout – as 'simple'. He meant this as a compliment, and Cassie took it as such, although she felt he was being slightly patronising.

He spent some time scanning the world outside through the windows, although there wasn't much to see, in the event. The rain had stopped but a mist had set in, shrouding everything in a haze of white. The courtyard below was visible, and next-door's slate-tiled rooftop, and the unlit gas lamp out in the street, but that was all.

Then, worn out, Az hit the couch again and collapsed into a deep slumber. The chuntering return of *Bertha* failed to wake him. Cassie, on the other hand, sprang to her feet the moment she heard the murk-comber's engine, and scurried downstairs to greet her family.

Four glum expressions told her it had been another fruitless day in the Zone.

Never mind. The news she had would cheer everyone up. 'Da? Boys? I's got something to tell you.'

Her father's immediate response, once Cassie revealed what she had discovered about the boy, was to purse his lips sceptically and suck his front teeth, all three of them.

'Bless my bum, him's been spinning you a yarn all right, girl. A neat one too. But where'm the proof?'

'Proof? Da, you should hear he. The sky-cities and that – nobody could make it up. Not in so much detail.'

'But the *proof*, lass. What's to say him's not just some nutter with a head full of fantasies about the Ascended Ones? Being as the lad was out there in a Shadow Zone, all on his own- some, I'd say "nutter" be a pretty fair description for he. And nutters make up stuff all the time, and they be convincing with it too, 'cause them's believing in it whole and full.'

'What about the weight of he, Da?' said Robert. 'You yourself said as how him be far lighter'n you expected. Now, if him comes from up there, where everyone flies, be'n't it likely that them'd have to not weigh as much? You know, like birds have hollow bones, or, not hollow, but what be the word? Porous.'

'No wings, Robert. That be what it comes down to. Where's the wings?'

'Come and see his shirt,' Cassie said. 'There be your proof.'

The Grubdollars went upstairs and tiptoed single-file into the lounge. Az, fortunately, was sleeping on his front, so that to expose his back all Cassie had to do was gently peel the blanket down to his waist.

Everyone took a good look at the sewn-up slits on the back of the shirt, then withdrew quietly to the kitchen. There, Cassie's father sat and ran a hand back and forth across his chin stubble, his eyes unfocused. You could see him slowly, slowly going over things in his head. Den Grubdollar was a man who seldom came to snap-decisions.

'Well now,' he said eventually, 'I be'n't saying you'm right, Cass. But I be'n't saying you'm wrong any more, either.'

'Reckon the Deacons will want he?'

'Maybe.'

'It'd be good money.'

'Maybe. But the lad be'n't just something for they to store in their Reliquary, if you take my meaning. He be'n't some mangled hunk of metal or the like. And us can't treat he as if him were. Not proper, that.'

'But what else is us to do with he?'

'There, Cass, you'm asking a fine question.'

Had Cassie been looking at one of her brothers just then, instead of concentrating on her father, she might have seen a strange light enter that brother's eyes.

Martin Grubdollar had had an idea.

No one else might know what to do with the boy, but Martin certainly did.

CHAPTER 33

A Day In The Life Of A World-Changer

Steamarm's plan had been to spend just twenty-four hours in Grimvale before moving on. Events, though, were racing ahead, requiring the plan to be revised.

The strength of pro-Humanist sentiment he had encountered in the township was extremely gratifying to him. What surprised Steamarm was just how widespread it was. It seemed that virtually everyone he met was a supporter of the movement, from shopkeeper to schoolteacher, from road-sweeper to notary. Even on the municipal council there were people with Humanist leanings, although being professional bureaucrats they couldn't simply come out and admit it. Instead, a delegation of councillors invited Steamarm to visit the town hall and, over lunch, expressed their approval for his aims in a coded fashion, by means of vague statements such as 'Far be it from us to stand in the way of your endeavours' and 'The public is free to demonstrate its will'.

Above all, Steamarm was aware of a definite restlessness in the air. The township was bristling with agitation, ready to take the next step, just awaiting the word *go*.

He had been scheduled to travel to this next stop on his itinerary, Darkham Crag, by overnight train. However, he sent a telegram to the local movement organisers there, tendering his regrets and saying he had been unavoidably detained. He then sent another telegram, this one to his colleagues at the Central Office of the Popular Movement For Radical Secular Change, a.k.a. Humanism HQ, in the regional capital, Craterhome. It read:

SEEDS SOWN IN GRIMVALE BEARING FRUIT AND RIPE
FOR CULTIVATION + STOP + METHOD OF COVERT
INGRESS ACQUIRED + STOP + STRONGLY URGE
BRINGING FORWARD TIMETABLE FOR ACTION + STOP
+ CONFIRM + STOP +

The clerk at the telegraph office did not charge Steamarm for sending the telegrams.

'What'm ours should be ours,' she said to him, brightly. She was a delightfully pretty, petite young thing, and she wore her hair in a tidy plait, which was just how Steamarm liked girls to wear their hair.

'The time is now, sister,' he replied, and beamed charmingly at her.

The clerk blushed and giggled, and Steamarm was tempted to invite her out for a meal, give himself a little treat. No, duty first. He couldn't allow himself to be distracted, not when the situation was reaching such a critical juncture.

'There'll be a reply to that second telegram,' he told her. 'Can you have it delivered to my hotel? I'm staying at the Pithead Inn.'

'Run it over there myself, I shall. Straight up.'

'Thank you, my dear.'

Next, Steamarm toured the local pickets and gave a speech of encouragement to the men and women standing there valiantly in the drizzling rain. It was the exact same speech at each picket, although there was no way the picketers could know that, especially as Steamarm recited it each time as though he was coming up with it on the spur of the moment. This was one of his many talents, making well-rehearsed words sound fresh and new to every pair of ears that heard them.

'... the hour is at hand ... overthrow the monopolistic tyranny of the Deacons ... the Chancels everywhere will fall ... days numbered ... twice as much wealth for the people ... casting off the shackles of moral oppression ...' And so on and so forth.

Back at the Pithead Inn, Steamarm found the reply from Central Office had been slipped under the door to his room. On the envelope containing the telegram, the clerk had scribbled a note. It said, 'Sorry I missed you, XXX'.

The telegram itself read:

```
TIMETABLE AMENDMENT APPROVED + STOP + ACTION
COMMENCES NIGHTFALL TOMORROW + STOP + FIRST
BLOW TO BE STRUCK AT CLIFFSIDE CITY CHANCEL +
STOP + FURTHER ACTIONS TO FOLLOW DEPENDING ON
LOCAL CONDITIONS + STOP + OPERATE AT OWN
DISCRETION + STOP + WHAT'S OURS SHOULD BE OURS
+ STOP +
```

Steamarm couldn't help grinning.

Down at the Logger's Head he assembled a small group of men, hardcore Humanists, the loyalest of the loyal. He plied them with beer and rhetoric, and watched them get drunker and more belligerent as the evening wore on. At the precise moment when they were still sober enough to take in and remember instructions, but not so sober that their consciences were functioning properly any more, he revealed what he wanted them to do for him.

To a man, they agreed.

Steamarm left the pub and wended his way back to the hotel. The rain had eased off and a chilly mist billowed through the streets of Grimvale, but he was warmed by a inner glow of triumph. As he walked he got glimpses through windows, hazy snippets of the domestic lives of the townsfolk. Families were preparing for bed. Parents were kissing children goodnight. Faces were being washed, teeth brushed, curtains drawn, lanterns snuffed. Hearth fires were banked up, their final flames flickering down. Grimvale was slowly closing its eyes and going to sleep, little suspecting the tumultuous events which lay in store just a few hours from now.

In his hotel room, Steamarm climbed into bed and willed himself to sleep too. He needed his rest. He had a very early start tomorrow.

He sank into slumber, and dreamed of a new world.

CHAPTER 34

Visitors At Dawn

Den Grubdollar, in a quandary as to the best way of dealing with the boy, determined that he would sleep on the matter before deciding. So Cassie spent another night in the armchair, keeping vigil over Az. This time she didn't nod off straight away. Her conscience plagued her. Was it right to try and sell Az to the Chancel? She looked at his prone, snoring form, outlined by the dim glimmer coming in through the window from the streetlamp. He seemed so ... frail. She hated the thought that he had put his trust in her and her immediate response had been to think of a way of exploiting him for money.

Money, though, would come in very handy indeed. The Grubdollars' outgoings were substantial, not least their diesel bill for *Bertha*, whose fuel tank was seemingly bottomless. Replacement parts for a murk-comber as old as *Bertha* was did not come cheap either. Right now, the family was deep in debt to several businesses in the township. The credit they were getting would not be extended indefinitely.

Guilt and self-interest warred within Cassie, until finally she reached a truce with herself. She would leave it up to her father. Whatever solution he settled on, she would go along with.

After that, she was able to sleep ...

... at least until shortly before dawn, when the entire household was woken by a strident hammering from outside. Somebody was thumping at the portcullis gate, hard.

'Who'm the hell can that be?' Cassie heard her father roar. 'Doesn't the idiot know what time it be?'

'I'll go see, Da,' Robert called from his room.

'Already on it,' said Martin, and there was the sound of his feet clattering down the spiral staircase, shortly followed by voices out in the courtyard and then the rattle of the portcullis gate being raised.

'Cassie, what's going on?' said Az in a slurred, sleepy fashion.

'Don't know. Visitors, seems like. Odd, though, at this hour.'

Out in the hallway Cassie found her father standing in his longjohns. He was stretching his arms and in the throes of a yawn so enormous it threatened to split his head in two.

'Martin's let they in, whoever them be,' she said. 'Must be someone him knows.'

Her father's face creased into a scowl. ''S not liking this, Cass. Maybe you should—'

The sentence terminated there, incomplete, as Martin came back up the stairs. With him there were a half-dozen men, locals. Cassie knew two of them by name – Fred Tollbeam and Lawrence Brace – and recognised the faces of the rest. They were all large, burly types, hard workers, lumberjacks, miners, quarrymen, pillars of the community. What did they want?

Behind them, someone else came into view, someone Cassie didn't recognise. He was definitely *not* a local. Tall and lean, he was smartly dressed and well groomed, patently the sort of man who took great pains over his appearance. He was clean-shaven, his teeth were white, and his fingernails were clipped and buffed to perfection. He must have been fiendishly handsome when he was young. Not so young any more, he did everything he could to maintain his looks, even to the point of dyeing his grey patches of hair. The brown at his temples did not match the brown on the rest of his head.

Cassie's immediate impression, apart from his looks, was that there was something slightly disdainful about him. He considered himself a cut above.

'Aha,' the man said to Cassie's father as he reached the top of the stairs, 'Mr Grubdollar I presume.'

'And who in the name of all that's bright and high be *you?*' was the growled response.

'Da,' said Martin, 'this'm a friend of mine and Fletch's.'

Fletcher, who had emerged into the hallway a moment earlier along with Robert, nodded. 'Good friend of ours,' he said.

'Friend?' said their father. 'Oh, don't tell I. This'm some ruddy Humanist, right? Them all is Humanists. Yes, of course them is. Now I see. Fred there, you'm notorious for having those tendencies. And this here clean-cut Mr Fancypants, him's the ringleader of the bunch. Got a name, sir, has you? I'd very much like to know it.'

'Steamarm,' said the well-dressed man. 'Alan Steamarm.'

'Good. Thanks for that. I always likes to know the name of the person whose face I be about to rearrange.'

So saying, Cassie's father drew back his hand, balling it into a fist.

The burly Humanists immediately closed ranks around Steamarm to shield him.

'Fred,' Den growled. 'Lawrence. All of you. I'll say this just once. Out of the way. I'll fight you all if I has to, but I won't have Humanists in my house.'

'Da, please,' Martin said. 'Nobody wants any trouble. Alan and the lads—'

Den rounded on his son. 'Shut up. I's going to deal with you later, you and Fletcher both. But first off I's going to show these here gentlemen what I thinks of their sort. Coming barging into a man's home like that . . .'

'I let they in, Da,' Martin said.

'I be well aware of that, more's the pity.'

'Mr Grubdollar, there's no need for threats,' said Steamarm from behind his barricade of thick torsos and muscular arms. 'In any case, you're outnumbered, and my colleagues won't think twice about—'

'Grraaarrghh!'

Cassie's father charged at the Humanists, barrelling into them like a bowling ball. The speed and ferocity of the attack caught them off-guard. He got in two good blows before they could muster a retaliation. Fred Tollbeam was decked by a single punch to the jaw. Another of the Humanists staggered backwards clutching his nose, from which blood was spurting freely. He caught himself on a small side-table, which collapsed under his weight. The sudden loss of support sent him sprawling to the floor amid wooden shards and splinters.

Even when the Humanists collected their wits and fought back, there seemed to be no stopping Den. He lashed out in all directions, catching one of the men under the chin with an uppercut and knocking the wind out of another with a jab of the elbow. He was rage incarnate, a force of nature.

Robert joined in the fracas, but was soon sent reeling and banged his head against a wall with concussing force. The impact dislodged a nearby embroidery sampler, whose stitched letters read 'HOME SWEET HOME'. It fell from its nail and hit the floor with a crash, frame splintering, glass shattering.

Den, meanwhile, for all his fury, was rapidly succumbing beneath sheer weight of numbers. After much grappling and struggling, two of the Humanists succeeded in pinning his arms behind his back. Then Lawrence Brace stepped forwards, fists clenched.

'Den,' he said, 'you'm a decent man, but you know what your problem be? You'm no friend of the modern age. You need to move with the times.'

So saying, he thumped Den in the gut, once, twice.

That was when Cassie finally roused herself from the state of horrified paralysis that had seized her. As Brace brought back his arm to punch her pinioned father a third time, she hurled herself at him. Leaping on him from behind, she wrapped an arm around his throat and squeezed with all her might. Brace, choking, flailed at her and swung around wildly, trying to dislodge her. Cassie clung on grimly, her only thought being to throttle the life out of this man who was hurting her da.

Eventually hands grabbed her and prised her off him. She kicked and shrieked in protest.

'Be still, Cass,' hissed a voice in her ear. Fletcher's voice. 'You'm only making it worse for everyone.'

'Traitor! Bloody buggering traitor! Let me go!' Cassie squirmed in her brother's grasp but couldn't break free.

'Everyone! Everyone! Please!'

This was Steamarm speaking. He lofted his hands in a peacemaking gesture.

'Please! This is all so unseemly. We mustn't fight one another. We're all on the same side here, united against a common enemy.'

'I be'n't on any side of yours,' gasped Cassie's father. A trickle of blood was flowing down from the corner of his mouth. He strained against the men holding him, but to no avail.

'Believe me, Mr Grubdollar, you are. Humanism is on the march. We're preparing to strike a blow for liberty. All across the world a revolution is starting. And whether you like it or not, you're a part of that.'

Den spat a wad of blood-flecked spittle at Steamarm's feet. 'What'm you wanting here anyways? Your lot's already poisoned the minds of two of my sons with your nonsense. You's taken *they* from me. What else of mine is you after?'

'Isn't it obvious?'

'Not to me it be'n't.'

'Well, if you can't work it out, you'll know soon enough. And after tonight you'll understand everything very clearly. After tonight, Mr Grub-dollar, we're going to be living in a different world.'

'Alan?'

Steamarm swung round.

Martin was standing in the doorway to the lounge. Cassie hadn't realised but he had slipped out of the hallway when the fighting started. Now he was back, and he had Az with him. Holding Az by the shoulders, he thrust him forward to show him to Steamarm.

'Who's this?' said Steamarm quizzically. 'I thought you said you only had two brothers, Martin.'

'This'm no brother of mine,' came the reply. 'Remember how I mentioned that kid we found in the Zone, day before yesterday? This be he. And guess what? Turns out him's one of them. Him's Ascended.'

'What? No. Surely not.'

'Surely yes.' Martin was grinning at Steamarm, gleefully, ingratiatingly, like a student with an apple for teacher. 'Bit of a prize, eh? Might come in useful. And him's yours, Alan. All yours.'

CHAPTER 35

Aftermath

Cassie, Robert, and their father were locked in their father's bedroom and one of the Humanists was posted on guard outside the door. Steamarm told them this was for their own good, to keep them out of harm's way. He insisted they shouldn't regard themselves as prisoners, but that was certainly how it looked to Cassie.

Her primary concern, though, was Robert. He was semiconscious from the bang he had received on the back of his head. She got her father to place him on the bed, where he lay burbling incoherently, like someone in the grip of a fever.

'His brains is all shook up,' her father observed.

Cassie fetched a damp washcloth from the basin on the dressing table, folded it into a roll, and draped it across Robert's forehead. Its coolness soothed him and he soon went quiet.

'Reckon him'll be OK,' she said. 'Him's breathing steady. Going to have a mighty headache when him wakes up, I reckon, but that be all. Now Da, what about you?'

'Fine, lass. Don't worry yourself about I.'

He wasn't fine, however. His lip was starting to swell, there were abrasions on his face, and every time he moved he winced. To judge by the way he held himself, his stomach was very tender where Lawrence Brace had punched him.

'Can't I just give you a quick look-over?'

'What for? It'm only bumps and bruises. Them'll heal. 's fine, I tells you!'

'No need to get shirty. I were only trying to help.'

'Yes. Sorry, girl.' Den turned down his mouth at the corners. 'Look, I'll be all right, honest I will. I been hit far worse in the past. Brace weren't really trying, I doesn't think. His heart weren't in it. What hurts the most be . . .'

He couldn't finish what he had been going to say.

'Martin,' said Cassie. 'Fletcher.'

'Yes. They. Can't bring myself to speak their names, I can't. Not now. But how could them do this? My own flesh and blood. It'm hard to believe.'

'Maybe them—'

He cut her off, jabbing a finger at her. 'Don't, Cassie. Don't say it. Don't even think about coming up with some excuse to justify what them did. There be'n't none. Them's brought shame on this household with their behaviour. As of now, I has two children only. Do you hear I, girl? Two children only. You'm forbidden from ever mentioning them other two again.'

With that, Den stalked off to a corner of the room and leaned against the wall, resting his brow on his forearm and staring morosely at the floorboards.

Cassie turned back to Robert. She sat on the bed beside him and stroked his arm. Poor Robert. Perhaps if she had got involved in the fight sooner, instead of standing there like a scared rabbit, Robert would now be all right. No, it wouldn't have made any difference. Probably *both* of them would have got hurt rather than just him. Besides, everything had happened so quickly. From start to finish the fight couldn't have lasted more than half a minute.

As she replayed the events over in her mind, she found herself wondering what the answer was to the question her father had asked Alan Steamarm: *What'm you wanting here anyways?* It wasn't Az, that was for sure. Steamarm hadn't known who and what Az was till presented with him by Martin. So, if that wasn't the original reason for the visit, what *had* he come for?

The answer popped into her head at the exact same moment that a roar of engine ignition came from down in the courtyard.

CHAPTER 36

Captive In The Larder

They hauled Az through the still-misty predawn streets of Grimvale Township. Gripping his arms, two of the Humanists frogmarched him across cobbles and flagstones, past houses whose darkened windows stared out like blind eyes, past shop-fronts with metal shutters closed to protect the wares inside, across a humpbacked bridge that traversed a stream of running water, down an alleyway so narrow that the buildings on either side appeared to touch heads. Everything seemed unreal to Az through the thickening and thinning of the mist, provisional, as though at any moment it could all fade into nothingness. A dirty twist of rag in a gutter – unreal. That long-tailed animal scampering for safety beneath a gate (from the Groundling exhibit, Az recognised it as a cat) – unreal.

Finally they arrived at a two-storey cottage with a whitewashed exterior and a sagging, deep-eaved roof. One of the Humanists escorting Az was called Lawrence, and this, apparently, was where Lawrence lived. Inside, the cottage consisted of small, dingy rooms with beamed ceilings. The doors had lintels so low that both Humanists had to duck to go through them.

Az was taken to a back room, a larder. It had a brick floor and a single, diamond-paned window set high up in the wall. The window lacked a handle and was sealed fast, never intended to be opened. Its purpose was to let in a wisp of light, not air, and its dimensions were so small that even if Az smashed out the glass he couldn't possibly squeeze himself through. Cobwebs hung over it like a net curtain, studded with fly husks.

There was no furniture in the larder apart from shelves which held jars of dried food and preserves and assorted items of grubby crockery, some of them greened with mould. In one corner of the floor there was a scattering of what looked like black grains of rice. Had Az known what a mouse was, he would have recognised these as mouse droppings.

The door slammed behind him, a key turned, and that was that for the next few hours. Az was left alone in the larder with nothing to do except squat cross-legged on the cold, bare floor and wonder what was going to happen to him. In an instant, his situation had gone from hopeful to dreadful. He despaired of ever being able to return to his own world. High Haven, home, his parents, Michael – all these seemed impossibly remote now, like a life that he had once imagined, a dream he had once had before waking into this harsh, grey reality. He hated the ground. He hated the people here, and he hated himself for ever having agreed to come down here. This was a ghastly place: no sunshine, everlasting gloom, everything damp and dank, and with a population who squabbled amongst themselves and double-crossed each other all the time.

As best he could judge, he had met just one halfway decent Groundling so far, and that was Cassie Grubdollar. One, out of who knew how many. And even her he wasn't completely sure about.

It might have been midday when someone finally came to look in on him. 'Might have been', because although Az was convinced that several hours had elapsed, the sky outside the tiny window didn't look a whole lot brighter than it had been at daybreak. The key clunked in the lock, and into the larder stepped the well-presented man who'd been giving the other Humanists their orders at the Grubdollars'. Az had overheard his name. Was it Alan Steerarm? Steelarm? Something like that. Groundling names were hard to get a grasp on.

'Good day to you, young man,' the man said to Az. 'Apologies for leaving you so long. I had things to attend to. Busy chap, you know.'

Az, out of a combination of stubbornness and apprehension, said nothing.

'Look, let's not be like that, shall we?' said the man. Steamarm. Yes, that was it. His name was Alan Steamarm. 'I'm here for a friendly chitchat, that's all. A little heart-to-heart. Because, as you know, the rumour is that you're an Ascended One, or at any rate you come from where the Ascended Ones live. Now, I've always been led to believe that to be an Ascended One you need wings. It's a basic requirement of "membership". Am I mistaken on that front?'

Az stared back at him, still saying nothing. What *could* he say? Telling anyone about anything seemed only to get him into trouble.

'Oh, come on,' Steamarm chided. 'I'm just after a few facts here.' He squatted down so that his and Az's eye-lines were level. 'Are you really from up there? And if so, what's gone wrong? Why have you descended to this lowly region? Not for a holiday, I'd hazard. Are you a reject, maybe? Have they exiled you? Chucked you out because you don't conform to their high standards? Is that it? Or is this whole thing just a story you've concocted, a prank, and you're actually an ordinary kid from around these parts who's got it into his head that it would be funny if he claimed he's Ascended? A stupid thing to do, if you ask me. What could you hope to gain?'

Steamarm's gaze was steady and unblinking. Az lowered his eyes and concentrated on the man's chin. It had a cleft in it, like the chin of a hero in a novel. It was a masculine, chiselled, good-guy chin.

'If I'm wasting my time here, Azrael, just say so. Did I pronounce that correctly – Azrael? The Deacons have long been telling us that the Ascended have exotic names. And your surnames are your father's fore-name suffixed by "son" or "daughter". Is that right? Is that how it works? Seems like a rather convoluted system to me. Must make life murder for your census takers, all those different surnames in one family. Do you even have census takers, I wonder. Come on, what's it like up there? Tell me a bit about it, Azrael. If you can.'

A chin like that ought to belong to someone you could trust, someone reliable. Not someone whose every word dripped with egotism and self-regard.

'You really should tell me now,' Steamarm insisted, 'because I'm starting to lose patience. If you're a liar, if this is all just some big hoax, I'll find out. Believe me, I will. I'm not one of these backwater simpletons like the Grubdollar family. You can't pull the wool over *my* eyes so easily. I'm a clever and some might say ruthless man. I'm also a man with precious little time to spare right now. So, if you aren't really Ascended, come clean and save yourself – and me – a heap of bother. If, on the other hand, you *are* what you say you are, and can prove it, then you could be very useful to me. You and I could even be friends. Understand? You could help me very much. Am I getting my point across?'

Yes, there were plenty of men who would give anything to have a chin like that.

'All right. I see.' Steamarm straightened up. 'So that's how its going to be, is it? Fine.' He smoothed out the wrinkles in his trousers with a sharp downward brush of his hands. 'I'm going to give you an hour, then. One hour to think about things. After that, I'm coming back with one of my pals. You know who I'm talking about. You've met them. One of those big fellows who like to use their fists. *Then* we'll see how long you keep up this silent act of yours.'

He swept out of the room. The door slammed.

One hour.

Az drew his legs up to his chest, buried his face against his knees, and wished he was elsewhere.

CHAPTER 37

What To Do Instead Of Sitting On Your Backside All Day

'Da? Da?'

Den Grubdollar was slumped in a wicker chair, as he had been for the past couple of hours. He didn't glance up but he did give a grunt, to indicate that he was listening.

'Da, us has got to get out of here.'

'Oh really, Cass? Why'm that?'

Cassie moved closer to him, keeping her voice low. 'For one thing, us has got to get *Bertha* back. I been thinking, and I reckon those Humanists is going to use she to worm their way inside the Chancel. Them be going to do that this evening. Remember what Steamarm kept saying? "After tonight . . . " It be the only reason I can think of for they taking her. With Martin or Fletcher driving . . .' She corrected herself, remembering her father's edict about mentioning those two of her brothers. With you-know-who or you-know-who driving, them could get through the gates easily. Deacons on guard duty'll recognise their faces. Won't look at they twice. Meantime there'll be a bunch of Humanists hiding in *Bertha's* loading bay. Them can be smuggled in that way, and then when them's inside the Chancel them can take over the place. I doesn't think the Deacons will put up much resistance. All a bit soft and weedy, be'n't them, from all that fine living. I mean, them'll try but it won't be a fair fight.'

Her father considered this, then nodded slowly.

'So?' he said. '*Cackling Bertha* be their ticket into the Chancel. So what? Why'm it up to we to stop they?'

'Not stop they, Da. I just wants she back, that'm all. I doesn't want she to be used like that. Her's family. I know that sounds daft-headed but it be true. Her's one of us, an honorary Grubdollar, and it be'n't right for they to drag she into their Humanist shenanigans.'

Den studied his daughter. His mood at present was aggrieved and distracted, and his face betrayed that but little else.

'You said, "For one thing",' he said. 'Be there a second thing?'

'Um, yeah. I reckons we should go get Az back too.'

'Beg pardon?'

'The boy. The Ascended One. Az.'

'I know who you be referring to. What I doesn't know is what you be on about. Az? What's us want he back for?'

'Da, it'm thanks to we that him's now a prisoner of them Humanists. I's no idea where them's got he or what them's after from him, but it be'n't' proper that us let they have he.'

'Weren't *us* that did that, lass. Weren't you and me. Were ... them who us be'n't mentioning.'

'All the same, him were in our care, him were our responsibility, and us let he down.'

'If I recall rightly, you was all after selling he to the Deacons.'

'Well, changed my mind, I has. Thinking about it, I reckon that it weren't proper to do that and that it *be* proper to rescue he now.'

Cassie's father looked inward for a while.

'Right,' he said, 'let's just I get this straight. You thinks us should somehow break out of here, somehow find where *Bertha* be, somehow get she back, then somehow firvl where Az be and someone get he back too. That about the long and short of it, lass?'

'Just about, yeah.'

'Lot of "somehows" there, you don't mind my saying.'

'I never said any of it were going to be simple, Da. But what else is us going to do? Sit here all day on our backsides, prisoners in our own house?'

For the first time since the Humanists had invaded his home, Den's gloomy demeanour showed signs of brightening. He even almost smiled.

'Well, when you put it like that, lass ...'

CHAPTER 38

Breakout

The Humanist guarding the three Grubdollars was a professional layabout called Colin Amblescrut.

He belonged to a family who were famous in Grimvale for many things, a fondness for booze being one of them, work- shyness being another. Mainly what the Amblescruts were noted for, however, was their failure to produce offspring who might be described as in the least bit intellectually developed. Indeed, there was a saying in the region: 'I may be dumb but at least I be'n't an Amblescrut.' Generation upon generation of Amblescrut youth had passed through the local education system without leaving a mark, apart from the odd scar or two on their fellow pupils. That, of course, was another notorious family trait: bullying. The Amblescruts took a particular pride in their liking for bullying and their proficiency at it. Bullying was their legacy, something handed down from parent to child, one might say dished out by parent to child. When they weren't doing their best to avoid earning an honest living, Amblescruts – alone or in packs – roamed about looking for victims to pick on. It whiled away the time between pub opening hours.

Alan Steamarm had left this particular Amblescrut in charge of the Grubdollars precisely because of his thuggish denseness. He would do the job he was assigned to do, unthinkingly, unquestioningly. Amblescrut was also the one person Steamarm felt he could spare, out of the squadron of Grimvale Humanists he had gathered around him. If he was going to leave behind one of the tools in his box, so to speak, then it might as well be the bluntest.

Truth was, Amblescrut was nursing a bit of a hangover today, after the pub session with Steamarm last night, where he had out-drunk everyone else by a margin of several pints. So his already far-from-sharp wits were further dulled by dehydration, a swirling stomach and a sore head.

This, in the event, would work very much to the advantage of Cassie and her father.

'Excuse me,' said Cassie, rapping on the inside of the bedroom door.

'Hmmh?' said Amblescrut, stirring from the bleary doze he had fallen into.

'I said excuse me.'

'What you be wanting?'

'My brother. The one in here, him that got knocked out. Him's taken a turn for the worse. Started bleeding.'

The note of panic in her voice sounded real enough. What Amblescrut couldn't know was that this was because it stemmed from a genuine sense of urgency.

'Bleeding?' he said.

'From his ear. That'm a bad sign. Someone needs to get he to a doctor.'

Colin Amblescrut cogitated very, very hard on this news. His thought processes were moving like porridge, not only slow but hotly painful as well. Bleeding? No, that was never good, was bleeding. Specially not from the ear.

Of course, it might be a trick.

Being who he was, Amblescrut was always on his guard for tricks. He had the bully's natural paranoia. He felt that anyone smarter than he was must be out to get him – and since there were few people who *weren't* smarter than he was, that meant just about everyone was out to get him. Which was why it was usually better to get them first.

'I be needing to see,' he said, 'with my own eyes. I be'n't just going to take your word for it.'

'Fine. Only, be quick about it. Him's losing blood fast.' Amblescrut went in search of a weapon. He wasn't about to enter the bedroom without some kind of hitting implement in his hand that would give him an edge. He remembered Den Grubdollar earlier on, fighting like a human cyclone. Grubdollar was old, and Amblescrut was both younger and stronger than him. Still, he knew it would be foolish to go in there unarmed.

He found a poker by the fireside in the lounge. Nice, stout lump of wrought iron. He gripped it in one hand and slapped it into the palm of the other.

Ouch.

But good.

'Right,' he said through the bedroom door. 'You and your da go to the far corner of the room and stand there facing the wall, backs to I, hands on your heads.' This was what they did at Grimvale police station when opening the cells to let detainees out. Amblescrut, having been arrested by the local constabulary on numerous occasions for drunk and disorderly behaviour and causing affray, was more than familiar with the procedure. 'I be opening the door a crack, and if I doesn't see you both standing there like I said, I's shutting it again straight away, and it stays shut and never mind your brother. Straight up?'

'Straight up.'

He waited a moment, hearing footsteps on the floorboards. Father and daughter were doing as asked. And why not? Amblescrut was used to getting his own way. When he made demands, people listened, and woe betide them if they didn't.

He turned the key, pressed down on the handle, and eased the door open.

First thing he saw was the young Grubdollar brother lying on the bed – and yes, there was blood trickling from his ear, and spots of blood on the pillow too.

Next thing he saw was that the other two Grubdollars hadn't gone to the far corner as instructed.

In fact, they didn't appear to be in the room at all ...

... unless they were hiding to the left of the door, out of his line of sight.

A cleverer man would have made this deduction more or less instantly, and hurried to take the appropriate countermeasures.

Not Colin Amblescrut, alas.

The sight of the blood had unnerved him, and then there was the fact that he had definitely heard footsteps, and the footsteps had got quieter, just as though they were moving away. But then what he had neglected to take into account was that footsteps could be made to *seem* as though they were moving away if the people generating them simply remained in one spot and trod more and more softly. An elementary ruse that wouldn't have fooled a child but *had* fooled him.

The door was yanked from Amblescrut's grasp. Next instant, he was being struck from the side with something large and heavy. He crumpled to the floor, the poker clattering out of his hand. He levered himself up onto all fours and scrambled to retrieve the weapon. Before he could reach it, he was struck again, this time squarely on the crown of his head. He went down but immediately got back up. It took a lot more than a couple of blows to fell an Amblescrut, particularly if the target was the head. Unusually thick skulls, the family had. More bone than brain, it was said.

The heavy object crashed down on his spine, flattening him.

For a third time he rose up.

He heard Den Grubdollar curse and say, 'What'm it take to stop the bugger?'

'How about this, Da?'

At the periphery of his vision, Amblescrut saw the girl pick up the poker – *his* poker – and toss it to her father.

Ah, he thought. *This'm going to hurt.*

He did his best to get himself upright before Den had a chance to wield the poker effectively. But he knew he wasn't going to manage it in time. There was a tragic, even poetic inevitability to the situation. By fetching the poker, he had brought this on himself.

He heard the poker swing. It made a sort of thrumming, humming *whoosh* through the air.

Then there was a lightning-like flash.

Followed by utter dark.

CHAPTER 39

No Either-Or

'I said, didn't I? I said us'd need something more substantial than that.'

Den indicated the wicker chair which he had used to thump Colin Amblescrut three times before having to resort to the poker. The chair was now looking rather sorry for itself. A dent had been gouged in the back of it, one of its legs had broken off, and another leg was hanging on by a splinter.

'You got he, that'm the main thing,' Cassie replied. She was winding a piece of cloth around her hand in order to bandage up the small gash in her palm which she had inflicted with the blade of her father's straight razor. The blood for Robert's ear had had to come from somewhere, and it was sensible that Cassie should be the source. Her father needed both hands unimpaired so that he could tackle Amblescrut. 'Now, let's tie he up before him comes round.'

They bound the unconscious Humanist's wrists and ankles with a length of strong cord from the storage area downstairs. Then, for good measure, they dragged him between them to the broom closet in the hallway, bundled him inside, and propped the door shut by shoving a kitchen chair at an angle up beneath the handle.

'Amblescruts,' said Den, shaking his head. 'Put three of they together, you still wouldn't have a whole brain.'

With a *tsk*, he turned away from the closet. All at once he staggered and let out a gasp.

'Da! What'm up?'

'Nothing.' He grimaced, clutching his side. 'Just overdid it, maybe, a little. Pass in no time, for sure.'

The pain did pass, but still Cassie insisted that her father sit down and let her examine him. She probed his chest and abdomen carefully with her fingers.

'*Aiiichh!*' her father hissed, as she found exactly where it hurt.

'Cracked a rib,' she diagnosed. 'Likely as not it happened when you'm got punched, and bashing Amblescrut made it worse. Da, you'm not going anywhere in this state. You won't barely manage to walk a hundred metres. I be going out after *Bertha* on my ownsome.'

'Uh-uh, lass. Face them Humanists without me to protect you? No way.'

'It be'n't no either-or, Da. You'm hurt too bad to be doing any protecting. Besides, somebody's got to stay here with Robert. Can't just be leaving he all by himself.'

'I reckoned a neighbour might—'

'Da.' Cassie scowled at him sternly. She had never loved him more and never before realised how vulnerable he could be. He was looking old. 'Be'n't often that I's the one what tells *you* how things is going to be, but that'm what I's doing right now, and no dispute. I'll find *Bertha* if I can, and if those Humanists is there when I finds she, I be dealing with they somehow. On my ownsome, a girl, there be less chance of fisticuffs breaking out than if I be turning up with my Da, who, let's face it, has a temper of him wouldn't shame a wild boar. Maybe I'll manage to get somewhere using subtlety and female wiles, and maybe not, but whatever happens, at least this way it be far less likely that anyone ends up injured.'

Den regarded his daughter. He had never loved her more and never before realised how grown-up she could be. She was looking old.

'Very well, lass,' he said with a sigh, and winced. Even sighing hurt. 'But you be careful, all right? Don't take any stupid risks.'

'Yes, Da.'

On impulse, Cassie leaned forward and gave him a peck on the cheek. Long after she had left the house, Den Grubdollar was still stroking the spot where she kissed him, with a faraway look in his eyes.

CHAPTER 40

The Hunt For Cackling Bertha

To track down a murk-comber even in a smallish place like Grimvale (population: 5,500) was not as straightforward a task as it might seem. There were four families with a licence to trawl the Shadow Zone for Relics, and a couple of professional businesses as well, so the sight of a murk-comber trundling along the streets was not an uncommon one. Added to that, there was the fact that the Humanists had taken *Bertha* in the early morning when most people were still fast asleep in bed. It was unlikely that there were any eyewitnesses to her departure, and even if someone heard her rumble past their house, they wouldn't necessarily know which way she had been heading or even be curious enough to draw back the curtains and take a look.

In Cassie's favour, a great big thing like a murk-comber would be very difficult to hide. It wasn't something you could just stash in your backyard under a tarpaulin or park out of sight down a side-alley. You'd need somewhere large, ideally an enclosed space or a place with stacks of equipment or raw materials to provide cover. A stockyard, a warehouse, somewhere like that.

And, logically, if you were going to drive your hijacked murk-comber to the Chancel later, you would want a site reasonably close to your destination, for convenience sake. You would probably choose a location either on or not far off one of the main roads into the Shadow Zone.

Based on this line of thinking, Cassie concluded that the Humanists would be keeping *Bertha* at one of the mines or lumberyards at the northern edge of town. Which narrowed down the field of search slightly, although not by a huge amount. There were two lumberyards and several coalmines all in close proximity to one another in that area, as well as a slate quarry and a couple of factories. What was she going to do, check them *all* out?

Well, yes. That was just what she was going to do. It was the only option open to her.

Cassie knew the countryside around Grimvale well. This had been her playground as a child. She had roamed far and wide through the forests and hills and was familiar with every back-route and every trail. She made her way up to a high ridge which ran parallel to the main road north out of town. It was hard going in places. The ground was sodden with rain. Ankle-deep mud sucked at her feet, trying to liberate her of her boots.

Once she had gained firmer ground she headed for one of the many clear-felled areas of forest. A swathe of treeless slope gave her an unimpeded view down to several of the industrial premises that were strung alongside the road.

There was the Filkshaw and Hawserdean Timber Mill, with its pyramid piles of tree trunks waiting to be sawn into planks, the piles laid out in a grid pattern like a miniature city.

There was the mine known as the Black Lake Lode, so named not because of any nearby body of water but because the seam of coal which the first prospectors had discovered there was so deep and broad that a lake was the only thing they could think of to compare it to, although it turned out to be even bigger than that, a seemingly limitless subterranean sea of carbonaceous rock.

Next door lay a rival mining concern, the Consolidated Colliery Collective. This was a communally-run enterprise where the workers were called stakeholders and where there was no disparity between the wages paid to labour force and management. Everybody earned the same basic salary, plus productivity bonuses.

The CCC had long been a hotbed of Humanist activity. It was there that the first pickets had been set up, there that the embargo on supplies to the Chancel was initially declared – and so it was on there that Cassie focused her fullest attention. In the leaden noonday light, gazing down across the expanse of dead stumps and spindly tendrils of new-growth, she surveyed the site. She observed miners – stakeholders – wheeling cartloads of freshly dug rubble out of the mouth of the mine. They deposited the contents onto conveyor belts, which fed into a large corrugated-iron building where the stuff was sorted by hand and sent up either of two distributor escalators. From the summit of one escalator, lumps of pure coal rained down; from the summit of the other, lumps of excess material, slag. Side by side, two conical heaps grew, respectively glossy black and drab grey.

There was a notable lack of urgency in the way everyone was working. A go-slow was in force at the CCC, as it was almost everywhere else. The pit was operating at 50% of full capacity, turning out enough product to cater to the needs of paying customers but no more. The extra coal that would normally have been donated to the Chancel was not being mined, and the trucks that would have transported it there were consigned to their sheds, not needed for the time being.

Unable to spot *Bertha* amid the coal heaps and slag heaps, Cassie homed in on the truck sheds. She saw that a couple of trucks were parked in front. Why leave them outdoors, she wondered, when they weren't being used?

Surely it would be better to keep them safely garaged, out of the elements.

Then she knew.

It was instinct as much as anything, a prickle at the nape of her neck, a tingling in the pit of her stomach.

Of course.

There was no direct evidence to corroborate her suspicion. It was perfectly possible that the trucks were parked outside because someone was planning to work on their engines or else they were old and decrepit and were going to be taken away and broken down for parts.

But she knew.

It was as though *Bertha* was calling to her from her place of concealment. Cassie had spent so much of her life in, on, around or under the murkcomber that she truly believed some kind of link had been forged between the two of them. Yes, *Bertha* was a machine, an inanimate thing. But she was so much more than that, too. Cassie knew her inside out, intimately. She knew her every mood, her every whim. When the Humanists made off with her, it was like having a beloved pet kidnapped. Worse – a close relative.

Bertha was family, just as Cassie had said to her father. She was like a maiden aunt, portly, sometimes cantankerous, with a hearty appetite and a wicked laugh, who worked hard and took care of all her kin, and asked only for a little care and kindness in return.

And she was down there in those sheds, taking up space normally occupied by the two trucks.

Cassie was sure of it.

Absolutely sure.

So sure that, without any further ado, she set off down the side of the ridge at a run.

CHAPTER 41

Crunch Time

The larder door opened. Az's hour was up. In came Steamarm, accompanied by Lawrence Brace. The latter seemed even larger and more hulking than before, an absolute giant of a man, with hands the size of dinner plates. Az saw that he was missing a finger. He hadn't noticed this earlier. The little finger on his left hand had been sheared off clean to the knuckle in some accident or other. Brace knew about pain, then. The receiving of as well as the inflicting of.

Az gulped. There was a constriction in his throat and a terrible dryness in his mouth. Up in the world he came from, that dream realm where the Airborn lived, it was hard to conceive of an adult ever deliberately harming a child. Down here, he didn't think the same rules applied. The ground was altogether a more brutal place.

Over the past hour he had had plenty of time to think. He had seesawed back and forth between defiance and submission. He had vowed not to tell Steamarm a thing, and to face the consequences. Then he had decided to give in and tell him everything. What had he got to lose? Then he had decided against *that*. Come what may, Steamarm wasn't getting a peep out of him. And so on. Back and forth, back and forth ...

Now it was crunch time, and he had to make a choice, fast.

'Azrael,' said Steamarm. 'Here we are again. So, are you ready to co-operate?'

'Please don't,' said Brace with a cruel leer.

Az's solution to his dilemma was a compromise: get in some defiance first, then submit.

'You're very brave,' he said. 'Two grown men threatening a teenager. You must be very proud of yourselves.'

'Oh, an attempt to make us feel ashamed!' said Steamarm. 'Well done, nice try. The fact is, Azrael, I have a calling, a cause that to me is far more important than the wellbeing of any single individual, be they adult or child. I don't care what I have to do in the name of that cause. Anything and everything is allowed if it gets me closer to my goal. Do you see what I'm driving at? I know no guilt, no shame. You can't appeal to my better nature because I don't have one.'

'What about you?' Az said, turning to Brace. 'You're the one who's actually going to ... to beat me up if I don't co-operate. How does that make you feel?'

Just a flicker of hesitation before Brace replied, 'Good. I be fine with that.'

'Really?'

Az knew that to tell if a person was unsure, you looked at the eyes. Whatever the mouth was saying, if the person didn't believe it then the eyes would not stay still.

Brace's eyes were darting to and fro.

This was a bluff. Brace was here only to intimidate Az. Steamarm had no intention of ordering him to use his fists.

'I'm not in much of a talking mood right his moment,' Az said, with a hint of gloating. He folded his arms. 'I think I'll just sit here and enjoy the solitude, and you two can go pluck yourselves.'

Steamarm looked him up and down, appraising him. A slow smile spread across his face.

Then he took two quick steps forward and whacked Az across the face, backhand.

Az crumpled to the floor and came up again pressing a hand to his cheek. It felt like it was on fire. Tears of pain filled his eyes, smarting. He couldn't stop them. His head reeled.

'You weren't listening, were you?' Steamarm said through clenched teeth. 'I made myself very clear. Anything and everything is allowed. So let's try once more, shall we? We'll start from the very beginning. Are you or are you not an Ascended One? Simple question. Yes or no? And I want the truth. No mucking about.'

The shock of the blow faded. Az's head settled. He felt his cheek starting to swell. The pain became less fiery but no less unpleasant.

Dully, miserably, he nodded. *Yes.*

'There,' said Steamarm. 'There we go. An honest answer, I'd say. Now we're getting somewhere. So, tell me more. Fill me in on the whole thing. Why, where and how. Leave nothing out. This ought to be quite enlightening ...'

CHAPTER 42

Inside The Shed

There were skylights in the shed roofs, and Cassie, keeping to the high ground at the rear of the Consolidated Colliery Collective, peered down through each, one after the other in a row. She moved stealthily, staying low, following the line of the sheds. The skylights were grimy, hadn't been cleaned in ages. At best she glimpsed dim outlines through them, silhouetted segments of vehicle, here the top corner of a driver's cab, there the tailgate of a flatbed. She was beginning to lose heart, fearing her instinct had been wrong.

Then, unmistakably: *Bertha*. Her rounded contours. Her turret and nacelles. Her big behind.

Cassie had to suppress a yelp of triumph.

She scrambled down the last section of mountainside; clambered over a tallish chainlink fence that was there mainly to keep forest animals out; scurried across a strip of open terrain; gained the shelter of the back of the sheds; pressed herself flat against the corrugated iron siding; took stock.

There was a taste in the air. She had noticed it a little while ago, but it had been faint then. Now it was strong. A slightly singed, oxidised taste that was nothing to do with her proximity to a coal mine. She knew what it meant.

A storm was on its way. Brewing up there in the clouds. Soon to be breaking.

All the more reason to keep moving, get this over and done with swiftly.

The sheds were arranged in threes, with narrow alleys running between each group. Cassie padded down the length of the nearest alley and peeked round the corner. Two miners were coming towards her, ambling along. They had evidently just finished a shift down the pit, to judge by their soot-smudged faces and forearms. Emergency breathing-apparatus packs were strapped to their backs. The masks and air-nozzles dangled from their belts, bouncing in time to their strides.

Cassie snatched her head back. Had the miners seen her? She didn't think so. She shrank into the alley's shadows, hearing the men's footsteps getting closer, their big workboots clumping.

She caught a snippet of conversation as the miners drew level with the alley mouth:

'Half the effort, same wages. Don't mind if this go-slow go on for ever!'

'But with them Deacons out of the picture, it'll be same amount of work as before, double the income. Look at it that way.'

They tramped past, lost in musings on a better future.

Cassie peeked out again. The miners were soon out of sight. The coast was clear.

She darted out from the alley and tiptoed past the broad, open entrance to the first shed. *Bertha* was in the next shed along.

There!

Cassie nipped in through the entrance and took another breather, hunkering against a toolbench. *Bertha* bulked in front of her, filling the shed with her presence, almost to the rafters. Her floodlight arrays seemed to be grinning.

'I be pleased to see you too,' Cassie whispered.

As far as she could tell, nobody was guarding *Bertha*. She took a couple of steps towards the murk-comber, thinking that the tricky part was over and from here on things were going to be plain sailing. She would climb in, start the engine up, and drive off. Once she got rolling, nothing and no one could stand in her way.

'Cass?'

She whirled round.

'Fletcher.'

Her brother had appeared from behind *Bertha*. He was carrying a large adjustable spanner. His hands were piebald with grease stains.

'What the hell is *you* doing here?' he said.

'Coming to take back what don't belong in this place,' Cassie replied, 'what else?'

'*Bertha?*' Fletcher hefted the spanner, weighing things up. 'Don't think I can let you do that, girl.'

'Yeah? Be that so?' She took another step in *Bertha's* direction.

Fletcher moved to intercept.

'Come on then, Fletch,' Cassie said, squaring up to him. 'Let's see what you'm made of. Hit I with that spanner. 'Cause that be what it'm going to take to stop I. You'm going to have to deck me.'

'Cassie ...'

'What?' she snapped.

'Please don't be like this. Just back off. Go on home. Don't make it hard for I.'

'Hard? Give me one reason to make it easy! Fletch, look at what you and Martin's done. Stolen *Bertha*. Got our Da and Robert beaten up –

who be both all right, thanks for asking, though neither of them's exactly what you might call chipper.'

'I didn't—'

'What? *You* personally didn't beat they up? No, but you might as well have. And you's helped split our family in two. Proud of yourself for that? Well? Eh?'

Fletcher shifted his feet uncomfortably. 'Cass, it be'n't so simple as you make out. This stuff, what us is up to, us Humanists, it'm important. It'm about more than just family or *Bertha* or any of that. It'm about ... a brighter tomorrow. For everyone. And maybe, in time, you'll come to realise that. Da too. When the dust's settled, maybe you'll both understand.'

'I tell you what I understand, Fletch,' Cassie said, tightlipped. 'I understand that you'm just spouting that old tosh what Alan Steamarm says. And I understand that Martin believes in it but you not so much. You want to because he does. You admire Martin. Of course you do. All of us do. Him's our big brother. Us has always looked up to he. And you'm closer to he than anyone 'cause there be only a year in age between you, while me and Robert, us has always been the babies. But you'm got to ask yourself, be this honestly what *you* want? This your own true dream? Or is you just going along with it to please Martin? 'Cause that be no reason for doing anything, just to please someone else.'

Again Fletcher hefted the spanner, gripping it tight as though it had all of a sudden grown much heavier. A V-shaped furrow appeared between his eyebrows.

'That be'n't it. That be'n't why I ...'

Her words were having an effect. He was probing inside himself, searching for his true feelings.

Finally, after what seemed to Cassie like an age, he said, 'She be misfiring a bit.'

Cassie blinked. 'Eh?'

'*Bertha*. She be misfiring. I been having a fiddle with her distributors. But I reckon some of her pipes is clogged too. Coke build-up.'

'They not have wire brushes here? What kind of mechanics they got working in this place?'

'Oh yeah, they got brushes. I were going to get round to it next. Clean off them spark plugs as well.'

'She still be roadworthy, though?'

Fletcher gave his sister a shy, sly wink.

'Roadworthy as ever, lass.'

CHAPTER 43

A Stranger To Storms

'One step at a time, Azrael,' said Steamarm. 'So you were born wingless, you say?'

'Deacons tell we,' said Brace, 'anyone who attempts to build a flying machine, him'll get Reconstituted without wings as a punishment.'

'Yes, that old superstition.' Steamarm gave a sneering laugh. 'Another little lie designed to keep us in our place. And of course the Deacons make sure that when a flying machine from above comes crashing to earth, the wreckage gets whisked off into their Reliquaries before anyone has the chance to get a good look at it. They wave a fistful of money at whoever finds it, and it's gone, never to be seen again. So the knowledge of how to make the damn things is kept from us. It's all about the Deacons preserving their position, hanging on to power, subduing the rest of us ... Sorry, started speechmaking there. Do carry on, Azrael.'

'What else do you want to know?' Az said, numbly.

'Anything. Everything. Let's try: why you're here.'

Az remembered his cover story, made up on the spot to dupe Cassie. It seemed a gossamer-thin confection now. It surely wouldn't hold up to Steamarm's abrasive scrutiny.

Still, he had to give it a go.

'I ... I came to be among my own kind,' he said. His cheek, where Steamarm had hit him, began throbbing more painfully, as if to remind him of the price of incurring the man's wrath. He forged on regardless. 'I wanted to see if I could belong here. You know, fit in, sort of thing. Like I couldn't up there.'

Steamarm leaned back, studying Az. He pursed his lips and tapped a forefinger against them.

Unconvinced.

'No,' he said. 'No, I don't reckon that's it. You want to know what I think? I think you were *sent* down here.'

'No, I wasn't, I came of my own accord. I—'

'Azrael.' Steamarm barked the word. 'It's very courageous of you to lie, when you know what the consequences are. It's also very stupid. It doesn't get anyone anywhere, and it only delays the inevitable moment when you *will* tell me the truth. So let's cut the nightsoil and get right down to it.

Spare us all a lot of unnecessary unpleasantness. You're a spy, aren't you?'

Az was a fraction of a second late in denying it, and that fraction of a second was all Steamarm needed to know that he had struck gold.

'Not a guess on my part, just a piece of logical deduction,' Steamarm explained. 'Who better to send to investigate when the supplies from down here get interrupted? Who better than someone who looks like one of us? Even if he is just a kid.'

Az considered trying to protest again, telling Steamarm he had got it wrong. But there was no point.

He felt dispirited but at the same time oddly relieved. He didn't have to keep up a pretence any more, however flimsy it was. That burden had been lifted from him.

What next, though? Just how much information about the Airborn world was Steamarm going to try to pump out of him?

'Now,' the Humanist spokesman said, 'I'm told by the elder Grubdollar sibling, Martin, that you were very sick when they found you. They feared a case of rattle-lung at first, but it wasn't that. You were nauseous, right? Dizzy? Had difficulty breathing?'

Az nodded, puzzled by the turn the questioning had taken. 'Interesting. And this state of feeling rotten lasted for roughly twenty-four hours?'

'Thereabouts.'

Steamarm turned to Brace. 'Remind you of anything, Lawrence?'

'Miners,' came the reply. 'Apprentice's bends.'

'Quite. Apprentice miners experience similar symptoms for their first few days on the coalface, especially if they start off working deep underground. Gradually they adjust. Their bodies acclimatise.'

Steamarm turned back to Az. 'But we shall say no more. This is of no concern to our young friend here. Not yet, at any rate. From you, Azrael, I think I require a little strategic intelligence now. For instance, your leadership. Who, exactly, commissioned you to come down here?'

'Her name is Serena, Lady Aanfielsdaughter,' Az said, 'and she is a great and wise woman.'

'She runs everything?'

'More or less.'

'A matriarch. Formidable, I should imagine.'

'She's a proper leader, not a longwinded, self-satisfied buffoon,' Az said.

Steamarm's right hand twitched, but he decided to be amused.

'I should like to meet this wonderful person someday,' Steamarm said. 'Apparently I could learn a thing or two from her. And perhaps I could teach *her* a thing or two in return.'

Just as he was saying this, there was a flicker of dazzling light at the window, followed a few heartbeats later by a deep, grinding rumble from above.

Az looked round in alarm. What was that?

'You seem startled,' said Steamarm. 'Just a spot of thunder. Surely you've heard thunder before.'

'"Thunder"?'

'Ah, an unfamiliar word. And "lightning" too, I suppose.'

Az shook his head to show that both terms were new to him.

'Really you do come from another world, Azrael. That flash of light, that rumble, they signify that a storm is coming. But of course, up above the clouds you don't have storms, do you? You're not affected by them. We down here, on the other hand, are. Sometimes severely. We get flooded, there are fires . . . All sorts.'

The electrostatic discharges in the clouds – those noiseless flickers of light – meant little or nothing to the Airborn. It was an event that happened far below, beneath notice. On the ground, however, it was obviously a matter of great importance.

There was another flash, and it filled the larder with a stutter of brilliance, making the shadows leap and writhe. The rumble that came after was like something vast being split asunder.

Lightning. Thunder. Mist. Rain.

All at once Az felt horribly, gut-wrenchingly homesick for the bright, sunlit, calm place where such ugly weather conditions were unheard of.

He was never getting back there. Not now. Once Steamarm was finished with him, once he had drained all the usefulness out of him, he wasn't simply going to let him go free, was he? No, either he was going to keep him here in the larder indefinitely, leaving him to rot, or . . .

Or dispose of him. In a more violent fashion.

Az felt a plunge inside, not unlike the horribly unforgettable sensation of plummeting through space with those copper wings on his back three years ago.

'Let us continue, shall we?' Steamarm said. 'Now that we've established you're a stranger to storms. I think we should turn our attention to defence matters. Specifically, what kind of military arrangement, if any, might one expect to find up in the realm of the Ascended Ones? Is there a standing army? Maybe some kind of aircraft-borne wing of the armed forces?'

'Wing!' said Brace, with a chuckle.

'Oh yes, a pun. Totally unintentional, I might add.' Despite that, Steamarm looked impressed by his own wordsmithery. 'Well, Azrael? Come on, I asked you a question. Don't start the silent act again. That would be a shame. We were getting along so nicely.'

Once more there was a rumble from outside.

Thunder again?

Az thought so, until he realised that it hadn't been preceded by a snap of lightning. And it wasn't a short, sharp burst of sound; it was continuous.

Continuous, and growing louder.

And louder.

'What the . . .' Steamarm looked around, perplexed.

So did Brace.

Suddenly a shadow loomed in the tiny window, casting the larder into darkness.

Next instant, the outer wall collapsed, erupting inward in a cascade of mortar and stones.

CHAPTER 44

Murk-Comber Versus Cottage

It hadn't been thunder, of course. Rather it had been the roar of a 500-horsepower engine propelling fifty tonnes of caterpillar-tracked vehicle at a sedate but remorseless speed across Lawrence Brace's back garden, straight towards his cottage.

The collision of murk-comber with external wall made both vehicle and building shudder. But only one of them suffered any harm.

And it wasn't *Cackling Bertha*.

Within seconds of the impact, Cassie leapt nimbly out from the loading bay and hurried towards the cottage. Meanwhile Fletcher threw *Bertha* into reverse, pulling her back to expose the large, jagged hole she had punched in Brace's home. Debris scattered from her nose. Chunks of plaster and stone tumbled to the ground, to be crushed beneath her treads.

'Az! Az!' Cassie stumbled across rubble and peered into the dark of the larder. 'Az, be you there?' She wafted away swirls of rising dust. 'Az?'

Lightning briefly whitened the world, and in its illumination Cassie made out three figures in the larder. Two were sprawled together, pinned by a fallen set of shelves, with an avalanche of crockery all around them. They were lying still. The third figure was slumped in the opposite corner, and was stirring.

'Az, that you?'

A cough came from the third figure, then a muffled 'Yes'.

'Up you get. Come on. Us is here to rescue you. You OK?'

Az got shakily to his feet. 'Think so.'

'This way then. Hurry.'

Az tottered towards her. There were fragments of mortar and plaster all over him, and his hair was whitened by dust. She noticed a couple of small cuts on his face, and a bruise- like swelling on his cheek. His eyes were glazed with shock.

'How ... I didn't think ... Why ...'

'No time for gab. Explanations later. Get yourself into *Bertha*.'

Cassie shoved him out through the hole and round to the side of the murk-comber. He clambered inside the loading bay, and Cassie jumped in behind him and hit the switch to shut the hatch.

She snatched up the speaker tube.

'Us is in, Fletch. Give she loads!'

Bertha let out an almighty cackle of delight and accelerated in reverse across the back garden, ploughing a fresh set of track furrows.

CHAPTER 45

A Heart-Rending Loss Of Marrows

Not long after, the two men left in the larder groaned and began to move.

Brace was the first to come to his senses fully, and as soon as he perceived that he and Steamarm were lying under a set of shelves, he set about remedying the situation. With a huge grunt and a flex of his shoulders he shunted the shelves off them, then he swiped away shards of broken crockery to clear an area of floorspace. He hauled himself upright, bent, and helped Steamarm to his feet. Tentatively, the two men made their way out through the hole, emerging into the open air.

'My house.' Brace surveyed the damage, his mouth down- turned mournfully. 'Look what them did to my house. 'you know how much that'm going to cost to fix? And my garden. Them drove straight over my vegetable patch. My precious veggies! My poor marrows!'

Brace was very partial to a marrow and very proud of the ones he grew, which he believed to be the largest and best in all of Grimvale. The sight of them smashed to a pulp by the murk-comber's treads was almost too much to bear. His eyes moistened.

'Never mind that,' said a still-dazed Steamarm. 'They've taken something I need, and I want it back.'

'You mean the boy?'

'No, not the boy.' Steamarm swore soundly through clenched teeth. 'And when everything was going so well, too! They'll regret it, though. You don't mess with Alan Steamarm and get away with it.'

The murk-comber,' Brace said, belatedly realising what Steamarm's 'something I need' referred to.

'Yes, the bloody murk-comber. *My* murk-comber. But it's all right.'

Suddenly Steamarm's voice was preternaturally calm; his face viciously determined.

'Yes, it's all right. They've got it now, but it won't be theirs for long.'

CHAPTER 46

Steamarm's Further Ambitions

'Figured you needed saving,' Cassie said. 'And being as it were our fault you ended up captured in the first place, it were up to we to get you out.'

'But your brother who's driving,' said Az, 'isn't he one of them? A Humanist?'

Cassie gave a wry shrug. 'Fletch and I had a bit of a chat. I set he straight on a couple of things. Got he to see sense. It were lucky, though, that him were alone when I reached *Bertha*. Martin were around at the pit but off having a bite of lunch. If *him'd* been in the shed, I wouldn't have stood a chance and I wouldn't be here now. Martin's a dyed-in-the-wool Humanist, while Fletch ... Well, him were open to persuasion, put it like that. And him knew where you'm being kept, and so here us is.'

Az eyed her by the glow of the single, low-output bulb that lit the loading bay yellowly. The pair of them were swaying to and fro in time to the ponderous sway of *Bertha's* progress, like dancers in some strange, non-contact waltz.

'I don't know what to say, Cassie.'

'"Thanks" would do, but actually I reckon this makes things even. Now all us has to do is return you to the Chancel so's you can get back up where you belong.'

'You'd do that for me?'

'Barring disasters, us can get you inside as far as the Relic sorting-house area. After that, you'm on your own. Think you can find them elevators again?'

Az wasn't at all certain, but he said yes.

'There you go then,' Cassie said. 'Done and dusted. Now, you'm really all right? What did our good friend Mr Steamarm want with you anyway?'

'Hard to say. He kept asking these random questions, wanting to know about our leadership, military capability and so on. He didn't get very far before you came crashing in. I don't think he learned very much.' This last statement was one which Az hoped, rather than felt, was true.

'Hmm,' said Cassie, musing. 'Sounds like ... No, him wouldn't. Would him?'

'Wouldn't what?'

Instead of answering, she grabbed the speaker tube.

'Fletch? After you lot was going to take over the Chancel, what then? What were your man Steamarm planning next?'

'Occupy it,' came the reply. 'Kick out the Deacons.'

'That'm it?'

'Far as I know.'

'No phase two?'

'Not that anyone told I about.'

Replacing the tube on its hook, Cassie said to Az, 'Maybe him was just being nosy. I mean, who wouldn't want to interrogate a real, live Ascended One if them got the chance?'

'But maybe not,' said Az slowly. He was catching her drift. 'What if Steamarm's ambitions aren't limited to occupying the Chancel? He mentioned our "flying machines", as he called them. And there was also some stuff about apprentice miners and "bends", although I can't say I completely followed it. You think he's planning an invasion, don't you? He's going to lead the Humanists up into the Airborn world.'

Cassie's frank, perturbed expression told Az that was precisely what she was thinking.

'So why hasn't he said anything about it to your brother? Surely he wouldn't keep his fellow Humanists in the dark about something as major as that.'

'Him might, especially with them who'm some way down the pecking order, like Fletch. So as not to alarm they. Telling they from the start that them's going to be mounting an attack on the Ascended Ones – it'd put a lot of they off. Them'd think it a step too far. But wait till the Chancels has fallen, and while everyone's flush with victory, tell they *then*, and him's considerably more likely to get they to go along with it.'

'The Humanists would really do that? Go up into the sky-cities?'

'I don't know, Az,' Cassie said, slightly testy. 'I be'n't one of them, be I? Also, Deacons say it'm impossible. Us can't survive up there. But judging from what Steamarm were asking you, all them things he were curious about, I'd say him be thinking about it.'

'A co-ordinated assault,' Az said, 'and nobody up there will be expecting it.'

'Them will be,' Cassie said, 'if you'm able to get there and give they a warning.'

Az squared his jaw and nodded. 'You're right. That's what I'm going to have to do, warn them. Straight up.'

Cassie peered at him askance.

'What?' he said. 'Why are you looking at me like that?'

'You said "straight up".'

'No, I didn't. Did I?'

'Yeah, you did.' She half smiled. 'How long you'm been here? Couple of days. And already you's picked up some of the lingo.'

Az half smiled back. 'Yeah. I *has* done and all.'

'Hey, watch it.'

'So, how long till we reach the Chancel?' Az's relief at being rescued was starting to ebb away as he considered the prospect of another run-in with the Deacons.

'An hour or so. *Bertha* be'n't the fastest thing on the road, but her's sure to get you there in the end.'

'What shall we do in the meantime?'

Cassie waved a hand. 'Want to take a tour?'

'Of the famous *Cackling Bertha?* Love to.'

CHAPTER 47

A Matter Of Perspective

They wriggled through *Bertha*'s crawl-ducts and up and down her ladders. Cassie showed Az each of the observation nacelles in turn, and the roof turret, and finally took him up to the driver's pod. There, they crouched behind Fletcher, and Az watched, fascinated, as the second eldest Grub-dollar brother manipulated the control sticks, guiding the murk-comber along the streets of Grimvale. Rain had begun to fall in heavy drops, spattering the windscreen. Fletcher engaged the wipers and switched on the headlamps. Lightning flickered every now and then, forking white through the inky blackness of the clouds. Each time, a thunder crackle resounded soon after.

Outside, Groundlings hurried through the rain, seeking shelter. Some huddled in doorways or under shop awnings. A few were carrying a protective device which Cassie told Az was called an *umbrella*. It was like a portable, foldable canvas roof, and it kept you from getting wet.

Soon *Bertha* was out of the town and beetling along through, a forest. The trees were tall and thick-trunked, giants compared with the tended, coppiced courtyard trees Az was used to. Even in the Airborn's parks there was nothing as towering as these evergreens, nor was there such a profusion of undergrowth. The Airborn favoured lawns and tidiness. Nature, in the sky-cities, was tamed and contained. It had to be. Down here, on the other hand, it had no confines. It proliferated wherever and whenever, without limits.

Even so, Az noted that there was something about the trees' foliage, a droopiness, a lack of vitality, that implied they grew tall only through great effort. Poorly nourished by the thin, cloud-filtered sunlight, it cost them everything they had to become as big as they did. Their needles were a yellowy green, nothing like the deep, vibrant, sun-drenched pine greens he was familiar with. Lichen covered their trunks, and moss, too, in thick, spongy blobs – parasites that thrived in the damp conditions.

At Cassie's suggestion, Fletcher took a detour, leaving the main road and heading off along a side road. The side road was windy and narrow and slowed them down, but, as Cassie explained, it meant they wouldn't be travelling past the Consolidated Colliery Collective, which was where the Humanists had been keeping *Bertha*. She didn't think it a good idea to parade the murk-comber in front of the noses of the people they had recently retrieved her from.

'Them wasn't too happy when us left,' she said to Az. 'Had to drive out through the front gate, and them picketers couldn't get out of our way fast enough. Scattered they like skittles, us did.'

'Them used some very colourful language,' said Fletcher, chuckling at the memory. 'Some even threw stones at us. Bounced off *Bertha*, of course. Doubt her barely felt it. But those people won't be any too happy to see we again, that'm for sure. Didn't make no friends there.'

'Plus, Martin's probably got they mobilised and setting up roadblocks, knowing him. Speaking of which, d'you think Martin'll ever talk to you or I again, Fletch?'

'Doubt it, lass.' Fletcher gave a rueful laugh. 'Maybe twenty years from now we'll get a "hello" out of he. Maybe. Martin be the type to hold a grudge all right.'

'Sorry to turn you against he.'

'Weren't *he* specifically, Cass. Was all of they. You just reminded me where my priorities lay. It were that and your poor hand.'

Cassie glanced at her bruised, verm-bitten hand.

'I looked at that,' Fletcher said, 'and remembered how you saved I the day before yesterday. Helped make sense of things, a bit. Truth be told, I were beginning to feel a bit queasy about it all anyway, not least when I saw they hitting Da. Didn't think it would come down to choosing sides, but it did, and I's glad I chose the right one.'

'Yeah, you did.' Cassie patted his shoulder – with her good hand.

'How about you, Mr Ascended One?' Fletcher said to Az, craning round. 'You'm going to be glad to get back home, I reckon. Tell you, life down here be'n't always this dramatic. You should come down another time when it'm calmer. You'll see us is an all right lot really.'

'I may take you up on that offer,' Az said. It didn't sound convincing even to himself.

They rejoined the main road at a point beyond the northernmost of Grimvale's industrial premises. Shortly, the landscape began flattening out, the mountainous terrain giving way to foothills and eventually a plain.

'The Shadow Zone,' Cassie announced.

Az leaned forward, peering even more attentively through the windscreen. The clouds were still black and rifted with forks of lightning, as though intermittently shattering. But ahead, there was a darkness that was deeper than that caused by the storm, a dreary, tenebrous gloom.

The last time Az was in the Shadow Zone it had been night and he had, moreover, been in no fit state to take stock of his surroundings. Now he saw a barren, broken expanse of landscape where scant vegetation grew and any that did was either low and mossy or tough and spiky. There were boulders and rough hillocks, and silvery flashes of waterway. Far, far in the distance Heliotropia's support column was visible, rising sheer into the clouds, finger-thin. In the low light Az could just make out the cluster of buildings at its base, the Chancel. Somewhere up above lay the sky-city itself, he knew, but there was no way you could get any sense of how it looked or even its size. It was visible only by the shade it cast through the clouds, the roughly circular penumbra that left several dozen hectares of the world below in perpetual eclipse.

'It's an impressive city,' he said in hushed tones, 'and yet down here you have no idea of that. All you get is what it isn't.'

'Yup, that about sums it up,' said Cassie, with more than a touch of irony. 'What us gets down here is what you lot up there be'n't.'

'Oy-oy.'

Fletcher was frowning up at a large convex mirror that was mounted to the left of the windscreen. There were two of these mirrors in the driver's pod, and if Az didn't miss his guess they reflected images conveyed from *Bertha*'s aft end along tubes via a system of lenses. Rearview mirrors with knobs on.

Fletcher turned to check the right-hand one.

'Oy-oy,' he said again, more emphatically this time.

'What'm up?' said Cassie. From any angle except from the driving seat the images in the mirrors were opaque; it was hard to make out what they were showing.

'Us is being followed. Two coal trucks. No, three. And them's gaining fast. Don't think the drivers is after checking our union accreditation, either.'

CHAPTER 48

The Low-speed Chase Begun

The coal trucks all bore the insignia of the Consolidated Colliery Collective – three C's, one inside the other. They were unladen and being driven at top speed. There was no question that they could catch up with *Bertha*, who couldn't manage more than 30 kph at full throttle. The question was, what were they going to do when they did?

'Steer off-road,' Cassie urged Fletcher. 'Them won't be able to follow.'

'Thought of that already, girl. If you take a look around, you may notice it'm too rocky out there. Us'll get stuck. First possible turning-off point be a good couple of kilometres ahead.'

'Block they, then. Get in the middle of the road.'

Fletcher eased the right control stick forward a notch. 'Think one of they will still be able to pull alongside. *Bertha*'s broad but maybe not enough.'

'What do they want with us, Cassie?' said Az.

'Best guess? Stop we. Run we off the road if they can. Anything, so long as they gets *Bertha* back.'

'Run us off . . . ? But we could be killed!'

Cassie's smile was grim. 'Not sure as that be too much of a worry for they.'

The leading truck swiftly closed the gap between it and *Bertha*, until its front bumper was less than a metre from her left-hand track. The driver nosed forwards into the space between *Bertha*'s flank and the edge of the road. Fletcher steered the murk-comber in that direction, narrowing the available room. The truck driver braked, falling in behind once more. As Fletcher straightened out *Bertha*'s course, the driver attempted the manoeuvre a second time. He was deterred again by the lumbering bulk of *Bertha* veering into his path.

The second truck arrived and took up position on the opposite side of the road. Using the mirrors, Fletcher nudged *Bertha* in front of it so that there was no way through. This, however, meant that the first truck now had a clear run. The driver seized his opportunity, gunned the engine, and accelerated past *Bertha* before Fletcher could swing back over to prevent him.

147

Now there was one truck in front, one behind, and the third zooming up to join them.

'Pull over,' Az advised. 'This is no good. Give them what they're after. It's all about me. Getting me to the Chancel. That's not worth risking your lives over.'

'What'm you talking about, boy?' said Fletcher. 'This be'n't about you. It'm about *Bertha*. And I'd sooner crash she in a ball of flames than let they have their way with she.'

'Fletch's right,' Cassie agreed. 'Took he long enough to realise it, but better late than never. No way is those Humanists having she. Besides,' she added with a tight smile, 'look at the size of what them's driving compared with *Bertha*. I don't know how them hopes to stop she with just trucks. Her weighs about five times as much. Them'd have to be crazy to—'

The truck in front braked sharply.

'Hold on!' shouted Fletcher.

Bertha rolled onward and collided nose-first with the truck's rear. There was a deafening screeching *smash*. The truck was shunted forwards, its tyres lost traction on the wet road, and it went careering this way and that till the driver regained control.

'Reckon him won't try that again in a hurry,' Cassie said.

'Let's hope not,' said Az.

The third coal truck at last joined the fray. All Fletcher could see in each of the mirrors was a driver's cab, a windscreen with the wipers working furiously, and a radiator grille with the three-C's logo embossed on it. The drivers themselves were hard to make out, blurry faces that appeared briefly each time the wipers cleared the windscreen before becoming lost again in the rain. He wasn't liking the fact that *Bertha* was boxed in, at the centre of a triangle of trucks. Even if the trucks were no match for her in terms of bulk, they might still be able to do some damage, enough to disable her. And as the somewhat foolhardy driver in front had just demonstrated, the Humanists were prepared to try anything to get her to stop, even at risk of their own lives.

The third truck suddenly veered sideways, slamming its wheel arch against *Bertha*'s caterpillar track. One of the sticks jumped in Fletcher's grasp but he regained control quickly.

The truck repeated the assault. The impact resounded through the murk-comber's frame.

'Him's a loony, that bloke,' Cassie said. 'Likely as not him'll kill himself, if him's not careful.'

'No, not a loony,' Fletcher said, coldly. He was staring hard at one of the mirrors. He had at last got a clear view of one of the drivers. 'It'm Martin.'

'Martin?'

'Him's the one ramming we. Because him knows. Knacker one of *Bertha*'s tracks, and her'll be crippled. Her'll stop dead.'

Cassie bent, trying to get a glimpse of the truck driver in the mirror. You'm sure it be he?'

'I know our own brother's face, girl.'

One more time, the truck hurled itself at *Bertha*. As it hit, its wheel housing was ripped away by the force of the collision. Metal twisted and tore. The truck slewed off the road, bumped and jerked crazily on the roadside rocks, and then, more through luck than anything, bounced back onto the tarmac and carried on driving. One of its front wheels was now uncovered, exposed by a section of missing bodywork.

And part of the section of missing bodywork was entangled in *Bertha's* track, being rolled around between the track links and the running wheels. This had been Martin's plan. If the shred of metal became caught—

It did. It jammed between two of the wheels.

All at once, *Bertha* began to skid.

CHAPTER 49

The Low-speed Chase Continued

Fletcher did everything he could to manage the skid. It happened with dreamy slowness, for *Bertha* never did anything in a hurry. Her front started to turn, sliding round in the direction of the tread that had seized up. Her rear end followed, lumbering outwards. Fletcher hauled back on one stick to counteract the rotation, but with minimal effect. *Bertha* had momentum, plenty of it, and all of it was going into the skid.

As for Cassie and Az, there was little else they could do but find something in the driver's pod to hang onto, and hang onto it tight.

Now *Bertha* was sideways on the road, still skidding. She was almost graceful in this moment of loss of control, ballerina-like as she pirouetted. Anyone watching from a safe distance might have been enchanted by the smoothness, the stateliness with which the sizeable vehicle spun.

She continued to turn, while the three trucks kept pace with her, as though this was all some prearranged formation exercise. *Bertha* had nearly about-faced when, through an abrupt stroke of good fortune, the piece of coal truck bodywork snapped loose from the wheels, pinging out onto the road. All at once, her jammed track was working again. Fletcher sensed it through the sticks and took the appropriate action. He had only one choice, if he wished to keep going at any speed. He lined *Bertha* up on the road and wrenched both sticks into reverse.

Bertha was still rolling. The three trucks were still with her, having failed to stop her yet. The only difference now was that *Bertha* was going backwards.

Through her windscreen, the two pursuing trucks were clearly visible. And yes, Cassie could see Martin at the wheel of one of them. The other driver was one of the Humanists who had invaded the Grubdollar's house that morning, one of the ones whose names Cassie didn't know. And beside him, in the passenger seat, was none other than Alan Steamarm.

A very angry-looking and unhappy-looking Alan Steamarm.

Cassie blew him a sarcastic kiss.

In return, Steamarm sneered.

'Perhaps you could stop flirting and start doing something useful,' Fletcher admonished her. 'Driving backwards like this be'n't easy. Why not find some way of messing they up like them tried to mess we up, eh?'

'What d'you mean?'

'Well, doesn't us have a javelin launcher on board?'

'You don't want me to—'

'Take out a tyre, that'm all.'

Cassie grinned. 'Fletch, genius!' She dived out of the driver's pod.

'What about me?' Az asked Fletcher. 'Can I help somehow?'

'Go aft to one of the rear observation nacelles. Tell I if I'm getting too close to the edge of the road.'

'No problem.' Az, too, dived out of the pod.

In the roof turret, Cassie primed the launcher and swivelled it round. Her priority, she decided, was the truck in front. She should clear the road.

The truck was perhaps thirty metres ahead. She drew a bead on it with the launcher's sights. What was it that Da said? Aim slightly high. A javelin never travelled in a dead straight line. There was always an arc to its flight.

She curled a finger round the trigger and squeezed. With a sharp propulsive hiss the javelin shot towards the truck's back wheel . . .

. . . and missed, hitting the road with a spark and spiralling away.

'Bugger!'

Ordering herself to keep her nerve, Cassie reloaded, primed the launcher again, and aimed.

She was about to shoot, but the truck hit a pothole and leapt out of the sights.

She centred the tyre again in the sights, then raised the launcher fractionally.

'You're mine,' she said. 'Pop!'

The javelin whistled across the distance between *Bertha* and the truck.

The tyre exploded. One instant it was there, inflated, full; the next it was just so much loose, shredded rubber.

The truck immediately went into a long, shuddering deceleration, throwing out fragments of tyre behind it. A moment after it came to a complete halt, diagonally across the road, *Bertha* went barging into it.

With so much weight behind her, *Bertha* wasn't going to be hindered by a mere truck. It was no obstacle whatever. She shunted it along for a hundred metres or so, pushing it up at an increasingly oblique angle, until the truck, as if deciding it had had enough of this undignified treatment, keeled over and tumbled off the road, rolling, bouncing, crunching onto the rocks, where it came to a standstill, upside down.

Bertha trundled past it, as did the remaining two trucks. Seconds later, one door of the overturned truck flipped open and the dazed driver hauled himself out.

'Good shot!' came Az's voice over the speaker tube.

'Yeah, lass, not bad,' said Fletcher. 'Now how about them other two?'

Cranking on a lever, Cassie spun the turret round. She grabbed a fresh javelin from behind her, slotted it in, and sighted on the coal truck Martin was driving.

No, she couldn't. In spite of everything, she couldn't fire on her own brother.

She swivelled her aim onto Steamarm instead.

No qualms about javelining *his* vehicle.

Suddenly: 'Left!'

Az, yelling urgently.

'We have to go left!'

Cassie felt *Bertha* start to turn.

'No, *my* left, not yours!'

Bertha lumbered the other way.

Cassie glanced out. They had reached a section of the road that had been carved into the side of a small hill, the last such hill before the Shadow Zone plain began. The ground fell away to the right in a steep slope some ten metres deep, a gradient of loose earth and gravel. On the left rose a bank of similar size and composition. It was like this for the next half-kilometre.

Slight subsidence meant that the road surface was very uneven and the camber more bowed than it should be. Additionally, the road started to curve round a bend here, following the contour of the hill.

In other words, it was a tricky stretch to navigate in *Bertha* even when you were going forwards and at a sensible speed.

Fletcher was tackling it in reverse and at full throttle.

No wonder he hadn't answered Az. He couldn't be bothering with the speaker tube. He had his hands full just keeping them on the tarmac.

Well, Cassie was in a position to give him assistance. She locked the javelin launcher back on her target: Steamarm's truck.

Martin, however, had other ideas.

CHAPTER 50

The Low-speed Chase Concluded

Martin stamped on the accelerator, ramming *Bertha* with his truck just as Cassie loosed off the javelin. The launcher jerked sideways and her shot went wild. The javelin lodged itself in the bank, quivering.

Another, unintentional, consequence of Martin's action was that *Bertha* was knocked slightly off-course. She was close to the bank already and the impact was just enough to shove her against it. She scraped the bank and rebounded with force, swerving slowly and inexorably across to the other side of the road. Her right-hand track left the tarmac and dug into the top of the slope. Earth and gravel churned out sideways.

Cassie could feel Fletcher fighting to keep *Bertha* steady. The murkcomber was shuddering and juddering. If she came off the road and went sliding down the slope, she would flip up when she hit the bottom and somersault end over end. Cassie had a stark vision of this happening. Everyone on board would be tossed around like beads in a baby's rattle. None of them would survive, and *Bertha* herself would be so much scrap metal.

Az was yelling frantically into the speaker tube, but to Cassie his words were meaningless gabble. His voice was just part of a tumultuous background cacophony, along with *Bertha*'s cackle anxious now – and the gruelling grind of gravel beneath her treads.

Inside, Cassie was weirdly calm. For seconds that seemed like minutes, she waited for the sudden sideways lurch that would mean *Bertha* was doomed. It was all she could do, wait. Wait, and wonder how much it would hurt when the moment of death came, and who would turn up for her Ceremony of Ascension. And what would become of Az? If an Ascended One died down here, could he or she Ascend? Did it work like that? It was an intriguing conundrum.

Then *Bertha* began to level out. Fletcher had her under control again. Both of her tracks were safely on tarmac, and the road was straightening now, and the slope on the right was gradually getting shallower.

When the slope was gone altogether, they would be properly in the Shadow Zone. At that point they could leave the road, striking out across the rugged open terrain where the coal trucks could not follow them.

153

Martin knew this. From the turret, Cassie saw him bring his truck in close, evidently contemplating one final assault.

He thought better of it. He eased off on the accelerator and the truck fell back.

She understood why. Just now, he had nearly killed his brother and sister. He had meant only to knock Cassie's aim off but he had come close to causing a disaster. No way did he want their deaths on his conscience. For all the differences between him and them, they were still family.

Alan Steamarm, on the other hand, had no such compunctions. Cassie saw him give Martin's retreating truck a furious stare. Then he gave an order to his driver, his gesticulations clearly saying that the driver should do what Martin had failed to earlier and snarl up the murk-comber's track with a bit of truck.

The driver steered close.

Fletcher, at that very moment, realised his chance to get away had come at last. He turned *Bertha* sharply. There was bumping, bouncing, thudding, thumping. Cassie was tossed around in her seat, so violently that she banged her forehead on the launcher handles.

Then they were moving away from the road. Fletcher had driven off it backwards, and now they were reversing across the raw terrain of the Shadow Zone. He must have felt confident that Steamarm would not pursue them any more, because he reduced *Bertha*'s speed to a crawl.

Steamarm, though, was not about to give up so easily. His truck braked, then ventured off the road in first gear.

'I don't believe it,' Fletcher said into the speaker tube.

'Don't believe what?' Az replied. 'What's going on?' Az was at the back of *Bertha*. He couldn't see the road.

'Steamarm thinks him can still catch we,' Cassie said. 'Him won't get far, though.'

If a vehicle could look tentative, that coal truck did. It resembled someone wading into icy cold water. The driver got all four wheels off the road, then pumped the accelerator experimentally. The truck lumbered forwards, and hit a snag. One of the front wheels rolled into a cleft, the kind of thirty-centimetre fissure in the ground that *Bertha* could pass over without even noticing. The driver shifted into reverse and, after several false starts, pulled out. With great care he navigated around the cleft – and promptly got a wheel stuck in another one.

Fletcher brought *Bertha* to a complete halt, putting her into neutral. 'This should be funny.'

The truck escaped the second cleft, but now there was a series of small boulders to be got around. The truck had a high wheelbase and good suspension but it couldn't ride a rock field the way a murk-comber could.

In all, the truck managed to struggle forward for a grand total of twenty metres before Steamarm admitted defeat and told the driver to turn around. Getting back to the road was another epic effort, and the truck almost didn't make it.

On the road, Martin was waiting. He had known better than to attempt what Steamarm had attempted. Steamarm climbed out of his truck and went over to Martin for a conference.

Az poked his head up through the turret entrance. 'Mind if I join you? I'm obviously missing out on some good stuff.' He clambered in. 'So what's up? Why aren't we moving any more?'

'Because us is safe, for now,' Cassie said.

'I must say, I thought we were goners back there.'

'You wasn't the only one.'

'I can laugh about it now.'

'But you was screaming like a girl earlier.'

Az looked sheepish. 'Yeah. Sorry.'

'Don't worry. Least you'm man enough to admit you was scared.'

Martin left his partly mangled truck, and he and Steamarm walked to the roadside. Martin looked towards *Bertha* and waved both arms in the air, the gesture of someone who wished to parley.

'What you reckon, Fletch?' Cassie said into the speaker tube. 'Go out for a chat?'

'Tempted, but I be'n't sure Martin has anything to say to I that I wants to listen to. Besides, us has the advantage here. Foolish to waste it.'

'My thoughts exactly.'

Martin's hands fell to his sides in disappointment as Fletcher started *Bertha*'s engine up. Fletcher brought the murk-comber around, beat out a cheeky toot-toot on the horn, and trundled away.

'That'm that then,' Cassie said to Az. 'Next stop, the Chancel.'

CHAPTER 51

Escape From The Chancel: The Blanks In Az's Memory Filled In

The Chancel boasted four entrances positioned equidistantly around its perimeter fence, one for each of the main roads that came in across the Shadow Zone. The entrances were fortified and patrolled. There were barriers, gatehouses, and even retractable ramps in the road which could be operated hydraulically to stop a vehicle from going in or leaving.

The Deacons took their security seriously. Or, to put it another way, they were very keen on protecting what was theirs.

The perimeter fence itself was a lofty steel stockade, crowned with outward-curving spikes. Looking at it, Az marvelled at the fact that he had escaped from the Chancel at all. He had no recollection of getting over such a fence.

'That'm because you didn't,' Cassie told him. 'I be guessing you went *through* it.'

'Through it? How?'

She showed him. Fletcher was making a detour around a shallow lake, crossing it at the far end where it dispersed into a series of streams and rivulets which ribboned out in all directions. *Bertha* splashed through them like they were mere puddles.

The lake's other end touched the Chancel's perimeter, and it was there that a water outflow pipe penetrated the fence, disgorging its contents into the lake in a pale brown cascade.

'You went out with the cleaned-up sewage,' Cassie said. 'Must have. That'm why you was so wet when us found you.'

This corresponded with Az's patchy memories of his last few moments inside the Chancel – the sewage treatment tanks, the rushing channel. He congratulated her. 'Brilliant detective work there, Miss Grubdollar.'

'Thank you.'

'So can't I get back in the same way?'

'Not unless you be a damn strong swimmer, and I's thinking you'm not. Actually, I doubt even a strong swimmer could get in that way. Doubt a fish could.'

'Fish?'

'Animal that— Never mind. Nope, only possible way in be by the front door, so to speak.'

'The Deacons'll let us in?'

'Don't see why not, us being in a murk-comber. And then, for afterwards, I's got a plan. Tell me, how big be your shoes?'

'How big?' Az was taken aback. What did the size of his shoes have to do with anything? 'I don't know. Medium large.'

Cassie studied his feet. 'Them look to be about the same as Robert's.' She hoisted herself out of the launcher seat. 'Let's go down to the loading bay, see if I be right.'

CHAPTER 52

A Sticky Moment With The Chancel Guards

Fletcher pulled up at the Chancel entrance. Cassie had anticipated that the guards in the gatehouse would simply raise the barrier and wave *Bertha* through, as normally happened. *Bertha* was a regular visitor. There was no reason for them to be suspicious.

But she was wrong. The barrier did not go up. Instead, the retractable ramps shot up behind and in front of *Bertha*, bookending her. She was trapped in place. Then the two guards emerged from the gatehouse and came striding over. The guards were ordinary Deacons, but armoured and armed. They had helmets on, breastplates over their robes, pikestaffs in their hands, handcuffs attached to their belts. One of them used the tip of his pikestaff to rap on *Bertha's* hatch.

Cassie motioned to Az: *get out of sight*. Az hurried up the nearest ladder. Then Cassie hit the lever for the hatch. As it opened, she greeted the guards with a beaming grin. 'What'm up, gents?'

'Afternoon,' said one of them. 'Haven't seen you Grubdollars here in a while.'

'That be because us has been having a run of bad luck. Not finding anything.'

'What a shame,' the guard said, although from the sound of it he couldn't have cared less. Both he and his colleague were looking past Cassie, scanning *Bertha's* interior.

Cassie knew these two. They were familiar faces to her. They were never friendly but they were usually a lot less frostily formal than this.

'Something you'm after?' she asked.

'No. No. It's just that we had a security breach here the other day.'

'Oh?'

'Yes. Someone got in who shouldn't have. A kid. So now we're under orders to check every vehicle that arrives, in case of stowaways.'

'Not that a lot of vehicles *are* arriving right now,' said the other guard.

The first guard nodded. 'Doesn't help that we're all a bit jumpy anyway, what with the Humanists and all that.'

'Ruddy Humanists,' Cassie said, encouragingly.

'Yes, quite. The Archdeacon is very concerned about them. Hence, extra vigilance. You can never be too careful. Even when dealing with the Grubdollars and *Cackling Bertha*. Where's your father, then?'

'My Da?'

'Yes. He not with you today?' The guard gestured up towards the driver's pod. 'I see your brother, but there's nobody in any of your observation nacelles. Is it just the two of you?'

'And have you had an accident lately?' the other guard asked. '*Bertha's* got a few new scrapes and dents, front and back.'

Cassie thought fast. The two Deacons were becoming too inquisitive for her liking.

'Yeah, would you believe it? Da had a prang with her yesterday. Him's OK but still puckered up about it. Said him didn't feel like coming out today. And Robert, him's come down with a touch of something. A cough. Don't think it'm serious, not rattle-lung or anything. And Martin ... Martin be looking after the pair of they at home.' How fluently she could lie, when she needed to. 'So that'm why it be just me and Fletch. And we found a Relic! Them'll be green with envy back home when us tells they about that.'

The guards didn't show any sympathy about her family's misfortunes, but at least they seemed to believe her. Perhaps it was the word 'Relic' that did it, reminding them that as well as protect the Chancel they were there to welcome valuable artefacts in.

'Relic, eh? Where is it?'

'Oh, it'm a small thing. Stowed somewhere up top, it be. I could go and get it for you if you like ...'

'No, no, won't be necessary.' The guards gave the loading bay a final once-over, then glanced at each other, satisfied. Shouldering their pike-staffs, they marched back to the gatehouse. A moment later, the ramps slammed flat and the barrier began to rise. *Bertha* rolled forward.

Cassie heaved a sigh of relief. She was glad she'd had the foresight to make Az hide. If the guards had spotted a stranger on board *Bertha*, there would have been all sorts of trouble.

And so the guards let in the very same kid who'd caused the security breach less than forty-eight hours ago.

CHAPTER 53

Difficult Farewell

All Relics were delivered to a sorting-house round at the eastern side of the Chancel. It was a large barn-like building with a rounded, ribbed roof, echoingly spacious inside. You drove your murk-comber in, parked, and showed your Relics to a Deacon, who assessed their worth and, if he wanted them, handed over a money chit which you took to another Deacon behind a barred window in a kiosk in an alcove. He exchanged the chit for cash. Since there was no strict itemised tariff for Relics, the transaction was sometimes open to negotiation. If the Deacon on duty was one of the more compliant ones, you could haggle with him.

The deacon on duty today *wasn't* one of the more compliant ones. Deacon Leavenscale was a hard bargainer, with an uncompromising, take-it-or-leave-it attitude. Cassie's father called him the tightest man he had ever met. 'Any tighter,' Den said, 'and him'd squeak when him walked.'

Cassie, however, couldn't have been more pleased. For Deacon Leavenscale, in addition to being extremely miserly, was extremely nearsighted. He wore spectacles with lenses like magnifying glasses, and in spite of this still had to hold an object up to his nose to see it clearly.

'T's known verms with better eyesight,' she said to Az. They were still inside *Bertha*, Cassie getting ready to exit.

'I take it verms are blind.'

'Spot-on.'

'So you think this gives me a chance?'

'You'd have to be pretty clumsy not to be able to sneak past Leavenscale.'

'I *feel* pretty clumsy in these clodhoppers.' Az indicated the boots he was wearing, which were the ones Robert used to go exploring outside *Bertha*. They were big, hobnailed, mud-encrusted things that came halfway up the shins. Az's own shoes, which Cassie was now holding, were delicate, almost slipper-like, in comparison.

'Them mayn't be as dainty as yours,' Cassie said, 'but them's a damn sight more practical.'

'By my people's standards mine *are* practical shoes. They're made specially for me by a cobbler. I walk a lot more than the average Airborn, so I need something tough on my feet.'

Cassie laughed, somewhat ruefully. 'Well, you'm going back up there now, where toughness be'n't all that necessary. Back to your old life.'

'I know.' Az hadn't thought he would feel anything except glad to be leaving the ground and its denizens. He was surprised to discover that this was going to be quite a difficult farewell after all. 'Listen, Cassie . . .'

Fletcher came shinning down into the loading bay from the driver's pod. 'You seen? It'm Leavenscale!'

'Yes, Fletch, us knows.'

'Blind old Leavenscale. Man wouldn't know where his own bunghole were if you gave he a mirror and a lamp and told he to . . .'

Fletcher's voice trailed off as he realised he was intruding on a sensitive moment.

'I'll, um, I'll just go and, er, do this thing over here,' he said, and ducked into a crawl-duct.

Az looked hack to Cassie. He groped for what to say. 'You've risked so much for me. I appreciate that. No, "appreciate" doesn't begin to cover it. Thanks to you I'm alive, and thanks to you I've got this chance of warning my people about the Humanists. Don't think I'll ever forget that, because I won't. I . . . I don't know if it's possible that I can come back down. I'd like to think I could, but . . . you know.'

'Come back down!' Cassie exclaimed. 'Why would you *want* to?'

'Well, er, to visit. Say hi.'

'Oh. I see. Sorry, I just couldn't think of a reason why you'm be considering making the journey here twice. Bad enough once. But you mean, like, a social call.'

'Yes.'

She understood then that Az wished to be friends with her, and perhaps more than friends. In a fumbling, roundabout way he was asking if she would like to see him again. Yet he must know that what he was suggesting was impractical, if not downright absurd. He must know someone like him and someone like her couldn't be anything more than footnotes in each other's life. He'd said what he had said because he had to say it. He'd had to get it out of him. But in a minute or so from now, he would be gone and there was never any chance they would lay eyes on each other again. Once Az was up where he belonged, among his own kind, he would quickly be reabsorbed into their way of life. For all his protestations, he *would* forget her.

And Cassie didn't mind that.

Did she?

She had rescued him, after all. She had put herself on the line for him. Was it just because she felt guilty? Because her sense of what was right had obliged her to? Or was there more to it?

Had she saved him because he needed saving, or because *she* needed to prove something to him by saving him?

Cassie confronted these thoughts in the space of a couple of seconds, then banished them. She was a pragmatic girl. She had little room in her for fanciful notions. She dealt in possibilities only, not impossibilities. In her next life, winged, Ascended, she would have all the time in the world for wondering and dreaming. Until then . . .

'Not going to happen, be it, Az?' she said. 'I mean, let's be realistic. Social call? You come down here to see I? About as likely as me going up there to see you.'

'Yes. Yes, of course.'

'Besides, us may have ruined things for the Humanists in Grimvale, but there'm other townships and other Chancels. This situation be happening everywhere, not just here. Sooner or later, probably sooner, there'm going to be strife. Your people against mine. Sky against ground.'

Punctuating her point, thunder rolled distantly, making *Bertha* vibrate.

'Not sure it can be avoided,' she went on. And I doesn't think there'll be much socialising going on then, if you see my meaning.'

'It can be avoided,' Az said resolutely, 'if everyone's prepared to negotiate. And I'm certain my people will.'

'Then you'd better hurry and get up there and tell they what'm going on, so's them can sort out their bargaining position.'

'Yes. You're right.' Az was disappointed, but her commonsense talk had blown through him like a sharp breeze, clearing his head. 'Well then. Pleasure to have met you, Cassie Grubdollar.'

'Likewise, Az Gabrielson.'

'Thanks for everything. And . . . and goodbye.'

'Goodbye to you too.'

They shared a handshake. She noted how soft his skin was. He noted how firm her grip was.

The handshake lingered.

Then Cassie disengaged her fingers from Az's and reached for the hatch lever.

CHAPTER 54

Distraction Techniques

'Hmmm,' said Deacon Leavenscale.

Fletcher winked at Cassie. They both could tell that it was a very positive *Hmmm*. Az's shoes intrigued him.

'Yes, I've no doubt they're authentic,' he said, holding one of the shoes so close to his nose it looked as if he was sniffing it. Distorted by his spectacle lenses, his weak grey eyes bulged like two mushrooms. 'The quality of the stitching tells me that, as does the nature of the leather. Tanned bird hide has its own peculiar pliancy and grain. I can't say I've seen soles quite as thick before, but perhaps it's a new fashion. But a pair. That's the remarkable thing. A *pair* of Ascended shoes. That's rare. Usually it's just the one.'

Cassie had taken a quick glance over her shoulder in *Bertha*'s direction. Realising that Leavenscale had stopped talking, she snapped her head back to face him.

Az had not made his move yet.

'Yeah, us was surprised about that too,' she said.

'Very surprised,' Fletcher chimed in. 'But, you know, us be'n't the sort to question what fate brings.'

Deacon Leavenscale laid the shoe carefully beside its counterpart on his desktop.

'Water-damaged,' he observed, 'and somewhat battered. That lowers their value.'

'Oh come on!' Fletcher said, genuinely indignant. 'It'm pissing down with rain outside. How's them *not* going to be water-damaged? Not to mention them fell who knows how many kilometres. When be the last time you saw a Relic that'm in a tenth as good condition?'

'True, true. It would, however, be remiss of me not to point out any flaws.'

Cassie sneaked another look over her shoulder. She glimpsed Az lurking just inside *Bertha*'s hatchway, poised to climb out. She took a stealthy step to the right, so that she was blocking Deacon Leavenscale's line of sight to the murk-comber. He might be a myopic old geezer but that didn't mean that his attention would not be caught by a distant blur of movement. She wished they could have parked *Bertha* the other way round, with her hatch on the far side, but the set-up in the sorting-house was such that this was impossible. There was a one-way system, from which you pulled off into angled parking bays that were clearly demarcated by white lines on the floor, with your hatch side exposed. There was no deviating from this arrangement.

At least there were no other murk-combers here at the moment, and consequently nobody present who was sharper- eyed than Deacon Leavenscale. The other Deacon, tucked away in his alcove kiosk, was in no position to see anything that went on in the main part of the sorting-house.

In the north-west corner of the building there was a swing-door, next to which were lined up the trolleys used for transporting larger, heavier Relics to the Reliquary. The door joined the sorting-house to the rest of the Chancel. Az had to make it there unobserved. He could do it, as long as he was careful.

Cassie sent him an encouraging thought: *You'll be fine, Az. Just take it nice and easy.*

Leavenscale bent his head, lowering his face to the shoes for another examination.

Az would not have a better chance than this to get going. Cassie turned and made a surreptitious flapping gesture to him.

Az nodded, taking the hint. He put one foot out from the hatchway, then other, and slithered to the floor.

'Miss Grubdollar?'

She spun round. 'Yes?'

Deacon Leavenscale blinked up owlishly at her. 'You seem ... pre-occupied. Is there something the matter?'

'The shoes,' Fletcher interjected quickly. 'What do you think them's worth?'

The Deacon turned his head. 'What? Oh, too early to say. I'll need to study them some more.'

'Rough estimate, though.'

'I do not give "rough estimates", Mr Grubdollar,' the Deacon said sternly. 'You know that.'

'Go on. Nearest round figure.'

'Young man, do not try my patience. I will not be hurried. And moreover ...'

Leavenscale began to lecture Fletcher on how the assessment of Relics was a highly specialised art that required practice and time. As he blathered on, Cassie canted her head to one side. By straining her eyeballs as far round in their sockets as they would go, she was just able to see Az at the periphery of her vision. He had sensibly frozen stock-still when he heard the Deacon addressing her. Now he began moving again. He crouched

164

low as he went, pressing himself against *Bertha's* side. He had fifty metres to cover to get to the swing-door, some distance, but between it and him there was a line of large concrete blocks which formed a cordon that ran almost the whole way. If Az stayed behind the blocks and kept his head down, he could follow them as far as they went, scurrying from one to the next, then make a final dash.

He must not be seen, though. There was a button on Deacon Leaven-scale's desk which operated a bell to summon assistance from the Reliquary, which was in the adjacent building. The bell doubled as an emergency alarm. If Leavenscale spotted Az, he could hit the button and there would be other Deacons here in no time.

Az stole across the gap between *Bertha* and the nearest of the blocks. He vanished from view.

In front of Cassie, Leavenscale was still droning on about the skill and precision with which he judged the value of Relics. It had been a smart move by Fletcher to ask for a rough estimate. It had pricked Leavenscale's sense of pride, and now he was too busy setting Fletcher straight to notice much else.

'... so you allow me to do my job properly, Mr Grubdollar,' Leavenscale said, concluding his sermon, 'and I shall not tell you how to do yours.'

'Yup. All right.' Fletcher sounded contrite, but he was having to hold back a smirk.

The Deacon flicked a hand, as though swatting aside Fletcher's little blunder like a fly. Now then, a moment or two's peace and quiet, please, so that I may continue my inspection.'

He picked up Az's shoes again, one after the other, and turned them over and over. He held them by his fingertips, handling them delicately, reverently.

Meanwhile the shoes' original owner crept, block by block, towards the door. Thunderclaps shook the sorting-house every so often, making the rafters groan. This and the drumming of rain on the roof provided camouflage for any scuffing sounds Az inadvertently made.

At last Leavenscale lined up the shoes on his desk, with a nod of finality. 'One hundred notes,' he said.

It was a lot of money, although Cassie knew that another Deacon would have gone higher.

Leavenscale sat back, confident his offer would be accepted.

'A hundred and fifty,' Cassie said.

Leavenscale blinked. 'I do not haggle, Miss Grubdollar. The Relic market is a buyer's market only. I'm saying a hundred and there's an end of it.'

'Hundred and fifty.'

Her last furtive look-round had told her Az wasn't at the end of the concrete-block cordon yet. She had to keep Leavenscale's attention fixed on her and not let it stray anywhere else.

'One hundred,' Leavenscale said, pronouncing each syllable crisply.

'One fifty,' she replied, mimicking his pronunciation.

'Or nothing. That's the alternative, Miss Grubdollar. You can keep the shoes if you don't want my money.' Leavenscale looked almost pitying. 'Don't think I don't realise that your family has been having a hard time of it recently. Cash reserves must be running low, eh? The cupboard starting to get bare. Now, I'm told that if you boil shoe leather in water for long enough, you can end up with a palatable and perhaps even nutritious soup. So there's always that option, is there not? Or there's money, plain and simple. A far surer way of getting hungry bellies filled. Which is it to be?'

Cassie gulped hard. No question, the family could do with that hundred. They could pay off their debts and still have a tidy sum left over.

Get a move on! she urged Az mentally.

'You yourself said a pair be a rare thing,' she said to Leavenscale. 'In my book, rare equals expensive.'

'And in *my* book, rare equals whatever I say it equals. I'm going to give you one last chance, Miss Grubdollar. A hundred notes. That's it. If you yet again come back with anything but a yes, the offer is rescinded, our business is over, you go home, 'bye-bye.'

'Cassie . . .' Fletcher said out of the corner of his mouth. His expression was pained. He was aware what she was up to, but he was envisioning all that ready cash, a thick sheaf of notes, wonderful folding stuff – seeing it there in his hand, in danger of being whisked away at any moment.

Az had reached the end of the cordon. Barely a half-dozen metres separated him from the door.

Cassie made a great show of rumination: scratching head, tapping feet, staring into space, humming. She was stalling for time, but she couldn't keep it up for ever.

Do it, Az!

If he didn't hurry up, she was going to have say it. Going to have to say no.

Do it!

Az was hesitating. She saw him peek round the edge of the block. Indecision was written all over his face.

Go!

'Miss Grubdollar? An answer.'

'Hundred it be,' Cassie said.

'Good. I thought you'd see sense.'

In the north-western corner, the swing-door squeaked. Cassie looked round. The door was closing, easing shut on its sprung hinges.

Az had made it.

Deacon Leavenscale was looking towards the door too. He squinted, frowned, then muttered something about draughts, and began filling out a chit.

It wasn't the best price she could have got, Cassie knew. Her father would have held out for 120 notes at least. But right now there were more important considerations than money.

Preventing a war, for example.

CHAPTER 55

The Reliquary

It was different this time, being inside the Chancel. Very different.

Last time, Az had been in a state of confusion and amazement. Dizzy, too. His head had been swimming.

Now he was clear-headed and suffused with a sense of mission.

Nothing was more important than reaching the elevators.

He proceeded along the corridor that led away from the sorting-house. Robert's boots were taking some getting used to. They felt like clamps on his feet. But apart from that he was in fine fettle, alert, ready for anything.

Almost anything.

Rounding a corner, Az came face to face with a pair of large doors. Each had a circular window inset into it, like a porthole. He knew he should move straight past the doors but he couldn't resist a quick glance through first.

His jaw dropped.

Beyond the doors lay a room, massive, but its massiveness was not its remarkable feature.

It was crammed. Crammed with stuff. *Stuffed* with stuff. From wall to wall, floor to roof, there were objects – objects on shelves, objects in cubbyholes, objects behind or under glass. The more Az looked, the fuller the room seemed. There wasn't a square centimetre that didn't have something in it, stacked, racked, piled up, or shoved in any old how.

Tiered galleries had been built to accommodate all the items, with a network of ladders affording access from one tier to the next. For all the apparent unruliness, there was organisation. Az saw labels on everything, and there were a couple of deskbound Deacons at work on ledgers, evidently in the process of cataloguing and cross-referencing. Other Deacons were dotted around the room, some on the ladders, many carrying clipboards and pens.

Az had a pretty good idea what this room must be: the Reliquary. It took him several moments, though, to adjust to the fact that its contents were bits and pieces which had fallen from above. Hearing about the Reliquary from Cassie was one thing, actually seeing it for himself quite another. Every item in the room was a scrap of what had once been Airborn property, an article that had been dropped from the sky-city overhead, come tumbling through the cloud cover, and wound up in the Shadow Zone, from where it was retrieved by the Grubdollars or by others in the same line of work.

The items included:

Clothing, some of it in shreds.

Tattered pages from books and newspapers.

Coins and paper money.

Hair combs.

Splintered twists of what must have been furniture.

Shards of glass.

Broken ornaments that had been pieced together painstakingly.

Cups, cutlery, crockery . . .

Centuries of accumulated detritus, gathered and labelled, hoarded like wealth. This was a second Museum of Airborn History, an upside-down version, a secret chronicle of the race told through dropped morsels and forgotten artefacts.

Az himself had doubtless contributed to a similar collection, not here but at a Chancel beneath High Haven. Once he had let the wind take hold of a sweet wrapper and whip it away. Then there was that sock of his that had inexplicably gone missing. Perhaps the wrapper and the sock had ended up in a Reliquary like this one, reclaimed from High Haven's Shadow Zone and squirreled away like treasure.

Horrifyingly, the Reliquary didn't contain just *things*.

Az's roving gaze came to rest on a series of padlocked, glass-fronted cabinets that held bones. Human bones. Airborn bones. They were dry and browny-white, and were sorted and stored according to type. In one cabinet there were femurs. In another, what looked like upper wing radii. Worst of all, one cabinet was host to a stack of skulls.

People. People fell and were never seen again. There were accidents – aircraft collisions and suchlike. The victims plummeted helplessly into the cloud cover, dead or dying, unable to save themselves, doomed.

This was where their remains wound up.

Az wished now he hadn't stopped to look in. He would have been content to go through life never having seen the inside of a Reliquary.

In a moment's time, there would be another reason for him to wish he hadn't stopped.

CHAPTER 56

An Unfortunate Coincidence

Deacon Shatterlonger was not a happy man. Although it had not been his fault, he was nonetheless being held responsible for the security breach a couple of days earlier. Archdeacon Corbelgilt needed somebody to blame, a scapegoat to take his anger out on. Deacon Shatterlonger had been saddled with that role.

The fact was, no one knew how the boy had got into the Chancel and found his way into the cupboard in the Ascension Chapel. Perhaps he had stowed away aboard the bus which brought the mourners in, and somehow sneaked out as they were disembarking, then hurried ahead of them to get to the room before they did. However, parties of outsiders visiting the Chancel were monitored from the minute they arrived and were escorted every step of the way, in and out. There were head counts and roll·calls. It was almost inconceivable that the boy could have slipped through unnoticed.

Nor could anyone figure out *why* he wanted to infiltrate the Chancel, unless, as Archdeacon Corbelgilt surmised, he was a Humanist spy. Understandably the Archdeacon was paranoid about Humanists at present, and the boy could well have been one, sent to eavesdrop on the Chancel's inhabitants and find out what effect the embargo was having on them. Shatterlonger had pointed out that the boy had seemed too nervy for that, too bewildered and skittish. And surely if the Humanists were going to choose a spy, they would go for a grown man, someone who could don a robe and pass himself off as a Deacon, rather than a boy in plainclothes. But there was no reasoning with the Archdeacon on the subject.

What had irked the Archdeacon above all else was Shatterlonger's failure to catch the miscreant. Shatterlonger acknowledged that he should have made good on the opportunity he had to seize him in the sewage treatment works. But who could have known the lad would do something as suicidally insane as jump into the outflow channel?

Now, anyway, Shatterlonger was in disgrace. Archdeacon Corbelgilt had given him a public dressing-down in front of all the Deacons and demanded penance from him. Penance entailed the shaving off of his hair, a diet of bread and water for a week, and one month spent carrying out the sort of duties that were expected of an initiate but not of a senior Deacon.

The loss of hair was tolerable (though his scalp itched and his head felt cold all the time). The subsistence diet was grim but also oddly bracing. What Shatterlonger really couldn't stomach was the demotion. Having been a favourite and a confidant of the Archdeacon, well in line to take over from Corbelgilt when he retired, he was now reduced to menial tasks such as doing the washing-up in the kitchen and helping out in the Reliquary.

Even once the penance was over, Shatterlonger would have to work hard to get back into the Archdeacon's good books and regain the status he had lost. In the meantime, he spent every spare moment fuming over the injustice of his punishment and musing on what he would do to the boy if he ever laid eyes on him again.

He was entertaining thoughts of revenge on the boy – physically abusive revenge – as he made his way towards the Reliquary to begin an afternoon shift there. Shatterlonger hated working in the Reliquary. Of all the aspects of his penance, it was by far the worst. He hated the dustiness of the place, and the fustiness of the Deacons who ran it. The Reliquary attracted a certain type of personality. Those who volunteered for full-time duties there were the sort of men who enjoyed indexing and numbers and bookwork. Librarian types. They had poor social skills and lax personal hygiene. Some of them loved being in the Reliquary so much, they seldom left it. They lived among the assembled Relics, constantly reshuffling and rearranging them and obsessively coming up with new ways to categorise them. They didn't see the Relics as Relics any more, as venerable reminders of the world above – they saw them as a large, complex taxonomical puzzle. Deacon Gnomoncast, for instance, the Head of Reliquary, had devoted the past decade of his life to establishing a precise set of formulae for the codification of carpet fragments, drawing up tables which ranged them according to size, colour, pattern, weave, texture, and so on.

A wasted decade, in Shatterlonger's view, although he would never have said this aloud to anyone.

Nearing the Reliquary, Shatterlonger felt his fires of revenge being stoked by the prospect of the coming work shift. It would be six hours of Deacon Gnomoncast and the others bossing him about, making him scuttle up and down ladders as though he was their personal dogsbody, and mocking his ignorance of their intricate classification systems.

He had, in fact, built up quite a blaze of vindictiveness inside as he reached the Reliquary doors.

And who should be standing there, peering in through the doors' windows?

Who but the source of his grievance.

The object of his violent revenge fantasies.

The boy.

Shatterlonger stopped in his tracks, overcome with disbelief. He had to blink several times to make sure his eyes weren't playing tricks on him. -

It really was the boy. He wasn't imagining it. This wasn't some vision conjured up by his thirst for vengeance. Nor was it a hallucination brought on by a lack of proper food. The boy was right in front of him, gazing into the Reliquary, oblivious to his presence. He had survived his plunge into the outflow channel, and now here he was, large as life, a sitting duck, a gift, an offering from kindly providence.

Shatterlonger thanked his luck, clenched his fists, and charged.

CHAPTER 57

The Drawbacks (And Benefits)
Of Robert's Boots

Something, some instinct, made Az turn at the very last second.

He recognised the Deacon who was bearing down on him at full tilt. The shaven head altered his appearance but the face was etched in Az's memory.

Shatterlonger.

Az sprang back from the Reliquary doors. He spun round and started to run ...

... and tripped over his own feet.

The boots! Robert's boots!

Even as he went sprawling to the floor, Az cursed his unfamiliar footwear.

Then hands grabbed him. He was hauled upright. Deacon Shatterlonger took hold of his shirtfront in one fist and bunched it tight. Knuckles dug into Az's throat. His collar began to constrict his neck.

'You have no idea what this means to me,' Shatterlonger said, breathing a blast of malodorous breath in Az's face. 'I never thought I'd get this chance. I'm going to make you suffer, you brat. I don't care who you are or why you're here. I'm going to make you wish you'd never been born.'

He slammed Az against the wall, knocking the wind out of him. Then he pushed upwards, and Az felt his feet leave the floor and his collar become even more constrictive. Suddenly it was getting hard to draw a breath.

Shatterlonger's eyes were insanely bright and joyful.

It was quite clear to Az that the Deacon intended to kill him. He didn't know what he had done to make the man so mad, other than escape from him. It didn't seem to matter anyway. Shatterlonger was bursting with murderous rage, that was all that mattered. He was going to choke Az to death.

Az tried to speak. He wanted to remonstrate with Shatterlonger and plead for his life. But his larynx was being crushed. He couldn't get anything out of his mouth except a hoarse hiss.

Shatterlonger shoved him further up the wall, so that Az was looking down on him, so close to him that he could see the broken capillaries that crazed the whites of the Deacon's eyes. Around the edges of Az's vision there were exploding sparkles of light. There was a roaring in his ears.

A tiny voice inside his head urged him to do something now or else he would die. The voice, funnily enough, sounded a lot like Cassie's. It was just the sort of thing she would have said.

Do something.

But what?

Az registered the fact that his feet were dangling and remembered that they were clad in heavy, hobnailed boots. The same boots which had caused him to trip had, he realised, the power to hobble someone else. All it needed was a good, hard kick.

Az kicked.

He didn't have the presence of mind or the coordination to aim. He kicked desperately, with all his might, hoping that his toecap would connect with Shatterlonger's knee, perhaps, or his thigh.

As luck would have it, he hit the jackpot.

Shatterlonger's face went white. His eyes rolled. A high-pitched whoop of pain escaped him. He dropped Az and his hands flew to his groin. Clutching himself there, he sagged to his knees.

Az, meanwhile, slid down the wall, holding his throat and wheezing.

For at least a minute neither of them could move. Az was having trouble getting air into his lungs. Shatterlonger was whimpering and swaying from side to side, racked with indescribable agony.

Finally Az managed to get himself upright.

He'd left it too late, though. Shatterlonger was starting to recover from the kick. As Az made to run past him, Shatterlonger reached out with an arm, barring his path. Az tried again, the other side. Again Shatterlonger blocked the way.

'You're mine,' the Deacon gasped. 'Little ... bastard. Mine.'

Az launched another kick at him but Shatterlonger managed to deflect it. Az realised there was no way forward.

He looked to his right.

The Reliquary?

A dead end, surely. He could hide in there, but he would still be trapped. And of course, the place was riddled with Deacons.

Back. That was his only option. Back the way he had come. Back into the sorting-house.

Maybe there was another route from the sorting-house into the Chancel.

It was a slim hope but it was all Az had.

He turned and lurched away from Shatterlonger.

The Deacon, hissing with pain, staggered to his feet and gave chase.

CHAPTER 58

Scuffle In The Sorting-House
(Grubdollars Against Deacons)

Cassie and Fletcher left the kiosk with their money and returned to *Bertha*. Their delight over the cash was mitigated by the sight of the murk-comber. This was the first chance they'd had to get a good look at her since the chase, and the recently-acquired dents and gouges in her bodywork gave her a bedraggled, hangdog look. To add to this impression, one of her floodlights had been broken during the chase. The empty housing dangled limply by a wire, like an eyeball that had been knocked from its socket and was dangling on the end of its optic nerve.

That's going to cost, Cassie thought. The Grubdollars could panel-beat *Bertha's* bodywork back into shape themselves and give her a lick of paint where needed. This would set them back next to nothing. The floodlight would have to be replaced, however, and lightbulbs and lamp glass did not come cheap. Some of the 100 notes would have to go on that.

Cassie's thoughts turned to Martin, who was in part responsible for the damage to the murk-comber. She couldn't decide whether she felt bitterness towards him or regret. The bond between siblings was a strong one, so that when it broke, it broke painfully. She would find it hard to forgive him for all he had done. But then Martin, in turn, would find it hard to forgive her for her part in thwarting the Humanists' plans.

Maybe, just maybe, the two of them would be able to patch things up eventually. But Cassie knew things weren't ever going to be the same. Like a shattered bone that had knitted back together, their relationship might work again, but never as well as it used to.

Reaching *Bertha*, Cassie tossed Az's shoes in through the hatchway. She was about to climb in after them when she heard a commotion over at the swing-door.

She turned in time to see Az bursting through the door, with a Deacon in hot pursuit.

Az!?

Cassie experienced a surge of pure resentment. Not two minutes inside the Chancel, and already Az had got into difficulties and come running back out with his tail between his legs. After all this! After all they had gone through to get him here!

Then the Deacon chasing Az let out an almighty snarl and lunged. He caught him around the midsection. They both went crashing to the floor together, Az on his front, the Deacon on top.

The Deacon straddled Az and began cuffing him around the head. The man's face was a contorted mask of hatred. Cassie could not help but wonder what Az had done to enrage him so much.

She also could not stand by and watch him beat Az up.

Fletcher clearly felt the same way, because as Cassie set off to help Az, so did he.

Az retaliated, flailing behind him, trying to parry the Deacon's assault. But the Deacon was a maniac. He rained blows on Az's head with mounting ferocity. He graduated from loose-hand slaps to clenched-fist punches. He would have ended up concussing Az, or worse, if Cassie hadn't intervened when she did. She dived at him sidelong, grabbing his wrists. As the Deacon fought to make her let go, Fletcher joined in, hooking an arm around the man's neck. The Deacon gave an infuriated grunt as Fletcher and Cassie together dragged him off Az.

Meanwhile, a startled Deacon Leavenscale groped for the button on his desk and pressed it three times. Far off in the Reliquary, a bell sounded. Three rings signalled an emergency in the sorting-house.

Between them, the two Grubdollars got the Deacon onto his back and pinned him down. Fletcher placed a knee on the man's chest while Cassie secured his legs. The Deacon bucked and squirmed beneath them but couldn't break free.

Cassie turned to Az, who was sitting up, looking stunned and battered.

'Go back in,' she told him. 'Now, while you can. Likely as not there'm more Deacons coming. Go! And don't screw it up this time.'

Her words galvanised him. Az stood and made his way back to the swing-door.

Leavenscale was still thoroughly perplexed by what was going on, but could not ignore the fact that a fellow Deacon was in trouble. He stumbled from his desk and went to assist Shatterlonger. He sized up the two Grubdollars and decided the sister was the weaker of the two, the easier to deal with. He took hold of Cassie by the shoulders and attempted to pull her off. Cassie lashed out, thumping him square in the belly. Leavenscale tottered back. His heel caught on the hem of his robe and he thudded backside-first onto the floor. Pain lanced up his spine. The impact also dislodged his spectacles, leaving him all but blind.

As he groped to find the spectacles, Leavenscale had time to regret getting involved in the fracas and regret even more picking on the girl.

He would be nursing a sore coccyx for days. The rough stuff, he concluded, was best left to others.

Cassie saw Az arrive at the swing-door, just as the door flew open and a half-dozen Deacons barged through. In their pell-mell haste they went straight past Az, not seeing him. The way was left clear. Az ducked into the doorway.

The Deacons summed up the situation in the sorting-house at a glance. They swarmed over Cassie and Fletcher, overwhelming them with numbers. In no time, the two Grubdollars were no longer holding down the Deacon on the floor; they themselves were the ones being held down.

Az was still in the doorway. His gaze locked with Cassie's. Two of the Deacons were holding her by her arms.

Her eyes told him not to hang about. There was nothing he could do for her and Fletcher. He should just make sure that this sacrifice of theirs wasn't in vain.

He acknowledged it regretfully, and disappeared.

At the same moment, the Deacon whom Cassie and Fletcher had saved Az from rose to his feet with a roar.

'You!' he yelled, gesticulating at one of the Reliquary Deacons. 'And you! Come with me. The rest of you, keep a tight grip on those two.'

With that, he wheeled round and stormed off after Az. The two Reliquary Deacons followed.

Run, Az! thought Cassie.

She hoped he would be all right.

But she feared he wasn't going to make it to the elevators.

CHAPTER 59

Az's Run

As he sprinted headlong through the Chancel, it seemed to Az that he was fated to spend his entire life running away from Deacons. Even though this was only the second time that it had happened, there was a nightmarish repetitiveness to the event. The corridors he passed through looked the same as last time; they linked and diverged in the same labyrinthine fashion. And it was the same Deacon behind him, Shatterlonger, with another two Deacons accompanying him, just like before. Az began to wonder if he'd actually escaped the Chancel after all. Perhaps everything he had done since then – wandering the Shadow Zone, meeting the Grubdollars, being taken captive by the Humanists, getting away from them – had been in his imagination. This was still the same chase as the first one. He had just experienced some sort of delusional lull in the middle of it.

Nevertheless, on he ran, his arms pumping, his feet pounding, his breath coming in rasps. Sweat began to dampen his armpits and dribble stingingly into his eyes.

Once or twice Az thought he had managed to shake the Deacons off his tail, but then suddenly he would hear them again – the clatter of their footfalls, Shatterlonger's urgent cries. They were never more than one turn of a corner behind him. If he paused even briefly to catch his breath, within moments one of the three would spot him and alert the other two, and the chase would resume.

How long could he keep running? How soon before exhaustion over-came him and he simply couldn't continue another step?

Az had a feeling he was going to find out. Unless he reached the elevator chamber in the next few minutes, he was going to use up the last of his stamina and collapse. He couldn't maintain this pace for ever.

Then he was in a red-lit area. He was scared to believe it but his surroundings somehow did look familiar. These were corridors he had been down during his previous visit, he was sure. The elevator chamber was close by.

But where? Where?

With his destination seemingly so near at hand, Az redoubled his speed. He quested this way and that, making frantic left and right turns. He recalled the door with the lever handle, which led off from the monitoring gallery in the elevator chamber. If he could just find *that* . . .

Another corridor. No such door.

Another one.

Now Az was aware of a burning sensation in his chest and a terrible bone-deep ache in his muscles. His legs were getting sluggish. Robert's boots seemed to weigh even more than before. Still he kept going, the exertion as much mental as physical. His body was close to conceding defeat. With his mind he forced it onward, telling himself to ignore the pain and the weakness he was feeling.

Shatterlonger and the other two Deacons were still hot on his heels. He could hear how tired they were. None of them was talking now. All three were panting hard. But they weren't giving up, so neither could he.

Then, dead ahead, as if by a miracle – the door! The door with the lever handle!

As he zeroed in on it, Az knew that it might be a different door, identical but the wrong one. It might open onto another room entirely, or onto a dead-end. In the time it took for him to struggle with the handle, the Deacons might catch up with him.

But he had no choice. This was it. All or nothing. He had to try it.

He grasped the handle, yanked down, put his shoulder to the door, pushed, fell through . . .

The monitoring gallery!

Moments later, Az was on the gantry in the elevator chamber. The drone of machinery hit him in a torrent of sound. In front of him were the whirling cranes, the thump-whumping pistons, the trundling pallets, the whole fantastic, intricate, clockwork-like array of moving parts which he remembered so vividly from two days ago.

Two days? It felt more like two *years*.

There was no time to stand and gawp. Az bounded across the gantry and scrambled down the ladder. As he reached the bottom, three faces appeared overhead. It was Shatterlonger and the other two Deacons, peering down at him. Their cheeks were scarlet, their skin polished with perspiration.

'Stop!' Shatterlonger gasped out. 'Stop! You can't go any further. It's – it's not allowed.'

Az stepped back from the foot of the ladder. What was and wasn't allowed had no relevance for him at the moment. His only concern was getting to the elevators.

'Forbidden territory,' one of the other Deacons said, between wheezing breaths. 'Only by special dispensation. The Archdeacon. Essential maintenance.'

So the Deacons weren't permitted to go any further than the gantry unless something in the chamber needed repairing. Az was on safe ground.

He started to walk backwards with slow, cautious steps, mindful that parts of the machinery around him might fling themselves out unexpectedly and send him flying. The Deacons on the gantry were aghast at what he was doing.

'Stop,' Shatterlonger said again. It was almost pleading. 'Or you'll never Ascend.'

Maybe so. But Az had every intention of ascending in the literal sense. First available upward-bound elevator – he was taking it.

Shatterlonger wrestled with indecision. Finally he placed a foot on the top rung of the ladder.

'Shatterlonger, don't,' warned one of his colleagues.

'It's not worth it,' said the other.

'I can't let him get away.' Shatterlonger grasped the ladder uprights. 'Not after all this.'

'It'll be penance for a year.'

'Weekly self-flagellation.'

'A stay in the Contrition Cells.'

'I know,' Shatterlonger replied. 'Even so ...'

He began climbing down, and there was nothing the other Deacons could do except look on, helpless.

Az knew his advantage was lost. He turned and staggered forwards, hurrying into the chamber. When he next glanced over his shoulder, he could see only the two Deacons on the gantry. Shatterlonger was no longer in view.

Az upped his pace. The frenetic mechanical tumult around him intensified, so he knew he was getting nearer the elevators. Then, there they were: some of them rising up the column, others coming down, their doors opening, empty pallets slotting in. Az had never been quite so grateful to see anything as he was those elevators. He was almost home.

Next thing he knew, he had collided with Deacon Shatterlonger.

He reeled back. The Deacon had popped up out of nowhere to obstruct his path.

'That's enough,' Shatterlonger said, voice raised in order to be heard above the background din. His face was haggard, his eyes wayward and wild. 'This ends here. You're coming with me.'

There was no way Az could let that happen.

Immediately to his left, he saw a set of rails. They ran towards the column base, but just before they reached it there was a junction and they fanned out into several subsidiary sets of rails. Each of these served a different elevator. Pallets rolled along the main set of rails and were distributed by a switching device to go down the subsidiary sets and feed into whichever elevator was ready and waiting.

Az took all this in at a glance. A pallet was approaching from behind him. He heard it hiss shimmeringly.

He knew, then, what he could do. *Must* do.

The move would have to be split-second perfect, though. If he stumbled or misjudged, he was likely to be mowed down by a heavy steel pallet travelling at speed. The result would be messy.

But he was worn out. His legs felt like rubber. Could he make it?

Suddenly Shatterlonger pounced, hands out like claws.

At the same time, Az sprang sideways.

He felt fingers brush his shirt. He seemed to be suspended in mid-air for hours. Then he landed awkwardly and was thrown over onto his side.

Propping himself up on all fours, he realised he had made the jump successfully. He was riding the pallet, and the pallet was racing away from Shatterlonger. The Deacon was frozen in a posture of bafflement, his arms embracing empty air. Shatterlonger couldn't seem to fathom how his quarry had evaded him *yet again*.

The pallet hurtled along the rails with Az aboard, clinging on. There was a moment of jolting and jouncing as it hit the switching device and was diverted down its allotted course. Then an open-doored elevator loomed like a hungry mouth. The pallet rammed inside. Az lost his grip and was bowled backward by the abrupt stop. He fetched up against the elevator's back wall, heels over head.

Upside down, dazed, he watched the elevator doors slowly slide shut. Through the narrowing gap he was treated to the sight of Deacon Shatterlonger clutching the air and stamping his foot in an ecstasy of despair.

Then, with a creak and a lurch, the elevator started to climb.

CHAPTER 60

The Taking Of RSE-2

Having lost *Cackling Bertha*, Steamarm returned to the Consolidated Colliery Collective in a foul temper. At the mine, he berated the picketers for failing to stop the Grubdollars when they made their escape bid with the vehicle. He knew that only a fool would stand in the way of a murk-comber rolling at full speed, but that wasn't relevant. He gave the picketers what-for, calling them cowards and incompetents. Afterwards, he felt better.

Martin came up to him when he had calmed down. He asked Steamarm if he had a back-up plan for getting into the Chancel. Steamarm, in a rare fit of honesty, admitted that he didn't.

'So what be them doing at the other Chancels?' Martin enquired. 'What'm going to happen there?'

'They'll be using brute force,' Steamarm replied. 'They'll ram the gates with trucks. Not elegant, not subtle, but probably effective.'

'Then why doesn't us do the same?'

'We could. I just prefer the murk-comber method. It has a greater guarantee of success, and there's less likelihood anyone on our side will get hurt in the process.'

'*Bertha* be'n't the only murk-comber in Grimvale.'

'I know.'

'Thought about commandeering one of the others?'

'I have,' said Steamarm. In fact, he hadn't. But I doubt there are any other murk-comber owners with Humanist sympathisers in their midst. I struck lucky when I met you and Fletcher. Well, *you*, at any rate,' he added bitterly.

'There doesn't have to be any sympathisers,' Martin said. 'There just has to be fewer of they than of we, if you get my meaning.'

Steamarm certainly did get his meaning, and in very short order he had rounded up a posse of Humanists. The same picketers he had yelled at half an hour ago he now coaxed and cajoled. Soon he had persuaded them to follow him to the headquarters of Relic Seeker Enterprises, a firm which operated not one but two murk-combers. The Humanists marched through the storm-lashed streets of Grimvale Township, assembled outside the Relic Seeker Enterprises building, and barged in. The firm's

182

proprietor, Peter Lumplaid, looked up from his paperwork to find several burly, sodden miners filing into his office, dripping rainwater all over the floor. He spluttered indignantly, demanding to know the reason for this ... this *intrusion*. Steamarm strode up to Lumplaid's desk and explained in simple terms what he was there for. Lumplaid blustered, postured, but inevitably gave in. The alternative was to have his premises vandalised and himself roughed up, and he valued his property highly and his own health even more highly.

One of the Relic Seeker Enterprises murk-combers was out at work, but the other was inactive today because it was having a new carburettor fitted. The job was complete, and down in the garage the firm's mechanic was giving the engine a test-run. It chugged smoothly. The mechanic congratulated himself on his handiwork, then looked round to find his boss and a whole bunch of men he didn't recognise coming towards him across the garage floor. Within moments, his newly repaired murk-comber was pulling out, with none other than Martin Grubdollar up in its driver's pod. The mechanic didn't know which was worse: having the murk-comber taken from him, or seeing one of his firm's main rivals at the controls.

RSE-2, as the murk-comber was known, crawled to the Consolidated Colliery Collective with its loading bay full of Humanists. There was a brief stop as they gathered up weapons – sledgehammers, crowbars, lengths of chain, fence- posts, shovels – a formidable makeshift arsenal.

Other Humanists were there at the mine, having assembled at a pre-arranged time. They boarded three coal trucks, carrying weapons too. *RSE-2* set off, leading the way. The trucks followed in convoy, like baby ducks behind their mother.

As they drove towards the Shadow Zone Steamarm listened to his troops in the loading bay, growling, cheering, and singing songs. He was in the driver's pod with Martin but the men's voices were so loud he could hear them even up there. They seemed not just ready for conflict but eager for it. Their blood was up. Finally, after all this time, it was starting. The Deacons' rule was coming to an end.

Steamarm pictured it: a spasm of rebellion taking place all across the Westward Territories more or less simultaneously. In other counties and countries Humanists were mobilising, making their way to the local Chancels, just as here. Steamarm felt part of a vast mass-movement, connected by a web of solidarity to thousands of likeminded individuals. All of them had but one incentive, one goal – to overthrow the Deacons. It was a marvellous thought, and it brought a tear to his eye.

And after the Deacons, what next?

Next, the sky-cities and the Ascended Ones.

Not every Humanist deemed it wise, or even feasible, to follow the invasion of the Chancels with an invasion of the sky-cities. To Steamarm, however, the second step was a logical extension of the first. When the Deacons had been displaced there would be no more supplies at all for the Ascended Ones. The Ascended Ones would not take kindly to this and would react aggressively. *How* aggressively, no one could say. Steamarm, in the light of his conversation with Azrael, thought there would at least be some form of concerted counterattack – and in order to prevent it, he felt the Humanists should get in there first. Hit the Ascended Ones before they could hit back.

Other Humanist leaders were uncomfortable with such an idea and balked at it. They still believed the Deacons' claim that it was death for a living person to go up above the clouds. Steamarm himself was convinced this was not true, especially now that he had met Azrael. Azrael had proved that what could come down could also go up – as long as you had the right equipment.

So Steamarm was resolved to show everyone else the way. Once the Chancel here fell, he would lead his men up in the elevators and overrun the sky-city above. Having set an example in this manner, he was sure all the other Humanist groups would copy it. Sometimes people lacked the courage or the imagination to follow things through right to the very end and needed a pathfinder, a trailblazer, a man of vision – in short, someone like Alan Steamarm – to demonstrate what had to be done.

In spite of all the setbacks he had suffered today, Steamarm was confident of victory. He had no reason not to be.

As *RSE*-2 reached the Shadow Zone, the trucks behind halted. This was as far as they went, for now.

Steamarm looked ahead through the windscreen at the distant Chancel. Soon, oh so soon, the Deacons would be confronted by the might of a creed more powerful and meaningful than their own – Humanism. Their long and unjust reign was coming to an end.

It was going to be a great day.

CHAPTER 61

An Audience With The Archdeacon

Cassie and Fletcher were bundled unceremoniously along corridors and up and down staircases. Two Deacons were holding each of them by the shoulders. Shatterlonger led the way. Leavenscale shuffled at the rear, wincing with every step. He had a hand pressed to his lower spine.

Shatterlonger had said very little when he returned to the sorting-house, but the fact that he had come back empty-handed spoke volumes, as did the blank fury in his face. Cassie knew then that Az had got away, and she had good reason to think he had actually reached the elevators.

That didn't help Fletcher's and her situation any, but it did at least give her a glow of satisfaction inside. Whatever else happened now, Az's people had some forewarning of what was coming.

Several disorientating minutes later, she and Fletcher were thrust into a beautiful chandelier-lit room. The place was cluttered with antiques and artworks, such an abundance of wonderful objects that the mind almost couldn't take it all in. Everywhere Cassie looked there was something expensive and ornate to admire, be it a painting or a timepiece or an item of furniture. There was more wealth on display in this one room than could be found in all of Grimvale.

Everyone knew the Deacons were rich but Cassie had never really understood what that meant until now. It meant the Deacons could surround themselves with centuries' worth of accumulated treasures and live with this kind of luxury as a matter of course. Any time of day or night they could come in here and feast their eyes on wonders.

For the first time in her life, she envied them.

Shatterlonger instructed one of the other Deacons to pay a call on Archdeacon Corbelgilt and request an audience. The man returned shortly, saying that His Grace was on his way.

The corpulent Archdeacon swayed in, looking both serene and inquisitive. Deacons scurried to find him a chair, then helped him lower his bulky backside into it.

'Well?' Corbelgilt said, lacing his fingers across the mound of his belly, comfortably cradling his own girth. 'What is it?'

'Your grace,' said Shatterlonger, 'first of all I have a confession to make. I have strayed onto forbidden territory without your permission.'

'Forbidden territory? You set foot on the floor of the elevator chamber?'

Shatterlonger bowed his head. 'I did, and I humbly beseech your forgiveness.'

'Forgiveness doesn't come into it, Shatterlonger!' Corbelgilt's fleshy double-chin wobbled in outrage. 'It's a year's penance. You know that. What, are you some kind of glutton for punishment?'

'Not at all, your grace. I committed the sin in question because I was pursuing a certain boy – the same boy who interrupted the Ceremony of Ascension three days ago.'

'Indeed? I thought the lad was dead.'

'I assumed he was, but it turns out I was mistaken.'

'So where is he?' Corbelgilt scanned the room. 'You caught him this time, I take it. He didn't elude you again.'

'No. No, unfortunately, he ... he did. But he's surely dead now, since he threw himself aboard one of the elevators. No one can make that journey and survive.'

Cassie allowed herself a quick, self-congratulatory grin. The Archdeacon noticed it. He fixed her with his piggy little eyes. 'You, girl. Who are you?'

'She's a member of a murk-combing family,' Deacon Leavenscale piped up. 'The Grubdollars. And that's her brother with her.'

'I recognise the name. You looked pretty pleased with yourself, Miss Grubdollar. Care to explain why?'

Before Cassie could say anything, Shatterlonger stepped in. 'It's my belief, your grace, that these two are in league with the boy.'

'And on what grounds do you base this assumption?'

'During my initial pursuit of the lad today, they interfered. I had him pinned down and would have been able to subdue him if they had not prevented me.'

'Subdue?' said Fletcher. 'You was killing he, more like.'

'So you don't deny you are associates of this boy?' said Corbelgilt.

Fletcher looked at Cassie, hoping she would know how to answer the question.

'Your grace,' she said, 'all that happened was that us was in the sorting-house and saw a youngster getting clobbered by a Deacon. Our natural reaction were to help he, as anyone's would be. Picking on a kid like that ...'

'Balderdash!' exclaimed Shatterlonger. 'You held me down deliberately so that he could get away. I'm not stupid, girl. I saw you look at him. You knew him. You were helping him. Deacon Leavenscale will back me up. He was a witness to the whole event.'

'Erm, I must admit I didn't see a great deal.' Leavenscale pointed at his magnifying-glass spectacles. 'I'm not so keen-eyed at the best of times, and there was a lot going on, it was very confusing . . .'

'Even so, I know what *I* saw,' said Shatterlonger, adamantly. 'Your grace, I'm sure the Grubdollars are lying, and I beg your leave to detain them and interrogate them so that I can get to the bottom of the matter. If the boy was, as you yourself have surmised, a Humanist spy, and these two are in cahoots with him, that would make them Humanists too. They could therefore have intelligence that could be useful to us.'

'Or you *wish* that to be the case, Shatterlonger, hoping it might mitigate your penance,' said Corbelgilt. 'Yours does strike me as the behaviour of a desperate man, someone who will say anything in order to get himself out of trouble.'

'I be no Humanist,' muttered Cassie.

'Quiet, girl,' said the Archdeacon. 'I'm not talking to you. On the other hand, Shatterlonger, there might be some merit in your claims. With that in mind, I consider it fair and reasonable that the two of them should be detained for a period of time.'

'You can't do that!' said Fletcher.

'My boy, I am Archdeacon of this Chancel and I can do whatever I want.'

'But – but us just *stopped* some bloody Humanists from getting in here. Us just foiled their plan. So us be'n't Humanists ourselves! How can us be? Don't stand to reason.'

'Really? Foiled a Humanist plan?' Corbelgilt sounded dubious. 'And how did you achieve that? Actually no, I'm not interested. Doubtless you'll spin me some cock-and-bull story, and I haven't got time for it. No, my decision is made. Deacon Shatterlonger, your second penance is deferred for now, and you will be exempted from it altogether *if* you can prove these two knew the boy and are Humanists. That's all. Good day.'

He tried to stand, only to find himself wedged in the chair. Resignedly he raised his arms and waited for a couple of Deacons to come to his aid. With grunts and groans they hauled on him until finally he popped free like a bung from a bottle. Then the Archdeacon waddled out of the room with as much dignity as he could still muster.

'Nice try,' Shatterlonger said to Fletcher. 'But a bit farfetched, don't you think? if I was going to dream up some, little fib to get me off the hook, it wouldn't be as preposterous as "we stopped the Humanists". It'd be something a lot more plausible.'

'But it'm true. Tell he it'm true, Cass.'

'Yes, of course it is,' said Shatterlonger with a sarcastic leer. He turned to the other Deacons in the room. 'All right, you lot, you heard His Grace. I believe we need to find somewhere to put these two. What do you think? The Contrition Cells?'

He looked back at Cassie and Fletcher.

'Not the cosiest of accommodation,' he said, 'but better you than me, eh?'

CHAPTER 62

The Contrition Cells

A rivet-studded iron door, bolted on the outside, with a spyhole at eye-level. A bare wooden bunk. A latrine bucket. A recessed ceiling light that burned no brighter than a candle.

This was what a Contrition Cell was like.

And then there was the heat. Sweltering heat. The air was so stiflingly, broilingly humid that the walls were slick with condensation, and Cassie herself, in a very short time, was slick with sweat.

She measured out the cell in paces: it was ten by five. She sat on the bunk and got jabbed in the thigh by a splinter. She put an eye to the spyhole but saw nothing. It was covered on the other side by a hinged shutter.

After that, there was nothing else she could think of to do, so she went and stood in the middle of the cell. Just stood. Not moving. Conserving energy. She didn't feel so hot and bothered if she stayed still.

'A Deacon spends time here to ponder on the error of his ways,' Shatterlonger had told her, shortly before slamming the door shut. 'If he has sinned or been disobedient, a spell in a Contrition Cell will soon sort him out. I'm hoping it will have the same effect on you and your brother. Now, how long should I leave you before you're ready to confess every-thing? How long do I think you need? Quite a while, I should imagine. Quite a while ...'

How long was 'quite a while'? Cassie dreaded to think.

'Cass ...'

It was Fletcher, very faint. He was in the next-door cell.

Cassie moved to the wall, putting her mouth close to it. 'I be here, Fletch.'

'This'm a pretty pickle us is in, straight up.'

'I know.'

'Why'm it be so hot in here?'

'Us is close to the furnaces, is what I reckon.'

'Infernally hot. I don't know how long I can stand it.'

'You'm going to have to. Just stay calm.'

'All right, I'll try. Though I reckon I be half-baked already.'

A little later, Fletcher spoke again. 'You think I should admit to they that I *be* a Humanist? Might save we, you never know. It'm the truth as well, sort of.'

'If it comes to that, I'll say I be one too. But let's hope it don't come to that.'

'Funny that us did help the Deacons and them wouldn't believe it.'

'It'm called irony, Fletch.'

'Irony. That be when it hurts to laugh about it, right?'

'Something like.'

A little later again, Fletcher said, 'Think Da be missing we?'

'Not yet, but when us doesn't come home tonight him will. Then him'll move mountains to find out what'm happened to us.

'Can him help we?'

'I hope so. Someone has to.'

There was another period of silence. Then: 'Cass?'

'Yeah?'

'I be frightened.'

'Don't you worry, Fletch. Just keep quiet and still and think cool thoughts. Us is going to be OK. Trust I. Us is going to be OK.'

Even as she said this, Cassie wished she felt half as certain as she sounded.

CHAPTER 63

Infiltration

The storm was reaching a climax as *RSE-2* pulled up at the Chancel's south gate. Rain was sheeting down, and the thunder-cracks came so thick and fast that barely had one finished rumbling before the next began.

Ramps shot up at either end of the murk-comber. Steamarm had not anticipated this. But it wasn't a disaster. His plan would still work. Everything else was on his side, even the weather.

A guard came out of the gatehouse and ran, hunching, over to *RSE-2*. He rapped on the hatch, and when it opened he leapt inside to get out of the rain. He looked around the loading bay and saw a dozen hostile faces peering back at him. He saw hands gripping implements – tools, shovels, that sort of thing – which glinted in the lightning flickers. He had just enough presence of mind to bring his pikestaff forward ...

... then he was flat on his back, out cold.

The other guard, who remained in the gatehouse, saw none of this. Apart from anything else it was hard to see more than five metres through the driving rain. He waited for his colleague to return and give the all-clear to let the murk-comber in. Soon enough, a robed figure emerged from *RSE-2* and loped back to the gatehouse. The second guard placed his hand on the lever, ready to lower the ramps. Then he sensed something was amiss. He scrutinised the other man's face. The truth dawned. Someone else was wearing his colleague's robe.

Too late. The impostor's pikestaff whistled through the air, haft first. The guard slumped from his chair, unconscious.

Ramps down.

Barrier up.

RSE-2 trundled through the gate.

Martin steered unerringly towards the sorting-house.

Meanwhile, at the very edge of the Shadow Zone, a Humanist with a telescope observed that the murk-comber had got inside the Chancel perimeter. He gave a signal, and the three coal trucks restarted their engines.

In the sorting-house, *Cackling Bertha* still occupied the frontmost parking spot. Martin drew in alongside her. *Bertha* looked abandoned. Her hatch was wide open.

'Why'd Fletch and Cassie come here?' he mused aloud.

'Obviously to send their Ascended friend home,' Steamarm said.

'Yeah, that'd make sense. Damn it, though. Trust they to be here when the trouble starts.' A bad thought occurred to him. 'You reckon them's told the Deacons about our plans?'

'I doubt we'd have got this far if they had.'

'Good point.' Martin killed the engine. 'Alan, promise I one thing. No one harms my bro and sis.'

'I can't make any guarantees, Martin. In the thick of battle . . .' Steamarm left the rest unsaid.

'Well, at least let me have first crack at they. If anyone be going to wring their necks it should be I.'

The Deacon on desk duty was a Reliquary junior who had been drafted in to replace Deacon Leavenscale. The junior Deacon had missed all the commotion earlier. He had been deep in the bowels of the Reliquary at the time, carrying out a survey of Ascended handkerchieves (the lace-trimmed ones were in the process of being subdivided into men's and women's, and sub-subdivided into used and unused). He regretted not being on hand to witness Deacon Shatterlonger getting into a fight with a couple of murk-comber folk. Life in the Chancel could sometimes get very boring, and the junior Deacon often longed for diversions and a bit of excitement in his life.

Little did he realise he was just about to get more excitement than he could ever have wanted.

Out of *RSE-2* stepped a large man. The junior Deacon was not experienced enough to know whether or not the fellow was a longstanding employee of Relic Seeker Enterprises. However, the man smiled as he approach the desk, and the junior Deacon was reassured. He smiled back.

Thwack!

The Deacon did not see the punch coming. Nor did he see the kick that followed. Nor the several kicks that came after the first one. He rolled up in a ball on the ground until unconsciousness finally, mercifully, claimed him.

Humanists piled out of *RSE-2*. Some went to the main entrance, others to the swing-doors, taking up positions there.

Martin was second-to-last to leave the murk-comber. Steamarm stepped out last of all. He checked his watch. Just about now the coal trucks would be nearing the south gate, where the Humanist in Deacon's clothing was waiting to wave them through.

Tick-tock, clockwork. Everything was going smoothly.

One of Steamarm's men came up, hauling the Deacon from the money kiosk behind him.

'It be just the two of them in here, be'n't it?'

'That's correct.'

'So what should I do with he?'

'D-don't hurt me,' stammered the Deacon.

Steamarm gave the Deacon a cursory once-over, then nodded to the Humanist. 'Hurt him. Just a little.'

He stalked off, leaving the Deacon to his beating.

The sorting-house had been secured. Within minutes the trucks appeared, and men clambered off the back, shaking rainwater from their hair. In all there were about seventy Humanists now inside the Chancel. Somewhere on the premises a hundred or so Deacons were roaming, oblivious to the danger they were in, utterly unsuspecting.

No big speech now, Steamarm thought. He was sorely tempted to give one, but there was no need for it. The Humanists were champing at the bit, eager for action. Why delay it any longer?

He kept it concise. 'Gentlemen,' he said, 'tonight we make history. Tonight we change the world.' He waved an arm. 'Off you go! Leave no Deacon standing.'

With a guttural massed roar, the Humanists swarmed towards the swing-doors, brandishing their weapons.

CHAPTER 64

Home

Az staggered out of the elevator and fell to his knees. The journey up through the storm had been a rocky ride, to say the least. The elevator shaking like a demented thing. The wrench of tormented metal. A tang of ozone. The thunderclaps like the planet splitting in two.

But home! He was home at last!

He could have kissed the floor of the supply-arrival depot. But instead he simply knelt there, grateful to be alive.

There was a *whoosh* of wings – a sound Az had once feared he might never hear again. He looked up, expecting to see the depot supervisor or a supply-arrival volunteer. But the person touching down gently in front of him was none other than Aurora Jukarsdaughter. Lovely, lovely Aurora Jukarsdaughter, smiling like a creature in a dream.

'You made it back,' she said. 'We knew you would.'

As she escorted him out of the depot, Az asked where everybody had got to. The depot was empty, the hover-lifters sitting idle, no one at work.

'We closed the place down temporarily,' Aurora said. 'No supplies were coming up anyway, so we invited all the volunteers to take time off. We didn't even need to invoke Silver Sanctum authority, just told them they'd be alerted when supplies resumed.'

'They didn't find that suspicious at all?'

'I don't think so. Mr Mordadson told the supervisor to pretend there was a technical fault. As a cover story it seemed to do the trick. As far as the volunteers are concerned, any excuse not to have to work is a good one.'

'And then you waited for me.'

'We decided we'd give you a week. Your brother, Mr Mordadson and I have been taking it in shifts, keeping watch over the elevators.'

'You were *that* sure I'd come back.'

'We were. Mr Mordadson especially. In fact, he was all for giving you longer than a week.'

'Really?'

'Oh yes. You may not realise it but that man has great respect for you.'

'Could have fooled me.'

'Didn't he give you that warning? When you went down?' "You're not alone."'

'He wanted to prepare you, so that it wouldn't come as a complete shock if ... Well ...'

'If I found people down there,' Az said. 'Which I did. He could have just told me straight out, though, couldn't he?'

'Not with Michael and the administrator within earshot. Besides, "straight out" has never been Mr Mordadson's way.'

'You can say that again. So everyone at the Silver Sanctum knows about the Groundlings, right?'

'Let's save the questions for now,' Aurora said. 'First things first, let's reunite you with your brother. Then, after that, we can go over everything you've seen and done.'

She took Az to a hotel, the Heliotropia branch of the Acme Inn chain. Michael was staying in a room on the fifth floor.

When he opened the door, Michael took one look at Az and said, mock-irately, 'You're late.'

Then he hugged him so hard, Az thought his spine was going to snap.

CHAPTER 65

How The Deacons Came To Be

The news of Az's safe return to Heliotropia reached Lady Aanfielsdaughter by carrier dove, which was the method used to transport all confidential Silver Sanctum communiqués. A dovecote official brought the message straight up to her as soon as it arrived, shortly after first light. Lady Aanfielsdaughter, still in her nightgown, unrolled the little slip of paper which had been coiled around the bird's leg and spread it out between the thumb and forefinger of both hands. The handwriting was tiny and cramped. She recognised it as Mr Mordadson's nonetheless, and as she read, a frown eased from her face. Muscles which had been tense with anxiety for the couple of days relaxed somewhat. It was a small ray of hope. Az had made it back.

She was glad, and relieved. She had not slept well recently. On her desk was a letter drafted during the small hours of the night before last, a particularly wakeful night. The letter was addressed to Az's parents and began, 'Dear Mr and Mrs Enochson, It is with the sincerest regret that I must inform you . . .' She had put off sending the letter, and now, thankfully, would never have to. Worry had a weight. Now that it was lifted from her, Lady Aanfielsdaughter felt several kilograms lighter.

However, there was a P.S. to Mr Mordadson's message:

Situation on the ground is in flux and potentially unfavourable. Will report to you in person ASAP.

Lady Aanfielsdaughter knew this meant the Silver Sanctum's worst fears were realised. Mr Mordadson was a master of understatement. When he said the situation was 'potentially unfavourable', he was actually saying 'we're in real trouble'.

For so long, Lady Aanfielsdaughter had been afraid the day would come when the Groundlings rebelled. In fact, she had dreaded it ever since she learned that the Groundlings still existed. She recalled Asmodel, Lord Urielson revealing the truth to her all those years ago, soon after she arrived at the Silver Sanctum and he took her under his wing. 'My dear,' he said, 'our entire society relies on the continued toil of those neglected folk beneath us. Were it not for them and the sweat of their brows, we would not survive. So far, without trying, without even realising, we have retained their goodwill. Let us hope that we can carry on doing so indefinitely.'

He then explained to her about the Deacons. In the period immediately following the Great Cataclysm and the building of the sky-cities, an elite class of engineers came to prominence on the ground. This was all a matter of record, part of an established oral history kept alive in the Silver Sanctum and passed down through generations of politician. The engineers ran things at the base of the columns. They oversaw the input and distribution of supplies. The job provided them with wealth and comfort, not to mention influence and power. Gradually they realised they should make the most of their position and at the same time ensure it for the future. To this end, they devised a cunning and cynical scheme. They decided to control not just the goods that people brought but the hearts and minds of the people themselves. So they began insisting that they could offer life after death. They, and only they, could guarantee that everyone's souls went up into the sky-cities, in much the same way that timber, coal and suchlike did.

It was a scam but an effective one. It was the promise of a reward which the engineers themselves never had to honour. Nobody could prove that the afterlife they were offering was a falsehood, and everybody was desperate to believe it was true. The engineers spun a yarn about rebirth above the clouds, and did it so brazenly and persuasively that their fellow Groundlings swallowed it whole. Over the centuries since then, little had changed except that the engineers took to calling themselves Deacons and their scam developed into a religion, with all the trappings and ritual that that entailed.

'But that's appalling!' Serena Aanfielsdaughter exclaimed. She was young then, and idealistic, not worldly wise. Everything Lord Urielson was telling her shocked her to the core. 'They're using others. *Exploiting* them. That's wrong.'

In answer, Lord Urielson merely shrugged. 'Perhaps, but if so then we are guilty of the same crime. It's beneficial to us that the Deacons maintain their hold over the rest of their kind. They are the buffer between the Groundlings and us. Should they fail in that role ...' He flourished his wings with a dramatic flap, loud as a whiperack. The action spoke of explosiveness and finality.

Lady Aanfielsdaughter flinched now, still able to hear that startling, ear-splitting *snap* even after all this time, so indelible was the impression it and Lord Urielson's words had made on her. She looked back on the conversation as the moment when she lost her innocence. She paid a price for entry into the Silver Sanctum, and the price was this knowledge.

Forty years on, the consequences implied by that wing-flap had never seemed more possible or more imminent. Lady Aanfielsdaughter had ended up in charge of the Airborn race at a pivotal time in history, when there was a risk that the centuries-long status quo was about to be overturned. Fate had decreed that an immense responsibility had fallen on her shoulders. She was facing the biggest crisis any Airborn leader had ever faced.

Was she up to the task?

Lady Aanfielsdaughter hoped so, and believed so.

But at the back of her mind lurked the fear that, ultimately, there was little she could do to alter the course of events. All she could do was manage the situation to the best of her abilities, while accepting that there was a very good chance that the Airborn race was doomed.

CHAPTER 66

Az The Ambassador

None of these concerns showed on Lady Aanfielsdaughter's face when, a short while later, she welcomed Az into her office, along with Michael, Mr Mordadson and Aurora. She betrayed not the slightest trace of distress or unease as she shook Az's hand warmly and told him how delighted she was to see him again. She was every inch the confident, charismatic politician. No one could have guessed the thoughts and fears that simmered within her.

'Look at you,' she clucked, eyeing Az's dishevelled clothing and his various scrapes and bruises. 'You've been through it, haven't you?'

'You could say that,' Az replied. 'It was ... interesting down there.'

'Interesting!' Lady Aanfielsdaughter laughed. 'I suspect it was a great deal more than interesting. Fill me in.'

Over the next hour, Az did. He described the descent in the elevator, the machinery he had found below, his encounter with the dead body, then the Deacons, the Ceremony of Ascension ...

As his tale unfurled, Lady Aanfielsdaughter grew more and more remorseful. She had known Az might run afoul of the Deacons, but she could never have foreseen the other tribulations he would have to endure. Nearly getting eaten by 'verms'. Being held captive and threatened by the Humanists. Being pursued by them. Managing to get back to the elevators by the skin of his teeth. Even the journey back up to Heliotropia had been a fraught one.

'Somehow, though, I knew I was going to be all right,' Az said. 'It would just have been silly otherwise. To go through all I did, only to die in the elevator on the way up? Wasn't going to happen.'

This was not the same boy Lady Aanfielsdaughter had sent off on a mission scant days earlier. He was stronger, she could tell, and wiser. He was also sadder. He had undergone the same change she had when Lord Urielson told her about the Groundlings, the same loss of innocence. It was haunting him, as it had haunted her. *She* had done this to him.

She said, 'It's only fair that I come clean and say we knew about the Groundlings all along.'

'Yes, I did gather that,' Az said.

'Me, I'm still finding the whole concept hard to get used to,' said

Michael. 'But right now, frankly, it doesn't bother me.' He scrubbed an affectionate hand through his brother's hair. 'This is all I'm bothered about.'

'Trust me, I share your sentiments, Michael,' said Lady Aanfieldsdaughter. 'And Az, while I'm coming clean with you, I should mention that the sickness you experienced wasn't wholly unexpected either.'

'Oh yes?'

'Yes. It's been theorised that there's a marked difference between the air pressure up here and down on the ground. The air up here is thinner, with less oxygen, and our Airborn lungs have evolved to cope with that. Down on the ground, the air is denser and oxygen much more richly available, and as a result your respiratory system became overloaded. That's why you felt the way you did. It took a day or so for your body to acclimatise.'

'But you didn't warn me beforehand.'

'We didn't know for certain. It was just a theory, an unproven, untested one. You have every right to be annoyed with me, Az. I sent you down there completely uninformed, and you may think you deserved better.'

'I think,' Az said, in measured tones, 'that you must have had your reasons.'

'That's true. You see, I needed you to be a blank slate. You had to go down without prejudices or preconceptions, so that you could form your own opinions, clear-eyed. Also, if you did run into trouble with the Groundlings, it was better that you had innocence and honesty on your side. Guile doesn't come as second nature to most of us, and I don't think the Groundlings would have appreciated you trying to hoodwink them. I think they would have seen through it very quickly.'

'Then I was supposed to be a sort of . . . ambassador? Is that it?'

'Well put. Yes. A dual-purpose ambassador-cum-spy, but more the former than the latter. Ambassadorship was your ulterior motive. Even though you didn't realise it, you were representing your race. You were intended to be the Groundlings' introduction to us, a way of easing them into an understanding of who we are, to show them that in many respects we're just like them.'

'Then I didn't do a very good job of it. Seems like most of them either wanted to use me or beat me up, or both.'

'Unfortunately, yes. But that wasn't your fault. Any of it.'

A shadow flitted across Az's features. 'Not even me blabbing to the Humanists about the sky-cities and everything? That wasn't my fault?'

'Az,' Michael said, 'I thought we settled this on the way over here. Two grown men were threatening to hurt you. You couldn't do anything except give them what they were after.'

'Agreed,' said Lady Aanfieldsdaughter.

'Mind you,' Michael added, 'if I ever get my hands on that Steamarm fellow . . .'

'Join the queue,' said Mr Mordadson.

Lady Aanfielsdaughter noted the remark. It seemed that relations between Az and Mr Mordadson had shifted since the last time she saw them. Her emissary appeared to have become very protective of Az. Az, in turn, seemed less resentful and mistrustful of the man. He had thawed towards him.

Mr Mordadson, she thought, I *hope you're not turning into a big softy in your old age.*

'In my view, I made a big mess of things,' Az said.

'In *any* view,' said Lady Aanfielsdaughter, 'you're a hero. Nothing less.'

Az didn't seem convinced. 'So what now?' he said.

'I was hoping you might have some suggestions.'

Az puzzled it over. 'We have to assume most of the Chancels, if not all of them, have been occupied. We also have to assume the Humanists are getting ready to make the next move, raiding the sky-cities. So we should put defences in place in the supply-arrival depots.'

'You truly believe the Humanists are going to invade?'

'If there's a leader like Alan Steamarm in every region, then yes, I do. Steamarm is ambitious and avaricious, and I don't think he'd have risen as far as he has if the other people at his level weren't the same. Birds of a feather flock together, and all that. So, sooner rather than later, they're going to be coming up. Probably Steamarm first, but the rest will follow. But there's something else.'

'What?'

'Lady Aanfielsdaughter, I probably shouldn't ask this, but – what the heck. You owe me one, I think.'

Lady Aanfielsdaughter raised her eyebrows, but then nodded. 'If it's a reasonable request, I'll do what I can.'

'I want to go back down.'

CHAPTER 67

Overstepping The Mark

Everyone looked surprised, even Mr Mordadson, who was in the habit of not revealing his emotions except through those smiles of his, and usually not even through them.

Back down? After Az had only just returned? *Eh?*

Az ploughed on, ignoring the astonished stares around him. The girl who helped me, Cassie Grubdollar – when I left her, she and her brother were in the clutches of the Deacons. That's bad enough, but if the Humanists have got into the Chancel, then the two of them are in double trouble. I wouldn't be talking to you now if it wasn't for them. I have to go back down and help them.'

'No,' said Lady Aanfielsdaughter, shaking her head. 'I'm sorry, Az, but it's out of the question.'

'You said you'd do what you can.'

'If it was a reasonable request. It isn't. It's madness. I understand your attachment to these particular Groundlings. You did well by them. However, I simply cannot sanction another trip down for you, especially with war brewing.'

'You say "attachment" like they're pets or something. Cassie and Fletcher are my friends, Lady Aanfielsdaughter, and they nearly got themselves killed helping me. What's more, they weren't helping just me, they were helping me, you, everyone in this room, the whole Airborn race. I hate to think what Deacon Shatterlonger's doing with them right now, or if not him then Alan Steamarm. We *have* to go down and get them out of there.'

'There are far more pressing concerns, Az.'

'Are there, Lady Aanfielsdaughter?' said Az, snidely.

'Az,' Aurora cautioned, 'remember who you're talking to.'

Az knew he was out of line, but he was too fired-up to care.

'I'm not asking for much, just four or five Alar Patrollers to go with me and—'

'Four or five Alar Patrollers!' Lady Aanfielsdaughter snorted. 'Why not a dozen? Why not a hundred? In fact, take the lot, Az, so there's no one left to defend the sky-cities. And while you're at it, why not take Troop-Carrier *Cerulean* as well? Honestly! Have you even thought this through?

You go down with some Patrollers, and then what happens? They reach the ground and experience the same low-altitude sickness as you did.'

'Not if they're only there for a short while.'

'And as if that's not enough of a disadvantage,' Lady Aanfielsdaughter went on, 'they'll be facing Groundlings in their own environment. I doubt wings will be much help on the ground. They'll probably be a hindrance, actually.'

'It might give them the element of surprise. It might even—'

'No, Az.' Lady Aanfielsdaughter wafted an imperious hand. 'That's all there is to it. No.'

Az opened his mouth to speak, but a withering look from Lady Aanfielsdaughter silenced him. He realised he had gone too far. In his bad-temperedness he had overstepped the mark and had alienated the one person who could have helped him. All was lost. Cassie and Fletcher were on their own and there was nothing he could do about it.

A soft cough came from behind him.

'Excuse me, milady, but might I put forward a suggestion?'

Lady Aanfielsdaughter switched her gaze from Az to Mr Mordadson. Her haughty expression faltered just fractionally.

'There might be a way in which we can combine helping Az's Groundling friends with forestalling a Humanist invasion,' said her emissary. 'Kill the proverbial two birds with one stone.'

Lady Aanfielsdaughter seemed as though she was about to tell him to shut up, but then, instead, she gave the tiniest of nods. 'Go on.'

'Something your ladyship said a moment ago has given me an idea. Would you permit me to elaborate?'

After a long pause, the answer came: 'Very well.'

Mr Mordadson flashed a smile and began to speak.

CHAPTER 68

Moving Mountains

The previous afternoon, Cassie had told Fletcher that their father would 'move mountains' to find out what had happened to them, but even as she said those words, Den was having difficulty moving even himself. His broken rib felt like shattered glass inside his chest, grinding excruciatingly if he so much as breathed the wrong way. He would have asked a neighbour to fetch a doctor for him, but Robert was still unconscious and he refused to leave his son unattended for even a few minutes. He kept hoping Cassie would come home soon, and nursed this hope throughout the day and well into evening.

At that point Robert came round, groggily asking for a drink of water, which his father brought him. Not long after, Colin Amblescrut came round too, in the closet on the landing. Immediately, he started whining. Den told him to shut up but it was no good. Amblescrut begged to be untied and let out. He promised he would behave. He was sorry, so very sorry, for everything he had done to the Grubdollars. He didn't like being trussed up like this. He didn't like small, dark spaces either. In fact, he hated them. He would do anything in return for being released – anything.

Den ignored him. He was far more worried about Robert, not to mention Cassie. Where had the girl got to?

But Amblescrut continued to whine, and then started to groan, and then sob, and Den realised he was in earnest. Amblescrut really was frightened of the dark and of confined spaces.

Unwillingly, against his better judgement, Den freed him. He did it holding the poker in one hand. 'For insurance,' he told Amblescrut, as he bent down and sliced through the Humanist's bonds with a kitchen knife. 'One wrong move and you'm getting a second bump on that thick noggin of yours to match the first one. And don't think I won't use this knife on you either, if I has to.'

Amblescrut was so relieved to have been freed, he looked as if he might kiss his liberator.

'Oh, thank you, thank you!' he cried. 'You'm a good man, a kind man, a decent man.'

'That I may be,' said Den. 'I'm also a man wondering how you can stand getting yourself in police custody so often if you'm so claustrophobic.

Don't it make you stop and think every time you be about to get into a fight? "Maybe I shouldn't, 'cause I hates being cooped up in dark cramped places, like police cells."'

Amblescrut heaved a morose, self-pitying sigh. 'Never be thinking too clearly, be I? Not at the actual moment when I get into trouble. That be on account of I may have had a pint or two first. And then next thing I know, I wake up the morning after feeling pretty rough, find Is been banged up in a tiny cell, and scream the whole police station down till them lets me out. I be'n't too proud of that. Any of it.'

'Nor should you be,' said Den. 'Well now, remember you promised you'd do anything for I in return for your freedom? I'm holding you to that promise. So here be what I want . . .'

Amblescrut left the house ten minutes later, meek as a lamb, and returned shortly with a doctor. The doctor bandaged up Den's chest tightly, so that the rib would stay put, and pronounced that Robert was fine and would make a full recovery.

Amblescrut was sent out again, having proved by his doctor- fetching mission that he could be relied on to do what he was asked to. This time, he went in search of news. Specifically, he was charged with the task of discovering where Cassie was and what the Humanists were up to.

He was gone for quite a while. The thunderstorm raging outside began to abate and had eased off completely by the time he came back.

The information Amblescrut managed to glean was that the Humanists had taken over the Chancel and that Cassie was believed to be there with them, along with Fletcher and Martin.

It was now nearly midnight, at the end of a long, weary day for everyone. Den nevertheless could not rest, and set about figuring out how to get into the Chancel and find his daughter. In this, he enlisted the aid of Colin Amblescrut yet again. By now Colin had become a sort of faithful hound. Like a dog, he had developed an admiration and a fear of Den Grubdollar that made him docile and obedient. Den, after all, had the power to hurt him and throw him into closets. Colin was keen to please his 'master', even if it meant acting against the man to whom he had previously pledged allegiance, Alan Steamarm.

For his part, Den did not like having Colin Amblescrut as an ally. He didn't trust the man any further than he could throw him (which, with his busted rib, was not far at all). However, as long as the fellow was scared of him, and as long as he didn't get drunk in the next few hours, he would serve his purpose. After that, he would no doubt revert to being the shiftless layabout he normally was.

So, while he could, Den was determined to get all the use he could out of Colin Amblescrut.

And not just out of Colin but out of the whole wastrel Amblescrut clan.

CHAPTER 69

The Amblescrut Army

That was how, at dawn the following morning, Den and Robert Grubdollar embarked on their rescue mission in the company of several dozen members of the extensive Amblescrut family.

During the night, Colin had gone round the Grimvale region and rousted cousins, uncles, aunts, nephews, siblings and step-siblings out of bed. Some of them he had bribed with promises of a beer down the pub later. Others he had boxed around the ears till they agreed to help. It was a crude but effective recruiting programme.

As daybreak suffused the clouds with a silvery glow, an Amblescrut army gathered in the Grubdollars' courtyard. They were a motley, shambolic bunch, hardly the kind of team Den would have selected for the job if he'd had any choice in the matter. They ranged in age from early teens to late sixties, although many of the younger ones had led such careless, dissolute lives that their bodies were prematurely old and had the wrinkles and sags more commonly found on the bodies of grandparents. Some of them were mangy, some were toothless, some sported all sorts of inexplicable bumps and knobbly bits here and there on their persons, and at least three of them had an extra finger on each hand. They came from outside town, the majority of them, from shacks up in the mountains and smallholdings deep in the woods, from remote spots where they led their aimless, self-contained Amblescrut existences with little disturbance. They had got here in a fleet of pick-up trucks and jalopies, now parked in the street outside – rusty, patched-together vehicles which seemed scarcely capable of staying in one piece, let alone being driven. Together the Amblescruts looked, to a large extent, as though they couldn't quite figure out *why* they were there, other than that cousin/nephew/brother/stepbrother Colin had muttered vaguely about the Chancel and getting into a fight, which in itself was a good reason. A fight was always an attractive proposition to an Amblescrut, and a fight inside the Chancel had an especially exotic allure.

So this puzzled but expectant crowd of relatives waited in the courtyard, murmuring among themselves and smoking pipes and home-rolled cigarettes, till Colin emerged from the Grubdollars' house along with Den Grubdollar and one of the Grubdollar sons. Then it was explained to them in very simple terms what they would have to do. The principle was straightforward enough. They were to gatecrash the Chancel and tackle all the Humanists inside. When one of the family, a third cousin of Colin's, asked why, he was told that he didn't need to know why. All any of them needed to know was that the Humanists were the bad guys.

'But be'n't you one of they yourself, Colin?' another family member called out, scratching her whiskery chin.

'I *were*,' came the reply, 'but I be better now.'

That seemed to clinch it. If the Humanists were the enemy, so be it. If one Amblescrut was against the Humanists, every Amblescrut was. End of story.

Engines coughed and revved. Exhaust pipes blurted out great sulphurous farts of fumes. Suspension springs creaked with the weight of people clambering aboard. Gears crunched. Threadbare tyres squealed for grip on the road surface.

The Amblescrut army, led by Den Grubdollar, with Colin as his lieutenant, got on the move.

CHAPTER 70

Meanwhile, At The Chancel . . .

. . . the Humanists were solidly entrenched.

It had been a rout, as Steamarm had predicted it would be. The Deacons had put up some resistance but not much. Overnight there had been a series of skirmishes throughout the building, each of which had ended with the Chancel's robed residents either surrendering or being beaten into insensibility. The Deacons had simply never countenanced being attacked in their own lair. They hadn't foreseen such a possibility. Over the centuries they had grown complacent, confident in their own security, sure that the world outside needed them so much and was in such awe of them that they would never be unseated. They had been wrong.

Even Archdeacon Corbelgilt, for all his anxieties about the Humanists, hadn't quite been able to believe that a day like this would come. He admitted as much to Steamarm when he was dragged into Steamarm's presence by a couple of Humanists. With his robe torn and his golden-arrowed mitre askew on his head, Corbelgilt cut a sorry figure. His shoulders were hunched abjectly and his voice quavered as he said, 'This . . . this cannot be happening. After so long, so many hundreds of years, so many generations of Deacons, so much respect paid to us . . . this isn't right. You've damned us all. Don't you realise that? You've upset the proper order of things and now we shall never Ascend, any of us.'

'Maybe *you* won't, Archdeacon,' Steamarm replied, 'but I certainly intend to.'

The Archdeacon didn't understand the remark, but then Steamarm hadn't intended him to. He snapped his fingers, indicating that Corbelgilt should be taken away. All of the Deacons, captives and casualties alike, were being held prisoner in a residential section of the Chancel. Archdeacon Corbelgilt was hauled off to join them, still protesting his disbelief.

That was late last night. This morning, Steamarm went on a tour of the Chancel, surveying his new domain. Everywhere he went there was jubilation and roistering. His men were making free with the Chancel's bountiful supplies of food and luxuries. Steamarm smiled fondly, indulgently, at their antics. Let them celebrate. They'd earned it.

Then he learned, to his dismay, that the Chancel had not been as comprehensively overrun as he had thought. A Humanist came to him with the report that a handful of Deacons had avoided capture and were still holding out, down at the Contrition Cells.

Irked, Steamarm hastened down there to find out what was going on.

There was only one door that led to the Cells and it was a massive thing of iron and rivets, thick as a brick. A half- dozen Deacons had barricaded themselves behind it and were refusing to come out. The door showed signs of Humanist efforts to break it down or pry it off its hinges. There were fresh scuffs, scratches, dents and gouges all over it. Yet it still stood in place, essentially unharmed, and several sweat-soaked Humanists were gathered around it, frowning, with hammers and crowbars hanging uselessly from their hands.

Steamarm approached the door, loosening his shirt collar. The heat in this part of the Chancel was ferocious! He banged the door with his fist and demanded to speak to whomever was within.

For a while there was no reply. Then a muffled voice said, 'Who's this?'

'My name is Alan Steamarm. I'm the leader of this group of Humanists, and I suppose you could say I'm the new owner of this Chancel. Who are you?'

'Deacon Shatterlonger, and while I live this Chancel will *never* be yours.'

'Big talk, coining from someone stuck like a rat in a hole.'

'It's no idle threat, Mr Steamarm.'

'Oh come off it!' Steamarm sneered. 'What do you hope to do from in there? Clearly there's no way in or out except via this door. You're our prisoner, Deacon Shatterlonger, and somehow you think you can still interfere with our plans?' He barked a laugh to show what he thought of *that* idea.

'I have something in mind,' Shatterlonger said.

'Do you? How interesting. Perhaps you're going to chant a few prayers to your precious Ascended Ones, get them to come down and save you. Is that it?'

'Do not mock my beliefs, Humanist.'

'I'm not mocking. Well, OK, I am a little bit. But honestly, I'm intrigued too. What cunning stratagem have you devised to turn the tables against us?'

'You'll find out soon enough.'

'Tell me now and spare me the suspense.'

'This conversation is finished. Farewell, Mr Steamarm.'

Nothing further was heard from behind the door. Steamarm called out Shatterlonger's name a few times, but to no response.

He turned to his fellow Humanists. 'That was a bit rude, wasn't it?'

'You think him's actually up to something?' one of the Humanists asked.

Steamarm shook his head. 'No. No, I think he's bluffing. Madly. He can't face the fact that he's been beaten and his cushy lifestyle is over, so he's deluded himself into thinking he still has a way of fighting back. It's pathetic, really.'

'So you wants we to just leave he and those other Deacons in there?'

'Of course not. We can't have any of them unaccounted for, and more importantly we can't let defiance go unpunished. I want them out. Ideally alive, but if not, dead will do.'

And how you'm proposing to get they out? Us has tried our damnedest to bust in. That door be rock-solid.'

'There's a truck about to depart for the Consolidated Colliery Collective to bring back certain supplies,' Steamarm said. 'I'm going to ask the driver to pick up a few small extras as well.'

'Extras? Like what?'

Steamarm beamed broadly, looking as if he could hardly believe his own ingenuity. 'You're a miner, correct?'

The man nodded. 'I be.'

'What do you do when you come across an immoveable object down the pit?'

'You mean like a rock or a big old wall of limestone or something like that? Something that'm in our way? Blow it up, of course.'

'And here we have a rock-solid door ...'

All of the Humanists began to nod, catching Steamarm's drift.

'Those few small extras I'm referring to?' Steamarm said. 'Dynamite, my friends. Sticks of dynamite.'

CHAPTER 71

Death By Dehydration

In her Contrition Cell, Cassie had been able to build up a picture of what was going on around her. It wasn't a pretty picture at all.

She knew the Humanists had invaded and taken over the Chancel. That came as little surprise. She knew how determined they were. Even without *Bertha*, they had found a way in.

What came as a surprise was when a number of Deacons had retreated here, to the Cells. She had heard their voices out in the corridor all night, and also dim scrapes and thuds which she presumed were the sound of the Humanists trying (and failing) to break in through the main door to the Cells to get at them.

What the Deacons hoped to achieve by burying themselves down here, she had no idea. Fletcher was as perplexed by it as she was.

'Nothing here but these Cells,' he said, 'and we.'

Fletcher claimed, however, that there was activity in the Cell next to his, on the other side from the one Cassie was in.

'Them's bashing and scratching away in there,' he said. 'I can't make it out clearly but them's working at *something*, straight up.'

Cassie had a bad feeling about it. Truth be told, she had a bad feeling about the entire situation. She and Fletcher were trapped, there were Humanists pounding away outside, Deacons beavering away inside, and no sign of her father coming to help ... what on earth was there to feel good about in any of that?

She was also desperately thirsty, and somehow that was the most worrying thing of all. She had sweated so much that her clothes were soaked through, and now she seemed to have no moisture left in her. There was an itchy, salty crust all over her skin. Her tongue felt dry and heavy, and a headache was starting to throb behind her eyeballs. She would have killed for a sip of water, and there was none to be found. She had tried licking off some of the condensation on the walls but the taste was repulsive and she would have had to lap up several square metres' worth even to begin to slake her thirst.

You could die of dehydration, she knew that.

It was a horrible thought, being slowly parched to death in this oven-like Cell, perspiring till she expired. It was the kind of thought which, if you weren't careful, could drive you crazy and make you start to scream and rave.

For some reason, Cassie's mind drifted to Az. She imagined him, up with the Ascended Ones, up among his own, safe and content in the cool, cloudless world of the sky-cities. Happy up there. Carefree.

Then she imagined him thinking about her.

And then she imagined him being not so happy, not so carefree.

And then, just like that, she knew he was coming back down. It wasn't a hope, it was a conviction, a certainty.

Az was not going to leave her here.

Perhaps it was delusion. Perhaps dehydration was making her believe things which had no basis in reality.

Still, deep down, in her gut, Cassie *knew*.

Az was on his way.

CHAPTER 72

A Rearguard Action

Deacon Shatterlonger had not forgotten that he had two prisoners in the Contrition Cells. Nor had he forgotten that he had been intending to interrogate Cassie and Fletcher Grubdollar this very morning. By now, after a night spent baking in the Cells' relentless heat, they should have been eager to tell him everything. Done to a turn, like turkeys. Crisp and ready to be carved.

The only problem was, Shatterlonger just didn't care about them any more. Other events had got in the way. Even the fact that the Grubdollar siblings had mentioned a Humanist invasion was of no concern to him. They'd said they had foiled it, but then it had happened anyway. This somewhat invalidated their claim and suggested, moreover, that they might actually have had some involvement with the invasion. They had concocted a lie about foiling it so that the Deacons would remain off-guard, while in truth they were part of it all along.

At any rate, it didn't matter now. The Grubdollar siblings were old news as far as Shatterlonger was concerned. He was focused on one main goal, namely making sure that the Humanists did not get the chance to enjoy their victory for long. He understood that he and the handful of men with him were the only Deacons left free in the entire Chancel. He understood, too, that it was lucky he had had the presence of mind to take refuge in the Cells not long after the invasion started. The moment he laid eyes on the Humanists as they came barging through the building, Shatterlonger had known the Deacons were facing superior forces and would be overwhelmed. The Humanists were larger, fiercer, tougher, and armed. Resistance, though noble, would be futile.

Hence he had taken the decision to retreat to the Contrition Cells. Along the way he had collected several Deacons, persuading them to accompany him. It wasn't an act of cowardice. The Cells were a defendable position, thanks to their stout main door with its many bolts and heavy lock. They were a good place from which to fight a rearguard action.

The reason for this was simple. The Cells were bang next door to the Chancel furnaces. The furnaces themselves were not a defendable position, since the chamber that contained them was accessible by a number of entrances and covered too large an area for a half-dozen men to guard effectively.

However, if the wall between the Cells and the furnaces was breached, then the furnace chamber could be entered that way. Someone could sneak in without the Humanists realising. Someone could then tamper with the furnaces, doing something to them which would force the Humanists to flee the Chancel in terror of their lives.

Breaching that wall was what the Deacons were up to right now, and had been up to all night long. In the Cell adjacent to Fletcher's, they were hammering and chiselling at the brickwork with a variety of makeshift tools: planks from a bed, the lip of a latrine bucket. They were even using bare fingernails to scrape away the mortar between the bricks.

It was painful, bloody, exhausting work, made still worse by the heat. Yet the Deacons, urged on by Shatterlonger, kept at it. They realised this was their one and only hope of ridding the Chancel of the invaders.

In the wall at the back of the Cell they had managed to gouge a hole a metre in circumference and nearly half a metre deep.

It wouldn't be long before they broke through to the other side.

CHAPTER 73

Travelling Out, Travelling In

Steamarm saw off the truck that was bound for the Consolidated Colliery Collective. The driver was Lawrence Brace, who had come to think of himself as Steamarm's second-in-command, although in truth Steamarm didn't see it that way. As far as Steamarm was concerned, all the Humanists he led were alike, an undifferentiated mass of footsoldiers. One in particular didn't stand out from the rest.

Brace steered through the Chancel gates and out across the Shadow Zone, tingling with a sense of purpose. He was on his way to collect dynamite from the mine. He understood that the explosives were going to be used to dislodge some Deacons who refused to surrender. The idea of blasting Deacons with dynamite was amusing, in a ghastly way.

However, the original and main purpose of his journey to the CCC was one that mystified Brace somewhat. Steamarm had told him to bring back as many emergency breathing-apparatus kits as he could lay his hands on. These were the cylinders of compressed air which every miner wore on his back in case of a release of poisonous fumes down the pit. Sometimes, when digging or drilling, miners hit a pocket of firedamp, that mix of deadly gases which could kill a man in seconds. The breathing-apparatus kits gave you a couple of hours of oxygen, and you could survive as long as you fitted on the mask quickly enough. The kits could also help if you got trapped by a cave-in and began to run out of air in the enclosed space.

What could Steamarm want so many of them for?

If Brace had been paying close attention during Steamarm's interrogation of the Ascended boy, Azrael, he would have realised the answer. And if Brace had really been a second-in-command, Steamarm would have *told* him the answer.

Well, the reason would be revealed soon enough, Brace decided. In the meantime he was happy simply to have a special job to do and to know that his leader trusted him enough to do it. Moreover, he was so keen on doing the job right that, for the time being, his mind was distracted from the matter of the sad fate of his homegrown marrows and the big hole in his cottage. That was a good thing, because Brace was still pretty sore about all the harm done to his property.

Hurtling along the road towards Grimvale, Brace crossed a bridge that spanned a narrow gully.

Had he looked down at that moment, he might have seen people hunkering in the gully, in the shadow of the bridge. But he was going too fast and his thoughts were elsewhere.

When the truck was long past the bridge and had become a mere dot on the horizon, the people in the gully began climbing out.

First of them to reach the top of the slope was Den Grubdollar. He scanned ahead. The Chancel lay less than two kilometres distant.

Robert appeared by his side. 'How long to get there, d'you reckon, Da?'

'Twenty minutes. Half an hour at most.'

'Still don't see why us is having to walk it. Would've taken no time by vehicle. Why'd us have to leave all them cars and trucks way back there at the edge of the Zone?'

'I told you,' said his father. The indirect approach. Us turns up in a convoy of backfiring old rustbuckets, it'm going to raise the alarm. The Humanists'll know us is coming long before us arrives. There be a better chance of we getting inside by sneaking up on foot.'

Robert cast an uneasy glance around. And then there be the verms

'Verms won't attack we, long as us is in a large crowd. Them's cowardly things and only goes for strays and singles.'

'Best listen to your Da, Robert,' said Colin Amblescrut, puffing from the effort of hauling himself out of the gully. 'Him's a brainy and sensible bloke, him is.'

Robert said nothing. Nor did his father, who simply waited till all the Amblescruts were up beside him. Then, with a loft of his hand, he set off across the plain, and his ragtag army straggled after him.

CHAPTER 74

Troop-Carrier Cerulean

She sailed out from Prismburg, stately lady, last of her line. For the past few decades, pleasure trips were all she had been used for, brief jaunts from her berth, circular journeys out, round and back in, none of them longer than a couple of hours. These kept her in working order, and the money from the paying passengers went towards maintaining her. She was costly to run. There had to be some way of making her earn her upkeep. So every day, she took tourists out, and airship enthusiasts, and nostalgia buffs, and anyone who had an interest in history or military hardware. She floated into the blue with these people in her belly, her propellers whirring, her graceful bulk bobbing in the jetstream currents, and showed them what she could do.

Once, she had fought in combat. She had manoeuvred against enemy airships. She had sent out boarding parties and siege squadrons. She had braved cordons and collisions.

But that was another time, a less settled time, when trade disputes between sky-cities were commonplace and when the smallest difference of opinion could trigger armed conflict. The Airhorn had put all that behind them when the Pact of Hegemony was signed. They had taken the collective decision to embrace peace, and had entrusted the Silver Sanctum with full responsibility for preserving that peace.

There were still trade disputes, of course, and other disagreements, but nowadays they were resolved at the Sanctum. Such matters were arbitrated on by the wisest and best among the Airborn. The Silver Sanctum's decrees were law, and the other sky-cities abided by them.

In a sense, then, Troop-Carrier *Cerulean* had been summoned towards the very place which guaranteed her obsolescence.

Except, now she was needed again. This wasn't any tourist outing. People were on their way to rendezvous with her, important people who wanted her and her crew to carry out a vital mission.

One of those people was Az Gabrielson, a boy who had longed all his life to fly in *Cerulean*.

CHAPTER 75

Martin's Unease

Martin Grubdollar found triumph to be a hollow feeling. It wasn't how he had imagined at all.

For one thing, the Chancel had fallen so easily. The Deacons were hardly any opposition. Throughout the night Martin had seen them cower before the Humanist onslaught. He had watched them behave like mice in a darkened room when you turned the light on, scurrying for cover or else just freezing on the spot and trembling in panic. The Humanists had attacked savagely, weapons flailing. Some of the Deacons had retaliated, but in vain. Most had curled up and allowed themselves to be pummelled and battered. Blood had been spilled, bones fractured. It had turned Martin's stomach. He could still hear, echoing in his memory, the cries of helpless pain and the pleas for mercy which had gone unheeded.

Why hadn't he joined in? Staunch Humanist that he was, he loathed the Deacons and all they stood for. Why hadn't he gleefully laid into them the way all his colleagues had? Why had he held back, stayed on the sidelines, looked on but not participated? Why had he started to feel sorry for the Humanists' foes and guilty for being involved in the violence against them?

These were questions Martin was still asking himself this morning, and the answers troubled him.

Everywhere he went now in the Chancel, he found Humanists vandalising and ransacking, or else evidence that they had vandalised and ransacked recently. There were men in the Reliquary, going through the shelves and smashing anything that could be smashed. In the library and the communal areas, pictures had been torn off walls, furnishings had been slashed and ripped, wooden tables had been reduced to kindling, and valuables that were small enough to fit in pockets had been pilfered (Martin saw empty display cabinets and Humanists bragging about their finds). A wine cellar had been plundered, and a few very drunk men were yelling along corridors, chanting victory slogans. In the kitchens, food was strewn about. Humanists had raided the Deacons' larders and feasted, and when they'd had their fill and couldn't eat any more they had chucked the leftovers around, just for the fun of it.

It was as if a herd of animals, not people, had stampeded through the place. Martin was not expecting that the Humanists should act in a civilised fashion during their takeover of the Chancel, but such a level of mindless barbarity was shameful and unnecessary. With every fresh example of destructiveness he came across, his unease deepened.

A further worry was that he hadn't seen Cassie or Fletcher all night long; hadn't even caught a glimpse of either of them.

Martin didn't know what to make of his brother's defection or his sister's efforts to derail the Humanists' plan of attack. As he had told Steamarm, he wanted to wring their necks. Yet at the same time, they were Fletcher and Cassie, blood-relatives, kin. Fletcher had always adored Martin, looking up to him as only a younger brother could, while Cassie was the baby of the family, the little girl Martin had felt protective towards all his life. He was stung that the two of them had turned against him. Hatred of them seethed within him – and yet the hatred would not have been nearly so strong if he didn't still love them too.

So where had they got to?

Now that the Chancel was securely under Humanist control, Martin made it his priority to track down his brother and sister. He searched every section of the building purposefully and methodically. The Chancel was truly a vast place. Fletcher and Cassie could be almost anywhere. But little by little Martin began narrowing down the possible locations, determined that he would get to them and confront them.

At one point his quest led him to the elevator chamber, and for a while he stood on the gantry, stupefied. The roar of the machinery, the turning of huge cogs, the slotting in and out ...

Then a thought occurred to him. Maybe Fletcher and Cassie had got on an elevator. Maybe they weren't in the Chancel at all. Maybe the Ascended boy had convinced them to go up with him above the clouds.

Martin dismissed the idea. They wouldn't be that stupid, would they? Go up in the elevators and die?

He resumed his search. Cassie and Fletcher were still somewhere in the building, he was sure. And when he found them, how he dealt with them would depend entirely on his mood. Either he would escort them to *Bertha* and tell them to get back home, or he would give them a piece of his mind and perhaps a few kicks in the rear end as well. Or he'd do both things.

Family!

Was there ever, Martin wondered, anything quite as confusing and exasperating as family?

CHAPTER 76

Breakthrough

In a section of wall in the furnace chamber, low down near the floor, a brick began to move. It shuddered, protruded by a centimetre, then by two centimetres, and all at once shot outwards. It landed on the floor with an almost musical *clink*, one corner of it snapping off.

In the aperture left behind, a pair of eyes appeared. They were Deacon Shatterlonger's. They scanned from side to side, checking if the coast was clear. As far as Shatterlonger could tell, there was no one in the chamber, not a Humanist to be seen.

Over the course of a couple of minutes, the gap left by the missing brick was widened. More bricks were knocked out, along with chunks of mortar. Soon there was a hole large enough for someone to crawl through. A short tunnel now connected the furnaces to the Contrition Cells.

Out from the tunnel came Shatterlonger on all fours. He straightened up, brushed dust and dirt from his robe, and looked around him. Definitely no Humanists in sight. They hadn't thought to post a guard here. Well, why would they? As far as they were concerned the Deacons in the Contrition Cells were stuck there with no way out. They hadn't reckoned on the possibility of them burrowing through to freedom like this.

But that didn't mean a Humanist might not by chance come along in the next few minutes. Shatterlonger knew he must work quickly.

The air in the furnace chamber was so hot, it was difficult to breathe. Covering his nose and mouth with a handkerchief, Shatterlonger crossed the floor.

The furnaces resembled a series of big brick beehives. Each rose to the ceiling and was crowned with ducts and flues. The flame glare from their inspection windows cast everything in a leaping orange light. Shadows stuttered and danced, making it difficult at times to see where he was going. The chamber was a world of brightness and darkness, two extreme opposites at war with one another. Shatterlonger trod carefully.

The furnaces weren't there just for burning the bodies of people Ascending. They were power. They provided the Chancel with heat and light, things that were needed at the epicentre of a Shadow Zone even more than they were needed anywhere else. The furnaces boiled water in pipes, which evaporated to steam, which turned turbines, which generated electricity, which ran everything.

At present, thanks to the Humanist embargo, the Deacons had been obliged to tap into their reserves of coal and other combustible material. The furnaces were still going full-tilt, therefore.

For Shatterlonger's purposes, that was perfect.

He reached a steel pipe which ran vertically from floor to ceiling, the size of a dinner plate in diameter. It had a wheel fitted to it at waist height – an air intake valve.

Shatterlonger started turning the wheel clockwise. It moved stiffly, stubbornly, with a protesting squeal. He kept turning it, grimacing with the exertion. Eventually the wheel hit a point when it could go no further.

There were several other identical pipes and air intake valves all around the chamber. Shatterlonger did the same with each of them, rotating the wheel till it could he rotated no more.

On a free-standing console in the centre of the room was a row of pressure gauges. As Shatterlonger went around the chamber turning wheels, the needles on the pressure gauges began to move. One after another, they slowly edged round from the green zones which denoted safety to the red zones, which were marked DANGER.

CHAPTER 77

Subtlety And Extreme Violence

Near the Chancel's southern gate, the Amblescrut army halted, regrouped, and debated their next move.

'Leave this to me,' said Colin Amblescrut, who was crouching behind a low ridge along with his relatives and Den and Robert Grubdollar. They had been observing the Humanist who was on guard duty, and Colin was convinced he could take the man down. 'Him be'n't exactly the beefiest fellow I's ever seen, and if I uses a combination of subtlety and extreme violence ...'

He was off before anyone could stop him. Den tried to object but it was no use. Colin leapt out from hiding and strode across the ground between the ridge and the gate with his arms swinging and an air of supreme self-assurance. Den was convinced that the self-assurance was misplaced. He had no doubt that Colin could manage *extreme violence*. It was the *subtlety* part of the plan that worried him.

'Oy-oy!' Colin called out. 'Be that you, Digby Sandwill?'

The Humanist in the guardhouse looked up, somewhat startled. 'Colin? What'm you doing all the way out here? Last I heard, you was back in town keeping watch over that murk-combing lot, the Grubdollars.'

'Change of plan. Fancied a bit of a stroll, I did. Stretch my legs.'

Behind the ridge, Den put his head in his hands. *Fancied a bit of a stroll!* Who would be dumb enough to fall for that?

Digby Sandwill, apparently.

'Oh? Well, I suppose it'm not a bad day for a walk. But you's come a long way, straight up.'

'Felt like seeing how things was going at the Chancel. Obviously it'm all gone well. You lot managed to take over the place, even without I.' Colin chuckled broadly.

'Yeah, it were pretty straightforward in fact.' Sandwill stepped out from the guardhouse. Colin was now less than five metres away. 'So, somebody else be looking after the Grubdollars then. I mean, you didn't leave they all by themselves, did you?'

'Of course not.'

'So who? Who'd you leave with they?'

Sandwill was not quite *that* dumb after all, then. He was peering at

Amblescrut with a half-formed frown of suspicion, and he knew his question had caught the other man on the hop. Colin did not have an answer ready.

'Maybe you should tell I what'm really going on, Colin.' Sandwill raised the weapon he was carrying, a pickaxe handle. "Cause something here just don't smell right.'

Den, listening to all this, knew that drastic action was called for. Otherwise the efforts they had made to reach the Chancel and get inside undetected would be in vain.

He popped his head up from behind the ridge.

'Digby Sandwill!' he yelled. 'Your mother be a monkey and your father has bandy legs and nothing hanging between!'

Sandwill spun round angrily, looking for the person who had insulted his parents.

Colin spotted his chance and seized it, just as Den had hoped he would. With Sandwill momentarily distracted, he was able to launch himself forwards and snatch the pickaxe handle away.

Then he clouted Sandwill with it, once, twice, three times, till the Humanist was battered into submission.

'See?' said Colin, as his family filed out from behind the ridge and headed for the now-unguarded gate. He tapped the side of his head. 'Not just a pretty face. I be smart too, in my way.'

Den resisted the urge to groan.

CHAPTER 78

Mid-Air Rendezvous

They met with Troop-Carrier *Cerulean* at a prearranged rendezvous point some forty kilometres west of the Silver Sanctum. They flew there in two small planes, with Lady Aanfielsdaughter and Mr Mordadson in one, Michael, Aurora and Az in the other. Each plane was piloted by a Silver Sanctum employee.

Az was first in their plane to spot *Cerulean* on the horizon. The great airship, with her pale blue balloon, was almost perfectly camouflaged against the sky. Az, however, was keeping his eyes peeled, and when he spied a distant, ellipse-shaped blur, he knew – just *knew* – that it was her. The long grey shadow she draped across the clouds below confirmed it.

They drew alongside her. *Cerulean* was enormous, bigger than Az could ever have imagined. He thought of the scale model he and his father were building. It could have fitted a million times over into the space the real *Cerulean* occupied.

The planes matched their speed to *Cerulean's* and nipped in under her hull. Docking clamps were ready, like open jaws. They latched onto the planes' wings, and the pilots cut the engines. Now they were the airship's passengers, clinging to her belly.

Overhead, hatches slid open and rope ladders unrolled. One after another, Lady Aanfielsdaughter, Mr Mordadson, Aurora, Michael and Az clambered up.

A crew member escorted them along the keel catwalk which ran the entire length of *Cerulean's* balloon, some 300 metres in all. Above, hundreds of gas cells were held in place by an intricate weave of struts and taut wires. The cells were made of rubberised canvas and bumped and swayed against one another, buffeted by the airship's progress. Together they held just over a million cubic metres of helium, providing over 200 tonnes of gross lift. Below the catwalk were the cabins where, in times of war, as many as 500 troops could have been quartered.

Down through an opening, the Silver Sanctum contingent entered the control gondola. There, they were greeted by Captain Qadoschson, a straight-backed, trim-bearded man with eyes that were pouched in wrinkles – eyes that had spent many a year squinting at bright, far horizons. He snapped a salute to Lady Aanfielsdaughter, as did his seven-man crew at their stations. All of them wore military dress uniforms which were smartly pressed and historically accurate right down to the Prismburg Air Force insignia badges sewn to the jacket sleeves. Captain Qadoschson had a gold-braided peaked cap on his head and impressive gold epaulettes on his wing arches. He looked like a veteran of countless wars, even though he had never seen a day's combat in his life.

'Milady,' he said, 'it's an honour to have you aboard.'

Lady Aanfielsdaughter returned the compliment. 'And I'd like to commend you and your crew for volunteering to take part in this expedition and for taking to the air at such short notice. You are all of you aware how risky a venture this is, and yet you've come without hesitation.'

'When the Silver Sanctum calls, one must answer.'

'Even so. You realise there's a good chance we may not make it back alive?'

Captain Qadoschson looked around the gondola, catching the eye of each crew member in turn. 'I speak for all of us when I say that we're ready to do whatever is necessary and face whatever dangers lie ahead. My understanding is that this is a matter of the utmost gravity and that the future of the Airborn race may depend on us.'

'Your understanding is correct.'

'Then we must do what we must do, milady. No question.'

'Thank you, captain,' said Lady Aanfielsdaughter. 'And now I'm going to hand over to this young man, Az Gabrielson, who is going to brief you fully on the situation and tell you what we can expect to find when we descend below the cloud cover. Az?'

Michael nudged Az from behind, and Az took a step forward and cleared his throat. He still could not believe that he was actually aboard *Cerulean*. It felt like a dream. Someone had taken his fondest wish and granted it. If only he could have been here under pleasanter circumstances.

The crew members were staring at him, as was Captain Qadoschson, all of them waiting for him to speak.

Az found his voice. 'It's like this,' he said, and started to explain.

He told them about his journey down in the elevator, about the Chancel, the Deacons, the Humanists ... He could tell from the crew's sceptical expressions that they didn't believe him, but he kept going and gradually the scepticism turned to cautious acceptance and then to full acceptance.

He then outlined the state of affairs down at the Grimvale Chancel, or rather at the base of Heliotropia's column. He stressed that he had no way of being absolutely sure about what was happening down there but he strongly suspected that the Humanists were in control of the Chancel and were soon going to be taking the elevators up, assuming they hadn't done so already.

Finally, he described the unpleasant physical symptoms which everyone was going to experience once the airship was below the cloud cover. The dizziness crept up on you slowly and was tolerable in the short term. With luck, they weren't going to be near ground level for long, so at worst they would feel mildly unwell, as if they had a stomach bug or a dose of 'flu.

'And that's the point at which you take over from me,' said Captain Qadoschson. 'You've experienced this ... this "ground-sickness" before, so you're likely to be hardened to it. If I'm incapacitated by it, you're the one who should take command of the ship.'

'Let's hope it doesn't come to that, sir.'

'But it may, so you'd best pay close attention to everything I say and do, just in case.'

'I think I can manage that,' said Az.

'Then let's start now.' Captain Qadoschson turned and barked out orders to his crew. 'All engines full ahead. Helmsman? Hold her steady on this course. Trim-master? Bring her nose up two degrees. Flight lieutenant? Keep an eye on the balloon pressure readings.'

With a low, keen murmur of power, *Cerulean* picked up speed.

CHAPTER 79

Aside

Mr Mordadson drew Lady Aanfieldsdaughter to one side for a private conversation.

'Milady, it's still not too late. Take one of the planes back to the Sanctum. Please. It makes me uncomfortable, having you here.'

'Why, Mr Mordadson? Because I'm a woman and this is men's business?' She spoke the last two words sarcastically. 'It's not like you to be so gallant.' This, too, was sarcastic, but teasing as well.

'That's not it at all, milady. Otherwise I would be recommending that Aurora go with you, and I'm not. To put it bluntly, I'm expendable. The airship's crew, Aurora, Michael, Az – we're all expendable. It doesn't matter what happens to us. You, on the other hand, as one of our highest-ranking government officials, are not expendable. We cannot afford to lose you.'

Lady Aanfieldsdaughter looked serene. 'I appreciate the concern, but I'm not going to run off and leave you now. What kind of leader would I be if I didn't take an active role in proceedings? Besides, I bear some responsibility for this crisis. If I hadn't sent Az down, perhaps the Humanists wouldn't have got it into their heads that they could come *up*. So I'm going to see things through to the end, come what may. It's only right and proper.'

'Well, I tried,' said Mr Mordadson, slumping his wings. 'And a very noble effort it was too. I have to admit to another reason for being here, though. I'm curious.'

'Curious, milady?'

'To see the ground. Aren't you? Finally to see with my own eyes what it looks like. I feel as if I'm about to break some great taboo, trespassing where I don't belong. It's been a long time since these old bones of mine felt quite so . . .'

'Excited?'

'Yes, that's the word for it. It seems inappropriate, but yes, I *am* excited.'

Mr Mordadson offered a vague smile. 'Me too. Although apprehensive as well.'

'Do you think this idea of yours is going to work?'

'Milady, I can't say.'

'Do you think the Groundlings are ready for us?'

Some certainty entered the smile. 'Long past ready, I'd say.'

CHAPTER 80

Steamarm And The Suspicious Steam

The first intimation Steamarm had that things were going awry was a sound. Something like a moan, albeit not one made by any human throat, it was so faint as to be only just at the threshold of his hearing. It seemed to come from everywhere and nowhere. It seemed to emanate from the Chancel itself, from the walls, the windows, the floors. It lasted only a brief time, there and gone in an instance, but after it had faded the atmosphere in the building was distinctly different. Something had changed, something small but vital.

Steamarm cocked his head and listened. The sound did not repeat itself.

Feeling unnerved, he went to the nearest window and looked out. He was in the apartment that belonged to the Archdeacon himself. It was a sumptuous set of rooms located high up, with a view of a large portion of the Chancel and, beyond, a wide southward expanse of the Shadow Zone.

Outside, Steamarm could see several of the furnace chimneys, as ever pouring dark smoke into the air. Next to one of them he noticed a vent which was sending up a furiously rippling white plume of steam. He frowned. That was odd. He was sure that last time he looked, no steam had been coming out. He hadn't even realised the vent was there until now.

Did this have anything to do with the sound a moment ago?

Before he could ponder the possible connection, Steamarm's eye was caught by movement outside. There were people down by the Chancel perimeter, on this side of the fence, not far from the southern gate. They were edging along in a line. He counted thirty of them, perhaps more.

They were too far away for him to make out their faces, but he knew they weren't Humanists. The way they were moving told him that: hunched over, treading softly, looking furtively around them as they went.

Someone had just invaded his Chancel!

Steamarm let out a growl of indignation and rushed out of the Archdeacon's apartment to round up Humanists.

Whoever the incomers were, he would make sure they got a very hostile reception.

CHAPTER 81

Under Pressure

In the furnace chamber, Deacon Shatterlonger beheld what he had done, and was pleased.

The other Deacons had joined him from the Contrition Cells and were on lookout at the chamber's entrances. They would warn him if anyone was coming.

A short while earlier, a deep, resonant moan had told Shatterlonger that the turbine system was starting to feel the strain. He imagined that steam vents all over the Chancel were wide open and doing their best to relieve the pressure. But the air intakes to the furnaces were fully open and the pressure was still building. The gauges indicated that. The needles were nudging remorselessly into the red zones.

It was awesome. He could feel the mounting power through his soles, through the floor. It trembled up his legs, flowing into his whole body, flooding through his veins. He was unleashing something incredible, a force with enough destructive potential to flatten the entire Chancel. The turbines were old and had, moreover, not been designed to operate at maximum output for any length of time. If pushed to the extreme, they would surely overload and break down. Then there would be unchecked steam coursing through the system, though aged and breakable pipes. Meanwhile the furnaces would continue to burn at temperatures far higher than their structural tolerances allowed. In other words, there was every chance of some kind of significant explosion.

Of course, it wouldn't come to that. Shatterlonger had no intention of allowing the overload to go beyond the critical stage. He wanted to put the wind up the Humanists, that was all. He wanted to scare them into quitting the Chancel.

But in order to do that they had to be prepared to believe that he *would* blow up the Chancel.

And if it came down to it, if he had to, really had to, he would.

CHAPTER 82

Into The Cloud Cover

Soon – far sooner than Az had anticipated – Heliotropia was visible from the forward viewing windows. *Cerulean* was not only graceful in flight, she was surprisingly fast. It helped that Captain Qadoschson understood the jetstream currents and knew how to take advantage of them. He had kept the airship at whatever altitude and whatever bearing would give her added velocity in the right direction. The jetstreams interleaved, running this way and that at different levels, and sometimes all it took was a 100-metre increase or decrease in height to go from struggling against a headwind to coasting along with a tailwind. *Cerulean*'s balloon acted like a sail. With a favourable following wind she could achieve speeds far in excess of anything a solely propeller-driven aircraft was capable of.

Az kept an eagle eye on everything Captain Qadoschson did, remembering it for later in case it was needed. *This, truly, is flying*, he thought. Compared with a plane, *Cerulean* was quiet, she was smooth, she slid through space as though cleaving the air open before her.

He was exhilarated. She was everything he had imagined, and more.

The sight of. Heliotropia brought Az out of his reverie, reminding him that this wasn't some pleasure cruise he was on.

'Commence descent,' ordered Captain Qadoschson.

The mood in the control gondola became perceptibly tenser as *Cerulean*'s nose dipped and she sank towards the clouds.

'This will get rocky,' Captain Qadoschson announced to his passengers. 'Best find something to get hold of.'

Az grabbed the brass handrail which ran all the way around the inside of the gondola, bolted to the bulkheads. He saw Michael, Lady Aanfieldsdaughter and Mr Mordadson do the same. Aurora did not. Instead, touchingly, she groped for Michael's hand and gripped it. Michael gripped back.

Az looked away, pretending he hadn't witnessed this. Michael wasn't the type who voluntarily held hands with a woman. He wasn't that kind of boyfriend. Az sensed that his brother had fallen very hard for Aurora and that he had at last met someone who wasn't bowled over by his good looks and cool job, who was in many ways his equal and in several ways his superior. Michael had, in other words, met his match.

There wasn't time to muse on this, however. The cloud cover loomed. It seemed to be rushing up to greet *Cerulean*, a rising field of torn white and grey. It looked solid, as though there would be an impact when the airship reached it, a devastating crash.

Nobody had ever done this before – willingly flown into the clouds.

At that moment it seemed to Az that they were attempting something insane.

'Steady does it,' said Captain Qadoschson. 'Steady.'

His voice didn't quaver in the slightest. His apparent nervelessness astonished Az. What self-control! Only the faint pulse of a tendon at the corner of his jaw betrayed the fact that Qadoschson was as anxious as everybody else on board.

Now filmy wisps of vapour surrounded the control gondola, and *Cerulean* began to buck and shake. Az could imagine her as a living creature, balking at the prospect of going where she clearly ought not to. He felt like patting the handrail to reassure her. He had never before quite understood how people could regard a vehicle or any kind of machine as a sentient being, the way Cassie regarded *Cackling Bertha*, for instance. It had seemed absurd and sentimental to him.

Not any more.

Cerulean immersed herself deeper in the clouds. Everything outside went pure white, then darker white.

This was it. No going back now.

Suddenly the airship lurched sideways.

'Helmsman! Correct her course!'

The helmsman counter-steered, spinning the large brass conn wheel. *Cerulean* resumed her original heading.

'Flight lieutenant. Readings?'

'All nominal, captain. Propellers working at ninety per cent of full thrust. Engine temps good. No red-lining.'

'Excellent. Notify me of any fluctuations. Trim-master? I think we're skewing a few degrees from true.'

'Aye-aye, captain. Fixing it.'

Az could tell that none of these commands was strictly necessary. Captain Qadoschson was keeping his crew's minds on their jobs so that they wouldn't have the leisure to think about anything else.

Cerulean plunged.

'Air pocket!' yelled one of the crew.

Az felt his stomach rise into his throat. At the same time, all the blood in his body seemed to rush to his feet. From several people in the gondola came an involuntary cry, almost as if the air was being shoved up out of their lungs. Wings flared to help maintain their owners' balance.

'Keep her nose up! Keep her nose up!' the captain ordered. 'More power to the forward props!'

Az clung to the handrail, fearing he would be thrown to the ceiling otherwise.

Then, as if nothing had happened, *Cerulean* settled.

There were white faces around the gondola. Even Aurora looked a paler shade of brown.

'We're all right,' said Captain Qadoschson. 'It was just a pressure drop. Happens even above the clouds. We probably fell about two hundred metres.'

'Two hundred and fifty, captain,' said the navigator, eyeing his instruments.

'Thank you, Mr Ra'asielson. Two hundred and fifty in a few seconds. An alarming sensation, but—'

Something seemed to strike *Cerulean* from outside, making her twist around her horizontal axis. The floor became a slope. Everyone leaned. Az found himself being squashed against the wall, the handrail digging into his side.

'Adjust! Adjust!'

'Trying to, captain!'

The slope steepened. *Cerulean* was pitching, slowly turning onto her side.

'Cut starboard props! Rotate port props to forty-five and down!'

'Sir . . .'

'Do as I say!'

Engines whined. The whole of *Cerulean*'s structure creaked and groaned. A mighty force had a grip on her and was rolling her over, rolling, rolling . . .

But the captain's countermeasures started to take effect. Slowly, strenuously, with so much effort that she seemed she might pop her own rivets, *Cerulean* righted herself.

There were relieved sighs all over the gondola, except from Captain Qadoschson.

'I don't think that's all you can do,' he said, addressing the cloud cover. 'Let's see what else you have in store for us.'

What came next was a bout of turbulence that rocked the airship from end to end, gusts of wind hurling themselves at her from a hundred different angles at once.

Overhead, in the balloon, there was a loud, sinister snapping *twanggg*.

'It's nothing,' Captain Qadoschson announced. 'Just a wire breaking. We've lost wires before. It's no big deal. Plenty of others to keep everything in place.'

The turbulence continued, and the clouds outside were getting darker and darker, the light in the gondola dimmer and dimmer.

Captain Qadoschson called for an altitude reading.

'Can't be much further,' he said. 'How thick are these clouds anyway?'

Cerulean fought her way onwards and downwards through the shocks and buffeting. Minutes passed during which not even her captain spoke. The crew members manned their stations in grim silence, the occasional twitch of wings betraying edginess and uncertainty. Outside the windows there was nothing but roiling, impenetrable greyness. Time slowed. To Az it began to feel like the turbulence would go on for ever. There would be no end to this tempestuous abuse. They had entered a kind of perpetual twilight existence, an eternity of shaking and gloom. He remembered this feeling from when he was in the elevator, this sense of being removed from reality, of being trapped in timelessness. They were nowhere, belonged nowhere, were going nowhere ...

And then, just like that, without warning, they were out of it.

The clouds were gone.

They were in clear air.

And below was the ground – the rough, rocky contours of the Shadow Zone.

And ahead, a little to starboard, lay the Chancel, that collection of jagged and bulbous buildings clustered at the column's base.

Cassie, Az thought, *I'm coming.*

CHAPTER 83

Cracks In The Coalition

The task of rounding up Humanists to repel the invaders did not go well.

What Steamarm had thought of as high spirits earlier, he now began to perceive was rowdiness. What had appeared to be jubilation was actually wanton, thuggish glee. His foot-soldiers were out of control. They were dispersed across the Chancel, doing pretty much as they pleased. A few were still more or less behaving themselves – the ones guarding the captive Deacons, for example. Most, though, were treating the fall of the Chancel as an opportunity to run amok. It hadn't been enough to take out their resentment of the Deacons on the Deacons themselves. They had to exact revenge on the Deacons' property as well. The result: a spree of looting and damage.

What prompted his realisation that things were degenerating into chaos was the discovery of several Humanists lying slumped in a corridor, dead drunk, snoring. The temptation to kick them was so strong Steamarm was almost blinded by it. In the event he didn't succumb. He left the slumbering men where they were, unharmed, and went in search of someone a bit more sober. He knew he had to reassert order, and quickly. He must rein his men in, or else.

'You there,' he said to the next lot of Humanists he found. They were in the Chancel library, systematically taking books off shelves and ripping the pages out of them. 'What's the meaning of this?'

The men looked up from the snowdrifts of torn paper around them. Their eyes had a strange, glutted gleam, like the eyes of children who'd indulged in too much cake at a birthday party.

'Just having some fun, that'm all,' said one of them.

'Being thorough,' said another. 'Be'n't fair that the Deacons has all this nice stuff. Reckon them can do without it from now on, like the rest of we.'

'Besides,' said a third, 'this all originally belonged to folk like we. Deacons blackmailed it out of they in funeral tithes. Them doesn't deserve to own it.'

'This is not what we came here for,' said Steamarm firmly.

'Be'n't it?' said the first Humanist. 'Well, maybe not you, Alan, but it certainly be what *I* came here for.'

There were low cheers of agreement all around.

Alan, thought Steamarm. *He called me Alan.*

He was disturbed, not so much by the use of his first name as by the way the man had said it. There had been no respect in it, nor even a kind of friendly disrespect. He had said it coldly and antagonisingly, in a belittling tone.

Steamarm began to wonder if he had made a serious miscalculation. He'd thought the Humanists were relying on him to rally them, to lead them, to help them achieve their aims. But what if they had merely been using him all along, without even consciously knowing they had? Could it be that, to them, he was just a convenient figurehead rather than an actual leader? Could it be that he had far less power over them than he thought?

Inconceivable!

And yet . . .

'Listen,' he said, with all the authority he could muster. 'I've spotted some people outside. I don't know who they are, but they've found a way onto the premises and I doubt their intentions are good. We have to see them off.'

The Humanists glanced at one another. Steamarm could scarcely believe that the idea of a fight did not appeal to them, and yet here they were, having to think about it. He reasoned that they had got a lot of aggression out of their systems over the course of the night. They hadn't yet worked up an appetite for fresh violence.

Or was he genuinely losing his grip? Were these men loyal to only one thing, their basest instincts?

'Who'd be coming to kick we out of here?'

'Seems daft. Deacons don't have friends out there.'

'You'm sure it be'n't more of our lot, come to see how us has got on?'

'Yes, I'm sure,' said Steamarm. 'Pretty sure. No, sure.'

'Don't sound it.'

'I'm sure. Straight up I'm sure.'

'Oh, "straight up", eh?' All of the Humanists chortled at Steamarm's attempt to sound like one of them. 'Well, if you be "straight up" sure, then who's us to argue?'

'So you'll do it then?' Steamarm had to struggle to keep the exasperation out of his voice. 'You'll see these people off?'

'If that'm what you want, Alan.'

This pattern was repeated elsewhere in the Chancel. It took Steamarm far longer than he would have liked, and was far more effort than he had anticipated, to gather together enough Humanists to confront the invaders (whoever they were). The situation was in danger of falling completely to pieces, and he pinned his hopes on the act of repulsing the invaders serving as the catalyst that would bring the Humanists back in line. For perhaps the first time in his life Steamarm was doubting himself. It was a feeling he did not relish in the least.

CHAPTER 84

A Building With Rattle-Lung

After hours of fruitless searching, Martin wound up in the bowels of the Chancel. He had looked everywhere else. By a process of elimination, Fletcher and Cassie had to be down here. Unless, that was, they were wandering around the Chancel too and he kept missing them. Which was possible but unlikely. If they *were* on the move, his path and theirs would surely have crossed by now. No, Martin was convinced that wherever they were, they would be staying put, lying low.

So he was left with just this one area to hunt through, the sweltering lower reaches of the building. The air smelled rank and humid here, and Martin was aware of a deep, vibrant rumble which pulsed around him, sometimes growing to a tormented roar then dwindling again. He could not identify the sound or pinpoint its origin, but he could tell it was not healthy, not the sound of things functioning well. It resembled the laboured breathing of someone in the throes of rattle-lung, that rasping, hiccupping inhale/exhale which Martin knew only too well. When their mother had been dying, the whole family had had to listen to her making that noise in the bedroom, night and day. It had filled the house and become the stuttering rhythm of their lives. Of all of them, only Cassie had remained oblivious to it, but then she had been too young to understand what it meant. She had been upset, but only because no one would let her into the bedroom to see their mother. She'd had no idea why she wasn't allowed in there and had thrown tantrums. She hadn't been able to connect the horrible wheezing and gasping that came from the room with the fact that she was being kept away from Ma. Infant innocence had protected her from the truth.

Now the Chancel seemed to be suffering from its own case of rattle-lung, and Martin wished he wasn't reminded of his mother. A building with a terminal illness? Not good. A sudden quake erupted all around him. He had to grab a wall to steady himself. The quake ebbed away, but the irregularly throbbing rumble continued.

Not long after that, Martin arrived at the furnaces.

He realised two things as he approached the furnace chamber. One was that he had finally found where the sound was coming from. This was its source. The very air around him seemed to churn with the noise. The flagstones underfoot trembled with it.

The other thing he realised was that there were Deacons still on the loose. It seemed impossible. He had been under the impression that they were all corralled somewhere upstairs. But he caught sight of a flash of robe in the entrance to the chamber up ahead and heard a muffled cry: 'Someone's coming!'

Martin quickly debated what to do. He ought to alert Steamarm. But that would take time, time he couldn't spare. Not with this worrisome rumble going on . . .

He made his decision and continued forwards. Maybe it was just two Deacons at the most. He could handle two Deacons. And they might have some idea of his siblings' whereabouts.

'Humanist!' yelled a voice ahead of him.

Martin halted.

In the entrance, a tall, lanky Deacon appeared. He had a shaven head and a weird kind of wildness in his eyes – the look of someone whose sanity had started to break loose from its moorings. Martin vaguely recognised him, but then he knew the faces of quite a few Deacons and had a hard time telling them apart sometimes. The robes made them all look alike.

'Don't come any further,' said the Deacon. 'Go back. Go back and tell your leader, tell Alan Steamarm, that he should leave the Chancel now, while he has the chance. All of you should. Tell him he doesn't have long. The furnaces are overheating and the turbine system is exceeding safe limits. He has perhaps just minutes before the entire Chancel is blown to smithereens.'

As if to underline the Deacon's remark, another short quake reverberated through the surrounding brickwork. The electric lights flickered. Dust sifted down onto Martin's head.

Martin raised his hands in a peacemaking gesture. 'Look, I don't want any trouble,' he said. 'I don't even much care if you want to blow this place up. I be looking for my brother and sister, Fletcher and Cassie Grubdollar. That'm all I want. Do you know where them might be?'

The Deacon peered at him appraisingly. 'Ah yes, a Grubdollar. Thought I saw the family resemblance. Well, I shan't lie. Your brother and sister are here, right here, not fifty metres from where we're standing. Right in harm's way. So you run off and find Alan Steamarm – and run quickly, mind – and if you reach him in time and if he vacates the Chancel immediately, then maybe, just maybe, I'll shut down the furnaces and we won't die, all of us, your brother and sister included.'

'Or maybe,' said Martin, starting forward, 'I'll just go past you and get they.'

The Deacon did not look too happy about this, but the wildness in him reasserted itself, fuelling his courage.

'I'm not alone, you know.' He nodded over his shoulder, and Martin noticed at least three other Deacons lurking behind him. 'There's several of us and only one of you.'

Martin didn't falter. 'My bro, my sis. Them's all I be after. Get out of my way.'

'And if I don't?'

Martin's answer was to snarl and break into a run.

CHAPTER 85

Fight In The Furnace Chamber

Martin charged headlong into the furnace chamber, ramming into the shaven-headed Deacon and sending him flying.

Two other Deacons set upon him, but Martin butted one sideways with an elbow and brought the other one down with a kick to the groin. Another Deacon grabbed his shirt collar. Martin spun round, twisting out of the man's grasp. He took hold of the Deacon's head with both hands and yanked down, at the same time bringing one knee up. Knee and nose collided, and there was a crunch of breaking cartilage and the Deacon let out a shrill, girlish shriek.

Martin turned, to find yet another Deacon in his way. This one was bulkier than average, with a bit of muscle on him. He looked as though he might put up more of a fight than the others.

Martin, however, was in a reckless, rushing whirl of action. His heart was racing, the blood pounding in his ears. The only way to win here was to be brutal and relentless. Without a second thought he crossed the gap between him and the Deacon and started punching. A straight shot to the midriff, another to the jaw. The Deacon punched back but without the same force or accuracy. His blows glanced off Martin's shoulder, scuffed the side of Martin's head. Martin drew his right arm back and landed a piledriver in the Deacon's midriff. The Deacon doubled over, clutching his belly, heaving for breath. Martin brushed him aside and continued on his way.

There was a howl from behind him that sounded more animal than human. Martin turned in time to see the shaven-headed Deacon sprinting straight at him. He managed to get his arms up in defence, then the Deacon hit him and together they went hurtling across the floor. Martin struck something spine-first. Next thing he knew, searing heat flared across his back, and with the heat, pain. He had been shunted up against a steam pipe and it was burning him through his clothes.

He flexed away from the pipe but the Deacon shoved him into it again. There was heat again, and pain, and Martin smelled scorching cotton. He gritted his teeth and arched his back and wrestled with the Deacon and strained, and eventually managed to thrust both of them away from the pipe once more.

The shaven-headed Deacon recovered his balance and went for Martin, hoping to push him against the pipe a third time, but Martin was ready for him now. He used the Deacon's own momentum against him. As the man lunged, Martin grabbed his robe and swung him round. The Deacon slammed sideways into the pipe. Martin didn't hesitate. He clamped a hand over the Deacon's ear, shoved the other side of his face onto the pipe, and held it there.

The Deacon's scream was horrifying. Worse, though, was the sizzle that his skin made as the pipe cooked it, and the stench that came off it, sweet and meaty and all too similar to the odour of bacon frying.

Nevertheless, Martin kept the Deacon's cheek pressed against the pipe, even as the man clawed at Martin's hand and lashed out at him desperately. Martin's lips peeled back in a grimace of disgust, but he had to do this, he had to do whatever it took to defeat the Deacon, because that was the only way he was going to be able to get to Fletcher and Cassie.

Finally the Deacon went limp and Martin let go. The Deacon collapsed to the floor in a dead faint, leaving a patch of fluid on the pipe which bubbled stickily. Martin stepped away, feeling sickened. Bile rose in his throat, and he bent over and vomited.

When he had finished he wiped his mouth with the back of his hand, then turned and looked at the other Deacons. Their faces were ashen, their mouths agape in shock. One of them had thrown up too. He could see they weren't going to give him any more trouble now. The shaven-headed Deacon was their ringleader, and they had watched how Martin had dealt with him. Also, they were still reeling from the punishment they themselves had received from him. The fight was over. Martin had won.

'Where be them, then?' he demanded. 'Cassie, Fletch. Where'm you keeping they?'

A trembling finger pointed him in the direction of a ragged hole in the chamber wall.

Martin set off towards it at a run.

CHAPTER 86

Outdoor Brawl

The clash between the Humanists and Den Grubdollar's Amblescrut army took place outdoors on a patch of ground between the Chancel and the perimeter fence. The fight went on for only a few minutes, but while it lasted it was fierce and most of the time it seemed an even contest, each side as likely to triumph as the other.

It began as a dozen over-zealous Humanists rushed out from the Chancel brandishing their weapons and yelling a wordless battlecry. They took one look at the opposition, realised they were outnumbered three to one, and turned tail and fled back inside.

The Amblescruts naturally gave chase. In spite of Den shouting at them to hold back, they charged forward yelling a battlecry of their own, which was a mix of phrases such as 'Get they!' and 'Bash their heads in!' with a sprinkling of crude insults thrown in. They piled through the doorway from which the Humanists had emerged, but then found themselves suddenly at a tactical disadvantage. They were in a passageway that was wide enough for two people to stand shoulder to shoulder, but no more than two.

This equalised things, and the Humanists knew it. They turned and confronted the Amblescruts. A pair from each side grappled in the narrow space. Meanwhile all the other Amblescruts were telling one another to retreat, get back outside, it was a bottleneck here, no good for anyone. Everyone was giving orders, no one obeying. It took some time for them to begin shuffling backwards out of the passageway, and four of them didn't make it, bludgeoned senseless by the Humanists.

Humanist reinforcements arrived in the interim, so that the battle which then took place was between forces of more or less equal strength. Humanists charged the Amblescrut army from two directions at once. Some came from the passageway, the rest attacked the Amblescruts from the rear, having exited the Chancel via the sorting-house nearby. The Amblescruts were caught in a classic pincer movement, but to their credit they collected themselves and fought back valiantly and effectively.

The two sets of combatants milled and mauled. For a time, Den could not tell which side was winning and sometimes could not even tell his forces apart from the enemy. From a distance, an Amblescrut and a

Humanist looked similar, and when they were all in a throng like this they merged together, becoming an amorphous mass of people. Whose hammering fist was that? Whose flying foot? There were no uniforms here to make distinguishing friend from foe easy.

That was one reason why he didn't get embroiled in the fray himself. The other was that his cracked rib was agony. Despite the bandaging it had been *giving* him grief all the way across the Shadow Zone, and now he could scarcely move his upper body without a burst of pain shooting across his entire torso. He knew, to his chagrin, that he was useless for fighting. All he could do was call out to his troops, encouraging them. He made sure that Robert stayed by his side and did the same. Robert was too young to get mixed up in this kind of carnage. He kept asking to be allowed to join in, and his father kept forbidding it.

Luckily the Amblescruts *could* tell friend from foe. Family member recognised family member, even amid all the chaos and confusion. It was almost instinctive.

Luckily, too, they didn't require much help. The addition of Den to their ranks wouldn't have made much difference. Although surprised by the Humanists' double-pronged assault, they soon had the measure of the enemy. They soon had quite a few of the Humanists' weapons as well, which they wrested from their hands and immediately used against them. Gradually the Humanists' strategic advantage was whittled away. They began to cede ground. They dispersed into small, separate pockets of men, losing unity. The Amblescruts clung together in larger groups. The battle broke down into a series of skirmishes, with two or three Humanists harrying a half-dozen Amblescruts and being soundly repulsed. Along the way there was attrition. Humanists limped off to the sidelines, some of them with broken limbs, some with deep gashes that would not stop bleeding. Several had to be carried off, concussed. Amblescruts likewise retired hurt from the battlefield, but in smaller numbers. It became a kind of running tally, a means of determining which way the fight was going. The side with the greater amount of casualties must be losing, and it was increasingly obvious that, in this instance, the Humanists were that side.

The Humanists had been weary to begin with, and they had won an easy victory over the Deacons, which had made them overconfident. The Amblescruts, by contrast, had come to the fight fresh and keen, and were considerably more skilled in the art of hand-to-hand combat than the Deacons were. Given those factors, the outcome should never have been in doubt, but Den remained unsure of success right up until the moment he realised that the Humanists were surrendering. Startled, he looked around and saw that everywhere, almost as one, they were throwing down their weapons and haggardly raising their hands. They had had enough. He then saw Amblescruts start to dance and cheer. The truth still didn't quite hit home until Robert tugged at his arm and said, 'It'm over, Da. Them did it. Them brainless hillbillies actually did it!'

'Best not call they that, boy,' Den replied in a growl. 'Like it or not, them's our friends now. Best get used to being a little more respectful to they.'

Colin came swaggering up and offered Den a jokey, exaggerated salute. 'General Grubdollar sir, I be pleased to report that us has engaged with the enemy and kicked their arses. What'm you wanting we to do now?'

'Round the Humanists up and put they somewhere safe. Then find out what them's done with the Deacons. Meantime, I'll be looking for Cassie.'

'Very well.' Colin snapped another salute and marched off to rejoin his rejoicing family.

'Haven't seen Martin or Fletcher anywhere, Da,' said Robert, surveying the defeated Humanists. 'Reckon them's inside the Chancel too?'

'Maybe. Not much bothered right now. Cassie's the one I be worried about.'

'You still mad at they?'

'Your brothers? I be waiting to have cause *not* to be. Now Robert, listen carefully. You stay here. You'm in charge now. Make sure them Amblescruts doesn't do anything too stupid.'

'*That'll* be hard.'

'Robert . . .'

'Sorry, Da. OK, I get it. I be in charge. You'm going off to rescue Cass. Good luck.'

'Thanks, boy.'

So saying, Den set off towards the Chancel. Meanwhile, just around the corner . . .

CHAPTER 87

The Blue Cigar

Lawrence Brace drove through the southern gate unchallenged. He was puzzled that there was no longer anyone on duty in the gatehouse as far as he could see (but then he could not see the unconscious Humanist whom Colin Amblescrut had dragged *behind* the gatehouse). The barrier itself was wide open, which also puzzled him, but he came to the conclusion that Steamarm must have decided that such security measures weren't necessary any more. And why would they be? The Chancel belonged to the Humanists now. Who would be foolhardy enough to want to break in?

Brace was feeling hugely pleased with himself as he steered the truck towards the Chancel buildings. He had obtained everything Steamarm had asked for: 50 breathing-apparatus kits and a box of 20 sticks of dynamite, with fuses. He looked forward to being showered with praise by the Humanist leader for having completed the errand so promptly and efficiently.

And lo and behold, here was Steamarm now, running to meet the truck. Brace had to admit that Steamarm didn't look like someone who was ready to shower praise. He looked agitated and panicky. Nevertheless Brace halted the truck, applied the handbrake, rolled down the window and waited to be congratulated on a job well done. Something of an optimist, was Lawrence Brace.

In the event, Steamarm charged straight past the truck's cab, barely giving its driver a second glance. He undid the tailgate and leapt up onto the flatbed where the items from the mine lay. He snatched up a breathing-apparatus kit, then opened the box of dynamite and began stuffing the sticks into the waistband of his trousers. By the time Brace had got over his bewilderment (and disappointment) and climbed out from behind the wheel, Steamarm had jumped down to the ground again and was hurrying back to the Chancel.

'Alan!' Brace called out. 'Alan? Alan, what'm up? Where you going? Alan!'

In reply, all he got was: 'They can't have won. Can't have. And they can't have it. It's mine. The Chancel is mine. I'll show them. I'll bring it down. Down around their miserable heads.'

Brace didn't think Steamarm was even speaking to him. Steamarm was speaking to himself. *Ranting* to himself.

Scratching the top of his scalp, Brace wondered what was going on. He had been away for a little over an hour. How much could have happened in such a short space of time?

The answer to that question, of course, was a lot.

But before Brace had a chance to find this out, something else happened – something which made him forget all about Steamarm's peculiar behaviour, something so extraordinary it had him wondering if he himself was starting to go a bit crazy.

A gigantic blue cigar came down from the sky and exploded with light.

CHAPTER 88

Five Minutes Earlier

On board *Cerulean*, Az observed the fighting at the Chancel, using a telescope that Captain Qadoschson had passed to him.

'What do you make of that?' the captain had asked, indicating the swarm of tiny, distant figures.

What Az made of it was that a third faction must have become involved in the takeover of the Chancel. There weren't any Deacons down there amid the melée. He could see no dark robes. It seemed to be Humanists versus ... whom? Az couldn't say. He couldn't even hazard a guess. A rival set of Humanists? That didn't feel like the right answer.

He confessed his ignorance. 'But it's good that they're out there in the open, because then our dramatic entrance will have more impact,' he said. 'And I think we should get on with it, too, before things spiral any further out of control.'

Captain Qadoschson gave a nod of assent. 'Let's take her down then, men,' he said to his crew. 'Two hundred metres above ground level should do it. How are we all faring? No ill effects yet?'

The crew members took it in turns to say they felt all right.

'Lady Aanfieldsdaughter?'

'Fine so far, captain. Yourself?'

'I must admit, I'm a little bit light-headed. But it could just be the excitement, the unfamiliar situation ...' He fanned his face with his cap, then resumed supervising the airship's descent.

Mr Mordadson appeared beside Az at the front of the control gondola.

'And how about you, Az?' he enquired. 'Everything OK?'

'I want to get down there. I want to find Cassie.'

'I know. Patience. We must stick to the plan. We're about to change the world for ever. That's not a thing you can rush.'

'Do you think the Groundlings will be frightened by us?'

'You'd be a better judge of that than me. You've met some of them.'

Az thought. 'Maybe they'll be frightened at first, but then they'll be intrigued. Glad, even. Finally to have actual contact with Ascended Ones, to meet them in the flesh ...'

'To see that, wings aside, we're just like them.'

'And they're just like us.'

Mr Mordadson aimed a smile at Az, and for once the smile included his eyes as well as his mouth. Behind the crimson spectacles, his eyes sparkled. It was a revelation. Briefly, while the smile lasted, Mr Mordadson seemed like an ordinary, normal, approachable person. He seemed like someone you could even *like*.

Az's feelings must have been clear on his face. 'There's more to me than meets the eye, Az,' Mr Mordadson said. 'I'm not as I appear. All my life I've done hard things, made hard choices, but invariably it's been for what I believe are the best reasons. I don't set out to be a nice person, I've never felt that life is a popularity contest – but I know right from wrong, and that's my overriding imperative, always to do what's right. *This* is right, what we're about to do. And for that' – Mr Mordadson lowered his voice – 'for that, Az, I have you to thank.'

'What? Me?' Az was no longer surprised, he was astonished.

'You, for wanting to save this girl. You, an Airborn, befriending and defending Groundlings. You, proving that our two races can and should coexist, that it's high time the division between us was ended. You've pointed the way, Az. People of your own race may have looked down on you because you don't *look* Airborn. But to me, you're everything an Airborn should be. As a matter of fact, you're one of our best.'

Before Az could even think of a response, Mr Mordadson added, 'But if you tell anyone I said what I just said, I'll deny it. I do have a reputation to uphold.'

He drifted off, leaving Az to question whether his own ears were working properly. Had Mr Mordadson really just called him 'one of our best'? It must be the low altitude. Either it was addling Az's brain or Mr Mordadson's.

'Approaching two hundred,' the navigator announced.

Captain Qadoschson acknowledged this, somewhat wanly. 'Very well. Chief engineer? Ready with the lights. Divert all surplus power to them. Done? Then on my mark ... Three. Two. One. Now!'

The chief engineer threw a series of fork-switches in rapid succession, and all at once, inside and out, *Cerulean* was ablaze. Floodlights within her balloon, searchlights attached to the hull of her gondola, running lights on her nosecone and tailfins, all burst into brilliant life. The glow lit up the ground below and was reflected in sparkles off the Chancel's windows. Az saw Groundlings recoil in astonishment, craning their necks and shading their eyes. He tried to imagine how *Cerulean* must look to them, floating majestically towards them like some gigantic blue lantern. He prayed they wouldn't panic. Panicking people could turn hostile. The purpose of turning on the lights was simply to draw attention to *Cerulean's* presence. This was the crucial moment. This was the fulcrum on which Mr Mordadson's idea teetered. If the Groundlings stayed calm, if they were fascinated by the sight of the airship rather than alarmed, then the plan stood a decent chance of succeeding. The Airborn would make a good first impression.

If not, then all was lost.

CHAPTER 89

First Contact

Humanist and Amblescrut peered upwards, side by side. There were gasps of amazement and muted murmurs of concern. People who a few minutes ago had been locked in conflict and had only just separated themselves into winners and losers, now stood united in awe. They watched the huge array of lights in the sky loom closer, squinting against the radiant dazzle. They perceived that this was manmade, a vehicle, some kind of aircraft. But weren't such things prohibited? Hadn't the Deacons decreed that aircraft were forbidden to exist anywhere except above the clouds? So what was one of them doing down here? Who could have built it and be piloting it?

Soon the aircraft was directly overhead, and the down- draught from its propellers set people's hair swirling and kicked up a thin cloud of dust. An urge passed through the crowd like an electric current. *Run. Scatter. Take cover.* But it was overwhelmed by a stronger urge, to stay put, to wait and see what the aircraft did next, to learn who was inside.

They didn't have to wait long.

A figure emerged from amidst the lambent blue glow that was at the heart of the phenomenon. To the crowd below it was a small dark silhouette, approximately human-shaped. A second figure joined it, then a third. Were they attached to the aircraft somehow? Descending from it on ropes?

No. No, the figures were moving away from the aircraft sideways, independently. Four of them. And they were people, yes, but they were more than that. Look how they moved. They were hovering, circling. They were coming down. They were like birds.

They had wings. People with wings.

Ascended Ones!

Now the crowd's consternation became a mutual buzz of excitement. Amblescrut turned to Amblescrut, Humanist to Humanist. In an instant, injuries were forgotten. So were animosities. Some Humanists found themselves sharing amazed looks with Amblescruts, and the other way round. Their expressions spoke eloquently. Ascended Ones? Here? Now? How could this be?

Down the Ascended Ones came with their wings outstretched, feathers splayed to create drag and slow the descent. Down, till the Grimvale residents on the ground could make out their individual physical details. There was a man with crimson spectacles. There was an elderly, elegant woman. There was a younger, dark-skinned woman. There was another man, also young. And in the arms of that man there was—

'Az!'

It was Robert who shouted this.

Az turned in the direction the shout had come from. Though he had only had the briefest of meetings with the youngest of Cassie's three older brothers, he recognised him nonetheless.

'Robert,' he replied.

Robert ran forward through the crowd, while the Ascended Ones covered the last few metres to the ground. Just as they touched down, the aircraft lights were doused and the Shadow Zone's habitual gloom returned. The aircraft spun slowly and pulled away, to take up position just outside the Chancel perimeter.

Robert reached the Ascended Ones. Az slipped from the arms of the man carrying him and greeted Robert.

'I owe you a pair of boots,' he said. 'I forgot to bring them back with me. Sorry.'

Robert frowned. 'Eh? What boots?'

'Never mind. How are you doing? Have you recovered from that knock on the head?'

'Got a bump there the size of a steamed pudding, feels like, but otherwise I be all right.'

Az scanned the crowd. 'So tell me what's been going on.' Robert gave a hollow laugh. 'What hasn't? But maybe first you should tell *we* about these friends of yours.'

'Ah yes.' Az got ready to make introductions. He sensed the significance of the occasion. It had fallen upon him to officiate at the first-ever formal encounter between Airborn and Groundling. For the moment his own personal desire, to find out about Cassie, had to take a back seat.

No sooner had he opened his mouth to speak, however, than there came a loud, ominous groan from the Chancel, followed by a flare of fire from one of the chimneys.

'That didn't sound good,' said someone in the crowd.

CHAPTER 90

Ground-sick

Flames continued to shoot up from the chimney. The groan repeated itself.

'What was that?' Az asked.

'No idea,' said Robert, with an anxious glance at the Chancel. 'Tut Da be in there, and Cassie too. And Fletch, Martin . . .'

'Then introductions can wait.' Az turned to his brother and the other three Airborn. 'Mike? I think you should move off to a safe distance. All of you. Whatever's going on in there, it sounds pretty serious.' He then turned to the crowd of Groundlings. 'In fact, I think everyone should evacuate the area. Now.'

The residents of Grimvale Township were still coming to terms with the presence of Ascended Ones in their midst, but they weren't so astonished that they couldn't see the logic in what Az was saying. Colin took charge, repeating the suggestion about evacuating. He had recognised Az as the wingless Ascended One whom the Grubdollars had been looking after (and whom Alan Steamarm had kidnapped from them). Any friend of Den Grubdollar was a friend of Colin Amblescrut.

'Come on,' he said, 'everybody head for the southern gate.'

Galvanised into action, people started to move. The uninjured helped the injured to walk. The crowd made its way in a shuffling, straggling mass towards the gate.

Az, meanwhile, set off towards the Chancel, with Robert in tow.

'Hey!' Michael took off, soared over Az and Robert, and landed in front of them, barring their path. 'Where do you think *you're* off to, Az? You just said we had to get to safety.'

'I said *you* did, Mike. *I'm* going in there.'

'Inside?' Michael frowned incredulously. 'That's crazy.'

'Maybe, but so what?'

'Look, I appreciate that you . . .' Michael shook his head. For a moment his eyes seemed to lose focus. His brows knitted. 'Uhhh, that was odd.'

'It's the low altitude. It's starting to get to you,' Az said. 'No, it isn't.'

'Bit of dizziness? Buzzing in your ears?'

Michael nodded.

'Told you. You're getting ground-sick. You have to go back to *Cerulean* while you still can, you and Lady Aanfielsdaughter and everyone. And I have to go in and get Cassie. That's all there is to it.'

Michael began objecting, but a second dizzy spell washed over him. The colour drained from his face.

'OK,' he said, reluctantly. 'But if I had any choice . . .'

'I know,' said Az. 'Look, don't worry, I'll be out again in no time.'

'You damn well better be.'

CHAPTER 91

A Grubdollar Thing

Cassie could hardly believe it when the door to the Contrition Cell flew open and there was Martin standing there, looking ruffled but stoic. All at once she forgave him everything. She threw her arms around him, thinking he was the best, the handsomest, the bravest big brother a girl could have. Martin returned the embrace, hesitantly at first, then warmly.

'I still be mad at you, you know, Cass,' he said. 'Just because I came looking for you don't change anything.'

'And I still be mad at *you*,' she replied, hugging him tighter.

They let Fletcher out of his cell. He whooped with joy at being free, then became somewhat sheepish as he remembered that he had helped Cassie steal *Bertha* behind Martin's back and had betrayed the cause which his older brother held so dear. Then he realised that frankly all he cared about right now was that he was no longer, trapped in a confined space being torturously slow-roasted, and he whooped with joy again.

'If you'm finished defeaning we, Fletch,' Martin said gruffly, 'maybe us could have a stab at getting out of here.'

'What'm the big hurry, Martin?' said Cassie. 'Be it something to do with all that grinding and shaking that'm been going on? Been scaring me half to death, that have.'

'It'm the furnaces, Cass. Deacons have sabotaged they.'

'What! Why?'

'Why d'you think? To destroy the place. If them can't have the Chancel, no one can.'

'Well, who be stopping they? Be'n't your lot trying to?'

'Not as far as I know.'

'Why not?'

'To put it plainly, things has got a little unruly around here. Which be all the more reason for us to leave, while us still can.'

Cassie nodded, but then shook her head.

'No?' said Martin. 'You don't agree?'

'No. Reckon us has something else to do.'

'Such as?'

'Not liking the sound of this,' said Fletcher, who had found a pitcher of water and was busy gulping it down. He handed Cassie the pitcher, and she drank deeply and gratefully.

'Us is bang next door to the furnaces,' she said, wiping her mouth. 'Therefore it'm up to we to do some unsabotaging if us can.'

'Don't be daft,' said Martin. 'It'm none of our concern.'

Fletcher agreed. 'Yeah. Let's just make for the exits like Martin says. What do you care if the Chancel get blown up, Cass? Be'n't as if the Deacons has been our best friends or anything. I don't know if you remember, but them's the ones as shut you and me up in these cells.'

'Think about it,' said Cassie. 'There be a sky-city directly up above. Helio-something-or-other. If the Chancel be demolished, the column might be demolished with it, and if that happens then down comes the sky-city with a ruddy great crash. Not only will Deacons die but Ascended Ones will die too.

'Oh. Yeah. Well, I see your point.'

'Plus, there be all sorts of folk in this building at present, not just Deacons. Us can't go rushing out, not when us is in a position to try and save everyone.'

Martin regarded his sister with a blend of admiration and despair. 'Cass, where'm it come from, this need of yours to always do what be proper?'

'It'm a Grubdollar thing, Mart. Us all has it. Even you. Just takes a bit longer to come out in some of we. Now, the furnaces. How's us best getting there?'

Martin wavered, but then, with a resigned sag of the shoulders, showed Cassie and Fletcher the cell he had come in by.

'So that be what Shatterlonger and the rest was up to all night,' Fletcher said when he saw the hole in the back wall. 'Burrowing away like moles.'

Without any further ado, Cassie ducked down to enter the hole.

Next moment, the floor leapt underneath them, as if a giant foot were delivering a mighty kick from below. The three Grubdollars were sent sprawling. A massive rolling shockwave of sound followed. For several seconds it felt as if the world was tearing itself asunder around them.

It passed. Cassie staggered to her feet, as did her brothers. Their ears were ringing.

Another, no less massive eruption came, knocking them flat again.

This time when they got up, not only were their ears ringing but their eyesight seemed to have been affected as well. Everything had gone hazy. It took them a moment to realise that this was due to the vapour that was billowing into the cell through the hole, filling it like a fog. It was a mixture of smoke and steam, and smelled oily and burnt.

'Cass,' Fletcher said, then repeated it as a shout because his voice sounded hopelessly muffled to him: 'Cass!'

'Yes?'

'Don't suppose *that* just changed your mind about all this, did it?'

Cassie shook her head with a grimace of determination.

'Didn't think so.' Fletcher coughed. The smoke and steam had begun to irritate his throat. 'Oh well, let's get cracking then.'

Cassie groped to find the edges of the hole, then lowered herself in.

CHAPTER 92

A Trouserful Of Dynamite

'Steamarm!' roared Den. 'Alan Steamarm!'

The Humanist leader halted in his tracks.

'Where'm you off to, you scumbag? Running away like a lily-livered coward, looks like. Now why'nt that surprise I?'

Slowly Steamarm turned to face him. They were at an intersection between four passageways. Steamarm had been heading along one of them, Den the other. The moment he spied Steamarm crossing in front of him, Den had felt a sudden and uncontrollable upsurge of anger. Now he stalked towards Steamarm, fists clenched, teeth tight. The pain from his rib was temporarily forgotten, obliterated by his loathing of this man who had barged into his home, hurt his youngest son, stolen his murk-comber, done who-knew-what with his daughter . . . and that was just the tip of the iceberg of his crimes. The fact that Steamarm had a breathing-apparatus kit strapped to his back was, at this particular moment, of no concern. Den was intent on exacting retribution. Everything else was incidental.

By rights Steamarm should have been trembling in his boots. The sight of Den hearing down on him in a passion of fury would have been enough to make almost any man quail. But in fact Steamarm seemed weirdly unperturbed. If his face showed anything, it was annoyance. He looked peeved to have been interrupted on his journey to wherever he was going.

'What?' he said testily. 'Just what it is you want from me, Mr Grub-dollar? I've a lot to do. State your intent, then leave me to get on with things.'

'State my . . .'

'Sorry, not plain-spoken enough for you, was I? Tell me what you're after. And make it quick.'

'I be after *you*, Steamarm,' Den said, halting in front of him. 'That be my "intent". I be after your head on a plate.'

'Oh really?'

'Yes oh really. I be after my girl Cassie as well, but now as I's come across you, I be looking forward to settling a few scores with the fellow who's mucked my life around so much this past couple of days. Maybe you'm seen how things has gone outside. Us has taught your Humanist chaps a lesson. Now it'm my chance to do the same to you.'

Steamarm studied Den's raised fists with a kind of weary contempt.

'Violence,' he said. 'That's how you solve everything, isn't it?

'On the evidence I's seen, it'm how *you* solve everything.'

'Violence is merely a tool, a means to an end. It's not a way of life with me as it is with some people.'

'Weren't a way of life with me till you happened along.'

'Mr Grubdollar...' Steamarm flung open the flaps of his jacket, revealing the top of his trousers. 'You're just not getting me. Look. Do you honestly think I'm scared of you beating me up? Do you honestly think I'm in any way bothered that some lumpen Grimvale no-account has "a few scores to settle"?'

Den gaped. At first he thought Steamarm wanted to show that he was wearing some kind of corset, which would have been bizarre in itself. But then he saw that the corset was in fact sticks of dynamite wedged between Steamarm's waistband and shirt. There were at least ten of them, protruding up like a set of slender, uneven brown teeth.

He was lost for words.

'Yes,' said Steamarm. 'As you can see, I've far bigger fish to fry. So if you'll kindly let me be on my way ...'

At that moment, two loud detonations occurred in swift succession. The first sent both men lurching to one side. The second sent them lurching to the other. It was as though the Chancel was being twisted one way, then the other, with appalling force.

On the second detonation, Den collided sideways with a wall. It was a tragically perfect mishap, since his ribcage took the brunt of the impact and, despite the bandage, his fractured rib was flexed inward. The agony was excruciating and all-consuming, like a flare of white light filling him from head to toe. He sank to the floor, almost weeping with the pain. By the time he regained any level of self-awareness, Alan Steamarm and his breathing-apparatus kit, not to mention his dynamite corset, were long gone.

CHAPTER 93

Inferno

Fires blazed. Smoke swirled. Steam hissed in jets. The furnace chamber was a nightmare of flame and heat and turmoil. The three Grubdollar siblings moved cautiously through it, groping their way like blind people. They *were* blind, almost. The smoke stung their eyes, forcing them to wipe them constantly and blink hard. Breathing was also a problem. At Martin's suggestion they tore off strips of shirt and wrapped these around their noses and mouths. Even so, they coughed and choked.

'Look for some kind of shutoff,' Cassie said. 'There'm got to be regulator controls or the like, something the Deacons opened which us can close.'

Martin nodded, but he himself was looking for a Deacon. Any Deacon would do. He could grab him and ask him to explain how to damp down the runaway furnaces, *force* him to if necessary.

But there were no Deacons around, and he could only assume they had fled the chamber once the explosions started. Even the shaven-headed Deacon, the one he had burned, was nowhere to he seen. Shatterlonger. That was his name, Martin remembered now. He guessed that the other Deacons had gathered Shatterlonger up and helped him to get out of there, leaving the furnaces unguarded. It wouldn't have occurred to them that anybody would be so foolish, so insane, as to enter the chamber and try to undo what they had done.

This guess was almost correct. Most of the Deacons had indeed fled the scene. One, however, remained behind.

Amid the seething smoke and steam, a single baleful eye was watching the three Grubdollars, staring out from a mangled face. The eye's companion had been baked in its socket and now, with its sightless yellow iris, resembled nothing so much as a cross-section of a boiled egg. The skin around and below was a rippled, glistening mess, wet with blood and lymph. The corner of the mouth on that side was tightened, pulled into a lopsided leer.

This distended, asymmetrical visage belonged, of course, to Deacon Shatterlonger, and ugly though it was, its ugliest part was the remaining good eye, which blazed with pure, undiluted loathing. All the hurts and humiliations Shatterlonger had suffered, not just recently but ever, were condensed in that eye. If emotions were visible things then the Deacon's hatred would have manifested as a beam of sheer malevolence, shooting in a straight line from his cornea to the trio of Grubdollars.

He tracked them stealthily, matching their steps with his, biding his time, waiting for the right moment to attack. From the moment he had laid eyes (or rather, eye) on them, it hadn't even bothered him to ask himself why they had re-entered the furnace chamber. All he knew was that he would have his revenge on the older brother for what he had done to his face. He would have his revenge on all of them.

When the three Grubdollars halted, Shatterlonger halted too. He heard them debating what to do. They had come to a stop next to one of the air intake valves, and the girl, Cassie, was suggesting to her brothers that this might be what they were after.

'That look like a ventilation pipe to you?' she said.

'Hard to tell in all this smoke and mess,' said Fletcher. 'There'm some sort of valve wheel there, straight up. But who knows if it be'n't to shut down the steam vents? If so, turning it'd only make matters worse.'

'Us has to do something,' his sister urged. 'And fast.'

'If it'm a steam pipe, it'll be hot. Touch it.'

'You touch it.'

Shatterlonger couldn't bear it. The Grubdollars, if they could finally make up their minds, might follow up Cassie's hunch about the wheel, and then he would be defeated. He couldn't let that happen.

His hands became claws, and with a cry of 'Nooooo!' he lunged towards the three siblings.

CHAPTER 94

Sacrifice

Martin turned in time to see the figure of Shatterlonger come hurtling out of the smoke. Without thinking he dived to meet the oncoming Deacon. They collided hard. Shatterlonger fell backwards but grabbed Martin's shirt as he did so, dragging Martin down with him. They crashed to the floor in a heap. Martin capitalised on the fact that he landed on top. He pinned Shatterlonger with his left hand and started thumping him with his right.

'Let's see if I can't make both sides of your face match, Deacon,' he growled as he punched Shatterlonger's unburnt cheek again and again.

Shatterlonger just took the blows, laughing. Laughing horribly. Insanely.

'What?' said Martin, pausing in his onslaught. 'What'm so funny?'

'Keep wasting your time on me.' The Deacon's voice was slurred, his distorted mouth unable to shape words properly. 'It doesn't matter what you do to *me*. I've got nothing to lose any more. This place can come down around our ears for all I care.'

'How does us stop it? Tell I!' Martin demanded.

'No.'

Martin struck him, viciously.

Shatterlonger just laughed again.

'Want I to take out that other eye of yours?'

'Threaten all you like. You'll not get any help from me.'

As Shatterlonger said this, however, he flicked a look with his good eye towards the air intake control.

It was an involuntary reflex, and it gave the game away. Martin, following the line of the glance, understood. Cassie was right. That valve wheel *was* the way to shut down the furnaces.

But before he could relay the information to her and Fletcher, his opponent acted. Martin's momentary distraction gave Shatterlonger an opportunity. He reached up, grabbed Martin's wrists, and thrust him off. Martin rolled over and came up onto his feet. Shatterlonger got to his feet too and closed in. He threw himself at Martin and began propelling him towards one of the furnaces, intent on scorching him on the hot brickwork and finishing the job he had started on the steam pipe during their earlier fight. Martin resisted, digging his heels in. The two men grappled, the one pushing, the other shoving back, their hands clasping and flailing. It was like some ghastly dance, a clumsy, desperate minuet of violence.

Fletcher moved in to help. His brother had lost the advantage and could do with a hand. Martin, however, saw him coming and shouted at him to back off.

'I can handle he,' he gasped. 'That wheel. Turn it. It'll do the trick. And there be others. I saw they when I were here the first time. You and Cass find they and turn they as well.'

Cassie wasn't convinced that Martin could handle the Deacon as he claimed. The injured Shatterlonger was possessed by madness, and that made him far more dangerous than he might otherwise have been. In his lunatic rage he was growing more and more feral with every moment. He raked fingernails at Martin's face. He even tried to bite him. Spittle flecked his lips and chin. It was all Martin could do just to hold him at bay.

'Don't just stand there gawping,' Martin yelled. 'I mean it. Turn that wheel or us is all goners.'

Cassie overcame her hesitation and grabbed the wheel. Anticlockwise was always the direction for shutting off taps and the like. She started hauling on the wheel with both hands, rotating it that way. At first it didn't want to move, but then bit by bit it budged. Fletcher stepped in to add his strength to hers, but she shook her head.

'You heard what Mart said. Other valve wheels. Go find they.'

Fletcher threw a last look over at his brother. Martin and the Deacon were still locked in their savage clinch. The strip of shirt over Martin's mouth had fallen away. His teeth were bared, just like Shatterlonger's, and clenched tight.

With a shoulder-shrug, a gesture of hapless resignation, Fletcher headed off into the smoke.

Cassie kept up her battle with the wheel, turning and turning it with all her might. She could hear grunts and gasps from several metres behind her, the sounds of the ongoing, toothand-nail struggle. Someone screamed, and she had a horrible feeling it was Martin. The wheel seemed to go round for ever, like an eternal punishment, a task without end. And what if it was all in vain anyway? What if it was too late to prevent all the furnaces from exploding?

The wheel halted. It could go no further.

Cassie spun round.

What happened next would remain etched in her memory till she died.

There was Martin. There was the burned Deacon. They were silhouettes in the smoke, outlines of men, with the furnace behind them. They were still wrestling for advantage, Martin bleeding from where a flap of skin had been torn from his forehead, Shatterlonger with his ruined face looking like something that should not be alive ...

Then fire erupted around them, engulfing them, and with the fire came a noise so loud it was like the world splitting in two.

Cassie was blown off her feet. When she staggered upright, there was no more Martin, no more Deacon, only their afterimages seared onto her retinas, two blue ghosts, hovering there, frozen in conflict, soon starting to fade ...

During the next few minutes of her life Cassie felt like a passenger in her own body. She moved around the furnace chamber, finding valve wheels, rotating them mechanically and methodically. Her ears were ringing. She was oblivious to the smoke, the flames, the piles of rubble on the floor, the general chaos. It didn't matter. Nothing mattered. She was tiny and insignificant. There was nothing to do but this: shut down the furnaces. There was nothing else to think about. If she thought about anything else, she would collapse in a sobbing heap. She was numb all over. She turned the wheels. Turned the wheels. Around her the pressure build-up perceptibly started to subside. The smoke thinned. Flames dwindled. The chamber's groans subsided.

She came across a control console and watched needles on gauges creep out of the red. She stared at them, understanding what this meant but not caring, not even caring that she understood.

Fletcher appeared. He was grey-faced, bloodshot-eyed. 'Cass, back there ... I saw two ... two bodies. I thought it were you and Martin, but ...'

He realised she knew. Their brother was dead.

They clutched each other, clung to each other, while the furnace chamber gave a last few rippling sighs and settled back into something like its usual operational rhythm, an uneasy and damaged beat which nonetheless conveyed a sense of things functioning again, still producing power. From the intact furnaces heat radiated once more, managed heat, the kind of heat which in the past had consumed countless bodies and sent their smouldering atoms spiralling up to the skies. Close to a gaping hole in the side of one of the furnaces that weren't intact, two charred corpses lay, joined in an embrace, flesh fused to flesh. Smoke drifted from them and was drawn by convection into the hole and up into the furnace chimney, up through the chimney, up and out into the open air. In a thin, almost invisible thread it continued to rise towards the clouds. In this way, together, wisps of Martin Grubdollar and Deacon Shatterlonger ascended, and Ascended ...

CHAPTER 95

A Sore Loser

Az and Robert almost collided with Den Grubdollar coming the other way. Robert's father was moving in a gingerly fashion, supporting himself on the wall with one hand.

He was annoyed to see Robert inside the building. 'Didn't I tell you to stay with them Amblescruts?' he growled. Then he looked at Az and his eyes widened. 'You? Why'm you still down here?'

Az quickly filled him in. Before he could finish the explanation he was interrupted by an immense *boom* which reverberated through the Chancel corridors. He just managed to keep his balance, as did the two Grubdollars.

'Third one of they,' Den said dourly. 'I be'n't liking our chances much. And then there'm that Steamarm and his dynamite.'

'What?'

'Just had a run-in with he a few minutes ago. Steamarm's got enough explosive attached to his body to take out half this building. Got a miner's breathing kit on his back too, for some reason. Haven't a clue what him wants *that* for.'

Az's face went hard. 'Oh no. He can't. Surely not.'

'Can't what?'

'Steamarm's going up.'

'Up where? Up how?'

'Up to Heliotropia, Mr Grubdollar. The sky-city at the top of the column. He's going to take the elevator up there.'

'What for? Wait, you don't think . . .'

'I do.'

'Bring down a whole sky-city? Could he do that?'

'If he has enough of this dynamite stuff, and if he sets it off at the top of the column, just underneath the city . . . it could work.'

'But surely him'll die on the way there.'

'This miner's breathing kit – it's designed to supply you with air, right?'

'Right.'

Az saw it all. Steamarm's talk of apprentice's bends, Lady Aanfielsdaughter's description of the differences in air pressure above the clouds and on the ground . . .

'Has he gone mad?' he wondered aloud.

Den weighed up the possibility. 'I saw his face. Spoke to he. Not mad, I don't think. Him just doesn't like losing. Doesn't like it one little bit.'

'So, because he's such a sore loser, he'll kill tens of thousands of people? Not to mention himself, more than likely.'

'Reckon so.'

Az went from incredulity to purposefulness. 'Robert. Mr Grubdollar. Keep looking for Cassie.'

He turned and started to run back the way he and Robert had come.

'Az!' Robert yelled after him. 'What are *you* going to do?'

'What do you think?' Az replied over his shoulder, not breaking stride. 'No one's destroying a sky-city if I can help it.'

CHAPTER 96

Taking Command

Out in the open, Az signalled desperately to *Cerulean*. He jumped up and down and fanned his arms above his head, praying that Captain Qadoschson or someone was keeping lookout and would spot him.

Someone did. A winged figure emerged from the airship and swooped towards the ground in a steep, breakneck dive, halting at the very last moment.

'You haven't found her then,' said Mr Mordadson.

'We've got to go up,' Az said. 'In *Cerulean*. Now.'

'Captain Qadoschson is extremely unwell. I don't think he—'

'Then I'm captain. Take me up there. There's no time to waste.'

'At least tell me why the great urgency.'

Az did in as few words as possible. In response, Mr Mordadson snatched up a crowbar that was lying nearby, left behind in the wake of the Humanist/Amblescrut battle. Then, with his other hand, he grabbed Az by the wrist and took off. Az was yanked into the air. The ground fell away beneath him. Mr Mordadson soared, his wings beating furiously. He was a much stronger flyer than Michael. The extra weight of his living cargo scarcely seemed to trouble him.

Moments later they were aboard *Cerulean*. In the control gondola, everyone was in various states of physical discomfort. Worst off was Captain Qadoschson, who was lying on the floor, moaning and looking very sorry for himself. Aurora was tending to him, although she herself seemed ready to keel over. Michael was putting on a brave face, as was Lady Aanfieldsdaughter, but in neither instance was it particularly convincing. The crew were still manning their stations but several of them would clearly rather have been lying down like their captain.

Of all of the Airborn present, only Mr Mordadson appeared unaffected by ground-sickness. Az suspected he was feeling as bad as anyone but refused to show it, such was his self-control, his iron willpower.

'Listen up,' Az said to the crew. 'We need to climb, and fast. We also need to get as close to the column as we can. Lives are at stake. There's no time to go into detail. You'll just have to trust me on this.'

The crewmen regarded him doubtfully. This kid, this wingless kid, was giving them orders? Some nerve.

'Do as he says,' came a weak voice from the floor. Captain Qadoschson rolled his eyes in Az's direction, then back at the crew. 'You all know how to fly her, and I believe Az has a feel for her. Whatever he asks of you, give it to him. That *is* an order.'

The crewmen exchanged uncertain glances. Then one of them nodded, and another offered a soft 'Aye-aye'.

'Then let's go,' said Az. Trim-master? Thirty-five degrees.'

'But that's—' The trim-master bit his lip. Thirty-five it is, aye-aye.'

'Engineer? Full thrust, all props.'

The chief engineer threw open the throttles.

'Helmsman? The column.'

The helmsman whirled his conn wheel.

Az looked round at the column and the elevators falling and rising on its circumference. Steamarm was in one of the ones going up. Az was sure of it. But which one?

It wasn't relevant just yet. What *Cerulean* had to go was gain height and reach Heliotropia before Steamarm did.

Could the airship outpace the elevators?

Az didn't know. All he knew was that she must, otherwise the sky-city was doomed.

CHAPTER 97

Race Against Disaster

When they hit the cloud cover, *Cerulean* was going so fast that for a time it was plain sailing. The turbulence couldn't seem to get a grip on her. She sliced cleanly through.

Then there was an almighty shudder and abruptly her nose began to lift. The floor of the control gondola, already at quite an angle, steepened severely. One of the crew lost his footing and went skidding backwards, fetching up against the gondola's rear wall with a thump and a burst of feathers. Everyone else clung on for dear life to the nearest fixture.

'Level her out!' Az demanded.

The trim-master replied that he was trying to, but if they hadn't been at 35° to begin with ...

'Az,' croaked Captain Qadoschson. 'She mustn't go tail-down. She'll drop like a stone.'

Az had a brainwave. 'Ballast,' he said to the chief engineer. The rear ballast tanks. Are they full?'

'Yes.'

'Jettison them. The lot.'

'But we'll be less stable after.'

'There might not be an after if we don't jettison them now.'

The flight engineer threw the requisite levers. Sluicegates opened at the rear of *Cerulean's* balloon and ballast water poured out in gushing, twisting streams. Seconds elapsed during which Az believed his drastic tactic hadn't succeeded. Then, with aching slowness, *Cerulean's* aft end started to rise; the angle of the control gondola floor became steadily less acute.

Az allowed himself a moment of satisfaction, but only a moment. The ascent wasn't over yet, and there could be any number of further challenges to deal with.

Cerulean battled on up through the clouds, until finally, with what seemed like a leap of exultation, she broke free. Brightness – the glorious brightness of the Airborn realm – surrounded her. Everyone on board experienced a lift of the spirits, however ill he or she was feeling. They had missed the sun. They hadn't realised till now just how much they had missed it.

Ahead, the column filled the viewing windows. Az ordered the helmsman to bring *Cerulean* alongside the column and keep her there while they continued to rise. 'Stay within fifty metres. Closer if you can.'

'Fifty, aye-aye.' The helmsman puffed out his cheeks, none too happy. Fifty metres was perilously close to the column. A stray gust of wind might catch the airship sidelong and send her crashing into the column, with fatal consequences for all. But he didn't cavil. As Az had said, lives were at stake. The helmsman chose to treat the exercise as a test of his skills, one he didn't dare fail.

'Mr Mordadson?' Az said. 'Are you all set?'

Grimly Mr Mordadson hefted the crowbar.

CHAPTER 98

Hard Choices

Holding the handrail, Az looked out through the viewing windows as Mr Mordadson winged his way across from *Cerulean* to the column. Az had done his part. Now everything depended on Mr Mordadson.

Briefly Az recalled his first encounter with the Silver Sanctum emissary less than a week ago. He remembered his initial mistrust of the so-called school inspector and his subsequent dislike of him when Mr Mordadson threatened his father. How things had changed. Now, all his hopes were pinned on Mr Mordadson. Everyone's hopes were. He alone stood between Heliotropia and its destruction.

As Mr Mordadson neared the column, Az thought that he looked pitifully small, dwarfed by the column's thickness and height. At the same time, metaphorically speaking, Mr Mordadson's stature had never seemed greater.

Mr Mordadson alighted on top of one of the rising elevators. Steadying himself with outstretched wings, he bent and inserted the tip of the crowbar between the doors. Straining with effort, he pried the doors apart. The elevator was empty. Mr Mordadson took to the air and circled round the column to the next rising elevator.

He tried three elevators in succession, without any luck. Az had time to doubt his own belief that Steamarm was riding up in one of them. He began to think he had misinterpreted the evidence and that Steamarm had something else in mind, some entirely different ploy. In which case, this desperate journey, with all its attendant risks, would have been in vain, and Steamarm would almost certainly pull off whatever lethal stunt he was attempting.

But the fourth elevator Mr Mordadson tried was occupied.

Lady Anfielsdaughter had joined Az at the viewing windows. So had Michael. Both were starting to recover from their ground-sickness. Az, however, was unaware they were even beside him. He was focused, with every fibre of his being, on what was happening outside.

He watched Mr Mordadson lever the doors apart, and there was Steamarm, crouching inside the elevator. He was wearing a sort of funnel-shaped mask. The mask covered his face completely, with two glass discs to see through. A flexible tube led from the front of it to a metal cylinder on his back. He looked inhuman with this device on, featureless and grotesque, not even a Groundling any more but something else, something less.

In his left hand he was holding what looked like a short length of wood. Az took this to be the dynamite. There were more such sticks around his waist. In his other hand was a match. Steamarm must have heard Mr Mordadon land on the roof of the elevator. He had had sufficient time to light the match. He now applied it to the dynamite fuse, which started to fizzle brightly.

Each of the next five seconds felt about a minute long.

One – Mr Mordadon somersaulted forwards into the elevator.

Two – in a single fluid manoeuvre he rolled out again, dragging Steamarm with him.

Three – he launched himself and Steamarm out into space.

Four – in a flurry of wing flaps, he put distance between them and the column.

Five – he continued to speed away from the column, with Steamarm twisting and writhing beneath him but still clutching the dynamite.

Then, with little ceremony, Mr Mordadson let go of the Humanist leader.

Steamarm fell. He fell with his arms flailing, frantically beating at the air, as though he thought they were wings, as though he himself could fly. He fell head-first, the dynamite fuse sparkling all the way like a star. By the way his mouth was wide open, you could tell he was screaming.

Hard choices, Az thought.

That was what Mr Mordadson had said. That was his philosophy.

Watching Steamarm plummet, Az understood exactly what he had meant. This was the right thing to do. It wasn't the kind thing or the moral thing. But it was the right thing. All those lives in jeopardy, set against the life of this one man.

Steamarm reached the cloud cover and vanished from view.

A split-second later, light blossomed within the clouds, a burst of brilliance, like a flicker of lightning, appearing and disappearing. After a short pause, a *bang* could be heard, faint and brief.

That was all.

That was the end of Alan Steamarm.

Hovering, Mr Mordadson looked down, then looked up towards *Cerulean*. He shook his head, adjusted his crimson spectacles on his nose, and with heavy wingbeats began making his way back to the airship.

CHAPTER 99

The Beginning

It was simply a continuation of what had been started, but not everyone was in favour of it. A couple of the crewmen grumbled. Hadn't they been through enough already today? A sharp rebuke from Captain Qadoschson soon brought them into line. He wasn't fully recovered but even so he could tell that what Az was proposing was worth doing. Lady Aanfields-daughter agreed, and that settled the matter.

So they descended again. They endured the cloud cover and the fresh onset of ground-sickness. *Cerulean* revisited the Chancel.

There, the situation had calmed. The Chancel buildings were no longer on the brink of tearing themselves apart. That particular threat had been negated, and Az quickly found out how and by whom. He also found out at what cost.

Cassie was softly weeping. Tears spilled down her cheeks, cutting trails through the smudges of dirt that covered her face. Fletcher was similarly distraught. Both of them looked tattered and battered. Bit by bit Az learned that Martin was dead, along with Deacon Shatterlonger. Martin had died buying time for Cassie and Fletcher to save the Chancel from Shatterlonger's sabotage attempt.

The member of the family hardest hit by Martin's death was his father. Den Grubdollar was in a state of shock, gazing into the middle distance, his face a mask of remorse. It wasn't simply that his eldest son was no more. He was remembering all the disputes they had had, the rows about Humanism, the rift that had yawned between them over the last few months. They would never be reconciled now. Neither would have a chance to apologise and mend fences. In the end Martin had been a hero and had done something which would have made his old man proud, but this was no consolation. It had come too late. Den was left with only regret and bitter self-recrimination.

Az felt awful for intruding on this family tragedy. He wondered if it would be best to postpone what he wished to do, or even abandon the idea altogether.

But then Cassie said, 'What did you come back down for anyway?'

'You,' he answered, simply.

She sniffed back tears and tried to smile. 'Yeah, I reckoned you would.

And that thing over there ...' She gestured towards the airship.

'That's *Cerulean*. She's my *Cackling Bertha*, I now realise.'

'She'm big. Makes *Bertha* look like a slip of a girl. That'd please *Bertha.*'

Even in her grief Cassie was able to make a joke. This instilled Az with renewed confidence. Cassie's strength gave him strength.

'Look,' he said, 'I know this is hardly the time, but there's something I'd like to offer. To everyone.'

'Go on,' said Cassie.

The offer was made. It was accepted.

Three dozen Groundlings were gathered together. Their numbers were drawn from the ranks of the Humanists and the Amblescruts, the uninjured ones, any of them who was still in reasonably healthy condition. The offer was also extended to the Deacons, who had been released from the Chancel apartment where they had been imprisoned. They turned it down point-blank. It was wrong. Blasphemous. The Humanists and Amblescruts, by contrast, were only too keen.

They were all equipped with breathing-apparatus kits, which were conveniently to hand because of course Lawrence Brace had collected a truckful of them from the Consolidated Colliery Collective. The chosen Groundlings were then escorted to *Cerulean*. The airship was brought down ground-scrapingly low, and they climbed aboard her using the rope ladders.

Cassie volunteered to come too. Az told her to stay with her family. She needed them right now, and they definitely needed her. But she said this was an opportunity she couldn't pass up, however sad she was feeling. She *had* to go.

With the Groundlings distributed among her troop cabins, *Cerulean* took to the air.

One relatively unbumpy flight later, she was above the cloud cover and rising towards Heliotropia.

It was unavoidably a short visit. The breathing-apparatus kits had a limited supply of air. *Cerulean* circuited the sky-city, and the masked Groundlings looked out from the cabin portholes.

In the control gondola, Az stood with Cassie, herself masked. Cassie didn't know whether to stare at Heliotropia or at the Airborn people in the gondola with her. She confessed to Az at one point that she had an irresistible urge to touch someone's wings. She wanted to know what they felt like. Az summoned Michael over and made him extend one wing to her. She stroked the feathers wonderingly. They were soft but real. They confirmed this was no dream. Then she turned back to Heliotropia and resumed gazing at it through the eye discs of her mask.

Az tried to see it as she was seeing it. Heliotropia was not the loveliest of the sky-cities. It was no Prismburg or Pearl Town or Silver Sanctum.

It was gaudy and overblown, suited to its role as a tourist resort but not refined or monumentally spectacular the way those other cities were. Even plain old High Haven had more class.

Still, it stood proud in the air. It brushed the firmament. It towered against the sun. It spread its immense, hotel-covered 'petals' in all directions. And there were crowds of Airborn in it and around it, winging between the buildings, sporting over the rooftops.

Not Ascended Ones. That was not how they were to be regarded. Just people with wings.

Cassie and all the other Groundlings were being shown the sky-city for that reason. So that they could return home and say, *We've seen the world above the clouds, and it's a beautiful place but it's just a place and the people who live there are just people.* They could tell everyone that, and word would start to spread.

There were tricky times ahead. Lady Aanfielsdaughter and the others at the Silver Sanctum would have much to do. There would have to be negotiations and careful diplomacy. Establishing a new form of relationship between Airborn and Groundling was not something that could be achieved overnight. The Airborn still needed their supplies from the ground, and with the Deacons' authority much diminished, if not utterly eliminated, that meant a brand new system would have to be put into place. Lady Aanfielsdaughter and Mr Mordadson were already conferring about this quietly in one corner of the control gondola, discussing the shape of the future.

That was none of Az's concern. He was content that Lady Aanfielsdaughter would do her best. She would try, and if she failed it would not be for lack of diligence or patience.

For now, taking Cassie and the other Groundlings on this trip to see Heliotropia was what counted to Az.

He felt Cassie fold her hand through the crook of his elbow. She squeezed his forearm. He wished he could see her face properly, but even just through the eye discs of the mask he could tell she was glad to be there with him. Not happy, because she couldn't be happy, not so soon after Martin's death. But glad.

Heliotropia shone in the sunlight, like a beacon.

Cerulean's Groundling passengers stared amazedly.

The world was changing.

It was a beginning.

Pirates of the Relentless Desert

CHAPTER I

The Black Cloud

The night sky above the Relentless Desert gave birth to a new cloud.

At first there was just the usual inky swirl of the cloud cover, palely marbled with moonlight. Then a long, rounded shape appeared, pressing itself out from the underside of the clouds. Black against blackness, the shape broke free, then rotated around its own axis and moved northward at an unhurried pace, emitting a low, droning hum as it went. Gradually it began to lose height. The faint, cigar-like shadow it cast on the sand below grew larger.

On the ground a few kilometres ahead, a small man-made spark glinted in the midst of the desert emptiness. It was a cluster of lights which shone out from a maze of criss-crossing roads that ran between drilling towers, distillation columns, 'nodding donkey' pump units, storage tanks, pipelines, derricks, and one-storey concrete housing blocks.

The lights belonged to Westward Oil Enterprises extraction and refining installation number 137, popularly known as Desolation Wells, and they burned all night long even though everyone on the workforce was fast asleep in bed. They burned to keep the darkness at bay – the vast, terrible darkness of the desert at night, which was as pure and unending as oblivion and could drive a person mad.

The lights were like a beacon. They drew the black cloud to them. The cloud vectored unerringly in the installation's direction, predator towards prey.

As it reached the perimeter of Desolation Wells, the black cloud came to a halt, its hum decreasing to a whisper. Suddenly dozens of winged figures emerged from it, one after another. They poured out in a stream and clustered together. Then, at a pre-arranged signal, they scattered. With near-silent wingbeats they fanned out across the installation. A few headed for the housing blocks. The rest made for the warehouses where refined oil was stored in steel barrels, ready to be transported by truck across the Relentless Desert.

The warehouses were not locked. There were no thieves out here in this remote spot, two days' journey from anything that might be called civilisation. At least, no thieves that the owners of Westward Oil Enterprises, WOE, could have anticipated.

The winged figures only had to roll open the warehouse doors, stealthily, to gain access to the hundreds of full barrels stacked inside. They set about removing as many as they could. Each barrel weighed several hundred kilogrammes and required the strength of three of them to lift it. Struggling with their burdens, the trios of winged figures bore the barrels to the hovering black cloud and deposited them inside.

The cloud – the pirate airship *Behemoth* – slowly filled up with plundered fuel. Over the course of an hour the airship's cargo holds were loaded to capacity. Softly she purged water ballast in order to compensate for the added weight.

Meanwhile groups of the winged figures stood guard outside the entrances to the housing blocks. Their colleagues were being as careful as possible with the barrels, but it was best to be prepared, just in case. Accidents could happen.

And eventually, one did. A barrel slipped from the hands of the threesome who were carrying it. Their arms and wings were aching after an hour of transporting so many gallons of fuel up to *Behemoth*; their fingers had begun to cramp. One of them lost his grip on the rim of the barrel. The other two could not keep hold of it between them. The barrel fell for fifty metres, tumbling end over end, and hit the ground with an almighty, booming *clonnggg*. It split open on impact and thick liquid slooshed everywhere.

The noise awoke the roughnecks – oil workers – who were sleeping in a nearby housing block. They leapt from their beds, threw on some clothes, and rushed to the main entrance to see what was going on.

Waiting for them outside the door were a half-dozen of the winged figures. To the roughnecks, still shaking off the fog of sleep, these looked like something out of a nightmare.

They were lean, nervy creatures, with sores and bad skin, and each wore a motley assortment of clothing. No two of them were dressed alike, some sporting bandannas around their foreheads, others scarves around their necks, others with sashes diagonally across their torsos, others with brocaded waistcoats, or any combination of these. Most had long hair, with beaded braids and brightly coloured streaks showing here and there amid the straggly curls and spikes. Most had ornate tattoos on their arms and faces, and metal piercings glinted in ears, noses, lips, and wings. All were bearing weapons – crossbows, sabres, daggers, maces – and they brandished these as they looked sneeringly at the roughnecks, their mouths curling up at the corners in contempt.

One, however, stood out from the rest. She was tall, sinuous, voluptuous, and clad solely in black leather, from top to toe. Even her face was covered. A black leather mask encased her head and a pair of smoked-glass flight goggles hid her eyes. Her wings, similarly, were black – black as a raven's.

She was like a silhouette, a shadow in the shape of a winged woman. Even the lance she carried was black. The only spot of colour on her was the patch stitched on her chest: a skull above two crossed feathers, picked out in black on red. The same motif, much larger, adorned the airship's tailfins.

'Air – Airborn?' one of the roughnecks stammered.

'Get back, emu,' barked the black-clad woman, waving the lance at him. The mask muffled her voice, making it sound distant and weird. 'Get back or I'll run you through.'

'What'm you doing? What *be* this?' another of the roughnecks asked.

The speaker was Magnus Clockweight, the 'toolpusher', or site foreman. He was a broad-shouldered, brawny, big-fisted fellow. All of the roughnecks were. You needed to be made of stern stuff if you wanted to work at Desolation Wells.

Yet, for all that, Clockweight's voice trembled as he phrased his questions. He was frightened, and so was everyone standing with him. These winged apparitions were shabby and unkempt and inhuman. They were *wrong*. The roughnecks had limited knowledge of what the Airborn looked like. Most, in fact, had never actually set eyes on a member of that race before. This was not how they expected them to be. This was almost the exact opposite of that.

'"What *be* this?"' one of the pirates echoed, with a high-pitched, demented laugh. His hair was a shock of green dreadlocks and his eyes rolled in their sockets like loose marbles.

'What does it look like it is?' the sinister, leather-clad woman said to Clockweight. She spoke with the unmistakable authority and assertiveness of a leader. 'We're taking what's rightfully ours. Taking what you Groundlings should still be giving us for free. Now shut up and behave. Be obedient little ostriches. Unless you want to know how it feels to have a lance skewer your guts ...'

None of the roughnecks was keen to experience that particular sensation for himself. They shuffled warily back from the doorway.

A moment later a loud horn blare sounded from overhead. This was *Behemoth* signalling that the raid was over and she had as much booty on board as she could handle. It was time to depart.

'Thank you so much for your cooperation,' the black-clad Airborn woman said to the roughnecks. 'Till next time!' She launched herself off the ground, and the other Airborn followed suit. The green-dreadlocked one was still giggling insanely as he took to their air.

The intimidated roughnecks peered out of the doorway, watching the winged figures disappear into the darkness beyond the glow of the refinery's lights. A huge throbbing beat filled the air, and rapidly faded. Then there was just the familiar hiss of the desert winds, the tickle of sand grains against windows and walls, and the far-off, plaintive howls of a pack of hackerjackals that had been startled by the huge, unfamiliar bulk of an airship passing above them.

'Them's supposed to be our friends now, be'n't they, toolpusher?' said one of the roughnecks finally. 'Trading partners at least.'

'Apparently not,' replied Magnus Clockweight. Grim-faced, he took charge of the situation. 'Right. Some of you go and check on the others, make sure there'm nobody been hurt. I want a full inventory of what those Ascended Ones' – he corrected himself – 'those Airborn have nicked off we. And somebody had better send a telegram to head office about all this.'

As the roughnecks rushed to obey his orders, Clockweight rubbed his brow worriedly.

'Already,' he said to himself. 'Barely a year gone and already there'm trouble. I might've known it wouldn't last.'

CHAPTER 2

A Day And A Half Later ...

... and half a world away, at the Silver Sanctum, Lady Aanfielsdaughter was saying much the same thing as Magnus Clockweight, although she was putting it somewhat less bleakly and more reassuringly.

'There were bound to be hiccups,' she said.

'Hiccups?' interjected Farris, Lord Urironson. 'If the reports we've been getting from the ground are even halfway true, then this is hardly classifiable as a *hiccup.*'

'Teething troubles, then.'

'Not that either, Serena. I honestly don't believe you can compare these incidents to – to the sort of ailments a small child might suffer.'

'Well, I do. After all, the new relationship between Airborn and Groundling is a fragile, tender thing, still taking its first baby-steps. We should treat it with the same sort of care and tolerance as we would an infant.'

Lord Urironson snorted. 'Infant. Baby-steps. Getting sentimental in our old age, are we, Serena? Maternal instincts coming to the fore? Rather late in life for that, I'd say.'

Lady Aanfielsdaughter fixed him with a frosty stare, but refused to respond directly to the taunt. Instead she said, 'Perhaps, Farris, you should give us the benefit of *your* opinion on this matter.' She indicated the other senior residents sitting in the preening parlour with them. 'We're all dying to hear it.'

Lord Urironson puffed out his wings self-importantly. The action meant that the preener who was tending to him had to dart sharply backwards so as to avoid getting smacked in the face. The preener gave a disgruntled pout, then resumed his work, using a teasing wand and a fine-tooth comb to neaten Lord Urironson's plumage.

A preening parlour might seem an unusual venue for a weighty political discussion, but that was how the Silver Sanctum operated. Government there happened casually – a lunchtime chat in the dining hall, a chance encounter in the macaw house, an impromptu get-together over a glass of wine or during a twilight flit around the turrets – although there was nothing casual about the content of these meetings. Serious topics were debated and solutions to knotty problems were thrashed out, even though to an outside observer it might look just like a few people having a bit of a chinwag while they did something else.

'I think,' Lord Urironson declared, 'that what we have here are the makings of a full-blown disaster.'

'Oh really, Farris!'

'No, no, hear me out.'

'Could you be any more melodramatic?'

'Serena, I insist on being allowed to have my say.'

'Very well.' Lady Aanfielsdaughter gestured to the preener who was ministering to her. The feathers at the tip of her right wing needed special attention, they were getting a bit dry, perhaps a touch of scented oil there? Yes, good.

'There are plenty of people who object to what you did last year,' Lord Urironson said, pointing an accusing finger at her. In his younger days he had been a lawyer and old courtroom habits died hard. 'They resent the way you took matters into your own hands, exposing us to the Groundlings and the Groundlings to us. They feel you overstepped your authority. You flung open a door which can never be closed again, and you did so without consulting anyone at the Silver Sanctum.'

'I discussed the matter at length with Mr Mordadson.'

'Ah yes. Mordadson. I hardly think he counts. He's just your pet hawk, trained to keep his beak shut and not argue. I mean us, your colleagues and peers. Had you deigned to talk about it with us first, we might have been able to warn you of the possible consequences. Consequences such as the rise of anti-Groundling feeling throughout the Airborn realm, which, as we are seeing in one sky-city in particular, has evolved into something more than mere protest.'

'What is it that you object to, Farris?' replied Lady Aanfielsdaughter. 'The decision I took or the fact that you weren't consulted?'

A couple of the other senior residents chortled softly. Lady Aanfielsdaughter had struck back well.

'Because you're wrong,' she continued. 'I thought long and hard before doing what I did, and I did it, moreover, because I had very little choice. The Groundlings were making their presence felt already with the embargo on supplying materials. By the time I became personally involved in the affair, they were on the point of making their presence felt – explosively. Heliotropia was under threat, and there was no way of saving the city without interacting with the Groundlings. Without opening that uncloseable door of yours. My hand was forced. I explained this to you immediately afterwards, all of you, at a grand assembly. You didn't seem to have a problem with it then, and I certainly don't remember hearing any dire prophecies of doom from you. And yet now that we face a minority protest group and a single sky-city going rogue, all of a sudden it's I-told-you-so and woe-is-me-all-is-lost.'

'To be fair, Serena,' piped up Alimon, Lord Yurkemison, 'one or two of us at the grand assembly did query the wisdom of your actions.'

'In the mildest possible terms. The overwhelming sentiment, however, was that I had performed a good and necessary deed.'

'And I'm startled to hear you describe the Feather First! movement as a minority protest group,' offered Faith, Lady Jeduthunsdaughter-Ochson. 'They're represented in every sky-city in every quadrant and their numbers are growing fast. I happened to get caught up in one of their rallies in Pearl Town the other day. Quite a gaggle! They brought traffic to a halt all along the city's Grand Concourse, and the Alar Patrol were very slow in getting them to disperse, which made me think the Patrollers themselves might be sympathetic to their cause.'

'But it's the situation at Redspire that's the real worry,' said Lord Urironson. He was surprised, but far from displeased, to find he had allies among his fellow nobles. Usually in discussions like this, everyone went along with whatever Lady Aanfielsdaughter said and his was the lone voice of dissent. This was no longer the case, which struck him as a mark of how grave the situation had become and how much worse it could well get. 'These cases of piracy we've been hearing about, Redspirian citizens raiding the ground. What if that acts as a catalyst? What if other people start to copy their example? Ultimately we could be looking at a war.'

'Honestly, Farris, you can be such an old woman at times,' said Lady Aanfielsdaughter, rolling her eyes.

Lord Urironson huffed and went scarlet. Several of the other senior residents, and a couple of the preeners, smirked. Somehow it was doubly insulting for a man to be called an old woman by a woman who was manifestly quite old, although in no way old-womanish herself.

'It's almost as if you *want* things to turn bad,' Lady Aanfielsdaughter went on. 'As if you're *willing* this whole venture to end in tears. That's not an attitude that's going to get us anywhere. Besides, you seem to forget that I prevented one war breaking out between us and the Groundlings. What makes you think I'd let another one start?'

'I don't know,' grumbled Lord Urironson. 'Maybe you enjoyed all the excitement last time. Maybe it gave you a bit of a thrill and you'd like to do it all over again.'

'Ridiculous! What a complete pluck-wit you are!'

Even as she snapped these words, Lady Aanfielsdaughter knew she shouldn't have. Her 'old woman' jibe had been fine, but 'pluck-wit' was altogether a cruder insult. She should simply have ignored Lord Uriron-son's comment; risen above it. Instead, she had finally allowed her irritation to show, which meant she had lost the upper hand in the argument.

She'd been unable to stop herself, however. Lord Urironson was always an irritant. On this occasion, though, he had really managed to get under her skin. Perhaps it was because, in spite of her supreme self-confidence in all matters, Lady Aanfielsdaughter still wasn't totally sure that she had done the right thing a year ago. Had there really been no alternative but to break the long-existing barrier between Airborn and Groundlings and put the situation between the two races on an entirely new footing? Couldn't a more elegant solution have been found, one with fewer and less far-reaching ramifications?

'So what do you propose, Serena?' enquired Pendroz, Lord Luelson. He was a good friend of Lady Aanfielsdaughter's and she knew she could always count on his support. 'I take it you have some plan of action in mind.'

'Naturally,' Lady Aanfielsdaughter replied, regaining a little of her authority. 'I'll be putting my top man onto it right away.'

CHAPTER 3

The Aforementioned 'Top Man'

Mr Mordadson stood ready, legs apart, wings splayed for balance, braced for the attack. A thin, sharp wind swooped across the high-level courtyard, ruffling his feathers and his short, dark hair. Behind his crimson-lensed spectacles his eyes glinted like a pair of fine-cut rubies.

He raised a hand and flicked the fingers against the palm twice – an invitation.

'Come on then,' he said to his opponent. 'Enough pussyfooting. Let's see what you're really made of.'

Az shook sweat from his eyebrows and moved forward, fists clenched. There was determination in his reddened face – determination and a hint of something harder and fiercer. He was aware that a handful of junior Silver Sanctum residents were looking on from the cloister at one end of the courtyard. They had been there for several minutes. Partly they were interested because a fight was always worth watching; but they were also there, Az knew, because of him. He was a novelty and a celebrity, even at the Silver Sanctum. Az Gabrielson – the wingless wonder who helped change everything.

He tuned out their presence. This wasn't about putting on a show for an audience. It was about him versus Mr Mordadson. About not letting Mr Mordadson win. Again. That was all that mattered.

He closed the distance between the two of them, then abruptly lunged. He feinted left and at the last second twisted to the right, aiming an upward chopping blow at the knot of nerves in Mr Mordadson's armpit.

Had the blow struck home, Mr Mordadson's arm would have been rendered numb and useless. But Mr Mordadson spotted the feint and parried with one wing, batting Az's fist aside. At the same time, he reached out and grabbed Az's other hand and forearm and wrenched the one backwards against the other.

The pain was excruciating. Az's wrist felt like it was about to snap. He was paralysed, his whole body locked down by the hold Mr Mordadson had on him.

He told himself to focus, take no notice of the pain, *think*. The hold was designed to hurt more if you tried to pull away. If you did the opposite, moved *into* it, it was no longer so effective.

Az thrust himself towards Mr Mordadson. Mr Mordadson, however, had anticipated the manoeuvre and released his grip at the crucial moment. He swung Az round, turning Az's own momentum against him. Next thing Az knew, he was plunging face-first onto the courtyard flagstones.

He managed to tuck and roll. Somersaulting, he came up lightly on the balls of his feet. Distant applause from the spectators told him the feat of agility had been impressive. He didn't let their clapping distract him. He wheeled round to face Mr Mordadson – *never turn your back on a foe* – only to find that Mr Mordadson was nowhere to be seen. The courtyard was empty. Where . . . ?

A fraction of a second too late, Az looked up. All he saw were the soles of Mr Mordadson's shoes descending towards him. Mr Mordadson landed on Az's shoulders with his full bodyweight, slamming him flat on his belly.

The wind was knocked out of Az. For several horrible, writhing moments he lay on the flagstones thinking he was never going to draw breath again. He heaved and gasped for air, uselessly.

Eventually his lungs began to work once more. He flopped onto his side. Panting, vision swimming, he saw Mr Mordadson's legs. They strode into view, halting just out of his reach.

'Had enough?'

'Only just started,' Az coughed out through gritted teeth.

'Then let me help you up and we can resume.'

Mr Mordadson extended a hand down to Az. Az groped for it clumsily, as if dazed. Then, quick as a flash, he kicked out at Mr Mordadson's ankles, swiping his legs from under him. Mr Mordadson toppled sideways but caught himself expertly with a beat of his outstretched wings, so that rather than hit the ground he merely brushed it with one elbow. An instant later, he was hovering five metres up, well out of harm's way.

'Sneaky,' he said to Az, with approval.

'If I hadn't tried that, you'd have done something similar to me,' said Az.

'Absolutely correct. You beat me to it, that's all. Well done. I see you've remembered the cardinal rule of combat: trust no one.'

'Least of all you.'

Mr Mordadson chuckled. 'Least of all me. Now, really – had enough? We've been at it nearly an hour.'

Wearily Az picked himself up and dusted himself down. 'Yeah, I reckon so. For today.'

'Very well.' Mr Mordadson alighted next to him. 'Then let's go and get a drink, and you can tell me what you're so angry about.'

CHAPTER 4

Angry? Who's Angry?

'You are,' said Mr Mordadson, sipping a glass of iced persimmon juice at a table in one of the Silver Sanctum's open-air cafeterias. 'You have been for several weeks. I've noticed it in our training sessions. You come at me with this mean look in your eye, like you plan on doing some serious damage.'

'Isn't that a good thing?' said Az, also drinking persimmon juice. 'You're always going on about the need for aggression.'

'*Directed* aggression. Aggression with a specific goal. Whereas what I'm seeing is a kind of unfocused, all-purpose aggression, which you're using your combat lessons as a convenient outlet for. Using me as a punchbag. Don't get me wrong, Az, your skills are improving. Even without the benefit of wings you're turning into a formidable fighter. But for all that, at present I don't think your mind is completely on the job. I beat you pretty easily today.'

'You cheated at the end. You flew.'

'Merely using the tactical advantages to hand. Any winged opponent would do the same.'

'But we had rules.'

'You don't think every opponent you come up against is going to abide by *rules*, do you? So come on. Are you going to tell me what the matter is?'

For a while Az said nothing. The sounds of the cafeteria filled the silence between him and Mr Mordadson: the chatter of Silver Sanctum residents and employees, the chink of cutlery and crystalware, now and then a flap of wings as somebody emphasised a conversational point or strongly disagreed with somebody else's opinion.

Finally Az said, 'It's complicated.'

Mr Mordadson nodded. 'It's Cassie, isn't it?'

Az failed to hide his surprise. 'How ...'

'Not hard. When a male seventeen-year-old is in a funk about something and doesn't want to talk about it, nine times out of ten the reason is girl trouble. Plus, I'm not stupid. I know how difficult it is for you and her. When was the last time you got together, the pair of you? A month ago?'

'More than that. Six weeks, nearly.'

'You went down or she came up?'

'She came up.'

'And the visit lasted how long? An hour?'

'If that.'

Mr Mordadson spread out his hands, as if to say *You see?* 'It was never going to be easy trying to conduct a meaningful, one-to-one relationship with a Groundling, Az. You must have realised that from the start. The obstacles that must be overcome. Not least, you having to acclimatise every time you go down to the ground and Cassie not being able to breathe properly every time she comes up here. In fact, all in all, it's almost inconceivable that you and she have any kind of long-term prospects as a couple.'

'Oh well, thanks for the encouragement.'

'Just telling it like it is.'

'I know, I know,' Az sighed. 'As a matter of fact, Michael said pretty much the same thing to me the other day. "Face it, Az, love's wonderful and all that, but three kilometres of altitude is a heck of a big gap to bridge."'

'Your brother has a knack for a colourful turn of phrase.'

'But . . .'

'But?'

Az shifted his head and neck, as if there were an uncomfortable weight on his shoulders. 'There's more to it. Lately I've been feeling like Cassie's pulling away from me. As if she's not interested in seeing me. Little things. Like, it's awkward when we chat. We don't know what to say to each other. I try and crack a joke; she doesn't laugh. I try and touch her; she shies away. Last time I was down in Grimvale, I really got the impression she couldn't wait for me to leave. I know she's having problems with her dad, and her family's finding it difficult to make ends meet. I know life isn't a barrel of laughs for her right now. Even so . . .'

Briefly Az wondered why he was sharing such personal stuff with Mr Mordadson. They were friends, yes, but hardly close ones. More than anything they were master and pupil now, thanks to their weekly combat training sessions. That lent their relationship a certain level of formality. Was it right that he should be confiding in Mr Mordadson about his love life?

But then Mr Mordadson *had* asked, and had seemed sincere in his interest. And somehow, talking about it did feel good.

'And then there's Michael's wedding.'

'Ah yes. The day after tomorrow, if I'm not mistaken,' said Mr Mordadson. 'What about it? Not written your best-man speech yet, is that the problem?'

'No, no. It's the Grubdollars. They've been asked to come and I'm hoping they'll be able to make it despite everything, you know, getting to the High Haven elevators, breathing apparatus, all the practical difficulties. Frankly I'll be amazed if they do. But I'm hoping. The thing is, I don't even know whether they're coming or not. When I invited Cassie, last time she was up here, she just shrugged and said she'd mention it to her dad and brothers and maybe they'd be there, maybe they wouldn't, it wasn't for her to say. Enthusiasm? Not much. We saw a sunbow and all she seemed to want to talk about was that.'

'Well, as you yourself said, the practical difficulties.'

'Mr Mordadson?' said a voice behind Az, a voice he knew well.

Mr Mordadson looked up. Az looked round.

It was Aurora Jukarsdaughter, Lady Aanfielsdaughter's personal assistant and Michael's fiancée.

Her expression could not have been any grimmer.

CHAPTER 5

A Summons

Aurora dipped her wings briefly to Az, an acknowledgement of his presence and also an indication that, under other circumstances, she would have greeted him more warmly.

Az, in turn, nodded to his soon-to-be sister-in-law.

'I've been sent to fetch you,' Aurora said to Mr Mordadson. 'You're to come to Lady Aanfieldsdaughter's office immediately.'

'I assumed as much. Something serious?'

Aurora did not reply, which was tantamount to a yes.

'Something to do with Redspire, I'll be bound.'

Again, no response from the ever-professional Aurora.

Mr Mordadson rose. 'Duty calls. Az? It's been a pleasure, as always, putting a few bruises on you. Same time next week.'

Aurora spread her wings and took off without a backward glance. Mr Mordadson made to follow but, before doing so, leaned back and muttered a few quick words to Az out of the side of his mouth:

'Or perhaps we shall get together sooner, if you can manage it.'

Watching Mr Mordadson soar to join Aurora in the air, Az's initial thought was: *Redspire? What's going on at Redspire?*

His next thought was: '*Or perhaps we shall get together sooner?*' *What did he mean by that?*

He puzzled over Mr Mordadson's parting comment. Was Mr Mordadson proposing that they have an extra training session, earlier in the week than usual? Was that it?

No, the way he'd said it, the intonation he had used, suggested more.

It implied a hint.

A challenge.

All at once Az recalled a conversation that had taken place not long after the events at Grimvale, when Mr Mordadson first said he was willing to school Az in hand-to-hand combat.

'*You're asking yourself, "Why me?"' said Mr Mordadson. '"Why is a high-ranking Silver Sanctum emissary offering to find time in his remarkably hectic schedule to teach a teenage kid everything he knows about self-defence and the fine art of duffing people up?"*'

'*Something along those lines,*' *said Az.*

'One reason: because you have no wings, and a person without wings is apt to get picked on.'

'I've been all right so far. A few people have made snide comments but' – Az shrugged – 'so what? Just means they're morons. That's not to say I haven't got into fights, but . . .'

'Quite,' said Mr Mordadson. 'We all know about your quick temper. But there may come a time when you'll need more than just a willingness to come out swinging. You may need some skill to back up the anger, to save yourself from real harm. Another reason: the way you handled yourself throughout this whole recent crisis, right from the start, impressed me. And I'm not, as you know, a man who's easily impressed. You have guts and integrity, which are rarer qualities than you might think. You also have a spark in you, Az, a faint glimmer of something that I believe, with the right encouragement, could be fanned into quite a flame.'

'What do you mean?'

'You'll see. Besides, be honest, what other plans do you have for your life right now?'

'Umm . . . I'm thinking of asking Captain Qadoschson if I can sign on with him as an airship pilot. You know, learn the ropes properly.'

'Very laudable. But otherwise?'

'There's school.'

'For a couple more years. And then?'

'Dunno.'

'Precisely. Az, I'm presenting you with the kind of opportunity the average man or woman in the street would pull out half their feathers for. Though I must admit to a selfish interest as well. I'd like to see if I can adapt the combat techniques I know to suit someone who can't fly. That should be a challenge.'

'Well, as long you get something out of it,' Az said.

Mr Mordadson flashed him a half-smile. 'Promise me you'll think about it.'

Az had promised he would, and had indeed thought about it, and had come to the conclusion that he had nothing to lose by learning a few combat moves, although he doubted he would ever need to use them. What had intrigued him about the offer was that it seemed to indicate that Mr Mordadson wasn't going to stop at teaching him how to handle himself in a fight. There was more to it, as though the combat lessons were just a first step and, if they went well, lessons in other skills would follow.

What those other skills might be, Az was not sure. But his suspicion was that Mr Mordadson could be grooming him for a role as a Silver Sanctum emissary like himself. That, surely, was the opportunity he had referred to, the one that 'the average man or woman in the street would pluck out half their feathers for'.

All of which led Az to believe that Mr Mordadson had issued him with an instruction just now – 'if you can manage it'. Mr Mordadson was telling him to tag along. He was telling him to find a way to get to Lady Aanfielsdaughter's office under his own steam and then surreptitiously listen in on their conversation.

Really?

Az shook his head. No, he was being crazy.

But why else would Mr Mordadson have phrased the remark so pointedly and said it under his breath so that Aurora wouldn't hear? What other interpretation could there be?

Az stood up from the table, sat down, then stood up again, this time with finality. He squared his jaw, resolute.

Mr Mordadson wanted him to prove himself? He wanted him to show he had the nerve and the cunning to eavesdrop on a private conversation between two of the Silver Sanctum's elite members?

OK then, he would. He'd make his way to Lady Aanfielsdaughter's office immediately.

Only one small problem.

How?

CHAPTER 6

How

To get to Lady Aanfielsdaughter's office, which lay halfway across the Silver Sanctum, Az would have to use a series of bridges and walkways, not to mention staircases. On foot, it was a lengthy, laborious journey, and by the time he reached his destination Mr Mordadson's meeting with her ladyship would almost certainly be over.

And even if he did manage to get there in good time, he couldn't eavesdrop on their conversation through the office door because the room was separated from the corridor by an antechamber, where Aurora worked. His only option was the balcony outside the office.

The office was near the summit of one of the Silver Sanctum's tallest towers. The sides of the tower were smoothly metallic. Climbing was out of the question, obviously. As, for that matter, was begging a lift off somebody. Az could just imagine the reaction when he went up to some random person and asked to be flown up to the office balcony and then had to give his reasons. *Why? Well, you see, I want to hang around outside and listen in as Lady Aanfielsdaughter briefs Mr Mordadson on some important affair of state, that's why. Perhaps you wouldn't mind hovering with me in your arms while I do it.* That was simply not going to work.

However ...

The Silver Sanctum was adorned with countless stained-glass windows. Some of them depicted renowned leaders from the past, others showed representations of notable historical events, while a few were simply abstract designs, gorgeous sprays and swirls of kaleidoscopic colour. Keeping the windows sparklingly clean was a full-time job and required the services of a dedicated team of washers armed with cloths and buckets of soapy water.

It would have tired the washers out, hovering all day long while they scrubbed and polished the glass. So, to conserve energy, they worked sitting in slings suspended from helium-filled balloons.

Just now, a few of the window-washers were taking a tea break in the cafeteria. Their balloons were tethered nearby.

That was the answer. Both of Az's problems were eliminated at a single stroke.

Having formulated a plan, Az moved quickly, before common sense could wag its finger at him. This was an insanely risky idea, he knew. But he was still on an adrenaline buzz from the combat session, and he found his own mood of recklessness rather pleasing. At the back of his mind, thoughts of Cassie simmered. In some obscure way he felt that this was how to show her that he didn't care about things stood between them. Was he bothered by her growing coolness towards him? No. He was so little bothered by it that he was happy to attempt something as daft as stealing a window-washer's balloon and riding it through the thorough-fares of the Silver Sanctum.

The balloons were lined up in a row, tied to the balustrade at the edge of the platform on which the cafeteria stood. They bumped against one another springily in the breeze.

Az stole a glance back at the window-washers. They were huddled around a table, heads down, engrossed in an anecdote which one of them was telling. Everybody else in the cafeteria was minding their own business. Nobody was looking his way.

Az slid himself over the balustrade and into the sling of the nearest balloon. It began to sink under his weight. He reached round and undid the line securing it. Then he pushed off from the platform. The balloon bobbed outwards, still descending until it settled into buoyancy. Az waited to hear a cry from above: *Hey! My balloon! Where d'you think you're going with that?* No cry came. A current of air snagged the balloon, moving it forward with some urgency.

He was on his way.

CHAPTER 7

The Consequences Of An Idea
Not Thought Through Fully

For a minute or so Az felt only exhilaration. He didn't think about the fact that he was hanging in midair with only a two-metre-diameter balloon keeping him there. The sheer drop below him didn't trouble him. It was a hundred metres straight down to an anvil-shaped plaza, a further fifty metres to a small domed structure, then a walkway, and beneath that nothing but empty air all the way to the cloud cover. He scarcely noticed. He was too busy revelling in his own boldness, too busy congratulating himself on his success at making off with the balloon without getting caught. He grasped the ropes which joined the seat of the sling to the balloon and he floated away from the cafeteria, letting the breeze coast him thrillingly along.

It was a minute or so later when he had his first misgivings, his first inkling that he hadn't thought this idea through as fully as he should.

For it was then that a sudden, strong air current came in and swept him off at right angles. It drove the balloon towards a tower, and there would have been a collision if the air current hadn't died down as abruptly as it had arisen. Az glided past the tower with centimetres to spare. A pair of storks, nesting near the tower's pinnacle, squawked and waggled their bills at him in protest.

Tingling all over, Az let out a laugh. *That* was a close shave! Except, the laugh did not sound very convincing, even to himself. And he found he was no longer grasping the sling ropes so much as gripping them.

It dawned on him that the balloon was all very well and fine as a method of transport, as long as you had a means of steering it. The window-washers used their wings for that purpose, employing them for propulsion and as rudders. In that respect Az was at a crucial disadvantage. Which left what?

His mind raced. He had visions of himself being buffeted around, helpless, till finally he was dashed against a building and killed. Either that or the winds blew him clear out of the Silver Sanctum and sent him gusting who-knows-how-far to who-knows-where.

Another sharp, fierce current of air seized the balloon and started twirling it around and around. The sling was flung outward by centrifugal force, and Az with it. He banged into the parapet of a jutting balcony, which hurt but had the benefit of halting the balloon's dizzying spin. With his shin scraped and throbbing, Az rebounded away from the balcony, not happy at all now.

He had to end this journey. He'd been mad to embark on it in the first place. The whole thing was a mistake. He was beginning to wonder whether he had misunderstood Mr Mordadson's remark after all, and even if he hadn't, still, was it worth getting himself killed for?

The balloon was picking up speed. It was tugging him along behind it with wicked gusto, as if enjoying its passenger's mounting sense of panic. Silver Sanctum towers whisked by on either side, faster and faster.

Think, Az!

Az thought.

He was suspended from a balloon. In the most basic sense there wasn't much difference between that and being in the control gondola of Troop-Carrier *Cerulean*. Az ventured out with Captain Qadoschson and his crew regularly, once a month on average, each time discovering a little bit more about airshipcraft and aerial navigation. *Cerulean* was, all said and done, just a big balloon with propellers attached. He knew how to fly her. Surely, therefore, he might be able to fly *this* balloon.

A one-person airship. That was how he should regard it.

He hurtled past the spire of another tower, coming within a whisker of impaling himself on its pointed peak. He noticed he was gaining height. The air current that had a hold on him was an updraught. Possibly he would be borne all the way up into the stratosphere if he didn't get a grip on the situation right now.

A one-person airship.

Here goes nothing, he thought.

He hauled down on the right-hand rope, hard. The balloon responded, dipping that way.

Yes!

He kept hauling down, gradually turning himself about.

Then he leaned back, straightening out his legs.

That worked too. All at once he wasn't ascending nearly as fast. He had, in airship terms, gained control of his trim.

Now: he knifed his body sideways at an angle. The balloon veered accordingly.

A human rudder.

A few more manoeuvres, a little more trial and error, and Az had mastery of his vessel. He wasn't beholden to the whim of the winds any more. He was in command.

He swooped. He sheared. He tacked into the breeze. He rose. He fell.

With a yank on the balloon here, a repositioning of his body there, he was able to guide himself in whatever direction he wished.

Soon he was heading for Lady Aanfielsdaughter's office. His course took him past a pair of Silver Sanctum residents flapping sedately along. He gave them a cheery wave. They did a classic double-take, looking at him first without interest, then with startled frowns. Az steered his balloon onward, grinning.

The tower loomed. There was a broad, semicircular balcony right outside Lady Aanfielsdaughter's office. Az aimed for it. The office windows stood wide open. Gauzy curtains billowed outward. Inside, Az glimpsed the Silver Sanctum's premier resident herself, along with Mr Mordadson. The balcony was below his feet. He slipped out of the sling, letting go of the ropes. He landed on the balcony softly on all fours. The balloon shot upward, racing towards the heavens. How was he going to get down from here again? Az didn't know, and it didn't matter. What mattered was that he had made it to his destination.

He waited, breath held, to see if his arrival had been noticed.

Lady Aanfielsdaughter and Mr Mordadson kept talking, uninterrupted.

Az crept forward, closer to the windows.

The voices became clearer.

Crouching behind a huge stand of potted pampas grass, Az listened.

CHAPTER 8

Overheard

'Piracy?' said Mr Mordadson.

'Well, how else would you describe it?' said Lady Aanfielsdaughter.

'I don't deny that technically it's the correct term, milady. But calling it piracy lends it a kind of glamour, when really it's nothing better than common thievery. So this will be their third raid, am I correct?'

'There have been three that we know of. It could be more. Accurate data from the ground is so hard to come by.'

'Three is enough. In fact it's three too many.'

'I agree.'

'And they're terrorising Groundlings, too.'

'That, to me, is the most serious aspect of the whole affair,' Lady Aanfielsdaughter said. 'Stealing is bad enough, but threatening lives – that's beyond the pale. It's a miracle no one's been harmed yet. I imagine it's only a question of time before someone is. All the more reason, Mr Mordadson, why the matter must be dealt with, and promptly.'

'I agree, milady. I've been waiting for you to bring me in on this.'

'What these people, these pirates, are doing flies in the face of everything we Airborn hold dear,' her ladyship continued. 'It makes a mockery of our beliefs and aspirations. *And* there's the danger that it could undermine everything we've managed to achieve this past year – the Bilateral Covenant, formalising relations with the Groundlings, trading with them rather than merely receiving supplies from them. I won't have that jeopardised!' She clapped the backs of her wings together. 'I won't.'

'Of course you've communicated your concern to the officials at Redspire.'

'Of course, in a strongly-worded letter.'

'But no joy.'

'They say they're not aware of any wrongdoing.'

'They say.'

'Quite.'

'And the pirates have an airship,' Mr Mordadson said, musingly. 'That's a puzzle in itself. Where did they get hold of one? Where did they find her?'

'Who knows? Does it matter? The main thing is, I want them stopped. Permanently.'

'You want me to head down to Redspire and sort the situation out.' This wasn't a question – Mr Mordadson was confirming orders, spelling out in precise terms what was required of him.

'I do.'

'May I ask then, at what level of authorisation will I be allowed to operate?'

There was a pause while Lady Aanfielsdaughter deliberated. 'What level do you feel you need?'

'Somewhere like Redspire – the place has long been a thorn in our side, an embarrassment to the entire Airborn community. I'm not surprised that's where these pirates hail from. If any sky-city was going to breed such criminals, it'd be Redspire.'

'Implying?'

'Implying, milady, that an example should be set. For everyone's sake, our own and the Groundlings', Redspire must be taught a lesson. A lesson it won't forget and neither will anyone else. We have to demonstrate that we have zero tolerance for this type of behaviour. Otherwise ...'

Lady Aanfielsdaughter's voice was sombre. 'I see where you're going with this.'

'Indeed. I'm asking to be given full discretion to act in whatever way I deem fit.'

'Yes. All right. Very well.'

'Up to and including extreme sanction.'

'I doubt there'll be any call for that.'

'With the utmost respect, I beg to differ.'

'Extreme sanction?'

'Extreme.'

Another pause from Lady Aanfielsdaughter, a long one this time. 'Well, if you feel it's absolutely necessary.'

'I do. So, whatever happens, whatever I do, you'll back me to the hilt?'

'Yes. Yes, I will.'

Mr Mordadson sounded satisfied. 'Thank you, milady. That's all I needed to hear.'

CHAPTER 9

Permission Not To Have
To Ask Permission

Moments later Mr Mordadson strode out onto the balcony, leaving Lady Aanfielsdaughter at her desk. He stood for a while with his hands behind his back, folded beneath his wings. He looked as if he was contemplating the view. Brilliant blueness stretched to the horizon where it met the creamy curve of the cloud cover. The spires of the Silver Sanctum shone.

Az remained in his hiding place behind the potted pampas. Should he come out? Or should he stay put until Mr Mordadson was gone?

Before Az could decide either way, Mr Mordadson turned his head and fixed his gaze on the very spot where he was crouching. Az gave a start. Mr Mordadson put a finger to his lips and nodded in the direction of the office. Az nodded back, understanding. Mr Mordadson walked over to the pampas grass in a nonchalant manner. Then, in a single, smooth motion, he grabbed Az by the wrists and at the same time stepped off the balcony's edge. Together they plunged in a steep dive, which Mr Mordadson converted into a glide ten metres down.

Once they were well out of Lady Aanfielsdaughter's sight and earshot, he spoke.

'So how much of that did you hear?'

'From "piracy" onwards,' Az replied.

'Excellent. You got most of it, then. Now I won't have to explain everything to you from scratch.'

'So you really did want me to listen in? That was the plan?'

'I thought I made that quite plain.'

'Well, you did, I suppose. I just wasn't sure why. Still aren't.'

'Partly, like I said, to save me the bother of having to repeat it all to you later. I'm lazy that way. Mainly, though, it was a test of initiative, to see if you could get to Lady Aanfielsdaughter's office under your own steam. And you did, so congratulations on that. A window-washer's balloon, right?'

'You saw me.'

'No. But the balloons were sitting there at the cafeteria. It seemed the obvious method. It's what I'd have done in your position. The only drawback, as you found, was having to abandon the balloon once you reached the balcony. You couldn't keep it. Something as big as that bobbing around outside would have given you away. So tell me, how were you proposing to get *off* the balcony afterwards? What would have happened if I hadn't come out to get you?'

'No idea.'

'Thought so. You left yourself without an exit strategy. That's bad. Never, ever, leave yourself without an exit strategy, Az. Always think one step beyond your immediate goal.'

Mr Mordadson canted his wings to the right. He dipped over slightly too far and adjusted with a grunt of effort. The extra weight he was carrying threw off his natural sense of balance.

Levelling out, he and Az swooped around the Hanging Garden, whose multi-tiered terraces spilled flowers like champagne frothing from goblets. There were so many blooms and they were so brightly coloured that it was almost painful to look at them. You had to squint to perceive their beauty.

'If you wanted me to know what Lady Aanfielsdaughter was going to tell you,' Az said, 'then obviously you want me to be involved in some way. Unless all you're after is my opinion on pirates.'

'Which is?'

'Pretty much the same as yours. Stealing is stealing, whatever name you give it. But pirates? Nowadays you only find them in history books and novels.'

'This Redspire lot seem to have revived the tradition, with a new twist. Instead of preying on other Airborn, they've elected Groundlings as their victims.'

'But it's more than my opinion you're after, isn't it?' Az said, as he and Mr Mordadson darted between the twin turrets of Silver Sanctum's public records office. The turrets' cupola roofs were covered with hundreds of roosting parrots, which made them look no less brilliantly gaudy than the Hanging Garden.

'Ever since a week ago, when I first got wind of what was happening at Redspire, I've had a feeling I might need your help. Now I'm certain of it.'

'And that would be because the pirates have an airship.'

'Full marks.'

'You're planning on going after them in *Cerulean.*'

'It makes sense. No other kind of vehicle has the range or fuel capacity. To find and confront one airship, we need another.'

Several more questions were jostling at the forefront of Az's mind, but one in particular begged to be asked:

'What's extreme sanction?'

Mr Mordadson flattened out his wings. They were approaching the landing apron at the city's perimeter, where a gyro-cab waited to take Az back to High Haven.

'What do you think it is?' Mr Mordadson said.

'Sounds to me like ... like permission to do anything you wish. Permission not to have to ask permission.'

'Hm. Nicely put. It also means I'm entitled to act without fear of reprisals or repercussions, especially legal ones. Remember Alan Steamarm?'

Az did. How could he ever forget? He remembered, all too clearly, watching Mr Mordadson hurl the Humanist leader down into the cloud cover and seeing and hearing the detonation of the dynamite to which Steamarm had strapped himself.

'That,' said Mr Mordadson, tight-lipped, 'is a perfect example of extreme sanction.'

CHAPTER 10

A Place Of Refuge

The moment Az let himself in through the front door of his house, his mother pounced.

'Azrael, good, you're back,' she said, bustling out from the kitchen. 'Now, firstly, I've given your father instructions about picking up the buttonholes and bouquets first thing on the morning of the wedding. We both know how forgetful he is, so I want you to make sure he does it, which means you have to go with him. They're at Celestial Florists on Sunbeam Boulevard, you know the place, next door to the wing jewellery shop. Also, I've been thinking about the music. Of course Michael and Aurora are insisting on having one of those four-piece close-harmony choirs rather than the traditional harp ensemble. That's all right, they're young, it's their wedding – but isn't a song like "Hearts Held Like Hands" just a bit too, well, contemporary? Too pop? What do you think? Oh, and the seating plan. I've been considering some revisions. Mainly I'm wondering if I should put the Grubdollars all together at one table or spread them out among the other guests. That way they could meet new people and our friends could get to know some Groundlings, which would be a good thing all round. That's if the Grubdollars are coming. Are they? Have you heard anything yet?'

All of this poured out from her in one go. She scarcely paused for breath, and Az just stood there in the hallway, pinned to the spot. His mother had been like this for at least a month, fizzing-full of plans for the wedding. Now, with just two days left, her enthusiasm was shooting off in all directions like fireworks. From dawn till dusk she was making arrangements, fine-tuning the arrangements she had made, and double-checking the arrangements she had fine-tuned. There was no stopping her. She was like a force of nature. Everything had to be perfect, everything had to go right on the big day, and all anyone else could do was going along with her demands and try not to get in the way.

'Erm, yes, no, don't know,' Az said. An opportunity to speak had at last presented itself.

'What's that?'

'Those are my answers to your questions, Mum. Yes, I'll go with Dad to the florists. No, that song isn't too contemporary. And as far as the Grubdollars go – I don't know.'

'Still?'

'Still.'

His mother's face fell. 'Oh dear. I do hope they'll let us know one way or the other soon. The elevator postal service isn't very efficient yet, is it? Perhaps that's the problem. They sent a letter but it hasn't got here. Or perhaps Groundlings aren't familiar with the social niceties, such as telling people whether you're going to be at a function or not. Is that it? Their ways and ours are so different. Maybe they'll just turn up anyway. I should probably go ahead and assume they will.'

'Where's Dad?' Az asked, changing the subject.

His mother rolled her eyes. 'Where do you think?'

In the basement, which Az's father used as a workshop, calmness reigned. The rest of the house crackled with the manic energy Az's mother was giving off, but none of that energy managed to penetrate down here. The tools which lined the walls and hung from the ceiling seemed to act like insulation. On any given day Az's father was happy to secrete himself in the workshop for an hour or two. At present, however, the place had become more than a place for tinkering with gadgets and ideas for home improvements. It had become a refuge, somewhere he – and Az too, if he wanted – could go to escape the wedding-preparation storm above.

'Lucky Michael,' Az's father said, 'living all the way over on the other side of town. There's the whole of High Haven between him and your mother. Whereas you and I, lad, we're right in the thick of things. She's running us ragged, and we're not even the ones getting married! Honestly, I don't know how much more I can take. Ramona's become this mad, organising machine. I swear, if she asks me again whether I've remembered to book a barber's appointment for tomorrow ...'

'And have you?'

'No, but that's not the point. Anyway, I'm sure I can just pop in for a quick trim.' Az's father rubbed his nearly-bald scalp. 'Won't take five minutes, with a threadbare bonce like mine.'

'Look on the bright side, Dad. Only one more day. Then it's the wedding, and then everything'll be over.'

'One!' Az's father pretended to break down and sob. 'I ... just can't ... go on, son. One more ... day of this! I don't think ... I can make it. Kill me. Please ... just ... kill me now.'

Az laughed, and the laugh turned into a yawn which he was helpless to stifle.

'Ah,' said his father, 'poor chap, you must be whacked. A ten-hour round trip, plus an hour of "exercise class".' He mimed quotation marks with the tips of his wings. 'That'll certainly take it out of you.'

'I am pretty tired.'

'How was it at the Silver Sanctum today? Mr Mordadson in good form?'

'Same as ever,' said Az.

His father detected something in his voice, a hint of evasiveness. 'What's up?'

'Nothing.'

But Az knew he wasn't going to be allowed to leave it at that. Gabriel Enochson might be pushing seventy but his mind remained as sharp as a quill tip. Az had never been able to fool his father and he was certain he never would.

'I'm going – I've *got* to go to Prismburg the day after the wedding,' he said, trying to make it sound casual.

A bushy white eyebrow rose. 'Oh?'

'Yes. For a week or so, maybe longer.'

'Silver Sanctum business?'

'No. Yes.'

'Involving *Cerulean*?'

'Yes.'

His father pondered for a moment. 'This is some kind of official assignment. Your friend Mr Mordadson has recruited you for something.'

Az gave a slow, reluctant nod.

Gabriel Enochson sighed. 'I suppose it was inevitable. Ever since you started combat training with Mr Mordadson, I've known the time was going to come when he would want more from you. It's clear he's got his eye on you and thinks you have great potential, and why shouldn't he? Wings or no wings, you're a star. We've always known that. We knew it long before you became Az the big, famous lad who went down to the ground. Without telling his parents.'

Az grinned sheepishly. It was still a sore point with his father and mother that he had agreed to go down in the elevators that first time, embarking on a journey which might well have killed him, and indeed nearly did, without their knowledge. To make matters worse, Michael had lied to them about it, sending them a message that Az was OK when he'd had no idea whether he was or wasn't. Although everything had turned out well in the end, Az's parents still hadn't quite forgiven him yet.

'But now,' his father went on, 'now, finally, old Mordy's decided to take things up a level, and I can't say I'm completely happy about it, Az. There's going to be some danger, right? Just like last time?'

'No, Dad.'

'Come on, be straight.'

The phrase *extreme sanction* ghosted through Az's mind. 'I don't think I personally am going to be in any danger.'

'But you don't know that for sure.'

'Do you not want me to go? Because I can say no. I can tell Mr Mordadson I've changed my mind and I don't feel ready. He doesn't *need* me to come along with him, I don't think. I mean, *Cerulean* is still Captain Qadoschson's vessel. I'm not even second-in-command.'

'That'd be your pal Wallimson.'

'Yes,' said Az ruefully. His father's 'your pal' had been more than a little sarcastic.

Gabriel Enochson glanced around the workshop. His gaze settled on the scale model of *Cerulean* which he and Az had not finished building. They had abandoned work on it a year ago, leaving it half done, after Az got his first taste of piloting the real airship. The model was redundant now and seemed more than ever a childish thing, a toy. Looking at it, Az's father realised his younger son was fast becoming a man, and this filled him with pride but saddened him as well.

'But still, you want to go,' he said.

'Yeah. Kind of. Yeah.'

The old man put on a brave smile. 'Then you should. You must. The only question is how to break the news to your mother.'

'I know.'

'Any ideas?'

'No.'

'Leave it to me. I'll come up with some excuse. You're taking *Cerulean* out for an extended trip, how about that? Putting her through some long-distance manoeuvres.'

Az shrugged. 'Sounds believable.'

'I'll make it believable. And I'll choose my moment. I'll mention it to her sometime tomorrow when she's right at the height of one of her planning frenzies. She won't be listening to me properly and may not even notice what I've said.'

'Thanks, Dad. You're the best.'

'Just promise me one thing.'

'Of course. What?'

With an index finger his father rubbed a lower eyelid, pushing the grey, pouchy bit of flesh back and forth. 'Promise me you won't ever forget your family.'

'How could I?'

'You say that, but for a while I've been feeling this sense of you gradually slipping away from us. There're your visits to the Silver Sanctum and down to the ground, your trips in *Cerulean*. Don't get me wrong, I'm not saying you shouldn't go out and explore the world and learn skills and make something of yourself. You're growing up, and growing up means growing apart from your family. It's natural and proper. That's what being seventeen is all about. And you're doing important things, and that's fine. Just ... just remember that we're important too. OK?'

'OK.'

'Not making you feel guilty, am I? I wouldn't want that.'

'No. No, I understand what you're getting at.'

'Do you? Good.' His father chuckled. 'Because I'm not sure *I* do. Maybe it's this wedding. One of my two lads is getting hitched and I'm starting to feel as if the nest is emptying. Even though Michael hasn't been in the nest for some time, he's still been around, he's still needed us – and now he won't need us so much, and I'm starting to get a bit soppy and sentimental about that. But still ... Oh look, forget it. Ignore me. I'm being daft.' He spread out his arms and his wings. 'Fancy giving your old dad a hug? I could really do with one. Or are you too grown-up for that now?'

'Not yet.'

The arms folded around Az and then the wings, a double layer of comfort. He felt enclosed and safe and loved. He became aware of the boniness of his father's body through his clothing: the ribs pushing against the skin, the muscles that were growing stringy and scrawny with age. With care, he hugged his father more tightly still.

CHAPTER 11

Pre-season Warm-up Friendly

The following day Az was too busy to think about anything except the wedding. Everything was a blur, a rush of preparation, with his mother alternately chiding and chivvying, not allowing anybody a moment's rest, least of all herself.

Az went over his best-man speech, rehearsing it out loud to his father, who laughed in all the right places. He tried on the smart suit which had been tailor-made for him (it was uncomfortable because it was new, but it fit). When Aurora dropped by in the afternoon to introduce her two bridesmaids to her fiancé's family, Az was polite and friendly, and Aurora was too. He assumed she didn't know he had been enlisted to help deal with the Redspire situation, and even if she did, he assumed she would keep quiet about it.

Then, in the evening, Michael took him out to the hoopdrome at Stratoville to watch the Shrikes take on the Azuropolis Bluejays in a pre-season warm-up friendly. The two brothers cheered as the Shrikes romped to a 37-12 victory. It was an easy win but also a good game of jetball, with some spectacular defensive work from the home side and a satisfyingly high quota of deep slams and horizontal drives. Both Az and Michael agreed that the prospects for the coming season were good, as long as the Shrikes developed their midfield play, especially at the lower levels where they weren't nearly as cohesive as they ought to be. A team like the Northernheights Goshawks, the division leaders, could rip them apart there if they weren't careful.

'You know that nothing is going to change between us,' Michael said as they flew back to High Haven in his new helicopter, an Aerodyne Aeronauticals Green Dart. It was just a few days old, hot off the production line, streamlined and shimmering. 'I mean, sure, my footloose-and-fancy-free bachelor days are over, but *we'll* still be the same, you and me. We'll still go and see the Shrikes at the 'drome every fortnight and maybe fit in some away matches as well if we can.'

'Of course,' Az said. 'Nothing's going to change. You're going to be an old married fogey, but apart from that ...'

'Cheek!' Michael reached across the cockpit, grabbed a clump of Az's hair and shook his head from side to side. The Green Dart sank sickeningly while his hand was off the collective handle, adding to Az's discomfort. Michael maintained control by applying pressure on the right anti-torque pedal, before grasping the collective again when he had finished roughing up his brother.

'And then kids will come along,' Az went on, 'and you'll be up half the night changing nappies and you'll be so tired you won't even remember you have a brother. But *apart* from all that ...'

Michael scanned the dashboard frowningly. 'Where's the damn ejector seat button? I know there's one here somewhere. It's fitted as standard on the Dart.'

'Oh yes, and just think, this is the last two-seater 'copter you'll ever own. Next aircraft you buy is going to be a nice, safe family-model front-prop.' Which, Az knew, was a fate worse than death as far as his brother was concerned. 'And also, you can forget about having a drink with your mates after work. You know what Aurora'll have to say about that. "Out again with those rowdy test-pilot friends of yours, Michael? I don't think so." No, from tomorrow onwards you'll be under curfew – home by six every evening or else.'

'Well, maybe not,' Michael said with a hopeful air. 'After all, Aurora's not giving up her job at the Sanctum, is she? She's going to be there four days a week, which means that for four days a week I'm going to be a free man.'

'She'll find ways of keeping tabs on you. She's not stupid, Mike.'

'That she isn't. She's incredibly smart.'

'Except,' Az added, 'she can't be that smart if she wants *you* for a husband.'

'Ejector seat, ejector seat, ejector seat.' Michael slapped the dashboard. 'Come on, work, pluck you, work!'

'I'd just hit the vanes anyway,' Az said in a smart-alecky voice.

'And they'd chop you to ribbons. Twice as effective.'

'Maybe, but they'd also break, and then you'd crash.'

'It'd be worth it.'

Az laughed. Michael laughed. It felt carefree. Their banter was the usual blithe brotherly banter. It felt like the two of them as they always had been.

And all at once Az found himself wanting to tell Michael about Redspire, about extreme sanction, about everything ...

... but he couldn't do it. He couldn't bring himself to tarnish the moment. As a rule he kept nothing from Michael. If he was gloomy, he would tell Michael so. If he was sad or anxious, he would tell Michael why. Suddenly, with Michael about to get married, it seemed that that option wasn't available to him any more. Michael was embarking on a new life and, no matter what he said, Az wasn't going to be a big part of it. His brother wasn't going to have as much time for him as he used to.

Meanwhile Az felt he was embarking on a new life of his own, one in which Michael and his parents were going to play an increasingly smaller role. In spite of everything he and his father had talked about yesterday, he couldn't ignore the fact that the drift of destiny seemed to be pulling him away from his family. The difference between him and them was no longer merely a matter of wings. He was becoming involved in affairs far removed from their simple domestic existence.

So really all he could do was lark about and laugh as if everything was the same as it ever was. Because in truth, despite Michael's claim that nothing was going to change, a great deal had changed already and a great deal more was about to.

CHAPTER 12

Visit Scenic Grimvale!

Cassie huffed into the speaker tube.

'Ladies and gentlemen,' she announced. 'If you'll kindly look to your left, you will observe the Thatcherhollow sawmill. Thatcherhollow is Grimvale's largest sawmill and one of the largest in all of the Westward Territories, turning out eighteen thousand tonnes of planks per year, on average, and a similar quantity of woodpulp, the basic material for making paper.'

Fletcher was in the driver's pod with her, seated at the controls. He let out a mocking laugh. 'A simi-larr ker-wantity of woodpulp! Hark at yourself, Cass!'

'Shh!' Cassie hissed, covering the speaker tube's mouthpiece with one hand.

'You know, every day you'm getting to sound more and more poncey when you'm on that tube.'

'Just speaking to they as them'd understand.'

'Oh yes, right. Of course, your highness. Pray continue.' Fletcher changed gear, and *Cackling Bertha* let out a laugh of her own – the chugging mechanical *clank-clatter-gurgle* which earned her her name.

'Thatcherhollow were established – *was* established in the early years of the last century,' Cassie said into the tube. 'The sawmill was one of the two main factors which helped turn a remote valley village into the thriving and successful township that we know today as Grimvale. The other factor, the Consolidated Colliery Collective, we will come to shortly. Thatcherhollow's sustainable pine plantations now cover almost half a million hectares of land and the timber which is derived from its hardy trees is as highly prized on the ground as it is up above the clouds. A great deal of your furniture is constructed from it, not to mention the elegant fretwork screens and the intricately carved statuettes which your race produces and which are now finding such favour down here.'

'Honestly, girl,' muttered Fletcher. 'This'm getting bad. You keep it up and I'll be checking your back for feathers.'

'Shut *up*, Fletch,' Cassie snapped out of the side of her mouth. 'I mean it. Elsewise you'm going to be finding this speaker tube rammed up somewhere you wouldn't want it rammed. Straight up.'

'If you did, them lot down in the loading bay wouldn't notice the difference. Just be getting one kind of hot air instead of another.'

Cassie clouted her brother.

Grinning from ear to ear, Fletcher steered *Bertha* around a corner. The forest-swathed slopes which clustered behind the sawmill fell away in the rearview mirrors. Ahead, a more industrialised section of Grimvale beckoned.

Cassie resumed her tour-guide monologue, doing her best to make what she was saying sound fresh and spontaneous. She had borrowed books from the town library and toiled to memorise a huge amount of facts and figures about Grimvale and the surrounded area until she could reel them off without thinking. To make the facts and figures interesting to her audience, however, she had to pretend that they were interesting to her.

And they weren't. After just a couple of months of running these sightseeing trips, Cassie was bored. It was the same journey every time, the same circuit through Grimvale and its outskirts, the same landmarks to be passed and commented on along the way – dull, dull, dull. There was no challenge, no excitement. It wasn't like murk-combing, where there'd always been the potential thrill of discovery, the chance (and hope) of coming across a Relic; where you'd had to rely on your wits and the sharpness of your eyes; where the many hazards of the Shadow Zone kept you constantly on your toes. Trundling along metalled roads, pointing out the 'highlights' of Grimvale to a handful of Airborn visitors who sat down in the loading bay on padded benches that Fletcher had installed and looked out through the rows of portholes that Fletcher had also installed, and who doubtless found what they were being shown was glum and grey and dismal and depressing – why did she do it?

Cassie knew why. She did it because she had no choice. It was this or she and her family starved.

That, though, didn't make the job any less boring or more bearable.

Soon *Bertha* was nearing the Consolidated Colliery Collective and Cassie found herself explaining to her passengers about the mine's shared-profits policy and about the so-called Black Lake Lode, the vast, apparently inexhaustible seam of coal upon which the pithead stood. She also mentioned the CCC's annual coal-output tonnage and various other fascinating statistics.

What she didn't tell them about was the attempted revolution which had sprung up at the CCC and almost brought down a sky-city. In all likelihood the passengers knew the story already. After all, that was how it was possible for them to be here now, sightseeing. Twelve months ago they would not even have realised that there were people down here to take them on a tour such as this. Now, since the events of last year, they could visit the ground and mingle with its inhabitants any time.

Not that many of them did. Today it wasn't bad. There were eight Airborn down in the loading bay: an elderly married couple, three university students and a mother with two young children. But most days the Grubdollars were lucky if they pulled in two paying passengers and some days they didn't get any at all. Cassie had done the maths and worked out that they needed two fares per trip just to cover their fuel costs. A third fare meant they had a bit of money to pay bills and buy food. A fourth, and they were turning an actual profit.

So, on average, they were just about breaking even, and good days like today helped with that. But breaking even wasn't enough. If you took into account the fact that she and Fletcher worked from dawn to dusk and didn't draw a salary for it, then they were actually running the business at a loss.

Resentment welled up inside Cassie. She swallowed it back down. Life hadn't been perfect back when murk-combing had been the Grubdollar family trade, but it had certainly been better than this. She must not allow herself to feel hard done by, however. That didn't help anyone.

'We'll shortly be coming to the end of our journey around the Grimvale region,' she announced. 'Our route now takes us back through the Shadow Zone to the Chancel at the base of the sky-city Heliotropia. You may wish to keep an eye out for the Shadow Zone's indigenous species, verms.'

'Indigenous,' Fletcher said, to himself. 'I doesn't even know what the word means.'

'As the daylight starts to fade,' Cassie said into the speaker tube, ignoring him, 'verms emerge from their burrows to forage for food. Totally blind, they hunt by —'

Clang!

Something small and hard struck *Bertha*'s side.

'What the —?' Fletcher peered out through the windshield and a sour look came over his face. 'Damn. Should have known.'

'Who be it?' Cassie asked.

'*They*,' came the cold reply.

CHAPTER 13

The Marquee

That morning, on their way to the Chancel to collect passengers, Cassie and Fletcher had spotted a marquee pitched at the roadside. It was large and weather-stained and its entrance flaps were tied open, revealing a shadowy interior. Inside, a man had been setting out wooden chairs, arranging them in rows in front of a rostrum. Outside, parked a few metres away, was a rusty, beaten-up old van with balding tyres and a tarpaulin covering half of its flatbed. The marquee hadn't been there the evening before. It had sprung up overnight, like a mushroom.

Both Grubdollar siblings had known what it signified. A travelling preacher had come to town. To be precise: a travelling Deacon.

Fletcher's first instinct had been to steer *Bertha* off the road and flatten the marquee. And if the man inside had happened to get crushed beneath *Bertha*'s caterpillar tracks too, so be it. Fletcher's loathing for Deacons ran that deep.

But he'd resisted the temptation and settled for a few growled threats instead. The Deacon, for his part, had glanced round at *Bertha* without curiosity, then resumed laying out the chairs. Fletcher had fired a rude gesture at him from the driver's pod but the man hadn't noticed. Cassie, meanwhile, had observed that the Deacon's hair was strikingly red and flared upward from his head like flames, but he hadn't been close enough for her to get a good look at his face.

It was clear what had happened since then. The red-haired Deacon would have gone into town to drum up custom. A recently-passed Grimvale bylaw meant he wasn't allowed to preach within the town limits. Nothing, however, prevented him from gathering an audience from the town and holding a meeting with them just outside.

What had he said at that meeting?

The precise words didn't matter. But if he was anything like other Deacons who had visited the region lately, he would have delivered a long, ranting sermon against the Airborn and against anyone who was friendly with them. He would have condemned the Bilateral Covenant and denounced the Groundling governments who had so willingly, blindly signed up to it. He would have lamented the fact that Deacons like him had been thrown out of their positions of authority and out of their

Chancels. He would have painted a picture of the world as it was now, emphasising the upheaval and confusion which were the result of contact with the beings formerly known as the Ascended Ones. 'So many people don't know where they stand any more,' he would have said. 'There's so much uncertainty now, and so little order.' And he would have gone on to conjure up images of a terrible future, with society breaking down, everything falling into chaos. War, disaster, death. All because the established way of doing things was gone. The division between the races was gone. The system which had been in place for centuries, and for centuries had *worked*, was gone.

And his audience would have lapped it up. They would have applauded throughout his speech. They would have grumbled their agreement with the Deacon's views on the present sorry state of the world and would have nodded dourly at his dark vision of what was to come. Gradually he would have stirred them into a froth of indignation and disgust. For his audience was made up of people who preferred the world as it used to be. They were unsettled by the drastic changes that had occurred. They pined for the not-so-distant past, a simpler time.

And then, just as the meeting was breaking up, what should these angry, seething folk see but a murk-comber growling its way towards them? A murk-comber which had been modified to carry Airborn tourists inside.

Little wonder that one of them picked up a stone off the ground and hurled it at *Cackling Bertha*. Little wonder that the rest of them started to do the same.

CHAPTER 14

The Effects Of Anti-verm
Countermeasures On Humans

A second stone hit *Bertha*, striking not far from the driver's pod.

'Bastards!' yelled Fletcher. 'What'm got into they?'

'That Deacon, that be what,' Cassie said. 'Filling their bellies with his own sour grapes. Just keep driving. Ignore they.'

'But them's pelting us with stones!'

'Can't hurt we or our passengers. Damage *Bertha*'s paintwork maybe, put a couple of dents in she, but then her be'n't a perfect beauty to begin with.'

'But —'

'Keep driving, Fletch. Only thing to do. Just not too fast. Make it as if us doesn't give a fig. So as not to alarm any of they lot down below.'

More stones came sailing in from the crowd that was clustered outside the marquee. They struck like gong beats on *Bertha*'s hull. Some missed. One rebounded off the curved windshield of the driver's pod, leaving a scratch on the glass. Dimly over the sound of the engine Cassie could hear the crowd shouting. She couldn't make out what they were saying but the tone was pure wild rage, like the baying of hounds.

A voice came through the speaker tube. 'Erm,' it said nervously, 'sorry to bother you, but might I ask what's going on? Why are those people attacking us?'

Cassie recognised the voice as belonging to the male half of the elderly Airborn couple.

'Nothing to worry about, sir,' she said. 'Please stay calm. It'm just some – some rowdy locals. We'll be out of their range soon enough. You're perfectly safe.'

But even as she said this Cassie observed that the stone throwers were now running alongside *Bertha*, keeping pace with her. And rocky missiles continued to bounce noisily off *Bertha*'s exterior.

'Chaff,' she said to Fletcher.

'What?'

'Let's see they off with some chaff.'

'Against people? But that'm for verms.'

'Still. Why not?'

Fletcher smiled. 'Yeah, why not?'

He pulled a lever. At *Bertha*'s rear a small panel slid open, exposing the end of a pipe. The next instant a fist-sized paper sphere shot out from the pipe with a *choom* of compressed air. It exploded above the heads of the pursuing crowd. Several of them were hit by tiny fragments of rock salt. They fell, clutching arms and faces.

Fletcher checked the lens-projected images in the rearview mirrors. 'Got some, annoyed the rest.'

'Smoke,' said Cassie.

Her brother pulled another lever.

A cloud of white smoke spurted violently from *Bertha*'s rear, enveloping the stone throwers. Some charged through it and emerged the other side unaffected. Others staggered and collapsed to the ground, choking and spluttering in the billowing fumes, tears streaming from their eyes.

Cassie debated whether to deploy another anti-verm countermeasure.

Fletcher was thinking the same thing. 'Let's electrocute they.'

'Us only wants to hurt they, Fletch, not kill. Besides, them isn't close enough for it to work. No, I reckon us has made our point and them's made theirs. Call it a draw.'

'Ahem, excuse me.' It was the elderly Airborn man again on the speaker tube. 'Sorry to bother you again, but those "rowdy locals" of yours managed to hit one of the portholes down here. There's a hole in the glass and, well, we're losing the pressure seal. Air's hissing in from outside.'

'Oh bugger it!' Cassie said under her breath. Into the speaker tube she said, 'Just sit tight, everyone. We'll get you back to the elevators in no time.'

She turned to Fletcher, but he didn't need telling. He thrust the control sticks forward to Full Speed.

CHAPTER 15

Under Pressure

The Grubdollars had converted *Bertha*'s loading bay into a self-contained, airtight compartment and had installed a vacuum pump so that it could be depressurised. That way they were able to replicate the thin, high-altitude atmosphere which their Airborn passengers were used to and the tourists would not suffer from ground-sickness.

With the seal breached, the air in the loading bay would return to normal ground-level pressure very rapidly. That meant the passengers were soon going to start feeling unwell. Cassie recalled Az's first time down on the ground. He had been near-comatose for twenty-four hours, on top of suffering from nausea and a splitting headache.

Then there were the two small children on board to consider. Ground-sickness might affect them even more severely than it did adults. It might even kill them.

'Faster, Fletch,' Cassie urged.

'Want we to crash? I be going as fast as I can.'

Cackling Bertha beetled along the Shadow Zone road, kicking up a plume of dust behind her. Dead ahead was the column which supported Heliotropia. Elevators shuttled up and down it, at this distance looking like aphids on a rose stem. To Cassie, the column didn't seem to be getting any closer, and she knew that with every passing second the air pressure in the loading bay was becoming denser and *Bertha*'s passengers were getting less and less comfortable.

'How'm you all bearing up?' she asked through the speaker tube, trying to sound upbeat. She wasn't aware that she had stopped imitating Airborn speech patterns.

'We're – we're OK,' said the elderly man. 'I can't say we're —'

Someone interrupted, snatching the speaker tube off him. 'Listen, Miss Grumdingle or whatever your name is. One of my friends has just been sick all over the floor. I'm starting to feel pretty dizzy. Why aren't you doing anything?'

Cassie guessed the person talking was one of the three university students. 'Us is trying to get you to the elevators quick as possible, sir, but *Bertha* be'n't exactly built for speed. Her top k.p.h. is —'

'I don't care about that! There are children here. There must be some way of keeping the air pressure down.'

'The vacuum pump be operating on full power but it'm not going to make much difference so long as that porthole be broken.'

'Then come down here and fix it somehow!' the student demanded.

'I can't,' Cassie said. 'To get into the bay I'll have to unseal the doors, which'll only make things worse for you. Maybe you could find something to stuff into the crack, like a piece of cloth or something.'

'We've already done that. It's helped, but not a lot.'

'That'm all I can think of. Sorry.'

A torrent of abuse burst from the speaker tube. Cassie hadn't known the Airborn could swear like that.

She looked at Fletcher.

All he said was, 'Well, there'm some new Airborn phrases you can use on the next tour.'

'That'm assuming there even be a next tour,' Cassie replied.

CHAPTER 16

Thanks A Lot

Fletcher steered *Bertha* into a parking space in the large, warehouse-like structure that used to be the Chancel's sorting-house. Cassie nipped out through an iris-style access point in the underside of the driver's pod, leaving Fletcher to hit the switch to open the loading bay.

There was a sigh of inrushing air as the hatch rose, although not the loud, sharp hiss that usually came. At the same time the fruity stench of vomit wafted out. Cassie had to force herself not to retch.

The Airborn passengers staggered out – the mother and children were first, then the students.

The mother said nothing. She just gave Cassie a dirty look, then hustled her children off towards the sorting-house's double-doored exit, herding them along with her wings. Council-appointed officials were waiting on the other side of the doors with a fleet of battery-powered carts to transport the Airborn visitors back to the elevator chamber.

One of the students hurried after the mother and children. He was green-faced and obviously was the one who'd been sick. He was keen to get to the elevator chamber as soon as possible.

The two remaining students rounded on Cassie angrily.

'Well, what do you call that?' the taller of them snarled. 'All part of the Groundling experience I suppose. A slice of life as it's lived down here.'

'We could have been killed!' said the other, who had flamingo feathers stitched into his plumage. These made him look very flamboyant, but their deep pink colour also matched the indignant flush that had come to his cheeks.

'I doesn't reckon you could have been killed,' Cassie replied. 'There were no real danger of —'

'Oh, you *doesn't*, does you?' snapped the taller one. 'So is it commonplace on these tours that one gets pelted with rocks? Or perhaps you arranged it. To add a little spice to the trip.'

'That'm just stupid.'

'Probably you'll start charging people extra now,' said the flamingo-feathered one. 'You know, to "guarantee security". This is a little protection racket you lot have set up.'

Cassie was finding it hard to keep an even temper in the face of such ridiculous accusations. These two were, what, nineteen? Not that much older than her, just a couple of years, and yet they were treating her like a child.

'I be truly sorry about what happened,' she said. 'It were circumstances entirely beyond our control. If there'm something I can do to make it up to you ...'

'There certainly is. A refund.'

'A full refund,' Flamingo Feathers chimed in.

'Would that make you happy?' Cassie said.

'No, but it would leave us feeling that we hadn't been ripped off.'

Reluctantly Cassie went to fetch the gifts with which the Airborn had paid for the tour. These were items of jewellery, silverware and small wooden statuettes, all of them beautifully crafted. The Airborn made artworks with a delicacy and elegance that Groundlings simply could not match.

'Which was yours?' she asked, holding out the box which contained the gifts, today's fares. It looked like a decent sum in total, although you never knew till you got to the gift-broker's shop. Cassie hated to lose any of it.

The two students plucked out a gold chain bracelet and a small mahogany figure of an eagle in flight. Flamingo Feathers also took an ivory-handled fan which the third student, the sick one, had paid with.

'I shan't be recommending you to any of my friends,' the taller student said haughtily, as he and Flamingo Feathers strutted off in the direction of the exit.

'Surprised if you's *got* any friends,' Cassie muttered under her breath.

The elderly Airborn couple had watched all of this in silence, and Cassie turned to them wearily, anticipating more of the same.

'Here,' she said, nodding to the box in her hands. 'Take what'm yours and go.'

'Young lady,' said the husband, 'I cannot apologise enough for those two.' He gestured at the departing students. 'Such ingratitude is unfor-givable. Believe me, they don't represent us all. Don't judge the rest of the Airborn by their example.'

'Oh,' said Cassie, taken aback.

'None of what happened was your fault,' said the wife, 'and I honestly don't believe we were in serious danger. The young man who was ill – that was fear and panic, not ground-sickness. He just worked himself up into a state.'

'So you doesn't want your gifts back?'

The husband shook his head firmly. 'On the contrary. In fact, I think Vesta has something for you.'

He pointed to his wife, who was undoing the clasp of her necklace. Cassie had noticed the necklace earlier when the tourists were climbing aboard. It was made of opals and gorgeous. Each white precious stone was carved into a rounded, asymmetrical shape. Strung together in irregular rows, they resembled nothing quite so much as a vista of glittering white clouds.

Now, the elderly woman took the necklace off and held it out to Cassie.

'Oh no, I can't accept that.'

'You can and you will.'

'But it'm much too nice.'

'It should make up for the refunds you handed out.'

'More than make up,' Cassie said. 'But still, I can't.'

'I won't take no for an answer.' The woman laid the opal necklace in the box. 'There. It's yours. And we have to go, don't we, dear?' she said to her husband.

'We do.'

'We *will* be recommending a Grubdollar tour to our friends,' the elderly woman said, as she took her husband's arm. 'Very enthusiastically.'

'Thank you,' Cassie said again, although the phrase scarcely began to convey what she was feeling.

The elderly couple headed for the doors, leaving her gazing at the necklace in awe. Flecks of colour shone within the opals' whiteness. If she tilted the box just slightly, a multihued shimmer rippled through the entire necklace.

All at once she thought of Az and the last time she and he had met, up overhead in Heliotropia.

They had been standing at the city's edge, looking out over the cloud-scape. Her visit was nearly up. There wasn't much oxygen left in her breathing apparatus. Az was asking her about Michael's wedding. Would she and her family like to come?

She made noncommittal noises. *Maybe. Perhaps. Depending.*

At that moment, the sunlight struck a gauzy peak of cloud and, out of nowhere, an arc of colours appeared. It remained there, transparent and shining, for just a few seconds, then vanished again. She asked Az what it was.

He told her: *a sunbow.* It was a trick of the light, something to do with refraction, the distortion of the sun's rays through cloud vapour.

He said it as though such a thing was commonplace, and to him, of course, it was. To Cassie, however, it was one of the most beautiful sights she had ever seen.

She knew then that there was too much separating them; too much in Az's world that he took for granted and that she never could. If this sunbow, this brief-lived miracle in the clouds, got nothing more from him than a shrug and a scientific explanation, then how could he and she ever hope to understand each other at even the most basic level? They were too unalike.

She'd recognised this as an excuse, even as she thought it. She was trying to find a reason not to be with Az any more, and the flimsiest of ones would do.

The opals reminded her of the sunbow, and that was all it took to make her happiness about the necklace vanish. The emotion popped like a balloon, punctured by a stab of guilt.

She still owed Az a reply to his invitation to Michael's wedding. It was tomorrow, and she hadn't given him a yes or a no. She had ducked the whole issue, ignored it, and it was too late now. She had left him in limbo and that was weak of her and she was ashamed.

If only things were simple! If only she didn't have all these worries, all these responsibilities!

If only, if only, if only.

'Penny for your thoughts?'

Cassie turned. Fletcher was standing beside her. She hadn't heard him walk up.

'Them be'n't even worth that,' she replied, then gave what she hoped was a breezy laugh. 'But hey, look at this!' She showed him the opal necklace. 'This be worth something all right.'

'Not bad.'

'Let's head back to town. Reckon if us makes good time, the gift-broker's might still be open.'

'You never know.' Fletcher sniffed the air, then leaned into the loading bay and recoiled with a disgusted expression. 'Phew! That'm *nasty*. Fains I doesn't have to clean it up.'

'Me either. I vote Robert.'

'Yeah. Least him can do, being as him gets to sit at home and twiddle his thumbs all day.'

'Motion carried then. Two to one. Robert it be.'

CHAPTER 17

Speaking Of Whom . . .

Robert did not actually 'sit at home and twiddle his thumbs all day'. For a start, he was still in school, so during term time he was out from eight till three each weekday being a reasonably attentive pupil at the Grimvale Central College on Loomshuttle Lane. Even during the holidays, though, he didn't get to go out in *Bertha* with his brother and sister, much as he would have liked to.

The reason was that someone had to stay home with their father, and Robert was the youngest and therefore, somehow, the job had fallen to him.

He wasn't quite sure how that had happened. Surely it was Cassie's duty, not his. As the girl in the family, she was the one you went to when there was looking-after and caring-for stuff to be done. But Robert was on the bottom rung of the Grubdollar sibling ladder, and youngest brothers and sisters tended to have to do what their elders told them to. It wasn't fair or democratic but it was the way things were. Hence, Robert was stuck with the dull and thankless daily task which he had taken to calling 'Dawatch'.

It was a necessary task too. Their father had to have someone there in the house with him. Nobody said it in so many words, but Den Grubdollar could not be left on his own.

Den was not a well man.

So unwell was he that sometimes, looking at him, Robert scarcely recognised him any more.

At this moment, Den was where he usually was: his favourite armchair in the corner of the lounge. He was just sitting there, staring into space, his hands resting in his lap, fingertip against fingertip. He wasn't talking or laughing, and at one time it had been rare to see him not doing either. Nor was he rushing around, busy with some job or other. For instance, you never saw him working on *Bertha*, which was once his favourite spare-time activity. His nails weren't permanently dirty from changing her oil; his hands weren't grease-stained from replacing gaskets and spark plugs. Nowadays, too, he barely ate, and didn't touch his beloved beer. Den used to have quite a belly on him, which he somehow managed to sustain even during the periods when the family's

324

fortunes had taken a downturn and food (and beer) were in short supply.

He had become thin, a shadow of his former self. His eyes were sunken in his face, as if he had grown hollow inside. Sitting and staring was what he mostly did during his waking hours, though he napped as well, either dozing in the armchair or sloping off to his bedroom in the afternoon for an hour or two. Occasionally he got up to look out of a window. Sometimes you could find him down in the courtyard, peering at the clouds or the ground. Very, very rarely he might step out through the front gate and stop and gaze one way along the street then the other, perhaps sighing as he did so. But that was as active as he ever got, and he never strayed more than a few metres from the house.

He stumbled through the days of his life, mute, lost.

It had been this way ever since Martin died.

All of the Grubdollars mourned Martin. His absence was a constant pang in their hearts. They missed him horribly. They remembered him as temperamental, hot-headed, opinionated – and ultimately brave and true, a hero. He could not be replaced and the pain of his death would not go away. The family was not the same without him. It functioned but only just. There was a vital component missing.

Their father, though, was taking it harder than any of them. He had lost his wife thirteen years ago, and now he had lost his oldest son. It had knocked the stuffing out of him. Robust, good-natured, cantankerous Den Grubdollar was gone, and in his place was an empty shell of a man, a shrunken effigy.

His children were worried that he might do something drastic and foolish one day, like kill himself. Even if he didn't go that far, they feared he might continue to neglect himself to the point where he would waste away to nothing. Perhaps rattle-lung or some other disease would invade him while his defences were down and destroy him from within; perhaps misery alone would be enough to do the trick.

So Robert was tasked with keeping an eye on him while Cassie and Fletcher were off conducting their tours, and when Robert was obliged to be at school, Colin Amblescrut filled in.

Colin had elected himself Den's faithful friend and was only too happy to keep him company when required. He probably – Robert thought ruefully – did a better job of it than he, Robert, did. Colin chattered all day long to Den, regaling him with story after story about the extensive Amblescrut clan and their unusual and frequently illegal exploits. The run-ins they had with the police were the stuff of legend. So were their skills at brewing moonshine and their artful methods of making money without doing any actual work. Colin's fund of Amblescrut tales was apparently endless. Whether Den enjoyed listening to them or not was unclear, but Colin certainly relished telling them. It entertained *him*, even if his audience seemed indifferent.

Robert, by contrast, just left his father to his morose staring while he himself got on with other things. He felt his dad couldn't be helped unless he decided he wanted to be. Until then, he checked on him at regular intervals, made him lunch and cups of tea, but otherwise stayed out of his way. It was odd how boring and irritating someone else's depression could be. Without question Robert still loved his father but he detested the surly, silent presence the old man had become. In Robert's view, if Den truly cared about his family he would make the effort to break out of the slump he had fallen into. Obviously he just didn't care enough.

The long trial of another day of Da-watch was coming to an end. As nightfall deepened the grey of the clouds to black, Robert heard a far-off clank-and-trundle which announced that *Bertha* was nearly home. He wondered what sort of a trip it had been, how many paying punters there'd been aboard, and how much cash Cassie and Fletcher had got at the gift-broker's in exchange for the Airborn's artefacts. He felt a keen edge of envy. At least his brother and sister got to tootle around in *Bertha*, even if it was along the exact same route every time. At least they got to see something other than the four walls of the family homestead, which were prison walls to Robert while he was on Da-watch. At least they *did* something with their days. Did they have any idea how frustrating his existence was right now?

It appeared to have been a good outing. Cassie emerged from *Bertha* clutching a sheaf of banknotes, which she eagerly showed off to Robert.

'Hundred and fifty!' she exclaimed. 'We had five tourists and one of they gave us a necklace that was real opal. Gift-broker were well impressed.'

'Strictly speaking it were eight, not five,' said Fletcher, coming up the spiral staircase behind her.

'What, you lose three of they halfway round?' said Robert. 'Pretty careless.'

The story came out: the Deacon's marquee, the enraged townsfolk, the hail of stones, the pressure-seal breach.

'Mind you,' said Fletcher, 'us may have made some decent money today but it'm going to cost us to get *Bertha* mended and shipshape again. New porthole, plus a lick of paint and some panel-beating to get the dents out of her.'

'Us can do that ourselves,' Cassie said. 'And maybe us can get the porthole glass at the reclamation yard, cheap and second-hand.'

'You'm certainly looking on the bright side today, sis,' said Robert.

'Someone has to,' Cassie replied, sounding determined and also ever so slightly desperate.

Robert was about to comment on this when a distant, deep voice spoke up from the lounge. Robert had heard the voice so seldom these past few months that he almost didn't know whose it was.

'Hurt *Bertha*?' it rumbled.

Den was up out his armchair. He was hunched and swaying, and in his sunken eyes there was a look which none of his offspring could remember seeing there before and none of them much liked. For once, his eyes were lively again, but the light that animated them was yellow and baleful. It spoke of curdled emotions and a despair that needed an outlet and had found one.

'Who,' Den intoned, growling out the words, 'hurt she?'

CHAPTER 18

Deacon Gerald Hardscree

Deacon Gerald Hardscree was reading to himself in his marquee by the light of a kerosene lantern. It was too early to get out his bedroll and turn in for the night, and anyway he wasn't much of a sleeper. His brain was always so busy that he had a hard time shutting it down. Thought after thought raced through it like the trucks of a freight train, keeping him awake with their rattle and clang.

The book in his hands was a slim pamphlet entitled *The Death of Faith, The End of Days*, written by one Archdeacon Corbelgilt. It was smudgily printed on cheap paper and not the sort of thing that could be found in an ordinary bookshop. Copies cost nothing and were distributed privately through a network of Deacons. One had come into Hardscree's possession a week ago when he was preaching thirty miles away at a town called Breaker's Harrow. There had been a Deacon in his audience, sitting there in plain clothes. He had come up to Hardscree after the meeting and pressed the book on him.

'You should read this, brother,' he had said.

Hardscree had known who Corbelgilt was. He had also known that he was planning to pass through Grimvale on the next leg of his travels. Grimvale, whose Chancel the selfsame Corbelgilt used to be in charge of. Hardscree had thought this an omen.

He studied the book, taking occasional sips from the hip flask of whisky by his side. Moths and other winged insects swirled in the lantern's orbit. Every so often one of them would hurl itself at the hot glass with a loud *plink* and sometimes a sizzle.

Corbelgilt wrote that the forced eviction of Deacons from their Chancels had been an act of gross heresy. Not only that but it was foolish and short-sighted and had damaged civilisation, perhaps beyond repair. For, if there was no promise of an Ascended life after this earthbound, cloud-shrouded one, then what did anyone have to look forward to beyond death? Nothing. All across the land, Corbelgilt said, people were slowly waking up to this dire fact. They had had hope ripped away from them. It surely wouldn't be long before they wanted it back, and the best way for that to happen would be to reinstate the Deacons.

Hardscree found himself nodding in agreement with Corbelgilt's book in some places. In others, he found himself shaking his head in strong disagreement. For instance, Corbelgilt insisted that the only way to normalise the world again was to tear up the Bilateral Covenant, break off relations with the Airborn, and put the Deacons back in the Chancels.

Hardscree didn't believe that that could be done. You couldn't have things exactly as they were before, not after such a fundamental shift in the way the world worked. A broken china cup could be glued back together but it would never be as good as it had been previously. A brand new cup was called for.

It so happened that Hardscree had an idea what that new cup should look like and how it might be fashioned. In the months that he had been roaming the Westward Territories, his thundering freight-train brain had been pondering the matter. Lately, an answer had become clear to him.

Footfalls outside the marquee caught his attention. Hardscree laid Corbelgilt's book down and looked out, shading his eyes against the lantern light.

A man appeared, panting. He was dishevelled and furious-looking. His eyes glared, his hair was scrubby, and he didn't have many teeth.

Hardscree sensed trouble but remained calm. He knew he and his kind weren't popular. That was why they were banned from preaching within town limits. For now, the public mood was against them and all that they stood for. Many wandering preachers didn't wear their Deacon robes any more for that very reason. A minority of people wanted to hear what they had to say, but the majority did not and could get quite aggressive about it. So it was wise to travel incognito whenever possible.

Hardscree himself was not ashamed of who he was and wore his robe openly and with pride. He had things to say, truths to spread, and didn't care if people were upset by that.

However, as a precaution, he wore something else too, beneath his robe: a sheath knife with a twenty-centimetre blade, strapped to his shin.

He didn't carry the knife idly, either. It wasn't for him to take out just for show, to try and scare people off with. He knew how to handle it and could do so with great skill. Before becoming a Deacon, Hardscree had been a huntsman. He had been born and raised in the Pale Uplands, that mountainous region where tracking and killing wild game wasn't a sport, it was a way of life. Hardscree was lethally accurate with a bow and arrow. He could hit a bullseye at a hundred paces. And he was no less deft with a knife. Once, he had skewered a rock hare from over sixty metres away, hurling the knife so that the blade impaled the fleeing creature in the back of the head, ending its life instantly.

Many times in his recent travels Hardscree had been underestimated by irate, indignant citizens. They thought that because he had spent much of his life in a Chancel, he was soft and pampered – an easy target.

They'd been wrong.

And this man was about to learn the same lesson, if he wasn't careful.

'Hello,' said Hardscree evenly. 'I'm afraid I've finished preaching for the day. I plan on holding another meeting tomorrow if you're interested. Perhaps you should come back then.'

'I be'n't after listening to your Deaconish jabber,' said the man, striding up the aisle between the rows of chairs. 'I want to know one thing, and that'm why you be stirring up all this trouble and getting folk to attack my *Bertha*.'

'Your ...' Hardscree deduced what he was referring to. 'Ah. The murkcomber.'

'Yes, the murk-comber,' growled the man. 'Where d'you get off, rabblerousing like that? Us has had enough trouble from your sort in the past, and here you come along raking up bad feeling again and preying on people's fears, and I won't have it!'

The man halted just a few metres from Hardscree. His fists were clenched and his body was quiveringly rigid. Hardscree assessed him carefully, thinking that the man had once been larger and sturdier than he was now. His clothes hung loosely off his frame. There was an unhealthy sallowness to his complexion. Once upon a time, Hardscree might have been wary of getting into a ruckus with this fellow, knife or no knife. As it was, he knew he'd have no difficulty subduing him, if it came to that.

But Hardscree didn't want it to come to that. The man seemed to deserve his pity rather than his hostility.

'Your name?' he enquired. 'At least let's introduce ourselves before this goes any further.'

The man blinked. 'Grubdollar. Den Grubdollar.'

'Pleased to meet you, Den. I'm Gerald Hardscree.'

He held out his hip flask.

'Fancy a nip?' he asked.

CHAPTER 19

Waking Up From A Long Dream

Den hesitated, then reached for the small, brushed steel container. It was almost a reflex. Someone politely offered you a drink, you accepted. At the same time he was confused by his own response. He'd come here to harangue the Deacon and maybe knock him around a little bit. Not give him a serious beating, just vent some frustration and indignation on him, a bruise here, a scuff there. Perhaps smash up a few of his chairs.

But now he wasn't even sure why he wanted to do that. It had struck him as a good idea when he learned about *Bertha* getting bombarded with stones, and he had felt a wonderful clear-headedness as he stormed out of the house and out of town. For the first time in ages he had something to aim at, something to do, a purpose. He'd felt as though he was waking up from a long dream.

And then, this.

He was abruptly deflated, empty. His fingers closed around the hip flask. He unscrewed the cap and took a swig. It was good whisky. Single malt, if he didn't miss his guess. Quality stuff.

A Deacon who drank whisky? Wine, maybe. That was a typical Deacon's sort of tipple. Port too, and brandy. But whisky?

'I'm from the Pale Uplands,' said Hardscree, as if reading his thoughts. 'Whisky's like water there. As babies we have a drop of it in our milk every night, or so it's said. I'm not convinced that's healthy but I imagine it ensures a good night's sleep for everyone, baby *and* parents.' He chuckled, then went serious. 'Now listen, about your murk-comber – I'd like to say sorry and ask your forgiveness. It was an unfortunate episode and I didn't mean for it to happen.'

'Yes? Really?' said Den. Half-consciously he took another swig from the hip flask.

'It all took place after I'd finished preaching. Everyone had left the tent and by the time I realised what was going on, it was too late. I shouted at them to stop but no one heard. For what it's worth, your murk-comber retaliated. Gave as good as she got. Chaff, smoke – it was pretty funny to watch, as a matter of fact. There were some sore feelings afterwards, I can tell you, but I managed to soothe egos and convince everyone that they had had it coming. You needn't fear any reprisals.'

'Still, none of it would have happened in the first place if you hadn't got those folk all so fired up with your speechifying and pontificating,' Den said.

'I agree. Guilty as charged. That's why I'm apologising.'

Den was more confused than ever. The Deacon seemed entirely sincere. That alone set him apart from every other Deacon he had encountered before. As a rule, a Deacon wouldn't know sincerity if it came up and bit him on the well-fleshed backside.

The other thing that distinguished this one was that hair of his. Like fire, it was. Den found himself mesmerised by it. He'd never seen hair quite so red, although he had heard it was a common feature of folk from the Uplands.

He cleared his throat. 'Well. Hmph. Apology accepted, I suppose. No real harm done. Not to *Bertha* at any rate. Them Airborn who was on board, them was all right too, apparently. Bit shaken, bit peeved, but no bruises, no bones broken. It'm just . . .'

'Yes?'

'Us has had some bad experiences with mobs and rabble-rousers here in Grimvale. Not so long ago . . . but you probably know the tale. Most folk does.'

Hardscree gave a nod. 'The Grimvale Humanist uprising. It was the catalyst, the reason why everything's the way it is now.'

'So you see, I fancied you was another Alan Steamarm. But you be'n't. You'm just another wandering Deacon.'

'From the way you said that,' said Hardscree, 'I take it you're no fan of Deacons.'

Den seesawed a hand in the air. 'Fair to middling about they. My son, see, my eldest boy . . . him were . . . him died. Died in a fight with a Deacon. A bad man, that Deacon were. Rotten and corrupt and, it turned out, insane. Martin, my son, died stopping he from doing something that'd've killed a whole load of people. No question, that were a reason worth dying for. But if it hadn't been for that Deacon, Martin'd still be . . . be alive.'

Deacon Hardscree gestured to a chair. Den accepted the invitation and sat. For a while he couldn't speak. He was lost in a swirl of memories, painful ones, guilt-ridden ones. Everything he had been brooding on and tormenting himself with this past year boiled up inside him. He tipped some more whisky down his throat without even thinking about it. What if he had got to the Chancel sooner on that dreadful day? What if he had been able to locate Martin in the furnace chamber? Would he have been able to save him? Couldn't he have sacrificed *himself* in the struggle with Deacon Shatterlonger? Wouldn't that have been infinitely better, him dying instead of Martin? Sons should bury their fathers, not the other way round.

And all at once Den was crying – crying so hard he could barely draw breath. Sobs coughed out of him. Tears coursed down his cheeks, burning like acid.

He felt helpless and hopeless. The impulse that had brought him to the Deacon's marquee had vanished utterly. It had been like a struck match, flaring briefly then gone.

He didn't know anything any more except his own grief and remorse.

He felt a hand on his shoulder.

'Tell me more, Den,' said Hardscree. 'Tell me everything.'

CHAPTER 20

'People Need Mystery'

The kerosene lantern guttered and hissed. More insects perished, drawn to its incandescence, flying too near, dying on singed wings. Outside the marquee, the clouded night was dark and still.

Much of what Den had to say was stuff Hardscree was already familiar with. The events at Grimvale had already entered into history, and into folklore as well. All across the world, people told one another about the Humanist siege of the Chancel and the arrival of the Airborn which quelled it, and with each telling they added their own invented details, their own embroiderings, and so the story mutated and got more complicated and grew.

Archdeacon Corbelgilt's book contained its own version of what had happened, although the account Corbelgilt gave was one-sided and concentrated less on description and more on criticism. Treachery! Outrage! Desecration! Those were the sort of terms Corbelgilt used, exclamation marks included.

Like Corbelgilt, Den had first-hand experience. He'd been an eyewitness to the events. He'd participated. And like Corbelgilt he had paid for his involvement, although far more dearly than the Archdeacon. In the end Corbelgilt had been deprived of luxury and prestige, whereas for Den the price of being caught up in the Grimvale Humanist uprising was nothing less than the loss of his eldest child.

Hardscree listened to him recount the whole tragic tale. Every so often he would stumble over some particularly difficult recollection, such as his arguments with Martin over Martin's Humanist beliefs. Hardscree would then coax the next portion of the story out of him with a soft query or two: *How did you feel about that? Do you think you can explain yourself a little better?*

Finally there was no more to tell. Den was left hoarse, drained, and somewhat bewildered.

'Never said it all like that before,' he said. 'Never been over the whole lot in one go, from start to finish. And telling it to a complete stranger, what'm more.'

'Sometimes it's easier talking to a stranger than to friends or kin,' said Hardscree. 'There's less at stake emotionally. You can open up without fear of hurting someone's feelings or irritating them or boring them or whatever.'

'But you'm a Deacon and all.'

'And I can see you'd have every reason to resent what I am. However, from what you said earlier I'm guessing that you feel, in a way, that Deacons aren't altogether a bad thing.'

'It'm odd, but I's always had the impression that us needed you lot. Personally speaking, I needed you, my family needed you, because us used to make a living off of you. But more'n that, us *all* needed you, all of us "Groundlings", as us is supposed to call ourselves these days. Us all needed you to be there between we and them lot above the clouds. A kind of . . . curtain, I suppose. A human curtain. Someone to keep the mystery a mystery.'

'People need mystery in their lives.'

'Exactly! Bless my bum, that'm just the phrase for it. People need mystery. And that be'n't there any more. Us meets the Ascended Ones all the time now. Us knows they on a personal basis. Us sees they, and them's much like we, apart from the, you know.' He mimed having wings on his back. 'Them may be a bit more highfaluting than most of we, and I won't deny that as a rule them's better-looking too. Not more handsome but just more . . .' He groped for a word to describe the Airborn's general appearance.

'Groomed?' Hardscree suggested.

'That'll do. Groomed, yes. Clipped fingernails, nicer clothing, suntans, all that. But still, them's just people. My daughter be pretty good pals with one, him's a good kid.'

'That's Az, right? The one you mentioned. The wingless Airborn boy.'

'That'm he. And the simple fact that her and him can be friends – it makes things all a bit too normal, you know what I mean?'

'You preferred it when you believed we could Ascend after death and become reincarnated as winged people and live a glorious second life in the sky-cities.'

'Yes. No. I were never too sure about it either way. It seemed kind of unlikely. A bit too far-fetched. But I felt it were important that us did believe it anyway, because then this life in this grey world where the sun never quite shines – it were bearable. It were like the savoury course of a meal, the part you have to get through so's you can then have the sweet. Do that make sense?'

'It makes an admirable amount of sense.'

'Don't get me wrong. The world weren't perfect the way it used to be. For starters, it were clear you Deacons were taking advantage of everyone else. You exploited we and you looked after what you had very carefully.'

Hardscree gave a shrug that said he agreed.

'You admit it?'

'Freely, Den. I was never comfortable with that aspect of our lifestyle. In my own Chancel I often clashed with the Archdeacon about all the creature comforts we surrounded ourselves with. I argued that we should be more restrained and self-denying. It would set a better example to everyone on the outside. But my Archdeacon never saw it that way, and I spent many a week in the Contrition Cells to atone for the sin of openly challenging him.'

'Know what?' said Den, looking Hardscree in the eye. 'I reckon you did and all.'

'Let me tell you, Den,' Hardscree went on, earnestly. 'You're not alone. I've travelled far and wide since I and all the other Deacons were thrown out of our Chancels, and everywhere I've been I've come across people who think the same as you, although few have expressed themselves anywhere near as concisely and even-handedly as you have. I've spoken with fishermen on the Granite Coast and farmworkers up on the Plains of Silence. I've met mayors and miners, manufacturers and musicians. I've pitched my tent outside countless cities, towns and villages, and preached to audiences as small as one and as large as a hundred and had their feedback afterwards. And what I've heard from them is what I'm hearing from you. "OK, the world wasn't perfect beforehand, but it's even further from being perfect now."'

Hardscree paused there, to make sure he had Den's full attention.

'But you know what?' he carried on. 'I think it could be perfect after all.'

CHAPTER 21

High Spirits

Later, Den traipsed homeward. The road was dark but he had the distant, glimmering lights of the township to guide him. He reached his house without difficulty, and once indoors he let his anxious children make a fuss of him.

'You's been gone for hours, Da.'

'You'm all right?'

'Us was worried. You said not to follow and us didn't, but the way you rushed off, it were hard to know what to make of it.'

'You didn't get into any trouble, did you?'

'Kids,' Den said.

The firmness in his voice, and the serenity, surprised them. But it was a pleasant surprise. Fletcher, Cassie and Robert looked at their father and realised that somehow, by some miracle, their old dad was back. He had gone off to remonstrate with the Deacon and had returned fuller-faced and brighter-eyed. He even looked a little taller than before. They hardly dared believe that he was himself again, but they could not deny the evidence of their own eyes.

'Kids,' he said again. 'I been a useless old lump lately. Don't say no. You know I has. No good to you nor anybody. That'm all done with. Never going to happen again.'

'What did you do with the Deacon, Da?' Robert asked. 'You give he a thrashing?'

'What went on between I and that remarkably red-headed fellow be my business. All I want you to know be that I love you, always has, always will, and thanks for putting up with I being such a miserable mope for so damn long. Like I said, never going to happen again. Straight up.'

'Oh, Da!' said Cassie, and leapt on him and planted a fierce kiss on his stubbly cheek.

'Now, how about us takes some of that hard-earned of yours and buys ourselves dinner at the Hole and Shovel? I know about saving money for our overheads and debts and that, but when were the last time us ate out? When were the last time us actually went out for a nice meal like an ordinary family? Let's *live* a little.'

It was late but food was still being served at the Hole and Shovel,

Grimvale's largest pub-cum-restaurant. The Grubdollars clustered around a table in the snug, and ordered pies, cake and beer. A band was playing jigs and reels in the next room, and the music spilled out through the doorway, jaunty and bright, a sound like a ray of hope. The food and drink arrived, and the Grubdollars pounced on it and devoured. Then, with gorged bellies, they sat back and chatted and bantered. For a time, they were once again a close-knit family unit.

'Cass and Fletch made I mop up Airborn puke!' Robert complained at one point. 'Why should I have to clean up Airborn puke? Be'n't fair. Tell they, Da. Tell they it be'n't fair.'

His father just laughed.

Back home, the three Grubdollar siblings went to bed in high spirits. Cassie in particular hadn't felt so optimistic in ages. Was it possible – just possible – that everything was going to be OK after all?

The next morning, she, Fletcher and Robert woke up to discover that their father wasn't there.

His bed had not been slept in. Clothes were missing from his wardrobe. His boots weren't where they should have been, at the top of the spiral staircase.

There was no note, or at least none that anybody could find in the house. He had left behind no indication of where he was off to or for how long or why.

He had simply slipped out of the house sometime during the night.

He had left.

Disappeared.

Gone.

CHAPTER 22

The Big Day

The wedding of Michael Gabrielson and Aurora Jukarsdaughter went smoothly, much to the relief of the bridegroom's mother. Ramona Gabrielson spent almost the entire day in the state of agitation, fretting over every single stage of the proceedings from the moment the High Haven Assembly Hall opened its doors to guests to the moment the newlyweds departed in Michael's helicopter (with ribbons and tin cans dangling from the undercarriage and a JUST MARRIED banner strung across the fuselage, courtesy of Az).

Mrs Gabrielson's nerves were not helped by the fact that Lady Aanfieldsdaughter was an invitee to the occasion, along with a number of other Silver Sanctum dignitaries and several members of management from Aerodyne. She feared that with such illustrious guests present, something was bound to go wrong and embarrass her. But Lady Aanfieldsdaughter, as if realising this, made a point of coming up to her just before the start of the ceremony and saying that the decorations looked marvellous and it was clear that every last detail had been taken care of. This did much to put Mrs Gabrielson's mind at rest.

And nothing did go wrong.

The ceremony itself was simple and beautiful. A local official intoned the rites. Rings were exchanged, and Michael and Aurora screened themselves behind their wings for their first, tender kiss as husband and wife. Meanwhile the close-harmony choir soared, and their voices soared too, filling the hall with song.

Then there was the traditional feather-blessing as the newlyweds wafted down the aisle. Each guest plucked a single feather from his or her wings and tossed it towards the happy couple. Az's father gave Az one of his own to use. Michael and Aurora passed hand in hand through a blizzard of slow-tumbling white down.

The reception was held at one of High Haven's fanciest restaurants, the Panorama. Encircled by views of nothing but sky, the guests tucked into sparrow pâté, honeyed duck breast, eggs Elysian and cloudberry ice cream. To wash it down there was wine from the Silver Sanctum vineyards, generously donated by Aurora's employers.

The speeches were good, and also short, which meant the guests paid attention and the less polite ones didn't start to yawn or heckle. Gabriel Enochson found himself too choked up with emotion to do much more than welcome his new daughter-in-law into the family and drop a broad hint about grandchildren. 'Look at me. How many more years do you think I've got? I can't hang on for ever.' To which Aurora, in her speech, replied that she and Michael would strive their utmost to see that he wasn't disappointed. She added that, having lost her own mother and father while she was young, she couldn't think of two people better suited to be her new parents than Gabriel and Ramona.

When Az's turn came, he had the room in stitches. He'd been nervous but as soon as he stood up and began speaking, the butterflies in his stomach vanished. If the purpose of a best man's speech was to keep everybody laughing, then unquestionably Az succeeded.

'I'm not here to make Michael look stupid,' he said. 'He's perfectly capable of doing that himself.'

And: 'I doubt Michael could love Aurora more – unless she was an AtmoCorp double-prop Bladecopter with radial fins, walnut dash, silver-chase detailing and flush-mounted teardrop undercarriage.'

And also: 'I can't possibly reveal what my brother's nickname at school was. He'd hate you to know that he was called Mike the Mirror because he used to spend all of break time in the boys' toilets getting his hair right.'

Not to mention: 'It's been said that marriage is a meeting of opposites. In which case, no wonder Aurora is beautiful, brainy, talented and thought-ful.'

'You are so dead,' Michael said mock-menacingly to Az during the applause afterwards. 'When I come back from our honeymoon, you'd better have found a good place to hide because I am going to hunt you down and kill you!'

'Az, I feel you and I need to have a chat sometime about my husband,' said Aurora. 'I'm already starting to think I may have made a mistake.'

'See, little brother? That's why I'm going to kill you.'

Then came the cutting of the cake, and following that the guests rose from their tables and mingled.

Lady Aanfieldsdaughter sought out Az.

'Excellent speech,' she said. 'Very droll.'

'Thanks.'

'I was expecting to see Cassie here today.'

'She couldn't make it.'

'Ah. Any reason why not?'

'Just . . . you know. Hard for Groundlings, being up here for any length of time.'

'Quite. A pity, though. I was looking forward to catching up with her.

340

Seeing how things are for her. I think fondly of Cassie and I'd like to believe she feels the same way about me.'

'Um, yeah. Yeah, she does.'

'She helped us so much, didn't she?'

'That she did.'

Lady Aanfielsdaughter's bright blue eyes narrowed. 'I'm getting the impression this isn't a thread of conversation you particularly want to follow.'

'No, no, it's not that.'

'What, then?'

Az racked his brains to figure out why he found it so uncomfortable talking to Lady Aanfielsdaughter. It wasn't anything to do with Cassie. He realised it was because he had crouched on the balcony outside Lady Aanfielsdaughter's office the day before yesterday, snooping like a spy. Guilt gnawed at him. He regretted what he'd done now and he wanted to confess to her about it but couldn't. She would be shocked and disappointed.

Lady Aanfielsdaughter decided not the press the matter. Instead, she peered across the roomful of guests and said, 'Oh look. There's an old acquaintance of mine. I must go over and say hello. Nice to see you, Az. Again, a fine speech. And well done on gaining such a worthy sister-in-law. Aurora will adorn your family.'

It was a neat, diplomatic way out of an awkward impasse. With relief, Az watched her ladyship flit off.

He spent the rest of the day avoiding Lady Aanfielsdaughter, and she managed not to bump into him either. Meanwhile, he continued to play his part as best man and bridegroom's brother. He chortled at a distant cousin's rude joke and let a blowsy great-aunt smother him with affection and the reek of too much perfume. He also dealt with the relatives from the further branches of his extended family who never quite knew how to feel about his lack of wings. Some pitied him and couldn't help letting it show; others strenuously tried to stick to topics of conversation that had nothing to do with wings and usually ended up talking about exactly that and stumbling horribly. Az faced them all with a tactful, patient smile.

There were plenty of guests who demanded he give them an account of his adventures down on the ground. He was used to telling the story now and could rattle it off in his sleep. The novelty of being famous had worn off long ago but he understood that other people were interested in what he had done, so he didn't treat them with disdain or an air of boredom. He answered their questions and modestly brushed aside their praise and their awe.

Throughout, he kept an eye out for Cassie, although he knew she wasn't going to come. He hoped she'd been delayed by some unexpected hitch.

He hoped she would put in a last-minute appearance. But at the same time he was reconciled to the fact that neither she nor her family were going to show up.

It told him what he needed to know and yet didn't want to know.

The next day, he was up at dawn and waiting out on the house's landing platform with a packed bag. The gyro-cab which was booked to take him to Prismburg could not have arrived too soon.

CHAPTER 23

A Fruitless Search

The Grubdollar siblings turned Grimvale upside down looking for their father.

On foot, Fletcher and Robert checked all of Den's known haunts – pubs, friends' houses, the skittles alley, even the bluff in the hills above town where he and their mother had courted. It was one of his favourite spots, somewhere he used to go when his mood turned melancholy and he wanted to recall happy times with his wife, when they were both young and nothing mattered more to them than each other. He wasn't there now.

Cassie, meanwhile, gave herself the job of searching further afield. She clambered into *Bertha* and started her up.

Or rather, tried to start her up.

With every press of the ignition button *Bertha* remained stubbornly silent. Not a cough, not a whine, not so much as a titter came from her, and certainly no cackle.

A quick rummage under the engine cowling identified the problem. *Bertha*'s distributor cap had been neatly removed and placed to one side. Without the distributor cap to direct the charge from the battery to the sparkplugs, *Bertha* wasn't going anywhere.

'Sabotaged she,' Cassie said to herself, her brow knitting in perplexed annoyance. 'How could you, Da? And why didn't you do a proper job of it, if you didn't want we to follow you?'

She picked up the dome-shaped cap in order to reconnect the wires. As she did so, something fell out of the cap: a small piece of paper, folded into a tight wad.

Cassie opened up the piece of paper. It was a note, and straight away she recognised the handwriting as her father's.

The note said:

Kids,
So sorry about this. I won't be gone long. You just carry on without I. I be off looking for a needle in a haystack. Which'm another way of saying I be looking for hope.
All my love,
Da

Cassie read the note several times and still couldn't understand what it meant, particularly that reference to a 'needle in a haystack'. What she did understand was that that her father had placed the note inside the distributor cap for a purpose. He was making a point. By removing the cap to disable *Bertha* (if only fleetingly), he was warning his family not to go searching for him.

That made Cassie all the more determined to do so.

She reattached the distributor cap wires, started *Bertha* up and trundled off through the outskirts of Grimvale, pausing to ask anyone she passed if they had seen her father. No one had. Eventually she made her way out to the Chancel. She couldn't imagine what reason the old man would have to go in that direction, but this was how desperate she was becoming.

No sign of him there. No sign of him anywhere.

Meeting up back at the house with Fletcher and Robert, she showed them the note. Together they racked their brains to fathom what it meant, and couldn't come up with an answer.

'Let's go over everything us knows,' Fletcher suggested. 'Might help. Last night Da went off to see that Deacon, then him came home and him were back to normal. His old self again.'

'In hindsight,' Robert said, 'anyone else reckon that were kind of odd? One moment Da's all doom and gloom, next him's all sweetness and light. Like somebody threw a big switch inside he.'

''Cause him took it out on the Deacon, that'm my theory,' Fletcher said. 'All the stuff inside that was bothering he. Sort of like squeezing a zit.'

'Squeezing a zit?' said Cassie.

'Yeah. All the pus and gunk spurted out.'

'Who'm the zit?' Robert wanted to know. 'Da? The Deacon?'

'No, the zit's the feelings inside Da.'

'So who were squeezing it? The Deacon?'

'No, it were — Oh, never mind. I were just drawing a parallel.'

'Bad one,' Robert muttered.

'Yeah?' said Fletcher, bristling. 'Well, pardon I for making an effort. Pardon I for trying to understand what might be going through Da's mind so's us can figure out where him's got to and why him doesn't want we knowing. Just trying to help, that'm all. But maybe you has some better idea, Bobby-boy. Being as you's clearly so much smarter'n I.'

'Never said I were smarter,' his brother replied. He was becoming annoyed too. One of Robert's pet hates was being called Bobby-boy, which, of course, was why Fletcher had called him that. 'But at least I be'n't talking gibberish about zits and pus and that.'

'No, you'm talking about big switches instead. That makes *so* much more sense.'

'Boys,' Cassie snapped. 'Enough. Bickering won't get we anywhere. For what it'm worth, I reckon there be truth in what both of you's saying. Obviously this comes down to the Deacon. But maybe it weren't something Da did to he, maybe it were something *him* did to Da.'

'Such as?'

'Not sure, Fletch. But I can tell you that his marquee be'n't there any more. I passed the spot in *Bertha* on my way to the Chancel. It'm gone, every last guy-rope and pole of it, and his van too.'

'You think Da and the Deacon has gone off *together*?'

'I be beginning to think it'm the only logical explanation.'

'But Da hates Deacons!' Robert said.

'But remember what him said last night when him came back? You asked if him'd given the man a thrashing, and Da replied, "That'm my business", or something more or less like that. Which weren't a no but neither were it a yes.'

'Da trotting off with one of them black-robed bilge-spouters,' Fletcher said wonderingly. 'Don't seem real. What if, instead, the Deacon kidnapped he?'

'Our da? Kidnapped? Never. Him'd never let it happen. Besides, the facts don't fit. Him left the house of his own accord. There weren't no struggle. And the note makes it clear him went off because him wanted to.'

'All right, not kidnapped then. Bad choice of word. *Persuaded.*'

'Yes,' Cassie said, slowly nodding. 'Those be my thoughts. Not liking to think they, but thinking they all the same. This Deacon somehow talked Da into heading off somewhere with he, to find this so-called needle in a haystack, whatever that actually be.'

'So if him doesn't want we coming after he,' said Robert, 'shouldn't us respect his wishes?'

'Nope,' said his sister firmly. 'Not if him's fallen under the Deacon's sway. That'd be —'

She was interrupted by a shout from the storage area at the bottom of the spiral staircase.

'Yoo-hoo! Grubdollars!'

It was Colin Amblescrut. They heard his heavy tread on the stairs, and then his melon-like head appeared above floor-level, followed by the rest of him.

'I banged on the front gate,' he said. 'No answer, so I let myself in. Thought perhaps you was still out and about and I'd wait for you to come home.'

'You know us has been out and about?' Cassie said.

''Course!' said Colin, beaming proudly. 'Be'n't much that goes on in this town that my family don't know about. The Amblescrut web's been

CHAPTER 24

Loaded For Battle

No sooner did Az get a glimpse of *Cerulean* than he knew that she had been modified. The airship had gained a number of add-ons which would have been almost undetectable to the untrained eye but which Az spotted immediately.

She bobbed at her moorings, a great oval of pale blue, with Prismburg's sun-shot glass towers and apartment blocks forming a gleaming, iridescent backdrop behind her. In her size and ponderous majesty she was unchanged.

However, set beneath the tip of her control gondola there was now a fan of small, forward-pointing steel tubes, which Az had a pretty good idea were grappling hook launchers; and just above her nose-cone a kind of gun had been mounted, one which – if Az knew anything about aerial warfare, and he did – fired bolas shells, weighted knots of steel cable that would snarl up an enemy airship's propellers and rudders.

'You've been busy,' he said as Mr Mordadson picked him up from the landing apron and carried him aboard.

'Haven't slept a wink in forty-eight hours,' came the reply. 'I've been charging around like a blue-bottomed bluebottle and I'm absolutely exhausted.'

'Where did it all come from? The weaponry?'

'Museums mostly. I had to call in a lot of favours and wave my Silver Sanctum seal under a lot of noses, but it got results.'

'And does it really all work? If those weapons have been mouldering in museums for decades, surely they'll have seized up and rusted.'

'We've overhauled them and greased them and replaced the parts that needed replacing. They've tested fine.'

'Well, maybe we won't have to use them anyway. Maybe we can get the pirates to back down simply by turning up in *Cerulean*. A show of strength.'

'Maybe, Az, and I admire your optimism, even if I don't share it. For which reason, I'm not relying on weaponry alone. I have a back-up plan.'

'Which is?'

'You'll see.'

Az did as soon as they entered by the aft hatch. A squadron of Alar Patrollers were billeted in the airship's cabins. For the first time since she was decommissioned all those years ago, Troop-Carrier *Cerulean* was carrying troops again.

One Patroller had quadruple-grooved gold wing hoops, indicating that he was a wing commander. He snapped a brisk salute at Mr Mordadson. Mr Mordadson returned the military gesture with a civilian one, a touch of finger to forehead. The wing commander went back to polishing his lance.

'That's Iaxson,' Mr Mordadson said. 'Good man. We were at Alar cadet academy together. He's in charge of the Patrollers and he answers to me. You should get to know him. You'll like him.'

Az wasn't so sure. Iaxson had a pinched, wary look about him, like that of a man who always saw the worst in people and refused to try to see anything else.

Down in the control gondola, a far kinder face was waiting to greet him. Captain Qadoschson clasped Az's hand in both of his and shook it warmly.

'A bit out of the ordinary, this, eh?' he said. 'Not the usual four-hour there-and-back with a load of daytrippers. Quite something else altogether.'

The crew were at their stations. Az returned their welcoming glances, pleased to see them. It had been nearly two months since his last visit to Primsburg. In the run-up to the wedding he hadn't been free to pop over and join *Cerulean* on one of her regular tourist outings. He'd missed being aboard the airship and he'd missed her crew, whom he counted as friends.

With one exception. A man whose absence in the gondola Az quickly noted, as he would have noted a rotten tooth that had at last been pulled.

'Is Flight Lieutenant Wallimson not here?' he asked the captain.

He was hoping the answer to his casual-sounding enquiry would be something like: *Oh no, Wallimson won't be coming with us today. In fact, we had to get rid of him.*

Instead, disappointingly, the answer was: 'He should be. I've no idea where he's got to. Notoriously unreliable fellow, as you know.' Qadoschson consulted his watch. 'Still, there's half an hour before cast off. I'm sure he'll make it.'

Az made a noncommittal sound, halfway between *ah* and *hmph*. It had been a nice thought that he wouldn't have to put up with Wallimson on the trip to Redspire, but that hope was now dashed. Oh well. You had to take the rough with the smooth, as the saying went, and in this case that meant Az had to accept that the pleasure of flying in *Cerulean* also brought with it the surly attitude of Captain Qadoschson's second-in-command. Unfortunately, he couldn't have one without the other.

He took the opportunity to quiz Qadoschson about various technical matters such as payload size and pressure height. This was so that he would have all the relevant data for this particular flight at his fingertips. If he was well-informed on *Cerulean*'s operational status, then Flight Lieutenant Wallimson, when he turned up, would have fewer excuses to criticise him or catch him out.

'I take it we'll be doing shifts,' he said once he had gleaned what he needed from the captain. 'Rotating command between you and Wallimson, with me pitching in between the two of you. I could oversee a skeleton crew at night, perhaps, if we're night-running.'

Captain Qadoschson turned to Mr Mordadson with a frown. 'You mean you didn't tell him?'

'Tell me what?' Az asked.

Mr Mordadson just smiled.

'Az,' said Qadoschson, 'all I'm here to do is supervise the arming and loading. Make sure everything's put together properly.'

'You're not coming with us?'

'I'm no spring chicken,' the captain said. 'I've a few too many grey hairs on my head and not all the feathers I should have on my wings. Time was, I'd have happily taken *Cerulean* out for a week or so. It would have been a treat. An adventure. But these days, at my age, I'm more of an early-to-bed-with-a-cup-of-cocoa kind of chap. Then there's the fact that we have weapons and Patrollers on board, with everything that that implies. We all know what could be waiting for us down at Redspire and, well, frankly I can't see myself taking part in that sort of malarkey. I'm too old and too tired and too keen on enjoying the life I have left. I made all this clear to Mr Mordadson the moment he got in contact with me. I told him I'd help outfit the old girl. I'd help him source weaponry for her. I'd see she had what she required. But as for actually captaining her ...' He shook his head.

Az's heart sank. 'So Lieutenant Wallimson's in charge?'

It was too awful to contemplate. *Captain* Wallimson?

Az could just see what was going to happen. Wallimson had taken a dislike to him almost from the outset, and it was obvious why. He felt Az was a threat. Qadoschson made no secret of favouring Az over him. Wallimson regarded Az as a usurper, someone who was after his job.

Without Qadoschson there, Wallimson would no longer have to confine himself to harsh stares and snide, just-audible comments. As captain, he could say and do whatever he wanted. He could give his spite for Az free rein. Az would be lucky if Wallimson let him take charge of *Cerulean* for even a minute. More likely, he would have him priming ballast tanks or unblocking latrines the whole way.

Az wanted to get off the airship right now. Forget the mission. Wallimson, captain? Having to answer to *him*? Follow *his* orders? No way.

'No,' said Qadoschson. 'Not Wallimson.'

'Who, then?' said Az, perplexed. 'Who's got the job? One of the crew?'

Mr Mordadson's smile broadened and sharpened.

'Isn't it obvious, lad?' said Captain Qadoschson. 'You have.'

CHAPTER 25

Feather First!

Prismburg received a higher than average number of Groundling visitors. There were three reasons for this. One: it was close to one of the largest and populous cities on the ground, Craterhome. Two: its architecture was a visual marvel. And three: *Cerulean* was berthed there, and Groundlings were keen for a glimpse of the famous and, until now, one and only Airborn airship.

Equipped with breathing-apparatus kits, Groundlings ascended by elevator, toured the sky-city via its walkways and bridges, and returned to the ground full of tales to tell their friends and families. The way the refractive-panelled walls of the buildings shone in every colour. The brightness of the sun and sky, so dazzling it hurt the eyes. The birdsong that in certain places was deafeningly raucous. The graciousness of the Airborn guides who ushered you around.

However, not every Groundling could manage the long journey up and back down in the elevators. Only the fit and healthy could endure the slow reduction in air pressure, which sometimes hurt the ears, and use the breathing apparatus, which could tax even the strongest of lungs. If Groundlings wished for a glimpse of how the other half lived, they had to be in good shape, not too old, not too young, with no history of respiratory problems. They had to be resilient and hardy.

Nevertheless those who could come came. They saw. They admired. And mostly they went home again happy, convinced it had been worth the effort.

Mostly.

Unless they happened to run foul of a group of Feather First!ers. That could soon sour the experience for them.

The majority of Feather First! demonstrations took place on six-way street corners or on public plazas and were relatively restrained affairs. Slogans were chanted. Placards were waved. GROUNDLINGS DOWN! AIR FOR THE AIRBORN! IF YOU CAN'T FLY, DON'T DROP BY! Traffic flow might be interrupted; ordinary sky-citizens might be inconvenienced; that was all.

Groundlings seldom got to witness these demos. They didn't occur often and they didn't last too long.

The Feather First! guerrilla protests, though, were a different matter.

On this day in Prismburg, for instance, a six-strong Groundling tour party was making its way along the prearranged route, heading towards Vitreous Park. Escorting the six were a pair of Airborn guides. The Groundlings were gazing around in wonderment and awe. They had the latest design of breathing-apparatus kits on. These were more comfortable than the old ones, with lightweight oxygen tanks and masks that covered just the nose and mouth rather than the entire face. In addition they were wearing tinted goggles, to protect their eyes from a degree of sunlight they simply weren't used to.

They were enjoying themselves. Everything was going fine.

Then, out of nowhere, a dozen Feather First!ers homed in. They encircled the Groundlings and began yelling insults.

'Emus!'

'Ostriches!'

'Go home! Go back down to your shabby hovels and stay there!'

Not content with that, the Feather First!ers began chucking handfuls of soil at the Groundlings. Dirt granules showered down on their heads. The Groundlings ducked and swore.

The guides rose to remonstrate with the Feather First!ers. They told them to stop. This was not the way to treat guests.

But the Feather First!ers just carried on. The guides tried to drive them away, but they were only two and the protestors were many. Each could tackle only one protestor at a time, which left the others free to continue hurling insults and soil at the Groundlings.

They kept it up till the bags of soil they were carrying were empty. Then, their malicious stunt complete, they zoomed off. Afterwards the guides could only express regret and the Groundlings could only shake the dirt from their hair and try not to feel offended and degraded.

Among the group of Feather First!ers was a man in his mid-thirties who flew a little more slowly than the others and struggled to keep pace with them. This was due to one his wings, the left, being malformed. It was crooked at the arch and did not flap as efficiently as the right.

As a boy he had been hit by an airbus when crossing a street and had broken the wing. Doctors had set it but, despite their best efforts, the bones had not knitted properly. Intensive physiotherapy had also not helped. The wing had healed badly, and the doctors had shrugged and told him it was 'just one of those things' and he would have to live with it.

Possessing a lame wing had done little for this man's self-esteem and character. He did not like being different from everyone else, being *less*. He held a grudge against the world for it. Permanently bitter, he purged his resentment by taking it out on others. In recent months he had developed a particular loathing for Groundlings. Such ungainly creatures. Coarse and crude. Cluttering up Primsburg's bridges and walkways. Stomping along.

The soil protest had been his idea. There was a pleasing symmetry to it, he felt. Sprinkling Groundlings with stuff from the ground.

Now, he called out to the other Feather First!ers. 'Good work, everyone,' he said. 'Well done. We'll meet up again soon. In the meantime, I'm running late. Must fly!'

With that, he parted company from them, banking left down a narrow alleyway which was a shortcut to the city's perimeter.

He knew he was cutting things fine, punctuality-wise. He would get into trouble for not being where he should be at the time he was supposed to be there. He didn't care, though. The guerrilla protest was worth any reprimand he would receive.

Besides, he wasn't looking forward to what lay ahead.

A lengthy trip in *Cerulean*.

With that little wingless plucker as captain!

Flight Lieutenant Wallimson's face hardened into a sneer as he wended his somewhat wonky way towards the docked airship.

CHAPTER 26

Leave-taking

As Wallimson entered the control gondola, Qadoschson gave him a withering look.

'Nice of you to show your face, lieutenant,' he said. 'Hope we weren't keeping you from anything important.'

'I was held up, sir. You know how hard it is for me to get around.' Wallimson flapped his bad wing feebly.

'Yet Az here hasn't got any wings at all, and he always manages to be on time. Funny, that.'

'Gabrielson is a better man than I am, captain. Clearly. After all, there's me with nine years of service on *Cerulean*, and yet *he* gets to take charge of the ship on this outing. A kid with less than a hundred hours of flying time under his belt, as opposed to a grown man with nearly a thousand.'

'Stop sulking, lieutenant. My decision is final, and I have the crew's full agreement. Don't I, men?'

The crew members assented.

'Aye-aye.'

'True enough, captain.'

They were as fond of Flight Lieutenant Wallimson as Az was.

'So let's not hear any more about this,' Qadoschson said to Wallimson. 'An order is an order. You are to regard Az as your commanding officer from now on and obey his every instruction and demand. Is that understood?'

Wallimson's reply came through clenched teeth. 'Perfectly, sir.'

Without so much as a glance at Az he stalked off to the forward viewing windows and stood there, grasping the brass handrail, his back hunched. You didn't have to be able to see his face to know he was scowling.

Az felt that, all in all, Qadoschson had let Wallimson off pretty lightly. The lieutenant had deserved a much more severe dressing-down than he had just received. Qadoschson probably hadn't wanted to antagonise him and deepen his resentment of Az. Still, Az sensed his and Wallimson's relationship wasn't going to get any sweeter in the foreseeable future.

'Az?' said Qadoschson.

'Sir?'

'*Cerulean*'s all yours. Look after her. Be as kind as you can with her.

And, if possible, do try and bring her back in one piece.'

'I will.'

Qadoschson took a last look around the control gondola, his lips pursed, his eyes wistful and tender. Then, with something like a sigh, he flapped up to the ceiling hatch and climbed through. Moments later Az caught sight of him out on the landing apron, gazing at his ship, hand to forehead in a salute.

'Right, men,' Az said, taking charge. 'Let's get cracking, shall we? Mooring lines detached and reeled in?'

'Aye-aye, sir. We're floating free.'

'Then give her quarter reverse thrust on the fore props.'

'Quarter reverse, aye-aye.'

Cerulean's engines started to hum. Gradually she began to pull back from Primsburg, although to Az it seemed more as if the sky-city was the one withdrawing, somehow shifting itself away from the airship. In the gut-knotting exhilaration of the moment, he felt that he was standing still and everything else was moving.

'Helmsman? Half a degree to starboard. Gently, gently. Easy does it.'

He uttered the commands with a calmness and confidence that surprised him. The launch procedures weren't new to him, but until today he had never had to execute them unaided, without Qadoschson at his shoulder, a reassuring presence. He realised that there was nothing to be afraid of. The crewmen were skilled, too, which helped. If he put a foot wrong, they would correct him.

'Bring thrust up to half. Disengage port fore prop. Engage starboard rear prop. Trim-master? Picking up some downward drift there. Fix it.'

'Aye-aye.'

Cerulean slowly came about. Presently the sky-city was behind them and there was nothing ahead but open sky.

Az glanced over at Mr Mordadson to see what he was making of the new captain's performance so far. But Mr Mordadson was sitting with his head canted against a bulkhead and his mouth agape, snoring softly.

'Take her up a hundred metres,' Az said. 'Let's sniff the jet stream currents, see which way they're running.'

The airship began to climb.

'And then,' he said, 'we plot a course for Redspire.'

CHAPTER 27

Desolation Wells Again

That night, the Airborn pirates returned for a second bite of the cherry.

This time, however, the cherry bit back.

Westward Oil Enterprises did not take kindly to having one of its assets raided and robbed. Magnus Clockweight's telegram to company headquarters had been received with astonishment and indignation in the boardroom, and also with consternation. WOE's executives were in a tricky position. Product had been stolen from them, and that was bad. But the people doing the stealing were Airborn and the executives found it hard to contemplate retaliation. The Airborn were everyone's new friends. More than that, they were officially WOE clients now. The company made money from them, as opposed to before, when half of its output had gone up the elevators for free. WOE's profit margins had swelled significantly since the Bilateral Covenant came into play. To fight back against the raiders would be to risk antagonising all the Airborn, and thus risk losing them as customers. The Airborn might decide to boycott Westward Oil Enterprises and take their business to another oil corporation.

All the same, the attack on Desolation Wells could not just be ignored and forgotten about.

So the executives did two things. First, they complained to the Airborn leadership through the proper channels. A message of protest was sent to the nearest Chancel, was relayed in letter format up via the elevators, and from there was transported by carrier dove to the Silver Sanctum. The reply followed the same route in reverse. It stated that the matter was being taken in hand and the culprits would be brought to justice. There were several signatures on the reply, including those of Lady Aanfieldsdaughter and Lord Urironson.

The WOE executives felt that this was satisfactory as far as it went. Their complaint had been noted and they had an assurance that it was being acted upon. Good.

But not good enough. Steps must be taken to show that a Westward Oil Enterprises extraction and refining installation was not a soft target. Nobody should be allowed to feel that they could swoop in and make off with a couple of hundred barrels of fuel any time they liked. It was just not on.

So the second thing the executives did was send a telegram to Desolation Wells, which read as follows:

```
INCIDENT OF ONE WEEK AGO MUST NOT BE REPEATED +
STOP + REASONABLE PRECAUTIONS ADVISED + STOP +
```

The message was very carefully worded, although it might not appear so. Nobody was saying that Magnus Clockweight and his team should do anything drastic or violent if provoked. Equally, nobody was saying they shouldn't.

The term for this was deniability. It was a corporate stratagem to provide a cover story for everyone involved. If something went wrong, the executives could blame the workforce for misinterpreting their instructions, the workforce could blame the executives for not making their intentions crystal clear, and that way no one had to take any actual responsibility.

Clockweight, at any rate, understood precisely what the suits in the boardroom were after. He knew he had been given carte blanche to defend Desolation Wells against the raiders if they came back, and defend it by whatever means he could manage.

So he and his men built a flamethrower.

A massive great flamethrower.

They took one of the installation's fire extinguisher trucks, drained the water from its tank, and filled it up with petrol instead. Thus a machine for stopping fires was transformed into a machine for starting them.

They tested the flamethrower out in the Relentless Desert. A pleasingly huge jet of burning liquid shot from the nozzle of the truck's hose. It arced fifty metres into the air, dripping small fiery gobbets onto the ground.

When *Behemoth* loomed once more from the night-dark clouds, the roughnecks were waiting and ready. This time Clockweight noticed the skull and crossed feathers on the airship's tailfins, visible even in the dark. He felt a surge of resentment, recalling that the pirates' leader bore the same motif on her chest. There was something aggravatingly brazen about it – the sheer shameless arrogance of it.

He tightened his grip on the control valve of the flamethrower.

Behemoth herself was too high to hit.

The pirates who emerged from her, however, were not.

As they came flying in towards the installation, Clockweight took aim and opened fire.

Literally opened fire.

He got three of the pirates with the first burst. They plummeted to the ground, spiralling down, wings burning.

The next few minutes were a frantic blur of driving and shooting. A colleague steered the truck crazily around, chasing after the scattering pirates. Meanwhile Clockweight, on the back, directed blast after blast of flame at them. At the same time, other roughnecks used portable, battery-powered searchlights to pinpoint the pirates in the sky and dazzle them. All of this took place some distance from the installation, of course, since it would have been madness to deploy the flamethrower on-site, near all that combustible material.

The flamethrower truck charged this way and that across the bumpy desert terrain, and the pirates darted this way and that overhead. Some attempted to attack the truck but Clockweight swung right and left, repelling them with devastatingly accurate shots.

In all, he brought down eleven of the pirates before *Behemoth*'s horn sounded, signalling retreat.

As the airship withdrew, the roughnecks whooped and cheered. Victory was theirs.

But only for now, Clockweight thought. The raiders would be back, and next time they'd be out for revenge. There was no real way of stopping them.

Unless, somehow, that airship could be destroyed.

CHAPTER 28

Coincidence And Bad Timing

'Explain to I once again, Colin, why you'm coming with we,' said Cassie. 'Just so's I be totally clear on it.'

Colin Amblescrut paused, about to load another carton of tinned food into *Bertha*.

'Den be my friend,' he said simply, then swung the carton effortlessly up to Fletcher, who was standing inside the murk-comber. Fletcher in turn passed the carton to Robert, who stacked it with others in a corner of *Bertha*'s loading bay. Both of them found the carton far heavier than the hulking, bulky Colin did.

'Also,' Colin added, 'I be the one who discovered where him's off to.'

'No, you didn't. You were told. It be'n't quite the same.'

Colin shrugged. 'Still and all. If I hadn't come and told you, you wouldn't have had a clue.'

'And,' Cassie went on, 'you doesn't know *exactly* where him and the Deacon is. All you said was them's headed out of town on the Craterhome road.'

'Yup.'

'And if it hadn't been for your relative – what'm his name?'

'John-John. My ma's aunt's brother-in-law's stepson.'

'If it hadn't been for he, you wouldn't have known at all. Now, you'm absolutely sure it were them him saw?'

'Absolutely. John-John were coming home from, er, from doing something near the Ridgerider farm, and an old half-tarp van passed he by. It were early in the morning and misty, but him got a good look at they inside, and it were definitely your da, and a Deacon alongside. John-John were with we during the attack on the Chancel. Him wouldn't mistake Den for anybody else. And as for the Deacon, him had the reddest hair John-John had ever seen, and as us all knows, that Deacon who were preaching outside town the other day were a ginger-nut.'

'It'm true,' said Fletcher. 'I saw that for myself. But what I want to know be what this John-John were doing out near the Ridgeriders' place at that sort of hour, Colin. Nothing illegal, I hope.'

'No,' Colin replied quickly. 'Not at all.'

'Nothing like poaching, perhaps?'

A firm shake of the head from Colin was followed by a reluctant, acknowledging nod. An Amblescrut's first instinct was always to deny accusations of wrongdoing, but with the Grubdollars it wasn't necessary. They knew as well as he did the sort of things his family got up to.

'What *I* want to know,' said Robert, 'is how come you actually know the name of your ma's aunt's – what were it again?'

'Ma's aunt's brother-in-law's stepson,' Colin said. 'And it'm easy. You see, him's John-John from the lower-township side of the family.'

'And?'

'Well, that means him be'n't upper-township John-John. Or John-John from the bunch who live out by Whitewater Rapids.'

Fletcher looked at Robert, Robert at Fletcher.

'Nope, still none the wiser,' Robert said.

'Suppose you has to be an Amblescrut for it to make sense,' Colin said. 'Suppose you does.'

'But Colin,' said Cassie, 'it be'n't that us doesn't appreciate you informing we about Da. Honestly, us is very grateful. It'm just that ... well, this be family stuff. Family deals with its own family things. You of all people should understand that.'

'And friends deal with friend things, Cassie. Your da, him once showed me kindness I didn't deserve. Robert'll tell you; him were there. I owe your da for that, and I's been trying to repay he ever since. This'm just a part of that.'

'I isn't going to be able to talk you out of this, is I?'

'Nope,' said Colin, hoisting another carton of tins onto his shoulder and carrying it over to *Bertha*. 'I be coming with you and there'm an end of it.'

You just can't argue with an Amblescrut! Cassie thought.

She tried to look on the positive side. Colin's muscle-power was coming in very handy right now. That was a point in his favour. And an extra person on board when they were out on the road meant the driving workload would be shared between four rather than three. Their father had a head start on them and was in a faster vehicle, and they had lost further time kitting *Bertha* out for a long journey. In order to have a hope of finding their da, wherever he was, they had to be prepared to drive round the clock, taking it in turns at the controls. Shorter driving shifts for everyone could only be a good thing. Cassie wasn't sure her brothers would like the idea of Colin taking *Bertha*'s controls, but maybe if they started him off an hour at a time, supervised, they could see if he could be trusted with the murk-comber on his own.

She turned her attention to the canisters of diesel fuel which had yet to be stowed aboard *Bertha*. These were for emergency purposes, in case *Bertha*, greedy old gas-guzzler that she was, started to run dry somewhere out in the middle of nowhere, with no filling station within range. For *Bertha*, the fuel canisters were the equivalent of the tinned food. They meant that, like the humans inside her, she could travel with the minimum number of stops for replenishment.

Cassie had bargained hard and got a good deal on the food and fuel. Even so, she only had a little of the tourist-gift money from two days ago left in her pocket. The cash they'd got for the elderly woman's opal necklace was all gone. In effect, the necklace was funding the whole trip. So if it hadn't been for the attack on *Bertha* by the Deacon's audience, Cassie and her brothers would not have been able to afford to go after Den. There was a kind of balance to that. It almost made her think that some things were meant to happen; that there was such a phenomenon as destiny.

Then again, destiny and coincidence could often be confused for each other.

Flap-flap.

Cassie looked up. What was that? Had she just heard —?

Flap-flap.

There it was again. The beat of wings. Airborn wings. Cassie had no difficulty recognising the sound. She was more familiar with it than most Groundlings.

'Hello down there?' called a voice from above. 'Hello?'

Cassie recognised the voice as well.

Two Airborn, a man and a woman, hovered into view above the courtyard. Their wings shone a shimmering white against the murky grey sky.

'Michael?' said Cassie. 'Aurora?'

'In the flesh,' said Michael.

'What'm you two doing here?'

'First, would you seal up that murk-comber and depressurise her?' Michael said, coming in to land. 'My head feels like it's about to burst.'

'Mine too,' said Aurora.

'Boys,' Cassie said to her brothers. 'Do as him says.'

At the same time, she restrained a sigh. This was all they needed, another delay. Talk about bad timing.

CHAPTER 29

Aurora's Offer

'We told everyone we were going to Heliotropia,' Michael said through the speaker tube. 'Only the most clichéd place in the world for a honeymoon. But it wasn't exactly a lie. We spent last night there. A very nice night it was too. Then today we came down in the elevators, because we actually want to spend our honeymoon in a less clichéd place.'

'You mean Grimvale?' said Cassie.

'The ground. We want to tour the ground for a week. And we'd like to hire you and your murk-comber to take us around.'

'*Bertha* be'n't for hire at present.' Cassie couldn't be bothered to put it less bluntly. 'Her'm already engaged. Us has business with she ourselves.'

'Oh. You sure about that?'

'Maybe if you'd given advance warning, Michael, us could have sorted something out. As it be, you'm out of luck. Try Roving Sightseer Enterprises, them that used to be Relic Seeker Enterprises. Them does tours too.'

'But we really fancied the idea of travelling with the Grubdollars. Seeing as you're Az's friends and all that. We'll pay well.'

'I told you,' Cassie said adamantly. 'You'm out of luck.'

'Well, that's nice, isn't it?' Michael's voice turned harsh. Even tinnily distorted by the speaker tube, Cassie could hear the sourness in it. 'You're not even prepared to think about it. A flat-out refusal. What is it with you, Cassie? What have you got against us?'

'What do you mean?'

'You know what I mean. Treating Az the way you have. Then simply not turning up to our wedding. Now this. Have we done something to offend you? Is that it?'

'No, that be'n't it,' Cassie replied, hotly, 'and you's no right making accusations like that. You know nothing about I or my life down here. Nothing. You may think you do but you don't. Anyways, don't bring Az into this. This be'n't about him, or you, or the Airborn, or anything of that kind.'

'Then what is it about?'

'None of your concern.'

Faintly she heard Aurora say, 'Give me that.' Next moment, Aurora was talking through the speaker tube, and her tone was measured and far mellower than Michael's.

'Cassie,' she said, 'look, Michael didn't mean any of that.'

In the background Michael grumbled, 'Oh yeah?'

'Ground-sickness, that's all,' Aurora went on. 'The air pressure in here is down, thank you very much, but our heads haven't quite cleared yet. That's why he's a bit grouchy. I just want to say, I appreciate the fact that you're unable to take us touring. We're disappointed, but you obviously have your reasons and I respect that. We're just grateful you've allowed us to use *Cackling Bertha* to catch our breath and straighten ourselves out. Once we're fully recovered we'll head over to the other tour company you mentioned. I'm sorry if we've inconvenienced you in any way.'

'You haven't, not as such,' Cassie said.

'I feel we have. I can see you're preparing to go somewhere. All this food you have here. Quite a long trip, I'd say. I can also see that … may I be frank a second?'

'Suppose.'

'Something's the matter. You're very tense. So are your brothers. And – well, I don't see your father anywhere. Now, I know your father's been a bit down in the clouds lately.'

A bit under the weather did she mean? That was putting it mildly!

'Him has,' Cassie admitted.

'And you're such a close family. Where is he? If he isn't here, where has he gone?'

Cassie was stuck to know what to say. It was uncanny. Aurora had diagnosed the Grubdollars' situation perfectly, from just one glance.

'My da,' Cassie replied slowly, 'has scarpered off somewhere and us is planning to find he.'

'Oh. How dreadful. You've no idea where he's gone?'

'South. Vaguely south. That'm all.'

'How do you intend to follow him?'

'Us'll ask around in towns and villages. Him's in a half-tarp van. That'm quite a recognisable vehicle. And him's with a Deacon. Also quite recognisable. People who see they two, them'll remember they.'

Even as she said this, Cassie was unconvinced. Yes, a half-tarp van and a red-headed Deacon were things that stood out. But they weren't *that* remarkable. Besides, if her father really didn't want to be followed, he would have the sense to keep a low profile. He'd make the Deacon stay out of sight as much as possible, and the two of them would stick to back roads and avoid highways and large towns. They wouldn't leave an easy trail of clues behind them.

The enormity of the task facing her, and the remote likelihood of success, suddenly weighed heavy inside Cassie. She was filled with a feeling that was close to despair. Her own phrase – *vaguely south* – resounded with a bleak hollowness. There was a vast amount of country *vaguely south*. A million roads to choose from. Endless land to get lost in.

'Let us help,' said Aurora.

'Huh?'

'We'd like to help you, Cassie. Let us. Let us come with you.'

CHAPTER 30

Cassie's Choice

Her first instinct was to reject the offer. What good would it do having passengers on board? Airborn passengers, what was more. All it meant was the food rations wouldn't go as far and *Bertha* would have a little more weight to carry and therefore use up that much more fuel.

She consulted with her brothers and Colin outside. She told them she could see no significant advantage to Michael and Aurora coming along for the ride, and several disadvantages.

Robert agreed. 'I's nothing against they. I just can't imagine them'll be much use to we.'

Fletcher, however, held a different view. 'For one thing, don't you reckon folk'll be more kindly disposed if us has Airborn with we? Whereas them mightn't tell the truth to *we* if them's seen Da, them might well to a couple of winged types.'

'And them has money,' Colin chipped in. 'You said them said them'd pay for a tour in *Bertha*, Cassie. With that cash us could travel further and for longer if needs be.'

'And I don't think us need really worry about extra fuel consumption,' Fletcher added. 'The Airborn doesn't weigh hardly anything, what with them porous bones of theirs. Remember, Robert, when you picked up Az and carried he? Barely had to bend your back to do so, and you'm such a weedy little tyke.'

'Oi!'

'So you both be saying you reckon us should bring them along?' Cassie said to Colin and Fletcher.

'I can't see it'll do any harm,' Fletcher replied.

'Me either,' said Colin.

'Myself, I doesn't exactly mind either way,' said Robert. 'There be room enough for all of we in *Bertha*. A tighter squeeze than before with them two aboard, but only slightly.'

'But in the end it'm your call, Cass,' said Fletcher.

'Be it?' Cassie frowned. It wasn't like Fletcher to defer a decision to her. Being older, he usually felt he outranked her and Robert, and whatever he said went.

'You know they better than us does, girl. You's met them up there in

High Haven a few times. You know their minds and characters. In practical terms, it can't hurt for they to come along with we. But if you reckon there might be problems personality-wise or whatever, then that'm a reason to say thanks but no.'

Cassie climbed back into *Bertha*, shinned up the ladder into the driver's pod, and unhooked the speaker tube.

'Mr and Mrs Gabrielson?' she said.

'Ooh, that's us,' said Aurora with a chuckle. 'It's weird to be called that.'

Aurora's remark made up Cassie's mind for her. She realised she would enjoy this woman's company on the trip – even if she wasn't so sure about Michael.

'Us has talked over your offer,' she said, 'and it'm a yes. Us would like your help.'

CHAPTER 31

Southward

An hour later, *Cackling Bertha* gave her signature mechanical laugh, spouted fumes from her exhaust, and pulled out of the Grubdollars' courtyard. Cassie was at the controls; Fletcher, Robert and Colin were ensconced in the observation nacelles; Michael and Aurora were sealed in the loading bay. It was late afternoon. The sky was shading from ash-grey to slate-grey, a change that was occurring earlier each day as autumn settled in. The darker half of the year brought more rain and also a spiritual dampness and gloom. Autumn and winter were the time when people were apt to contract rattle-lung and other fatal diseases; the time when life on the ground became least bearable. The sun was a pallid wraith, showing itself for just a few hours and shedding little light and no warmth at all through its veil of cloud. Shadows hung everywhere. The world was cobwebby and dim.

Cassie switched on *Bertha's* headlamps, casting a yellow glow on the road ahead. She was grappling with wintry thoughts herself, with feelings of hopelessness and foreboding. She steered through the town's outskirts and joined the Craterhome road, which ran arrow-straight for four kilometres before unravelling into a series of twists and turns as it climbed over the southern hills out of the Grimvale region.

A hundred kilometres to the east, and a couple of thousand metres above, *Cerulean* was also wending its way southward.

Had Cassie known this, would it have made any difference to her mood? Had she known Az was guiding the airship in a similar direction, on a journey with no more certain an outcome than hers, would it have helped comfort or console her in any way?

Who could say?

Night was falling.

Bertha's cackle grew subdued in the thickening twilight.

Cassie drove on.

CHAPTER 32

The Rudiments Of Falconry

Lord Urironson knocked and entered.

'Farris,' said Lady Aanfielsdaughter. Her voice carried a hint of quizzicality, just enough to leave him in no doubt that she found it odd he was visiting her in her office. One-to-one conversations, unless they were of a non-official or friendly nature, were frowned on at the Silver Sanctum, and she couldn't imagine Lord Urironson had anything to say to her that was non-official or friendly. Their mutual animosity ran too deep for that.

'I'll get straight to the point,' Lord Urironson said, with a businesslike flourish of wings.

Lady Aanfielsdaughter slid the paperwork she was perusing to one side. It was a pile of written applications from people wishing to join the Silver Sanctum. Dozens of these arrived every day and each had to be assessed impartially and carefully before an invitation to come for an interview was sent out.

'Please do,' she said.

'You're aware there's been a second attack on that Westward Oil Enterprises installation?'

'I have heard about it.'

'And the workers there retaliated?'

'So I understand.'

'I'm very concerned by this development.'

'As am I.'

'The Redspire pirates won't take it lying down, you know. Up till now they've raided with impunity. They hit that small Groundling village first, didn't they? Took some timber, some coal. No casualties on either side. Then they went for a steelyard. Again, no casualties. Now, if what we're hearing from the ground is true, ten or so of them are dead. Burned to a crisp, by all accounts. They'll want to get their own back, you can bet your pinfeathers on that.'

'I won't deny, it is a regrettable escalation of the problem,' Lady Aanfielsdaughter said. 'But one can see the Groundlings' point of view. The pirates stole from them. Little wonder they decided to strike back.'

'You're siding with them? Condoning what they did?'

'I never said that, Farris.' Lady Aanfielsdaughter's eyes flashed like chips of ice. 'And I feel this discussion is at an end. If you have anything further to say to me on the subject, say it in a public place with other people around.'

'I would, Serena, if only I weren't trying to help you.'

Lady Aanfielsdaughter blinked. 'I'm sorry, I didn't quite catch that. Did you just say "help"?'

Lord Urironson moved closer to her, his wings furling behind his back to indicate submissiveness and a lack of threat.

'Listen to me,' he said. 'You may not realise it but the atmosphere around this place is getting pretty anxious, and what the Silver Sanctum feels is a pretty fair reflection of what the Airborn in general are feeling. We're the barometer of the race's mood, or at least we should be. People here are talking in frightened tones. I hear them. Maybe you don't because they don't dare do it around you. They put on a brave face because you're the mighty Lady Aanfielsdaughter and they don't want you to think them weak or alarmist. But I hear what they're saying, and what they're saying is that Airborn are dead, killed by Groundlings. Never mind the circumstances, never mind the provocation – Airborn are dead, and that cannot simply be ignored.'

'What would you have me do about it?'

'What *are* you doing?'

'You know full well. *Cerulean* should be arriving at Redspire within a few days.'

'And your Mr Mordadson will solve the pirate problem?'

'Indeed. I have every faith in him.'

'Well, good. Let's hope he does. But even so, it still won't address the issue of Groundlings murdering Airborn. That's what's critical here. The pirates stole but they didn't kill. The Groundlings killed. Granted, they were defending themselves and their livelihoods, but instead of a proportionate response they overreacted. Which leaves us with a stupendous mess.'

'What would have been a proportionate response? Stealing something of the same value off us?'

'I don't know. But not murder.'

'And how is it helping me, telling me this?'

'Isn't it obvious?' said Lord Urironson. 'The whisper running round the Sanctum is that you've gone soft, Serena.'

'Soft. Really.' Lady Aanfielsdaughter arched an eyebrow. 'I despatch *Cerulean* south with Patrollers on board and with extreme sanction authorised, and apparently I've gone soft. How interesting.'

'The feeling is that more affirmative action is required.'

'Such as?'

'At the very least, a proclamation to the Groundlings. A strongly worded statement to all their governments letting them know that attacks on our kind will not be tolerated.'

'I can't see the benefit of that. It would smack of self-righteousness and hypocrisy.'

'We need to be firm with the Groundlings. We need them to respect us. It's like training a hunting falcon. The bird is a wild creature, a law unto itself, and in order to tame it you have to bend it to your will. You must teach it to obey your commands first and its own instincts second. Otherwise it will never do as it's told.'

'Ah, an aviary analogy,' said Lady Aanfieldsdaughter with a sardonic twist to her lips. 'You do realise you're talking to a fowl-farmer's daughter? Someone who knows more about the rearing and taming of birds than you ever will?'

'I don't know anyone at the Sanctum who *isn't* aware of your humble origins, Serena. You never tire of telling us about them.'

'Then you'll bow before my expertise on the subject. You've clearly had no experience of falconry, whereas my father was a skilled falconer and I learned the rudiments of the art from him. One doesn't bend the bird to one's will, as you claim. One works in harmony with the bird. A falcon is naturally aggressive and the whole point is to harness that aggression and make use of it. In the process, one should be prepared to receive the odd scratch or peck. It's only to be expected. But the injuries would be that much worse if one were actually trying to break the falcon's spirit using punishment and scare tactics. It wouldn't respond well to those at all, and in the end there'd be a disgruntled, petulant bird that won't hunt and a falconer covered in cuts and blood. One must woo the bird and gain its trust. Then it will be a loyal partner for life. Do you see what I'm saying?'

'With great clarity,' said Lord Urironson. 'But I believe you're wrong. I believe that showing the Groundlings any kind of weakness, any level of tolerance, will simply encourage them to behave worse. Give them a centimetre and they'll take a kilometre, to coin a phrase.'

'Not everyone perceives tolerance as weakness, Farris.'

'Many do. Not least in this very city.'

Lord Urironson thought this a nice line to exit on, and so about-turned and did. Outside Lady Aanfieldsdaughter's office he paused long enough to grin to himself, then leapt into the tower's central shaft and plunged twenty floors, braking at the last moment before he hit the bottom, his wings catching him with a *whoomph*.

As for Lady Aanfieldsdaughter, she sat for a long time staring into the middle distance. Try though she might, she couldn't dispel Lord Urironson's comments from her thoughts. He had touched a nerve. Were people talking behind her back and lying to her face? Did they really think she wasn't doing enough to contain the situation? Or was Lord Urironson merely stirring up trouble? Muck-raking? Seeding doubts in her mind? If so, why? What did he hope to gain?

For the first time in her long and distinguished career, Lady Aanfielsdaughter wondered if she wasn't getting too old for this job.

CHAPTER 33

City Of Number-crunchers

A brilliant sunrise shot the surface of the cloud cover with streaks of pink and blue. The dawn light was so pristine that almost every fold and billow seemed perfectly delineated, as though the clouds were etched on glass. To starboard, *Cerulean*'s shadow moved ripplingly, broad and elongated, like a bizarre follower, a warped second airship faithfully dogging her tail.

Gazing out from the viewing windows with bleary eyes, Az fought the urge to yawn. He had managed four hours' sleep last night and not much more the night before. It was all he could allow himself. *Cerulean* was running constantly, twenty-four hours a day, and her crew were on overlapping double-shifts and taking naps when and where they could. Az could do no less himself.

They were all exhausted – all except Flight Lieutenant Wallimson, who had no qualms about leaving the control gondola whenever he felt like it and retiring to his cabin for a nice long snooze. 'Someone has to be fresh and alert', was his excuse, but that cut no ice with the crew. 'Just plain lazy', was their view, which they expressed in several different ways, although never within Wallimson's hearing.

Several kilometres ahead, rising from the pink-blue clouds, lay the city of Gyre. *Cerulean* was already scheduled to make a refuelling stop there. Az had decided a rest stop would be a good idea as well. There was no way the crew could maintain this pace indefinitely. Better that everyone got a period of uninterrupted downtime before carrying on. Otherwise they would be beyond exhausted by the time they reached Redspire and unable to perform effectively.

Gyre was helical in shape, a single cone-like spiral three kilometres in diameter at its base, mounting to a sharp apex. All its buildings faced outward in rising, terraced tiers. It was home to mathematicians and accountants, statisticians and actuaries – a city of number-crunchers. The arithmetically-minded gravitated to Gyre and lived there in almost total isolation. They had little contact with the outside world except to take in bookwork. Otherwise, they spent their days lost in the realms of abstract calculation. By and large, it was a city of weirdoes, or so its reputation went. Az would have chosen anywhere else to halt, except that would have meant a significant and time-consuming detour. Gyre was directly on the route to Redspire.

One further unusual feature of Gyre was that it still had a mooring mast at its summit. Most other sky-cities had dismantled theirs long ago. With officially only one airship in existence, the masts had become a skyline-cluttering waste of space. Gyre lacked either the will or the manpower to take its one down.

Docking at a mooring mast was a tricky procedure and Az had never practised it. Now was not the time to try. *Cerulean* would use the landing apron at the sky-city's base.

He pressed the button which rang an alarm in the crew-members' cabins. Within minutes he had a full complement of crew on deck, rather than just the night-time skeleton crew of three. They manned their stations, rubbing their eyes. A few of them had buttoned up their uniform tunics the wrong way.

When Az announced that they would be taking some time off at Gyre, a low cheer went around the gondola.

'Nice one, skipper,' said the navigator, Ra'asielson. *Skipper* was what the crew had taken to calling Az. It was deferential but not quite *captain*.

'Time off?' Mr Mordadson had arrived. 'Are you sure?'

Az explained his reasons. 'Unless you want them men nodding off at their stations while we're hunting the pirates' airship, I'd say a rest period was utterly necessary.'

'Fair enough. We've made good progress so far. I think we can spare a few hours. And it's hard to imagine a more soporific place than Gyre. Ideal spot for a bit of shut-eye.'

As *Cerulean* drew nearer the city, Flight Lieutenant Wallimson put in a belated appearance in the control gondola.

'Mooring mast,' he observed, peering out. 'There's something you don't see every day. I don't suppose you've ever docked at a mooring mast, Gabrielson.'

Az was irritable with tiredness. It was an effort to keep his cool and not snipe back at Wallimson.

'I haven't and I don't plan to today.'

'Really? Why not? It's far from difficult.'

'That's not what I've heard.'

'All it takes is nerve and a good command of your vessel. But perhaps you don't have either.'

Az threw a look at Mr Mordadson, as if to say, *Can't you do something about this pain-in-the-backside?*

Mr Mordadson's response was a slow, neutral blink. It told Az that Wallimson was *his* concern, no one else's. Mr Mordadson couldn't fight his fights for him. It was up to Az to sort Wallimson out.

'If you're so keen on using the mast, flight lieutenant,' Az said, 'why not take over and manage it for me?'

'Oh, I couldn't. Captain Qadoschson made you boss, not me. I couldn't go against his wishes.'

'Well, I'm not going to do it.'

'A pity. The crew would think more of you if you did.'

Az knew he was being goaded. Wallimson was trying to shame him into attempting the manoeuvre.

Unfortunately, the tactic was working.

'All right,' he said, as coolly as he could. He thought he could see a way of turning Wallimson's act of provocation to his own advantage. 'Men? We're going to aim for the mast. Start unspooling the mooring line and take her up a hundred metres.'

To Wallimson he said, 'You, flight lieutenant, are going to help. I want you to be my co-pilot. You'll be my eyes at the front. You keep us on track.'

Wallimson made a show of considering this, as if it was an offer rather than an order. Finally he gave a nod.

Cerulean lifted her nose, her propellers canting downwards. Decelerating, she zeroed in on the mast. Az dished out commands, listening to what the crew were telling him. He was careful to consult Wallimson on each phase of the manoeuvre. The flight lieutenant curtly corrected him once or twice, otherwise saying nothing.

If this worked as Az hoped, Wallimson would perhaps feel more involved in the running of the ship. He might even come to respect Az more.

There was a catcher at the top of the mast, a V-shaped metal armature mounted on a swivel. It swung in the prevailing wind like a weathervane and was fitted with a spring-loaded pressure switch which snapped the catcher shut as soon as a mooring line touched it and triggered it. *Cerulean*'s course of approach had to be directly into the wind and at the correct height so that the line, trailing below her, slotted into the catcher.

Steering headlong into the wind meant she began to jump and lurch about. The mast, her target, seemed to dance this way and that.

'Hold her steady,' Az said. 'Steady.'

He was starting to wonder if he hadn't bitten off more than he could chew. But he couldn't back out now. He was committed. If he called off the manoeuvre and went down to dock at the landing apron instead, he feared it would do irreparable damage to his standing with the crew.

He glanced over at Mr Mordadson. The Silver Sanctum emissary's expression was unreadable.

'Two degrees to port,' he said.

A hush had settled over the control gondola. Everyone was concentrating hard. Wings were tensely folded.

'Another two. That's it. Bring the engine power right down. Let the wind brake us.'

'Gabrielson, we're a little too high,' said Wallimson.

'Are we? Doesn't look it to me.'

'Trust me. The line will miss if we don't come down slightly.'

Az hesitated, then said, 'Down ten metres.'

'Aye-aye, ten metres.'

'More,' said Wallimson.

'More?'

'You asked me to co-pilot. I'm co-piloting. We need to go down more. The wind's strong and it's blowing the line beneath us at an acute angle. It won't reach the catcher.'

'Rigz? Can't we pay out more of it?'

'It's at its fullest extent, skipper,' said Chief Engineer Rigzielson. It was Rigz's duty to operate the mooring line winch during launches and dockings.

'Then, another ten metres,' said Az.

The top of the mast seemed alarmingly close to the airship. The catcher loomed like a pair of metal pincers.

'All engines, full stop.'

Cerulean drifted forward under her own momentum, still juddering in the headwind. The mast was now twenty metres away.

Fifteen.

Ten.

The wind dropped.

Cerulean lost lift. Her nose dipped.

'Up!' Az yelled. 'Bring her up! Bring her up!'

The crew reacted, but just too late.

Time slowed to a crawl. Everything that happened next, happened with a kind of appalling leisureliness – a snail's pace disaster.

One side of *Cerulean*'s balloon rubbed against the top of the mast.

The catcher dug into the balloon canvas.

The canvas split and the catcher dug deeper. It scored a gash that lengthened and widened. The tearing sound was horrible, like a deep groan of pain.

The catcher continued to rip through the canvas until it hit one of the main frame sections, the giant circular braces which gave the balloon its cylindrical roundness. Steel screeched on steel. Then the catcher snapped shut, and *Cerulean* rocked to a halt. Everyone in the control gondola who wasn't seated staggered forwards a step.

For several seconds there was silence. The crew waited to see if that was the end of it; if the crash was over or there was more to come.

It was over. *Cerulean* was stuck fast, her balloon impaled on the mast.

'Oh well done,' said Flight Lieutenant Wallimson, and he started a slow handclap. 'Bravo, "skipper". Nice going.'

Az, mortified, did not know where to look.

CHAPTER 34

Damage Assessment

It was bad but it could have been a great deal worse.

The catcher had failed to penetrate any of *Cerulean*'s gas cells. They were all intact, no helium leaking.

Which still left a gash in her canvas 20 metres long, but that could be mended relatively easily. The result would be unsightly, like a newly stitched scar, but would not affect *Cerulean*'s flight performance.

What was a problem was the structural damage to the balloon's frame. Where the catcher had collided with the circular brace, the brace had bent and twisted. Rivets had popped out and several of the support wires strung within the brace had snapped. A large section of the thing was deformed and needed to be straightened out before *Cerulean* could continue on her way.

'At least two days' work,' said Rigz, lugubriously eyeing the broken, dangling cables. He was standing with Az and Mr Mordadson in the airship's axial corridor, a skeletal steel tube which ran the length of the balloon from stem to stern. A chilly wind was hissing in through the tear in the canvas. 'We'll have to cut out the bent bit, hammer it straight and weld it back into place, then reattach all those cables. I suppose we could manage it in a day and a half, if we bodge.'

'We can't just fly with it as it is?' Mr Mordadson asked.

'Not unless we want *Cerulean* to keep corkscrewing. The distension in the balloon would drag on that side, creating a torque effect. We'd have a struggle to keep her from turning upside down.'

'Tell me, Rigz,' said Az, although he didn't want to hear the answer, 'was it my fault?'

The chief engineer scratched the back of his head and let out a whistle through his teeth. 'Yes and no, skipper. Yes, because maybe you shouldn't have attempted docking at the mast. No, because nobody could have foreseen that sudden wind drop. That's what knackered us. That and ...'

'And what?'

'And the fact that we were coming in too low.'

'But Wallimson said —'

'Wallimson misjudged,' said Rigz. 'Not wishing to cast aspersions or anything, but the flight lieutenant obviously didn't gauge our height right.

He should have given us more leeway, in case of exactly what occurred, the wind letting up. He had us in too tight, no margin for error.'

'Then I'm not to blame.'

'Afraid so. See, it's your responsibility as captain, or whatever you are, to double-check all the information you're given by the crew. You can trust us but you can't *rely* on us. Because we're fallible. We're only human. We make mistakes. You have to know better than us and not accept everything we tell you at face value. Tough, I know, but there it is. Someone has to be the big fellow who makes the decisions and lives with them. Someone has to carry the can. That, for better or worse, is you.'

Az swallowed hard, the chief engineer's words a bitter pill. 'Let's get started on the repairs immediately. I'll go and tell the Alar Patrollers what's going on. And then Mr Mordadson and I will head down into Gyre and explain things to people there. Is that a good —?'

He had turned to address Mr Mordadson, only to find him gone. At some point while he and Rigz were talking just now, the Silver Sanctum emissary had flitted off without a sound. He was nowhere to be seen.

Az hoped there was an innocent reason for his abrupt departure, but, knowing Mr Mordadson, there probably wasn't.

CHAPTER 35

The Sound Made By Someone With A Thumb Digging Into His Throat

'Ghnnk!' said Wallimson.

Mr Mordadson ground his thumb harder into the flight lieutenant's windpipe.

'What was that?' he said. 'Didn't quite catch it.'

'Ghnnk!' said Wallimson again. His eyes were bulging and his face had gone purple.

'Nope. Still not making yourself clear. You want me to pull my thumb out of you neck? Is that it?'

Frantically Wallimson nodded.

'I don't know. I'm having such fun watching you squirm. I think I might leave my thumb where it is till you stop squirming altogether. How about that? Good idea?'

Wallimson gave a pitiful shake of his head. He was terrified. All he could see in Mr Mordadson's crimson-shaded eyes was implacable determination. The man was going to kill him, he was quite sure of that. Already he could feel his lungs bursting for breath. His vision was growing hazy. It would be a miserable death, here in *Cerulean*'s latrines, where Mr Mordadson had lured him with a request for 'a quick word'. What a sordid and unseemly way to go, being throttled in a toilet cubicle with your head pressed up against the lavatory cistern.

He pleaded with his eyes, begging the Silver Sanctum emissary to let him live.

Mr Mordadson cocked his head, seemed to ponder for a moment, then withdrew his thumb.

With a gasp, Wallimson collapsed onto the toilet seat. He took several raspy gulps of air, sitting limp, overjoyed to be alive.

'Right,' said Mr Mordadson, 'here's the deal. I know you deliberately sabotaged Az's attempt to moor at the mast.'

'I didn't —' croaked Wallimson.

Mr Mordadson poised his thumb over Wallimson's throat. 'Shut up. I'm talking.'

The flight lieutenant clamped his lips tight together.

'I don't believe you meant for us to crash,' Mr Mordadson went on. 'I do believe, though, that you were hoping we would miss the mast or perhaps scrape it. Then you'd put a dent not only in *Cerulean* but in Az's credibility. You'd make him look incompetent, you'd undermine his authority, and in the process you'd make yourself look like a better candidate for captain. Well, congratulations. You succeeded. Trouble is, you've delayed us now. In messing with Az you've messed with *my* mission, and as you can see I'm not best pleased by that. I'm taking what you did very personally.

'I want to make one thing clear,' he continued. 'I don't care what your beef is with Az. I know you don't like him and he was promoted over you. That's got to hurt. But maybe what you really hate about him is that he has no wings and manages fine, while you have two wings – OK, one and a half – and still find life a struggle. Maybe it's jealousy, the worst kind of jealousy, the kind that has a little bit of admiration mixed into it.

'Thing is, I *just don't care*. All I care about is fulfilling my mission, and anyone or anything that gets in the way of that, I will deal with harshly. You've been given a warning, Wallimson. Buck up your ideas, or the next time this thumb gets planted in your epiglottis, it stays there. Understood? You may speak now.'

'Understood,' said Wallimson, coughing out the word.

'Bear in mind, I'm not doing this to protect Az. He has to learn to stand on his own two feet where you're concerned. He has to work out his own strategy for dealing with you. All this is about is you and me. And I think we've straightened things out between us, haven't we?'

'We have.'

'If I had my way, I'd bung you off this airship right now, but we need a back-up captain, someone who can take over if Az is indisposed. So I'm stuck with you. And you're stuck with me. But that shouldn't be a problem for either of us any more, should it?'

'No.'

'Good man.'

Mr Mordadson patted Wallimson on the cheek, as though they were close chums. The flight lieutenant flinched.

'Now, clean yourself up and get back to work,' Mr Mordadson said, and he stepped out of the cubicle.

Seconds later, Wallimson heard the door to the latrines swing shut. Only then was he able to relax.

He was puzzled by Mr Mordadson's remark about cleaning himself up, till he noticed that his trousers were soggy at the crotch.

In his terror, Wallimson had wet himself.

He staggered to his cabin and changed clothes. While he was doing so he thought of the moment he had stared into Mr Mordadson's eyes and seen his death in them. He felt he would carry the memory of those eyes for the rest of his life – the memory of his own helplessness and dread.

There was a small vanity mirror mounted on the cabin wall. Wallimson looked into it. He saw his face, pale in the aftermath of his near-murder. He saw his crooked, lame wing.

The last of his fear sank away and his old, ingrained resentment resurfaced.

Mr Mordadson was right in one respect, Wallimson thought. Wallimson hadn't intended to harm *Cerulean* as badly as he had. He'd been hoping for a collision with the mast but a glancing one, nothing quite as drastic as what did happen. He loved *Cerulean*, in his way, and he regretted the damage he had helped cause.

But Mr Mordadson was wrong if he thought their encounter in the latrines was going to persuade him to mend his ways.

All it had done was sharpen his hatred of Az. What was that kid? Nothing more than a jumped-up Groundling lookalike, that was what. Everyone thought of him as a somebody, a hero, because he had played a part in saving Heliotropia and bringing the Airborn and the Groundlings into contact with each other.

Well, big deal. Wallimson had played a part too. He'd been on *Cerulean* when they flew down through the cloud cover. He'd been there when they carried a bunch of Groundling passengers up to Heliotropia and given them their first glimpse of a sky-city. Yet no one was calling Wallimson a hero and giving him plum jobs on Silver Sanctum missions! No, all the honour and glory went to Az Gabrielson, a snotty wingless teenager who just got lucky.

If it hadn't been for Az, there might not be Groundlings roaming the sky-cities now.

If it hadn't been for Az, the Airborn might not have to share their space and their wealth with those ostriches.

Yes, when you got down to it, Az Gabrielson had a lot to answer for.

'And you won't always have mean old Mr Mordadson to look out for you,' Wallimson said to his reflection in the mirror, as though he were addressing Az. 'He can't be there the whole time, hovering at your shoulder. A moment will come when you're on your own and at my mercy. You can count on it. For the time being I'll play nice. I'll simper along all meek and mild. I'll be the finest flight lieutenant you could wish for. But when the moment comes . . .'

Wallimson didn't need to complete the threat. His reflection's grin said it all.

CHAPTER 36

Harried By A Potter

The Grubdollars picked up their father's trail in Timberwolf Knoll, thirty-five kilometres southeast of Grimvale. Then, promptly, they lost it again.

The half-tarp van had been spotted near Timberwolf Knoll heading for the Fishkill River, but once they crossed that by the bridge at Ladenford they couldn't find anyone who had seen the van coming that way. For lack of an alternative, Cassie decided they should follow the river east, but a day of driving along bumpy roads and halting at every steamboat landing and mill town along the way yielded no results. They doubled back and went west, travelling as far as Glass Lake and the Heartberry Dam. No sign of the half-tarp that way either.

Then a ferocious rainstorm broke. They had to halt because the down-pour was too torrential for *Bertha's* wipers to cope with and there was a risk she might pitch sideways into a drainage ditch.

Down near Hillcrest they had what they thought was a stroke of luck, although it proved to be a false alarm. Robert was at the controls, when Colin, in one of the front observation nacelles, started yelling over the speaker-tube system: 'There! There! A half-tarp! There'm a half-tarp parked by the roadside!' Robert slammed on the brakes and all four of *Bertha's* Groundling occupants piled out and hurried over to the van.

It certainly was a half-tarp and in shabby condition, just like the Deacon's. Unfortunately it didn't belong to him but to a potter who used it to transport his earthenware urns and flowerpots to the weekly market at Croaker Gulch. His house was up a small path in the woods and he was busy ferrying his produce between it and the van. He was not happy to come down the path and find a quartet of youngsters clustered around the vehicle, peering into it. He thought they were about to steal his merchandise, so he set down all but one of the flowerpots in his arms and charged at them.

Sensibly he elected to tackle the largest of the four kids first, and swung the pot at Colin's head. He couldn't have known that Amblescruts were born with notoriously thick skulls. The pot shattered, and Colin turned round to look at his attacker with a puzzled frown, as though he'd just been tapped on the shoulder. The potter peered at the fragment of clay remaining in his hand, then got very afraid.

But Cassie stopped Colin before he could give the potter too severe a beating. The man got away with just a few lumps and bruises, and knew he had been fortunate.

They carried on their quest through the Diamondcrop region and further south into Harkaway, not far from Craterhome itself, capital of the Westward Territories.

Meanwhile, inside *Bertha*'s loading bay, Michael was growing increasingly bored, and then frustrated, and then annoyed.

'Some honeymoon,' he said. 'Cooped up inside this blasted lumbering hunk of junk. Nothing to do but stare out of the windows all day. Whose idea was this again, Aurora?'

'Yours.'

'You sure?'

'Quite sure. You said, and I quote, "Let's do something no one else has done. Let's have an adventure."'

'Yeah. And I meant it and all. I just didn't imagine an adventure could be quite so – well, so unadventurous. Not to mention so claustrophobic. I'm going nuts in here. I need to be out for more than a few minutes at a time. I want to really spread my wings. I'm sick of this.'

'You think I'm not?' said Aurora. 'Apart from anything else I'd be glad of some time alone, so that I don't have to keep on listening to you whinge.'

'I don't whinge.'

'What do you call this, if it isn't whingeing?'

'Just stating how I feel.'

'Also, if I recall rightly, you had an ulterior motive for hiring the Grubdollars to take us on a tour. You were going to use the time to work on Cassie and find out why she's been making Az so miserable. I haven't seen you doing much of that.'

'Haven't had the chance, have I?' Michael said. 'She's been so wrapped up in looking for her dad, I've barely managed to talk to her for more than a couple of minutes. And that damn tube isn't the ideal medium for in-depth heart-to-hearts.'

'Do you want to give up? Call this off as a bad idea? We could ask to be dropped off at the nearest Chancel and then go up and find ourselves a nice hotel and spend the rest of our honeymoon honeymooning properly.'

'Do *you* want to do that?'

'I'm sorely tempted. We're not being much use to the Grubdollars, except maybe financially, and we're taking up all this room while they're stuck in those cramped observation-bubble things.'

The decision was more or less made. Michael and Aurora agreed to speak to Cassie about being offloaded at a Chancel. The Grubdollars would still get paid in full, but would be able to go on without the inconvenience of Airborn passengers on board.

Then Fletcher had a brainwave.

CHAPTER 37

Fletcher's Brainwave

'Pressure,' he said to Michael and Aurora. 'I's been thinking about it and what to do about it. Be'n't kind or fair that you two's hunkering inside *Bertha*'s belly all the time so as you won't be ground-sick. Us could simply open up the loading bay and you could be ill for a day till you acclimatise, like Az do on his visits. Or . . .'

'Go on,' said Aurora into the speaker-tube mouthpiece.

'Or us could equalise the pressure between you and the outside little by little. Lower the pump speed a notch at a time. Make the adjustment a gradual thing. Then you mightn't feel too unwell. Mightn't feel unwell at all, in fact.'

'Do you think that'll work?'

'Us can only try. Question be, you'm up for trying?'

Aurora turned to Michael, who nodded. For the first time in several days he looked almost enthusiastic.

'Why not?' she said to Fletcher. 'Let's give it a bash.'

They gave it a bash, and it was successful. While the search went on, Fletcher decreased the power on the air pump at half-hourly intervals. To begin with Michael and Aurora found this uncomfortable. Their ears popped painfully and they complained of a buzzing, headachey sort of dizziness. However, Fletcher found that if he increased the pressure slightly for a quarter of an hour, the next half-hourly decrease was easier to bear. And so it went, in a kind of two steps forward, one step back pattern. Gradually the air pressure in the loading bay became denser and more closely equalised with the air pressure outside, and the Airborn newlyweds experienced no further ill-effects.

In all, the procedure took seven hours. At the end of that period the pump was turned off and the loading bay hatch opened. Michael and Aurora stepped out and waited to feel ground-sick, and waited, until eventually it became clear they weren't going to. Then Michael launched himself into the sky and turned cartwheels and spun around and around in loop-the-loops and figure-of-eights, whooping and cheering.

'You're a genius,' Aurora said to a blushing Fletcher. 'I was beginning to think our marriage was over almost as soon as it had started. We weren't even going to make it through the honeymoon without coming to blows.'

'Divorce avoidance – all part of the service, ma'am,' Fletcher replied.

In truth, he was pretty pleased with himself. He had hit on a way of making the transition between sky and ground much easier and more comfortable. It was so simple and obvious he was surprised nobody had thought of it before. Already he could see the technique being applied at every Chancel, and at the top of every elevator column as well. After all, if it worked for the Airborn coming down, might it not also work in reverse for the Groundlings going up? People could acclimatise before they made their journeys, or else just after they arrived, reasonably quickly. He needed to put his mind to it a bit more. Special tanks could be built. They could be called Fletcher Tanks . . .

'Shall us be on our way?' said Cassie, intruding on Fletcher's thoughts. She was watching Michael's aerial antics in an impatient stance, hands on hips. 'Time be wasting.'

'It'm all go-go-go with you, be'n't it?' her brother said. 'Give he a little longer to frolic. Him's been going stir-crazy.'

'Well, 'scuse I for my sense of urgency,' Cassie shot back. 'There'm I thinking us is trying to find Da and every second counts as him gets further and further away. *Obviously* us should let Michael doodle about up there for as long as him likes. Matter of fact, why doesn't us jack in looking for Da altogether and just do whatever them ruddy Airborn feel like doing.'

'*Cass*,' Fletcher hissed. Aurora was within earshot. 'Clip it down, girl. A few minutes won't make any difference. Besides which, the trail's gone cold. You's no more idea where Da be now than any of we.'

'All the more reason to keep searching.'

'Where? How? Do you even have a plan? Or is us just going to carry on thrashing around the country hoping to get lucky again?'

'Yes!' said Cassie hotly. Then: 'No.' Her eyes brimmed with tears. 'Oh Fletch, it'm useless, be'n't it? Da's really pulled a vanishing act. Us is chasing after shadows.'

'No, lass.' Fletcher reached for her and enfolded her in an embrace. 'No, that be'n't so. Us is going to find he, I swear. Don't know how, but us is.'

'I hope you's right, really I do.' She buried her face in her brother's chest, sniffing. 'If only Martin was here. Him always knew what to do. I miss he, Fletch.'

'I miss he too,' Fletcher said, thick-voiced. 'Every day. It'm odd but I keep thinking him's still around. You know, at home I walk past his room and I think, *Oh, Martin must be in there, that'm why the door's shut.* Then I remember him be'n't in there and it just hits me, hard, this twisting feeling in my guts, like someone be digging a knife there.'

'Yeah, same with I. It'm like him died only yesterday, not a whole year ago. Even remembering what an old bossy-boots him could be – I don't mind. I'd give anything to hear him boss I around again.

'Martin mayn't have been right all the time but more often than not him was,' Fletcher said, with a rueful nod.

'So what do you think him would have suggested us do?'

'Now?'

'Yeah. With Da.'

'No idea. Let I think. Maybe – maybe him'd've said something like go to Craterhome.'

Cassie stepped back, wiping her face with a hand. 'Craterhome? Why would Da be there?'

'Why not? Great big city. Lots going on. Whatever him and the Deacon be after, Craterhome be as likely a place as any for they to find it. And also, Da's note said a needle in a haystack. Well, haystacks don't come much bigger than Craterhome. Metaphorical haystacks, I mean.'

'Reckon?'

Fletcher was starting to like his own idea more and more. 'Crowds of people, too, in a city. That'd help we. Loads of pairs of eyes that might've seen they if them's there.'

'That'm not bad thinking at all,' Cassie said, brightening. 'You know, Fletch, you'm not nearly as dumb as everyone says.'

'All depends on how dumb them says I be, doesn't it?' Fletcher retorted with a grin. 'And being as I's actually the smart one in the family, however dumb I be, that'd make you even dumber.'

'The smart one? Oh yeah?'

'Oh yeah!'

'Says who?'

'Says me,' declared the inventor of the Fletcher Tank, a device he was confident would revolutionise the way the two races of the world travelled to and fro and interacted.

But that was for later.

For now, Fletcher and his companions' immediate goal was Crater-home. And as soon as Michael had had his fill of aerobatics, Craterhome was where they set off to.

CHAPTER 38

The Outlier

The Count of Gyre was old and as thin as it was humanly possible to be without actually being a skeleton. His cheeks were sunken and cadaverous, his shaven head skull-like. The white toga he wore, with its purple hem and gold braid, revealed knobbly shoulders, stick-thin legs and in general more of his scrawny, mole-riddled, lived-spotted physique than you might care to see. It swished around him as he ushered Az and Mr Mordadson through a series of adjoining chambers to his private office.

In each chamber, Az saw scores of men and women working in large cubbyholes stacked a dozen high. Every one of them had an adding machine or an abacus in front of him or her, along with reams of graph paper and a plethora of pens, and every one was tapping away and jotting down intently. The adding machines' keys clacked, the counters on the abacuses clicked, and these noises built up into a insistent background clatter-chorus which was counterpointed by the wingbeats of clerks who flitted from cubbyhole to cubbyhole, delivering or gathering documents.

Like the Count, all these people had shaven heads, male and female alike, and were clad in white togas, albeit without the trimmings. Az noted a peculiar serenity about them. They were industrious but at the same time tranquil. It was as if they found the act of compiling figures and making calculations hypnotically soothing. Many had blissful smiles on their faces as they toiled away.

Maths was not one of Az's strong subjects at school. That made it all the more extraordinary to him how the citizens of Gyre could derive such happiness from their jobs and why they loved providing accounts and statistical analysis for the whole of the Airborn realm. Basic algebra alone was enough to give him a headache.

Definitely a city of weirdoes.

And the Count of Gyre, governor of this place, the arch-calculator, was the biggest weirdo of them all.

'Now,' the Count said, after he had despatched a minion out of his office to fetch herbal tea for his guests. 'What can I do for you again?'

'This is a courtesy call,' said Mr Mordadson. 'We need to berth for a couple of days here at your city while we carry out repairs on *Cerulean*.'

'Of course. You are welcome. A couple of days? Can you be more precise with that estimate?'

'I'm afraid not.'

'Oh dear, oh dear,' said the Count, fluttering his wings. Somehow even his wings looked bony and skeletal. 'Too vague. I find vagueness distressing. But I shall try to accommodate.'

'We'd also like to buy fuel.'

As he said this, Mr Mordadson produced his Silver Sanctum seal. Normally the sight of the seal was enough to prompt people into doing their civic duty and willingly providing whatever goods or services the bearer asked for.

In this case, however, it seemed not to have the desired effect.

'That thing,' the Count said with a dismissive sniff.

'You have a problem with the Silver Sanctum?' said Mr Mordadson, his eyes narrowing.

'Not as such. We do your book-keeping. You're a major client. There is no lack of respect here for the Sanctum. No, my problem is with the seal itself.'

'What about it?'

'Its influence is out of all proportion to its intrinsic value,' the Count said. 'Even if we factor in its net worth as so many grammes of precious metal, it still represents far more than it is, to an absurd degree. Can we assess, in real terms, how much it can obtain? No. Can we provide a clearly itemised bill for all the services that have been rendered gratis over the years, every time one of those seals is shown? No. Can we know if its usage obtains us taxpayers a fair outlay-to-reward ratio? No. The seal is problematic because it cannot be quantified with any accuracy. It is of no establishable cost-effectiveness.'

'It's an emblem,' Mr Mordadson replied. 'You can't quantify emblems. By definition they have to be more than they actually are. A flag, for example, can't just be thought of a rectangle of printed cloth. It has to embody everything that the people who it stands for feel. Otherwise, what's the point?'

'What indeed? Hence Gyre has no flag, no insignia, unlike every other sky-city. Because we cannot see the point. We cannot assign a direct value to it. However, let us not argue about this. You will get your fuel. We shall provide it. Grudgingly, but we shall. It so happens there's something I am more interested in.'

'And that would be?'

The Count swivelled round and pointed at Az. 'You.'

Az mirrored the gesture, pointing at himself. 'Me?'

'Yes, you. The great Az Gabrielson. The wingless wonder. Don't look so surprised. Of course we've heard of you, even in Gyre. You're well-known throughout the Airborn realm, and on the ground too, I should imagine. But we have taken a particular interest in you, ever since your exploits first came to our attention. And now lo and behold, at the extremity of all the laws of probability, here you are, arriving right on our doorstep.'

'We had to stop here. It was expedient.' The Count was fond of long words so Az thought he would match him with a little verbosity of his own. 'It so happened that our flight path —'

The Count bared his teeth, an arresting sight. His teeth were yellow and unusually long, poking out from their gums like clothes pegs.

In fact, he was grinning.

'Expediency, coincidence, accident, happenstance,' he said. 'Let me tell you, young man, none of these things exists. They are merely names people give to varying contingencies of measurable probability. There is no turn of luck, no chance meeting, no confluence of events, which cannot be rationalised and accounted for by means of figures and statistics. There is no outcome that cannot be predicted with the proper calculation, and thus no set of circumstances that is not preordained.'

'I don't understand.'

'I didn't think you would. Let me put it more straightforwardly. You stopped here because you were meant to stop here. You crashed your airship on our mast because you and I were meant to have this conversation.'

'Meant by who?'

'By *whom*,' said the Count, correcting his grammar. 'And it's the wrong question. You should be asking, by *what*?'

'All right then. By *what*?'

'By the underlying order of numbers. By the tendency of mathematics to work out. By the arithmetical structure which underpins the world's apparent randomness. Hence the *what* rather than the *whom*. That which I'm talking about is not an entity, not a guiding sentience, although some have mistaken it for that and called it God. It's at once simpler and more intricate. It's the dimension of pure mathematics, that whole beautiful para-realm where one and one always equals two, two and two four, and so on ad infinitum. Where every fraction can be reduced to its lowest common denominator and every equation can be balanced and every theorem can be proved. Where the —'

'Sorry to butt in.' Az was feeling a mixture of bafflement (*para-realm?*) and boredom. He suddenly seemed to have become stuck in the worst maths lesson ever. 'You said you've taken a "particular interest" in me.'

'Indeed.'

'Well, why? Because I was the pioneering sky-ground go-between?'

390

'Partly that,' said the Count, 'and also because you are what's known as an outlier.'

'Beg pardon? Did you just call me a liar?'

'Outlier,' the Count reiterated patiently. 'Something which lies outside the norm. In the strictly statistical sense it means a value that is extraordinarily large or small and does not fit into the data set as a whole. It cannot even be accounted for by standard deviation. In the broader sense, I'm talking about an anomaly. One of a kind. Unique, even.'

'Ah. The no-wings thing. As a matter of fact, I'm not unique there. Apparently there's this woman in the Cumula Collective. Mr Mordadson here told me about her. No wings, eighty years old, half-blind. They had to decide which of us to send down to the ground, her or me. Funnily enough they plumped for me.'

Either flippancy was lost on the Count or he would not deign to acknowledge it.

'We know of her too,' he said. 'She does not matter, except in so far as her lack of importance points up *your* importance the more greatly. In contrast with the relative uneventfulness of her long life, your short life has already been packed with incident. As an outlier, that makes you statistically significant and impossible to ignore. It points to a qualitative purpose to your existence.'

'Oh?'

'Yes, Az. May I call you Az? You see, we at Gyre have an inkling that you are pivotal to the future of the Airborn race, and the future of the Groundling race too.'

Az groped for something further to say but couldn't find it. No more facetious comments sprang to mind. The Count's words, and the utter solemnity with which he spoke them, had set the skin on the back of his neck crawling. He felt he had strayed into uncertain territory. This wasn't a situation ripe for poking fun at any more. Things had taken a turn for the strange.

'And I can prove it to you,' the Count went on. 'Would you care to come with me? You too, Mr Mordadson. It's not far but some flying is required.'

CHAPTER 39

The Ultimate Reckoner

As the Count led them along a series of winding, cross-connecting corridors and shafts, deeper into Gyre, Mr Mordadson bent his head close to Az's and whispered: 'I wonder if he's taking us to see what I think he is.'

'Which is . . .'

'Something I've heard only rumours about. Something I didn't believe really existed.'

'Tell me.'

'No. Let's just wait till we get there.'

At last they arrived at a spacious hallway which was, Az guessed, close to the centre of Gyre, if not right at the city's core. As Mr Mordadson set him down, he became aware of a low, churning, clanking background clamour. He could feel the sound as well as hear it. It made the polished marble floor tiles beneath his feet vibrate.

At one end of the hallway were a gigantic pair of doors, each so big it could let an army through. This was a portal designed to dwarf you and make you feel awestruck and insignificant. All over the doors there were mathematical symbols, inlaid in gold. Az recognised many of the symbols: $+$, $\div$, $=$, $>$, $<$, $\neq$, and so on. Some, though, were not so familiar, for instance $\approx$, and ∞, and Δ, and $\cap$. And a few were so ornate and exotic-looking he wasn't certain they were genuine mathematical symbols at all.

The Count threw a large lever, and the doors started to grind ponderously apart, sliding sideways into recesses.

Az knew that what lay on the other side was a vast chamber full of machinery. Judging by the racket coming from there, it had to be. He imagined it to be similar to the supply-arrival depot at Heliotropia or the elevator chamber in the Chancel below, an immense space filled with moving, whirring, thundering technology.

He was surprised, therefore, when the doors opened to reveal . . .

. . . a room not much larger than the living room at home.

The walls, floor and ceiling were bare and white, and there were just two items of machinery visible, right at the centre. One of them was a kind of pedestal, on top of which was a sloping panel with buttons on it, which reminded Az very much of the adding machines he had seen earlier.

Larger, slightly more complicated-looking, but essentially the same.

The other was a freestanding printing device, which was busy turning out a ribbon of tickertape that gathered in loose, unruly coils on the floor. The tickertape was four centimetres wide and covered in rows of numbers.

With a flick of his hand, the Count invited Az and Mr Mordadson to follow him into the room.

The thrum of machinery came from all around them but was barely any louder here than in the hallway. The Count had to raise his voice in order to be heard, but only a little.

'This,' he said to his two guests, 'is the Ultimate Reckoner.'

'Doesn't look like much,' Az remarked. *Ultimate Reckoner* seemed a grandiose name for just those two pieces of apparatus.

'What you're looking at is simply the Reckoner's input and output portions,' the Count explained. 'They represent a small fraction of its full bulk. All around us, if you'd care to imagine it, is a system of brass rods, linked by sprocketed flywheels. Each rod is thirty centimetres long and contains ten dials numbered with the digits nought to nine. In all, there are fifty thousand rods. The machine as a whole extends a hundred metres in every direction, give or take a metre or two. As such, the Ultimate Reckoner represents forty years' worth of construction by a total of more than three hundred residents of Gyre. Forty-three years, to be exact, and three hundred and twenty-nine residents in all. A million-plus man-hours of labour. To be exact, one million, one hundred and seven thousand —'

'Yes, yes, we get the picture,' said Mr Mordadson. 'Tell us what it *does*.'

'Why, it's nothing less than the most sophisticated calculating tool ever built. It is to the ordinary adding machine as a human brain is to the brain of a common-or-garden sparrow.'

'And what's all this?' Az said, indicating the growing pile of tickertape on the floor.

'That is the task the Reckoner is currently engaged on. At present, we have the machine working out π to a trillion decimal places. That's its default setting, a calculation we use to keep it ticking over, so that the sprockets and rods don't seize up with disuse. We're collating and analysing the results, looking to see if there are cycles of repetition within the number string. It's something of an outlier in itself, is π. A mathematical operation which refuses to conform to any rules. Circles and spheres occur spontaneously in nature. That means π is a biological construct and therefore, to our way of thinking, ought to demonstrate a pattern and be finite. In the end, seven *must* go into twenty-two. The division *must* be achievable. And if anything can prove that, the Ultimate Reckoner can.'

'A *trillion* decimal places?' said Az.

'We're not there yet but we're well on the way. And if, after a trillion, we haven't shown that π has repetitions and is finite, we'll try a trillion

CHAPTER 40

The Sealed Envelope

Az assumed he must have misheard.

'Seriously? Tell the future?'

'Destiny, for want of a better word, is simply a product of inter-dependent chains of event,' the Count of Gyre said. 'One thing leads to another. If we translate that in terms of sequences of probability, it means the likely thing leads to the next likely thing, and so on and so forth. I could explain about continuous and discrete random variables and probability density function, but I'd doubt I'd leave you any the wiser. What it boils down to is that the Ultimate Reckoner has the computational power to determine the course of a plan of action, a city's fortunes, or even a person's life.'

'I don't believe it.'

'It doesn't matter whether you do or not. The Ultimate Reckoner works. It is a divination tool. It can prophesy. It predicted your coming here.'

Az was sceptical and didn't hide it.

'Oh yes,' said the Count. 'We perform regular data surveys with the Reckoner. It helps us map out our upcoming workload so that we can deploy our personnel resources with the greatest efficiency. We feed in information – in the form of graphs, tabulation, Venn diagrams, flow-charts – via the control panel on that pedestal. The Reckoner then returns its outcome-prediction, which we call an evaluation, through the ticker-tape printer. Twelve days and nine hours ago, we ran one of our usual surveys and received an evaluation strongly indicating that you, Az Gabrielson, the Airborn outlier, would be paying us a visit.' He folded his hands together. 'And here you are.'

'And now you're asking me if I'd like my fortune told by this – this big whizz-bang bunch of cogs and dials?'

Az was starting to think the Count of Gyre wasn't just weird. The man was downright mad. Being fanatical about figures and calculations, amid a city full of people who were similarly obsessed, had messed up his brain.

'No, not in the slightest,' the Count said.

'Well, that's a relief.'

'No, because we knew you were coming, Az, and because you fascinate us, we took the liberty of setting the Reckoner to construct an evaluation for you in advance.'

'Riiight.'

'Believe me, it spent a long time coming up with a result. What with you being an outlier, it had to reach far beyond the normal parameters and the standard quartiles and percentiles to plot your evaluation.'

The Count reached into a fold of his toga and produced a somewhat crumpled envelope.

'And here it is,' he said.

He held the envelope out.

Az deliberated for several moments before finally taking it from the Count.

'It's sealed,' the Count said.

'Have you looked at it?'

'I have.'

'And?'

'I found it striking and intriguing, although hard to fathom fully. But you should not have a problem interpreting it. It is specific to you, after all. You know more about yourself than I do, therefore you will perceive nuances and levels of meaning in it that I cannot.'

'Can't you even give me a hint about it?'

'No. It is your evaluation. It's up to you whether or not you look at it, and it's up to you whether or not you act on what it tells you.' Gravely, the Count added, 'I would rather, though, for the sake of all of us, that you did.'

CHAPTER 41

Tickertape Prognostication

Az returned to *Cerulean* with the envelope still unopened. The meeting with the Count and the trip to the Ultimate Reckoner had left him with a queasy feeling in his stomach. He didn't know what to think. On the one hand, he simply couldn't see how a piece of machinery, however cunning and intricate it was, could foretell the future. But on the other hand, what if it could? Did he really want to find out what lay in store for him?

'What would you do?' he asked Mr Mordadson as they arrived at the airship.

'Me? With a "prophecy" like the one you have there? Read it, laugh, and chuck it in the bin.'

Az didn't do that. Instead, he left the envelope in his cabin and went to see how the repairs were coming along.

Under Rigz's supervision the crew were slicing away the bent section of brace using blowtorches. While one crewman did the cutting, another three hovered around him with fireproof blankets to catch and smother any stray sparks. The helium gas which gave *Cerulean* her buoyancy was not itself flammable – in fact, it was a natural fire retardant. However, if her canvas caught alight, the whole ship could burn, so the sparks from the blowtorches had to be carefully contained.

By afternoon the section of brace was ready to come away, and all hands were put to work levering it free and then lowering it to Gyre's landing apron, where a space had been cleared in readiness. Some of the Alar Patrollers helped with this. Then Rigz and the rest of the crew set about pounding the brace back into shape with mallets.

Flight Lieutenant Wallimson joined in, which was unlike him. He usually regarded any form of manual labour as beneath him, and yet there he was, down on the apron, hammering away and meekly doing whatever the chief engineer told him to. How had this remarkable change of attitude come about? Az didn't like to think that Mr Mordadson had had something to do with it, but that seemed the most plausible explanation.

At dinner in the crew's mess, Rigz pronounced himself pleased with the day's efforts. They were making good progress. Az commended everyone on their hard work, but otherwise he was quiet and subdued at the meal.

The crew assumed he was still feeling guilty about the crash (which he was), and they teased him in the hope of cheering him up.

'Don't worry, skipper. There'll be other masts.'

'Don't say that! You'll put him off ever trying to moor again.'

'Yeah. No more mooring for Az.'

'Never*moor* will he moor!'

'*Moor's* the pity!'

'The *moor* the merrier!'

Az smiled gamely. If they were ribbing him, at least it meant they were halfway to forgiving him.

Guilt, however, wasn't the reason he was subdued.

The envelope still waited for him in his cabin.

And eventually, when everybody went to bed for the night, he was confronted by it. It sat on top of the tiny, tubular-steel desk in the corner of the cabin. Just an oblong of gummed paper, but it seemed to taunt him. It seemed to say, *Don't you want to know? Aren't you even a little bit curious about what's inside me?*

Az remembered the Count of Gyre telling him he would be pivotal to the future of both races. He also remembered Mr Mordadson's recommendation: *Read it, laugh, and chuck it in the bin.*

With a sudden burst of recklessness, he snatched up the envelope and tore the flap open. He fished out the short length of tickertape inside and spread it out on the desktop.

He didn't laugh.

Neither did he chuck the tickertape in the bin.

He scowled.

A prophecy?

If so, it was one he couldn't make head or tail of.

What the Ultimate Reckoner had produced for Az was a symbol that looked like this:

It was meaningless as far as he could see. A two-way arrow? Up and down? With a question mark? What did that represent? What sort of a prophecy was *that*?

After a while he slid the piece of tickertape back into the envelope and stashed the envelope away in the desk drawer, out of sight. He resolved not to think about it any more. It was a joke. A hoax. The Count was either a charlatan or deluded, or both, and the so-called evaluation was pointless, nothing more than machine-generated nonsense.

Az lay down to sleep, and sleep came, though not till after he had lain awake for over an hour, wondering, pondering.

CHAPTER 42

Craterhome Sweet Craterhome

The seven boroughs of Craterhome were named, imaginatively, First to Seventh. They occupied a septet of immense cauldron-like depressions in the ground, clustered close together and linked by a series of tunnels through which road traffic and trams passed to and fro constantly. The smallest borough was three kilometres in diameter and 200 metres below sea level at its base. The largest, the Third Borough, had a span of nearly eight kilometres and plunged to a depth of one and a half kilometres below sea level.

Six of the boroughs were mainly residential, and one in particular, the Fifth, considered itself Craterhome's most gentrified area, with grand apartment blocks decked around the inside of its rim and beautiful mansions nestling in its interior, each set in its own grounds, encircled by lavish, mossy gardens.

The Third Borough, by contrast, was the city's commercial and industrial hub, and was a warren of shops, factories, foundaries and tenements. Day and night it teemed with activity. It never rested, never slept. Its streets and alleyways were perpetually packed with people and threaded by vehicles and clanging trams. A tide of workers flooded in at dawn and flooded out again at dusk, and after dark the borough played host to rowdy throngs of drinkers and fun-seekers who filled the pubs, clubs, restaurants and music venues to bursting. With them came an attendant swarm of thieves and muggers who preyed on the merry revellers like parasites. Crime flourished at night in the Third Borough, under a sickly gas-lamp glare, and prospered only slightly less during the dimness of day.

There were mazy covered marketplaces in the Third Borough. There were teetering-tall curiosity shops and basement-based antique stores. Cobblers and shoeshine men operated out of kiosks that were effectively alcoves in walls. Dodgy doctors hawked potions and nostrums on street corners. Purveyors of 'quality second-hand goods' peddled their wares from the backs of pushcarts, vanishing at the faintest whiff of a police constable. Newsboys roved, yelling out headlines as they brandished copies of the latest edition of the *Craterhome Messenger* and the *Westward Territories Gazette*. One-man bands shuffled from place to place, strumming, bass-drumming, tooting, hooting, cymbal-crashing. Hand-wound barrel organs churned out tunes. Beggars sat slumped, caps ready for coins, showing off the mangled limb or blinded eye or missing hand which prevented them from holding down gainful employment.

It was —

'Mad,' said Robert

'Like an Amblescrut get-together, times a hundred,' said Colin

'Damn hard to drive through,' said Fletcher.

'Scary,' said Michael.

'Bewildering,' said Aurora.

Cassie herself said nothing. She was too busy scanning the crowds to comment. A river of bodies flowed around *Bertha* as the murk-comber crawled along. Cassie, in one of the front nacelles, flicked her gaze from one face to another, hoping, hoping, that suddenly she would spy her father. But stranger after stranger passed by, and several of them glared back up at her and shouted snarky comments which she couldn't hear through the glass. Residents of Craterhome's Third Borough did not, it seemed, take kindly to being peered at.

'Seen a place to park yet?' she asked Fletcher.

'Not a chance round here. There'm barely a scrap of roadway without somebody on it.'

Eventually Fletcher found a spot for *Bertha* in a broad alley, next to some overflowing dustbins and an open drain which carried a trickle of sludgy, lump-filled water towards a sewer grating.

As Cassie clambered out, the stink of putrid garbage and human waste hit her. These smells mingled with a darker odour, an acrid background miasma of coal smoke and other burnt fuels. She coughed and spluttered. Parts of Grimvale were bad, but never *this* bad.

Fletcher emerged after her. He coughed too, and spat out a wad of phlegm. 'Filthy place. How does them stand the stench?'

'Live here long enough, suppose you must get used to it.'

'Well' – Fletcher glanced around the alley – 'I be'n't leaving *Bertha* here unguarded, straight up. Reckon just you and me should go out and everyone else stay behind.'

The proposal was put to the other four and met with no objections. Robert was entrusted with responsibility for keeping *Bertha* and her Airborn passengers safe and secure. Colin was assigned patrol and lookout duties. He would wander around and keep an eye out for potential trouble. He was not, though, to stray far. He should remain within sight of *Bertha* at all times.

'Within sight, right you be,' he said.

'Can I use anti-verm countermeasures if I has to?' Robert asked.

'Yes,' Cassie said. 'But only if you absolutely have to.'

'Ace!'

'Michael? Aurora?'

The Airborn honeymooners stood just inside the loading bay hatchway. Michael had a handkerchief pressed over his mouth and nose. Aurora was gripping the doorframe with one hand, as if to anchor herself.

'I doesn't know how long us'll be,' Cassie said. 'I'd suggest you don't go off exploring, in case you get into difficulties.'

'Don't worry,' Aurora replied. 'I think Michael and I will be very happy staying right here.'

'Good.' Cassie turned to Fletcher. 'OK then, big brother. It'm you and me. Let's see what us can turn up.'

CHAPTER 43

Hundred Ways

No member of the Grubdollar family had visited Craterhome before except Den, who had come here once, long ago, in a fit of youthful curiosity. He'd stayed for a very short time, and all he would ever say about the city was that it was a squirrelly kind of place and he never wanted to go back.

By 'squirrelly' Cassie took her father to mean frantic and devious, and Craterhome was. If she hadn't realised that from her first exposure to it while inside *Bertha*, she certainly did now. She and Fletcher hadn't walked more than a couple of hundred paces before someone tried to sell them a man's wallet, complete with a small lithograph of a woman and two children inside, and someone else invited them to come and watch a 'bed show' (Cassie wasn't sure what this was, but she had a pretty good idea it didn't involve sleeping). A few paces further on, and a basket of laundry tumbled from a fourth-storey balcony and crashed at their feet, scattering clothes everywhere. Fletcher had come within a whisker of being hit, but when he and Cassie looked up they didn't receive an apology. Instead, they were subjected to a torrent of abuse from a waspish-faced woman leaning over the balcony rail. She yelled at them for failing to catch the basket and preventing her laundry from being strewn all over the pavement. Look at it! It was getting trampled! And whose fault was that? Theirs, not hers!

They hurried on. They were heading for a place called Hundred Ways, the nucleus of the Third Borough, a large open square where a number of streets converged, although not actually a hundred; more like twenty. It was renowned as somewhere you could go and spout an opinion on any topic you liked. People would gather and listen, and if they approved of what you were saying they might throw money at you. If they didn't approve, then they would throw other things – rotten vegetables, bad eggs, stones, and worse. Plenty of wandering Deacons came to Hundred Ways. Perhaps *their* wandering Deacon was there now, or had preached there recently.

Having obtained directions from a passably civil passer-by, Cassie and Fletcher soon reached Hundred Ways. A tumult of shouting and jeering echoed around the square. Individuals stood perched on chairs and crates, holding forth on a variety of subjects. Some spoke softly and with a measure of restraint, while others hectored and harangued till they were red in the face. Some pleaded intelligently on political issues such as greater electoral transparency and the reform of prison conditions, while others were clearly madmen and argued, for instance, that fish should be treated as honorary humans or that everyone should build themselves wings made out of wood and feathers and flap up through the clouds to join the Airborn. Each had drawn an audience of anything up to three dozen, and the audience members seemed not to care too much whether what they were being told made any sense or not. They abused the speakers and attempted to drown out their voices with booing and catcalls. Occasionally a decaying-food missile flew through the air, lobbed more for comic effect than with accuracy.

There were several Deacons to be seen, and the two Grubdollars made a slow circuit of the square, stopping to look at each one. On the way they passed a Humanist, who was busy proclaiming his particular creed. Humanism had become widely discredited since the Grimvale uprising. Most people considered the movement and its followers to be irrelevant and out-of-date, in much the same way that Deacons were. The world had moved on.

But if so, no one had told *this* Humanist, who was delivering a scathing attack on the Deacons as if they were still lording it over everyone in their Chancels and the upsets of the past year had never happened. The Deacons who were close enough to hear him would pause from their preaching every so often to tell him to shut up. The Humanist, in return, would advise them to 'shove it up your robes'. The crowds loved it and egged the two sides on, hoping the verbal clash would turn into something more physical.

Cassie sensed Fletcher stiffening as they came near the Humanist. His hands became fists.

'Let it go,' she said, placing a hand on his arm. 'It'm in the past. Him's just a clapped-out windbag with nothing to say.'

Fletcher's fists unclenched. His face was rueful.

'Can't believe I ever thought him and his kind was the way forward,' he said. 'How wrong can a bloke be?'

They completed their circuit of Hundred Ways without seeing a Deacon who matched the description of the one they were looking for. Cassie felt her heart begin to sink.

She also felt a hand delving into the back pocket of her trousers.

Without thinking, she spun round and thumped the owner of the hand.

He, a nine-year-old boy, fell to the ground with a yelp. He was clutching a wad of banknotes which just a second earlier had been in Cassie's pocket. As he scrambled back up onto his feet, Cassie grabbed hold of him by the shirt collar. He struggled to get away, but she shook him roughly till he stopped squirming. Then she plucked the money out of his hand.

'Cass? What'm you doing?' said Fletcher. He had seen nothing except his sister hitting the boy and taking the banknotes off him.

'Him were trying to steal from I,' she said. 'Wasn't you?' she snarled at the youngster.

The boy shook his head vigorously.

'Want I to hit you again?'

The boy shook his head even more vigorously.

'Then 'fess up.'

Slowly, hesitantly, the boy nodded. 'I *were* trying to steal from you. Only, it weren't supposed to go like that.'

'What d'you mean?'

'You wasn't supposed to catch me. And you wouldn't've, either, if I'd been using my proper hand.'

He held up his right hand. The index finger was wrapped in a thick, grubby bandage.

'It'm hard for a pickpocket to make a decent living,' the boy said, 'with his finger busted and his pinching hand out of action.'

CHAPTER 44

Pickpocket With A Broken Finger

Cassie couldn't believe it. 'So you admit you'm a pickpocket.'

Neither could Fletcher. 'Brazen little tyke, be'n't he?'

'Look around,' the boy said with a shrug. 'See all those folk? See how none of they is looking at we? Not even curious, despite all the hollering and frothing you's made? That'm because at least one in ten of they be in the same trade as I or something similar, and the rest'm so used to it them doesn't care when one of we gets caught. It'm only people like you who makes such a big song-and-dance about being thieved from.'

'People like we?'

'Out-of-towners. Country bumpkins.'

Cassie gaped at him. Not only was this boy unashamed about being a professional thief, but he had the nerve to insult her, his intended victim.

'Don't mean it harshly,' he went on. 'But it comes off of you like a reek. The way you was staring around all bug-eyed and baffled. The fact that you had that money making a big fat bulge in your pocket. Nobody in Craterhome carries cash in their *pockets*. Nobody be that stupid. This'm your first time in town, eh?'

Dumbly, Cassie nodded.

'Well, it could be you's been very fortunate, then. Think of I as your wake-up call. From now on you'll be a whole lot more city-savvy, unless you want the same thing to happen again in an hour or so, or less.'

Fletcher burst out laughing. Cassie looked daggers at him, but then she too saw the funny side.

'Got to admit, sis, him's a live wire.'

'I know. I be'n't sure whether to drag his sorry bones to the nearest police station or just give he a pat on the head and let he go.'

'Oh, I wouldn't bother taking I to the cops,' the boy said, tugging himself free of Cassie's grasp and straightening out his shirt. It was a cheap woollen shirt but he smoothed it down like it was a tailored garment woven from the finest silk. 'Them's no better than anyone else in this town. All I has to do is offer they a small, ahem, contribution and I'll be on my way in no time, free as a bird.'

Cassie couldn't help but think that this must be true. In Grimvale the police were reasonably honest, but then that was down to there not being much wealth around. No one could afford to bribe them, so the constables had no choice but to do their job properly. Here in Craterhome, where money abounded and thievery was commonplace, all sorts of opportunities for police corruption were available.

'Tell me then,' she said, 'how come you got your finger broken? Were it an unhappy accident or did someone else catch you trying to nick from they?'

'The second one,' the boy replied, with a hangdog look. He eyed his bandaged finger as if the unfortunate digit had somehow let him down.

'Really?' said Fletcher. 'So maybe you'm not as skilled at the old pocket-picking as you thought.'

'No, I be pretty damn good at it,' the boy said with some force. 'Had plenty of practice. Been doing it since I were four. It were just that this Deacon I were snatching from – him were something out of the ordinary.'

'You tried to steal from a Deacon?' said Cassie.

'I be liking this little pipsqueak more and more,' said Fletcher.

'Yeah, well, I had to, really. The man had this lovely-looking knife strapped to his ankle. A hunter's knife. I saw it when him were going up some steps into a shop. His robe flapped up in a breeze, and there it were. I only caught a glimpse but I knew that knife were worth something and I knew I had to have it. So I waited for him to come out, and him was carrying all this stuff him'd bought, whole big bunch of it in brown paper bags, so I saw this were my chance and I snuck forward, got in his way, bent down like I were tying my shoelace, and made the grab as him stepped around me. Only . . .'

'What?'

'It were uncanny. That'm the only word for it. Uncanny. It were like him *knew* what I were going to do. I mean, Deacons, right? Not exactly worldly-wise, is them? Fresh out of the Chancels and all naïve and clumsy. So I thought him'd be an easy mark. Why not? But him weren't at all. Kicked me here.' The boy pointed to his chest. 'Didn't even see his foot move, I didn't, and next thing I know I's flat on my arse and the wind's knocked out of me and the Deacon's put down his shopping and him's got hold of my finger and hand and . . . *snap*.'

Cassie and Fletcher winced in empathy. Whatever else he was, the kid was still just a nine-year-old.

'"There," him says to I,' the boy went on. '"You won't be trying that again in a while." And here I be, just three days later, back in the game, sort of. But even so, him were so cool and calm about it. Just yanked back my finger quick as you please, like pulling a wishbone. Then him stood up and smoothed out that red hair of his and picked up his bags and waltzed off, and I be left there with a finger pointing up in a direction it had no right to and with enough pain coming from my hand to make me dizzy and feel like throwing up, and —'

'Hold on,' said Cassie, interrupting. 'Back up a moment. Did you say *red* hair?'

'Bright orangey red, it were, and all sticking up like flames.'

She glanced at Fletcher and could tell that he was thinking what she was thinking. Neither could quite believe it. Their Deacon? It couldn't be. Could it?

'Were there another fellow with he?' she asked the boy. 'Tallish, stubbly chin, not too many teeth?'

'Not that I saw.'

'Then did the Deacon by any chance have a van?'

'Yup, that him did.'

'What type?'

'It were a cruddy old half-tarp. I saw it from behind. Barely roadworthy, by the looks of it. And a pile of stuff bundled up in the back, like canvas or something, ropes, poles.'

Cassie stared the boy in the eye. 'Where precisely did you see he? What shop were him buying stuff from?'

The boy stared back. 'I'll show you – for a tenner.'

They held each others gazes for a long while. Then, reluctantly, Cassie peeled off one of her banknotes and waved it front of him. He snatched it from her and tucked it inside the waistband of his trousers.

'Take we there,' she said. 'And if there'm even a hint of any funny business, you'll have another broken finger to go with the one you's already got.'

CHAPTER 45

The Ignorance-Is-Bliss Imperative

Colin Amblescrut was taking his sentry duty very seriously indeed. He marched up and down the alley, performing a smart about-turn at each end. He bore in mind the instruction not to let *Bertha* out of his sight, so that even when he was walking away from her he kept his head swivelled at an angle to make sure she was always within the scope of his vision. Once or twice he collided with a wall because he wasn't properly looking where he was going, but this was a small price to pay. The main thing was that he was following his orders to the letter. He wouldn't let anyone down.

Up in *Bertha's* javelin turret, Robert sat and lovingly fingered the auxiliary set of anti-verm countermeasure controls. He was envious of Fletcher and Cassie, who had had the opportunity to use the countermeasures against people. It wasn't that Robert had a burning urge to hurt anyone, just that he was tickled by the idea of exploding a chaff bomb, say, in the face of some deserving human victim. That would be much more satisfying to watch, he thought, than doing the same thing to a dumb old verm.

As for Michael and Aurora, she was giving him a lecture on the origin of the craters in which Craterhome was built and he was nodding and seemed to be very interested in what she said, although in fact he was already developing the ability common to many husbands, namely the knack of appearing to listen to a wife's comments while not actually listening at all.

'They were formed during the Great Cataclysm,' Aurora was saying. 'The whole of the ground is pocked with them, although it's rare to get so many all in one spot like this. As best we can tell, they're the result of gigantic rocks which hit the planet from space. The impacts left these immense dents and also threw up a thick pall of dust and debris, which collected vapour around it and formed the cloud cover. No one is a hundred per cent certain this is what happened but it's the fairest guess, based on the evidence. People remember the Cataclysm as a time when fire fell from the sky, but the fire was those rocks burning up as they entered the atmosphere.'

'Atmosphere, yes,' said Michael.

'It's fascinating, isn't it? The thought of rocks out there among the stars, big as city blocks, hurtling through space. What were the chances of them hitting us? What did they come from originally? Why were they out there in the first place? Nobody knows. But whatever life was like beforehand, the Cataclysm changed it in a flash. Literally.'

'Literally.'

'Lady Aanfieldsdaughter says there's a huge amount of history that was eradicated by the Cataclysm. There's also a huge amount of Airborn history that has been forgotten or else lies buried so deeply in libraries and archives that it might as well have been forgotten. A lot of it's kept at the Sanctum and there are scholars whose job is to excavate and study it – but what they find out always remains in the Sanctum. The rest of the race doesn't need to know about these things and probably doesn't want to. Lady Aanfieldsdaughter calls this the ignorance-is-bliss imperative. The Sanctum harbours secrets which the general population is better off not having revealed to them.'

'Them.'

'It's like the way we used not to know about the Groundlings. I'm not saying we're worse off now. It was a phase that had run its course. It had to end. But while it lasted, it made the Airborn's lives that bit easier. And the same with all those other secrets. I'm told that the higher up in the Sanctum you are, the more of them you learn. Someone in Lady Aanfieldsdaughter's position is privy to a whole host of facts about our race that would weigh heavily on a lesser person's shoulders. It's almost like the Sanctum elders know about these things so that no one else has to. Which makes me wonder about my own ambitions. Do I want to get to the top, if getting to the top means finding out all sorts of dark, hidden truths? What do you think, Mike?'

'Oh yeah. Definitely.'

Aurora frowned at him. Then her expression turned sly. 'Yes. And I suppose when we have children you'll be happy to look after them full time. You wouldn't mind that?'

'Hmm? No, wouldn't mind.'

'So that I can be free to pursue my career. That's excellent. You promise? Even though I want to have at least ten kids. That won't be too much for you?'

'No way. Too much? No.' Michael glanced up, suddenly worried. 'Wait a second. What are we talking about?'

'Oh, nothing, dear.'

'No, tell me.'

'You just made a promise, that's all.'

'To do what?'

'You don't remember?'

'No.'

'Well, a promise is still a promise. It's not my fault if you weren't listening.'

'You can't hold me to something I said if I didn't know what I was saying.'

'I can and I will.'

Michael rose up, wings outstretched. From tip to tip they spanned half the width of the loading bay.

'You better tell me what I just agreed to,' he said, moving towards Aurora mock-menacingly. 'Or else.'

'Or else what?'

'I may be forced to feather-smother you.'

'For one thing, don't you dare,' said Aurora, grinning. 'For another thing – feather-smother? How old are you? That's straight out of the playground!'

Michael bent his wings towards her, as if intending to cocoon her in them. 'Tell me.'

'Never!' Aurora leapt backwards, propelling herself out through the loading bay hatch.

Michael followed, and together they spiralled upward, batting each other with their wingtips as they went. Peals of laughter spilled from them. It was the sort of blithe, young-couple horseplay which wouldn't have garnered much attention in a sky-city.

But of course, they weren't in a sky-city.

CHAPTER 46

Barnswallow's Practical Goods Emporium

'Hoo. Hum. Yes,' said Cyrus Barnswallow, proprietor and sole sales representative of Barnswallow's Practical Goods Emporium. 'The Deacon. I've had a few Deacons come through my door lately, but how could one forget *him*? Such hair! Like a burning brazier atop his head. A northerner, if I'm not mistaken. There was a hint of the Uplands in his accent, a whisper of the snows and frost.'

'There, can I go now?' said the pickpocket. 'I's done my bit.'

Cassie shushed him. 'Him were on his own?' she asked Barnswallow. 'There weren't anybody with he?'

'I told you —' the boy began, but Fletcher poked him and he fell silent.

'On his own?' said Barnswallow. 'Hoo. As far as I recall, yes.'

'And what did him buy, if I might ask?'

'What did he buy? Huhhh. Hmm. Let me think.' Barnswallow looked around at the tall, tightly packed shelves of his shop, blinking through his brass-rimmed pince-nez spectacles. The room bulged with apparatus and paraphernalia of all kinds. There were fire irons and fishing rods, umbrellas and thermal underwear, gumboots and galoshes, towels and trowels, mousetraps and catflaps, baking trays and camping stoves, fly swatters and ink blotters, binoculars and bin bags, doormats and hardhats, paintbrushes and painkillers … In fact, rather than list what the Practical Goods Emporium sold, it would be easier to list what it didn't.

'I remember he bought a compass,' said its owner. 'A Magnet Opus, what's more. Top of the range. He bought a quantity of beef jerky. He bought some hardtack biscuits. Bags of raisins. What else? Hoo. My memory – it's not what it was, you know. Ah yes, a shovel and a mattock.' Barnswallow pointed to a rack of tools which looked like pickaxes with flattened blades. 'In fact I think he bought two of each. And flashlights. It was quite a shopping list he had, let me tell you. Insect repellent. A first-aid kit. Did he buy a first-aid kit? Yes, he did. One that included antivenin for snakebites. He was very specific about that. Huhhh. There was more, I'm sure.' Barnswallow levelled his gaze sternly at Cassie. 'But what I'm wondering, young lady, is why you're so keen to know. What business is it of yours, the purchases a certain Deacon made?'

Before Cassie could answer, the pickpocket piped up. 'Them's chasing he. I heard they chatting about it on the way here. The Deacon's taken their da hostage or something like that. Them's been looking for he all over, and I be the first real lucky break them's had.' He beamed with pride, as if the small matter of his attempted larceny meant nothing now that he was being so useful.

'Well, there's a thing I never heard of before,' said Barnswallow, stroking his chin. 'These Deacons are a funny lot, eh? Hoo. It's almost as though they're beginning to go crazy, now they don't have a clearly defined role any more. You listen to them preaching at Hundred Ways and their words seem to smack of desperation. So, somehow, it doesn't surprise me to learn that one of them has resorted to kidnapping, or whatever it is he's done with your father. I am surprised, though, that he would be taking him where he appears to be taking him.'

'Him said?' Cassie asked, excited. 'Him told you where them was going?'

'Not as such. I'm merely inferring from his selection of purchases. Hoo. I could be completely wide of the mark, of course. But . . .'

Barnswallow paused for a long time, uttering a stream of those peculiar throat-clearing noises. Cassie was afraid he had become stuck and would simply *hoo* and *huhhh* and *hum* from now till he died. She fought the urge to snap him out of it with a kick in the shins.

Finally he said, 'A map of the south. Did I mention that earlier? He bought one of those. A map covering the area from Craterhome all the way down to the shores of the Centric Ocean. That and the snakebite antivenin . . . Yes. Do you see?'

Cassie thought she did.

'Him's going into the desert,' she said.

'Must be,' said Barnswallow.

'The Relentless Desert,' the pickpocket said wonderingly. 'Be him some kind of nutter? Has him got a death wish or what!'

CHAPTER 47

The Power Of The Press

Yesterday, the *Craterhome Messenger* had carried the following headline on its front page:

CRATERHOMERS
ASSAULTED
BY AIRBORN!

The article below began:

A grotesque prank was played on a group of Craterhome residents visiting the sky-city of Prismburg last week.

The incident, which has only just come to light, involved a tour party whose number included several prominent Craterhomers. Among them were two prosperous local industrialists and the undersecretary to the mayor.

In a wholly unprovoked attack, at least a dozen Airborn descended on the tour party and showered them with dirt. The Airborn also hurled racist abuse. They were heard to use such terms as *ostrich* and *emu*, a reference to the legendary flightless birds of those names.

The victims of the attack were unhurt but were left shaken and distressed.

Inside the paper, an editorial piece tried to strike a note of conciliation but could not quite manage it:

This newspaper abhors conflict of any kind and has been a keen promoter of harmonious relations with the Airborn. We praised the Bilateral Covenant and we have openly welcomed the new economic circumstances that exist between the inhabitants of ground and sky.

We even changed our title from *Examiner* to *Messenger* and redesigned our masthead to feature a winged figure, all in the name of fostering closer ties between us so-called Groundlings and those formerly known to us as the Ascended Ones.

However, the recent unpleasant incident at Prismburg (reported on today's front page) has left us fearing that we might be forced to reconsider our views. Although no one was physically harmed, nonetheless this malicious violation of the newly formed trust between the two races leaves a nasty taste in the mouth.

Are we to accept the Airborn leadership's assurances that it was an isolated event, unlikely to be repeated?

Not if stories the *Messenger*'s newsdesk has been receiving from other regions are true. We are aware of at least three separate accounts of similar outrages being perpetrated on innocent visitors to the sky-cities – tourists whose 'crimes' were nothing more than inquisitiveness, and an absence of wings.

Craterhomers are well known for their tolerance and generosity of spirit. This paper would urge the people of our great city not to do anything in retaliation for the indignity committed upon their own kind. Acts of petty vengeance will help nobody.

At the same time, we must not allow the Airborn to feel that further such attacks will be graciously endured. The insult should be forgiven, but not forgotten.

As a point of interest, one of the 'prominent Craterhomers' who was bombarded with soil by the Feather First!ers in Prismburg was a close friend of the owner of the *Messenger*. He, in fact, brought the incident to the newspaper's attention and had a hand in writing the editorial. He sincerely did not want to stir up trouble but he also could not help letting his chagrin show through.

Consequently, the *Messenger*'s readers – the paper had a circulation of some 200,000 – were infected with a similar sense of hurt and indignation. Contrary to the editorial, Craterhomers were *not* well known for their tolerance and generosity of spirit. They seethed at the thought of Airborn treating their fellow citizens with such contempt. The seething had spread through the city, until it became a pulsing undercurrent of anger that ran everywhere, from borough to borough, mansion to tenement, factory to pub.

So when several people spotted a pair of Airborn sporting around above the rooftops, it didn't take long for news of the sighting to travel the length and breadth of the Third Borough. Nor did it take long for an irate mob to form.

Airborn? Right here in the city? Flying about, free as you please?

Time for a little payback.

CHAPTER 48

The Mob

Outside Barnswallow's, the pint-sized pickpocket raced off without so much as a goodbye. Cassie watched him go with a mixture of amusement and pity. She was dismayed that a kid his age was forced to steal to survive. However, he was a sparky little tyke and seemed to relish his precarious criminal lifestyle, and for that she almost admired him.

A moment after the pickpocket vanished around a corner, Barnswallow came puffing out of his shop.

'Which way did he go?' he demanded, looking right and left.

Cassie pointed.

'Little monster! Hoo! Nabbed a handful of cigarette lighters while I was distracted talking to you. I just noticed.' He lumbered off in pursuit of the boy, shouting over his shoulder: 'If I don't catch him, I'm holding you two liable!'

'Then it'm best if us be'n't here when him comes back,' Fletcher said to Cassie with a chuckle.

'Him's a cold-hearted bastard, though, that copper-topped Deacon,' he added as they set off back in the direction of Hundred Ways. 'Even by Deacon standards. Snapping the kid's finger ...'

'Da wouldn't stand for that,' said Cassie, firmly. 'Which makes me wonder if him's still with the Deacon.'

'I think him is. I think Da were in the van and didn't see what happened. Also, Barnswallow said him bought *two* shovels and mattocks, remember? Why'd him want two if it were just he travelling alone?'

'Good point. Still, more and more I be thinking them makes a strange pair, him and Da. What does them have in common? What be them after together?'

'Dunno,' said Fletcher, 'but I reckon us'll see soon enough.'

Locating Hundred Ways again was not as simple as they thought. Streets seemed familiar but weren't. Distinctive urban landmarks were few and far between. One factory or tenement block looked much like another. The two Grubdollars soon became disorientated, and finally found their destination more by accident than on purpose. Once there, it took them a while to identify which of its converging thoroughfares was the one they had originally entered by earlier.

They both observed that the square was half as full of people as before. There were the same number of speakers but they were addressing significantly smaller audiences.

Cassie then became aware of a rumble of noise. It was coming from some distance away, roughly the direction in which she thought *Bertha* lay. This made her apprehensive.

Fletcher had noticed the noise too. 'What'm that?' he wondered, cocking an ear.

'Not sure. Sounds like voices. Shouting. I reckon us should go and see.'

Other people were heading towards the rumble, and Cassie's apprehension deepened as she joined them. No one was running but equally no one was walking. They were all moving at an eager jog, as if summoned towards something exciting.

She quickened her pace to match theirs. Fletcher did so too. Cassie was picking up murmurs around her. One word she kept hearing was 'Airborn', and it was being said in a fierce, sneering way. She knew now beyond any doubt that *Bertha* was at the centre of the source of the noise. This wasn't premonition; it was a horrible logical deduction.

Finally she and Fletcher arrived at the alley where *Bertha* was parked. They had to fight their way through a milling, baying throng to get within sight of her. All around them fists were being shaken and mouths were yelling with spittle-flecked fury: 'Birdbrains out!' 'Back up where you belong, you wingnuts!' 'Fly away home!'

Bertha was totally surrounded. Hands were hammering on her. Some of the mob tried rocking her from side to side but she was too heavy for that, so they swarmed over her instead and began pounding on her windscreen, portholes and nacelle bubbles.

Cassie caught a glimpse of Robert in the javelin turret, peering out with panic in his eyes.

'Come on!' she urged Fletcher.

The alley was packed tight with people. It was hard to make headway through the crush of jostling bodies. Cassie trod on toes, clambered over shoulders, jabbed with her elbows, but even so she struggled to get any closer to *Bertha*. It was like some nightmare where she needed to move but was stuck fast and no amount of effort could help. She knew – *knew* – that the situation, which was already dire, was about to get a whole lot worse. She might just be able to prevent that, if she could make it to *Bertha* in time.

She couldn't, and the dire situation did indeed get worse.

CHAPTER 49

Bertha Besieged

It had happened appallingly fast. Colin was striding the length of the alley for the umpteenth time, with no less enthusiasm than when he had started out. Michael and Aurora had returned to the loading bay, their brief, japesome jaunt over. Everything seemed calm and normal.

Then Colin saw a half-dozen people appear at the end of the alley. Then a dozen.

'Oi!' he called out. 'What'm you wanting?' He didn't like the way they were looking at *Bertha*.

'Be there Airborn in that murk-comber?' one of the people asked.

'What if there be? What of it?'

The people exchanged looks and muttered to one another, too low for Colin to catch what they said.

Colin puffed out his barrel chest and flexed his arm muscles.

The people melted away.

Job done, thought Colin.

But a few minutes later they returned, and there were more of them this time. Many more. They started to stalk towards *Bertha* purposefully.

Colin gulped. Not good.

He set off towards *Bertha* at a sprint. He was nearer to her than the small crowd of Craterhomers were. They broke into a sprint too, but Colin got to the murk-comber several seconds ahead of them. He leapt aboard, startling Michael and Aurora, who were having a nice, cosy cuddle in the loading bay.

'Us has got trouble,' was all he said, and he hit the button to close the hatch.

The hatch came down painfully slowly. There was still a metre-wide gap left when the frontrunners of the crowd reached *Bertha*. Two of them hurled themselves through into the loading bay, and a split-second later the hatch shut tight with a *clang*.

Colin knocked the first of the intruders cold with a single punch to the head. The other one made for Michael and Aurora with a growl, but Colin grabbed him by the belt and yanked him back, sending him crashing against a bulkhead. The man staggered upright.

He was similarly proportioned to Colin, slightly shorter but no less stocky. He punched Colin twice in the face. Colin shrugged and punched him back twice as hard. Blood spurted from a broken nose. A dislodged tooth went flying. But the Craterhomer didn't seem fazed. With a roar, he launched himself at Colin, arms outstretched.

Michael and Aurora looked on as a brutal fight ensued. Colin and the Craterhomer slammed each other around the loading bay, trading blows. A knee to the groin. An elbow in the stomach. A head butt. Both of them seemed to relish the carnage, baring grins at each other and grunting deliriously as they grappled.

Then an uppercut from the Craterhomer caught Colin under the chin. The legendary thickness of the Amblescrut cranium couldn't protect him there. Colin reeled dizzily, stumbled against a seat, and fell to the floor. The Craterhomer loomed over him. Colin was trying to get up. His opponent raised a leg, ready to stomp his face.

A carton of tinned food came thudding down on the Craterhomer's head. He staggered, his eyes rolled up, and he crumpled like a marionette with cut strings. He landed beside Colin on the floor, unconscious.

Michael dropped the carton, bent down, and helped Colin to his feet.

'I had he,' Colin insisted, between gasps for breath. 'I were just ... lulling he into a ... false sense of security.'

'I know,' said Michael, with a smile.

That was when the hammering outside started, dozens of fists beating against *Bertha*'s bodywork. Within the loading bay the sound resounded deafeningly. It was like being inside a vast kettledrum.

Robert shouted down through the speaker tube: 'There'm hundreds of they! All over the place! And more coming!'

Furious faces glared in through the portholes. The hammering intensified. Aurora ran to Michael and they clung to each other. Colin, still dazed, bellowed abuse at the mob through the porthole glass. There wasn't much else he could do.

Robert's voice came over the speaker tube system again, now scarcely audible above the thunderous racket.

'OK, it'm OK,' he said. 'I's got a plan. Hang on. Watch this.'

Next moment, there was a colossal

ZZZZZAP!!!

followed by a massed shriek from the mob, then a quieter aftermath of groans and moans and pitiful sobs.

'Oh bugger,' said Robert. 'I didn't mean to press *that* one.'

CHAPTER 50

Trail Of Carnage

Nobody was killed, a small miracle for which Robert would be forever thankful. So many Craterhomers were clustered around *Bertha* that, when he accidentally hit the button to electrify her hull, the charge was shared among all of them. Nobody received a dose of voltage large enough to die from. The people closest to *Bertha* got the biggest shocks, and several of them were knocked senseless and suffered superficial burns. The people touching those people were stunned but unharmed. The worst that happened was that their hair shot straight upwards and stayed that way for hours. Further outwards, members of the mob leapt and yelped, but more in surprise than pain.

To Cassie, it was like watching a small earthquake sweep out from the murk-comber, losing strength as it spread. People fell, jumped or twitched according to how far they were from the quake's epicentre. By the time the electricity touched her and Fletcher there was scarcely any power left in it at all. Cassie felt nothing more than a nipping sensation in her palms, which were pressed between the shoulderblades of the person in front of her. Bee stings hurt worse.

She saw her chance.

'Now!' she said, grabbing Fletcher by the wrist.

While the mob was still reeling from the electric jolt, Cassie lunged towards *Bertha*, dragging her brother behind her. They shoved some of the Craterhomers aside and stepped on others, and within seconds they were standing below the driver's pod, which stuck out from *Bertha* like a head on a neck.

A short metal ladder hung from the pod's underside, leading to the access point. Fletcher gave Cassie a boost. She climbed the three rungs and grasped the recessed handle above her. A half-turn clockwise and three half-turns anticlockwise unlocked the access point. It dilated, triangular steel plates retracting with a scraping screech. Cassie hauled herself inside. Fletcher leapt for the ladder and followed her in.

The mob was beginning to stir. People were recovering their wits and stoking up their anger afresh.

Cassie slipped into the driving seat and fired up the ignition. *Bertha* cackled into life. Cassie honked the horn long and loud to warn everyone to get out of the way. She gave them five seconds to do so, then engaged gear.

The mob scramble-tumble-dived clear of *Bertha* as she moved forwards. The murk-comber sliced through the crowd like a plough through soil. The mob shoved themselves up against the walls of the alley and clambered on top of each other to avoid her, or else scattered ahead of her, spilling out into the street at the end.

Soon *Bertha* was in the street too and trundling along at speed, slewing this way and that as her tracks slithered and freewheeled on the cobblestone roads. Cassie didn't much care what *Bertha* hit, as long as it wasn't a person. Her sole concern was leaving Craterhome as fast as possible. Thus a greengrocer's stall was overturned, strewing fruit and vegetables everywhere; a barrel organ got flattened; a stack of baskets containing live chickens received a glancing blow and freed birds fluttered briefly into the air, clucking and squawking; and there was a glancing, sidelong collision with a tram which dislodged that vehicle from its tracks and sent it skidding into a piece of municipal statuary, a stone effigy of one of the city's foremost sons, a long-dead field-marshal who had commanded his army to victory a century ago in the War of Intervention between the Westward Territories and the Axis of Eastern States. The tram shunted against the statue's plinth, and the field-marshal and the horse he was riding slid forwards and landed nose-down on the cobbles. Both broke into chunks.

Cassie winced and drove on. What else could she do? Stop and say sorry?

Shortly afterwards she arrived at a stretch of dual carriageway. Signs pointed a way out of the Third Borough and out of Craterhome. Cassie joined the road, entering the flow of traffic which was heading for one of the tunnels between boroughs. Just before she reached the tunnel, a light on the dashboard came on. It indicated that the loading bay hatch was opening.

'What'm you doing down there?' she asked through the speaker tube, as she applied the brakes.

'Just getting rid of some excess cargo,' Colin replied.

In a rearview mirror Cassie saw him dump the limp form of a man onto the roadside. Seconds later, a second man was dropped out the same way.

'There,' said Colin. 'Much lighter load now. On you go.'

Cassie shoved the control sticks forward and *Bertha* rolled on into the tunnel. In roaring darkness she switched on the floodlights.

The tunnel was two kilometres long. Now at last there was time to think.

And all she could think was: *the Relentless Desert.*

A vastness of rocks and sand, howling winds and lethal wildlife.

A huge, hostile emptiness at the heart of the Westward Territories.

And somewhere in it – who knew where? – was her father, and with him the finger-breaking, knife-carrying Deacon.

Fletcher, crouching beside her, picked up on his sister's mood. 'Things be looking up,' he said.

'How d'you reckon that?'

'Out in the desert there'm only a limited number of roads them can travel on. So our job be that much easier now.'

'What if them doesn't stick to roads, though?'

Fletcher gave the dashboard a pat. 'Where can them go in a half-tarp that a murk-comber can't go better and faster?'

It was a tiny crumb of comfort but Cassie took it and fed on it as though it were a feast.

CHAPTER 51

Desolation Wells, A Final Time

Night after night Magnus Clockweight watched the skies, waiting for the airship to return.

Night after night it failed to appear.

Had he and the other roughnecks won? Had they really driven the pirates off?

His men certainly thought so. They were swaggering around, crowing about their victory over the Airborn. They'd shown those winged raiders a thing or two. You didn't mess with Groundlings and get away with it.

Clockweight himself wasn't so confident. He insisted that the flame-thrower truck remained at the ready and he posted night-time lookouts around the perimeter of the installation. The men called him over-cautious, but he wasn't taking any chances.

The desert had taken care of the burned Airborn bodies. Scavenging animals, hackerjackals most likely, had picked the remains clean. All that was left was a few chewed bones.

Clockweight didn't believe the pirates would let these deaths go un-punished. The leather-clad woman, their leader, had struck him as forceful and ruthless. Even though he had had only the briefest contact with her, he knew she was someone not to be taken lightly.

That was why, although the pirates had not yet got around to taking their revenge on Desolation Wells, he was sure it was only a matter of time until they did. And that was why he was formulating a back-up plan to defend the installation.

The day before yesterday he had sent out a couple of men in a company dune-buggy, with a map and precise instructions. Clockweight knew of a rumour, one that had circulated in this region for decades. He had no idea if the rumour had any basis in truth or not. The mission of the two men was to find out either way.

Strange stories abounded in the Relentless Desert. An area like this – largely uncharted, mostly uninhabited – was rife with tales that stretched credibility, tall stories of the sort that travellers loved to tell. There were unexplained disappearances, isolated tribal communities surviving through cannibalism, valleys haunted by ghosts and ghouls, holes in the ground which were the lairs of giant fire-breathing termites, lakes of quicksand which shifted from place to place as though alive, that sort of thing.

This particular rumour could just be one of those.

But if it wasn't, it might hold the key to combating the pirate airship, and so it was worth investigating.

Another night had fallen, and the two-man search party had not yet returned. Clockweight was expecting them back soon. They'd be here by tomorrow at the latest. Unless, that was, they had fallen foul of a giant fire-breathing worm or a roving quicksand lake!

Clockweight prayed that the black airship would not make its reappearance tonight. If the pirates were to hold off for just a couple more days, he and his men might have a better chance of fighting back.

But his prayer, alas, was not answered.

Around midnight, *Behemoth* descended from the clouds.

Directly above Desolation Wells.

One of the lookouts spotted her. Scarcely had he raised the alarm, when an object fell from the airship's rear hatch.

It tumbled lazily, like it had all the time in the world. It was an oil barrel, and there was a bright white flame at one end of it, sparking and sputtering – a fuse.

The barrel hit one of the storage tanks and exploded.

A split-second later the storage tank itself exploded. A million litres of crude oil ignited at once. The fireball was the size of a city block and illuminated the desert landscape for kilometres around. The thunderclap of detonation was loud enough to burst eardrums.

Then the adjacent storage tank went up. Another city-block-sized eruption of fire tore the night air apart. The shockwave shattered every pane of glass on the site that hadn't been shattered by the first explosion. It also blew the installation gates clean off their hinges.

Men ran out of the housing blocks. They scurried this way and that like ants whose nest had been stamped on. Deafened, dazzled, dazed, they didn't know where to go. Clockweight tried to marshal them, directing them towards the fleet of tanker trucks. He knew Desolation Wells was doomed. Fire was everywhere. The inferno at the storage tanks was spreading to the refinery and the drilling towers. Lesser explosions thumped all around, one after another. The only sensible course of action was to abandon the installation.

But the pirates had anticipated this. *Behemoth* turned towards the area where the trucks were parked. Another of those homemade oil-barrel bombs was jettisoned from her rear hatch. It landed in the midst of the trucks. The ground rocked as it blew up. Most of trucks were destroyed instantly; the rest caught light and burned to charred wrecks.

Clockweight ordered the men to head for the desert. He could barely make himself heard above the roar of flames. The air was searing-hot and filled with black, choking smoke. Clockweight grabbed workers by the scruff of the neck or gave them a kick up the backside. Get moving! Get out! Go!

To venture into the Relentless Desert after dark, on foot, was the next best thing to suicide, which was why many of the men hesitated even though the installation was coming down around their ears. They had an ingrained fear of what lay out there beyond the perimeter fence. Nevertheless, it was certain death to stay put. They hurried towards the gates, with Clockweight urging them along every step of the way.

Behemoth hadn't finished with them, however.

Gliding serenely above the blazing chaos on the ground, she dropped three further barrel bombs. Each was aimed at the fleeing WOE employees. Each found its mark.

Men died screaming. Some were incinerated on the spot. Some ran with their clothes and hair afire, like human torches. They rolled on the ground and beat at themselves to put out the flames, but with little success. The lucky ones got away with patches of scorched flesh and blistered skin. No one was left unscathed.

Behemoth performed a circuit of the installation, as if gloating over the devastation she had wrought. Here and there, fresh fires were breaking out. Gouts of flame shot upwards. A derrick keeled over with a huge crash, like a dying dinosaur. A drilling tower collapsed in on itself. Smoke billowed. Flame-light cast everything in an eerie, pulsing yellow.

Finally the airship lofted her nose and slipped up into the clouds.

Down on the ground, a safe distance from the immense, twisting funeral pyre that had been installation number 137, Clockweight gathered the survivors together and counted heads. Barely fifty remained alive, out of a workforce of almost two hundred.

Before dawn, twenty of those fifty succumbed to their injuries. They shuddered and gasped on the sand, and there was nothing their toolpusher or anyone else could do except watch them expire, slowly, in agony.

Clockweight himself had lost most of the skin off his left arm and cheek. One eyebrow had been singed off. He was dizzy with pain and shock.

But even as Desolation Wells was reduced to an expanse of smoking rubble, a fire of a different kind was kindled in his belly.

CHAPTER 52

Two Pieces Of Very Bad News

She couldn't get it out of her thoughts. She tried to dismiss everything Lord Urironson had said to her, and couldn't. His words had bored into her brain and were gnawing at her like a worm.

Every corridor Lady Aanfielsdaughter walked down, every shaft she flew through, every room and chamber she entered, she felt that she was being surreptitiously watched. People she passed glanced at her then glanced away again, furtive. Anyone who greeted her seemed to mean more than he or she actually said. Every *hello* and *how are you?* seemed pregnant with implication. Even friends and close confidants were wary around her, or so she felt. Their talk was guarded, as though there was a lot they had to say but they were holding their tongues for fear of upsetting her.

She thought she heard whispering behind her back. At times she thought she heard giggling.

No matter how often she told herself she was being silly and paranoid, she just could not shake the notion that Lord Urironson was right. The mood around the Sanctum was uneasy, jittery. People were worried, and they blamed her for it. No one accused her directly of anything. No one came out and said what they were feeling. But she could see it in their eyes.

Not everyone perceives tolerance as weakness, Farris, she had said.

Many do, Lord Urironson had replied. *Not least in this very city*.

The situation wasn't helped by the arrival of two pieces of very bad news from the ground.

In the city of Craterhome there had been an incident involving two Airborn. Reports were sketchy but it appeared that a rabble of locals ganged up on the Airborn and some kind of retaliation occurred, resulting in a number of minor injuries among the Groundlings. Something to do with a murk-comber.

Lady Aanfielsdaughter wasn't sure what to make of this story but some instinct, some intuition, told her she knew the people concerned. There were plenty of murk-combers around. This one didn't *have* to be the Grubdollars'. Yet somehow she was convinced that Cassie's family were mixed up in the affair.

426

The other piece of news was that Westward Oil Enterprises had lost all contact with installation number 137. Telegram messages weren't reaching it. Truck shipments of refined oil had stopped coming from it.

There was cause to be alarmed, the WOE executives said.

Lady Aanfieldsdaughter concurred.

Every hope she now had was pinned on *Cerulean*. If Az and Mr Mordadson failed in their mission, her position at the Sanctum was in jeopardy but, more importantly, so was the entire fledgling relationship between Airborn and Groundlings.

She waited for some good news to come from Redspire.

And waited.

CHAPTER 53

Dangers Of The Relentless Desert: A Field Guide

It was a hard journey.

Once civilisation petered out and there was only desert, the roads dwindled to dirt tracks (and frequently were not even that). There were gravelled patches where the bigger potholes had been filled in; otherwise it was just a bumpy, rock-strewn surface all the way. Now and then the edges of the road blurred into the surrounding terrain so that it was almost impossible to tell where one ended and the other began. Now and then, too, the rusted hulks of trucks loomed at the roadside, half buried in sand, testament to the desert's power to conquer even the sturdiest means of transport.

The half-tarp kept trying to join the ranks of those abandoned trucks, breaking down an average of three times a day. Dust would clog up the engine air intakes, or the radiator would overheat, or sand would get into the brake cylinders and jam a wheel. The van was not at all suited for this kind of environment. But Den kept it going. His skills as a mechanic were repeatedly put to the test but each time he rose to the challenge and triumphed.

On one occasion he was lying on his back beneath the van, plugging a crack in the oil sump, when he felt something touch his ankle. It was a brushing, tickling sensation.

Immediately he froze. 'Gerald?' he said softly. 'You there?'

Deacon Hardscree was standing at the rear of the van, taking sightings with his compass while also keeping an eye out for predators. 'Yes.'

'There'm something on my foot.'

Hardscree went round to where Den's legs were sticking out from under the van.

'Well? What be it?'

Hardscree's answer was barely a whisper. 'Don't move, Den.'

'I be'n't moving.'

'Stay like that.'

'All right, but what be it?'

No reply.

The tickling sensation grew worse. Something was exploring the skin around his ankle – something small with sharp little claws or feelers.

Den was very frightened. All at once he was sweating from every pore and his mouth had gone bone-dry.

For what seemed like ages, nothing happened. He couldn't see Hardscree and he began to wonder if the Deacon was actually doing anything.

Then there was a scrabble of activity, a thud, a wet squelchy sound, and finally the words he had been longing to hear: 'It's OK now. You're safe.'

He slithered out, to find Hardscree holding up a hunting knife. Impaled on the blade was the ugliest creature Den Grubdollar had ever clapped eyes on. It was so loathsome it made a verm look like a cute fluffy kitten.

'Scorpipede,' said Hardscree.

The thing was still alive, thrashing and writhing around on the knife. It was a handspan in length from end to end and had four sets of pincers, a dozen little blue-black eyes like elderberries, and a segmented body with a pair of legs on each section. Its abdomen tapered then forked into three tails. Each tail had a barbed, semi-transparent bulb at the tip and each bulb contained a venom of a different colour: one yellow, one red, one black. The venoms were dripping out through the barbs and splattering uselessly on the ground. Thick dark goo was oozing down the knife blade from where it pierced the scorpipede's thorax.

'It uses a particular venom according to its prey,' said Hardscree, gesturing at the tails. 'Yellow for other insects, red for reptiles and black for mammals. Each is designed to kill that particular species in an instant. You, for instance, would have been injected with the black stuff, and it'd've stopped your heart in a few seconds. Ingenious creature, really.'

'Maybe so,' said the scorpipede's intended victim, 'but I'd be happier if that "ingenious creature" were a lot more dead than it be now.'

'Of course.'

Hardscree flicked the scorpipede onto the ground and crushed it underfoot.

'Nice knife, by the way,' said Den, mopping his damp forehead with his sleeve.

'Isn't it? I was given it by my father when I turned twenty-one.'

'You Uplanders. It'm all weapons and hunting with you lot. Surprised you still carry it, though, being as you'm a Deacon and all.'

Hardscree grinned. 'You can take the boy out of the mountains but you can't take the mountains out of the boy. Now, how are the repairs coming along?'

'Should be done soon.' Den crouched down to crawl back under the van. He paused to check there weren't any more scorpipedes lurking in the vicinity, then nodded at the knife. 'Best keep that handy, eh? Just in case.'

Hardscree wiped the blade clean on his robe. 'Don't you worry, Den. You're far too valuable for me to lose you.'

There were plantlife hazards as well as wildlife hazards in the Relentless Desert. Early the next morning, after breakfast, Den went off in search of a place to relieve himself. A large clump of bushes seemed the ideal spot, providing shelter and a little bit of privacy – until he heard the Deacon call out, 'I wouldn't go there if I were you.'

'Why not?'

'Weltwort. Releases a puff of caustic mist when disturbed. We have a similar species in the Uplands. It burns like the blazes and the blisters last for days. All you have to do is brush against it and you'll get a squirting.'

'Ah. Understood.'

Den tiptoed delicately around the weltwort bushes and found somewhere else to do his business, far away from any vegetation.

Not all the difficulties they encountered were living ones, either. Late one afternoon a sandstorm of staggering ferocity rose up, engulfing the half-tarp and shaking it so viciously that driving became impossible. There was no alternative but to pull over and wait for the storm to pass.

It raged for an hour, buffeting the stationary van and its occupants. Den watched particles of sand etch tiny scratches in the windscreen glass. Every so often the van felt as though it was about to be plucked off the ground and sent rolling over and over. Somehow it stayed put.

While the sandstorm was at its height, a grim-faced Hardscree said, 'You must be wondering right now whether any of this is worth it.'

The thought had crossed his companion's mind. 'I don't known which'm tougher,' Den replied ruefully. 'Getting to where us is going or the fact that I had to leave my kids behind and keep they in the dark about it all. I's never deceived they before in any way.'

'It was necessary. We both agreed on that. You wouldn't want them to face these risks you're facing.'

'But if I dies out here and them never knows what became of I . . .'

'We aren't going to die, Den.'

'You sound pretty certain.'

'Trust me,' said Hardscree, with a skewed smile. 'I'm a Deacon.'

'But what if, after everything, this place us is looking for – what if it don't exist?'

'It does.'

'But you's never seen it. You's never been there.'

'Deacon after Deacon has told me about it over the years. It's an open secret among our fraternity.'

'And you really believe the stuff that'm kept there be what us needs?'

'I do. I believe it's "stuff" that will pave the way to a better tomorrow. It will put us on a fairer footing with the Airborn. It will enable us and

430

them to interact as equals – true equals. It's our race's best chance of safeguarding our future. You see, Den, as long as the Airborn look down on us, literally look down on us as well as figuratively, we're never going to be more to them than something unpleasant beneath their feet. Rather like that scorpipede of yours. Something they'd much rather squash than embrace. But we, you and I, can change that, and will.'

Den thought of Az, the one Airborn he knew at all well. The lad wasn't the type to look down on anybody. But then Az wasn't representative of his kind, was he? He was himself looked down on by other Airborn. So there was no reason to think the rest of Az's race weren't just as Hardscree described. After all, they'd spent centuries not even acknowledging that Groundlings existed. They had lived off the sweat of Groundling backs, conveniently forgetting who it was that was making their lives so easy for them. Now, everyone on the ground was meant to be thankful for no longer being taken for granted – but the fact was, Groundlings were giving away as much of their material wealth as ever, and receiving just trinkets and knickknacks in return. It wasn't right.

All the way from Grimvale through Craterhome to here, Hardscree had quietly but insistently reiterated these arguments. He'd claimed his proposed solution would work. It would be the first step towards evening up the scales, which were at present heavily weighted in the Airborn's favour.

Den was once more convinced. Even with the sandstorm still battering away at the half-tarp, he felt a renewed firmness of purpose. He had already decided he liked this Deacon. Now, more than that, he was starting to admire the man.

The sandstorm ebbed and subsided.

With the shovels and mattocks purchased from Barnswallow's Practical Goods Emporium, the two men dug the van's wheels out from the drifts of sand that had banked up around them. Den cleaned out the air intake filters, yet again.

The journey across the Relentless Desert continued.

CHAPTER 54

Absence Of Evidence

Redspire, unsurprisingly, was red and consisted of lots of spires.

Legend had it that you couldn't accurately count the spires. Anybody who tried to ended up with a total that was either one more or one less than the previous total somebody had arrived at.

Legend also had it that Redspire was the first of the sky-cities to be built. Or the last. One or the other.

What was certain about Redspire was that it lay at the extreme southern tip of the Western Quadrant. It was the remotest sky-city. It stood at the very edge of the Airborn realm.

An outlier, Az thought. *Like me.*

Then he told himself to shut up. He was determined not to think about Gyre, outliers, or anything connected with the Ultimate Reckoner's so-called prophecy. He shunted all such thoughts to the back of his brain and left them in the darkness there to wither and die.

So: Redspire.

Like a huge scarlet pincushion.

No, like an upturned hairbrush with hundreds of bright red bristles.

Whatever it resembled, there it lay, dead ahead. Destination. Journey's end.

And *Cerulean* was approaching it at low speed, with an escort of Alar Patrollers around her. This was a necessary precaution as well as a show of strength. No one knew what to expect from Redspire. No one had any idea what sort of reception *Cerulean* would receive.

'I don't see any airship,' observed Rigz, scanning the city.

'She could be berthed on the far side,' Az said. 'That's why we're going to do a circuit.'

Cerulean was also going to fly once around Redspire to let all the inhabitants know she was there.

It took half an hour to complete the orbit of the sky-city. The Alar Patrollers maintained perfect formation the whole way. They flew in V-shaped units, seven men per grouping. Wing Commander Iaxson used shouts and a whistle to keep them tightly together. He didn't allow any Patroller to deviate more than a metre from position. It was configuration flying at its finest and most precise.

No airship could be found. Redspire's civic landing apron had the usual complement of single-seater planes, airbuses, cargo transporters, helicopters, autogyros and private passenger craft, but nothing that even remotely resembled a lighter-than-air troop carrier.

'You don't suppose this was all a false alarm?' Az asked Mr Mordadson.

'No, I do not,' came the thin-lipped reply. 'Absence of evidence is not evidence of absence. Let's move in and dock. The airship may not be here but someone in the city will know where she is.'

CHAPTER 55

A Huge Collective Hangover

The silence was eerie. The whole of Redspire appeared to be asleep. Or worse.

Az, Mr Mordadson, Wing Commander Iaxson and a trio of Patrollers padded across the landing apron, waiting for someone to hail them and ask what their business was.

No one did. The landing apron was populated only by parked aircraft. There wasn't a living soul in sight. The Patrollers gripped their lances, looking around, wary and uncomfortable.

'Eleven-thirty a.m.,' said Mr Mordadson. 'You'd have thought there'd be *somebody* up and about.'

They ventured further into the city. Everywhere, there were indications that Redspire was usually an inhabited, bustling place. Shops, though shut, had merchandise on display in their windows. Municipal fountains gurgled. The greenery in public parks had been tended to, more or less.

Yet, for all these signs of normality, no people. Where were they?

Finally, on a triangular plaza suspended between three spires, people were sighted.

Three men and two women lay sprawled together in a heap. Their heads touched and their arms and wings were thrown around one another.

Dry-mouthed, Az asked, 'Are they ...'

'Dead?' Mr Mordadson stepped closer to the jumble of bodies, sniffed, then straightened up again. 'No. Dead drunk. Look.' He pointed to a litter of empty wine bottles strewn around the slumbering figures. 'They've been having quite a party.'

'Want us to wake them up?' asked Iaxson.

'Why not?'

The Alar Patrollers took great delight in prodding the sleepers with their lances.

'Come on, you lazy lot!'

'Wakey-wakey, rise and shine!'

Soon all five were blearily on their feet and standing in a dishevelled line. Mr Mordadson flashed his Silver Sanctum seal and started interrogating.

It turned out that not just these five but the whole of Redspire had been carousing the night before. Apparently, this wasn't uncommon. Roughly once a month Redspire went on a massive bender. The city's population danced and drank from dusk till dawn, then spent all of the next day in a state of disarray, nursing a huge collective hangover.

'How nice,' said Mr Mordadson. 'Do these celebrations commemorate anything in particular?'

'No,' said one of the bloodshot-eyed citizens with a shrug. 'We just like to do it.'

'Tradition,' said another.

'What about your kids?' Az asked. 'What happens to them while the grown-ups are boozing themselves into a stupor?'

'Where are your wings? Are you a Groundling?'

'No, I'm not. Now answer me.'

'Our kids? We keep them up. They're usually so exhausted by morning that they sleep late, so their parents get a lie-in too, much needed. Now, is that everything? Only, my head's killing me and I'd really like to close my eyes and get a bit more kip, if you don't mind.'

'Oh, that's definitely not it,' said Mr Mordadson. 'I have plenty more questions to ask. However, out of respect for your delicate condition, I'll confine myself to one. Where's the airship?'

All five of the Redspirians shuffled their feet and fluffed their wings. None was keen to answer.

'Come along,' said Mr Mordadson. 'You all know what I'm talking about. But it appears I'm not speaking clearly enough. Perhaps it would help if I RAISED MY VOICE SLIGHTLY.'

In fact, he shouted these words, and the five Redspirians flinched and grimaced. Loud sounds were unpleasant when you were suffering the after-effects of too much alcohol.

'SO?' Mr Mordadson went on. 'WHICH OF YOU IS GOING TO TELL ME ABOUT THE AIRSHIP? EH?' He was yelling right in their faces. 'OR WOULD YOU LIKE ME TO **REALLY TURN UP THE VOLUME?**'

'All right, all right,' said one of the women, clutching her brow as though trying to prevent her brains from spilling out. 'Please. We'll tell you anything. Just . . . please keep it down.'

'It's all Naoutha's doing,' said another of the five. 'Naoutha Nisrocsdaughter.'

'Her and her gang,' said another. 'They're the ones to blame.'

'Interesting,' said Mr Mordadson. 'Explain.'

Between them, haltingly, the five did.

CHAPTER 56

Prodigal Daughter

Redspire had long harboured a grudge. Because it was so far from any-where else, it always felt neglected and overlooked. It felt that the rest of the Airborn race didn't care about it and preferred to pretend it didn't exist.

The city was fine with that, mostly. It took a perverse pleasure in being on the fringes, isolated and ignored. That was why it would do things like hold mammoth monthly parties – to show how little concern it had for conventional behaviour and the niceties of polite society. It regarded the other sky-cities as a snooty club to which it had no desire to belong. They rejected it, it thought, so it rejected them in return.

All the same, deep down, Redspire resented the way it was sidelined and disregarded. It had a long list of complaints, many of them legitimate grievances. For instance, every time one of its citizens applied to join the Silver Sanctum, he or she was turned down (the reason usually given was 'irreverent attitude'). And then there was the fact that Redspire alone, of all the sky-cities, did not receive supplies from the ground and therefore had to rely on imports from its neighbours. For this it was charged a steep mark-up, which was justified on the grounds that everything had to travel a long distance and there were transport costs. However, goods exported out of Redspire fetched the same prices as those from anywhere else. Was that fair? No, it was not.

Redspire, then, was in a dilemma. It yearned for respect and proper treatment, but at the same time couldn't bring itself to act in a responsible manner which would guarantee those things.

The city's sense of injustice was sharpened when the presence of Groundlings was acknowledged officially and the Bilateral Covenant was signed. Suddenly Redspire was having to pay a further premium on incoming supplies of daily necessities, to compensate for the amount the other sky-cities were now having to pay.

That was when Naoutha Nisrocsdaughter decided to take matters into her own hands.

Naoutha was a rebel even by Redspire standards. One of that rare minority born with black wings, she had been insolent as a child and a hopeless tearaway as a teen. By the time she reached adulthood she was completely out of control, and had gathered a gang of like-minded types around her, a good forty or fifty of them. While the city was content to enjoy a major shindig once a month, Naoutha and friends made it their goal to drink and be merry every single night. They were troublemakers and vandals, and the city had tried its hardest to tame them but without success. You just couldn't control Naoutha. All her life she had stood out thanks to those black wings. She had been bullied at school because of them and had learned to fight back. She had embraced Redspire's outcast ethic and taken it to the next level. She was a source of eye-rolling despair to most people, but those who admired her, admired her ardently. Her young band of followers worshipped the air she flew through. They were disciples as much as partying pals. She ruled them, and they loved her and would do anything for her.

Not only that but they were into pterine.

Pterine was a recreational drug, a stimulant derived from a hormonal secretion contained in the gall bladders of eagles. Powerful stuff, it sharpened the reflexes and increased the body's strength and endurance. While its effects lasted it was like having an extra set of wings. You felt wonderful. Invincible. Indestructible.

It was terribly addictive, of course. It was also terribly expensive. Naoutha and her gang got into pterine in a big way and, since none of them was any good at holding down a job, they needed to find some other method of funding their habit.

That was when they started making trips to the ground.

Having learned there were people down there after all, Naoutha spied a commercial opportunity. She started to go exploring, and more often than not her gang went with her. They descended in aircraft and overcame ground-sickness through sheer willpower, or so they claimed, although it was reckoned that they medicated themselves with pterine beforehand to armour themselves against the worst symptoms of the condition. Either that or their hard-partying ways had increased their tolerance to dizziness, nausea and fatigue.

They returned with extraordinary tales of what they found down there in the vicinity of Redspire. Largely they found wilderness – vast tracts of uncultivated land, rugged, barren, intimidating. There were pockets of Groundling habitation, but these were few and far between. The rest was just emptiness.

Then one day they came back with an airship.

She was old and decrepit. That she could fly at all was nothing short of a miracle. Naoutha and co. managed to get her up to Redspire, just. They refused to say where they had found her. Instead, they set to work fixing her up. They toiled zealously, patching the holes in her balloon canvas, reconditioning her ailing engines, and replacing her broken propeller arms with new ones they forged themselves. They scavenged and borrowed the materials they needed. They spent weeks making the airship as good as she had ever been, and then, doubtless as a tribute to Naoutha's wing colour and peculiar dress sense, they painted her matt black all over, adding the black-on-red skull and crossed feathers motif to her tailfins.

It was safe to assume that the airship must be a troop carrier from the wartime era, although nobody knew which one she was or how she had survived when all the rest had been decommissioned. The only clue to her origins was the sky-city insignia on her tailfins. Before being covered with Naoutha's own emblem, the fins had sported the colours of Brightspans.

Whatever the airship had been called formerly, Naoutha had dubbed her *Behemoth*, and that seemed as good a name as any.

In *Behemoth*, Naoutha and her gang took off one evening and weren't seen again for several days. When they sailed home, they brought with them a substantial cargo of timber and coal. They offered this to the city for a reasonable sum, less than the usual asking price for such items, and the city, reasonably, bought it. No questions were asked. Among Redspire's officialdom the opinion was that Naoutha had struck a deal with some Groundlings somewhere. That was what they told themselves, at any rate. They were getting a bargain, so they didn't want to dwell too hard on the matter of where the stuff was coming from or how Naoutha had obtained it.

They felt the same way when *Behemoth* came back with a consignment of steel.

And, even more so, when she came back with barrels of fuel.

Above all else, Redspire was pleased that Naoutha appeared to have mended her ways. She and her gang were still into pterine, but that aside, they had transformed themselves into enterprising individuals who wanted to help out their hometown. Naoutha was coming good after all. The prodigal daughter had become a proper Redspirian.

That said, she had not been seen for nearly a week now. It was assumed *Behemoth* was off scouting for further supplies; Naoutha was trying to locate more Groundlings to do deals with.

And that was everything the five hung-over citizens knew about the airship and its crew.

Or almost everything.

CHAPTER 57

The Aircraft Mausoleum

'What if I told you this Naoutha of yours wasn't buying these supplies but *stealing* them?' said Mr Mordadson. 'What would you say to that?'

The five Redspirians exchanged looks. Then one of them said, 'Well, it would explain why you're here with Patrollers.'

'Stealing?' said another. 'For real?'

'But you knew all along,' Mr Mordadson said. 'There's no point trying to act surprised. You didn't want to think it, you certainly didn't want to say it aloud, but you knew. Your city had got a nice little black-market thing going, so nobody was willing to ponder too deeply on the whys and hows.'

'Didn't the local Alar Patrol get even a tiny bit suspicious?' Iaxson asked. 'I'd have thought they would have questions even if no one else did.'

'This is Redspire,' came the reply. 'We barely have an Alar Patrol.'

'The bats,' said another of the five, with a sheepish grin. 'That's what we call them, bats. As in blind as. Because they never quite manage to see any crimes happening.'

'They're bribed to be that way,' said a third. 'No one really wants the Patrollers sticking their beaks into other people's affairs. A little extra cash in their wage packets every month makes sure of it.'

'It's our system,' said a fourth. 'It's always worked OK.'

Iaxson scowled and spat. 'Yes, that makes sense. A place like this gets the policing it deserves.'

The five nodded in agreement, as if the wing commander had spoken approvingly.

Mr Mordadson turned to Az. 'What do you reckon? Do you think we've been given enough information to find this *Behemoth*?'

'Not really, but I don't feel we're going to get anything else useful from this bunch.'

'You may be right. I fear even shouting at them again won't help.'

One of the men said, 'For what it's worth, I bumped into one of Naoutha's gang recently and we had a brief chat. It was in a bar, as a matter of fact.'

'In a bar,' said Mr Mordadson, deadpan. 'Why am I not shocked?'

'This was shortly before *Behemoth* last went off,' said the Redspirian, unfazed. 'This guy was there in the bar along with a few of his mates. They stand out because they dress pretty outlandishly. Silks, scarves, brocade waistcoats, beads in their hair, plenty of leather. That's on top of all the tattoos and piercings they already had.'

'Playing at being pirates,' said Mr Mordadson, with a sneer. 'And still no one stopped to think, "Hang on, where are they getting this stuff they're selling to us so they can buy their next pterine fix? Can their source really be legit?"'

'Do you want me to tell you this story?'

'Oh, yes please. Do proceed.'

'So anyway, it so happened that we were ordering drinks at the same time,' said the Redspirian, 'and I told the guy what a good job he and the rest had done with that airship, fixing it up the way they did. It's not as if there are airship maintenance manuals you can just buy in any bookshop, are there? And he scratched at the scabs on his face – pterine scabs, they all get them if they use it too much – and then said, "Labour of love. Plus, we improvised a lot."'

'Is that it? What a charming anecdote.'

'No, that's not it. I'm trying to remember how the conversation went after that. He started going on about how he used to be a professional aircraft mechanic but got the sack because his boss said he was unreliable. And he said he did most of the repair work himself, with the others helping. They didn't want to but Naoutha bullied them into it, telling them she'd withhold their pterine if they didn't make themselves useful. You can work extra hard if you're on pterine. You can also work extra hard if your pterine supply is under threat.'

'I almost admire the woman,' Mr Mordadson commented drily.

'So then I think I said something like, "So why's it such a big secret where you got the airship from?" And the gang guy said – now I remember, his name's Abuzaha Biletson – he said, "It's only a big secret because we don't want anyone else finding the place." I said, "Why not?" and Biletson said that there were other items there which he and his friends might like to use in future so they wanted to keep the place's whereabouts to themselves.'

'Go on.'

'So I said, sort of making a joke, "Come on, you can tell me." I thought maybe I'd pushed it too far and he would just clam up, but he was pretty far gone and he did reveal something about the place. He used the phrase ... oh, what was it?'

The Redspirian racked his aching brains. Mr Mordadson struggled to contain his impatience.

Finally the man said, 'An aircraft mausoleum. That was it. I'm sure that was how he described it.'

'An aircraft mausoleum.'

'Right, and he said it was this weird mix of junkyard, museum and, you know, tomb. Then his drinks arrived and that was the end of the chat.'

'Biletson didn't give any clue where this place was? Direction? Distance? Anything?'

'Somewhere south, that's all I know. Quite a way south, I think.'

Mr Mordadson sighed. 'Fair enough. It's a lead, although not much of one. I'd like to thank all of you for being such fine upstanding citizens. You're a credit to your race. You can collapse now.'

With grateful groans the five Redspirians sank to the floor.

CHAPTER 58

The Fate Of The Brightspans Empress

'Brightspans,' said Az as he, Mr Mordadson and the Patrollers made their way back to *Cerulean*. 'Then the airship would have to be the *Brightspans Empress*.'

'You think?' said Mr Mordadson.

'Stands to reason.'

'The *Brightspans Empress*,' said Iaxson. 'Rings a faint bell. How come she wasn't decommissioned like the rest?'

'She was meant to be,' Az explained. 'She was on the list. But her captain was a sentimental old sort, couldn't bear the thought of her being torn apart and sold for scrap, so shortly before the decommissioning was due to begin he hijacked her. That's if you *can* hijack your own airship. At any rate, he and a few other crewmen sneaked into the breakers' yard and made off with her. Then they abandoned her somewhere far out from the airlanes, letting her fly off unmanned into the sunset while they went home in another aircraft. She was never seen again, so presumably she must have gradually lost height, sunk through the cloud cover and floated to the ground more or less intact. Of course nobody knew back then that there were people down there. The captain just thought he'd rather see her go all in one piece, with some dignity. I can see his point. I'd feel the same way about *Cerulean*.'

'Did he get into trouble?'

'He certainly did. He was stripped of his rank and pension and had his pilot's licence torn up. Same with his accomplices. They ended their careers in disgrace. But even so, I bet they thought it was worth it.'

'And now the *Brightspans Empress* is back,' said Mr Mordadson, 'and under the control of a bunch of pterine-heads.'

'Yup,' said Az. 'So what's our next move?'

'Fancy a trip below the cloud cover?'

'Not much,' Az replied, 'but I reckon we don't have a choice.'

CHAPTER 59

The Maze

Bertha loved the desert. This was her kind of terrain. This was what a murk-comber was built for.

The cruder and more uneven the roads became, the deeper and throatier *Bertha*'s cackle grew. She hadn't been particularly happy on ordinary roads, asphalt too smooth and slippery for her liking, and she hadn't relished the cobbles of Craterhome at all. Here, though, with grit and sand and sprigs of scrubby vegetation beneath her tracks, she thrummed along, kicking up a joyous cat's tail of dust in her wake.

Her good mood wasn't shared by most of her passengers.

Robert was in the doghouse with Cassie after the incident at Craterhome. No matter that it had been an accident, his sister still couldn't get over the fact that he had electrocuted all those people, including her and Fletcher. She suspected that there had been no serious casualties and thought Robert had been very fortunate in that respect. She appreciated, too, that he had been frightened and flustered. Nonetheless it had been a grave mistake, and she was sure there would be unwelcome consequences for the Grubdollars further down the line.

Meanwhile, as a result of the same incident, Colin had become insufferable. It didn't take much to give an Amblescrut a swollen head. The clan had an inbuilt streak of pride which emerged at the least excuse. In Colin's case, he couldn't stop bragging about protecting Michael and Aurora, his 'Airborn pals', from the two Craterhomers who'd got into the loading bay. Each time he told the story, the fight became longer and more violent. In addition, he could not forget that Michael had saved him at the last moment, so some of the slavish devotion which he felt for Den Grubdollar was now transferred to Michael. He kept badgering Michael to reminisce about the fight. He felt that the pair of them had been bonded by battle.

'Be'n't it amazing?' he said. 'You and me, Mike, us comes from different worlds, and yet us is so close now. Like brothers. Brothers in arms.'

Michael found it highly irritating. Aurora found it highly amusing, at least to begin with, although she, too, grew weary of Colin's incessant chatter. It didn't help that she appeared to be suffering from a slight touch of ground-sickness again. She complained of feeling faintly nauseated but told Michael not to make a fuss or bother Fletcher about it. She was sure it would pass and she would re-acclimatise soon.

With Cassie annoyed at Robert and with tension in the loading bay, Fletcher took on the role of cheerleader, trying to keep everyone's spirits up. From the driver's pod or his observation nacelle he would deliver droll, sarcastic comments about what he saw outside. 'Oh look, there'm another rock,' he would say, or 'Interestingly, us is passing another large patch of sand.' Sometimes he managed to raise a weary laugh or two.

All of them could feel it, however, as they voyaged further and further into the desert – a mounting sense of futility, of despair.

The Relentless Desert was huge, its vistas impossibly distant. The emptiness was relieved by an occasional outcrop of boulders or a towering mesa, here and there a scrubby shrub or some kind of twisting cactus, and perhaps the hollowed wreck of a vehicle. But otherwise it was a flat expanse of brown nothing beneath a similarly flat expanse of sullen grey sky. Being in the middle of it was like being sandwiched between two immense voids.

This landscape stared in through *Bertha*'s portholes and windscreen. It stared into her passengers' hearts and oppressed them.

The roads were straight and monotonous, long scratches in the sand that extended from horizon to horizon. Sometimes a junction would appear without warning, a two-way fork marked by a metre-high cairn of stones. There was never a signpost. There was just a choice: right or left. It was up to whoever was at *Bertha*'s controls at the time to make the decision. Then, soon, the junction would be far behind and the road had become another straight stretch virtually indistinguishable from the last.

At each turning, *Bertha*'s passengers knew they weren't getting any-where, even though the junctions gave the illusion that they were. Simply, they were driving around in a vast maze whose layout they had no con-ception of. Somewhere else in the maze was Den Grubdollar. In trying to find him, they were becoming lost.

They kept going regardless. They had to. They had come too far to give up.

With *Bertha*'s cackle as encouragement – their only encouragement – they travelled on.

CHAPTER 60

The Smoke Pillar

It was Robert who spotted the smoke, and in doing so he managed to redeem himself in Cassie's eyes.

'Hey! What'm that over there?'

Cassie peered. All she could see was a tiny, curving black line like an apostrophe on the eastern horizon.

'Don't know,' she said. 'Looks like smoke. Some kind of bonfire or cooking fire, maybe.'

'Worth investigating?'

'Definitely. Those'm some sharp eyes you's got there, little bro.'

Robert felt a warm glow. It was the first nice thing anyone had said to him in four days.

Cassie steered off-road, making a beeline towards the smoke. *Bertha* growled with glee as she tackled terrain that was even bumpier and rougher than before.

Soon it became clear that the source of the smoke wasn't some minor conflagration. Distance had made the size of the smoke pillar hard to judge. In fact it was massive, bridging the gap between earth and sky. Its dimensions were those of the column of a sky-city, although of course it lacked the smoothness, straightness and solidity, and its head flattened and fanned out as it hit the clouds, dispersing into them like ink into water.

On board *Bertha* there was speculation as to what was generating the smoke. Whatever it was, Den and the Deacon might have seen it too and gone in for a closer look. The smoke was visible from a long way away in all directions. Anyone who caught sight of it would be drawn in, out of curiosity if nothing else.

Shortly another road appeared ahead. It arrowed straight towards the smoke, with a line of telegraph poles running alongside which from a distance looked like a stitch sewn across the desert. Cassie drove onto it.

A large metal sign by the roadside read:

WESTWARD OIL ENTERPRISES
EXTRACTION AND REFINING
INSTALLATION
137

At the bottom someone had added, in slapdash paint:

DESOLATION WELLS

Half a kilometre further on, the road ended at a tall chainlink fence, the perimeter of an enclosure covering several hectares of land.

Much of the fence lay flat on the ground. Beyond was a scene of devastation.

Ruined buildings.

The shattered, charred remnants of cranes and steel-girder towers.

Storage tanks like huge, cracked-open eggs.

And everywhere, fires. Small ones, large ones. Some were low and pulsing like furnaces, others jetted into the air like geysers. Each sent up a plume of smoke which merged together overhead with the others to form the single billowing pillar.

Cassie halted outside the entrance to the installation. For a while no one aboard *Bertha* dared speak. They all looked out at the carnage in awestruck silence.

Finally Fletcher said, 'What be this? How did it happen? Were it an accident or what?'

'Dunno,' Cassie replied, 'but I vote us should get out and look for survivors.'

CHAPTER 61

Bodies

The three Grubdollar siblings put on the retrieval suits which were still stowed aboard *Bertha* even though they hadn't been needed in over a year. The last time any of them had worn one of the suits was when they discovered Az out in the Shadow Zone, being pursued by verms. Since then there hadn't been any Relic-hunting for the Grubdollar family and the suits had lain in their lockers getting musty and creased. Cassie felt a pang of nostalgia as she wriggled into hers. The stiffness of the padding and the coldness of the chain-mail gloves evoked a purer, happier time in her life. Even the helmet, with its narrow slit of a visor, felt somehow cosy.

Michael insisted on coming out to help. Aurora did, too. Her mild dose of ground-sickness had eased and she was feeling more like herself again. They took off and flew in criss-crossing patterns to reconnoitre the area. Meanwhile Cassie, Fletcher and Robert trudged on foot through the entrance to Desolation Wells. The installation's gates were lying several metres from where they should have been, tangled and twisted like crumpled paper. Colin, in the driver's pod, tooted *Bertha*'s horn to let everyone know he was there if they needed him.

Even through the retrieval suit's padding Cassie could feel the heat of the fires. The acrid stench of the smoke was thick in her nostrils, despite the helmet. She and her brothers roamed the site, keeping clear of the largest and fiercest of the various infernos. They didn't come across any survivors but they did see dead bodies – twisted, half-cremated forms which only just resembled human beings. Cassie flashed back to Martin's burned remains. The memory made her horror that much greater but also filled her with compassion for the dead people, whoever they were. She felt as though she knew them. They weren't just strangers.

Every so often she checked the sky to see if Michael and Aurora had found anyone alive. Finally she spotted Aurora waving to Michael. He flew to his wife's side, looked down to where she was pointing, then soared over to the Grubdollars.

'Over that way,' he said. His eyes were red and streaming from the smoke. His mouth was hard and sombre. 'I've got to warn you, though. It's not pleasant.'

'Be'n't all that nice here either,' Cassie replied.

447

With Michael leading them, the three Grubdollars trooped back out of the installation and headed for the spot above which Aurora was hovering.

On the ground, in a neat row, lay twenty or more bodies. These were not as severely burned as the ones inside the installation. They had, however, been left there for at least a day and were starting to bloat and putrefy. Their limbs were contorted with rigor mortis, their eyes were pale and bulging, and their skin bore a hideous purple-black mottling. Even worse than the sight of them was the smell. Cassie got no closer than ten metres from them, and still the stench was atrocious. Her helmet did nothing to keep it out. Bile rose in her throat. It was an effort not to retch.

'Someone laid they out,' Fletcher said. 'Them didn't die in the fire, them died out here afterwards.'

'So there *be* survivors,' Cassie said. 'Just not here. Them's gone on somewhere else.'

'Stands to reason. And, hey, look over there.' Fletcher indicated a patch of ground not far away. A large quantity of pebbles had been set out, carefully arranged to form words. It was a message, accompanied by an arrow pointing off towards the south-west.

Before Cassie had a chance to go over and read it, however, she was distracted by a shout from above.

'Down there!' Michael yelled. He was gesticulating wildly at something he could see, and the Grubdollars couldn't, on the other side of a nearby ridge.

'What be it?' Cassie called up.

'I don't know. I don't have a name for it. I've never seen anything like it. But there are lots of them and they're coming fast.'

A sudden coldness filled Cassie's gut.

'Run,' she said to her brothers. 'Run like you's never run before.'

Moments later, a pack of dog-like animals came bounding into view. Hackerjackals.

CHAPTER 62

Attack Of The Hackerjackals

The hackerjackals would have smelled the roughnecks' corpses sooner and come to eat them, but the smoke and fire had confused their senses and scared them away from the area. Only now had they plucked up the courage to return.

The alpha male, the pack leader, was the first of them to catch a whiff of rotting meat in the air, and with a soft yelp he conveyed this information to his wives, offspring, cousins and the couple of young pretenders who had attached themselves to the pack and would one day fight with the alpha male in the hope of usurping him and becoming the new dominant member. As one, the pack moved off, following the scent trail. With the alpha male at the fore, they homed in unerringly on the gorgeous, delicious odour of death-decay. Bellies rumbling, mouths slavering, they gouged furrows in the desert sand with their sickle-like claws. The black hackles along their spines bristled with eagerness.

Eagerness turned to joy as the hackerjackals crested the ridge of rocks and spied not just dead creatures but living ones too. There was only thing hackerjackals liked more than the taste of carrion, and that was the taste of freshly killed prey. To wrench flesh from bone while it was still springy and moist, to lap up blood as it poured hotly from torn veins – this was truly heaven.

With bloodlust lighting up their pus-yellow eyes, the pack hurtled past the row of dead humans, making straight for the three who were alive.

The three Grubdollars, naturally enough, had no desire to be chomped on, and turned and fled from the hackerjackals as fast as their legs could carry them. The bulkiness of the retrieval suits hampered their progress. Nonetheless they ran, skidding, slithering, arms pistoning, thinking only of getting to *Bertha* and safety.

Above, an alarmed Michael and Aurora knew they had to help. They might never have laid eyes on a hackerjackal before but they recognised a carnivorous predator when they saw one. They'd watched kestrels dive on sparrows, hawks sink their talons into pigeons. These large, fanged mammals were the same, just without feathers.

Michael folded his wings and plunged towards the hackerjackal at the front of the pack. His feet collided with its back, slamming it flat on the ground. The hackerjackal shrieked, rolled over, and leapt up snapping. Michael just managed to hoist himself out of range in time. The hacker-jackal's teeth clacked on empty air.

Aurora came down too and kicked one of the hackerjackals in the side of the head. It responded by pouncing at her with its claws outstretched. It slashed a hole in her shirt, missing her skin by mere millimetres.

The hackerjackals were quicker and tougher than the Airborn newly-weds had anticipated.

They were also a whole lot smarter.

The alpha male yipped, giving orders. Two of the larger bitches broke away from the pack. One went after Michael, the other Aurora. Snarling, fangs bared, they sprang at the winged humans, driving them backwards and higher and higher into the air.

The rest of the pack bounded on after the non-winged humans.

Cassie's frantic, panting breaths echoed inside her helmet. She didn't know if the retrieval suits would protect her from the hackerjackals' wicked claws and finger-length fangs, and she didn't want to find out. The suits were designed for dealing with verms, whose teeth were comparatively small and whose claws were blunted from burrowing. The beasts pursuing her and her brothers looked like they'd have no difficulty tearing the padding apart. Even the helmets and the chain-mail gloves might not deter them.

Bertha still seemed far away. Cassie was sprinting with all her might and the murk-comber somehow didn't get any closer. She prayed that Colin would see what was going on and would start *Bertha* up and drive to meet them. It was perhaps their only chance. A swift glance over her shoulder told her that the nearest of the hackerjackals was now less than twenty metres away. It was the biggest of the pack and it moved with a sinewy grace and purposefulness. Its eyes met Cassie's, and she saw a horrible intelligence in them. In that moment it seemed to lock onto her, making her its sole target. Cassie had the impression that this hackerjackal, obvi-ously the leader of the pack, had singled her out as the leader of *her* small pack. Therefore, out of a sense of symmetry, it had resolved that it ought to be the one to eat her.

She dug deep inside herself, finding an extra level of speed. Robert was just behind her, Fletcher just behind him.

She was aware of a scream building in her throat.

Colin! she begged mentally. *Colin! See we and start the bloody engine!*

CHAPTER 63

Banjo Musings

Colin was sitting with his feet up on the dashboard. He was picking at a scab on his knuckle, a legacy of the punch-up in the loading bay. He was humming the tune of a folksong one of his quarter-brothers liked to play on the banjo ('My Heart's Been In The Coal Pit Since My Girlfriend Got Her Wings' was its title). He was thinking that he would like to learn the banjo himself one of these days. He was thinking that he would like to do a lot of the things which he never actually got around to doing.

Colin was supposed to be monitoring the situation outside, in case the Grubdollars got into difficulties. But then Amblescruts were not famous for the length of their attention span.

Then something – a flicker of motion at the periphery of his vision – prompted him to glance up.

Next second, he was scrambling to hit the ignition.

Unfortunately Colin didn't know *Bertha* like the Grubdollars did. She didn't always fire at the first attempt, unless you leaned on the ignition switch for just the right amount of time. Panicked, he gave her too little juice. Then, when he tried again, he gave her too much. Both times *Bertha* spluttered but didn't start.

Third time, he got it right. *Bertha* roared. Colin shoved the control sticks fully forwards. *Bertha* ground dirt and accelerated skiddingly.

'Idiot!' Colin berated himself as he made for the Grubdollars and the ferocious canids that were pursuing them. 'Numbskull! Moron! Poop-for-brains! Mule-head! Useless, woolgathering, all-the-sense-of-a-cheese, dribble-mouthed dingbat!'

No amount of self-recrimination, though, was going to make up for lost time or get *Bertha* to go any faster. Judging by the Grubdollars' speed compared with that of the animals, Colin estimated they had less than five seconds before the animals caught up with them. And he was at least half a minute from reaching them.

CHAPTER 64

Joining The Airborn

Robert felt himself being grabbed from behind and knew he'd had it. The hackerjackals had caught up with him. He had a strange sensation of being lifted, his feet parting company with the ground. Everything was syrupy-slow and surreal, as in a dream. He waited for the pain, the crunch of hackerjackal teeth sinking into his neck, the agonies of death. Maybe it had already happened. Maybe he'd already been attacked and killed, and this feeling of lightness was his soul slipping free from his body and Ascending. People said that often when you died violently, you didn't feel a thing. Shock numbed you. You drifted away.

So this was it. He was going up into the next life. He was going to join the Airborn, if that was what really happened.

Then, at the corner of his restricted field of vision, Robert glimpsed Fletcher. His brother was beside him, rising into the air too. But that was because Michael had his hands locked under Fletcher's armpits and was carrying him.

Belatedly Robert realised that he himself was being carried in the same fashion, by Aurora.

He looked down and saw Cassie was on her own, still running, with the entire hackerjackal pack at her heels, bounding after her.

Then he was borne over his sister's head, in the direction of *Bertha*. He could feel Aurora was struggling with the extra weight. The two of them kept dipping downwards, and then Aurora would grunt as she strained to haul them aloft again. Michael seemed to be having similar difficulties with Fletcher, and Fletcher wasn't helping matters by thrashing around in Michael's clutches. Faintly Robert heard his brother yelling at Michael: 'Put I down! Get Cass! Don't worry about I! Cass!'

They flew over a rift in the ground, a jagged scar that had been carved in the earth by a river, long since dried up. It looked to be about seven or eight metres deep. *Bertha* lay on the other side. Aurora was almost sobbing with effort as she covered the last stretch to the murk-comber. She deposited Robert on *Bertha*'s roof, then collapsed beside him in a heap, heaving for breath, wings limp.

Michael dropped Fletcher beside them, and instantly flipped around in midair and made his way back towards Cassie.

She was just a couple of strides from the rift. The hackerjackal pack was almost on top of her.

Michael was exhausted from carrying Fletcher. He flapped as hard as he could, but everyone, including him, could see that he wasn't going to reach Cassie in time.

CHAPTER 65

Try Or Die

The rift had to be at least five metres across. Cassie didn't know if she could leap such a distance, even with a run-up. She didn't think it mattered. There was no choice. It was try or die. If she turned left or right along the edge of the rift, the hackerjackals would catch her. Straight over was the only way.

The thumping lollops of the hackerjackals' paws rumbled behind her. Ahead, on the other side of the rift, Cassie could see *Bertha*, with Aurora and her brothers safely on the roof. Michael was flying towards her.

Reaching the rift, she didn't hesitate. She kicked off with her right foot and launched herself into space.

She made it.

She didn't make it.

One moment, her left foot landed squarely on the far edge. The next moment, the ground gave way, her leg shot from under her, and she was slithering helplessly downwards.

She caught herself with her arms. Her chain-mailed fingers clawed for purchase in the crumbly soil. Her toecaps dug frantic grooves in the sheer wall of the rift. There was an immense thump as one of the hackerjackals hit the edge of the rift right next to her. It had jumped after her but its leap fell short. It tumbled down into the riverbed, rolling end over end and hitting the bottom with a yelp. When it tried to get up, it stumbled and whined. One of its hindlegs was broken.

All the other hackerjackals stopped at the rift. All but one. The alpha male swiftly assessed the situation, turned and took a short run-up. Its leap was more successful than that of its over-eager packmate. It touched down gracefully on the other side, next to Cassie, and spun round.

Cassie was still trying to fight her way out of the rift, but the bulkiness of her retrieval suit hampered her movements. In fact, it was all she could do just to stop herself sliding further down.

The alpha male seemed to feel it could take its time. It padded over in an almost leisurely fashion and lowered its muzzle to Cassie's face. The slit of her helmet visor was filled entirely with the sight of two rows of fangs. The creature's teeth slotted together almost perfectly, a solid mesh of lethal sharp ivory, glistening with saliva. The hackerjackal's breath was like a gust of wind from hell.

'Hold on, Cassie!' Michael yelled. But he sounded like he was a million kilometres away.

Cassie closed her eyes. There was only one thing for it.

She let go of the rift's edge and fell.

CHAPTER 66

Out Of The Blue ...

On top of *Bertha*, Fletcher was kneeling beside the javelin turret with his arm thrust into the slot through which the javelin launcher protruded. He was trying to grab one of the spare javelins that were racked at the back of the turret. It was futile, he knew, but he had to try and do *something* to help Cassie. Reaching in as far as he could, he managed to brush the shaft of the topmost javelin with his groping, gloved fingers. He almost had it – then he dislodged the javelin from its mounting and it rattled onto the turret floor.

He howled with frustration.

'Fletch ...' said Robert softly.

'I can do this,' Fletcher said. 'Shut up. Let I do this.'

'No, Fletch,' said Robert, tapping him on the shoulder. 'Look. Just look.'

Something in the tone of his brother's voice made Fletcher turn. Robert's gaze was directed straight upwards. Aurora's was too, and there was a hint of a smile on her face.

Smile? thought Fletcher. *How can her smile at a time like this?*

Then he became aware of a sound – a sound he recognised. A steady, reverberating drone.

Overhead, casting a huge shadow before it, was the very last thing Fletcher would have expected to see and perhaps the very best thing he could have hoped to see.

Huge, stately, graceful, descending ...

Cerulean!

And out from the airship, uniformed men were pouring in a stream. Alar Patrollers.

Lances poised, the Patrollers descended on the hackerjackals at the rift's edge. One after another they hit the pack. One after another the hackerjackals were impaled with lance-thrusts. They squealed and yelped as they died. Some of them retaliated, leaping at their attackers, but the Patrollers quickly learned to stay out of range. Their lances were long enough for them to be able to inflict fatal wounds with minimal risk to themselves.

It was brisk, efficient, methodical slaughter, and Fletcher was overjoyed to see the hackerjackals getting their comeuppance.

Finally the hackerjackals' collective spirit was broken. Pack unity gave way to panic. The few surviving beasts scattered in all directions, and the Patrollers gave chase, picking them off individually.

Fletcher surveyed the scene of carnage that was left behind. Dead and dying hackerjackals lay strewn alongside the rift. One of them snapped angrily at the blood-gushing hole in its own flank. Another struggled to walk, but with each trembling step more of its entrails spilled out from its ripped-open belly and dragged behind it in a clump.

He searched for Cassie, but could see no sign of her.

Where was she?

And where, for that matter, was Michael?

CHAPTER 67

Down In The Rift

The alpha male hackerjackal escaped the cull.

It did this simply by plunging after Cassie. Digging its talons into the side of the rift, it slid and skidded downward in a reckless headlong rush. It ended up at the bottom in one piece, with a landslide of loosened earth and stones spilling behind it.

Its packmate with the broken hindleg crouched nearby, whimpering. The alpha male strode past, pausing only to tear out the other hacker-jackal's throat with a single, almost casual snap of its jaws. An instinctive habit. A wounded hackerjackal was no use to the pack. Better off dead.

The alpha male homed in on Cassie, its eyes glowing like lamps in fog.

Cassie lay stunned on the floor of the rift. Her retrieval suit had protected her from serious harm, but her slithering, precipitous descent down the wall of the rift had left her bruised and shaken. She wanted to get up but neither her arms nor her legs seemed to have any strength in them.

The alpha male knew it had been overconfident before, when the human pack leader had been clinging onto the edge of the rift for dear life. Then, it had let its prey get away. It was not going to make the same mistake twice.

With a low, hungry snarl the hackerjackal bent its head over Cassie's neck and opened its maw wide.

'No!'

Michael came crashing down feet-first on the beast's back.

Last time, this had worked for Michael, knocking his victim flat. But that hackerjackal had been one of the smaller members of the pack. The alpha male was much larger and stockier, a hefty brute, and scarcely seemed to feel the impact. With startling speed, it turned and lashed out with a forepaw.

Michael cried out as the talons raked his calf. The pain was blinding, red-hot. He flew up several metres, blood pattering down from his leg onto the hackerjackal's spine bristles. The alpha male, with a kind of rolling shoulder shrug, lowered its head again over Cassie and gave a growl. This was unmistakably a sound of gloating satisfaction. *No more interruptions*, it said. *Now you're mine.*

Michael's intervention, however, had alerted Cassie to the danger she was in. A rush of fear lent her the co-ordination she needed. Her hand found a rock the size of her fist. She swung it round with all her might, slamming it into the hackerjackal's snout.

Blood spurted. Fangs splintered. The alpha male yowled and recoiled. Cassie drew the rock back for a second strike.

Then there was a *whump* of wings and the hackerjackal shot into the air.

The beast gave an almost comical yelp of surprise as it hurtled vertically upwards, suspended by its hindlegs. Cassie had a glimpse of the person who was carrying the hackerjackal aloft, and was surprised to see that it wasn't Michael. She saw dark clothing, close-cropped hair and . . . crimson spectacles?

Up they went, Mr Mordadson and the upside-down dangling hacker-jackal, zooming up out of the rift, shooting skyward, heading for the clouds. Now they were 100 metres high, now 150, now 200. By the time the startled animal had gathered its wits enough to bend round on itself and start snapping at Mr Mordadson's hands, the two of them were at least 250 metres above the ground.

The alpha male didn't seem to realise that it was putting its own life at risk by attacking the human who was holding it. All it wanted was to make him let go.

For reasons of self-preservation as much as anything, Mr Mordadson did just that.

The hackerjackal plummeted to the desert, howling and flailing the whole way.

The impact was loud and wet and messy, a great blood-spattering *thud* which cut short the hackerjackal's cries, and also its life.

Mr Mordadson floated down into the rift and landed beside Cassie, brushing his palms together.

'Cassie,' he said. 'It is Cassie inside that outfit, isn't it?'

Cassie nodded.

'Are you all right?'

She nodded again.

'Then come with me. There's someone who'd like to say hello to you.'

CHAPTER 68

Reunion # 1

Az folded his arms, unfolded them, put his hands in his pockets, took them out again, leaned against a bulkhead nonchalantly, decided this didn't work, and was still trying to figure out what sort of stance he should adopt as Mr Mordadson ushered Cassie into the control gondola.

In the end, instead of looking in any way cool or casual, Az stood there, arms hanging by his sides, and said, simply, 'Hi.'

Cassie, with her retrieval suit helmet tucked under one arm, said 'Hi' back.

'So,' Az said. He was conscious of the presence of the crew. They weren't looking at him but he knew they were listening. If only this meeting could have taken place somewhere else, somewhere private. But Az had thought that it might impress Cassie, seeing him in the control gondola, in an obvious position of authority. He realised he should have known better. She was never the type to be easily impressed.

'It's funny,' he said, after an awkward silence.

'What'm funny?'

'Me saving you from a pack of wild animals. It's like the first time we ever met, only with the roles reversed.'

'Except,' Cassie pointed out, 'it were Mr Mordadson and those Patroller fellows who saved we. Not you.'

'Let's not split hairs. If I hadn't spotted *Bertha* when I did, and then you, you'd be those creatures' lunch by now.'

That came out sounding more brutal than he intended.

'What were those things anyway?' he asked in a placatory tone of voice.

'Them's called hackerjackals.'

'Nice name. Sounds like the way they look.'

'You wouldn't think it so nice if them was chasing you.'

'I wasn't saying *they* were nice. I just meant the name is — Oh, never mind.'

Az told himself he wasn't going to get spiteful or peevish. He had every reason to be annoyed, he felt. Cassie had treated him unfairly and now, against all odds, here they were, the two of them, reunited. They had run into each other in the middle of nowhere, he had saved her life (or at any rate *helped* save her life) and she was repaying that by continuing to be as difficult and defensive as she had been during their last few get-togethers. She could at least have said thank you. Was that too much to ask?

But then he looked at her, at her tousled, chunkily-cut hair, her large brown eyes, the soft contours of her face, and he remembered everything that he liked about her – her courage, her humour, the kindness that lay just beneath that couldn't-care-less exterior, the way she used to touch him, how it felt to kiss her and be kissed by her . . .

He remembered all of that, and knew he couldn't bear a grudge.

'We don't have much time, I'm afraid,' he said. 'We have to get back above the clouds soon before everyone on board starts feeling unwell.'

'Yeah,' Cassie said, and in that single syllable Az heard, or thought he heard, a profound sorrow for all the things that divided him and her. It was more a sigh than a word.

It gave him hope.

'Yeah,' he said, echoing her tone. 'We're hopping up and down, you see, spending a few minutes below the clouds every hour. We're searching for someone. Or rather, some*thing*. Another airship.'

'I thought *Cerulean* were the only airship in service.'

'So did I. So did we all. But apparently not. Somehow, some Airborn have got hold of another one. They're a bad lot and they're using the airship to raid the ground. We suspect this may be their handiwork.' He indicated the smouldering ruins below. 'That's why, as soon as we saw the smoke, we came in for a look. We thought they might still be here. And instead we found you.'

'Quite a coincidence,' Cassie said.

There's no such thing as coincidence, Az thought, then cursed himself. The Count of Gyre had really got inside his head, hadn't he?

'Maybe,' he said. 'The smoke was pretty hard to miss, though, and we couldn't ignore it. I assume it's what brought you and your family here too.'

'To this spot, yes.'

'Why *are* you here, by the way? I mean all the way out here in this wasteland. We're a long way from Grimvale.'

'Us has . . . reasons.'

Az waited for her to elaborate. 'But you're not going to tell me them,' he said, when she didn't.

'It'm a private matter,' Cassie said.

'Right. I see.'

Mr Mordadson coughed. 'Sorry to butt in, but I'm curious. Just wondering, Cassie – do you know anything about the raids this airship's been doing? Have you heard about them?'

'Honestly, no. Until now I hadn't heard a thing. But that'm not saying much. I's been kind of busy with other stuff lately.'

Az hated it that Cassie seemed much more comfortable speaking to Mr Mordadson than to him.

'So your reasons for being out here would have no connection with our mission?' Mr Mordadson said.

'Not as far as I be aware.'

'Fine,' said Mr Mordadson. 'Only, if you told us what you were after, perhaps we could help.'

'Doubt it. Besides, you's got this big, important mission you be on, whereas us has just a little personal business to take care of, that'm all. No need to waste your time on we.'

'We'd like to help, Cassie,' Az said, taking his cue from Mr Mordadson.

'I'm sure you'd like to,' she replied curtly, 'but you can't.'

Az lost patience. He'd had enough of Cassie's surliness. He was about to give her a piece of his mind – but then someone else entered the control gondola.

'Little brother!'

CHAPTER 69

Reunion #2

Michael? Michael as well?

'I don't believe it,' said Az.

'Me either,' said Michael. He came limping across the control gondola to brace his brother by the shoulders and give him a loving shake. 'But here I am. And here you are. How you doing?'

'Not bad. What's up with your leg?'

'This? A scratch. One of those beasties got me. Aurora bandaged it up. She did a good job.'

'Aurora's here too?'

'Why shouldn't she be? We are on honeymoon after all.'

Michael filled Az in on his and Aurora's decision to stay for only one night at Heliotropia, then spend the rest of the time travelling on the ground.

'You lied to us,' Az said, amazed but also admiring.

'We didn't want anyone worrying, specially not Mum and Dad. And as honeymoons go, this one's certainly had its worrying moments. Hasn't it, Cassie?'

She nodded.

'So you're the reason *Bertha*'s here,' Az said. 'You're exploring the desert. You're the "personal business" Cassie's taking care of.' He glanced at her, looking smug.

'Huh?' said Michael. 'No. That's not it. Actually, we're searching for her father.'

'Her ...'

Now it was Cassie's turn to look smug. 'Don't know everything, do you, Az?'

'But ...' Az floundered. 'Why didn't you just say so, Cassie? Why be so secretive?'

'Maybe it be'n't the same for you Airborn, but for we, family deals with family stuff. No one else gets involved.'

'Michael's involved. Aurora's involved.'

'Yes, well, them made we an offer us couldn't refuse.'

'*I'd* have got involved, if you'd asked me. What's happened to Den? Where is he?'

Cassie explained as briefly as she could. Az could see that it hurt her to admit to the breakdown within her family. Her pride was strong, he thought. So strong that she found it hard to allow herself any failure. So strong that she automatically spurned offers of assistance from anyone but her immediate kin.

'Ahem.'

This came from Flight Lieutenant Wallimson.

'Yes?' Az said. He had been trying to figure out if there was anything he could do for Cassie. Given that *Cerulean*'s goal was stopping the pirates, he doubted he could be sidetracked from that. The mission came first. He couldn't see any possible overlap with the hunt for Den Grubdollar.

'The last of the Patrollers are back on board,' Wallimson said. 'I hate to break up the happy meeting, but if we don't get up above the clouds again soon, we're going to have a ship full of very ground-sick people.'

'Of course. You'd better head back down, Cassie. Mike? What about you? Do you want to come with us or stay with the Grubdollars?'

'Haven't asked the missus,' Michael said, 'but I imagine we'll carry on with the Grubdollars for the time being. If I know Aurora, she'll want to see this through to the end. I know I do.'

The parting was over with quickly, a few goodbyes, then Michael and Cassie were gone. Az watched his brother descend with Cassie in his arms. Michael strained against gravity with laborious downbeats of his wings. He looked exhausted by the time he alighted close to *Bertha* with his dense-boned cargo of Groundling.

'Set a course for the clouds,' Az told his crew.

He kept his gaze fixed on the tiny figures below until *Cerulean* nudged up into the cloud cover and the ground disappeared in a white haze.

CHAPTER 70

The Shape

During *Cerulean's* turbulent ascent through the clouds, Flight Lieutenant Wallimson had his second glimpse of a large, dark *something* out there in the whiteness.

His first glimpse had come during *Cerulean's* last but one trip through the layer of vapour. Since Wallimson was not assigned to any particular station in the control gondola, his duties as flight lieutenant consisted of keeping lookout at the viewing windows. Two hours ago, as the airship was bumping downward for yet another recce of the ground, he had spied a vague shape, a distant dim blot, roughly elliptical in outline, a few degrees off starboard.

He had been about to say something but held his tongue. The other crew members were concentrating on their controls and instruments, and the 'skipper' was busy doling out commands. Wallimson had felt he was better off not mentioning the shape. He had probably imagined it anyway. It had appeared fleetingly, there one second, gone the next.

The second time, he was certain he was not imagining it. Although the shape flitted into view for just an instant, Wallimson knew now that his eyes were not playing tricks on him. This wasn't some optical illusion brought on by the juddering of the airship or the roiling of the clouds or even mild ground-sickness. There was definitely a murky, elliptical silhouette out there, and Wallimson had absolutely no doubt what it was.

Report it?

Again, he nearly did. He was minded to. For everyone else's sake, he knew he ought to have.

But then he had, just a few minutes earlier, witnessed a nauseating display of friendliness towards a Groundling. He'd watched Az, Mr Mordadson and Az's brother all speak to that Groundling female as though she were their equal and in some way worthy of respect. They'd grovelled to her, in fact. That ... that *ostrich* had had them behaving in a manner that was wholly unbecoming of their race.

Traitors, that was what they were. And Az Gabrielson, he was the worst of the lot.

Whereas the pirates ...

Flight Lieutenant Wallimson was forming the view that the Redspire pirates, far from being renegades or criminals, were a credit to the Airborn. They knew exactly how to treat the Groundlings. None of this pussy-footing around, no 'please', no 'thank you', no squandering money on supplies, no pretending the two races were the best of chums now. They went down, took what was rightfully theirs, and that was that. And if the pirates *were* the ones who'd destroyed that oil refining place, they had clearly had good reason to.

All in all, he was thinking he had more in common with them than he did with the bleeding-heart, Groundling-loving do-gooders aboard *Cerulean*. If the opportunity arose, he would gladly defect to the other airship and join the pirates' cause.

So, although he was sure *Behemoth* was stalking *Cerulean* through the clouds (and he was the only one aboard *Cerulean* who realised it), Wallimson kept the information to himself.

Life, he thought, was about to get rather interesting.

CHAPTER 71

But What Of The Roughnecks?

With Desolation Wells destroyed, Magnus Clockweight and his men were left facing a stark choice: stay put and wait for help, or find some means of transportation and get the hell out of there.

Staying put was not really an option, not in the Relentless Desert. A rescue mission would surely be mounted, once the WOE executives realised that contact with the installation had been lost. But who knew how long it would take for the rescuers to arrive? The desert might finish off the roughnecks long before help came.

So a brave team of volunteers, led by Clockweight himself, ventured into the still-burning installation. They foraged for food and found some, but their main task was to see if any motor vehicles had escaped the catastrophe.

Somehow, a few had.

Desolation Wells possessed a fleet of eight dune-buggies. These were short-range vehicles intended for use in and around the installation. For instance, visiting geologists would go prospecting in them, looking for fresh oil deposits in the vicinity, and the workers themselves employed them to get from one corner of the site to another quickly.

One of the dune-buggies was already spoken for, of course. Clockweight had no idea what had become of the two men he had sent out in it on a search expedition. He hoped they were OK but was beginning to fear the worst.

Three of the remaining seven dune-buggies were damaged beyond repair.

That left four workable, serviceable vehicles. Clockweight and team drove them through the installation, avoiding piles of rubble and the gouts of flame flaring from decapitated wellheads. Avoiding, too, the corpses of friends and co-workers.

The roughnecks outside the installation were delighted to see their toolpusher emerge through the gateway in a dune-buggy, accompanied by volunteers driving three others. They did have a chance of getting back to civilisation after all.

But then Clockweight confronted them with an offer.

'Us can run home, tails between our legs,' he said, 'or us can get our own back on the buggers who did all this to we.' And he explained how.

While the workers deliberated, who should turn up at that moment, as if on cue, but the two men whom Clockweight had begun to despair of ever seeing again?

They were breathless, wind-burned and dust-caked. Once they had got over the shock of seeing what had happened to Desolation Wells, they were only too happy to announce that their expedition had been a success.

'Us found it!' one exclaimed.

'Can't believe it'm there, but it be!' said the other.

'Us looked but didn't go in, toolpusher, as per orders.'

'But if outward appearances be anything to go by, it'm huge. Huge!'

Clockweight turned to the thirty-odd survivors. 'Up to you, lads,' he said. 'No shame, whichever way you decide. Home, or vengeance? Let's put it to a vote.'

The vote was passed without objection or abstention.

Vengeance.

Immediately Clockweight told his men to gather up pebbles. They would leave a message for the rescuers, telling them where they had gone. Using the stones, Clockweight laid out five words on the ground not far from the bodies of his fallen comrades:

GONE SOUTHWEST
LOOK FOR NEEDLE

He added an arrow pointing in the right direction, just to leave no room for error.

Then the roughnecks piled into the dune-buggies. It was a tight squeeze. Each car was designed to carry no more than four people and had only the smallest of back seats. Several of the men had to perch on the rear spoilers and cling to the roll bars for support.

The crammed dune-buggies set off in a convoy, the one with the two explorers leading the way. Thick tyres churned sand. High, fat exhaust pipes spewed smoke.

A thirty-six-hour trek that began at Desolation Wells ended at a distinctive, teetering mesa which lay due southwest.

The mesa was shaped like a gigantic sewing needle. Eons of desert wind had worn a hole through the summit and eroded its base to a remarkable thinness. It was a unique and striking geographical feature and a very handy landmark, one that was visible from several kilometres away, one that could not possibly be mistaken for anything else.

The convoy of dune-buggies drew up in front of it. Clockweight climbed out and addressed his two explorers.

'Out of curiosity,' he said, pointing towards the mesa's base, 'were *that* here last time?'

'No, boss.'

'You'm sure about that?'

'Quite sure.'

Clockweight frowned.

Between the time his explorers had left the spot and now, someone else had arrived.

Sitting parked at the foot of the mesa was a half-tarp van.

CHAPTER 72

Cavern

'Echo,' said Den.

Echo … echo … echo …

'Knock it off, Den.'

'Sorry. Just trying to keep my spirits up. I doesn't much like this, being underground. I could never have been a miner.'

'Keep walking. Watch your footing. I don't think it's far.'

Den grimaced and shone his flashlight upwards, hoping to see the ceiling of the cavern. But it was too high for the beam to reach, so he had no alternative but to imagine what lay overhead: sheer rock, with wickedly sharp stalactites suspended here and there.

Not a comforting thought – all that tonnage of rock, all those jagged stalactite points, seemingly ready to fall onto him and Hardscree. He knew the cavern was vast. The size of its entrance had told him so, as did the way his and the Deacon's voices and footfalls echoed once they were inside it. Nevertheless he was beginning to feel cooped up and claustrophobic.

Nope, he could definitely have never been a miner. Lucky for him that murk-combing was the trade he'd been born into.

He and Hardscree were following the course of a broad-gauge railway track which ran from the cavern's mouth deep down into the ground. They had put daylight (and that extraordinary needle-like mesa) behind them half an hour ago. They were walking through pure darkness, with just their flashlight beams to guide them – and the illumination from those beams seemed pitifully wan, barely adequate to the task. There was so much darkness for the flashlights to hold back. Thick darkness, which seemed to get thicker with every step.

The track itself gleamed dully whenever the flashlights played across it, two parallel lines of iron that hugged the shallow downward gradient of the cavern floor. It originated beside a broad, sloping concrete platform just outside the cavern entrance.

Den wondered how long the track had been in place. The aridity of the desert air meant that rust formed slowly, if at all. He reckoned it could have been at least a couple of centuries since those rails were laid down, maybe even three.

Something must ride up and down the track, but he had no idea what.

He and Hardscree continued to descend further and deeper. Den was just starting to think that the cavern went on for ever, right into the bowels of the planet, right to its very core, when abruptly Hardscree halted.

'There,' he said.

The glowing yellow cone from his flashlight picked out a large diesel-driven generator. Seventy, eighty horsepower output, Den estimated. A lot of energy.

After a few false starts and quite a bit of un-Deacon-like cursing, Hardscree got the generator running. As it chugged into action, lights came on. Here, and now here, and now here, one after another, dozens of bulbs began to brighten. Soon a whole section of the cavern was lit up brilliantly by the electric constellation overhead.

And, blinking, dazzled, Den and Hardscree saw things – wonderful things.

The two of them were standing at the edge of a big dome-like area, a natural subterranean hollow which had been enlarged and improved by human hands. Steel joists helped support and brace the roof, while all of the rocky surfaces had been sanded and smoothed to a near-gemlike sheen.

The floor of this area was filled with flying machines.

Most consisted of just parts and portions. Here a random wing, there a rudder, the odd propeller, a segment of fuselage.

A few, however, were complete.

There were helicopters and autogyros, some with solid, umbrella-like rotors, and there was a range of fixed-wing aircraft, including a few elderly-looking biplanes made of wooden frames covered with a skin of canvas. There were a couple of larger planes – airbuses, Den thought they were called – multi-passenger public transport vehicles. And there were a number of strange things that were scarcely recognisable as flying machines. Early models, he guessed, from far back in Airborn history.

He let his gaze roam over them all, wide-eyed like a treasure hunter who'd just discovered the ultimate trove.

Hardscree's face bore a similar expression.

'You told I,' Den said at last. 'You described it. But you didn't do it justice.'

'How could I? I didn't know. I was only going by what others had said. It's a whole different thing to see it for oneself.'

'Relics. Them's all Relics.'

'Decades' worth.'

'And some of they is intact, all but,' Den said, scratching his head. 'Bless my bum. How come that happened? Given how far they has to fall, you'd have thought them'd end up as nothing but flinders.'

'It's amazing but some of these planes practically glide to earth.

Especially the earlier models, the ones made of wood and canvas – their lightness saves them from harm. Although not so the people in them. When it comes to crashes, even the canvas aircraft turn out to be a lot more robust than their porous-boned pilots.'

'Us picked up bits of aircraft ourselves, me and my kids, in the Shadow Zone, once or twice. Just fragments. I presumed them got stowed in the Chancel Reliquary.'

'Maybe temporarily, but in the end they'd have been brought here. Every piece of Airborn aircraft that ever came down anywhere in the Westward Territories wound up here. We were running out of room for them in the Reliquaries so we started shipping them out from the Chancels on articulated lorries under cover of darkness, driving them to this cavern, and depositing them out of sight.'

'So's us Groundlings couldn't have they.'

'Precisely. So that Groundlings would not be able to fly. It was in our own interest, as Deacons, to ensure that nobody else got their hands on any of this.'

'But the Deacons doesn't rule the roost any longer.'

'Which means these planes are up for grabs.'

'What used to be *there*, I wonder.' Den indicated a large gap near the middle of the aircraft collection. It was approximately 300 metres long and shaped like a stretched-out oval, with stanchions at both ends from which ran thick lengths of hawser. Now lying limp on the floor, the hawsers had clearly been used to secure something once.

'No idea,' said Hardscree, with a shrug.

Den was reminded of *Cerulean*. An airship would have fitted neatly into a space like that.

'But our job,' the Deacon went on, 'is to see how many of these craft are fit for purpose and figure out how to make them fly.'

'How's us supposed to get they up to the surface?'

'Easy. They can go out the way they came in.' Hardscree directed Den's gaze to where the railway track terminated. Resting against a set of buffers was a large flatbed rail trolley. 'It uses a pulley and counterweight system, much like one of the sky-city elevators. There's a release mechanism at the top so that it always returns down here after use. That way it won't ever be left sitting out exposed to the elements for months on end.'

'What about actually loading the planes onto the trolley?'

Hardscree gestured to the cavern roof. Up there was a hoist which operated on a grid pattern of metal runners. Hook-tipped chains dangled from it. The hoist could reach any part of the cavern.

'There's a control console for it somewhere,' Hardscree said.

'It'm all pretty much sorted then, be'n't it?' said Den. 'So when does us get started?'

Deacon Hardscree started rolling up the sleeves of his robe. 'No time like the present.'

CHAPTER 73

Hamstrung

'Skipper?'

'Yes, helmsman?'

'I'm ... I'm having a spot of bother here.'

'What sort of a spot of bother?'

'The rudder's behaving oddly. I'm not getting much response from it.'

'Problem with a cable?'

'Could be.'

Cerulean had just emerged above the cloud cover and was at cruising speed. Az had been looking forward to a brief respite from turbulence, a stretch of plain sailing.

No such luck.

'Keep trying. Rigz? Could you go aft and check the rudder cables? Maybe one of them snapped or came loose while we were being shaken around just now.'

The chief engineer was on the point of carrying out the order when he hesitated. He'd spotted something peculiar outside.

'Skipper? You ought to take a look at this.'

Az joined Rigz at the viewing windows. He saw a patch of darkness down on the clouds to starboard.

'That? That's just *Cerulean*'s shadow, Rigz. Been with us all the way!'

'With all due respect, skipper, it isn't. The sun's high and we're heading east. Our shadow should be portside, and is.'

A prickle of fear ran up Az's spine.

Before his very eyes, the patch of darkness began to rise. It wasn't *on* the clouds, it was *in* them. And it was gradually surfacing, breaking through the topmost layer, starting to open up a V-shaped furrow in the white.

Behemoth.

Up she came. The cloud cover parted around her nose-cone, flowing back along her balloon in gauzy ribbons. Up she came, trailing skeins of vapour from her tailfins. Up, with her black-painted canvas shining dully in the sunlight.

'We didn't find them,' Az breathed. 'They've found *us*.'

'Skipper?' said the helmsman. 'I have no control at all any more.' He spun the conn wheel to prove it.

'They've severed the cables,' said Rigz.

'But how?' said Az. 'They're nowhere near us.'

The answer came a moment later. A garishly dressed man winged up to the viewing windows and waved to everyone inside the gondola. He had wild eyes and shaggy, lime-green dreadlocks, and in his hands were a large pair of bolt cutters. He mimed using the bolt cutters, gave a gleeful giggle, then darted down towards the still-rising *Behemoth*.

Rigz swore.

Mr Mordadson smiled mirthlessly.

Unseen and unheard by anyone, Flight Lieutenant Wallimson snickered.

'In midair,' Az said, disgusted and incredulous. 'He flew across while we were in the clouds, latched on and started snipping.'

'He's crippled us,' said Rigz. 'We're hamstrung.'

'Perhaps so,' said Az, 'but we still have Patrollers on board. Let's sound the alarm and send them out. The pirates won't be expecting that.'

No sooner had the words left Az's lips than the viewing windows shattered inwards.

Three pirates had darted up in front of the control gondola from below. Using short-handled maces, they knocked out all the windows in swift succession. The crew ducked as shards of glass sprayed in all directions. Freezing-cold air whistled into the gondola.

The pirates clambered through the empty window frames. Each tucked his mace into his belt and drew out a long-bladed dagger. Their eyes were crazy and bloodshot, their cheeks were sallow and acne-pocked, and their movements were jerky and agitated. These were the familiar indicators of sustained, long-term pterine abuse.

Mr Mordadson stepped forward to intercept them, but Az grabbed his arm.

'Let go, Az.'

'No. There's three of them and they're armed.'

'So? I've faced worse odds before.'

'And they're off their faces on pterine. I can't risk you getting injured.'

Mr Mordadson sneered, as if to say he thought the chances of *that* happening were pretty slim.

Then two more pirates entered the gondola.

Glass crunched as the new arrivals strode past the other three pirates, heading straight for Az and Mr Mordadson.

One of them was the grinning, dreadlocked creature they had seen earlier, the one who'd appeared outside with bolt cutters. He tittering softly to himself, as if at some priceless private joke.

As for the other ...
Leather trousers creaked.
Black wings unfurled.
'Gentlemen,' said Naoutha Nisrocsdaughter. 'Let's parley.'

CHAPTER 74

Ultimatum

She was tall, brawny-shouldered, statuesque. The all-over leather she wore hugged the contours of her body, showing off a curvaceous figure. Her wings were as glossy as a raven's and shimmered with highlights of midnight blue.

The crew stared at her, awestruck. Az found it impossible not to do likewise. Even Mr Mordadson seemed startled and a little bit tongue-tied at the sight of her.

What was her face like behind that mask and those goggles? One could only assume that it matched the rest of her and was stunning.

'Your ship is useless now,' Naoutha said. 'We have you at a complete disadvantage. I am giving you one chance. If you agree to turn home and cease all efforts to interfere with what we're doing, we shall leave you alone.'

'And if we don't agree?' said Mr Mordadson.

'So far we've done nothing that can't be fixed. Keep pursuing us, however, and we'll do something ... unfixable.'

Her green-haired sidekick tittered loudly at this.

'Not much of a choice, is it?' said Az.

'No, Azrael Gabrielson, it isn't.'

'You know my name?'

'Don't be flattered, boy. How many wingless teenage airshipmen are there? Though, in truth, I suppose I should say thank you to you.'

'What for?'

'You visited the ground and opened up all these possibilities for us. In a way, you're responsible for me and my friends becoming what we are. Without you we'd still be frittering away our lives at Redspire. We'd be just another bunch of dead-end layabouts, doing dull, stupid jobs so we can enjoy ourselves a little in the evenings. Whereas now, look at us. Pirates! Actual, living, breathing pirates! We used to be so bored and lazy, and now we've found a dramatic new purpose in life, and it's all down to you.'

'I'm honoured.'

'You should be.'

'But if you're so pleased with yourself,' Az said, 'why wear that mask?

Do you have something to hide? Are you secretly ashamed of what you do, maybe?'

Naoutha lowered her head so that there was less than a hand's breadth between her face and his. Az saw a mirror-image Az reflected dimly, twice, in the goggles' black lenses.

'I wear it to intimidate,' she said. 'Is it working? Are you intimidated?'

Az shook his head, but in truth he was. The mask and goggles, in combination with the leather outfit, made Naoutha look less human and more like an insect – a large beetle, perhaps, or an oversized flying ant. She was sexy but at the same time very creepy.

'Your eyes say you are,' she said. 'And if *you* are, imagine how Ground-lings must feel when they see me.'

'We've a ton of Alar Patrollers on board,' Az said, hoping to intimidate Naoutha in return if he could. 'Some of them are probably coming for'ard right now to see why we've stopped.'

'So what?' Naoutha replied. 'We aren't planning on staying long. We're just here to —'

Mr Mordadson had been waiting for an opening, a moment when Naoutha was distracted. That moment had come, and he sprang at her, fists clenched.

But Naoutha was not caught unawares. Her pterine-enhanced reflexes worked at lightning speed. Blocking Mr Mordadson's fists with her forearms, she lashed out with her left wing. Its upper arch smacked him across the nose. His spectacles flew off. Blood spurted. Mr Mordadson grabbed his face in pain. Without pausing Naoutha brought her right wing around, low, and swept his legs out from under him, toppling him onto his back.

The other pirates were on him in a flash. Kneeling, they pinned down his limbs and wings. The green-haired, giggling one straddled his chest and placed a dagger against his neck.

'I only have to give the word,' Naoutha said, 'and Twitchy Ziz there will carve you a new smile. Won't you, Twitchy Ziz?'

Twitchy Ziz tittered and mimed throat-cutting with the index finger of his free hand. His bulging eyes dared Mr Mordadson to resist. He clearly yearned to do some bloodletting.

'He's never been right in the head, has our Zizulph,' Naoutha added. 'Born an addled egg, as the saying goes. As a boy he used to torture birds.'

'Pull their legs off,' said Twitchy Ziz with relish. 'Twist their heads round. Squawk! Crunch! Robins especially. Friendly little fellows. So trusting. Redbreast, deadbreast.'

'And he's no better now,' Naoutha added, almost fondly.

Mr Mordadson glared up at the madman leaning over him, but he did not struggle. He knew it was useless.

Naoutha swivelled her head, looking around the control gondola in an imperious manner. 'Any more have-a-go heroes here?'

The crew looked at their hands or inspected the floor.

'Didn't think so,' Naoutha said.

Az was tempted, but thought better of it. Not while Mr Mordadson had a dagger to his neck. Then there was the fact that Naoutha had bested his friend in hand-to-hand combat so easily. If Mr Mordadson couldn't win against her, what chance did Az have?

'You know we can't let you and your pirates just carry on raiding,' he said defiantly. 'We have clear instructions from the Silver Sanctum. You're to be stopped at any cost.'

'And how are you going to do that with your rudders out of action?' Naoutha retorted. 'You can't even steer now.'

'We'll find a way.'

'Is that so?' She cocked her head, as if studying him. 'Well, we shall see. You've had your ultimatum, at any rate. How you choose to proceed from here on is up to you.' She snapped her leather-gloved fingers. 'Guys? Time to go.'

Twitchy Ziz kept his dagger against Mr Mordadson's throat while the other three pirates let go of his limbs and wings and stood up. Then, carefully, Twitchy Ziz himself stood and backed away, leaving his blade in contact with Mr Mordadson's skin till the last possible moment.

He joined Naoutha and the other pirates at the shattered windows. Then, together, all five back-flipped out into the open air. They kept pace with *Cerulean* for several wingbeats, then peeled off in a line towards *Behemoth*.

Mr Mordadson staggered to his feet. He was bleeding profusely from the nose. He drew out a handkerchief, wadded it up and pressed it to his nostrils to stem the flow

Az picked up his spectacles and handed them to him. Mr Mordadson tried to put them on but winced and hissed.

'Broken,' he said thickly.

'They look fine to me.'

'No. My nose. She broke it.'

'Oh. Ouch.'

'Ouch is the word.'

Outside, *Behemoth* gathered speed, drawing ahead of *Cerulean*. The latter airship was starting to veer to starboard, and there was nothing anyone could do to correct her heading.

'So,' Mr Mordadson said through the handkerchief, 'are we just going to let them sail away?'

'Of course not,' said Az. 'Rigz? Can you fix the rudder?'

'Sure. It'll take a while, though. If they had any sense, they'd have cut

479

out a whole section of each cable – as much as is exposed between the balloon and the tailfins. I'll have to find some extra from somewhere and patch it in.'

'How long?'

'Three or four hours.'

'Get on it,' said Az.

Rigz flew up through the ceiling hatchway.

'In three or four hours' time they'll be long gone,' said Mr Mordadson. 'In fact, less than that.'

'Maybe,' Az said. 'But not necessarily.'

'You have an idea?'

'I think I do.'

CHAPTER 75

Common Ground

The trolley trundled up the final section of track towards the light at the cavern mouth. The brightness ahead was blinding. Den and Deacon Hardscree squinted as their eyes adjusted.

The cavern mouth formed an almost perfect semicircle. Just outside, where the desert began, Den thought he saw figures moving. Rapidly they swam into focus. He counted ten men. No, twenty. No, more.

'Gerald?' he said in a low voice.

'I see them,' said Hardscree.

'Who be them?'

'Wish I knew,' said the Deacon, and reached down to his ankle.

As the trolley drew out into the light, the strangers swarmed around it. The trolley rolled along the last few metres of rail, coasting to a halt next to a short section of raised platform with a ramp at the end. The plane which Den and Hardscree had loaded onto it was one of the newer and more airworthy-looking models, a single-seater craft with swept-back wings and a raised cockpit. The strangers were fascinated by it – and warily curious about the two men who had brought it up from the cavern depths.

'Who'm you?' one of the strangers demanded. The skin on his face and arm was red raw with burns.

'I could ask you the same question,' replied Hardscree.

'The name's Clockweight,' the other man said. 'Toolpusher of Desolation Wells. That's foreman, in common parlance. Or at least, I was toolpusher of Desolation Wells, till just recently. And you, it goes without saying, be a Deacon.'

'Obviously.'

'And you'm stealing from your own stash of aircraft, I see.'

'Not exactly. It can't be stealing if it's *my* stash, now can it?'

Den guffawed.

Clockweight's expression hardened. He leapt nimbly onto the trolley and walked towards Hardscree with an air of unmistakable menace. 'You'm a smart-mouthed one, eh, Deacon? Snooty, too. Think you'm better than the rest of we, just like all your kind does.'

Hardscree whipped out his knife.

'One step closer and I'll gut you,' he said, levelling the knife at Clockweight's stomach.

Clockweight froze, then laughed. 'Reckon you'm bluffing. Reckon you doesn't have the first clue how to use that.'

'Try he,' said Den. 'Just try he and you'll find out. Him's a Pale Uplander, see. Up there in the north, folk gets knives as birthday presents.'

Clockweight frowned at him, then at Hardscree. 'Really. Well, it doesn't make much difference. Us is here for the aircraft, and there'm thirty of we and only two of you. You could kill I but I doubt you could kill all of we. So drop the knife and surrender. That way nobody gets hurt.'

Hardscree did not drop the knife but he did raise it to vertical, an indication that he didn't necessarily wish to see anyone hurt either.

'Might I ask what you want the aircraft for?'

'Don't see as it'm any of your business,' was Clockweight's reply.

'You never know, it may be very much my business. It may even be that you and I, Mr Clockweight, have some common ground.'

'How d'you suppose that?'

'Logic. Intuition. An understanding of character. Evidently you want these aircraft for a specific purpose, and from your body language I'm guessing it isn't, for instance, to take them and sell them to someone else. There's a determination about you, an aggression, which suggests a less mercenary motive. Am I right so far?'

'Go on.'

'You said you were foreman of Desolation Wells "until just recently". Judging by your burns, and the similar injuries I see among your colleagues, I'd say something regrettable happened at your oil refinery.'

'That'd be an understatement.'

'A tragedy of some kind.'

Clockweight blinked and said, softly, 'Yes.'

Den looked from Hardscree to Clockweight and back again. The Deacon was working his wiles and Clockweight was being swayed. Den recalled how Hardscree had won *him* over when he'd gone to the tent to remonstrate about the attack on *Bertha*. Whatever charisma was, Hardscree had it in bucketloads.

Den began to feel uncomfortable, however. He knew the Deacon a lot better now. He knew him as a person. Watching someone else get charmed by him was like watching a conjuring trick when you were in on the secret behind the illusion. The magic was still there but you were aware of the deceit as well.

He saw himself in Clockweight's place. He saw himself being disarmed just as Clockweight was being. Somehow it seemed patently obvious what Hardscree was up to. He was using words to defuse a sticky situation. He was manipulating Clockweight, saying whatever he had to in order to get Clockweight on his side.

Was it that easy? Could Hardscree make anyone fall for him like that, at the proverbial drop of a hat?

'Care to tell me about it?' said the Deacon to Clockweight, oozing empathy.

Clockweight scratched his singed forearm, then nodded. 'Yeah. All right.'

CHAPTER 76

Disenchanted, Disenfranchised
And Discarded

Soon, the roughnecks were busy fetching aircraft up from the cavern and wheeling them off the trolley, onto the platform, down the ramp, out onto the sand. Hardscree looked on with a satisfied air. When Den came up to him, the Deacon offered a quick arch of the eyebrows as a greeting.

'So what do you think of our hard-working new friends, Den?' he asked.

'I be thinking them seems a decent enough bunch as far as it goes. But I also be thinking us has rather strayed from the point, Gerald.'

'Meaning?'

Den hesitated. How to put this?

'When us set out on this exploit of ours, I were under the impression the plan were to liberate the Airborn's flying technology. Our ultimate goal were going to share it with everybody, make it accessible to everybody. Balancing the scales and all that. People could take the planes and back-engineer they and build planes of their own.'

'And?'

'And now us is giving it to these roughneck chaps so's them can get their own back on the airship that blew up their refinery and killed their mates.'

'So?'

Den tried to honey his words with a laugh. 'Well, don't that strike you as a misuse of it? Be'n't that precisely the wrong way to go about making the world a better place? Us is encouraging violence against the Airborn.'

'Airborn who've murdered people.'

'Yes, but from what Clockweight said, them's the one that started it. Those roughnecks. *Them* murdered first.'

'Under provocation.'

'Even so.' Den gritted his teeth. 'Look, Gerald, I be'n't saying this'm a mistake, just saying this be'n't what I signed up for.'

'No, Den, you *are* saying this is a mistake,' said Hardscree coolly. 'You're too polite to tell me flat out but that's the gist of it. You want me to stop what's been started here. But I'm not going to. Would you like to know why?'

'Sure.'

'Because, for one thing, I couldn't even if I wanted to. Clockweight said it himself. Thirty of them, two of us. Overwhelming odds. We've no choice but to let him have his way. But you know what else? I believe they have a good case. The people in that black airship cannot be allowed to get away with theft and mass killing and destruction. Someone has to bring them down, and if these planes' – he waved an arm at the fleet of aircraft which was steadily being amassed outside the cavern – 'if these planes are the means of achieving that goal, then so be it. To my mind, that *is* balancing the scales.'

Bitterly Den replied, 'I thought you was a moral man. Even for a Deacon. I thought you had a fair grasp of right and wrong. I had you pegged as somebody who looked a bit further, saw the bigger picture.'

'I am. I do.'

'Then how come you can't see that there'm a cycle of violence spiralling out of control here? And d'you know where it'll end? *I* do. It'll end in just more people dead. Like my son. It'll end in pointless, futile, stupid bloody slaughter. It'll make a whole lot of corpses, like my Martin's, and nothing will be gained. And maybe worse'll happen. Maybe it'll anger the Airborn and them'll retaliate somewhere else, and our governments'll feel the need to fight back, and then where will us be? I's seen this sort of thing before, and I tell you, Gerald, us has to prevent it, not aid and abet it. And you *can* prevent it. I's sure of that. With your speechifying and your talent for persuasion, you can talk these men round, knock some sense into they. If you try to. If you want to.'

Hardscree looked him up and down, as if seeing him in a whole new light. He was silent for a while. Then, one hand smoothing back his brush of flame-orange hair, he said, 'The aircraft will need a thorough overhaul before they can be flown. Clockweight and his men have the knowhow, but I'm certain your additional expertise would be welcome.'

Den knew in that moment that he had been downgraded from close companion to mere motor mechanic. Perhaps that was all he had been all along.

And guess what? He didn't care.

'No, Gerald,' he said evenly. 'Them'll just have to muddle through without I. As of now, I be officially out. I want nothing to do with this any more. Nothing. I quit. Hear I?'

'Loud and clear, Den. Loud and clear.' Hardscree smiled without warmth. 'You've made your position known. I'd recommend, though, that you don't try anything rash.'

'Such as?'

'I shouldn't have to spell it out. Just don't get in the way. Let things run their course. I'd take a dim view of any opposition from you, and so, I feel, would our newfound allies.'

Den said nothing, merely snorted.

'Stick around,' Hardscree went on. 'Like it or not, we're in this together, all the way. Stay and see the Groundling race take its first steps to becoming airborne like the Airborn. I think it's going to be quite a show, Den!'

Hardscree gave another warmth-free smile.

Den, in return, spun on his heel and stomped off.

CHAPTER 77

Ruminations Of A
No-longer-useful Tool

Den walked as far away from the activity at the cavern mouth as he dared –
which was not far. The yells and banter of the roughnecks, as they unloaded
the planes, afforded a kind of protection. While he remained within sight
and sound of other people, the dangers of the Relentless Desert were held
at bay, or so it seemed.

He halted in the shadow of the needlelike mesa and gazed out into the
surrounding emptiness.

What a fool he'd been!

He had learned just how little Hardscree actually thought of him. If the
Deacon could switch allegiance away from him so quickly and readily,
that told him he had meant nothing much to the man in the first place.
He'd been a useful tool, that was all, a way of ensuring Hardscree and his
half-tarp got to where they were supposed to. His usefulness was now at
an end. Hardscree had altered his plans, and the new plans did not include
him.

'Kids,' Den said to the desert, his voice a lonely croak. 'Fletch, Cass,
Robert, I be so sorry. What must you think of I? Your da's been a sad,
deluded old prune. Him ran off and left you in the lurch, and what for?
For a dream that'm gone and turned into a nightmare. If only I could see
you all now! If I did, I'd chuck myself down at your feet and beg you to
forgive I, straight up.'

But his children were hundreds of kilometres away. There was half a
desert, and a lot more besides, between him and them.

It seemed scarcely plausible to Den that he was going to see his family
again any time soon.

CHAPTER 78

Riding The Jet Streams

Cerulean continued to climb, her propellers vertically downturned for maximum lift. She was still skewing to starboard, however, and *Behemoth* was a shrinking black speck on the horizon.

'There's a crosscurrent up here,' said Az, tight-lipped. It was more a prayer than a statement of fact. 'There's got to be.'

The jet streams varied at different heights. At any given altitude you might find one running northerly, southerly, south-easterly, or from any other direction. They interleaved in layers, invisible sheets of wind sliding silkily across one another.

Captain Qadoschson had explained this to Az, saying that clever use of the jet streams could lessen journey time considerably. He'd added that, in the event of rudder failure, you could also use the jet streams to steer. The principle was simple: find one that was going the way you wanted to and stick with it, letting it blow you along. If it changed heading or petered out, then all you need do was rise or fall until you found another.

'It isn't an exact science,' Qadoschson had said, 'but in case of emergency it'll do.'

And if this wasn't an emergency, Az didn't know what was.

But *Cerulean* couldn't seem to locate a jet stream that was travelling the same way as *Behemoth*. So far she'd gone up nearly 1,000 metres, and the prevailing wind was still driving her on a course perpendicular to the other airship's. If she didn't hit a useable crosscurrent soon, *Behemoth* would be lost from sight.

'Come on, come on,' Az intoned. His voice trembled in time to his shivers. Everyone in the control gondola was shivering. Somebody had fetched blankets for people to drape around their shoulders, but even so warmth was hard to come by. With the windows gone, there was nothing to keep the sub-zero air outside from entering. Ice crystals were forming on dials and metal surfaces. Breath was visible.

Az reckoned if they didn't get lucky soon, he would have to abort the manoeuvre. *Cerulean* couldn't go much higher without risk of someone in the crew succumbing to frostbite or even hypothermia.

Just a few more metres. Surely, surely, the wind would change.

Az became aware of a rocking motion. *Cerulean* was being gently nudged from behind.

Could it be ... ?

It was!

The airship was turning round towards *Behemoth*. She had penetrated into a new jet stream and it was pushing her on almost exactly the right heading. It was strong, too. Seventy knots, according to the navigator's wind-speed gauge. *Behemoth* appeared to be managing less than sixty.

'Brilliant,' said Mr Mordadson, with an approving nod. His nose had begun to swell and was turning an ugly shade of mauve. Without his spectacles on, his eyes had a diffused, lost look to them. For the first time in Az's experience, the mighty Mr Mordadson seemed vulnerable. Az knew, though, that in his heart he was scheming away. Naoutha Nisrocsdaughter had got the better of him once. It wasn't going to happen again.

'We should be able to make up lost ground,' Az said. 'As long as this jet stream keeps up, we'll be within striking distance of *Behemoth* in about four hours.'

'And then there'll be a reckoning,' said Mr Mordadson.

He didn't have to say any more.

It wouldn't be long before extreme sanction was due.

CHAPTER 79

Preparation For Assault

Slowly but steadily the gap between *Cerulean* and *Behemoth* narrowed. The black airship grew from a speck to a dot to a blob, and was soon close enough that Az could make out details such as her propellers and her tailfin assembly with the skull and crossed feathers on it. *Cerulean* was still a thousand metres above her, more or less. She was also coming towards her out of the sun. In other words, it was unlikely anyone aboard *Behemoth* would spot *Cerulean* approaching until it was too late.

This time, *Cerulean* had the advantage, not the pirates.

She also had steering again, to a certain extent. Rigz had cannibalised support wires from the balloon frame in order to replace the missing sections of rudder cable. He had plaited the wires together for strength before welding them into place. The helmsman reported that he had approximately 75 per cent of full control. Not bad, under the circumstances. Enough to do the job.

The crew were now swaddled in several layers of blankets, but were still blue-lipped and shuddering.

Az assured them they would be descending to warmer climes shortly. 'We can't afford to lose the boost we're getting from the jet stream just yet,' he said.

Then, looking around the control gondola, he added, 'I need a volunteer to go out and man the grappling hook.'

Really there was only one logical candidate, only one crewman who could be spared. Az's gaze zeroed in on him.

'Me?' said Flight Lieutenant Wallimson, pointing at his own chest.

'You,' said Az. 'Are you up for it?'

Wallimson considered, then gave a grin. 'I'd like to make myself useful,' he said. 'Count me in.'

He headed for the ceiling hatch.

Az was a little taken aback by how eager Wallimson was to help. He'd expected some grumbling at the very least. Then again, the flight lieutenant had been nothing but reliable and conscientious since Gyre. Once such a thorn in Az's side, he had metamorphosed into a trustworthy crew member. Whatever Mr Mordadson had done or said to get him to change his attitude, it had, in spite of Az's initial misgivings, done the trick.

Behemoth loomed closer, and closer still.

'We're nearly within range,' Az said. 'Descend.'

Cerulean sank.

'Sound an alarm.'

A klaxon hooted back near the cabins.

'Action stations.'

At the aft of the ship Patrollers formed a line to the rear hatch, clutching their lances. Mr Mordadson was with them. They dived out in pairs, somersaulting then righting themselves and peeling off to the left and right.

In the control gondola the crew tensed. Az himself found he no longer felt cold. Adrenaline was rushing through his body, making his pulse race and his blood pump faster, warming him.

'Here we go.'

CHAPTER 80

Treachery, Sabotage, Betrayal,
Undermining, Double-cross, Deceit, Etc.

Cerulean slotted in at *Behemoth*'s rear, bumping in her wake. Wallimson was gliding outside the control gondola, holding on with one hand, priming the spring-loaded grappling hook launcher with the other. The Patrollers and Mr Mordadson, meanwhile, flanked the airship in attack formation. Mr Mordadson had borrowed a spare lance. He wasn't going to miss out on the chance to strike back at Naoutha.

The pirates still didn't appear to have spotted *Cerulean*. Obviously they believed they had sorted her out and left her far behind. Their overconfidence, Az felt, would be their undoing.

'We still have the element of surprise,' said Rigz, tentatively, as if he didn't want to jinx things.

'Let's hope so,' Az said. Raising his voice, he called out, 'Wallimson? I want you to —'

That was when everything started to go wrong.

From outside the gondola came a hollow, metallic *choomph* sound, and Az saw a grappling hook shoot towards *Behemoth*, trailing a wriggly line of rope. *Cerulean* was still slightly higher than the other airship, too high for the hook to find anything to latch on to. Az had been about to tell Wallimson to hold off from firing for at least another minute. Now, he watched in dismay as the grappling hook reached its limit. The rope snapped taut and the hook fell, landed flat on *Behemoth*'s balloon, slithered down the canvas, bounced outward, plummeted past the propellers, and continued in an arc down past *Behemoth*'s control gondola. From there it flopped back towards its point of origin, *Cerulean*.

'Wallimson!' Az shouted, running to the viewing windows. 'You moron! I never said fire.'

But the flight lieutenant wasn't beside the launcher any more. He was making for the grappling hook, which dangled below the gondola, swaying around like a useless pendulum. He grabbed the hook and flew with it strenuously, lopsidedly, towards one of the forward propellers.

Az's jaw dropped.

No.

No!

No, he wouldn't!

But he would. With an almost casual flick of the arm, Wallimson tossed the grappling hook at the propeller, then darted to safety.

The hook itself overshot the propeller but its line got snagged in the whirling blur of the blades. It wrapped around them, yanking the hook back. Metal screeched against metal as the blades chewed into the hook's prongs. Next instant, the whole propeller disintegrated in a burst of twisted fragments.

Some of the fragments tore holes in *Cerulean*'s canvas. Others bombarded the control gondola like lethal hail. Ra'asielson the navigator cried out in pain, as did Rigz. Az saw the chief engineer slump to the floor, steel shards sticking out of his arms and chest.

The propeller mounting was bent out of true, and the drive chain broke. It flailed around its cogs before unravelling and spinning off into space.

Az yelled out an order to stop the other forward propeller so that *Cerulean* would not veer off-course.

Then he saw that the pirates were emerging from *Behemoth*.

The misfired grappling hook had warned them of *Cerulean*'s approach. Naoutha and her gang were coming out to meet their enemy.

Clash At Sunset

The pitched battle between the pirates and the Patrollers took place in late afternoon, as the sun was sinking. Its reddish rays formed a fitting backdrop to the proceedings, staining sky and clouds the colour of blood.

The initial wave of pirates from *Behemoth* unleashed a volley of crossbow fire. Steel-tipped hickorywood bolts whisked through the air towards the Patrollers, forcing Wing Commander Iaxson to give the order for evasive manoeuvres. His men broke formation, scattering in all directions.

The pirates kept up the barrage. Their crossbows were short-range weapons, ineffective at more than fifty metres. None of the Patrollers was hit or hurt. But that wasn't the pirates' goal anyway. They were buying time, keeping the Patrollers busy while reinforcements appeared from inside *Behemoth*.

Soon there were equal numbers of pirates and Patrollers in the sky. The pirates put away their crossbows, and Iaxson blew the whistle command for his men to re-form. The Patrollers rapidly arranged themselves in neat ranks and files, lances at the ready. The pirates, meanwhile, gathered in clusters and brandished their own weapons – a daunting array of close-quarter implements, some sharp such as swords, daggers and axes, some blunt such as maces and clubs, and some, such as spiked iron balls on chains, that were both.

The motley throng of pirates jeered at their uniformed opponents, calling across to them, making coarse gestures of invitation, telling them to come and get it. Some of them howled with derisive laughter, others chanted rude rhymes. Leading the insults was the pirate called Twitchy Ziz. He danced a war dance in midair, jerking his limbs up and down and shrieking like a macaw, his dreadlocks flopping around his face.

'Kind of reminds me of the Sinking Cities Panic,' said Iaxson to Mr Mordadson. 'Remember, just after we graduated?'

'Yes, except those people weren't armed and they weren't hopped up on pterine. It was a wave of mass hysteria. They hardly knew what they were doing. This lot not only know what they're up against but think the drug will give them the edge. And they could be right.'

'But we have discipline and training on our side. Given a choice between that and drugs, I'll go with discipline and training any day.'

'Me too,' said Mr Mordadson, then narrowed his eyes. He had just located Naoutha Nisrocsdaughter in the pirates' midst, distinctive with her black wings. She was his primary target. He and she had unfinished business.

Iaxson readied himself to order an attack, but Naoutha got there first. She let out a high-pitched, ululating scream, and the pirates took it up and flew towards the Patrollers, coming at them in a swarm. All at once the Patrollers were on the defensive. Each found himself on the receiving end of a flurry of sword slashes or axe blows and was so busy using his lance to parry that he couldn't deploy it in attack.

Several of them perished under the onslaught. The pirates hacked wings and stabbed bellies and clouted heads. Dead or dying, their victims fell towards the clouds.

Finally Iaxson was able to establish control again. He ordered the Patrollers to withdraw and regroup, and then gave the signal for a counter-attack. The Patrollers hurtled at the pirates in a Flying Spearhead, a configuration shaped like a pyramid on its side and famously effective in dispersing crowds of rioters. The pirates scattered but some were not fast enough and ended up with lances through their torsos. They too fell, figures who became doll-sized then dot-sized as they descended, like the recent Patroller casualties, who still had not reached the cloud cover yet.

The pirates' response was to fight dirty. They assembled in pairs and trios and then picked on single Patrollers. One pirate would come at the Patroller from above, another from below, and, if there was a third involved, he would attack from behind. Pincered in this way, beleaguered on at least two fronts, the Patroller was hard pressed to protect himself.

The skies around *Cerulean* and *Behemoth* became a torment of shrieks, grunts, growls and clanging metal. Loose feathers swirled. Blood rained. Chaos reigned.

In the thick of it, Mr Mordadson battled as fiercely as anyone. He ripped the jaw off one pirate with a sideways swipe of his lance. He despatched another pirate by grabbing the man's hair braids and swinging him round and round till a section of his scalp tore away. Blinded by the blood streaming down his face, the pirate blundered through the air until, accidentally, he flew into the arc of a sword being wielded by one of his friends. An artery was severed, and the pirate spiralled downward, leaving a dotted spray of crimson in his wake. Mr Mordadson threw the handful of scalp and hair after him.

All the while, Mr Mordadson was keeping an eye out for the pirates' leader. He had lost track of her in all the confusion.

Finally he spied her, not far from *Behemoth*. Naoutha was clinging to a Patroller's back, her legs scissored around his waist. The Patroller was struggling to break free from her grip but could not. As Mr Mordadson looked on, she seized the man's head with both hands and wrenched it round. The sound of neck vertebrae snapping was audible even about the tumult of battle and the drone of the airships' engines – a sharp, sickening *crack*. She let the dead man go, and his limp form began its long, inexorable plunge to the ground.

With a cry of fury, Mr Mordadson flattened his wings and dived at her.

Naoutha saw him coming and went into a steep dive herself, chasing after the Patroller she had just killed. She snatched the lance out of the dead man's clutches and rose again to meet Mr Mordadson. She had a sword as well, and launched herself at him with both weapons to the fore.

The impact of lance against lance shivered up Mr Mordadson's arms. An instant later, Naoutha's sword slammed down, hitting the spot on his lance where his right hand had been holding it. Had he not snatched the hand back just in time, Naoutha would have chopped it off at the wrist. In return, he lashed out with his foot, catching her a glancing blow on the thigh. At the same time he tried to strike one of her wings with one of his. He was aiming to numb the wing and paralyse it, if lucky break a bone, but Naoutha's pterine-fired reflexes enabled her to anticipate and deflect the shot. His wing tangled with hers. Feathers meshed, white and black. Then Naoutha planted her feet in Mr Mordadson's chest and kicked, separating them.

The two adversaries circled one another warily. Mr Mordadson feinted with his lance. Naoutha feinted with hers.

'I'll grant you this,' Naoutha said. 'You're a worthy opponent – for an old geezer.'

'Middle-aged geezer, if you don't mind,' Mr Mordadson replied.

'Whatever. How's the nose, by the way? Hurting?'

'The pain is a useful reminder why I have to kill you.'

Behind her mask Naoutha laughed, raucously and contemptuously. 'You can try, middle-aged geezer.'

She lunged at him abruptly. If her face had been visible Mr Mordadson might have had an inkling that the attack was coming. The face gave subtle cues – a narrowing of the eyes, a tightening of the mouth – which foreshadowed an opponent's intention.

As it was, Mr Mordadson managed to twist sideways as her lance jabbed at him ... but he was a fraction of a second too slow. The tip of the lance skewered his left arm at the biceps and gouged out a chunk of flesh.

He bit back a scream. Agony flared up from his arm, but he forced himself to ignore it. Bringing his own lance round, he thrust it at Naoutha. He was aiming for her chest emblem or thereabouts.

The thrust found its mark, but Naoutha's leather, and the fact that one of his arms wasn't fully-functioning, saved her from serious harm. He managed to embed the lance tip a couple of centimetres deep into the top of her pectoral muscle. She shrugged off the wound, knowing that the injury she had inflicted on Mr Mordadson was far more severe.

She sliced at him with her sword. Mr Mordadson parried with the lance handle. By dint of good fortune more than anything, he knocked the sword from her grasp.

Now, armed equally, the two of them went for it, using their lances like quarterstaffs. They collided and collided again in midair, the lances thudding together in an X-shape each time. Mr Mordadson drove Naoutha backwards; then it was Naoutha's turn to drive Mr Mordadson backwards. Locked in this ferocious private struggle, they hammered at each other. They pounded at each other. They matched blows like for like. Mr Mordadson's features were set in a contorted, spittle-flecked snarl. Naoutha's, presumably, looked similar.

It could perhaps have gone on for ever. Neither one seemed able to gain the upper hand; neither one was willing to weaken.

Then, suddenly, Mr Mordadson felt someone grab his wings from behind and pin them against his back. He stretched his wings out, shaking the person off. It was just a brief distraction.

Naoutha didn't hesitate.

She whipped the butt of her lance across Mr Mordadson's skull.

Mr Mordadson, knocked cold, began to fall.

CHAPTER 82

The Bolas Gun

Az sprinted along the axial corridor towards the nose-cone. He couldn't tell how well the battle outside was going but he knew he had to do something other than simply keep *Cerulean* on a steady course. He had to help in a more proactive way.

By doing some harm to *Behemoth*, for instance.

Reaching the nose-cone, he pulled out a box knife which he had taken from Rigz's storeroom.

Rigz. Was the chief engineer all right? He had looked badly hurt, as had Ra'asielson.

Az told himself he could worry about that later. Crew members were administering first aid to the two stricken men. There was nothing he personally could do for them right now.

He began cutting the canvas. It was tougher than it looked and he had to saw at it holding the knife with both hands. Eventually he succeeded in hacking a jagged sideways tear in the canvas, large enough for him to push through. He forced his head into the tear, then wriggled his shoulders and torso through after it.

He emerged just below the bolas gun which had been screwed onto the nose-cone. While still half inside the balloon, he grabbed the framework of the gun and hauled the rest of his body out. His legs swung free and for a terrifying moment he was supporting the whole of his bodyweight with just his hands. His grip started slipping. Scrambling frantically, he gained a foothold on the gun. Then he pulled himself up and over, and collapsed, panting, into the gun's seat.

No time to rest.

The gun's mechanism was straightforward enough and it was already loaded. He pumped the air compressor arm till the gauge read green. Then he grasped the guide-handles and swivelled the gun barrel round, taking aim at *Behemoth*'s rear starboard propeller. He peered down the sights and curled his finger around the trigger.

A pirate soared into view directly in front of him.

The pirate raised his weapon, a mace, and heaved it down towards Az's head.

Instinctively Az pulled the trigger.

The bolas slammed into the pirate, hurling him back. The five steel strands coiled around his body and wings, wrapping him tight. One of them encircled his neck, strangling him. The pirate plummeted, choking, clawing madly at his throat.

Az never found out if the pirate managed to unpick the bolas strands and save himself. He fell rapidly out of sight and Az did not see him again.

He guessed, though, that he had just killed someone.

Extreme sanction, he thought.

But it was him or me, was his next thought. *He'd have smashed my skull open if I hadn't done what I did.*

That eased his conscience a little. But only a little.

He reached for another bolas round. Each bolas was kept in a compact cylinder which slotted into the gun breech.

Load.

Pump.

Aim ...

Shoot!

The bolas whirled towards *Behemoth*, its strands unfurling till it was like a five-pointed star with a spherical weight at each tip.

Az's aim was good. The bolas struck the propeller and snarled it, bringing it to a halt. The result wasn't as explosive as Flight Lieutenant Wallimson's act of sabotage, but it would do. *Behemoth* was hobbled, like *Cerulean*. One prop down, three to go.

Just as he was about to load another cylinder, Az spotted two figures fighting not far from *Behemoth*.

Both were clad in black. One of them had white wings, while the other's wings matched her outfit.

Mr Mordadson and Naoutha Nisrocsdaughter.

They were going at each other mercilessly and unrelentingly with their lances. The skirmishes that Az could see elsewhere were vicious enough. The Patrollers and the pirates were not holding back. But these were nothing compared with the tussle between Mr Mordadson and Naoutha. Every blow, every lunge, every strike spoke of a deep and abiding enmity, and also of the combatants' evenly matched skills. As much as each of them wished the other's death, neither could find a way of bringing it about.

Then a third figure entered the fray.

Even if this third party had not been wearing a *Cerulean* crew uniform, Az would have identified him by his unique flying style. He approached Mr Mordadson from behind in an awkward, effortful fashion, twisting himself sideways with each wingbeat to compensate for the reduced thrust he was getting on his left-hand side.

Az yelled out a warning which he knew wouldn't carry as far as Mr

Mordadson's ears, but what else could he do? Apart from that he could only watch in helpless horror as Flight Lieutenant Wallimson seized Mr Mordadson's wings. Mr Mordadson shrugged Wallimson off but was momentarily unbalanced, and Naoutha was quick to make the most of it.

Next thing Az knew, he was watching an unconscious Mr Mordadson fall, helpless, towards the clouds.

CHAPTER 83

Defection

'Who the hell are you?' Naoutha demanded, turning her lance on Wallimson.

'A friend,' he replied. 'Someone who just saved you and who wants to join your group.'

'You didn't save me. I'd have beaten him anyway, in the end. All you did was take away the satisfaction of a proper victory. For that I ought to run you through.'

'Didn't you hear what I said?' Wallimson pushed the lance aside. 'I want to join you. I want to be one of you.'

'But you're one of *them*,' Naoutha said, gesturing at his uniform.

'Which would make me a valuable asset to you. I know their methods. I know how they think. I know their weaknesses. I can help you defeat them.'

'We are defeating them.'

'No, Naoutha, with the greatest respect, you're not. Look around.'

Naoutha quickly scanned the battle scene.

Wallimson was telling the truth. While she had been focused on her fight with Mr Mordadson, the tide had turned against her and her gang. There were more Alar Patrollers left in the air than pirates. In the end, discipline and training had paid off, even against pterine users. They were hounding the pirates, gradually herding them back towards *Behemoth*.

'Here's what you need to do,' said Wallimson. 'Retreat and take me with you. Pull back to fight another day. *And* – take Mordadson hostage.'

'Who?'

'That's the name of the man you've just been having your little set-to with.' Wallimson pointed down at the dwindling form of Naoutha's adversary. 'Catch him, get him onto your ship. He's more use to you alive than dead, believe me. Think about it. A Silver Sanctum emissary in your clutches. Think of the power that'll give you. Think of the demands you can make then. He's a valuable bargaining chip.'

'Don't presume to give me orders.'

'I'm not. I'm pointing out a golden opportunity, that's all. But be quick about it. If you're going to catch him, you'd better get after him right away.'

'You go.'

Wallimson extended his lame wing as far as it could go. 'Can't. Sorry.'

Naoutha debated the sense of his words. Finally, with a *tsk*, she jack-knifed forward and went into a sheer vertical dive. Within seconds she caught up with Mr Mordadson, whose wings, loosely extended, were acting as a brake on his descent. She veered beneath him, scooped him up in her arms, and soared back towards *Behemoth*.

Wallimson followed her into the black airship. She hadn't invited him to, but she had taken up his suggestion about Mr Mordadson, and from that he inferred that he was now on her team.

How things could change.

A Feather First!er and former airship flight lieutenant had just become a pirate, a renegade, an outlaw.

Wallimson was thrilled.

CHAPTER 84

Who'd Have Thought A Hostage Would Come In Handy Quite So Soon?

The Patrollers continued to chase the pirates towards *Behemoth*, trying to pick off as many as possible before they gained the safety of the airship.

Wing Commander Iaxson led the pursuit on board. He wasn't happy about taking the battle into a confined space but he wanted to carry out a thorough mop-up operation. Not one of the pirates was to be left alive.

Entering *Behemoth* via the rear hatch, he was prepared to have to claw through the opposition, fighting hard for every centimetre of ground gained. He anticipated that the pirates would close ranks and come at him and his men in a rush.

What he wasn't expecting was to find *Behemoth*'s keel catwalk all but deserted. The pirates had dispersed into other sections of the airship, leaving a lone representative on the catwalk.

It was Naoutha Nisrocsdaughter, and she was crouching over a man's body with a knife poised at his heart.

Iaxson saw that the man was his friend Mordadson and that he was alive but unconscious.

Calmly Naoutha said, 'You have three seconds to get off my ship. Otherwise he dies.'

'You wouldn't —' Iaxson began, but Naoutha dug the knifepoint into Mr Mordadson's lapel.

'One,' she said. 'Two.'

Iaxson had a moment to decide, and decided.

'Fall back!' he called out to the Patrollers behind him. 'Off the ship. Return to *Cerulean*.'

'A wise move,' said Naoutha.

'This isn't over,' Iaxson told her, retreating. 'Not by a long shot.'

'Of course it isn't over,' she replied. 'But for the moment I think it is.'

CHAPTER 85

Back In The Control Gondola

Quarter of an hour later, Az was finding it hard to believe that Iaxson had simply left Mr Mordadson there.

'He wouldn't want that,' he said. 'He'd want you to finish the job.'

'She was going to stab him through the heart,' said Iaxson.

'It was a bluff.'

'No, kid, it wasn't. I've more experience with this sort of thing than you. She'd have gone through with it, no question.'

'So we just let them waltz away?' Az flapped a hand towards the viewing windows. *Behemoth* was putting air between her and *Cerulean*, creeping off into the twilight. 'With Mr Mordadson as their captive?'

'I can't see an alternative,' said Iaxson.

'But we had them on the run. When I saw you and the Patrollers board *Behemoth*, I thought that was it. You'd rescue Mr Mordadson, deal with the remaining pirates, commandeer the ship, hurrah, end of story, let's go home. That's why I didn't fire another bolas. I assumed we'd won. But then you all came out again, looking downcast and slack-winged ...'

'You think I'm not frustrated too? Not as disappointed as you are?' There was steel in Iaxson's eyes. 'I lost good men out there. I'd gladly see every last one of those pirates exterminated.'

'And don't you think Mr Mordadson would agree?' said Az. 'I reckon he'd rather you let him die than have the pirates get the better of you.'

'Then lucky for him it wasn't your call to make. How long have you known Mordadson? A year or so? I've known him for twenty. We bunked together at cadet academy. I wouldn't sacrifice him. I couldn't. It was a life-or-death situation, and I chose life. You, kid, are probably not familiar with life-or-death situations.'

'Oh, I know about them all right,' Az retorted, thinking of the pirate he had shot with the bolas gun. 'I also know that we're not leaving Mr Mordadson. We're getting him back.'

'No.'

'Yes, wing commander, we are.'

'No. There's another way. There must be.'

'There isn't. I'm in charge of this airship. I say where she goes, and right now, where she's going is wherever *Behemoth* is going.'

'Mordadson will die!'

'Not necessarily. Think about it. Naoutha saved him. Wallimson must've convinced her she needs him alive. As long as we chase them, then, he has his uses to her. He's her trump card. I'm betting that while we're on the pirates' tail, she'd kill him only as a last resort.'

'That's a twisted sort of logic.'

'Maybe, but Naoutha's a twisted sort of person. Wing commander, us staying with *Behemoth* is Mr Mordadson's best chance of survival. I'm sure of it.'

'Perhaps we should ask your crew for their views,' Iaxson said, looking around the gondola. 'After all, we're in a pretty sorry state here.'

There was no disputing that. Wind was now hissing in not only through the empty windows but also through the debris-impact holes in the gondola's starboard wall. Broken glass littered the floor, and with it were spatters of blood from Rigz and Ra'asielson. Those two had been taken to the cabins, so the crew was down to just four, not including Az. Plus, a propeller was missing and the steering had been compromised.

It would have been the easiest thing in the world just to admit defeat and give up. Enough was enough. The ship couldn't – shouldn't – have to take any more punishment.

'Guys,' Az said, addressing the remaining crewmen. 'It's up to you. I have no idea what Captain Qadoschson would say or do under these circumstances. To me, it's simple. The pirates have caused us no end of grief, and it doesn't seem right that they should get away with it. Flight Lieutenant Wallimson nobbled us, and he's now on their side. Naoutha Nisrocsdaughter has Mr Mordadson captive, and there's no telling what she'll do to him. Those are the facts.

'Then there's *Behemoth* herself. She was once the *Brightspans Empress*, a troop carrier like *Cerulean*, a sister ship. I know transporting soldiers is hardly a peaceful occupation, but that was a long time ago. *Cerulean* may not have had a spotless past but she's made up for it since, whereas the *Brightspans Empress*, as *Behemoth*, is being used solely to plunder and kill. I don't know about you but it pains me to see her the way she is. She's a mockery, a black-painted perversion of an airship. Like a sick cage-bird, I think she ought to be put out of her misery.

'What it comes down to is whether you have the heart to carry on and see this to its conclusion. Whether you, like me, want to put right all the wrongs that have been done. Whether you feel, after the battering we've taken, that you've enough left in you for a last, determined push.

'This wasn't meant to be a big motivational speech,' he concluded. 'I just wanted to say what I'm feeling. The choice, really, truly, is yours. Whatever you lot decide, we do. But you have to decide quickly, before *Behemoth* sails out of sight.'

The crew were silent.

Then the trim-master said, 'We'll go on.'

The helmsman said, 'Let's get 'em.'

The other two agreed.

Az turned to Iaxson. 'Well?'

Reluctantly, sombrely, the wing commander nodded. 'All right.'

'Full speed,' Az announced. 'All engines.'

'Aye-aye, captain,' said the helmsman.

Only Az noticed. Nobody else even batted an eyelid.

Not *skipper*.

Captain.

CHAPTER 86

A Groundling Gains His Wings
(Though Not In The Metaphorical,
'Ascending' Sense)

The roughnecks worked hard all afternoon, using toolkits from the dune-buggies, and by early evening their efforts bore fruit when the engine of a biplane let out a spurt of fumes and started to roar. Other planes swiftly followed suit. Choked carburettors coughed, clearing the sediment from their barrels. Seized-up propellers turned, slowly and stutteringly at first but soon with a smooth, pearly whir. Once-awkward ailerons articulated and angled on demand.

The first attempt at flying took place at dusk. Magnus Clockweight settled himself in the cockpit of a single-seater, pulled the glass bubble-canopy shut over his head, and hit the ignition. The plane rolled towards open desert, gathering speed.

Clockweight and Hardscree had pooled their knowledge of aeronautics, such as it was. Neither was in any way an expert but between them they were able to establish a solid theoretical base to work from. It was all about lift. A plane's wings were shaped so that the air flowing over the top of them was faster than the air flowing underneath. The rounded upper surface of the wings meant the air travelled slightly further than it did below the flat underside, but at the same speed. The difference between the two rates of flow created a partial vacuum above the wing and thus provided lift. It raised the plane off the ground.

In order to achieve lift, though, you had to be going quickly. Clockweight leaned on the throttle and the single-seater juddered forward, faster, and faster still. The tail end kept skidding and he had to maintain a firm grip on the joystick to stay on a straight course. All the while, his heart was in his mouth and his belly ached with fear. This was madness, utter madness!

Suddenly, unexpectedly, and all too briefly, the single-seater took off. Clockweight had a delicious, tingling sense of weightlessness. Flying. He was *flying*.

Then the undercarriage touched down and he was rumbling along the ground again.

He gunned the engine. He'd had a taste of being aloft. He liked it. He wanted to get back up there.

The single-seater gave a lurch and a leap, and all at once become airborne and this time stayed that way. Clockweight let out a whoop of joy. The watching roughnecks did the same. Hardscree smiled.

Clockweight flew for less than a minute, remaining at a height of ten metres or so. He experimented tentatively with steering, but for the most part he concentrated on keeping the single-seater up and going. At last he pushed down on the joystick and descended. He realised, almost too late, that he also needed to decrease his speed. The ground was rushing up to him at an alarming rate. He pulled back on the throttle, hit the desert with an almighty bang, and lurched frighteningly upwards again. His stomach did a weird kind of flip-flop. For several seconds he feared he had lost control and the plane was going to roll over and land on its top. But the single-seater then seemed to take command, levelling out, as if it wanted to touch down safely as much as its pilot did. Its wings stopped seesawing, and Clockweight was able to bring it down to the ground bumpily but in one piece.

The roughnecks were clapping one another on the back and cheering as their toolpusher taxied to a halt in front of the cavern. Clockweight stepped out of the cockpit a bona fide hero. All of his men wanted to be next to have a turn, to follow the boss's example and shake off the bonds of gravity. Only a couple got the chance before the last of the daylight leaked from the sky and it was too dark to see.

With the onset of night, the roughnecks retreated to the shelter of the cavern, lit a fire, and cooked their supper on it. Hardscree had gone out and caught over a dozen patchrabbits, little burrowing mammals with piebald fur that were native to the desert and considered, by some, to be a delicacy. Though their meat was stringy, it was also tangily tasty, and while the roughnecks gnawed, they talked eagerly about tomorrow. Come tomorrow, they would all be pilots. They had plans for weapons, too, cunning improvised devices which they could use to attack the black airship with. They would find the pirates and give them what-for. Those Airborn scumbags would have no idea what hit them.

While the roughnecks schemed and predicted, Den Grubdollar kept himself to himself, chewing quietly on a patchrabbit leg. He had plans of his own.

CHAPTER 87

Dishonourable Men

It was midnight, or later. Den had lost track of time. Finally, finally, the last of the roughnecks had stopped chatting and dropped off to sleep. Now was his chance.

He stole out from the cavern and moved towards the needle mesa. The moon was fingernail-thin and the little light it shed was further dimmed by the clouds. He walked like a blind man, arms feeling in front of him, every footstep careful and considered. Now and then he tripped on a patch of uneven ground. Each time, he stood stock still, listened out, and heard nothing but snores from the cavern. Bit by bit the snores got further away. The needle mesa loomed closer, a giant, shadowy obelisk rising against the field of faint silver that was the sky.

Would it be the half-tarp van? Or one of the dune-buggies?

Den still hadn't made up his mind which type of vehicle to take. He would surely get further in the half-tarp, but then a dune-buggy was better suited to the rough terrain and therefore faster in the short term.

Before he set off in either, though, he had to disable all the other vehicles so that nobody could go after him. Removing the distributor caps would do the trick (with regret, Den remembered how he had immobilised *Bertha* that way).

Only problem was, taking out a distributor cap was a labour-intensive procedure and difficult to accomplish quietly, especially in the dark. A simpler, better solution was to let down the tyres on each vehicle. There was a foot-pump in the half-tarp. He would leave that behind so that the tyres could be reinflated. He doubted whether anyone would even think it worthwhile to pursue him, but if they did, he wanted a decent head start.

He located the first of the dune-buggies by blundering straight into it and barking his shin on its front bumper. Cursing under his breath, he rubbed the shin till the pain faded. Then, crouching down, he groped for the valve on the nearest tyre.

He didn't understand why his neck suddenly felt odd. There was a line of coldness running along the side of it, across his jugular vein, as though someone had placed an icicle there.

'Den, Den, Den . . .' said a voice right next to his ear.

Deacon Hardscree's voice.

And then Den knew that the line of coldness was the blade of Hardscree's hunting knife.

He hadn't heard a thing! The man had crept up on him in the dark without making a sound.

'I knew you'd do something like this,' Hardscree carried on, with soft menace. 'I just knew it. Even though I told you you'd have to stay, you couldn't, could you? But where did you think you could go? There's a huge amount of desert to cross. Did you think you could just drive out of here, putter along for a couple of days and then, hey presto, you'd be back in civilisation? You must know how unlikely it is that you'd have made it.'

'That'm no reason not to try,' Den growled. 'Somebody in authority needs to know what you's doing. Somebody needs to be told so as you can be put a stop to, straight up.'

'And you'd be the one to do the telling? How brave, Den. How noble. I'd admire you, if I didn't think you were so misguided. Can't you see that this, what we're doing, *this* is how to realise our dream of equality with the Airborn? Not merely by using their aircraft but by using their aircraft against them. It's completely logical, completely appropriate. It's —'

'Oh, bless my bum, just kill I,' Den snapped. 'Do it. Get it over with. Anything rather than have to listen to your long-winded, pontificating guff for one more moment.'

Hardscree chuckled cruelly. 'I think I may kill you at that. You're proving to be a nuisance and frankly we'd all be better off without you. Hmmm. Yes. I'd have to make it look like an accident, like some wild beast got you – but I'm sure I can manage that. The right sort of slashes here and there. Clockweight and his men would be none the wiser. I could even make myself look good by saying I heard your screams and rushed out to help. I wasn't able to save you, alas. I didn't get to you in time.'

'My screams,' Den said in soft, chilled tones.

'Oh yes. Being savaged by a wild beast – of course you'd scream.'

Den's right hand began to move, picking its way sidelong across the ground like a crab. There must be something around here, something he could use to defend himself.

'You'd murder I in cold blood,' he said, stalling for time. 'And here I were, having you pegged as an honourable man.'

'Mostly I am,' said Hardscree. 'But sometimes there comes a point where honour meets practicality head-on and one of them has to give way to the other. This is one of those times and I've reached that point with you. I'm indebted to you for all you've done to help, Den, but as of now you've become unhelpful and you're in the way.'

'Be that so? 'Cause I reckon' – Den's exploring hand came across a narrow, sharp-edged stone – 'I reckon all that'm happening here is you's taken a fancy to the notion of killing a person.' His fingers closed around the stone. 'As opposed to an animal, I mean. You'm a Pale Uplander, you's used to killing animals. But here be a human being, and you's got an opportunity to do away with he and not face any consequences, and you'm going to go ahead with it. And you know why?'

Hardscree heaved a sigh. 'I'm sure you're about to enlighten me.'

'Because I were wrong about you. You doesn't have a scrap of honour after all. Turns out you'm just a psycho-nutter fanatic like all them other Deacons. But that'm OK.'

'OK?' echoed Hardscree, quizzically.

'Yep.' Den picked the stone off the ground. 'When it comes down to it, you see, I doesn't have a scrap of honour either.'

So saying, he lashed backwards with the stone, ramming it with all his strength into Hardscree's knee. It wasn't a knife but it was almost as good as. He felt it pierce the Deacon's robe and cut through into his kneecap. He heard Hardscree give a sharp cry. Thrusting the knife away from his neck, he sprang upright and started running.

There was no direction to his running, no specific objective he was heading towards. He ran through the dark, stumbling across sand and scrub, simply in order to get away and be somewhere, anywhere, that Deacon Hardscree wasn't.

He continued to run long after he would normally have collapsed from exhaustion. Panic and fear carried him far, far into the night-shrouded wastes of the Relentless Desert.

CHAPTER 88

Point Of No Return

Cerulean dogged *Behemoth* through the night. Az kept the running lights off so that everyone's eyes would remain dark-adapted. It was just possible to make out the shape of *Behemoth* ahead. She was visible despite her coloration because she stood out against the stars. Where there was an oval hole in the starfield, that was where *Behemoth* was.

Both airships were operating at half capacity, so their mean speeds were the same. Thanks to Az's handiwork with the bolas gun, the pirates would not be able to outrun *Cerulean*.

Or so he hoped.

Cerulean, however, had started to make some very unhappy noises. Creaks and groans shuddered through her frame, and every so often the usually steady rhythm of her propellers skipped a beat. For all her size, she was a delicate thing. She had taken a battering, she had wounds, and now she was being pushed to her limits. She couldn't carry on like this indefinitely, and Az knew there was a real risk of her suffering a breakdown, potentially a catastrophic one.

The issue of fuel consumption was also raising its head. The gauges showed that the tanks were running dry, and although *Cerulean* had reserves, it was debatable how far they would get her. With a favourable tailwind, back to Redspire, possibly. But not necessarily. Ra'asielson would have been able to give Az a precise estimate of the distance involved and a formula for optimal speed and altitude ... but the navigator was lying comatose in one of the cabins, close to death.

Az was aware that the outcome of the entire mission now rested squarely on his shoulders. But more than that, lives were depending on him, and he knew that in this respect he would shortly be facing a stark and awful dilemma. At some stage he was going to have to weigh up the safety of one person, Mr Mordadson, against the safety of many, the crew and the remaining Patrollers. He was going to have to choose whether to keep pursuing the pirates for as long as it took or cut his losses and turn for Redspire. If he did the former, there was a good chance *Cerulean* might run out of fuel and fail to make it back to civilisation. But if he did the latter, Naoutha would doubtless see that her hostage was surplus to requirements and get rid of him.

Soon the point of no return would come, the moment when the fuel gauges said it was Az's last chance to make a bid to reach Redspire, now or never.

Twelve hours, he reckoned. That was how much longer he could afford to stay on *Behemoth*'s tail. That was how much longer this pursuit could continue. After that, he would have to break it off and abandon Mr Mordadson to his fate.

CHAPTER 89

'A Lovely Chat'

Mr Mordadson came to with a start.

His skull ached. His brain was a fog.

He breathed evenly and carefully, long slow ins and outs, restoring his equilibrium.

The ache lessened. His thoughts became clearer.

He assessed his predicament.

He was tied to a chair. Ropes bound his arms and wings tightly to the chair's back. His ankles were fastened by more ropes to its legs. He twisted and writhed, but the knots were good and there was no slack to work with. He was held fast, for the duration. The lance wound in his biceps blazed excruciatingly.

He was in a cabin, and by the starlight glow coming in through the porthole he was able to confirm that it wasn't one of *Cerulean*'s cabins. The place was a mess, particularly the floor, which was littered with empty booze bottles and also with drug paraphernalia – discarded hypodermic syringes and little glass ampoules with their caps snapped off. These various glass containers rattled around, tinkling musically with the vibration of *Behemoth*'s engines.

The engines themselves, Mr Mordadson could tell, were going flat out. That might mean the airship had somewhere she urgently had to get to or it might mean she had someone she urgently had to get away from.

Before he could ponder more deeply on this matter, the cabin door was flung open and in came Naoutha Nisrocsdaughter, along with Twitchy Ziz and Flight Lieutenant Wallimson.

Mr Mordadson was startled to see Wallimson in Naoutha's company, but immediately worked out what must have happened. The flight lieutenant had swapped sides. And it was a fair bet that Wallimson was the one who had grabbed him from behind during the fight, giving Naoutha the window of opportunity she needed to knock him out.

'Ah, awake!' said Naoutha. 'Shame. I was looking forward to rousing you with a couple of slaps. Oh, what the hell. I will anyway.'

She cuffed Mr Mordadson twice, a sharp backhand blow to each side of the face.

This amused Twitchy Ziz greatly. 'Thwack! Thwack!' he exclaimed, flipping his head from side to side as if he, too, had been hit.

Mr Mordadson smiled at Naoutha. 'Thank you. Very refreshing. I feel much better now.'

Naoutha studied him for a moment, then struck him again, this time with a firm fist.

'Ooh!' said Twitchy Ziz, wincing delightedly.

Mr Mordadson swivelled his head back round to look at Naoutha. A line of blood started to ooze from the corner of his mouth.

'What a tease you are,' he said. 'All this caressing. When are you going to start hitting me properly?'

Before Naoutha could react, Wallimson stepped forward and slammed his fist straight into Mr Mordadson's swollen nose.

It was agony, like splinters of glass being driven into his sinuses, but Mr Mordadson refused to give anyone the satisfaction of knowing how much it hurt. Even as fresh blood began trickling from his nostrils, his smile became a grin.

'Such a lovely chat we're having, isn't it, Naoutha? The four of us, getting along so nicely. We must do this more often. You, me, the flight lieutenant, and that – that *pet* of yours there.'

Twitchy Ziz bristled. 'Pet!?' He stepped forward to take his turn hitting Mr Mordadson, but Naoutha stayed his arm.

'No, Ziz. He's goading us. He wants us to keep hitting him till he passes out from the pain, and then he won't be any use to us.'

'Curses, you've foiled my cunning plan,' said Mr Mordadson.

'I know this man, Naoutha,' said Wallimson. 'He won't cough up information willingly. Beating it out of him is the only way.'

'Depends,' said Mr Mordadson. 'What do you want to know? I'd be happy to tell you all about the flight lieutenant here, for instance. Couldn't handle someone else getting the captain's job when he felt it should have been his. That's all it took to drive him into the arms of our enemy – resentment because someone else got promoted over him. That's the type of man your new ally is, Naoutha. Pathetic, eh?'

'That's not the only reason I decided to throw my lot in with Naoutha,' Wallimson said, stiffly.

'No, I'm sure your personal dislike of Az was also a factor. Anything to get back at him. But you know what I think, above all, convinced you you wanted to be a pirate?'

Mr Mordadson left a pause, so that the flight lieutenant had no choice but to ask, 'What?'

'You're a freak. And look who you're with now. *Look* at them. Where would a freak like you feel more at home than in the company of other freaks?'

With a grunt of rage, Wallimson flew at Mr Mordadson and began pummelling him mercilessly. The helpless captive's head snapped from side to side as Wallimson punched him, right hand then left, over and over – mouth, nose, cheek, eyes. It took all of Naoutha's strength to pull him away.

'No!' she said. 'No. Don't let him get to you. There'll be plenty of time for that later.'

Wallimson struggled in her grasp. His cheeks were flushed with humiliation and spite. 'Bustard!' he yelled at Mr Mordadson. 'Call me a freak? You try going through life with one working wing. See how *you* like it.'

Mr Mordadson could feel the skin of his face tightening. Contusions were starting to form in all the places where he had been hit. His head throbbed all over, pulsing in time with his heartbeat. The pain of the wound in his arm added to his general agony. He felt near to vomiting.

Nevertheless he forced his mouth to bend once more into a smile, or as close to a smile as his mashed and swollen lips could manage.

'You're enjoying this, aren't you, Wallimson? Settling scores with me. Getting your own back for what I did to you at Gyre. Well, make the most of it. I won't be tied to this chair for ever, and then I'll show you a thing or two about inflicting pain. That goes for you too, Naoutha.'

Wallimson made another lunge forward, but Naoutha swung him round and bundled him out of the cabin.

'Stay there,' she ordered. 'And you too, Ziz. Out.'

The skinny pirate whimpered pleadingly.

'No,' said Naoutha. 'I think I'll get better results on my own.'

Twitchy Ziz left the cabin with a sulky pout.

Slamming and locking the door, Naoutha turned back to Mr Mordadson. 'Now then. It's just you and me ...'

CHAPTER 90

Bait

'So this is what it's all about, eh?' Mr Mordadson said, clucking his tongue. 'You've a thing for older men. I knew it! And here's me without a bunch of flowers or a bottle of wine or anything.'

'That's enough cheap bravado, Mordadson,' said Naoutha. 'I'm not here to be impressed by how well you can withstand punishment. I'm here for facts, and I will get them.'

'Surely Wallimson's been an excellent source of intelligence already.'

'He has been helpful, yes, but there's still one or two things I need to clear up.'

'Well, seeing as it's just you and me, as you say, Naoutha, I'll do what I can.'

'Sarcasm,' Naoutha said with an audible sniff. 'Delightful. Now tell me, why is *Cerulean* persisting on chasing us?'

That explains why Behemoth's *flying hard*, Mr Mordadson thought. *Az is behind her and he's not giving up. Good lad.*

He said, 'Maybe there's some irresistible attraction between *Cerulean* and *Behemoth*. Airship love! After all, *Cerulean*'s been one of a kind for so long. She must have got lonely. Horny, too. And then another airship comes along. Not much to look at, but beggars can't be choosers. And so —'

'Stop it,' said Naoutha. She was starting to sound annoyed, in spite of herself. 'I mean it. This is pointless. This whole situation is pointless. Don't you see? You can't win. You'll never be able to bring us down. However many Alar Patrollers you send, you'll never succeed. We'll always beat you, because we're younger and we're faster and most of all we have nothing to lose.'

'Now who's indulging in cheap bravado?'

'It isn't bravado if you believe in it.'

'So how come you're still fleeing from *Cerulean*? That would suggest your side didn't actually win the battle. I'm guessing you forced a standoff, using me as leverage, but even so *Cerulean*'s still on your tail and you can't shake her off.'

'Well deduced. And so nearly correct. You don't think we're genuinely *fleeing*, do you?' Naoutha had recovered her poise. From her tone of voice, it was easy to picture a triumphant sneer behind the mask and goggles.

'What would you rather I called it? "Tactical withdrawal"?'

'The commonest word for it is trap.'

'Trap,' Mr Mordadson echoed. His stomach felt as though someone had dropped a large stone inside it.

'We're leading *Cerulean* a dance,' Naoutha went on, 'and at a certain point we're going to dip into the clouds, lose her, and hide somewhere where she can't easily find us. And if she does eventually manage to find us, by then we'll have augmented our attack capability . . . and that will be the end for your precious airship. Then there'll be nothing to prevent us from going about our business.' She straightened her shoulders, pleased with herself.

'You didn't really come here for information,' Mr Mordadson said, with cold certainty. 'You came here to gloat.'

'Guilty as charged. But in a way you *are* providing me with information, Mordadson. Your reaction speaks volumes. It says that you understand that you're the bait in the trap and that you think *Cerulean* won't be able to resist being lured. The Gabrielson boy won't abandon you, meaning he's going to play right into our hands.'

'No, no, Az will give me up if he has to. He's no fool. He'll realise I'm expendable. We're far out from the airlanes here, a long distance from the nearest refuelling stop. He'll soon take the decision to leave me and head for home.'

'Too late to bluff. You've already given away your true feelings. First responses never lie.' Naoutha rubbed her gloved hands together. 'A very satisfactory outcome. And I didn't have to resort to violence after all. All I did was use my wits. Maybe you could learn from that.'

Her captive barked a rancorous laugh. 'The day I've something to learn from *you*, Naoutha Nisrocsdaughter, is the day I die.'

'Let's not get too hasty here. No one said anything about dying – at least not just yet. Although I do have to ensure that you don't attempt anything tiresome, such as escaping. Those ropes are all well and fine, but even trussed up like a turkey you might find a way of slipping out of them. If I could only think of some means of rendering you helpless . . .'

She pretended to rack her brains and come up with a solution.

'Ah! Of course.'

From her trouser pocket she took out an ampoule of clear liquid.

'Pterine,' said Mr Mordadson. 'Fine. Go ahead. Increase my strength and resilience. I'll stand a far better chance of freeing myself.'

'A single dose would certainly benefit you.' Naoutha produced two more ampoules. 'But a triple dose?'

Mr Mordadson's eyes went flinty hard.

'I'm sure you know what pterine in excess does to the human body,' she said. 'Too high a concentration in the bloodstream produces all sorts of nasty effects. Heart palpitations. Uncontrollable tremors. Loss of muscular control. In some extreme cases it can even lead to death. But let's hope that's not the case here. All I want is for you to be a gibbering, shuddering, incontinent wreck for the next few hours, nothing more spectacular than that.'

She bent down, rooted around on the cabin floor, and selected one of the used hypodermics. Breaking the caps on the three ampoules, she inserted the syringe needle into each one in turn and drew the contents into the tube using the plunger. Then she held the full syringe with its needle upwards and tapped the tube so that the tiny bubbles in the liquid rose to the top, forming an air pocket. She got rid of the air pocket by depressing the plunger gently till a droplet of pterine beaded at the needle's tip. She did all this slowly, in full view of Mr Mordadson, taking her time. She hummed a tune to herself throughout.

Finally she brought the syringe over and pricked the needle into his neck.

'There?' she wondered. 'Or the arm?'

'Just get on with it,' Mr Mordadson snapped.

'Patience. One mustn't rush these things. Yes, the neck. That way the drug'll reach your brain sooner.'

Mr Mordadson braced himself.

'Now, you may feel a slight scratch,' Naoutha said, and jammed the needle all the way in.

Seconds later, Mr Mordadson started to scream.

CHAPTER 91

Yes Or No

A long, long, lonnnng night. *Behemoth* always ahead, a blankness in the sky, a blot against the stars. *Cerulean* heaving and moaning, like an exhausted person eager for sleep, begging for rest. Az himself barely able to stay awake, eyelids drooping, head nodding. Somehow forcing himself not to succumb. Knowing that Mr Mordadson was counting on him. And all the while, the fuel gauges creeping down, heading for the red zone and E for Empty. And the bitter, knifing cold of the high altitude winds. And the no less icy fear inside – fear of failure, fear of disaster, fear of letting down a friend in his hour of need.

As a mental exercise to keep him from dozing off, Az picked out and named constellations, all the star shapes he knew, each representing a character or creature from Airborn mythology, each with its own story. He recalled doing this on his first ever visit to the Silver Sanctum, up in the Astral Dome, shortly before he gave his decision to Lady Aanfields-daughter on whether he would accept her assignment to travel to the ground. The immense changes that had taken place in his life since had all stemmed from that moment.

That moment . . .

It was late, time was short, and Lady Aanfielsdaughter couldn't wait any longer. She needed an answer. 'Yes or no?'

Az said no, and from then on he was ordinary. A boy without wings, yes, but otherwise just a seventeen-year-old, leading a normal, average, humdrum seventeen-year-old Airborn's life. He never had to deal with Humanists who wanted to bring the sky-cities down. He didn't confront the mad Deacon Shatterlonger, who tried to strangle him. Nor was there any of this stuff now – pitched battles with pirates, death in the air, shooting a man with the bolas gun, pursuing *Behemoth* interminably through the dark. Az finished school. He found himself a job somewhere. He was just another citizen.

He said no, and Lady Aanfielsdaughter nodded but she was clearly disappointed, and standing nearby in the Astral Dome was the Count of Gyre. The Count held up the strip of tickertape with Az's prophecy symbol on it. He pointed to the question mark in the centre of the double arrow.

'Up or down?' he said, peeling back his lips to reveal his yellowy clothes-peg teeth. 'Light or dark? Right or wrong? Yes or no?'

Az's decision remained firmly no, and he didn't go to combat lessons with Mr Mordadson and he never became captain of an airship and he stayed at home with his parents and he never learned of the term *extreme sanction*. He said no because that was the easier option, the answer which didn't scare him, the choice which brought the fewest unwelcome implications and complications. Why volunteer for danger? Why open yourself up to threat and misery and pain and death?

He said no, and the Count tore the bit of tickertape to shreds and bowed his head.

Mr Mordadson was in the Astral Dome too. He looked away, refusing to meet Az's gaze. Michael was ashamed of him. Aurora dipped her wings in regret.

Still Az said no, and there was no Cassie. There was never any Cassie. He never met her. She ceased to exist.

He wanted to be glad about that. He could think of her only with hurt feelings and a sense of dismay. Without her, wasn't his life cleaner and simpler? Wasn't he better off?

Yes.

No.

Az looked Lady Aanfieldsdaughter in the eye and gave her his final answer, the one he had known he was going to give all along, the one he was meant to give. With an emphatic nod of the head, he said —

'Sir? Captain? Did you hear me?'

Az snapped alert. Idiot! He *had* dozed off!

'Sir?'

'Yes, trim-master?'

'*Behemoth*'s going down.'

'Down?'

'Into the clouds, it looks like.'

The black shape ahead was indeed descending towards the moon-silvered cloud layer. Soon her propellers were whipping its upper tufts into vaporous whorls.

'Should we follow?'

Az thought hard. 'We follow her in there and we'll lose her for sure. That's what the pirates want. So instead we stay put and wait for them to come back up. Go into a holding pattern. Halt engines. Use them only if we start to stray from position. We stay here and we keep watch.'

The propellers stopped turning and *Cerulean* drifted.

Az peered down at the cloud cover as it parted silkily to let *Behemoth* in. All the once, the black airship was engulfed. The clouds closed over her. She was gone.

He was gambling on her resurfacing, as she would have to sooner or later. Was this the right thing to do?

He remembered the dream he had just had.

Decisions.

Yes or no.

In the end, that was all life was: an endless succession of alternatives. Do this or do that. You couldn't ever know which was the correct path, you could only trust your instincts and judgement and make a choice and hope that hindsight would prove you had chosen well. There was no going back once you'd settled on a course of action. There were no second chances.

In other words, if this gamble of his didn't pay off, Mr Mordadson was dead.

CHAPTER 92

The Razorweed Vortex

Daybreak greyed the world, and Den Grubdollar crawled out from under the rocky overhang beneath which he had hunkered for the past few hours, clutching his knees and shivering. The night-time cold had penetrated to his bones, and his body felt as stiff as sticks. He spent several minutes stretching and bending and massaging some life back into his muscles. He was hungry and thirsty, and during the small hours he had developed a racking cough which was chillingly reminiscent of his beloved Orla's final days. It didn't take much to bring on a case of rattle-lung. The disease was latent in most people and could emerge with very little provocation, when you were already ill with some other sickness, for instance, or when you had allowed your core temperature to drop low for a sustained period. The cough might be just a cough, of course, his lungs troubled after a night spent out in the open, nothing more sinister than that.

But wouldn't that take the biscuit, Den thought, to be lost in the Relentless Desert *and* come down with rattle-lung. Wouldn't that be the icing on the cake.

Biscuit and *cake* sparked an image in his mind's eye – a host of delicious, sugary teatime treats piled high on a table – and his stomach grumbled. He ordered himself not to think of food. Not to think about eating in any way. He mustn't torment himself with what he couldn't have.

A coughing fit overcame him, bending him double. He hawked up and spat out what felt like several lungfuls of phlegm.

Then, straightening up, Den started to walk.

It was hopeless, he knew. This was the Relentless Desert, one of the most inhospitable environments on earth, and he was in the middle of it without victuals, without transportation, without any means of protecting himself. He was as good as dead.

But he walked nonetheless, and vowed to keep walking till he couldn't go another step. Where the clouds were lightest at present, that was east. Therefore he knew roughly where north was, and he aimed his footsteps in that direction. He would continue going north, using the sun's position as a guide, because it was the only bearing worth following. North, ultimately, meant civilisation. Civilisation was impossibly far away. He would never reach it. But still, nonetheless, north.

Den had no idea how long he'd been walking when he first heard the strange sound. Nor did he have any idea how long it took him to arrive at the sound's source. He was already losing track of time. Seconds were footsteps. Minutes were the intervals between coughs.

The sound started as a faint rustling hiss and from there evolved into a deeper, skittering scurry, like fallen autumn leaves fluttering around in a breeze. Soon it had grown to a loud, resonant, strident crackle, which was reminiscent of the noise of a large bonfire but which could almost, almost, have been electrical in origin.

Den headed towards it with some eagerness, his pace quickening. If the sound was electrical, that meant machinery, and machinery meant the possible presence of people. But even if it wasn't machinery, he still had to know what was generating the sound. Hope and curiosity drove him to find out.

He came to the rim of a deep depression in the ground, a sloping-sided canyon shaped like an elongated horseshoe. Down in the rounded end of this rift, not far from where he was standing, was a throng of moving objects. At first Den took them to be animals of some kind, further examples of the bizarre types of wildlife that were unique to the Relentless Desert. They shifted around one another, climbed on top of each other, jostled for position, collided, bounced, tumbled, exactly in the manner of sentient creatures. Somehow they had become stuck up one end of the canyon and couldn't find a way out, and in their agitation they were rolling around and mauling one another and growing desperate.

On closer inspection, however, it became apparent that they weren't animals at all. They were balls of razorweed.

Den recalled Hardscree pointing some razorweed out to him a few days earlier. It was a scrubby, thorny shrub, and it propagated itself, the Deacon had said, by dying and letting the wind uproot it and bundle it into a ball, which would then roll across the desert, popping out seed pods along the way. Razorweed's thorns were huge and brutally sharp, hence the name. It was said that one clump, if you didn't get out of its way as it hurtled towards you, could fillet the flesh from your body.

Here, hundreds of razorweed balls had collected in the base of the canyon like litter in a dead-end alleyway. The same wind that had blown them there was now harassing them mercilessly, propelling them round in circles to create a whirling vortex of barbed brown vegetation. Now and then the wind would lift one of the razorweed balls up, bring it near the canyon rim, offer it a tantalising glimpse of liberty – only to let it fall back down again at the crucial moment and rejoin its companions below.

To Den, the razorweed vortex was a mesmerising sight, and also a discouraging one. It spoke of trappedness and futility.

It also spoke of death. Imagine if someone were to fall into that spinning soup of tangled branches with finger-long thorns . . .

He shuddered. It didn't bear thinking about.

'Doesn't bear thinking about, does it?' said Deacon Hardscree.

Den spun round.

Hardscree was standing a few metres away, poised on the canyon rim. The knife was in his hand. The hem of his robe was dusty and torn. He wasn't even looking at Den, just peering down at the endlessly swirling, circulating razorweed.

'You – you —'

'I've been following you, yes, Den. Tracked you all this way. Not difficult for an Uplander. I could track a mouse in this desert if I wanted to, so you were no challenge at all. Only thing that made it hard was my knee.' He moved a couple of paces closer to Den, demonstrating a severe limp. 'You made a serious mess there. Tore a ligament, I think. It hurts like a son of a bitch. Every step of the journey has been agony, and for that you're going to pay – dearly.'

The knife blade glinted.

'Prepare to Ascend, Den,' said Hardscree. 'No, why sugarcoat it? Prepare to *die*.'

CHAPTER 93

Brawl On The Canyon Rim

Briefly Den thought, *Ah well, the desert'll kill I anyway, may as well let Hardscree do the honours instead. Might even be quicker his way, you never knows.*

But no. He wasn't going to grant Hardscree the privilege of ending his life. At least, not without putting up a fight.

Hardscree came at him, knife raised. Thanks to his damaged knee, he wasn't as quick or as co-ordinated as before, and Den was able to intercept his knife-holding hand, grabbing it by the wrist. Hardscree bore down with the weapon. Den resisted. Seconds passed, the two men grappling next to the canyon. The knife was between them, its point quivering mere millimetres from Den's face.

Then Den kicked out, and the toecap of his boot made contact with Hardscree's bad knee. Hardscree shrieked and hopped backwards, but rapidly recovered and prowled towards Den once more, slashing the knife from side to side.

Den backed away from the scything swipes of the blade, and all at once he found himself teetering on the edge of the canyon. One foot was half on the ground, half not. His heel had nothing beneath it but space, and the earth under his instep was crumbling. His arms windmilled. Down below, the razorweed vortex revolved, sounding almost greedy in its crackling, like someone smacking their lips before a meal.

Then the crumbling earth gave way and Den's leg shot downwards. At that selfsame instant Hardscree lunged, aiming to stab him in the throat. Den slithered far enough down the canyon slope that the knife thrust passed harmlessly over his head. While Hardscree regained his balance, Den grabbed the ground with both hands, dug his fingers in and pushed with all his might, shoving himself up out of the canyon before he could slide any further in. Rolling away from the brink, he leapt to his feet, and scarcely had time to catch his breath before the Deacon's next assault. The knife slashed towards his belly but he managed to sidestep out of the way and the blade caught only his clothing. It lacerated his shirt but not him.

Hardscree, fiery hair flapping in the breeze, went onto the offensive yet again. Den, even as he continued to dodge and dive, felt a horrible sense of inevitability. Injured knee or not, Hardscree would not let up. He would keep on coming, keep on coming, until his knife finally found its target. Den didn't have the energy to fight him for ever.

Again he entertained the notion of simply letting the Deacon do his worst. Get it over with.

And again, he rejected such fatalism. Give in? Not while there was a breath left in his body.

Hardscree stabbed, and Den made a desperate grab for the knife. He wasn't quick enough. Hardscree yanked it back and Den's hand closed around the blade rather than the handle. A fierce pain lanced up his arm. He recoiled, hand bleeding. A glance showed him his palm had been opened up to the bone. He had no idea anything could hurt quite so much.

Hardscree paused for a moment to crow. Tossing the knife from hand to hand, he said, 'First blood to me. And if you think that's bad, just you wait. There's worse in store.'

Den glowered at him, the breath rasping through his lips.

'Oh, don't be like that,' Hardscree said. 'You didn't expect this little scuffle of ours was going to have any other outcome, did you? You surely didn't think you could *win*.'

Den cocked his head. He had just heard something above the massed susurration of the razorweed. The noise was familiar. Absurdly familiar. He knew it as well as he knew the sound of his own voice.

No, not possible. It couldn't be what he thought it was. He was imagining things. The pain was fuddling his senses.

'What?' Hardscree demanded, with a frown.

Den listened harder. The noise was definitely real. He just couldn't quite pinpoint where it was coming from.

'Why are you looking like that?'

Den turned his head, scanning the horizon.

'Answer me!'

Den's gaze alighted on a far-off shape. It was heading this way, growing bigger, getting rapidly nearer.

Hardscree, scowling, followed his line of vision.

'Know what, Deacon?' Den said. 'All of a sudden I reckon I *can* win after all.'

And he started to cackle.

Just like *Bertha* was cackling.

Trundling across the desert plain, her throttle wide, her tracks churning up rocks and sand.

Bearing down on Den and the Deacon.

Like some lumbering fifty-tonne mirage, a glorious, smoke-spewing vision of salvation ...

The most wonderful thing Den Grubdollar had ever seen.

CHAPTER 94

A Predator At Bay

Den had every reason to think that Hardscree would now surrender. The Deacon seemed utterly flummoxed by *Bertha*'s appearance. The knife drooped in his hand. Surely he would have to admit defeat. Reinforcements had arrived. Somehow, in the vast, trackless wastes of the Relentless Desert, against all the odds, Den's family had found him. Hardscree must realise that now he was outnumbered and outflanked.

Which was true, and he did.

But he was also outraged. Den hadn't reckoned on how deep the Deacon's animosity towards him ran. When it finally dawned on Hardscree whose murk-comber this was and he understood that the balance of power had shifted decisively in his enemy's favour, he responded not with a sigh of surrender but with a surge of resentment. Hot on the heels of that came a resolve to finish what he had started, while he still could.

And so he rounded on Den once again.

And so he sealed his own fate.

Hobbling towards Den with his knife aloft, Hardscree looked a lot like a predator at bay, wounded, crazed, certain of nothing except the urge to lash out at those who had him cornered and harm as many of them as he could. His eyes bore a feral gleam and his red hair flamed wildly. The sophisticated, articulate Deacon he had been was very little in evidence now. He seemed to have reverted to a more primitive mode, his Uplander heritage showing through. Here was a man of the mountains, someone raised to stalk and catch and kill, someone who was close in temperament to the very beasts he routinely used to hunt.

Briefly, Den marvelled at how easily a man's civilised veneer could be stripped away. Then he stirred himself, summoning up the energy to repel yet another attack.

And then he didn't need to.

A javelin slammed into Hardscree from behind, skewering him through the shoulder, its tip emerging with a spurt of blood just above his collarbone. A perfect shot, hitting the Deacon where it would disable him but not cause a fatal injury.

Reeling under the impact, Hardscree dropped the knife and groped behind his back with both hands for the shaft of the javelin. He was so intent on pulling the weapon out that he wasn't looking where he was going. He staggered blindly towards the canyon edge. On impulse, Den yelled out a warning. He would never fully understand why he did this, why he tried to help somebody who just moments ago had been hell-bent on murdering him, but then that was what made him different from Hardscree – his humanity.

At any rate, Hardscree didn't hear the warning, or if he did, didn't heed it. He blundered straight over the rim of the canyon, still pawing desperately at the javelin's shaft as he fell.

The razorweed made short work of him. His screams lasted half a minute at most, as the wind-whirled thorns flayed him to ribbons.

When the screaming had stopped, Den took a reluctant peek into the canyon. One glimpse at the shuddering, bloody mess that had been Deacon Hardscree had him tottering away wishing he had never looked.

Bertha chuntered to a halt close by, and Den turned towards her. He tried to move his feet but all at once he felt drained, utterly depleted. Instead of rushing to meet his family, all he could do was sag to his knees.

He saw *Bertha*'s loading bay hatch open and Cassie spring out. She launched herself towards him at a run. Fletcher and Robert were not far behind.

Then, for a while, Den saw nothing. He was blind; couldn't focus. His eyes were too full of tears.

CHAPTER 95

The Merits Of Collaboration
Over Confrontation

When Den had finished weeping, when his children had finished weeping too, when Cassie had treated the gash in his hand with disinfectant and bandaged it up, when Den had (with some puzzlement) greeted Colin Amblescrut and (with even more puzzlement) Michael and Aurora, when he had gulped down some water and found this eased his cough, when he had had something to eat, when he began to regain his strength – then came the time for explanations and justifications and, above all, for apologies. Endless, profuse apologies, which his children batted aside, saying it didn't matter, he had nothing to be sorry for, they didn't care about any of that, they had their da back, that was all they cared about.

'Him seemed to have the answers, that Deacon,' Den said. 'With he, everything seemed to make sense. Even Martin dying. Hardscree made I think I could turn that to the good, make it mean something. I were ... vulnerable, I suppose the word be. I were so desperate to feel optimistic about life again, to feel hope, that I stopped thinking straight. I fell for his lines, his Deaconly patter, even though it weren't all that different from the crap the Deacons used to spout in the old days. It were the same old sales pitch given a bit of a tart-up and a polish. That were how them used to get to we all, offering us promises of better things, better days ahead, and I always thought I were smarter than that. Always. And what should happen but, at a low point, I turned into a dumb old sucker like everyone else. Let my guard down for a moment, and that were that.'

'What did him offer you, Da?' Cassie asked. 'What was you chasing after all the way out here?'

'Illusions,' Den said bitterly, and told them about the cavern full of aircraft and then about the arrival of the roughnecks from Desolation Wells and how Hardscree chose to side with them because, never mind his big talk of raising Groundlings up, all he really wanted was to bring Airborn down. He was interested in creating equality but only the kind that came from confrontation rather than collaboration.

'Compare that with you lot and Michael and Aurora here,' Den said.

'From the sound of it, you all worked together and that'm how you found I.'

'That and pure dumb luck,' said Fletcher.

Colin nodded. 'Us was starting to lose hope, but Cassie insisted us keep at it.'

'Flogged we on like a slave-driver, she did,' said Robert. 'I don't think she'd ever have let we give up.'

'It weren't completely luck,' Cassie said. 'There were the message left at Desolation Wells. You left a hint about "a needle in a haystack" in your note to we, Da, and the message on the ground mentioned a needle too. It were a long shot but I reckoned it were worth taking. That'm why us came this way. And I were right. Your needle weren't just a figure of speech. It were this mesa you just told we about.'

'Nice piece of figuring-out, girl,' Den said, patting his daughter. 'I didn't leave that note as a clue, just as a way of letting you know I hadn't gone off my rocker. At least, not completely off my rocker. I'm glad I wrote what I did now, though. Straight up.'

He turned to the two Airborn. 'And congratulations be due, be'n't they? On you getting married. Sorry us couldn't make it to the wedding.'

'Think nothing of it,' said Michael.

'Didn't even get you a gift.'

'Knowing you're safe and well is gift enough.'

Den laughed for what felt like the first time in weeks. 'Well, I doesn't believe it for a moment, Michael, but it'm kind of you to say so. Now then.' He clapped his hands together, and instantly regretted it. 'Yeow. Won't do that again in a hurry. Now then,' he repeated, this time keeping his hands well apart, 'shall us get going? I'd like to be saying 'bye-bye to this desert, and I expect you lot would as well.'

'Erm, just one thing, Mr Grubdollar,' said Aurora.

'Call I Den, Aurora.'

'Den it is. You mentioned that these roughnecks plan on taking on the airship which destroyed their oil installation.'

'In the planes, yes.'

'In your view, do you think they stand a chance?'

'From what I saw, I'd have to say the answer be no. When I left, them was barely able to get those aircraft off the ground. I can't deny that them showed some guts in trying, and maybe guts will be enough. But even so . . . Oh. Ah. I think I see where you be going with this.'

'Let's say, for argument's sake,' said Aurora, 'that they become reasonably good at flying and then go after the airship. I know a bit about the people who are in that airship. Before the wedding, Lady Aanfielsdaughter told me about them, and since then, of course, we've witnessed ourselves how aggressive and ruthless they can be. The state of the installation is testimony to that. So, the roughnecks take them on, in vehicles they know next to nothing about, and . . .'

'A massacre,' said Michael, picking up her thread. 'But then that's what Az and Mr Mordadson and all those Patrollers are out here to deal with. They're hunting the Redspire airship, and we know she's in the area, so there's every chance they've already brought her down by now.'

'But what if they haven't?' said his wife. 'Worst-case scenario, the pirates go head-to-head with the roughnecks in the air. They'll surely win. That's thirty more Groundlings dead, to add to the death toll of who knows how many at Desolation Wells. And a whole lot more anti-Airborn resentment is created as a result.'

'This be another one of those dangerously escalating crises, be'n't it?' said Fletcher. 'It'm the Grimvale Chancel all over again.'

'I'm afraid that's how it's looking.'

'And you'm thinking us should get involved,' said Cassie. 'Again.'

'The way I see it,' said Aurora, 'the roughnecks could do with some help, and here we are, not that far away from them, with two people who happen to know their way around a plane.'

'One of them's a genius when it comes to aircraft, actually,' said Michael.

'Even if he does say so himself,' said his wife. 'Now, I'm suggesting this very tentatively. I don't want to put pressure on anyone. Least of all you, Den. You've been through so much. If it's your opinion that enough's enough and it's time to go home, fine by me. Then again, as you say, this could be a chance to demonstrate how collaboration is much better than confrontation. Airborn helping Groundling.'

'Even if it'm helping them against other Airborn?' queried Den.

'Against rogue Airborn. Dangerous Airborn. A mutual enemy. So, what do you think?'

Robert piped up. 'Nobody ever asks I my view,' he said, 'but I be with Aurora. It sounds like something us ought to do.'

Den appraised his youngest son. Boys his age were so gung-ho, so reckless when it came to answering the call to action. 'Well, that'm one firm vote in favour,' he said. 'Fletch?'

'Not sure, Da. I suppose us could at least drive Aurora and Michael to where these planes is and see how it goes from there.'

'That'm a yes then?'

'A qualified one.'

'Colin? Only fair to ask you too, since you's been a part of this from the start, as I gather.'

'Den,' said Colin, 'I be your pal and I be a pal to our Airborn chums here. My answer has to be a yes.'

'Cass?'

Cassie bit her lip. 'I be'n't sure either, Da.'

'What'm the matter?'

'Nothing. I just reckon Fletch has it right. Us could just drive them there, limit it to that. There be'n't much else us could do beyond that, anyway, being as none of we Groundlings knows the first thing about flying a plane.'

Den turned back to Aurora. 'There you has it. The Grubdollar/Amblescrut consensus appears to be: us'll help up to a point.' He shrugged. 'OK with you?'

Aurora gave a gracious bow. 'It's absolutely OK. It's plenty. I couldn't expect more.'

'Then let's get cracking,' Den said, clapping his hands together again. 'Agh! Yowch! *Got* to stop doing that.'

CHAPTER 96

A Future Lady Aurora Gabrielson?

As the Grubdollars and Colin scrambled to various positions within *Bertha*, Michael wrapped his arms around Aurora and planted a huge, proud kiss on her cheek.

'You can do better than that,' Aurora teased, and there followed several moments of passionate, lip-locked snogging. Wings splayed in shivery delight.

'Pretty pleased with yourself, aren't you?' Michael said, drawing back to look at her.

'As a matter of fact, I am.'

'And so you should be. You did some good leadership stuff there. Persuading others. Winning them over. You spoke like a true Silver Sanctumer.'

'I did, didn't I?'

'Am I looking at a future Lady Aurora Gabrielson?'

'You could well be.'

They both laughed. It seemed a fantastical prospect – Aurora one day joining the exalted ranks of the senior residents at the Sanctum – and yet at the same time, thanks to her confident, commanding performance just now, it seemed utterly plausible.

'And you,' Aurora said, 'are pretty excited at the thought of getting your hands on some vintage aircraft, aren't you?'

'Can't deny it. I can't imagine what's been stored down there in that cavern but I'm looking forward to finding out.'

'Then,' Aurora said, with a slight clearing of the throat, 'I suppose now would be as good a time as any to tell you that I think I'm pregnant.'

Michael: jaw open to the breastbone, eyes standing out on stalks, voicebox rendered incapable of speech.

Bertha: ignition, rumble, cackle.

CHAPTER 97

Little Miss Deadeye

Den occupied one of the front observation nacelles, and Cassie squeezed herself in behind him.

'What'm up, lass?' he enquired, as *Bertha* trundled southward, retracing roughly the same journey he had made coming the opposite way this morning and last night. Soon, surely, the needle mesa – that vast place-marker – would hove into view.

'Nothing, Da. Just wanted to be with you.' Cassie slipped an arm around his neck and Den patted her hand.

'But you'm troubled about something. Come on.'

She hesitated, then said, 'It be that Deacon. I didn't mean to kill he.'

'It were you that fired the javelin? I should have guessed. Little Miss Deadeye. That were fine aiming.'

'But I killed he all the same.'

'No, lass,' said her father, with finality. 'No, you didn't. You shot to wound, and if you hadn't done that him would've killed I for certain. Him would've gutted me open like a fresh-caught trout, quick as you please. You shot to wound and that means you did nothing wrong. Him's only dead because him fell into that razorweed. Don't even ask yourself twice about it. Your conscience be clean.'

'I – I saw he charging at you, and it were like Martin all over again. Somebody I love, fighting with a Deacon. Only, this time I could do something about it.'

'And you did.'

'I be guilty that him's dead but I be'n't sad. That make sense?'

'Does to me.'

'And ... and that has something to do with why I doesn't want we to help Aurora. At least, not as much as us maybe could. Because, last time us helped Airborn, Martin ended up dead. And just now us so nearly lost you as well. I doesn't want to risk any of my family's lives ever again.'

'Understandable.' Den fixed his daughter with a gaze of stern fondness, or fond sternness. 'Let I tell you something, though, girl. You'm sensible and you'm responsible, and those be just two of the many, many things that I love about you and that make I so proud of you. But you also takes on too much responsibility sometimes. You can be too hard on yourself.

I be'n't saying you should lighten up, just saying you might want to switch your priorities around a little. You always put others first, and that'm noble and laudable, but why not put *yourself* first for once? Accept that what *you* need be as important as what others need?'

'If I hadn't put you first, Da, us wouldn't be having this conversation now.'

'Agreed. That aside, though, there'm no shame in being selfish now and again. And if that means not volunteering to fight the good fight this time around, so be it.'

Cassie grinned with relief, and put her other arm around her father's neck and hugged him hard enough to choke him. When he pointed out that he was having a spot of bother with the whole inhaling, getting-oxygen-to-his-lungs process, she slackened her grip but didn't let go.

Nor did Den want her to let go. Not for a long time. Maybe not ever.

CHAPTER 98

Planespotter

It was well past midday by the time the needle mesa appeared on the horizon. Den had run and walked much further than he had thought. Such was the combined power of blind panic and blind faith.

Out of nowhere, a snub-nosed little plane appeared and buzzed *Bertha*. The plane shot past her on the right, its stubby wings seesawing in salutation.

'Pluck me gently!' exclaimed Michael. 'That's a Metatronco Condor. The most misnamed light aircraft in aviation history. Pathetic range, unlike a real condor. Pathetic fuel consumption too. The first production run was five hundred and they didn't manage to shift even half of those. There was this whole load of jokes about it, remember? The plane that nearly sank Metatronco. "What do you call a dustbin with wings?" "A Condor." "Name a bird that has to have a drink every half an hour" ...'

'Michael,' said Aurora, 'there's no point showing off. I already know what an aircraft nerd you are, and there's no one else around to be impressed.'

'Mike!' said Colin through the speaker tube system. 'Did you see that? That were amazing, that plane. Zoom! Whoosh! Went by so fast.'

'No one else around to be impressed, eh?' Michael said. He picked up the speaker tube. 'That was nothing, Colin. Just you wait. There's bound to be something better in that cavern. At least, I hope so. Otherwise, we're in for a big let-down.'

There *were* other planes, happily, and as far as Michael was concerned all of them compared favourably to the Condor, even the ones that were certifiable antiques. The sky around the needle mesa teemed with low-flying aircraft. None of the pilots appeared very confident, however. The planes bumbled along anxiously, and often strayed into one another's paths, resulting in some hair-raising midair near-misses.

For Colin's benefit, Michael identified each one they saw. That was an Aerodyne Striga II limo, with that pair of owlishly round viewing ports at the front. That was a Solarsoar C-class Cleaver (distinguishable from the B-Class model by the scalloping of its ailerons and the extra stabilising fins midway along the fuselage). That clattering antique rattletrap over there was a Blackbird ('Basically a box kite with a propeller attached,'

Michael said). And that one there looked like an AtmoCorp 9-5, although someone had bolted the tail assembly from a Metatronco Shooting Star onto it.

Before *Bertha* even reached the cavern entrance, Colin had had a thorough grounding in the art of planespotting and was avid to learn more. Michael seemed to him just about the cleverest and most knowledgeable person alive, and if he loved aircraft, then Colin was resolved to love aircraft as well.

A small posse of roughnecks came out on foot to meet *Bertha*, with Magnus Clockweight at the fore. When Den emerged, shinning down the ladder from the driver's pod, Clockweight's expression went from wary to confused.

'Us thought you'd done a runner,' he said. 'You and the Deacon both. Only, where you'd have gone without taking a vehicle, that were a mystery to we all. And now you'm back in ... a murk-comber? Where on earth did you get hold of that?'

'It'm a long story,' Den said, 'one for another time.'

'Be the Deacon with you?'

'Er, no. No, him and I got – ahem – separated. Cut off from one another, you might say. I doesn't expect to be seeing he again.'

'Oh.' Clockweight frowned, evidently sensing that he wasn't being told something; Den was leaving out some crucial detail. Clockweight, however, had other things on his mind, so he confined himself to saying, 'Pity. Him seemed a reasonable enough guy. For a Deacon and all.'

'Seemed,' said Den.

'And a useful ally, too.'

'You want useful allies?' Turning towards *Bertha*, Den put a thumb and forefinger in his mouth and whistled. 'I's got a pair of those for you.'

The roughnecks gasped as two Airborn stepped out from the loading bay. Several of them, still traumatised by their previous encounters with members of the winged race, raised the tools they were holding, ready to defend themselves.

'Now calm down,' Den said. 'These be friendly ones. Everyone, meet Michael and Aurora Gabrielson.'

The roughnecks gradually lowered their weapons.

'It'm obvious that you lot has found your feet, so to speak, with these here aircraft,' Den went on. 'But how much higher does you think you'll be able to fly with a couple of Airborn showing you the way? One of they is even a professional test pilot. How about that? How much of an advantage does you think *that'll* bring you?'

It was a rhetorical question. To Clockweight, the answer was abundantly clear: the advantage would be significant.

He had his misgivings, though. As with his men, his view of the Airborn had been coloured by recent events. Could he trust these two?

'I were under the impression you didn't approve of what us is up to, Den,' he said. 'Deacon Hardscree were all for it, and I got the distinct feeling you disagreed with he.'

'Him and I had our differences of opinion,' Den replied, 'but that'm in the past.'

'And you,' Clockweight said, addressing Michael and Aurora, 'you'm really willing to chip in and help?'

They nodded.

'Might I ask why?'

Aurora took the lead. She explained that she was a Silver Sanctum resident and therefore, in effect, an ambassador for the Airborn. She spoke with the authority of the Airborn race's ruling body and her view was that the Redspire pirates – whose airship *Behemoth* had inflicted such misery on Clockweight and his men – constituted a grave threat to the stability brought about by the Bilateral Covenant. They should be considered enemies of both races. Hence, it was her and her husband's moral duty to assist the roughnecks in their resistance against the black airship.

'Besides,' she added, 'by the looks of things, if some of you don't get proper flying instruction soon, there's going to be a nasty crash.'

'Us is doing OK,' said Clockweight defensively, but just then another of those close shaves occurred overhead as a puttering Wayfarer narrowly avoided ramming into a sleek Skylark sideways on. Michael winced and clutched his face, appalled almost as much by the potential damage to the Skylark as by the potential loss of life. There could have been no more undignified fate for such a beautiful plane than to be T-boned by that which was the very definition of aeronautical mediocrity, the Metatronco Wayfarer.

'Wow, do you need me,' he said to Clockweight, pain in his eyes.

The roughnecks' toolpusher couldn't help but burst out laughing. 'Said with real feeling, that were.' He extended a roughened, grease-smeared hand to Michael. 'All right then. Seeing as you'm so keen to join in, it'd be foolish of I to refuse. Welcome to the team.'

Michael shook the proffered hand, without hesitation. He wasn't the slightest bit bothered by the grease that transferred itself from Clockweight's palm to his.

Getting his hands dirty – Michael had an inkling that there'd be plenty more of that to come.

CHAPTER 99

Developments

Michael worked with the roughnecks all afternoon. When he wasn't huddled with a group of them near the cavern mouth, peering under the engine cowling of a malfunctioning plane and offering repair tips, he was aloft in another plane, demonstrating to a passenger or passengers the basics of flying, then letting one of these amateur pilots take over and put into practice what he had just learned. This resulted in a few nerve-jangling moments, not least when one of his pupils stalled at a height of 800 metres and the plane went into a nosedive. Michael seized the controls and managed to re-start the engine and pull out of the dive, but with just seconds to spare.

Aurora also conducted lessons, about which Michael was less than happy. The revelation that she was pregnant hadn't fully sunk in yet, but it had sunk in far enough for him to realise that he wasn't comfortable with the idea of her going up in a plane with an untutored co-pilot. It wasn't only her life at stake, it was the life of their unborn child. He took her to one side and tried to explain this to her, but Aurora told him not to be silly. She said he couldn't treat her as though she needed to be wrapped in cotton wool, and if he insisted on trying to, their marriage would go down as one of the shortest on record. Besides, if it ever looked like she was in danger, she would simply eject herself from the plane and fly to safety under her own wingpower. Any poor Groundlings with her would have to fend for themselves, but that was their problem. She wasn't going to be *completely* reckless. She, too, understood the importance of the fact that she was carrying another life inside her.

'It's sweet of you to worry, Mike,' she said, 'but don't. I can take care of myself. Anyway, I think you need to worry more about the child you've already got.'

She was referring to the childlike Colin, who had decided that he wanted to fly planes too and went up with Michael at every opportunity, whenever there was a spare seat available. He drank in every word Michael said, soaked up every drop of information that fell from Michael's lips, absorbed the rudiments and refinements of aviation technique with sponge-like thirstiness and retentiveness, until finally he demanded to be allowed to have a go himself. Michael said no in a dozen different ways, but Colin persisted. Pestered. Badgered. And in the end, what else could Michael do but give in?

They went up together in the Skylark, which, of all the available planes, was the one Michael had not flown yet and the one he was itching to get his hands on. The last ever Skylark had rolled out of the factory gates four decades before he was born, and many of them remained in use even now, lovingly preserved by their owners. Occasionally he would glimpse one scudding along a sky-city thoroughfare, and he would stare in envious awe at its arched wings, its blue and silver bodywork, and its unique four-finned tail design. Although he was a helicopter man through and through, if he had to own a plane and money was no object, Michael would have had a Skylark.

This one, despite having fallen through the clouds and sat in a cavern for umpteen years, flew like a dream. The joystick had just the right level of responsiveness, the engine purred, and the plane as a whole had a kind of buoyancy, a lightness, as though exulting in every moment it spent in the air. While Colin crouched attentively in the passenger seat, Michael put the Skylark through its paces. He didn't want to hand over the controls. But eventually, with great reluctance, he did.

He feared that Colin would mishandle the Skylark and, through sheer clumsiness and inexperience, somehow mar the plane's perfection. Not by crashing it, simply by not flying it properly. He was regretting his eagerness now. He should have insisted that Colin have his first bash at being an aviator in another plane, any other plane. But Michael hadn't been able to wait for a spin in the Skylark any longer.

His fears proved unfounded. Colin was a natural. Almost as soon as he was in the pilot's seat he was guiding the Skylark along with ease, like a seasoned cockpit jockey. He was nervous to begin with, constantly seeking reassurance from his instructor, but in no time he had relaxed and was chatting casually, mentioning altitude and attitude readings, and commenting on geographical features below and the other planes that passed by.

Michael was forced to revise his opinion of Colin. Where he had once seen a good-natured but none-too-bright chap, lazy and fond of a fistfight, now he was looking at somebody with an enormous capacity and aptitude for learning who'd clearly had few chances to show off these attributes before. Within that dense-boned Amblescrut skull lurked a brain. It was the kind of brain which didn't respond well to schooling (assuming Colin had ever gone to school) but which grasped certain practical subjects instantly and intuitively. If something fascinated Colin, he would latch on to it and concentrate on it with remarkable focus and will. As he did with the Skylark.

He brought the plane smoothly back to earth, executing a soft, three-point touchdown that Michael himself would have been hard pushed to equal.

'Were that OK?' Colin asked, as he killed the Skylark's engine.

'Yeah, Colin,' said Michael, nodding, 'I think you could safely say that was OK.'

'Goody!' Colin leapt from the Skylark and ran over to *Bertha* to tell the Grubdollars about the flight. After that, like a contented puppy, he settled down inside the murk-comber for a nap.

Colin's desire to be a pilot was one reason the Grubdollars had delayed their departure. Their plan, of course, had been to drop Michael and Aurora off at the cavern and then be homeward bound. They'd stayed on, however, partly because Colin was so mad-keen on having a chance to fly. They'd stayed, also, because to turn and shoot off so abruptly struck them as somehow wrong. Now that Colin had fulfilled his wish and actually piloted a plane, strictly speaking there was no reason for them to linger. They could start *Bertha* up at any time, make their farewells and head north.

And yet they didn't.

For one thing, they had an obligation towards Michael and Aurora. How were the Airborn couple to return home without the Grubdollars' help? Maybe they would find a way. Possibly they could take one of the planes. But the only surefire, guaranteed, 100 per cent risk-free method of getting back up to the sky-cities was via the elevators at a Chancel, and to reach one of those, ground transport was required. There was a half-tarp van going begging, but it wasn't anywhere near as desert-capable as a murk-comber. Michael and Aurora's best bet – perhaps their only bet – was to travel with the Grubdollars.

So *Bertha* could not leave just yet.

And then there was Den, who found himself gravitating towards the roughnecks and the aircraft they were fixing, the planes which either no one had been able to start yet or had flown but come back down to earth spouting smoke or making some very disconcerting noises. The mechanic in him wouldn't allow him to stand idly by while others tinkered and mended and got smudged with grease and grime. Nor would it allow him to pass up the opportunity to inspect some exciting new machine technology. He sidled towards Clockweight, enquired airily if there was anything he might do, and in no time was up to his elbows in aircraft. Adjustable spanner in one hand, screwdriver in the other, he took engines apart component by component, identified the problem, and then put the engines back together so that they were as good as new.

Robert joined him in this. He said he wanted to show solidarity with the roughnecks, and Den agreed, saying he felt much the same way himself. He wanted to prove that he had come round to their way of thinking. The Airborn pirates *were* a threat that needed to be confronted. Before, he hadn't been in possession of the full facts, or at any rate his falling out with Hardscree had prevented him from perceiving the full facts. He'd not been in a position to accept that the roughnecks had a case, that their grudge against the pirates was a valid argument for fighting back and their methods for doing so were appropriate. Now, thanks to Aurora, he saw matters in a fresh light.

Clockweight acknowledged Den's and Robert's contribution to the cause, understanding what it was intended to represent. He also was filled with admiration for the two Grubdollars' mechanic skills, Den's in particular. Here was a man with a clear affinity for machinery, a flair for finding out why it didn't work and making it work again, a talent that bordered on genius.

When he wasn't surveying Den's handiwork with professional approval, Clockweight was busy supervising his men both at the planes and else-where. A secondary effort was under way, just inside the cavern mouth. There, several of the roughnecks were piecing together their improvised weaponry.

Principally, they were building bombs, incendiary devices similar to the ones the pirates had dropped on Desolation Wells but portable. Scavenged glass bottles were pressed into service as casings and filled with petrol. For fuses, the men used twists of petrol-soaked rag, secured in place in the bottles' necks with plugs of dried mud. Nuts and bolts were taped to the exterior of the bombs to form makeshift shrapnel.

A few of the more enterprising roughnecks set about making catapults out of scrap metal and lengths of fan belt. They tested these outside, using the hubcaps from random broken-off sections of landing gear as projectiles. The hubcaps sliced keenly through the air, and their aero-dynamicity was improved (and so was their lethal potential) by filing their rims to a blade-like sharpness.

Amid all this industrious activity, Cassie and Fletcher kept to themselves and minded their own business. They had no wish to participate. They'd done what they agreed to do, transport Michael and Aurora to the cavern, and from here on whatever happened was none of their concern.

Or so they told themselves. As the day wore on, however, both felt the tide of commitment growing stronger and becoming harder to resist. Colin had been up and down in planes all afternoon. Robert and their father were engineers at large. The involvement of Michael and Aurora was a given, but even so, it was slightly shaming to watch these two beavering away on the Groundlings' behalf while Cassie and Fletcher, Groundlings themselves, just moped around inside *Bertha* or sat on her tracks, looking on.

At last they both came to the conclusion that they were either going to stop feeling guilty that they were the only ones not making a positive contribution to the anti-pirate preparations, or they were going to make themselves useful.

As Fletcher put it, 'It'm time for we to poop or get off the pot.'

Cassie nodded but remained unsure. 'Da told I it were all right to be selfish sometimes. So how come it *don't* feel all right now? How come it seems childish?'

'Because us has got consciences,' said her brother.

'But this be'n't our fight.'

'Don't make any difference, ultimately. At some point, you always has to choose a side. Remember in the truck sheds at the CCC? When you talked I out of being a Humanist?'

Cassie did.

'It weren't really a choice at all,' Fletcher said. 'I knew that all along. I just couldn't see it till you showed I. Same here. Everybody be knuckling down, mucking in. Us has been watching from the sidelines, pretending us be'n't part of the deal, but deep down us knows us is. It'm just taken we a while to recognise it.'

'And now us has?'

'Now us has,' he confirmed. He stood up.

Cassie stood too. 'So what be on the agenda? Mechanic work, like Robert and Da?'

'Most likely. There be more than enough mechanics to go round but I guess two more won't hurt. Cass?'

'Yeah?'

Fletcher's tone of voice had suddenly changed, becoming low and slow. 'You know those floaty little specks you sometimes get in front of your eyes? Not sure what the proper name be for they, but you can get them when you'm tired or when you sort of half close your eyelids.'

'I know they. Why?'

Fletcher was staring out into the desert, squinting, his eyebrows knitted. 'Well, I's got one now. Only I don't think that'm what it actually be.'

'What do you mean?'

'Take a look. There.' He pointed into the distance. 'Tell me if you sees it too. If you does, then it'm no floaty speck.'

She followed the line of his finger.

Just above the seam where clouds met landscape, she made out a tiny dark dot.

She knew instantly, almost instinctively, what it was, and her stomach tightened into a knot.

'Fletch, go and tell Da and that Clockweight fellow.'

'Huh? Tell they what?'

'The black airship. *Behemoth*. It'm here. It'm coming this way. Go! Now!'

Scramble!

While Fletcher ran towards the cavern entrance and the planes that were being serviced, Cassie sprinted in the opposite direction, towards the area where the airworthy planes were parked.

'Aurora!' she yelled. 'Michael! Everybody! The pirate airship! Over there!'

Shouts of alarm passed among the roughnecks. Heads turned and hands went to foreheads to shade eyes. Michael darted up into the air to get a better perspective and came down with grim confirmation on his face.

'It's *Behemoth* all right,' he said. 'At least, it isn't *Cerulean*, so it's got to be the other one.'

'How come them's coming here?' asked one of the roughnecks.

Michael shrugged. 'Your guess is as good as mine. Maybe they spotted us and want a closer look. Or maybe they're after spare parts. After all, the cavern's where got the airship from in the first place.'

Clockweight came charging over. 'What be you lot standing around scratching your behinds for?' he demanded of his men. 'This'm it. Let's get up there and attack.'

The roughnecks looked at Michael, who realised they were seeking his blessing. If he, the aviation expert, thought they were ready and skilled enough to take on *Behemoth* in the planes, then they were.

'Your boss is right,' Michael said. 'This is it. You may feel you could do with more training.' He himself certainly felt they could do with more training. At least a month's worth. 'But there isn't time. Think about it this way. The pirates aren't going to be expecting an attack, and they're certainly not going to be expecting an attack from a bunch of Groundlings in aircraft. So you may not have much flying experience but you do have the element of surprise, and that counts for a lot. Do what you can up there. But above all else, leave the way clear for me. Get that? I stand a far better chance of planting a bomb in the right place than any of you. You lot run interference, keep the pirates busy, attempt a hit if you can . . . but leave the fancy stuff to me.'

Clockweight glanced at Michael in surprise. Then he nodded to him, to show that he acknowledged and appreciated what Michael had just volunteered to do.

'Good strategy,' he said. He turned back to his men. 'There'm nothing more to be said. Hop to it. Scramble!'

The roughnecks let out a loud hurrah and ran for the planes. Other roughnecks came from the cavern clutching armfuls of bottle bombs and matches with which to light them. The catapults had already been mounted on the backs of some of the older aircraft, the ones that had uncovered cockpits and room for more than one person on board.

Men slid into pilot and passenger seats. Engines gunned. Propellers whirred.

Colin arrived at Michael's side, panting.

'Here I be, Mike,' he said. 'Which plane d'you think I should take?'

'What? What are you talking about?'

'I be going to go up and give those pirates a bloody nose, of course.'

'Colin, it's dangerous. You'll more than likely kill yourself.'

'Think I don't know that? But it'm what needs doing.'

'No,' said Michael. 'No, you're just not ready.'

'Neither's them oilmen,' Colin protested.

'They have a personal stake in this. They care more about getting their own back on the pirates than anything else.'

'But didn't I just hear you say you be flying with they?'

'Yes, but —'

'How about I join you then? As your co-pilot. You fly, I'll drop bombs.'

Michael could see some sense in this, not much but some, and he didn't want to stand around all day arguing.

'All right,' he sighed. 'Go and get into the Skylark.'

'Yippee!' yelled Colin. He dashed off towards the vintage silver-and-blue aircraft. One of the roughnecks was going in the same direction but Colin bumped him out of the way. 'That'm ours. Find your own plane.'

Michael was about to follow when a stern voice stopped him in his tracks.

'Hold on there, Mike Gabrielson,' it said. 'I heard what you just said to Colin. When did you agree to be a part of the attack? And at what point were you planning on telling me?'

'Aurora ...' Michael turned to his wife and flattened his wings to show resignation. 'I've got to help. These Groundlings haven't a prayer without me.'

'You're not even prepared to discuss this?' said Aurora.

'There isn't anything to discuss. You've seen how those men fly. This is a suicide mission for them. I can make the difference, maybe even save a few of them from getting themselves killed. I have to think about them.'

'You have others to think about too.' She touched her stomach, a coded gesture which only Michael could interpret.

'Listen,' he said, 'earlier today you told me you could fly yourself to

547

safety if things got hairy. Well duh, so can I. Trust me, this is going to be fine.'

Aurora looked very doubtful but eventually she nodded, giving her consent. 'I love you,' she said.

'Likewise!' Michael shouted over his shoulder, as he took off and flew to the Skylark.

Cassie saw the concern on Aurora's face and the compassion in her eyes, and something clicked.

'Gabrielson boys,' she said. 'Them can be annoying, can't them?'

'*Really* annoying,' said Aurora. 'Impulsive. Wilful. Obstinate. But they have a strong moral compass. They do what's right, and you have to admire them for that.'

'And forgive they too.'

'And make them forgive *you* if your moral compass points in a slightly different direction.' Aurora smiled briefly, ruefully. 'Cassie, we should have had this conversation days ago.'

'Days ago I wouldn't have been interested.'

'And now isn't the time, alas.'

'No, it be'n't,' Cassie said. 'Now'm the time for we to take refuge in *Bertha*. If us has to be bystanders, best do it somewhere safe.'

As they hurried towards *Bertha*, Aurora said, 'Just promise me one thing. When all this is over, you'll sit down with Az for a good long chat. Ask him and yourself a few honest questions.'

'Yeah. Yeah, I reckon us'll do that.'

'Good.'

One by one the planes taxied out into the open desert. Then, one after another, they rose to the skies. Some of the roughnecks managed the takeoff better than others. A few climbed at too steep an angle and nearly stalled. One scraped a wingtip on the ground just as his plane began to lift, although he recovered from this near-fatal mishap and still made it up into the air.

Eventually they were all aloft. They adjusted course till they were heading on the same bearing. The faster aircraft reduced their speed so that the slower aircraft could catch up.

A mismatched, maverick fleet assembled, and made its way in loose formation towards the oncoming black bulk of *Behemoth*.

The Skylark was among the last to get airborne. With Colin in the passenger seat beside him, Michael followed the roughnecks towards the airship, thinking that if any of those brave, foolish Groundlings made it back to earth safely, it would be nothing short of a miracle.

Men Against Aircraft

Michael had predicted the pirates' reaction accurately. The last thing anyone aboard *Behemoth* expected was to see planes come swarming up from the ground and home in on the airship with obvious aggressive intent.

In the control gondola, amid various expressions of shock and amazement, Naoutha alone stayed silent. She was too outraged to speak. Those were *her* planes. She had returned to the cavern precisely in order to retrieve them and use them against *Cerulean*. She had boasted to Mr Mordadson about augmenting her pirates' attack capability, and these aircraft were it, her means of gaining an edge on the other airship – and now somebody else had got hold of them and was about to use them against *Behemoth*!

The pirates had had their hoard pirated. The raiders had been raided.

But Naoutha was in no mood to appreciate irony, and her sense of outrage only deepened when Flight Lieutenant Wallimson said, 'Are those pilots . . . Groundlings?'

Everyone in the control gondola peered forward, and soon the conclusion was reached that yes, they were Groundlings all right.

'Groundlings flying? But . . . that can't be,' said Wallimson. 'It's just not right.'

A dreadful, cracking noise filled the gondola, and everyone turned towards its source, Naoutha. She was grinding her teeth, so loudly that not even her mask could muffle it.

'They may be in planes,' she said, 'but can they truly fly? Do they have the instinct for it? I think not.'

'What do you want us to do, Naoutha?' asked one of her gang. It was Abuzaha Biletson, the mechanic largely responsible for the *Brightspans Empress*'s resurrection as *Behemoth*.

'What do you think? Go out there and fight them, of course.'

'But – but they're in planes. Men against aircraft? That's madness.'

Naoutha's arm flashed out, grabbed Biletson by the collar, and yanked him towards her.

'How dare you!' she shouted, shaking him. 'How dare you question my orders! Those are *Groundlings*. You are Airborn. You were born to fly.

They weren't. You can run rings around them. Shoot the ones in planes with open cockpits. Otherwise, dodge around them, distract them, throw them off-course, do whatever you have to – just make sure those mother-plucking aircraft don't get anywhere near *Behemoth*. Do I make myself clear?'

Meekly Biletson nodded.

'Good. Now go and tell the others.'

She shook Biletson once more then let go. He scurried aft to relay his leader's orders to the rest of the gang.

Moments later, pirates left *Behemoth* to confront the planes. They were armed with crossbows and fortified with shots of pterine.

They clustered at the front of the airship, matching their speed to its. As the planes neared they muttered among themselves, wondering if Naoutha really expected them to play chicken with aircraft travelling at around 100 knots. Then, as they watched, two of the planes veered towards each other, getting closer, closer, dangerously close, until abruptly they collided. In a tangle they spun out of the sky, tumbling to the desert earth, where they exploded in a mushrooming fireball.

Another of the Groundling pilots, observing this calamity, panicked and lost control of his aircraft. He went into a tailspin which he couldn't get out of. His plane, too, hit the ground and burst into flame.

'See that!' shouted Twitchy Ziz with a shrill chortle. 'They're useless! They really can't fly!'

The other pirates let out a jeering yell. All at once it was clear to them that they had the advantage. The Groundlings barely knew what they were doing.

They flew forward to meet the planes.

Naoutha looked on from the control gondola. Three of the aircraft were down already, and combat hadn't even begun. Even though those were her planes, she decided she didn't care if every last one of them was destroyed. No one had the right to steal from her. She'd found the cavern, she'd staked a claim on it, she was the rightful owner of everything in it – and she was damned if she was going to let these Groundling thieves take any of it away from her. If she couldn't have the planes, they certainly weren't going to.

The roughnecks saw the flock of pirates coming towards them. Half immediately took evasive action, peeling off from the formation. They were anxious enough as it was, simply being at the controls of a plane several hundred metres up in the sky. On top of that, having to try and dodge around living obstacles was too much.

The remaining roughnecks kept their nerve. Though inexpert aviators, they knew enough to realise that smashing your plane into a human-sized object in midair would be fatal for both parties. The pirates, though, surely wouldn't sacrifice themselves like that ...

Would they?

Clockweight led by example. He was piloting the Metatronco Condor. For all that Michael despised it, Clockweight liked the Condor for its straightforwardness and the sturdy utility of its design. It looked like how a child might draw a flying machine, all squared-off edges and blunted ends, and it didn't ask for a fine touch at the controls. The opposite, in fact. You had to ram the joystick and throttle in their slots to get any response from either, and Clockweight found that comforting. The Condor was an uncompromising, no-nonsense aircraft – his kind of ride.

He aimed straight for the centre of the cluster of pirates. Behind, the half of his fleet that was still in formation followed.

The pirates loomed in the Condor's windshield, wings flapping, wild-eyed. They scattered at the very last second, either darting into open space or seeking refuge in the shelter of *Behemoth*.

The planes passed over, under and alongside *Behemoth* in a wave. One of the roughnecks misjudged the gap between him and the airship. His port wing clipped *Behemoth*'s rear starboard propeller, the one that Az had knocked out of commission. The wing crumpled and his plane went whirling through the air like a boomerang. It crashed into another plane, all but chopping off that aircraft's tail section. Momentum carried both of the stricken planes onward for a full minute, as each fell meteor-like in a long, graceful arc to its inevitable, punishing impact with the earth.

Meanwhile a roughneck, passing above *Behemoth*, managed to drop a bottle bomb on the airship. But the bomb simply bounced off the balloon canvas and fell, burning uselessly, dripping globs of fire into the air.

The roughnecks banked and turned, grouping for a second run at their target. They were joined by the stragglers who had balked at the start of the first run. Although they had taken casualties and *Behemoth* remained intact, the roughnecks had reason to feel encouraged. The pirates weren't going to be the formidable opposition they had feared.

The pirates felt encouraged too. It seemed that men *did* stand a chance against aircraft, especially when the pilots of the aircraft were so easy to spook.

Michael, in the Skylark, could see that the roughnecks had grown in confidence. He was holding off at the periphery of things, biding his time, waiting for an opportunity. As the ragtag roughneck fleet headed for *Behemoth* on a fresh sortie, he could tell they were keener than before. The planes drew tighter together. They upped their airspeed.

Now the pirates rushed to intercept, swooping at the planes with insane glee. The pterine was well and truly kicking in. The pirates' perceptions had become diamond sharp. Their brains bulged with the enormity of what they were capable of. They felt all-powerful. Nothing could harm them. The rest of the world, as far as they were concerned, was full of slow, stupid things that were easily evaded and bested.

Crossbow bolts were nocked. The pirates targeted the planes with open cockpits and fired as they zoomed past. Pterine improved their accuracy a hundredfold, and many of the bolts found their mark. All at once, several aircraft were zigzagging erratically or dipping towards the ground. In one case, a roughneck passenger had just lit the rag fuse of a bottle bomb when the pilot took a crossbow bolt in the throat. As the plane swerved out of control, burning petrol spilled everywhere. The plane was a streak of fire as it hit the desert.

Then Michael spied his chance. In the wake of the second run, the pirates regrouped at *Behemoth*'s nose-cone. Because Michael had held back, they hadn't spotted him. Now he steered the Skylark at the airship's stern.

'Colin,' he said, 'it's up to you. Don't miss.'

Colin grabbed a bottle bomb and lit the fuse. As the rag flared, he thrust open a small side window. A torrent of wind rushed in, like a hammer to his face.

'Wait,' said Michael. 'Waiiit . . .'

It took every scrap of willpower Colin had not to toss the bomb out immediately.

The Skylark overtook *Behemoth*'s skull-and-crossed-feather tailfins and Michael yelled, 'Now!'

Colin hurled the bottle bomb with all his might.

It was a dud. The fuse fizzled out before the bomb even reached the airship. The bomb rebounded off the balloon and tumbled from view.

On their third attack run, the roughnecks did their best to out-manoeuvre the pirates. They'd learned their lesson. Those crossbows were deadly. Now, in return, they brought the onboard catapults into play. Sharpened hubcaps zinged through space. Most went wide. The pterine-enhanced pirates saw them coming as if in slow motion and got out of the way. A few of the hubcaps did hit home, however. One beheaded a pirate cleanly. Another disembowelled its victim. He plummeted with his innards uncoiling and flailing bloodily around him.

This time, Clockweight in his Condor managed to score a direct hit with a bottle bomb. It exploded across the upper surface of *Behemoth*'s balloon in a burst of fluid fire. He really thought he had done it, and let out a whoop of triumph. The airship was doomed. Revenge was his.

But then, looking over his shoulder, Clockweight groaned. The fire failed to take hold. The flames dwindled and petered out. All that was left was a patch of grey charring on the canvas.

Clockweight had been afraid of this. The bottle bombs, even when they worked as they were supposed to, weren't enough. He circled the Condor round, avoiding a pirate who lunged recklessly close to the plane. His injuries throbbed and ached, and he wondered, miserably, just how in hell he and his men were going to bring down that airship. They were like mosquitoes buzzing around an elephant. They stood little chance of piercing its hide, let alone causing it a fatal injury.

Even with Michael Gabrielson assisting them, it seemed hopeless. Clockweight was close to despair.

Naoutha, on the other hand, felt elation as she surveyed the action from inside the control gondola. *Behemoth* had taken a couple of hits but was essentially undamaged. Her gang were repelling the attackers and thinning their numbers. If things went on like this, victory would soon be hers.

All at once Naoutha experienced a sharp pang, a sensation she knew only too well. It was mainly in her stomach but it affected the rest of her body too, a general, nervy ache, a system-wide yearning, like an all-over itch that must be scratched. How long had it been since her last pterine hit? Too long. Yesterday evening, it had been, shortly before she and her gang engaged with the Alar Patrollers.

She craved the drug. She longed for the alertness, the clarity, the invincibility it brought. Whenever its influence faded, the world seemed dull and slow and pointless. She needed more of it, always more. With it, she was Naoutha Nisrocsdaughter, pirate queen. Without it, she was nobody, nothing, a void.

But she was reluctant to leave the control gondola while the battle was still raging outside. Who could go and fetch her a syringe and an ampoule of pterine? Which of the gang members currently crewing the ship could be spared to run an errand?

'Wallimson . . .' she said.

CHAPTER 102

Biting Wit

Wallimson traipsed along the keel catwalk, disgruntled. He didn't mind doing Naoutha a favour but he did mind the way she had asked for it. She'd spoken as though he was some sort of flunky, there just to do her bidding. *Get me pterine. You'll find some in my cabin.* Wasn't he her newfound friend? Hadn't he helped her in all sorts of ways? Yet he was beginning to feel that he meant nothing to her or to any of the pirates. They were treating him here much as he had been treated on *Cerulean*, as redundant, just so much lame-winged ballast.

A touch of ground-sickness was adding to Wallimson's bad temper. *Behemoth* remained quite high, not far below the clouds, so the symptoms could have been worse, but he nevertheless felt muzzy-headed and not-quite-all-there. Pterine would no doubt have helped, but he wasn't a drugs type of person. Never had been. Nasty stuff. Didn't do you any good in the long run.

Speaking of which . . .

Wallimson reached the cabin where Mr Mordadson was being held. Pausing at the door, he listened out. Not a sound from within. Sometime during the small hours Mr Mordadson had stopped screaming, but his moans and the thumps of the chair legs on the floor had continued for a long time afterward, echoing along the catwalk. Now, those had stopped too. There was only silence.

Was he dead?

Wallimson hoped so, but also hoped not. While he wished only bad things for Mr Mordadson, he wanted him to remain alive at least long enough that he could have another crack at him. Last night Naoutha had intervened before he could really get started. He felt he still owed Mr Mordadson a lot of pain.

Yes.

Wallimson reached for the cabin door.

This wasn't what Naoutha had sent him back for. Equally, the temptation was too great to resist. Just a brief detour from his journey. A couple of minutes alone with Mordadson. No one would mind. With all the fighting outside, no one would even know.

Wallimson turned the key in the lock and opened the door.

554

Mr Mordadson was sitting slumped. The ropes were the only thing holding him up. His head drooped, and his face, what Wallimson could see of it, was a mass of pulpy red flesh, barely recognisable. There was a circle of dried bloodstains around the base of the chair, like a dark spattery halo on the floor.

'Mordadson?' said Wallimson softly, with a singsong inflection. 'Mordadso-o-on?'

The head stirred. The eyes flickered between their swollen lids. The distended lips mumbled something unintelligible.

'How are you feeling?' Wallimson shut the door behind him. 'Pretty rotten by the looks of it. Have you heard what's going on outside? Another fight – this time against Groundlings, no less. Flying Groundlings! Wonders will never cease. Everyone else is busy with that, anyway, so I thought you and I might have some together time, just the two of us. Now, refresh my memory. Didn't you promise you'd show me a thing or two about inflicting pain? Did I remember that right? I'd love to know more. Do tell me.'

With a wicked grin, Wallimson moved closer to his helpless target.

Again, Mr Mordadson mumbled.

'I'm sorry, you'll have to speak up. I can't make out a word you're saying.'

Mr Mordadson tried to talk clearly but still all Wallimson could distinguish amid the string of burbled syllables was the phrase 'listen in' – although it might have been 'glistening'.

He leaned down, putting his ear next to Mr Mordadson's mouth. It wouldn't hurt, would it, to discover what his intended victim wished to say, before the savage beating commenced. Famous last words and all that.

'Come on, Mr Silver Sanctum Big Shot. What is it? Spit it out.'

Next thing Wallimson knew, his ear was clamped between Mr Mordadson's teeth. The whole ear, right to the root, and Mr Mordadson was biting, biting, and Wallimson was howling in agony and blood was pouring down his neck and he pummelled at Mr Mordadson, battered him with his fists, but he would not let go. The pain was excruciating. A shrilling sound filled Wallimson's head. He felt himself becoming faint. He couldn't even manage to hit Mr Mordadson any more. He just wanted the pain to stop. Stop. Stop. Please stop.

It didn't stop but it did lessen. Mr Mordadson relaxed his jaw-grip slightly, although his teeth continued to dig in.

Wallimson's thoughts cleared. He grabbed hold of Mr Mordadson's head to push it away. Immediately, the teeth sank deeper again.

The next time the pressure of the teeth abated and the pain dulled, Wallimson tried to wrench his own head away.

More agony. Fiery agony.

Finally it dawned on him: resistance only brought suffering. Compliance, however, had a more positive result.

'What – what do you want?' he stammered.

'Uh ooh ooh ink I onh?' Mr Mordadson said, his voice reverberating down Wallimson's ear canal with horrible vibrancy.

What do you think I want?

'You want me to untie you.'

'Eh-eh eh-oh.'

Clever fellow.

'But . . .'

Pain, drilling into Wallimson's skull. Not as bad as before. Bad enough, though.

Obviously no *buts* were allowed.

'Naoutha will —'

Pain!

'I can't —'

Pain!

Wallimson realised, miserably, that objections were futile and he was likely to lose the ear if he carried on lodging them. He had no choice. He was going to have to do as Mr Mordadson asked.

He reached round the back of the chair for the first of the knots that secured Naoutha's prisoner.

Shortly they were undone and Mr Mordadson was free. He maintained his tooth-hold on Wallimson's ear right up until the last rope came loose. Then he opened wide and Wallimson staggered away, clutching the side of his head.

Mr Mordadson spat and spat till he had rid his mouth of Wallimson's blood and all that came out was pinkish saliva. Then he eased the cramps out of his wings and limbs. Then he strode towards Wallimson.

Cowering in a corner of the cabin, the flight lieutenant looked up as Mr Mordadson loomed over him.

'What are you going to do to me?' he moaned, still pressing his hand flat against his head. It numbed the pain a little. 'You can't just leave me here. The pirates will kill me if they find out I released you.'

Mr Mordadson's bruised, battered, bloodied face was inscrutable.

'Please. Please forgive me,' Wallimson begged. 'I never meant for any of this to happen.'

And implacable.

'I just needed to belong somewhere. I —'

Mr Mordadson cut him off. 'It's not what happens to you . . . that makes you who you are,' he said, shaping the words with great effort. 'It's how you . . . deal with it.'

'Yes. Yes!' said Wallimson, like a man in the throes of an epiphany, flooded with clear-sighted understanding. 'I've dealt with it badly. That's it. I accept that. I should have been better. I'll try to be better from now on. I'll try to be a good person.'

'No, you won't,' said Mr Mordadson, kneeling down. 'Believe me, I've ... tried to be a good person too, and it ... hasn't worked. Some have the capacity for it, others ... don't. I don't. I am ... what I am, and I've learned to deal with it ... and live with it.'

Wallimson looked deep into the other man's eyes, and what he saw there left him helpless with terror.

Mr Mordadson seized the flight lieutenant's head in both hands and slammed it against the bulkhead behind.

Slammed it and slammed it until Wallimson's body finally stopped twitching and shuddering and lay still.

CHAPTER 103

Leap Into The Dark

Az's self-imposed time limit of twelve hours was up, and his gamble had not paid off. *Behemoth* had not resurfaced. Naoutha and co. were still down there below the cloud cover, somewhere, and Mr Mordadson with them.

Az was beyond exhaustion now. He'd entered a dreamlike state of suspension where everything seemed real but existed just out of his reach, as if behind an invisible wall; everything he did or said seemed to be someone else's deeds or words. He found himself, at one point in the middle of the morning, having a blazing row with Wing Commander Iaxson, and as soon as it was over he couldn't recall what it had been about. About Mr Mordadson, probably, and about heading home. All he knew was that he had won the argument. At least, he thought so, on the strength of the look Iaxson had given him as he left the control gondola – a steely glare that said, *If you were a grown-up, I'd have punched you.* Iaxson had agreed to his time limit? Probably. Reluctantly.

Az wasn't sure that he knew what he was doing any more. He was operating on automatic, with all his systems shut down but the essential ones. His inner reserves were as near-empty as *Cerulean*'s fuel tanks. Some dim, distant part of his brain was telling him the mission was over, it was a failure, *he* was a failure. He tried not to pay it any heed but it was hard to ignore. The truth was hard to ignore.

Cerulean was drifting. Had been for some while. Az had ordered the crew not to correct the drift, not to waste precious fuel trying to stay put. One of the less dynamic jet streams had the airship in its grasp and was nudging her gently but insistently – which way? Az could have checked the compass on the navigator's station. He could have found out her bearing. He just couldn't be bothered to. Some direction. Whatever. Didn't matter.

Now was the time. He knew it. Now he had to admit defeat, abandon all hope of rescuing Mr Mordadson, and make the run for Redspire. The four crew members, sleep-starved zombies, were waiting for him to give their command. *Let's go.* That was all he would have to say. Two words. Two simple syllables.

He tried. He couldn't.

Visions paraded through his brain. People he knew. People he loved. His parents. Michael. Lady Aanfielsdaughter. The Grubdollars. Cassie. Dominating everything was the Ultimate Reckoner's prediction, the allegedly significant symbol. It hovered in his mind's eye like the after-image of a glimpse of the sun. Wherever he looked, whatever he tried to think about, there it was, gibbous and ominous.

The Count of Gyre's voice echoed insinuatingly.

Up or down?

Right or wrong?

Light or dark?

Yes or no?

'Descend,' Az said abruptly.

The crew's heads turned. Their grey-ringed eyes blinked. Their brows furrowed.

'Sir?'

The question mark, poised between one thing and another, in that grey zone of uncertainty, pure quandary . . .

'Descend. Go down. Lose height. Sink. How many ways can I put it?'

'Through the —?'

'Right through the clouds.'

'But —'

'An order. Do it.'

The crew eventually, and grudgingly, obeyed. *Cerulean*'s rear propellers started to spin. Helium was vented to increase the rate of decline.

Az clambered up the ladder to the control gondola's ceiling hatch. He swung the hatch shut and turned the wheel that slid the locking bar into place. The hatch could not be opened from above. This was a security measure dating back to the airship's troop-carrier days, to seal off the gondola against enemy boarders and give the crew time to make a safe exit.

Moments later, Iaxson came storming along the keel catwalk, as Az had known he would. Finding his access to the gondola barred, the wing commander pounded angrily on the hatch.

'Gabrielson!' he roared. 'Open up! Let me in!'

'I can't do that,' Az replied evenly.

'You damn well can. Open up, or I'll force my way in.'

'Do what you have to. I have to see this through first.'

'This? See what through? Why are we descending? If we're going anywhere, it's to Redspire like we agreed. Exactly what are you up to here?'

'I'm answering the question,' Az said. It sounded ridiculous even to him, and yet it was the truth.

'Question? What question?'

The crew's faces were asking much the same thing.

'Just ... the question,' Az said.

Cerulean was touching the cloud cover already. Tendrils of white vapour were snaking in through the broken windows.

'All right,' said Iaxson from above. 'That does it. I'm taking over this vessel. By the powers vested in me by the Alar Patrol Statutory Authority, I am relieving you of your command, Azrael Gabrielson, effective as of now.'

'Not without entering the control gondola you're not,' Az replied. 'It's ... it's the Custom of the Skies. In order to revoke his command, you must formally confront a captain face to face.'

'Custom of the Skies? Never heard of it.'

Hardly surprising, since it was something Az had just invented. It was a blatant bluff, but he was hoping it would buy him time, both with Iaxson and with the crew. He could not expect the crewmen to be willing to defy the law the way he was, but if he could just keep them on his side long enough, and keep Iaxson at bay, everything might pan out the way he wanted it to.

'Stripping an airship captain of his rank must be done in person,' he said. 'Otherwise it's considered mutiny.'

'Oh really?' said Iaxson.

'Captain Qadoschson had to tell me in person that I was to take his place. He couldn't surrender his position by, for example, writing me a letter. It's standard practice on airships. Custom of the Skies.'

The crew were now sure that Az was talking nonsense, but their expressions said they weren't *completely* sure. Maybe Az knew something they didn't, some arcane piece of airship lore. For that reason, they were prepared to give him the benefit of the doubt, for now.

After a lengthy pause, Iaxson said, 'Fine. Then I'm coming in. If I can't break through the hatch, I'll exit the ship and get in via the windows.'

'Suit yourself,' said Az.

The control gondola was now flooded with whiteness, a whiteness so dense that the crew had to strain to see anything, even the gauges and instruments in front of them. *Cerulean* shuddered with a mild tremor of cloud cover turbulence, a taste of worse to come.

Az was counting on Iaxson being unwilling to fly outside *Cerulean* while she was in the clouds, and on the hatch proving difficult to bust open. Iaxson would find his way into the gondola eventually, of that there was no doubt. All Az wanted was to get below the clouds first. One glimpse of the ground, that was all he was after. One look, to see if this leap into the dark he was taking was a leap of faith, or a leap in logic.

Skyjack

The pirate gang saw the Groundlings repeatedly fail to make any impression on the airship. Their bombs either didn't go off or, at best, merely scuffed the surface of *Behemoth*'s balloon. Any advantage their planes gave them was cancelled out by the ineptness with which they flew them.

Brimming with bravado and pterine, the pirates scaled greater and greater heights of mad daring. Twitchy Ziz led the way, by commandeering one of the enemy aircraft. It was an almost impossible feat which no sane person would have even dreamed of attempting, but then Twitchy Ziz was long past sane.

A roughneck made a bombing run at *Behemoth* but got it badly wrong. He hit the flaps too hard and his plane, the AtmoCorp 9-5 with the Shooting Star tail welded on, shot upwards in a sheer, near-perpendicular climb. Inevitably, he stalled. The 9-5 slowed as it reached the peak of its steep rising curve, and for a brief moment, the merest fraction of a second, came to a full stop.

By chance, Twitchy Ziz was just metres away when this happened. He spied his chance and lunged for the 9-5 as it began to descend, tail first. He latched onto the cockpit canopy and wrenched it open, one-handed.

Inside, the terrified roughneck was slamming the joystick around as if this might save him – as if he could somehow fight the pull of gravity by making the ailerons flap like a bird's wings. Twitchy Ziz reached in and hauled the man bodily out of his seat. Pterine-strong, he flung him aside and took his place at the controls.

Side by side the roughneck and the 9-5 fell. The roughneck screamed and windmilled his arms. The 9-5 was silent and inert, just so much dead weight. Twitchy Ziz let the plane tip forward, the heaviness of its engine bringing its nose down. Then, as the 9-5 began to dive, he hit the ignition. The propeller screeched into life and the plane corkscrewed crazily, till Twitchy Ziz brought it under control. The 9-5 flew. Its erstwhile roughneck pilot continued to fall.

Twitchy Ziz giggled gibberingly as he swung the plane up and around. In no time he was gunning for the Groundling aircraft. He buzzed them and swerved at them. The roughneck pilots took drastic action in response. At the sight of the 9-5 rocketing towards them, they barrel-rolled out of the way, or nosedived. Most of the time they were able to correct and carry on flying, but now and then Twitchy Ziz got one of them to go into freefall. Then there was nothing the doomed pilot could do but watch the ground wheel closer and closer, and cover his face with his arms, and scream, and perish.

Inspired by Twitchy Ziz's example, other pirates tried to take over planes too. They weren't as successful. Twitchy Ziz had been able to skyjack the 9-5 only through a set of exceptional circumstances. The other pirates' attempts ended in gory disaster. After four of them would up mashed against windshields or mangled on propellers, the rest gave up. Even though each death also brought down one of the planes, it didn't seem a worthwhile price to pay.

They resumed using their crossbows, while Twitchy Ziz battled on with the 9-5, scattering the Groundling planes, creating havoc, an eagle amongst pigeons.

Until he came up against Michael.

CHAPTER 105

A Bonkers Plan

Michael watched the commandeered AtmoCorp 9-5 devastating the roughneck ranks. The pirates definitely had the upper hand now. Only he could even up the balance again.

'Colin,' he said.

'Yup?'

'That Nine-Five. The red plane with the yellow tail section. It's making a right mess of things.'

'I know. Somebody should do something about it.'

'Yes. Us.'

Briefly, Michael outlined what he had in mind.

'That be a bonkers plan!' Colin exclaimed.

'You have a better one?'

The big, spherical Amblescrut head rotated from side to side. 'Not as such. But you must admit it'm crazy.'

'Crazy as a headless hen. I reckon we've a one in ten chance of getting through it alive. But we can't let that pirate keep scaring the roughnecks out of the sky.'

Colin heaved a sigh. 'All right. But I be trusting you not to screw up.'

Michael half-laughed. 'I'll do my best.'

He spun the Skylark in a dizzying loop, then dived towards the 9-5.

Colin clamped a hand over his eyes. 'Can't look.'

They zoomed past the 9-5's nose, missing it by a whisker. The 9-5 shuddered in the Skylark's slipstream.

Michael peered upwards as he recovered the Skylark from its dive.

The 9-5 was coming round.

'That got your attention, didn't it?' Michael said to the pirate. He poured on speed. 'OK then, come and get us!'

Only Flesh

Magnus Clockweight had come to a decision.

It was seeing the pirate in the red-and-yellow plane that did it. He recognised those green dreadlocks. He remembered all too well the man's demented laughter during the first attack on Desolation Wells. Now he was watching this same pirate cut a swathe through the roughneck fleet. The roughnecks were dropping like flies. Clockweight's workmates, his friends, the people who were his responsibility, were being killed mercilessly.

Too many of them had died already at the pirates' hands. Here, during this futile assault on *Behemoth*, and back at Desolation Wells. Too many.

Enough.

Clockweight knew what he had to do.

He banked and turned, moving away from the mêlée around the black airship. He felt suddenly, sublimely calm. The low pain from his injuries melted away. He looked down at his burned arm, and the blistering and scabs and redness meant nothing. It was only flesh, and flesh was just a temporary shell. It was the casing that your soul walked around in. The body had no value in itself. Its value lay in the things your mind could make it do – the deeds it could carry out, the purposes to which it could be put.

The sacrifices it could make.

When he was a couple of kilometres out from *Behemoth*, Clockweight turned the Condor again, through 180 degrees.

He lined the airship up in his windshield and throttled forward. The Condor gathered speed unenthusiastically, as though it knew what its pilot intended and wasn't at all pleased.

Then, one-handed, Clockweight lit the fuse of a bottle bomb and tossed it over his shoulder. With a *whoof*, flames flared behind him, and the cockpit rapidly began to fill with heat and smoke. Clockweight focused on nothing but the oval silhouette of *Behemoth* as it grew larger in his field of vision. The smoke thickened. Soon his eyes were streaming, and he was choking for breath. But he kept the plane steady.

In a way, it was a relief. Moments from now, everything would be over. Of course Clockweight was dreading death, but somehow it wasn't so bad, when his death would help save the lives of the remaining roughnecks and finally avenge those who'd been murdered.

He was the toolpusher. The boss. Head honcho at Westward Oil Enterprises extraction and refining installation number 137.

He had always done his job dutifully and to the best of his abilities.

This was his last ever task.

Fear and joy wrestled in Clockweight's heart as he aimed the burning Condor for the exact centre of *Behemoth*'s balloon.

Precision Timing

Michael drew the 9-5 away from the fray, out into the open air. He wobbled the Skylark a few times, to give the pirate the impression that an untrained Groundling was at the controls, not an expert Airborn pilot. It would aid his plan if the pirate underestimated what he was up against.

Abruptly he flung the Skylark into a sharp turn, bringing it about to face the 9-5.

He lined up with the other plane and shot towards it on a direct collision course.

'Ready, Colin?'

'Nope, but let's do it anyway.'

The gap between the Skylark and the 9-5 narrowed at an astonishing rate. Colin groped for the door latch. Michael's bonkers plan required precision timing. Opening the door would create a sudden sideways drag and throw the Skylark off-kilter. Michael would factor that in to their line of approach, but even so, they could not bail out until they were close enough to the 9-5 to guarantee a direct hit.

'Wait for it,' Michael said, clenching his teeth. 'Only when I give the word.'

Colin knew he had to have perfect faith in Michael. There was no alternative. His life was now in his new friend's hands. That was scary but also oddly thrilling. Colin felt giddy.

The pirate, at least, seemed to be playing along. He kept the 9-5 on course, no doubt confident that in a test of nerves between him and a Groundling aviator, he stood to win.

Then ...

'Dammit!' yelled Michael.

The 9-5 had swerved away. Far too soon.

'I didn't think him'd wimp out like that,' said Colin.

'Me neither. Not his style. Oh, I see.'

The pirate hadn't taken fright, although it looked like that at first. In fact he had spied another target, one that was of more pressing concern than the Skylark.

Clockweight's Condor, spewing smoke from its cockpit as it arrowed towards *Behemoth*.

Michael didn't hesitate. He understood at a glance what Clockweight was up to. He knew, too, that the pirate in the 9-5 recognised the threat to *Behemoth* and would stop the Condor by any means possible.

The bonkers plan was still in effect, although Michael reckoned the survival odds were now down to something like one in twenty.

He homed in on the 9-5, wringing every last scrap of speed he could out of the Skylark. Both were swift planes, but while the 9-5 was closer to the Condor, the Skylark had the lighter airframe.

Michael thought he could just reach the 9-5 – just – before it reached the Condor.

If he was lucky.

CHAPTER 108

Enlightenment

Twitchy Ziz shrieked at the Condor's pilot.

'No no no no nonononono nooooo!!!'

He'd forgotten all about the Skylark. *That* little escapade was in the past. This other enemy, in his bumbling old clunker of a plane, was going to ram *Behemoth*. The Condor was alight. The Groundling pilot was on a suicide run.

Twitchy Ziz would not stand for that.

A ribbon of spittle froth snaked from his lips as he swooped to intercept the Condor. He didn't even check behind him once to see what had become of the Skylark. He continued to shriek in fury at the Groundling in the Condor, and the words merged together, becoming one long senseless howl.

In the seething turmoil that was his brain, Twitchy Ziz had devised a plan that was much the same as Michael's. Namely, fly at the enemy at top speed, bail out at the very last instant, and *blam*.

He nearly managed to pull it off, too.

He was metres away from the Condor. But just as he was starting to undo the cockpit canopy . . .

The Condor jerked upward, out of his direct line of sight.

Twitchy Ziz didn't hear the impact of the Skylark striking his plane. All he was aware of was a plunging sensation, his stomach slamming into his throat. The Condor and its streaking trail of smoke kept getting smaller and smaller, further and further away.

The 9-5 was shaking and rattling around him.

Cracks crazed the glass of the canopy.

Then, suddenly, Twitchy Ziz understood everything with pin-sharp clarity. He was fully conscious of his predicament. He knew his aircraft had been hit and downed, he knew he was about to die, and he knew there was not a thing he could do about it.

During the final few seconds of Twitchy Ziz's existence, he was perhaps the sanest he had ever been.

All those birds he had tortured and killed as a boy.

He remembered every single one.

Now he knew how they had felt, what they had gone through, as he'd clasped them tight and wrenched off their wings and snapped their skinny little legs. The helplessness. The abject terror.

He could almost hear their shrill squeals and squawks, coming back to haunt him.

These, though, were the sounds of metal rending and tearing, an aircraft disintegrating, with Twitchy Ziz trapped inside.

And the sounds of Twitchy Ziz himself, in an agony of enlightenment, screaming.

The Men Who Fell To Earth

'Now!'

Colin yanked down the latch and opened the door, swinging it outwards against the onrushing force of the Skylark's airspeed. It took all his considerable strength to keep the door from slamming shut in his face. Wind hammered into the cockpit and the plane lurched sickeningly, yawing and rolling at the same time. All at once the doorway framed a view of nothing but ground.

'Jump!' Michael shouted.

Colin hesitated.

Then a hand shoved him between the shoulder blades and he tumbled out.

Colin had vowed to himself that he wouldn't scream, but he did. He screamed like a girl. He knew Michael was right behind him. Or rather, he didn't know it but had to believe it. Michael had jettisoned himself out of the plane in Colin's wake. Any second now, Colin was going to feel Michael's hands grabbing him. That would happen.

Nevertheless Colin screamed. The desert below him seemed an awful lot nearer than it had any right to be. His eyes were screwed up, his vision a blur. All the same, it was plain to him that the rocks and scrub and sand were rushing up to meet him with terrifying speed.

There was a *boom* of impact from above. Colin had no idea if this was the Skylark colliding with the 9-5 or the 9-5 colliding with the Condor, and he didn't care.

Where was Michael?

Where ...

Was ...

Arms banded around Colin's chest. Legs fastened around his midriff. The breath was wrenched from his lungs as his freefall was halted with a powerful jerk.

Clinging to Colin, Michael beat his wings with all his might. The root muscles in his back groaned with the strain. The secondary flight muscles in his chest throbbed in protest too. He felt something tear – a sharp grind of pain low down in his spine. He'd never carried anything this heavy. Even Fletcher Grubdollar was a featherweight compared with Colin. The man was solid bone, it seemed.

Michael flapped and flapped, and the pain intensified, and he knew this wasn't going to be a flight; it was going to be a more or less controlled plummet. That was all he could manage. And he and Colin were going to ...

... hit ...

... the ...

... ground ...

... *hard.*

Dust blossomed in a cloud.

Both Michael and Colin lay still for a long while. They were dazed. They were tangled together so tightly, neither was sure whose limb belonged to whom. Each was scared to move, in case it hurt. Right now they were numb. There was no pain. It was weirdly comfortable to lie there in a heap while the dust cloud thinned and settled around them. If either of them moved, that was when they might find out if they were injured, and how badly.

At last Colin said, 'Mike?' His face was buried in the sand, his voice muffled.

'Yes?'

'Not that you weigh a lot or anything, but ...'

'What?'

'Would you mind getting off I?'

'OK.'

'Just because, you know, it be'n't very dignified. Two grown men, all hugger-mugger together like this. If you know what I mean.'

'Yeah, I get you.'

Slowly, stiffly, carefully, Michael stirred himself and clambered off Colin. Colin, in turn, picked himself up off the ground, brushing dust from his clothes and spitting out grains of sand. Each checked himself for injury, but everything seemed in working order. Scrapes, bumps and bruises they had in quantity, but nothing more serious than that.

'Did us ...?' Colin began.

'Get the Nine-Five? We did,' Michael replied.

'And did the Condor ...?'

Michael peered upwards to find out.

CHAPTER 110

A Mortal Blow

Choking and spluttering, Clockweight steered his plane headlong into *Behemoth*.

The impact stove a hole in the balloon and sent a shock wave rippling out across the canvas. The Condor fragmented. Its engine was rammed through the dashboard and into Clockweight's torso, killing him instantly. The plane's wings folded backwards. Its fuselage crumpled concertina-fashion. The remaining bottle bombs in the cockpit shattered and petrol spurted everywhere. The fire Clockweight had started became a billowing inferno. Flames erupted in all directions, leaping onto the balloon canvas and also onto the walls of the gas cells which had been exposed when the Condor ploughed into the airship.

Behemoth shuddered from stem to stern and lumbered sideways. She had been dealt a mortal blow. Her frame was breached. Her structural integrity was fatally compromised. What the impact of the plane had started, the fire would finish.

From now on, the lifespan of the former *Brightspans Empress* could be measured in minutes.

CHAPTER III

Stowaway

Aurora and the Grubdollars watched the battle around *Behemoth* with their hearts in their mouths. From time to time Aurora spotted the Skylark at the fringes of the frenzied swirl of action, and she would let out a hiss of relief. There was dismay aboard *Bertha* too, as assault after assault on the airship met with failure and Groundlings fell from the sky. Cassie and Aurora were gripping each other's hands, and the longer the struggle went on, the tighter the knot of their fingers grew. *Behemoth* sailed on through the chaos surrounding her, apparently immune to harm. She seemed as relentless as the desert beneath her, a vast, indomitable, unstoppable thing.

No one in *Bertha* saw the Condor strike the airship. It happened on the far side of her balloon, out of their line of sight. Nor, for that matter, did they see the Skylark crash into the AtmoCorp 9-5, or Michael and Colin hurtling to the ground.

Immediately, though, they perceived that something significant had happened. Things had changed. All at once *Behemoth* was lurching rather than gliding. She rolled slightly, like a wounded whale. Then smoke appeared from behind the crown of her balloon, soon followed by fire, licking upwards, churning in coils and spirals. The blaze spread quickly, heading fore and aft. In no time the black outline of the airship had a corona of flame, like some elliptical solar eclipse.

Den led the cheers. 'Them did it!' he exclaimed. 'Bless my bum, I didn't rate their chances, but them did it!'

'I don't see Michael,' Aurora said softly, anxiously, scanning the sky through a porthole.

'Him's fine,' said Cassie. 'I be sure of it.'

Aurora said nothing.

Meanwhile, secreted in one of the murk-comber's crawl-ducts was a figure who should by rights have been dead and yet was still, miraculously, alive. A figure who was more a walking wound than a whole person. A figure sustained and animated by hatred alone.

Centimetre by suffering centimetre, Deacon Hardscree had hauled himself out of the razorweed canyon. He had wrenched the javelin out of his back and then tottered, hobbled, shuffled, often crawled across the desert, following the distinctive pattern of dual furrows churned into the ground by *Bertha's* caterpillar tracks. Though in unimaginable agony, Hardscree had trailed the murk-comber all the way to the cavern and had slipped aboard, unseen, shortly before the air battle got under way. He'd hidden himself inside and lain still for a while, to recover from the ordeal of the journey. He was summoning his strength for a dying deed, a lethal swansong, one final outburst of violence.

Now, the vengeance-crazed stowaway stirred himself and began to slither out of the crawl-duct, knife gripped beneath his teeth.

Hardscree knew he didn't have long left to live. Minutes at most.

But in that time, while he was still capable of it, he vowed he would slaughter as many Grubdollars as he could.

Desperation + Lack Of Alternative = Extraordinary Feat

Turbulence subsided, cloud dispersed, and *Cerulean* was in clear air.

This coincided with Iaxson and several fellow-Patrollers finally making progress with the hatch. It had defied their best efforts during the journey down through the cloud cover. They had stamped on it and thumped it with the butts of their lances, gradually bending the locking bar and loosening the hinges. Still the hatch had stood firm. Now, at last, it budged. Suddenly it was hanging part-way out of its frame, twisted. It wouldn't hold out much longer.

While the barrage of blows continued overhead, the crew stared out through the windows, astonished.

'Planes?' said the trim-master. 'What are planes doing down here?'

'Never mind that,' said another crewman. 'Look over there. *Behemoth*. And she's on fire!'

The airship lay some five hundred metres off the port side. Everyone clocked her, then turned and stared at Az.

He was no less astonished than they were. How had he done it? How had he pulled off the extraordinary feat of bringing *Cerulean* down in exactly the right spot, getting her to exactly where she ought to be, and, it seemed, just in the nick of time?

He wasn't sure himself. He had obeyed an impulse, that was all. Desperation and a lack of alternative had played a part, but what it boiled down to was that he had surrendered to luck, fate, chance, whatever you cared to call it – all those things that the Count of Gyre claimed didn't exist. He had chosen without trying to make a choice. It had just ... *happened*.

He tried to fathom what this meant, and couldn't.

Then the hatch was finally bashed free from its frame and fell to the floor with a clang. Iaxson dropped down into the gondola. Without any further ado he pounced on Az, seizing him by the shoulder and swinging him round.

'Right, sonny. Enough's enough. *My* ship.'

'Erm, maybe you should take a peek out there, wing commander,' Az said, with a jerk of his thumb.

'Don't give me any more of your guano. There's nothing out there but ...'

The sentence tailed away as Iaxson realised that there was, in fact, an awful lot out there. Namely: a number of planes engaged in aerial combat with Naoutha's pirates, and a certain black airship whose balloon had a huge hole in the side and was on fire.

'Pluck me gently!' the stunned wing commander swore. 'How the —? What the —?' He peered at Az in frank disbelief.

'I've no idea myself,' Az said, 'but we have to get across to *Behemoth*. She's going down, and Mr Mordadson won't thank us if we just stand here and let him go down with her.'

'Men!' Iaxson called up through the hatchway. 'Down here. We're boarding *Behemoth*.'

'And I'm coming with you,' Az said.

'Don't be daft, kid.'

'Wing commander,' Az said, with steel in his voice, 'let's not waste time arguing. I'm coming with you.'

Iaxson looked Az up and down. He realised the boy wasn't going to take no for an answer. And Az had, somehow, given him a chance to rescue his old friend Mordadson. He owed him for that.

'All right. But don't expect me to nursemaid you. Once we're on that airship, you take your chances like the rest of us. You fend for yourself.'

Az nodded. 'Gotcha.'

'Then hold on tight,' Iaxson said, and he scooped Az up in his arms and launched himself out through the viewing windows. Patrollers, lances in hand, followed.

CHAPTER 113

Cheap Psychoanalysis

Mr Mordadson could barely think straight, but he knew two things for certain. One, *Behemoth* was in dire straits, and two, he wasn't leaving till he had dealt with Naoutha Nisrocsdaughter.

He had felt the airship rock just a couple of minutes ago as something smashed into it from the side.

Now, staggering along the keel catwalk, he could hear and smell *Behemoth* burning. Smoke was creeping down into the lower reaches of the balloon, and from above came shrieks of metal warping with heat and firecracker-like bangs as rivets popped from their sockets. In her distress *Behemoth* swayed and wallowed, and the catwalk kept canting at an angle, now one way, now the other. Mr Mordadson tottered from side to side, using his wings to prevent him from being thrown completely off-balance. He would have flown, except his brain was still reeling with the aftereffects of the triple dose of pterine and he was generally in too much pain. He could only just muster the wherewithal to walk.

And he thought he was in a fit state to tackle Naoutha?

He wasn't. But if there was one personal characteristic which Mr Mordadson prized above all others, it was his willingness to keep plugging away till the job was done. Whatever the cost to him, Naoutha would not survive to fight another day. Not if he had anything to say about it. And not if the contingency weapon in his coat pocket had anything to say about it either.

As he neared the entrance to the control gondola, there was a tremendous *crump* as one of the gas cells imploded, emptying itself flat in a second. *Behemoth* lurched downward, engines whining. Mr Mordadson thought she had embarked on a final, fatal, irrevocable plunge, and clung to the catwalk railing and braced himself. But somehow she stabilised and stayed afloat. Truly these troop-carriers were a hardy breed. They had their weaknesses but it took a lot to kill one.

Traversing the last few metres of catwalk, he readied himself to jump into the gondola. If Naoutha was down there, his one hope of defeating her lay in catching her by surprise. All he needed was to get in two or three good hits before she could retaliate, then he could finish her off with the contingency weapon while she was still reeling.

In the event, it was Mr Mordadson who was caught by surprise. A crushing weight struck him from above, sending him sprawling face-first onto the catwalk. He thought he had been hit by some chunk of falling debris, till he tried to rise and was knocked flat again.

Then a pair of leather-encased legs touched down in front of him, and the owner of the legs, in mocking tones, said, 'Well, I went aft to find you, Mordadson, and you've saved me the trouble. How obliging. Now I can kill you and have done with it, and still get off this ship with time to spare.'

'Glad I could ... help, Naoutha,' croaked Mr Mordadson.

He made a grab for her ankle, but she swatted his hand aside with a sweep of one wing.

'I take it old Wonky Wallimson is no longer with us,' she said.

'I talked him into ... setting me free. Bent his ear, in a ... manner of speaking, till he ... gave in.'

'No great loss. He was an idiot. I was going to get rid of him myself, when I had a moment. Again, you've been very obliging.'

She kicked Mr Mordadson in the temple, with casual malice, how you might kick a piece of furniture you'd just stubbed your toe on.

Mr Mordadson rolled with the impact, fetching up with his wings against the railing.

Naoutha squatted beside him, resting her forearms on her thighs. 'Do you ever wonder,' she asked, 'why you do all this? Why you fight and kill on behalf of the Silver Sanctum? I bet you do sometimes, maybe at night when you can't sleep. I bet you lie there in bed and think, *I'm just a paid thug. They don't care about me, those high-and-mighty Sanctum types. They use me to do their dirty work and they're polite to me, but deep down they despise me because my existence reminds them that their world isn't perfect. They'd like it to be perfect, but to achieve that they'll always need people like me, and they hate themselves because of that and hate me for making them hate themselves.'*

'Spare me the ... cheap psychoanalysis, Naoutha,' Mr Mordadson said. 'Your airship's doomed. Your little pirate game ... is over. Face it, you've lost.'

'*I've* lost? So says the man with the face like minced giblets and less than a minute to live.'

'Less ... than a minute? Better hurry ... up, then. I don't think your ... airship's got even ... that long.'

Naoutha bent her head sideways, acknowledging the point.

'Very well then. This may hurt.'

She grasped Mr Mordadson's head with both hands, planted the tips of her thumbs in the corners of his eyes, and got ready to dig them in.

CHAPTER 114

Under Threat

Den Grubdollar saw which way the stricken *Behemoth* was heading, extrapolated her trajectory, and announced to Fletcher, via speaker tube, that perhaps now might be a good time to start *Bertha* up and move her.

Or as he put it: 'That airship'm coming straight for we! Reckon us should shift our ruddy arses!'

Fletcher, seated up in the driver's pod, agreed. *Behemoth* was drawing near to the needle mesa. If she continued on the same course at the same rate of descent, she was going to plunge into the cavern mouth, and that meant she would come down close to, if not right on top of, *Bertha*. Fletcher started up the engine and engaged gear, and *Bertha* lumbered away from the cavern.

'Be that ... be that *Cerulean*?' said Robert, as *Bertha* slowly gathered speed. 'Just past *Behemoth*? Anyone else see that?'

The bright blue airship had appeared just above and behind the black one. It was like some strange optical illusion, *Cerulean* a ghostly double image, shimmering in the heat-haze generated by *Behemoth*'s flames.

Cassie pressed her face to the glass of a loading bay porthole. She could make out a column of winged figures moving across from *Cerulean* to *Behemoth*. One of them, the man in the lead, was carrying a non-winged figure in his arms.

'Az.'

Even as she whispered the name, Cassie felt a surge of fear and impotence.

Az had entered the fray, and was rushing headlong into danger. In a flash, Cassie regretted all the obstacles and misunderstandings and antagonism that the two of them had allowed to rise up between them and cloud their relationship, and she wanted nothing on earth so much as to have that talk with Az, the one Aurora had recommended; to have an opportunity for them to clear the air and start over. She feared she might never get it now.

The boarding party from *Cerulean* entered *Behemoth* at the rear and disappeared from view. The burning black airship continued her slow, inexorable downward progress. Streamers of smoke were billowing back from her nose-cone. Fully half of her balloon canvas was aflame.

Meanwhile, unbeknownst to anyone in *Bertha*, Deacon Hardscree was hauling himself forward through the crawl-ducts. His legs had ceased to work properly so he used his arms only. The razorweed had flensed the skin and meat from one of his elbows. Bare bone bonked every time he jabbed down the elbow and pushed off with it.

At last he made it to the end of the crawl-duct. It opened onto a small storage area which afforded access to the loading bay and also to the driver's pod. Hardscree slithered out. A glance up the shaft into the pod showed him there was just one person there. He could see boots, trouser legs, an arm. They belonged to a young man. Den Grubdollar's elder boy, he assumed. Fletcher was his name? Yes, Fletcher. As good a place as any to start his Grubdollar massacre.

Hardscree grasped the lowest of the rungs and heaved his body up the shaft bit by bit, till his head emerged into the pod. Hooking one arm over the top rung to anchor himself, he took the knife from his teeth with the free hand. He flipped it over, catching the tip in his fingers. The nape of Fletcher's neck was exposed between the back of the seat and the headrest. The range was a little over two metres. An easy throw. An easy kill.

Hardscree angled the knife so that the haft was beside his ear. The blade would enter between two vertebrae and its point would exit through the throat. Fletcher wouldn't feel a thing. He wouldn't even know he was dead.

Muscles contracted. Wrist flexed and straightened. The knife zinged through space.

CHAPTER 115

The First Rule Of Punching

'Spread out!' ordered Iaxson. 'Check every cabin and cranny within a hundred metres. We're here for one minute and not a second longer. If we don't find him within a minute, we bail out. No delaying. No heroics.'

The Alar Patrollers fanned out along the keel catwalk, darting down side-corridors and kicking open cabin doors. A pall of smoke hung in the air, thickening rapidly. Az felt his eyes start to water and his nostrils start to sting. It wouldn't be long before no one was able to breathe or see. Nevertheless he joined the Patrollers on their search. The airship was dying around them. Her groans of suffering merged with the roaring crackle of flames. A minute wasn't enough. There were so many places Mr Mordadson could be.

Soon, all too soon, Iaxson blew a long peep on his whistle, signalling a pull-out.

Ignoring the order, Az picked up his pace. He heard Iaxson shouting for him, and then telling him he was on his own. Fine by him. He plunged still further into *Behemoth*. He continued to try door after door along the catwalk, only to find empty cabin after empty cabin. He yelled out Mr Mordadson's name, but it came out more as a cough than speech. The smoke was becoming chokingly dense. Sparks and embers – scraps of burning canvas – had begun to drift down from above, like a glowing snow. They singed Az's hair. His eyes were streaming with the smoke. He was stumbling, half-blind.

Then, ahead, dimly through the haze, he glimpsed two figures. One was crouching over the other. Black wings. It could only be Naoutha, and by the looks of things she was about to sink her thumbs into Mr Mordadon's eyeballs.

Az didn't hesitate. He charged along the catwalk and ran full-tilt into Naoutha, barging her away from Mr Mordadson. He knocked her over but was going too fast to halt himself and went crashing down with her. Limbs tangled. Az managed to extricate an arm. He began raining punches on Naoutha. Instinct and combat training took over. Mr Mordadson had once urged him to memorise the first rule of punching: *hard to soft, soft to hard*. He couldn't impress on Az enough the importance of that. Unless you wanted to break your own knuckles, you should ease up when hitting an opponent's face or ribs. Anywhere else – stomach, neck, groin – you should feel free to hammer as violently as you liked.

Az hammered. But Naoutha's leatherwear absorbed much of the force of the blows. And Naoutha had wings.

One upward flex of her left wing, full in the face, sent Az reeling. He got to his feet, stunned and groggy, in time to see Naoutha lunging at him. He was able to get his forearms up in a standard block, but the collision was brutal. His forearms took the brunt of it but still he was slammed backwards against the catwalk railing.

'Little wingless brat,' Naoutha intoned. She grabbed him by the neck. 'You've been an absolute pain in the tailfeathers. I'm going to rip the heart from your chest.'

She meant it literally, as well. Az felt her fingers poke into his solar plexus. She fully intended to tear his ribcage open with her bare hands. And he was too dazed to prevent her.

He glimpsed movement over Naoutha's shoulder. A silhouette, rising. Mr Mordadson. Something in his fist. Small. Glinting. Sharp. A hypodermic syringe?

'A taste of ... your own ... medicine, Naoutha,' Mr Mordadson said, and jammed the syringe into her back and depressed the plunger.

And Naoutha ...

... *howled.*

And let go of Az and staggered backwards, tugging out the hypodermic.

And lurched towards the control gondola hatch.

And toppled over the edge and fell in.

And landed below with a thump, out of sight, still howling.

'What was in that syringe?' spluttered Az.

'Mega-dosage of pterine. Six times ... the usual,' said Mr Mordadson. 'Now let's get ... out of here.'

'Yes,' said Az. 'Exit strategy.'

'You have one?'

'You're it. But we have to go out that way.' Az pointed towards the control gondola. Somewhere down there, Naoutha continued to howl, as though her very soul was in torment. Her heels beat out a jagged rhythm on the floor. 'Quickest route. Back along the catwalk's too far.'

Mr Mordadson winced. 'I don't know ... if I can ... fly.'

Through the smoke, Az could see that Mr Mordadson was in dreadful shape. Injuries aside, it seemed that the simple act of standing upright was taking everything Mr Mordadson had. He looked ready to pass out at any moment.

From somewhere outside came a vast, thudding, grinding *boom*. The whole of *Behemoth* was racked with convulsions.

'Tough guano,' said Az, grabbing Mr Mordadson by the sleeve. 'Whether you like it or not, flying's our only hope.'

CHAPTER 116

Near-Miss

Behemoth had hit the needle mesa, just next to its 'eye'. She scraped her starboard flank along it, losing both propellers on that side. Balloon canvas peeled back in strips. The propeller mountings snapped off and tumbled down, ending up as twisted metal wreckage on the ground.

Behemoth carried on, her terminal plunge slowed but not arrested. Skewing sideways, she continued to fall at an acute angle towards the cavern entrance.

The mesa, however, came off rather worse. It shivered with the impact all the way down to its narrow base, and then, with epic slowness, began to topple. The 'eye' section fell first, and the rest of the mesa followed in layers, like the tiers of a tall cake that had been shoved sideways. Slab after immense slab sheared off and came thundering down.

Bertha was not directly in the path of the falling mesa but was close enough for Fletcher to feel the need to take evasive action. He jammed down on the left-hand control stick, and *Bertha* skidded to one side. The 'eye' of the mesa landed not far in front of her, striking the earth with enough force to make the murk-comber jolt. A huge cloud of dust was kicked up, swamping *Bertha*.

The sudden sharp turn saved Fletcher's life, for he performed it at the exact same moment that Hardscree launched the knife at his neck. Hardscree's aim had been true, but *Bertha*'s unexpected jerk to the left meant the knife thudded into the headrest rather than Fletcher's neck. Fletcher escaped death by a margin of three centimetres.

He felt the impact behind his head. Puzzled, he looked round.

And wished he hadn't.

The face that glowered up at him from the shaft was like something out of a nightmare. Torn, mangled, caked in dried blood – Fletcher had never seen anything so hideous, and the sight made every hair on his body stand on end and turned his guts to jelly. He lost his grip on the control sticks. *Bertha* started to decelerate and he didn't even notice. All he could do was stare in numb, abject horror at the head that had protruded into the driver's pod – the head attached to a body that, even as he watched, began to lug itself out of the shaft and pull itself with clawed fingers across the floor towards him. Every movement this *thing* made was shuddery and spasmodic and yet determined too. Grimly determined.

The clumps of red hair still clinging to the torn scalp, and the tatters of robe that wreathed the body, informed Fletcher that he was looking at his father's Deacon. But the man had been hit with a javelin and fallen into a canyon of razorweed. He ought to be dead. How could he still be alive? And how did he come to be here in *Bertha*?

As if from far-off, Fletcher heard his father's voice over the speaker tube, demanding to know why they had slowed down. They'd had a near-miss with the mesa but now they were closer than ever to the airship.

Fletcher could do nothing about that. He couldn't even move himself, let alone *Bertha*. The living ruin that had been Deacon Hardscree had reached his seat and was dragging itself up by the armrest and groping for the knife that protruded from the headrest. The stench of blood and death was awful. The half-dead abomination was almost, almost touching him. Fletcher longed to shrink away from it. But it was as if he was paralysed. His body would not obey the messages his brain was sending it. He could only sit, frozen with fear.

Now Cassie was calling up to him from the loading bay. He tried to answer but his throat was locked tight. He heard her start to climb up towards the pod. He tried to shout out a warning. He couldn't.

Hardscree yanked the knife out. He raised it above his head. Fletcher watched the blade tremble in the air. He knew he was about to die.

Rendered (H)armless

Den Grubdollar scrambled along a crawl-duct from the rear observation nacelle to find out what was going on with Fletcher. The lad would get them all killed if he didn't buck up his ideas and give *Bertha* some juice.

Cassie, meanwhile, sprang up into the driver's pod just in time to catch Hardscree before he could bury his knife in Fletcher's chest. She didn't allow herself to wonder how the Deacon had got there, or to feel any squeamishness. She seized hold of his slashed-up forearm and wrenched it back. Hardscree fought her with maniacal strength, trying to bring the knife down and stab Fletcher. Cassie refused to let him. She would not permit another of her brothers to die. She had saved her father's life. She would save Fletcher's. With every erg of strength she possessed, she hauled back on Hardscree's arm. Her hands became slippery with his blood; it was dripping down her wrists. She clung on all the more tightly.

They were locked in struggle, stalemated, Hardscree trying to force the knife forward, Cassie forcing it back. This couldn't go on indefinitely. Something, Cassie knew, had to give.

Something did.

Hardscree's arm, to be precise.

To be absolutely precise, his shoulder joint.

The muscles surrounding the joint had had all they could take. Shredded, brutalised, under strain – suddenly, with supple slickness, they snapped. Tendons broke. The arm came free from its socket.

Cassie was flung backwards, still clutching the arm, which was still clutching the knife. Hardscree screamed and collapsed in the opposite direction, blood jetting from the ragged hole from which the limb had been uprooted. He landed on top of the access point in the floor of the pod. Cassie fetched up just behind the driver's seat.

She tossed the arm aside in a convulsion of disgust, then shouted at Fletcher: 'Him's lying on the access point! Hit the switch!'

Though her brother was still in a state of shock, he managed to galvanise himself into action. He slapped the switch on the dashboard. The triangular plates beneath Hardscree irised open, and the Deacon fell through.

But not without grabbing Cassie first. His one remaining arm reached out and seized a handful of her shirt. As he plunged through the hole, he dragged her with him. Fletcher made a bid to catch her. He got a hold of her blood-slicked wrist but she slid out of his grasp. Together, Hardscree and Cassie tumbled out of the driver's pod and onto the desert earth.

At that same moment, Den came scrambling up the shaft. He saw the detached arm, blood spray everywhere, Fletcher bending over the open access point. He took the situation in at a glance.

Then he saw *Behemoth* looming. The burning airship filled the windscreen.

Twenty seconds to impact.

Twenty Seconds

20 ...

The crew of *Behemoth* had sensibly abandoned ship several minutes earlier; they'd realised there was no hope of saving the airship. The control gondola was now empty except for Naoutha, who was howling and writhing on the floor in the throes of her extreme pterine overdose. Az and Mr Mordadson skirted around her thrashing form and made for the viewing windows, which the departing crew had bashed out in order to escape.

19 ...

On the ground, Cassie lay on top of Hardscree. His body had absorbed the force of the fall, saving her from harm. His arm, however, was clamped around her like an iron band. She struggled but couldn't break free. She could feel his chest rising and falling and hear his breath coming in raspy wet heaves. He was on the brink of death – but he would not let her go.

18 ...

Abruptly Mr Mordadson collapsed against the trim-master's station, where all of the dials and gauges were going wild. He looked at Az with eyes that were so bloodshot, their whites were crimson. It was almost as if he had his spectacles on again. 'I ... can't,' he gasped to Az. 'You'll have to ... jump. I just ... can't.'

17 ...

'One,' sighed Hardscree in Cassie's ear. 'Just one of you will do.' And then he let out a croak and his body stiffened beneath her. But his arm did not loosen. It locked her tight against him. A death grip.

16 ...

'You fly or we both die,' Az said, pulling Mr Mordadson upright. 'Got it?' Feebly Mr Mordadson nodded, and together they staggered towards the windows, with Az supporting most of his friend's weight. And then, behind them, Naoutha's howling sharpened, becoming a keening shriek of fury.

15 ...

'Cass!' Fletcher yelled down from the driver's pod. 'Cass! Get up! Grab a hold on *Bertha*! Us has got to get out of here!' But Cassie shook her head forlornly. 'I can't break free,' she shouted back. 'Just drive, Fletch. Get everyone to safety.'

14 ...

Naoutha, standing tall, her wings out wide, snatched the mask and goggles from her face. What she exposed was not the vision of beauty Az had assumed lay behind her disguise. Far from it. The face might have been beautiful once, but now it was ravaged and half eaten with sores. In places the flesh had rotted away completely, revealing the bone beneath. The toll taken by prolonged use of pterine was terrible to behold, and Az, in spite of everything, was transfixed with horror.

13 ...

Fletcher was about to jump down to the ground, but his father stopped him. 'Drive, boy,' Den said, thrusting him towards the controls. Fletcher protested that they couldn't just leave Cassie lying there, but his father had already leapt down through the access point.

12 ...

Rage, as well as the pterine sores, disfigured Naoutha's features. She lurched towards Az and Mr Mordadson, fully resolved to stop them getting away. If she was going to go down with her airship, so were they.

11 ...

Landing next to his daughter, Den bent down and tried to prise her from Hardscree's clutches. The arm clung on with inhuman tenacity. Meanwhile, Fletcher brought *Bertha* back to life and shoved down hard on the right-hand control stick. Tears were pouring down his cheeks, but he knew his father was right. For Aurora's and Robert's sakes, he had to drive.

10 ...

Az went into a crouch. Naoutha took off and swooped at them. Az knew he had just one shot at this, one chance to get it right. His leg flashed out in a roundhouse kick. His foot slammed into Naoutha's midriff and she went hurtling backwards, crashing against the gondola's aft wall.

9 ...

Den grimaced with effort. He pulled. Cassie pushed. The arm bent, bent further ... Something creaked. Something cracked. Suddenly Cassie was free.

8 ...

Outside the viewing windows, the cavern entrance gaped like a dark, hungry maw. Az bundled Mr Mordadson over to the shattered frames. Pterine-crazed Naoutha was screaming senseless words of vengeance, flailing as she tried to get up.

7 ...

Bertha slewed to the right, her left rear track missing Den and Cassie by centimetres. Den grasped his daughter's wrist and dived for the back of the murk-comber.

6 …

Az shoved himself and Mr Mordadson out of the gondola. His last glimpse of Naoutha showed her rising to her feet while burning debris began to pour down through the hatchway. She stood, a black silhouette against a backdrop of tumbling flames.

5 …

Den latched on to a projecting piece of *Bertha's* bodywork and clung on by his fingertips. With his other arm he swung Cassie round and up. She landed on the mudguard above the left rear track.

4 …

For a second, it seemed to Az that he and Mr Mordadson were suspended in midair. They floated in space while *Behemoth* sailed above them, a vast blazing fireball, like the sun brought to earth.

3 …

Den's grip slipped. Cassie viced a hand around his wrist before he could slide off *Bertha* onto the ground. Sprawled on the mudguard, she held him while Fletcher poured on the speed, trying to outrace *Behemoth*. The airship was so low that Cassie could feel the heat from its flames. The crackle of burning was deafeningly loud.

2 …

'Fly!!!' Az yelled, and Mr Mordadson flapped his wings, weakly at first, but then with more force. Az clung on to his arm, as Mr Mordadson's wings carried both of them out from under the belly of *Behemoth*.

1 …

Cassie looked up.

Az looked down.

Each saw the other lit up by the glare of the airborne inferno that was *Behemoth*. Illuminated.

Then …

Crash.

CHAPTER 119

Simultaneous Burial And Cremation

Behemoth died amid fire and fury.

As she rammed head-first into the cavern, her fuel tanks ignited. The explosion cracked her apart in the middle, sending sheets of flame in all directions and shattering the rock around the cavern entrance. The roof of the cavern immediately began to crumble, coming away in boulder-size chunks. While the front portion of *Behemoth* rolled down the incline with a slow, elephantine grace, the rear portion was buried in a cascade of stone and stalactite. Framework was crushed, cables snapped, metal spars splintered, fins were flattened, all amidst bulging gouts of smoke and flame.

As the cave-in continued, gathering speed, the front portion of the airship rolled on, also gathering speed. Like some immense wheel of fire it hurtled through the subterranean darkness, following the course of the railway track, downward into the deeps of the earth where the aircraft mausoleum lay. It disintegrated as it went, shedding segments, losing shape, till by the time it reached the Deacons' depository of fallen planes it was more like an avalanche, a tidal wave of burning bits and pieces, a torrent of fiery fragments, which broke over the collected aircraft and parts of aircraft, and over the joists and the generator which the Deacons had installed, setting everything alight.

In short order, the dome-like chamber was ablaze. The place became one large conflagration which burned rapidly and steadily, destroying planes and infrastructure, laying waste to the handiwork of Airborn and Groundling alike.

Up above, the cavern mouth flattened with a titanic *boom*, sealing itself shut for ever.

The smoke and dust took an hour to disperse.

The Talk

The Aerodyne Striga II rose till it scraped the base of the cloud cover. This was a safe, neutral zone, high enough for an Airborn not to get too ground-sick, low enough for a Groundling not to suffer altitude-related problems.

Michael put the Striga into a circling pattern, and for a while he and his two passengers, Az and Cassie, surveyed the scene on the ground.

Down there, the surviving roughnecks were gathered in a rapturous huddle, celebrating the demise of *Behemoth* and their part in her downfall. At the same time they mourned the death of their toolpusher, Magnus Clockweight. Their cheers were tinged with sorrow as they spoke of his heroic act of self-sacrifice, and the sacrifices of all their colleagues who hadn't made it safely back to ground.

Colin was in the midst of the roughnecks, and was enjoying the praise he got for his part in helping clear Clockweight's path to the airship. Michael didn't mind Colin taking the much of credit. The lad had done well. Besides, Michael would much rather be up here, scooting around in the Striga. It wasn't the Skylark, of course, but it was almost as good as. And, being a limousine-class plane designed to be chauffeur-piloted, it had voluminous seats in the back and a partition that could be raised between cockpit and passenger section for privacy.

Cerulean hovered at a similar height to the plane. The Alar Patrollers had rounded up *Behemoth*'s crew and locked them in *Cerulean*'s cabins. Once the pirates had realised that *Behemoth* was doomed, the fight had gone out of them. They had nothing left to defend, the whole pirate escapade was over, and so they'd surrendered meekly to Wing Commander Iaxson. Iaxson wished that their ringleader, Naoutha, was in his custody as well, but he appreciated that that would never be. He and Mr Mordadson were both quite convinced that she had perished along with *Behemoth*. No one could have survived that explosion or the cave-in that came after.

Bertha was parked not far from the ruins of the cavern. She waited to take Cassie back to Grimvale. Michael and Aurora would be hitching a ride home with Az in *Cerulean*. The (now quite definitely) last surviving troop-carrier airship was due to depart within the hour. Rigz and Ra'asielson were showing signs of recovery and Aurora was attending to them. Their wounds remained a cause for concern, however, and getting them to a sky-city for proper medical attention was a high priority.

Az and Cassie did not, therefore, have long. But then, they were used to that.

Michael, with a sly smile, pressed the switch to raise the partition between him and them. The strained muscle in his lower back was hurting like crazy, but he wasn't going to let it stop him giving his brother and his brother's girlfriend this private time together.

The Striga completed another full circuit before either Az or Cassie could think what to say. Then they both blurted out something simultaneously.

'Cassie, I think I should —'

'Az, it'm probably —'

They stopped.

'You go ahead,' said Az.

'No, you.'

'No, *you*.'

'Don't be so damn polite.'

'Why not? I was brought up well.'

'What, and I weren't?'

'Don't get all snitty. I didn't mean it like that.'

Cassie relented. 'You'm right. Sorry. So, anyway. You got your bad guy, then.'

'I did. And so did you.'

'Yeah. Mine was a real creep.'

'Yeah, but mine was ugly.'

'Mine were pretty ugly too. Not to begin with, but him ended up a right old *urrghhh*.' She shuddered at the memory of the maimed and mutilated Hardscree.

'But mine had only half a face,' said Az.

'Yeah, but mine ... Well, maybe us shouldn't get into a whose-bad-guy-were-uglier competition.'

'Agreed. On the plus side, you found your dad.'

'I did. And you found your pirate airship.'

'Which your side destroyed.'

'Which us'd wouldn't have managed if you hadn't chased her here.'

'Funny how we both wound up homing in on the same spot in this desert.'

'Yeah, funny.'

'Separate quests, same destination.'

'If you want to be all fanciful about it.'

'I can't help it. I'm feeling a bit odd and fanciful about the entire situation. Like there's something more to it all, something I can't easily explain.'

'Such as?'

Az frowned, searching inside himself for how he felt and a means of expressing it. 'When I came down through the cloud cover, I . . . I somehow knew that that was what I had to do. It was a statistical improbability that we'd end up almost on top of *Behemoth*. It was absurd, a million-to-one chance. I was winging it completely. But it makes you wonder, doesn't it?'

'It makes *I* think you were just phenomenally lucky.'

'Could be that's all there is to it,' Az conceded. But the faraway look in his eyes suggested he thought otherwise.

'Whereas I,' said Cassie, 'had to track down my da through detective work and sheer hard slog. Nothing more'n that. No luck involved. Well, not much.'

'Oh, you had it easy, definitely,' Az said with a laugh.

'Cheek!' Cassie gave him a playful punch on the arm. 'Traipsing halfway across the Westward Territories, getting caught up in a mob in Craterhome and nearly eaten by hackerjackals and nearly killed by a raving-mad Deacon – and you's the nerve to call that *easy*???' She hit him again, and then a third time, for good measure.

'Stop that!' Az said, rubbing his arm. 'You don't know your own strength.'

'You Airborn be soft, that'm the problem.'

'Soft? I'd punch you back, if you weren't a girl and I wasn't a gentleman.'

'Go ahead,' said Cassie teasingly.

'I'm trained in combat, you know.'

'Don't care.'

'I could kill you without meaning to.'

'You and whose army?'

'Just me. I'm a living weapon. You should have seen the kick I nailed Naoutha with.'

'Ooh, you're such a big hero.'

'I *am*, though.'

'Such a bighead too.'

'Hey!'

They both started laughing, and suddenly, in the middle of the laughter, they both caught themselves and halted. They looked at each other.

'This . . .' said Az. 'This feels good.'

Cassie nodded. 'I know.'

'This is us. This is how we are together. How we should be.'

She nodded again. 'Stuff got in the way, Az.' She laced her fingers into his. 'I shouldn't have let it but it did. You know how important family be to I. That'm my only excuse but I reckon it be a good one.'

'Family's important to me too, Cassie. But you didn't have to shut me out. I'd have helped. You know that. Right from the start. All you had to do was ask.'

'Next time I will.'

'And don't you get the impression that someone's trying to tell us something?'

'Huh? Who d'you mean?'

'Not a person. Just – I don't want to use the words fate or destiny, but look how all this turned out. Your and my paths got drawn together, despite us. It's like we couldn't do anything about it. Even though we had our differences, we still got pulled into the same adventure. Doesn't that tell you anything?'

'Only that you be reading too much into things. You see destiny working, I just see life doing what it does, which be flowing together sometimes, falling apart at other times, coming back together once more, and so on. Just the usual give-and-take, that'm all. You'm a hero all right, Az, I be'n't denying that. You's done good stuff. Old Mordy owes you his life. But little things, ordinary things, can make a hero as well. There don't have to be an airy-fairy something like destiny running the show. It'm *people* who run the show. You, me, everyone. And us can be heroes in all sorts of ways.'

'But there's a grand scheme, isn't there? A bigger picture?'

'If so, it'm made up of lots of people. Humans. Groundlings, Airborn, whatever. Just we, all interacting and clashing and working together. That be your bigger picture.'

'I . . .'

Cassie rapped him on the forehead, as if to knock all the difficult thoughts to the back of his brain. 'Az, time's short. Let's make the most of it.'

'Eh?'

'I said, shut up and snog I.'

The Striga circled and circled until the needle on the fuel gauge hovered near zero. Then Michael brought the plane down for a smooth, perfect landing. It and its occupants touched ground as though as light as a feather.

CHAPTER 121

First Epilogue:
Lady Aanfielsdaughter And Aurora

'I understand congratulations are in order,' said Lady Aanfielsdaughter. 'We're expecting to hear the flutter of tiny wings.'

'That's right,' said Aurora, with a slight blush. 'It's early days yet, but still ...'

'But still, thrilling news. Anyone in mind for godparents?' Lady Aanfielsdaughter gave her a significant look.

'Milady, you are top of the list. Of course, I shan't let the baby interfere with my work. I'd like to continue at the Sanctum full-time, or as close to full-time as I can manage.'

'We can't function without you, Aurora. You'll have your maternity leave, and then I'm sure we can work out amenable hours.'

'I've been talking to Michael about his moving here, so he can help out with the childcare.'

'Let me know if he agrees to it and I'll help you find a nice large apartment.'

'*When* he agrees to it, don't you mean?'

Lady Aanfielsdaughter smiled. 'My mistake. I wasn't taking into account your formidable powers of persuasion. Which reminds me. I've just received a letter from the WOE executives expressing gratitude for our assistance in halting the pirates. They've lost their installation, of course, and we're working on a reparations package of some kind. But there'd have been a lot less compliance from them and a whole lot more complaint, I'm sure, if it weren't for your decision to get involved and coax your husband and the Grubdollars into helping out the oil company employees. You judged it brilliantly. It was a wise move, both tactically and diplomatically. Well done.'

'Thank you, milady.'

'And now that you've been back at the Sanctum for a few days, may I ask you something?'

'Please do.'

Lady Aanfielsdaughter rose from her desk and went to the windows to take in the view. 'How are people reacting to this whole Redspire business, now that it's over? How well do they think I handled it? What's your opinion on the general mood here? Be candid.'

Aurora considered her answer. 'There's some concern still. Not about what we did but about what the long-term consequences of the pirate attacks might be. I understand there have been reports of unrest in several Groundling cities, and up here the Feather First!ers are becoming ever more vocal and gaining new recruits every day. Those are worrying developments. But on balance I think the mood at the Sanctum is favourable. We did what we did, and it worked out OK.'

'And me?' said Lady Aanfieldsdaughter, still looking away so that Aurora could not see the troubled light in her eyes. 'What are they saying about me?'

'Milady . . .'

'Ah. That bad, is it?'

'You're still the most popular senior resident by far,' said Aurora. 'But I've heard grumbles here and there, people saying you should have cracked down harder and sooner on the pirates. Some are even saying you should have done something about Redspire long before the pirates reared their heads.'

'Hindsight is a wonderful thing. What, am I supposed to anticipate every crisis before it happens? Am I supposed to have precognitive powers? And if a place like Redspire misbehaves but doesn't actually break any laws, I'm still expected to send in the Patrollers? Isn't that a bit, well, draconian?'

'I wasn't saying the criticisms are fair, milady. And they're coming from a small minority. I'd ignore them, if I were you. They'll die down soon enough.'

'I only wish I *could* ignore them, Aurora, but a minority grumbling today can become a majority calling for my head tomorrow. I need to take these detractors seriously if I'm to stay in this job.'

What Lady Aanfieldsdaughter left unsaid was that she wasn't sure how much longer she actually wished to stay in the job. Instead, she turned back to Aurora, looking as regal and in-control as she always did.

'But let's just bask for now in the glow of achievement,' she said. 'There could be trouble ahead, but for the moment we've won. Let's enjoy that. Moving on to more important matters . . . Have you thought of names yet? If it's a girl, I think Serena has a nice ring. Don't you?'

CHAPTER 122

Second Epilogue:
The Grubdollars

Rubbing sleep-grit from his eyes and yawning, Robert shuffled downstairs to the courtyard. Someone on the other side of the solid, portcullis-style gate was pounding away, hard enough to rattle the hinges.

'Who'm there?' he called out. 'You know what time it be?'

'Grimvale constabulary. Open up.'

'What does you want?' Robert asked, suddenly alert and on edge.

'Open up,' came the curt reply, along with more pounding.

Robert obeyed, and found half a dozen policemen standing outside. Two of them he recognised – local coppers. The rest were unfamiliar, from out of town.

'Robert Grubdollar,' said one of the locals. 'These gents with I be from the Craterhome police department. Them's here in connection with an incident that occurred a fortnight ago, involving your murk-comber.'

'What?'

'Son, don't play games,' said one of the Craterhome policeman, a cynical-looking sergeant. 'Us has a large number of eyewitness and victims, all of whom has given sworn affidavits testifying to the fact that on the date in question a murk-comber caused widespread bodily harm to a number of Craterhome citizens. There'm also the small matter of damage done to a piece of civic statuary, repairing which be estimated to cost five thousand notes. It'm taken we a while to establish whom the murk-comber in question belonged to, but following extensive investigations, and with the assistance of our Grimvale brethren here, us has narrowed down the list of suspects to one. To wit, the murk-comber under the registered ownership of Dennis Grubdollar and family.'

'But – but – them was all in a mob around us' said Robert, wide-eyed. 'It were self-defence. And that statue – that were a total accident.'

'So you be'n't denying either of the incidents took place.'

'No. Yes. No, I be ...' Robert was flustered and didn't know what to say.

He was rescued by his father, who appeared in the courtyard, dressed in his pyjamas, with Cassie and Fletcher in tow.

'What'm all this about?' Den demanded. 'What be you lot doing here at crack of dawn? Be'n't decent folk allowed their kip?'

'Put plainly, Mr Grubdollar,' said the sergeant from Craterhome, 'you and your family's in deep, deep trouble. You may consider yourselves under house arrest for the time being, and us is impounding your murk-comber as evidence of a crime.'

'House arrest? Impounding *Bertha*?' Den spluttered.

'Now, I be sure you'm willing to do this quietly. No fuss and nonsense.'

'Da!' said Cassie. 'Them can't take *Bertha*. Us can't let they.'

Den looked at her, and at his sons, and then at *Bertha*, and finally back at the policemen. His shoulders rose and fell in a gesture of defeat.

'Actually, I don't know how us can stop they,' he said.

At an order from the sergeant, two of the Craterhome policemen moved towards *Bertha*. Cassie ran to prevent them getting aboard, but her father grabbed her and pulled her against him. She struggled but he wouldn't loosen his grip.

Dismayed, the Grubdollars watched the policemen enter *Bertha*, start her up (on the fifth attempt), and drive her out of the courtyard.

Cassie was in floods of tears as the murk-comber disappeared down the street. *Bertha* herself seemed unhappy about this turn of events. Her cackle held none of its usual glee.

'It'm just a misunderstanding, girl,' her father said softly. 'Us'll sort this out in no time.'

But his face told a different story.

CHAPTER 123

Third And Final Epilogue:
Lord Urironson And ???

The visitor came at the prearranged hour. It was long after nightfall and the Silver Sanctum was dark. Lord Urironson was waiting on the balcony outside his apartment, and no sooner had the visitor alighted than he ushered him hastily indoors, closing the windows behind him. For several moments the two of them stood in Lord Urironson's sitting room, saying nothing, while the mynah bird that occupied a cage in a corner eyed the new arrival warily, cocking its yellow-flashed head from side to side.

'You're here,' Lord Urironson said at last. 'You actually came. I must admit, your request for a meeting surprised me. Not so much the request itself, more the way it was phrased. The tone. It sounded almost conciliatory. As if you aren't here to upbraid me, or even – and I hope I'm right about this – hurt me.'

'Hurt me, *awrrk*,' croaked the mynah, accurately mimicking its owner's rich, fruity tones.

The visitor answered Lord Urironson with a curt nod, nothing more.

'In fact,' the senior Silver Sanctum resident continued, surer of himself now, 'although I have every reason to fear you, I suspect that you come in peace. Would I be correct in that surmise?'

'Correct in that surmise,' the mynah cawed.

Lord Urironson silenced the bird with an irritable gesture. The mynah, miffed, turned round on its perch and began to nibble at the underside of one wing.

The visitor nodded again.

'I thought as much,' his lordship said. 'You see, had your intent been hostile, you would not have requested a meeting at all, and your message certainly wouldn't have asked me to keep it a secret from your immediate superior. In the normal course of events I'd have consulted with Lady Aanfielsdaughter beforehand, as soon as you got in touch, to establish if you were acting on her behalf or independently. By telling me not to, you were letting me know that you are acting of your own volition. Which is interesting indeed. Am I detecting a schism? A breaking of the ranks? Is there a whiff of betrayal in the air?'

The visitor gave a calm, discreet smile.

'Then elucidate,' said the senior resident. 'Tell me what you want from me.'

With a slight bow and a small fluffing of the wings, the visitor did.

'Yes, I agree, Lady Aanfielsdaughter *is* a spent force,' said Lord Urironson when the visitor had finished outlining his motives and intentions. 'You're wise to be distancing yourself from her. But what about Az Gabrielson? How will your young protégé feel about this – this change of heart?'

'Az?' said the visitor. 'Az could be a problem. But he'll be *my* problem, and when the time comes ...' The smile on the visitor's bruised, black-and-blue face widened, turning cruel. 'When the time comes, I will deal with him. You can count on that.'

'Then,' said Lord Urironson, extending a hand, 'let us shake on it. A new partnership. An alliance. A clandestine one for now, but not for long.'

'*Thweep*, a new partnership,' echoed the mynah softly, still with its back turned to the two humans.

'Indeed,' said Mr Mordadson, and he reached out and firmly shook Lord Urironson's hand.

The End